The Agapéd Bearer

Books by Hannah Taylor Lindsey

The Agapéd Bearer Saga
The Agapéd Bearer: Wishing Stars
The Agapéd Bearer: Paragon Games

THE AGAPÉD BEARER

WISHING STARS

BOOK I

HANNAH LINDSEY

STARNATE PUBLISHING

For those in need of someone who can save their weary heart,
in need of a celestial escape, or simply in need of a friend,
this book is for you.

PART I

RANEMIR

"My dear Ariela, I have heard your call... and because of your loyalty to me, I will bestow to you a power to stop your Fallen Elysian brethren—a magic superior to everything you have known, for its origin is from me, and its light is of my light.

"Know this: the power that Darkness has over the Fallen is one that is now of Man. This magic I gift to stop their destruction is not for you, Ariela... it is for the human heart of *its* choosing; for though many hearts may be weak to Darkness, there are those who are even stronger with light. This magic—this light—will be unlike any other in the history of time. This magic... the Agapéd Magic... will choose a heart to home, one that is *good* and has the strength to face calamity.

"For as long as there is Darkness among Man, the Agapéd will be called. The heart of Man is stronger than you and your Guardians may know, so do not fret my dear Ariela, and know that I love you, for even a glow from the smallest star can be a guiding light in the deepest dark."

For over 500 years, Ranemir's gift of the Agapéd has saved our worlds from the Fallen, and now, it must do so again... lest calamity consumes all.

I

FALLEN STAR

Without a doubt, there were two things I knew to be one hundred percent true: First, that middle school was the absolute worst, and second, that magic was real.

You could be new to the neighborhood, like me, already have a kid of your own, like Mom, or be as old as dirt, like Grandma, and agree that middle school—at any time period—was never the best experience. You looked forward to turning thirteen, finally discarding the title of "kid" and being able to watch PG-13 movies without hiding it from your mom, but then, you realized it was just a number. One foot onto the grimy floors of an educational building that could pass as a prison with poorly drawn artwork hanging on every brick wall, and you were still as pathetic as before. Someone was already older than you, mentally or physically, or both. Judgment came from the teachers and the little sixth graders alike, making you feel even worse about your already low self-esteem. There was always someone prettier than you, no matter what class you were stuck in, and to top it off, there was no escape.

Maybe for some, middle school was a good experience. They must have had what I called "confidence." I had never seen it when I looked in the mirror, and every time I tried to find some, fear squashed it like an ant and scraped it off on the curb outside of the school doors. The teachers would try and pull it out of me, but even after being in Keyport, New Jersey, for almost four years, none had succeeded.

It was partially my fault. I chose to be quiet in fear of being made fun of for something as silly as playing video games daily, and I chose to listen more than talk when in group settings. In class, I would rather another student answer out loud even if it meant my participation grade dropped; saying the wrong answer and getting laughed at was not something my heart could handle. I didn't think my voice sounded funny, and I normally knew the answers, but I would rather not be labeled a Know-It-All either. I didn't want the whole class to think I was super smart—because I wasn't. I just studied the average amount, paid attention when the teacher's notes said "THIS IS IMPORTANT" written across the top, and wrote down the things I knew I would forget later—all to get that good grade. And *that* was all the confidence I needed. Plus, Mom loved seeing me do my best.

I truly believe, though, that even if I was confident, had the prettiest brown hair, wasn't covered in freckles, or didn't have glow sticks for legs... I would still be that unspecial, second-choice-of-a-girl. No matter what I did or what hobby I liked in any school I was in, everyone already seemed to have someone they would rather spend time with. I would try to be kind as Mom taught me, but kindness didn't have the same value as luck did in middle school. Some people were simply born to be talented and adored, and some happened to show up at the right place, at the right time, with the right people. The winning lottery ball for a life of uniqueness was never in my pot, and yet, I still tried to grab it every day.

But, I couldn't complain too much. I had a great mom to come home to and two *decent* friends who didn't mind me joining their duo.

"Aw, Mom packed me regular chips," Lily complained, dumping her pink lunch box's contents onto the cafeteria table, her blonde hair trailing off her shoulders. "Lisa, can you trade me for your Gushers?"

This was a weekly occurrence of Lily's personality, and normally, I wouldn't have minded trading... but I packed those Gushers this morning, *specifically* just for me. They were my favorite snack at the moment, and nothing was going to make me trade them.

Her face wasn't scary at all, but those pursed pink lips of hers sucked out all my confidence, and I couldn't handle the pressure. I caved. "Sure."

"You can't just keep taking Lisa's food, Lily," Jenny Kim exclaimed, half an Oreo cookie chewed inside her mouth, sitting across from Lily and me.

"Lisa doesn't care and could've said 'no,'" Lily interjected, eating my Gushers.

"I'd rather have the chips anyway. Mom never buys this kind." I kind of lied, but it was true that Mom never buys Lays chips. Always Doritos. *Always.*

"What did you guys get on your English final?" Lily asked us.

"85," Jenny Kim said, sounding like she didn't really care but happy enough it was a B.

"I misspelled 'Italian'," I said, taking a bite of my ham and cheese sandwich, chuckling a bit.

Lily let out a laugh. "AH–Me too!" We both started guffawing at our stupidity.

"It was in the *prompt!*" Jenny Kim remarked. "You guys are *so dumb!*"

Jenny Kim and Lily were two of my closest friends at school... and kind of my only friends.

Lily was a teacher's favorite, always answering questions and asking to help with everything. She was, however, pretty picky... about everything as well. She liked the nicest clothes, wore fake nails every day, and didn't like it when her food touched. Her personality wasn't one I would choose to be around, but Lily was the first one I met when I moved to New Jersey; therefore, I was thrown in with the cool and pretty girl group even though I didn't feel like I fit in. Small body, no tan, one default hairstyle—the complete opposite of the word "popular." Lily taught me a lot: how to do my makeup, what clothing was in style—even though I never noticed I was "out of style" before—and what TV shows were the best to watch. However, the most crucial thing Lily taught me was how to blend in and be liked. It just sucked that you couldn't try something new without the fear of being judged and called "a freak."

Jenny Kim was the opposite of Lily, with only confidence and gorgeous hair in common. She was friends with Lily before I was, so they were much closer. She's Korean but was born in New Jersey, which seems to have helped her popularity in our small-town school. Unlike Lily, she was high up in the socio-educational food chain, not because she had the prettiest clothes or a blemish-free face but because she was amazing at basketball. Her best quality, the one I admired most but one nobody seemed to care about, was that she never was afraid to voice her opinion or live in fear of what her peers thought of her. I looked up to Jenny Kim because I wanted to be as confident as she was.

Though Jenny Kim and Lily invited me to join their friendship circle, I always could tell they didn't care for me as much as they cared for each other... but, then again, it could've just been my self-doubt talking.

"What are you doing over the summer?" Lily asked us. Before we could answer, she had already decided to voice her plans. "*I'm* going to the Camp of the Arts."

I was a little curious. "Isn't that super expensive?" I took another bite of my sandwich.

"Has to be," she responded, seemingly proud of the fact that it was. "It's where you spend your whole summer with professional designers, musicians, and painters. I told Mom I needed to go if I wanted to become a fashion designer one day, so she is paying for me to go the whole summer." She ended her declaration by taking another sip of her strawberry milk.

"You're gonna be gone for two months?" I said, shocked.

"It's in Philadelphia, so it's only, like, two hours away. I can come see you guys on the weekends unless the designers need me there to model their new clothes."

Jenny Kim rolled her eyes before making eye contact with me. "Lisa, what about you?"

Next to Lily's summer plans, mine seemed so lame to say out loud. I had about one second to think of a better way to say "nothing."

"My mom normally plans something fun for the two of us. I think she might take me to the beach or something." I lied again, sort of. I mean she *could* surprise me with a beach trip, but the possibility was quite low since she hates traveling and sand. I quickly turned the attention back to Jenny Kim. "Are you going to visit your dad's family this year?"

"Nope, Mom's." She popped a cocky grin before taking a bite from her PB&J like she wanted us to be impressed.

It worked. "*You're going to South Korea?*" I exclaimed.

"Uh-huh! It's going to be so freaking cool! We leave in mid-June and will stay for about a month."

I was about to say something when Lily took back the conversation. "You better get a picture of the main city because no one will believe you when you get back."

"Duh—we are going to visit Seoul, and all the celebrities live there, too!

Mom even booked us a tour at one of the agencies where Korean pop stars work!"

"No one will know who they are, so it's not really gonna matter if you show off pictures of seeing them," Lily retorted.

Jenny Kim looked at me, then at Lily, and then at me again. We both started to snicker. Jenny Kim was not afraid to point out Lily's jealousy, and laughing at it was the best way to do so.

Lily's ears turned red, and she scrunched up her glossy lips. She stared at us holding in our laughs, pausing for a long time. "... *Stop it!*" Her smile broke free from her spiteful stare, and she immediately grabbed her trash and headed to the garbage can.

Jenny Kim and I lost our composure, and the laughs wouldn't stop.

The lunch bell rang as Lily threw away her trash, and Jenny Kim ran after her as I tagged along. Her black hair swooshed in her ponytail as she jumped against the back of Lily and pushed on her shoulders before sticking her landing. "Just admit you're jealous!" she said for all those around her to hear, though not many cared to notice.

"You're the worst friend ever," Lily remarked in her high-pitched voice.

I continued to follow behind them, giggling when I had perked up enough courage to attempt to join in. I was about to grab Lily's arm and tell her I'd be her friend if Jenny wasn't when all of a sudden, Jenny Kim nudged me to the side. It was by accident, seeing as she didn't pay attention to me almost hitting the brick wall.

My chuckling became more discrete.

"*Jealous~*" Jenny Kim sang, not letting Lily get away with her envious attitude.

Lily pushed her shoulder against Jenny Kim, which caused her to almost knock me into John Peters—right into the lockers.

"Sorry, John!" I quickly said, feeling the embarrassment turning my face pink.

"You're good," he said, never looking in my direction.

Lily and Jenny Kim didn't even notice the incident, continuing their happy stride down the hall—laughing and locking arms.

I hunched my shoulders, gripping the straps on my backpack. All the confidence I had to join in on the escorting down the hall was gone. I had hoped they'd notice, but like always, it seemed I was third-wheeling again to the next class.

As far as friends went, it wasn't like they were the best, but they didn't call me ugly or tell me to leave when I was around. They were the only ones, too, who bothered to give me the time of day when no other students did.

Would I choose them in a line-up of thirteen-year-olds to be my friend if a complete new girl said, "Hey, you seem pretty cool"? No, but our school was small... and I was shy. They were the only friends I had.

I quietly trailed behind them like I always did, keeping thoughts of Summer Break swimming through my mind to bring my mood back up.

One by one, kids started jumping into their assigned vehicles, fleeing the school car rider line as fast as possible. I took out my MP3 player and placed my earbuds in my ears, so I didn't have to wait in silence for my mom to arrive. Lily and Jenny Kim's moms had already picked them up from school, and I was stranded to wait by myself for the rest of the duration of 3:00 p.m. This was normal for me, though.

Mom didn't get off work until 3:00, and it took her about 20 minutes to get from the office to the school. She was an underwriter, but to be honest, I had no clue what she did. Something to do with math and accounting, but it was a little over my head. She used to work from home, and I enjoyed that, and I'm pretty sure she did, too. She loved picking me up early, spoiling me when I was sick, and spending all the school holidays with me.

Almost four years ago was when she started working from the corporate office near Keyport. I remembered her asking me if moving was okay, which was odd because I was just a kid. We lived in a dinky two-bedroom apartment in Lexington, Virginia. I was coming out of fourth grade, still questioning if Santa Claus was even real or not, and she asked *me* if it was okay. She didn't sugarcoat anything—didn't even bother to cover up her distraught emotions.

She just said, "Lisa, work offered me a better job, but it is all the way in New Jersey. I don't know what to do, so I want *you* to decide for Mom, okay?"

This was the first time I saw tears in her eyes. I thought only kids and actors in movies cried, so I knew it meant a lot to her.

I nodded my head, and she continued. "If we move to New Jersey, I will be able to buy us a nicer house, and I'd be able to have the weekends off with you, but I won't be able to work at home. If we *stay*, I will have to take up some work on the weekends, but we will be here with all your friends, and I can work from home." She was sitting on the couch with both of her legs crossed like a toddler in kindergarten. My hands were grasped in hers as she waited for my answer.

Most kids would've said whatever their parents wanted to hear or would've made some type of deal where if they move, they will get more toys or the best room in the house. Kids would've merely picked the option that the parent convinced them to sound the best. Mom was right: I would still have her there and all my friends if we stayed.

I remember looking at Mom and telling her my answer. "I wanna move."

Little nine-year-old-me thought about the pros and cons and ignored them. I was a child, but that didn't mean I was inconsiderate. Mom clearly wanted more money for us and to be away from Grandma—starting a new life with just the two of us. Maybe she thought I wouldn't understand the true worth of money, or maybe she just wanted to have an excuse for why she shouldn't take it, but I could feel the worry coming through her words when she asked me. I was already happy where I was, not because of my friends. It was her. Choosing something to make Mom happy wasn't a hard choice at all—

"*Lisa!*" an all too familiar voice shouted, interrupting my thoughts outside of school.

I paused my music and put away my MP3 player as a white Corolla came to a stop right in front of me. Sounds of old 80s music were playing out of the rolled-down window. I walked a couple of steps, opened the door, and slung my backpack to the car floor, and Mom started to drive off.

"Hey, sweetie! How was school?" Mom said cheerfully, turning down the music. She wore pastel green work pants with a white blouse and matching shoes. Her hair was clamped back with loose strands dangling beside her clay-made earrings. She only had a little mascara on, and her peachy lipstick had faded away since early that morning. She still looked as pretty as ever.

Mom was born with a type of coveted natural glamor, more so than most moms I knew. She didn't need makeup—never wore much, to begin with—and was skinnier and more toned compared to my friends' moms, but that also had to do with her age. She had me when she was only nineteen years old, and whenever we were out together, a lot of people would think she was my aunt or much older sister.

People say we looked extremely alike, but I didn't see it. She had thicker hair, tanned skin, and a narrower jaw, while I was stuck with a baby face covered in freckles. We both did have the same eye color, but boring blue was nothing to brag about, and we both held the same destiny: never to reach above the height of five-foot-four without high heels.

"Good," I responded.

"Oh really? So your English final went well?"

Most parents would stop after their kid says "good." I thought most people assumed that "good" was code for "don't talk to me," but it wasn't. It was more like a test to see if you genuinely care about the person's day or if you're just trying to break the silence. Mom always cared.

"Yeah, except I did such a stupid thing," I said.

"Oh, don't say stupid—did you spell your name wrong or something?"

"I misspelled Italian…"

"That's not so ba—"

"The prompt was 'Write a short narrative about an Italian chef.' "

Mom paused.

"Italian is in the title, Mom."

"Ah, and you—"

"*Misspelled it!*" I huffed.

Mom tried to hold in her giggles but couldn't help it. Her laugh seeped through her teeth, making her sound like an elephant with its nose tied, causing us both to laugh even more.

"I'm sorry, sweetie," she said, her laughter dying down, "but I'm glad you still did well. I'm making enchiladas tonight. Is that alright with you?"

"Sounds perfect, actually."

The drive home beamed with serenity more than usual, making it perfect for daydreaming. All the clouds were plump and puffed, forming various shapes in the deep blue sky, a perfect near-summer day. The ports were packed with boats, most of which had just come in after a long day at sea, and many people walking their dogs flooded the sidewalks as we started to come to the heart of Keyport.

Our neighborhood was toward the end of the crowded area, right where the trees popped up and the tall buildings dissipated. It was much nicer compared to our small apartment back in Virginia. Finally, we had a dining room and a garage instead of street parking. We now lived in the middle of the suburb—the house with the only light blue door—but it was surrounded by trees, providing us with just enough seclusion from the rest of our neighbors.

For it being only me and Mom, our little home was perfect, especially the laundry room—never thought I'd say that in my lifetime. This was where you'd find the prettiest view of the sky. The two skylights angled with the roof perfectly, and tonight—after enjoying the *best* enchiladas in the world—the moon was shining bright enough to paint the walls with a blue light.

I was removing my clean clothes from the dryer, admiring the summer night sky. It was rather beautiful, so I glanced up for a while, not worrying about all the soon-to-be wrinkled clothes brushing against my bare feet. Thousands of stars were visible, forming various constellations, but I could only point out the Big Dipper.

When I threw my favorite light blue hoodie into my plastic hamper, a star twinkled—winked at me from the window.

Stars glimmer, but this one kept shining. Its glow grew bigger and bigger until it was the brightest one in the sky.

I didn't pay attention to the shirt I grabbed or if I even was holding a shirt. That star wasn't growing; it was *falling*.

As if it saw me gawping at its glow—a *purple* glow and not the usual yellow or white—that iridescent star *shot* out of the sky like a celestial bullet. Cosmic lightning of bright magentas and sunset oranges flared from the fiery orb, leaving a luminescent trail as it poked through Earth's atmosphere.

What the...

I thought it would do what shooting stars do, vanish as quickly as a blink. But then that pluming wisp of alien lights plummeted into the forest of my backyard. Crackles of thunder *boomed* when it landed, causing me to drop the clothing in my hand. The light fell about 100 yards away, but I swear I heard debris hit and bounce off the windowpane as the trees danced from the crash of the fallen light.

My eyes stayed wide. My stance was frozen. *Was that... Did I just see a shooting star? Things like that don't happen—things like that* can't *happen... right?*

"Mom! Did you hear that?" I shouted through the house, my view cemented to the window. I knew she was still sitting in front of the TV, so she had to have heard the *boom*. I stayed paused but didn't hear her respond.

My leg hit the plastic hamper as I rushed out of the laundry room and through the kitchen, turning right to go toward our living room. Mom was lounging on the couch on her cell phone. By the irritating tone, I knew it had to be Grandma, which meant she probably wouldn't mind if I interrupted.

"Mom," I started again, "did you not hear that?"

"Hear what?" she asked, turning her attention to me.

"The huge *boom* that just happened in our backyard." My voice was growing louder. I walked past her to go toward the window near where she sat and peered through the blinds, thinking maybe some neighbors would be outside to investigate. "Something fell from the sky and hit our backyard. There was a huge purple light and everything—"

I stopped my sentence when I turned back toward Mom. The side window, directly behind our couch, had purple light glowing through it. It wasn't the best view, but the light was shone just enough to prove to Mom I wasn't seeing things.

"Something *did* fall!" I started running back to the laundry room, gesturing for her to follow. "Mom, come on! It's in the trees behind our house! You can get a better view from the laundry room!"

I heard Mom close up her flip phone, but she didn't follow. She instead went out the back door and stood on our small concrete patio that faced the forest of trees. After I noticed, I ran out to join her. Right amid our forest, the purple light was fading in and out like a candle's flame. *I can't believe this is happening!* My smile was so big. *I have to be the luckiest girl in the world right now—I cannot wait to tell Jenny Kim and Lily about this!* Finally, *something exciting happened to me for once!* When I glanced back at Mom to see her reaction, she did not seem impressed. She rubbed her eyes and furrowed her brows.

"I don't see anything."

2

THE DREAM

The relationship between Mom and I had always been pretty great. We liked mornings, binge-watching movies, eating pineapple on pizza, and most of all, we *always* saw eye-to-eye on everything—except on mushrooms (Mom thought they tasted gross, and I didn't understand why at all). If I thought a new movie was lame, Mom did, too. If I thought the cashier at the grocery store was intentionally rude to Mom for trying to find the exact change at the bottom of her purse, Mom thought the same.

The biggest thing—and, quite frankly, the most important thing—was that I would *never* put on an elaborate show to play a joke on Mom, and she was the same. Pranks were something our family didn't do. We enjoyed watching others pull pranks on TV, laughing until we cried, but that was all. Personally, it was not in my nature to be the center of attention or risk being yelled at by planning out some crazy lie just to say "I'm kidding" at the end. I would only fib a little to cover up my staying up late or procrastinating my homework, but that was *it*.

So, Mom not believing me about the *giant purple beacon in the middle of the forest* did not compute in my mind.

"What do you *mean* you don't see anything?" I shouted, baffled. "Mom, there is a giant glowing purple light out in the middle of our backyard!"

Mom rubbed her eyes again, middle fingers squishing near her tear ducts, and traded stares from the forest back to our neighbors' houses. "I don't see what you're talking about, sweetie, and what were you saying about before—about that loud noise?"

I was starting to lose it. "Something *literally* fell from the sky, Mom. It landed and made a huge booming sound—" I started adding hand motions to prove my point.

All the while, Mom just kept staring at me with her arms crossed.

I gestured toward the laundry room window to finish my argument: "—debris even *hit* the window!"

Mom's cell phone started ringing in her pocket, distracting her from my evidence, but my focus was back on the window. Outside the laundry room, Mom had this gnome, a kitsch form of art if there ever was one. It came with the house, and we never bothered to get rid of it when we moved, so it was now a staple of our garden. The gnome stood right next to these blue flowers, and it was the *most* unstable thing ever made. A bird could knock it over if it even just perched atop the gnome's hat, but at that very moment, it was standing perfectly straight, proudly watching over the garden. The mulch around the gnome even looked properly placed.

This should've fallen over from the wind alone. I could've sworn that rocks and dirt hit the window. I was now starting to question if I was going crazy or not. Turning around, I also noticed everything was really quiet. *Where are the neighbors?* I could only hear Mom answering her phone and an owl cooing in the distance. *Shouldn't the Chambers' dog be barking by now? Why does it seem like I'm the only person who saw anything?*

"Hey, Ma, can I call you back? Give me one minute," Mom quickly concluded, closing her phone before returning to me.

I was now standing in the grass, barefoot with my long hair tangled at the curled ends, looking pretty stupid, glancing back and forth from the gnome to the window to the neighboring houses.

"Lisa—" she started, but I couldn't stop talking about the phenomenon.

"Look, Mom, I *swear* something crashed to Earth! It's out there—look it's *still* glowing—and I promise you I heard a loud noise, too. Are you *sure* you don't see a purple light out there?"

Mom looked again, but I could tell she had already given up after seeing nothing the first time.

"I think all those late nights playing video games have gone to your head,

Lisa. Grandma just called, and I better call her back before she gets upset, and *you* still have school in the morning. Let's just go inside and call it a day." She had already left the back porch before I could even respond.

I waited a couple more seconds to see if something would happen. I thought about running out there, grabbing whatever it was, and bringing it back to prove I wasn't lying, but that idea was interrupted by her yelling, "Lisa, come on!" through the screened door. I walked back inside like she said to avoid getting into trouble. My mind was just not ignoring it, though.

The purple light still glistened from behind the trees as though it were reaching out to me—taunting me with its mysterious aura—but I slowly shut the door.

I waited patiently on my bed, squeezing my plushie stuffed cat, listening for all the cues Mom gave off to signal she was about to go to sleep. I heard the five creaks from the stairs leading up to the house's second floor, trailing toward the bathroom. After about ten minutes, I saw the bathroom light go off; she had just finished her nightly routine and brushed her teeth. Her door then shut, and the white noise machine turned on, which meant I had about ten more minutes of being in silence before I could make my way to the back door.

A constant plethora of questions ran through my mind in those bitterly slow minutes. *Why couldn't Mom see the light? Can only certain people see it? Maybe this is a good thing—maybe it is a star!* I fiddled with the toes of my stuffed cat. *Wouldn't it have made a bigger crash? Can it be an alien, like in the movies?* I eventually got up and paced the diameter of my purple rug, going back and forth from wall to wall, and every couple of seconds, I would check my window to see if the light was still glowing amid the trees.

It was still there, providing a dim, jeering light to my bedroom.

As the last minute of my countdown began, I threw on my oversized sky-blue hoodie and some white socks. *20 seconds left.* I grabbed my black sneakers, but instead of putting them on just yet, I held them close to my chest to subdue as much noise from the floorboards as possible. *8 seconds left.* I sat on the edge of my bed.

3... 2... 1...

The ten-minute mark had now passed. It was time.

Quietly, I opened my bedroom door and started to head downstairs. I knew exactly how to step onto the stairs without creating any noise (due to the many midnight Oreo runs to the pantry), leaning toward the wall and skipping the fourth one down. Once downstairs, I had a little more freedom to move around swiftly since I knew Mom wouldn't be able to hear me too well with her white noise humming. So, I laced up my sneakers and went straight to our garage in search of our flashlights. Found them and picked up the biggest one, testing it to make sure it worked by flashing it once along the wall. It worked as it should. Slowly, I opened the back door, giving myself just enough room to slide by. Beyond the trees, the purple flickered bright, making the shadows of the lush branches softly dance in the breeze. *It's still there.*

I ran, not very fast… but fast enough to avoid being seen by any night-owly neighbors. The yellow beam from the flashlight began to grow steadier as I inched closer and closer to the trees.

The cool magenta hues beamed softly through every tree branch, teasing, calling out to me.

How can Mom not see this? There wasn't a definite entrance to the midst of the trees, but to my right was more worn down than the rest. I took a deep breath and stepped forward, following the amethyst glow.

My heart started to race. Normally, I would be hesitant to run straight toward the woods—too many spiders and unknown animals waiting to crawl on me without my consent—but not this time. Over and over, ideas ran through my mind of what the light could be. *It's gotta be a star! But wouldn't it be bigger? Is it a part of a satellite—could it explode? Why didn't it burn through the trees?* I picked up the pace, getting snagged by branches and tripping over more tree roots. *How many more steps? Ten? Twenty? I want to see it! I have to!*

I reached the middle—a small, treeless circle of the forest with patches of grass growing at random in the dirt—and there it was. The purple glow came from a… floating light not but three feet off the ground, wafting, beaming, no bigger than a basketball. I couldn't tell if it was a star, but the center of the light glowed a soft white, fading from orange to magenta, and then to a neon purple. Warming energy plumed off the flame like fire, but after stepping closer, it was more like warm-blanket heat: comforting. It moved delicately like loose ink in water, dancing up and down with its light flares, the prettiest thing I had ever seen in my life.

"Wow," I said softly. I couldn't take my eyes off of the light and slowly started to pace around it. I circled the glowing flame two times, then three, then four, checking to see if it was an illusion or something real. *It's real, alright.* I didn't see any weird space debris, so it being an alien or a part of some satellite seemed unlikely. My next guess was that it had to be a fallen star. *Is this what shooting stars really look like up close? Aren't they supposed to... shoot away and not float in slow motion?* I waited a bit longer to see if it would move, make noise, or do something weird, but it just kept floating in the same spot. Kept taunting me— *begging* me to inch closer.

So, I did.

Still, the hovering orb of quiet flames didn't budge, and the only sounds to be heard were from the crickets hidden in the grass and my heartbeat blaring in my ears.

I didn't see anything threatening about it, and honestly, it was quite soothing to admire. *Kind of looks like the glowing jelly in a lava lamp this close... Wonder... Would it burn me? Wait—no, it didn't burn the trees or singe a single leaf...* I then moved even closer, extending my arm slowly. "What happens if I touch—"

The moment my index finger made contact with the light, something pushed me back onto the grass—stronger than a mere gust of wind—and I saw the light coming straight toward me. It all happened so suddenly that I was unable to react, dropping my flashlight and falling on my back hard. Twigs snapped beneath me, and my spine ached from the tree root I thundered upon. When I recollected myself, I stood up quickly.

The light was gone.

"Where did it—"

At that moment, I remembered what had just happened. I didn't even dust off the dirt from my thighs or get the mess of leaves out of my hair. My eyes grew wide, and I started patting myself down as if I would somehow find the light pocketed in the seams of my hoodie. My frantic search soon became a frantic realization. The light... it was what zoomed toward me. It was what pushed me down and had now vanished. *What if... it's in me—inside my chest right now!*

I wanted to shake off that assumption, seeing as I wasn't glowing and felt completely normal, but I knew what I saw.

Though, what followed was nothing but woodland stillness, as if a free-floating flame didn't just smack me to the ground. The trees were quiet, and the crickets continued chirping. Just like before, it seemed I was the only one who saw or heard anything. *I'm not crazy, right? That just happened. No wind pushed me—there isn't even a gust of breeze hitting the trees. I clearly saw a light fly into my body... So why does everything look and feel so normal?*

With the night continuing its midnight humming, I picked up my flashlight I dropped when I fell and started walking home. I followed the path I formed in the weeds of the forest floor to make it to the back door, but my mind was not resting. *Did I really see something? I had to have! What if something happens to me? I can't tell Mom. She'll think I'm crazy. Plus, she won't believe me anyway. She will just think I'm lying and get on to me about going out past 11 p.m.*

Just like before, I took off my shoes before going up the stairs—skipping the fourth one down and hugging the wall—and headed to my room. I went straight for my full-length mirror to see if I looked any different. Besides my ankles and knees being dusted with dirt and scratches from the trees, I still looked like a normal, though slightly over-freckled girl. I saw the time reflected in the mirror. 12:01 a.m.

I thought going to sleep would stop the worry, so I quickly wrapped myself in my blanket and shut my eyes, faking sleep until I drifted off. *Just sleep it off until tomorrow. Everything is fine.*

The worrying couldn't wait until tomorrow. I could *not* fall asleep. Perhaps, it was fear or some form of excitement, but my heart and mind were working together to make me continuously relive what just happened. *What if that light is just swishing around in my bloodstream right now—what if the government does experiments on me? Would they know—what if they know right now—*

I grabbed my stuffed cat to see if it could offer comfort.

Nothing. Its too-cute face stared lifeless into my conflicted soul, making my worrying even worse than before.

Just go to SLEEP!

I made a cocoon out of my blanket with me inside, ignoring the smell of grass still in my hair as best as I could, but forcing myself to sleep had never been this difficult before, even on Christmas Eve. *You're fine, you're fine! Stop thinking about it for now!* I was not sure when my mind stopped chasing the unknown answers, but I soon tired myself from worrying enough to fall into a deep sleep.

An eternity of nebulas and stars surrounded me—vast outer space—as I stood on an island made of black sand. Planted on a barren land floating freely amongst the galaxy.

Where am I?

I turned around on the dune of onyx pebbles to see Earth behind me, so close I could practically touch the planet and ripple the oceans with my finger. Cosmic colors of the universe hummed music in my ears. Peaceful melodies, resembling a theremin's waves moving in slow, deep rhythms, played, mixed in with delicate violin strum patterns.

A force—my heart—yanked my attention away from the star's view of Earth, forcing me to face the center of the onyx-colored island.

The flame of purples, magentas, and sunset oranges was there—what I saw in my backyard—and it was held in a figure's palm. The silhouette wasn't dark or shadowy; it was bright. It resembled a human but the intensity of the light covered all sense of detail encased on its body.

I ran toward the bright figure, and upon reaching their presence, they held out the warm light to me, like a gift.

"What's this for?"

They didn't answer but nudged the purple floating orb they held closer to me.

I extended my hand, and the ground shattered like glass beneath my feet. I free-fell into darkness—nothing but the glow of purple falling with me—and the figure of light vanished. I didn't scream but focused on grabbing the glowing light.

I grasped the flame and pulled myself toward it, cradling it as a toddler does with her favorite toy. As my hand held the flames, I stopped falling. I was now floating—flying.

And the light started pulling my hand in the direction in front of us.

"Where are you taking me?"

It didn't respond or change speed. The darkness started to reveal objects again, bits and pieces of shadows forming in the distance. A dark blue night sky came into view, followed by clouds, then houses, and soon...

"My backyard? But why?"

I flew to the edge of the forest, and the orb, shining with gradients of a sunrise, went into the midst of the trees like before. I took one step forward in hopes to catch it again—

BEEP! BEEP! BEEP!

My alarm clock pierced my ears, jolting me awake from sleep. I hadn't felt that tired in a while, rubbing my eyes and stretching my arms as I slammed on the "off" button. I lay on my back, looking up at the ceiling as memories of last night resurfaced. Memories of the dream that was so bizarre it truly felt as if I were in space, following after the orb of light into my backyard forest.

I rarely dream, and when I do, it's always something simple and usually makes sense. This was by far the craziest dream I ever had, and the only explanation was because of what happened last night.

My palms rubbed deep into my eyes as I sat upright in my bed, the sun beginning to peek through my window. *Dreams don't mean anything. Just gonna go to school today, make it through the weekend, finish school Monday, and enjoy the summer—just Mom and me.* I jumped out of bed and decided to just spend the day like a normal Friday.

<hr />

Mom came around 3:30 p.m., and our ride home was a pretty normal one for a Friday night. We grabbed some fast food, made it home, reheated the food, and watched TV as we ate. When all the to-do list items were checked off for the day, my mind remembered the dream I told myself to forget.

Mom had been sitting in our tiny dining room since finishing dinner, working on budgets and card payments on her work laptop. I was fidgeting with the idea of telling her about the dream. She didn't believe me about the light. No *way* would she even consider my dream to mean anything significant either.

After a couple of minutes, I came up with a solution. I got off our couch and slowly went to the kitchen to dispose of my trash and wash my dishes.

"Hey, Mom?" I asked quietly, still walking toward the kitchen. "Do you ever have dreams that seem... real?"

She didn't break her stare from her computer—the glow enhancing the sapphire hues around her pupils. "Yeah, of course. Everyone does at some point."

So far, my brilliant strategy was working.

"Well, what if you had a dream about something that happened recently?"

I threw my trash away and casually walked to the sink. "Like, if you went to the store and saw something suspicious, and then, that night, you dreamt about that same moment again... would that mean something?"

"Did you have a weird dream about that glowing light you were talking about last night?"

My heart had never leaped so fast in my life. *Did she somehow know?* I just acted calm about it while I started rewashing all the forks in the sink again.

"Oh, that was just the neighbor's car," I lied. "I—I just had a dream about school and my classes and stuff. It just seemed really real, like I relived it all over again."

Mom must have been pretty distracted because that had to be the worst lie I've ever told. My face was directed toward the sink, and I could only hear the slow sounds of typing coming from the keyboard. For about five seconds, that and the running sink water were the only noises filling our house. I was starting to think she didn't hear me.

"So, Mom," I continued, "what do you think?"

"Oh—sorry, sweetie!" Mom responded. She sat back in her chair and picked a spot in the room to ponder over my question. "Well... I think when you dream about something you experienced before, it just means you are conflicted about something during that time. It could also mean that something about that day was important to you, and your mind just replayed it. Then again, it could *also* just be that it was the last thing on your mind before bed—all of this is subjective and just my opinion. I wouldn't read too much into it if you only dreamed about it once."

Hearing Mom tell me not to worry about it gave me some relief, and that was all I was hoping for. I accepted her advice with a smile and an "Ah, that makes sense" reply, and we continued with our night.

The last time I checked the clock, it said 11:45 p.m. I had spent my night gaming—forgetting about the freak experience in my backyard and the dream—but soon, my eyes started becoming lazy, and I couldn't focus on what my character was doing anymore. I shut off the console and quickly crawled into my unmade bed before my drowsiness wore off.

My eyes shot open in view of my dark bedroom. My back was all sweaty. My heart was pounding hard and quickly. *Thud, thud, thud*—thumping loudly in my ears. I had the same dream *again*, only this time the orb hit me with a cannonball of light when we landed in my backyard, jolting my eyes awake and out of the dream world.

My clock beamed 2:20 a.m., the only light visible besides the faint moon glow through my window.

I rubbed my face with both hands. *Why am I dreaming this? Why does it feel so real?* I was frustrated with everything that was happening, and I didn't know what to do. I tried to ignore it—tried to act like I wasn't going crazy, but this… this happening *twice* was no mere coincidence. I had to accept the fact that something *did* happen to me the night before, a glowing ball of light *did* fly into my body, and my dreams *did* have something to do with it.

I sat up in bed with my feet hanging off the side, hair tangled and damp from sweat. I remembered what Mom said about dreams, that they could show me I'm conflicted about something. *Duh, Lisa, but why the forest?* I glanced outside my window.

The forest looked completely normal.

Then—call me crazy—I thought my dream was telling me to go back out there.

It was the middle of the night, and I was about to run out to the dark woods alone because my dream told me to. Everything about the situation screamed, "main character of a horror movie," and nothing was rational. But I just had a gut feeling that something out there was waiting for me.

The heart-compelling forest glared at me through the window.

Lisa, you are officially insane.

With a deep breath and a head full of questions, I headed back downstairs.

I grabbed my flashlight, put on my shoes—not bothering to tighten the laces—and rushed out the back door in my pajamas. Summer dew seeped through my sneakers as I ran to the trees again. I regretted not putting on socks, but that feeling was overshadowed by thoughts of the strange fallen star and my otherworldly dreams. Reaching the forest's edge didn't slow my pace, and I sprinted down the same path as before, avoiding the roots I tripped over the first time. Before, I had a glowing light to follow, but this time, I was running blind.

I figured I would skim past something—anything that would help answer my questions as to why this all was happening.

I made it to the flat clearing, the small perimeter that grew no trees. The moon was shining brightly above, making it easy to see everything around me without much use of the flashlight.

There was nothing: just dirt, rocks, and the sounds of the wind hitting the trees. I paced back and forth a bit, waiting to see if something would happen. Crickets chirped, owls cooed, and my shoes crunched on the dirt. Nothing otherworldly or sounds of mysterious creatures to be heard.

Darkness shadowed me, and the comfort of the moon diminished the more my eyes surveyed the space beyond the trees. *Come on, light—dream—weird fallen star thing—show me something, please?* The sense of being alone in the woods was starting to creep up on me, sending rivers of chills down my arms and legs as the summer breeze blew in. I began to hear twigs breaking in the distance, shooting my head left and right. My body wanted to leave, but my heart said stay—*stay just a little bit longer.*

After a few minutes of walking in circles with nothing but the woods turning eerier by the second, I dropped my flashlight to the ground and squatted down on my feet with knees and hips bent, covering my face with my hands. I didn't cry but sunk into a sense of defeat—a sense of pure agitation.

"Can someone, *please*, just tell me what I am supposed to do?" I exhorted softly, feeling my frustration begin to take over in the form of tears.

A fluorescent blue glow started to peer through the space between my knees and drooping hair. I uncovered my distressed face from my hands to see flowing rivers of aquamarine light forming about ten feet before me. The glowing ribbons were drops of liquid crystals, flowing and dancing like saturated dye through clear water, but with a sense of direction—all gravitating toward a set axis point that was in a random spot in the air, three feet above the ground.

I stood up, bewildered at the phenomenon.

The glowing azure aura grew to the height of an average adult in just a matter of seconds. Blue ribbons transformed into sheets of light. As the last strand of blue met the axis point, they all combined and beamed a bright glow. An unusual soft chiming sound was made when the light glowed brightest, but before the realm of blue vanished, an ethereal figure came walking out of it.

She was the most beautiful lady I had ever seen. Her stature was tall with perfect posture, and her long, rose gold hair was styled in a thick braid over her shoulder, swimming past her waist. The moonlight glistened off of her layered garment, which consisted of a thick, cyan leotard underneath multiple sheer fabrics. Her forearms, ears, and ankles were embellished with dainty bands of strawberry gold, almost matching her hair color. An intricate belt hung around her thin waist, but the moonlight's radiance wasn't strong enough to show all that was attached to it.

I stood still as I watched her appear in front of me. I was not about to be the first one to speak—I was too scared and intimidated to even think of something profound to say.

Luckily, she broke the second of silence. "Oh, I hope I didn't frighten you," she said, slightly bowing as she spoke. Her voice was soft, sincere. Celestial.

Quickly, I shook my head before saying, "No, I'm fine." My voice was pathetic compared to hers.

I guess that was all she needed to grow more comfortable with me because she just started walking toward me, exclaiming, "That's so good to hear. I am Inna, a Keeper of Stars. I was not told we would be meeting out here, and I was worried you might run away after seeing someone appear out of nowhere. I am glad, though, it has worked out for the best."

When she spoke, she was very articulate and took the time to say each word perfectly, ending her speech with a glossy grin.

The angelic lady was now standing about six feet in front of me. Any normal person would have been conscientious about this whole situation—a glowing ball showing up, a stranger walking out of it asking if you're okay—but I had one question I wanted answered. If anybody could do that, it would be *her*.

"Do you know why that star fell from the sky and why it flew into my chest?" I asked. I sounded silly—a toddler telling her daydreams—but the lady dressed in the colors of the ocean smiled and knelt in front of me, making me just barely taller than her. Her face was glossy and wrinkle-free, and her eyes—the color blue never looked more enchanting until I saw the hues underneath her long eyelashes—complemented her tan, glowing skin.

She stared at me and made a smile, the kind of smile that was half-happy and half-sympathetic. "I do."

My heart and mind were finally released from their burden of uncertainty. I didn't have to guess whether I was just seeing things or if something was wrong with me. That internal worry I felt for two days was transformed into excitement, taking my mind on a ride of all the possibilities of what a fallen star could mean.

"So it *was* a star!" I said, smiling at the newfound answer.

Inna replied, "In a form, yes. A Wishing Star fell, not to be confused with a normal star."

"But I didn't make any wishes the night it fell—do they do that often, fall from the sky like that? Are you from a star, too?"

She quietly giggled at my questions, staring at my freckled, enthusiastic face, making the sweetest laugh. "You said it 'flew' to you, correct?"

"Yes! Flew right into my chest." I pointed to my heart.

Inna held out her left hand, palm facing up, her knees still bent. "Lend me your hand."

I did as she asked, placing my palm upwards as well. She took her free right hand and moved her fingers above my palm in an "S" shape. A glow trickled from her fingers, bringing forth a blue ball of light. It was similar to the purple and orange one I saw in the forest and in my dreams, but hers floated in the shape of a teardrop. It glistened like the ocean, radiating a gloss of seafoam green and turquoise blue.

And she just formed it out of thin air.

"What you saw, was it something like this?" she asked.

"Yes, but it was more like a purple and orange flame," I uttered, mesmerized by the sparkling wonder floating above our palms.

"What you saw that night was magic. It does take the form of stars in the night sky, but once that magic has fully formed, it will burst and find the first vessel it has a magical connection with. All magic looks different, and this is just the essence of mine—what it looks like in a physically projected form. Normally, when a Wishing Star releases its magic, it does not show a physical form like this; it will be unseen and can only be felt in the heart and mind of the person who possesses it. The magic that came to *you* is much more enigmatic and unpredictable."

She smiled softly, letting me glimpse her perfectly white teeth beneath her pink lips. "It *chooses* its vessel, whereas all other magic is drawn to a specific person based on their magical connection and lineage." The lady paused for a moment and took a deep breath. "I came here because this magic, the Agapéd Magic, finally chose its heart to fill, and it just happened to be *you*—a curious, young girl from Earth. I suppose that makes you quite exceptional, does it not?"

I never thought I was born to be something extraordinary. I grew up hearing adults and celebrities always pounding on the idea that you can be whatever you want to be with just enough hard work, and I believed that for the most part. You can work hard to live a happier life—relatively speaking—but hard work doesn't determine the correct timing, and you simply can't be something great without being in the right place at the right time. I lived in a small family in a middle-class neighborhood full of average people, *all* of whom resided in an averagely middle-class small town called Keyport, New Jersey. Nothing remarkable had ever happened in this town, so the chances of me being born in the time period when something *did* happen would be one in a billion. I could be the smartest kid in school and rank varsity on all the coveted sports teams and *still* never be known as "The Great Lisa Robbie," all because the timing wasn't perfect.

And yet, here I was being told—right in my backyard of all places—that my heart was chosen, out of every living person on Earth, to home magic.

"Magic... but why me?" I asked, speaking slowly while admiring the blue light floating on my palm.

Inna let go of my hand and grasped both in hers, making the ball of light disappear. "Where there is goodness in one's soul, there lies one's unwavering strength, and a heart is no different. What is your name, I should have asked earlier?"

"Lisa, ma'am."

"Lisa, it chose you because your heart is strong and good. You may not see that yet, but in time, you will. I promise." She smiled at me again, making me feel important and wanted. I had never felt that feeling with anyone besides my mom. It was a lot to take in, but this lady made it seem so real, and I was overjoyed.

"Wow..." I breathed and smiled back at her.

"Now then," Inna continued. She shot back up to stand in her perfect posture again. "Back to the reason I came here—we have to get going. I'm not usually the one they ask to bring the Agapéd Bearer, so I don't want to keep them waiting any longer than intended."

"Wait—we're going somewhere?" I uttered. She started walking away from me to the middle of the clearing, right where she appeared.

"To Haim Gana," she declared. She held out her hand as if she wanted me to hold it.

I hesitated, glancing back and forth between her elegant hand and eyes, wiping my sweaty palms on my track shorts. I turned my head and looked in the direction of my house. Sure, this lady gave me her name, but I truly didn't know who she was, and *what was Haim Gana?* I wasn't dressed for anything but sleep, and I wasn't allowed to leave my house without Mom or another adult—an adult who wasn't a *stranger.* Mom would have a fit if she didn't find me the next morning... but this... something in my heart told me this was right.

"Will we be back before morning?" I inquired timidly, fidgeting with my fingernails. "I just don't want my mom to think I'm missing."

Inna thought about my question for a moment before responding in her serene, positive voice. "I'll make sure you return before sunrise, okay? No need to worry."

With her affirmation and a smidge of trepidation, I took her hand. "Okay."

"Alright!" she said in a perky voice. "Since you have never evanesced before, be sure to hold on tight to my hand and stay close."

My answer was my grip around her left wrist, tightening, and my heart pounding against my ribcage.

Inna looked down at me, her voice squeaked. "Not that tight," she said, and I instantly loosened my grip. She smiled, helping my embarrassed heart not feel guilty for almost squeezing her wrist off. "Just do not let go, okay?"

I nodded, pressing my lips together to form a thin line.

She lifted her right arm, forming a fist. Blue lights—ribbons of liquid *magic*—radiated between her fingers and knuckles. She then gripped tighter and *punched* the air. Light encased the surrounding area—encased all the space my eyes could behold—and a rush of wind zoomed around us, causing me to shut my eyes tight. The sound of nocturnal creatures in the trees was replaced with chimes and claps of thunderous booms.

My feet were weightless as if gravity did not have any effect on me. I wanted to open my eyes, but the rays of magic prevented even the smallest peep. When the light took over the atmosphere, I could tell the scenery around me had completely changed. The teleportation only lasted a matter of seconds, and when I felt solid ground again, I opened my eyes—in view of an ethereal planetary kingdom.

3
I CAN DO IT

The sky was a gradient of blues and greens, patterned with silken clouds and doves with wings like dragonflies as we stood in the middle of a lush field. Breezes blew soft and light, carrying scents of sweet peony and rose water along their path. Stone mountains, covered in moss and succulent greenery, stood stories high, poking the clear atmosphere; I never thought rocks could be that tall. The plains expanded wide—farther and farther the more my eyes lingered—shifting from blades of rich emerald grass to flower-covered fields, all intertwined with quartzite and chalkstone pathways. Purple-petaled trees stretched with the fields and mountain tops, and when the wind blew, it strung along the loose blossoms to detail the earth. Rays of warm light peered through the clouds and the mountain gaps, resembling blurred, transparent rainbows. I wanted to touch each strand of the sun's beauty—to drink the colors it poured over the endless abundance of verdure.

Is this actually real?

My brown hair whipped off the shoulder of my hoodie, wafting the sweetness of the land into my nose and mouth. Something caught my gaze to the left of me, and I thought it was a bug. I turned my head to see a flower floating at a mere two inches tall. It landed in my hand and uncovered two little black eyes from underneath its pastel petal in its center.

It was the cutest thing I had ever seen. I thought it stood up, but its little green legs were so short that I couldn't tell. It waved at me with its petals before the wind carried it off.

A flower just greeted me! "This place is amazing!" I said, smiling from the pure excitement and bliss. I didn't even notice my hand wasn't holding Inna's anymore.

"Welcome to the realm of Haim Gana," she happily affirmed.

"This is where you live?" I inquired, stopped in place, feeling the thin strands of the plush grass grazing against my calves, still admiring the scenery.

"My home is on planet Kalm," she said. She looked back at me, gesturing for me to walk alongside her and down the knoll of purple flowers. "However, this is not Kalm. You are in a realm not to be confused with a physical world you're familiar with. While planets are tangible, physical places, realms are metaphysical worlds. They exist in between the reality and fantasy of one's mind—through one's magic... but only if their magic is strong enough, enabling them to manifest an entire world completely constructed from their magic pulse. I have been here in Haim Gana many times, though, so I learned the ways around the courtyard grounds and outer fields."

"Whoa—so is this place actually... *real?*" I asked Inna, tagging along beside her as she began to walk through the thin grass and purple petals, the little bug-flowers gliding by us on the strands of the wind.

"Of course! Just because it's made of magic doesn't mean the grass beneath us isn't soaking in the sun's rays or that the birds flying aren't beating with hearts. The maker of the realm brings in whatever they would like, adding a hint of their magic within each crevice and creation. Haim Gana is the purest realm, thriving from an immortal heart—a 'magic core' you could call it—because of Lady Ariela."

Everything Inna said was brand new, like a different language being spoken to me, so when I didn't respond, she looked down at me, seeing a freckled face completely lost in the dark.

Inna giggled. "Don't worry, Lisa. Everything will make sense soon enough. For now, just think of this place as a world within the world: completely real but living in and through magic."

We made it to one of the tiled, chalkstone paths and followed it toward the right. Each stone was clean—no weeds cracking their way through—and glistened pearly white from the light in the sky. There were not any signs of direction as I would normally see on a road or trail, making me clueless as to where Inna was taking me.

"We aren't too far from the Elysium," Inna stated as we started our path down the perfectly slated trail.

"What's that?" I asked, staring up at her sea-blue eyes and sparkly, dainty nose.

"It's the Great Pavilion's main domain for the Guardians and Elysians. It's a place of dignified meetings, discussions of magic, and a carrier of vast knowledge. Today, there will be a meeting about you and the Agapéd Magic."

Again, nothing she said made sense in my mind. *Is this basic knowledge that everyone is meant to understand, or am I just missing something?*

Inna turned toward me, smiling gently. "Don't be nervous, Lisa. In time, this will all make sense, but please, ask as many questions as you need."

Feeling more at ease, I asked, in mind of her first statement, "What are these Guardians and, uh... *Elysians,* you mentioned?" I had never even heard that word before.

"They are here to keep the balance between magic as it travels through nature and its creatures. Good magic is birthed from The Light, known as Ranemir amongst us few. Dark magic conflicts with light magic, causing ripples of imbalanced magic. Creatures become fiends, and nature falls prey to death, so the Guardians are here to rectify that."

"So, they are like protectors for magic?" I said, squinting confusedly.

"In a way, yes. For all planets in all four universes, actually."

The gentle wind tickled my nose, and I blinked rapidly. *"Four?"*

"Ah, I forgot! Your earth only knows of itself and its universe's planets. There are, in fact, four universes: Novatear, Cassiopeia, Luna Theta—Andromeda Galaxy is the name Earth is more familiar with—and the Milky Way."

We started to walk through a canopy of purple blossom trees as the path grew wider—curving alongside one of the tall stone mountains. Birds were chirping new songs, and more of the little flower fays floated by, making subtle glances at me and Inna. Despite my awe, I remembered why Inna came to me and why I was here.

"Do you know what they want to talk to me about?" I asked.

Inna let out a perplexed sigh as we continued down the chalkstone path.

"Honestly, I do not know the true intentions of the meeting. I was only sent to accompany you here."

"But aren't you a Guardian?"

"Oh—no, no, no," she reacted quickly, her hands moving in the air and jingling the rose-gold bracelets around her wrists. "I am a Keeper, one of the three Keepers of Stars. I apologize for the miscommunication. Like you, I am human, just with the magic of a Keeper. Guardians were crafted by The Light and the Elysian Lady Ariela, so they are not fully human nor fully celestial beings."

More bewilderment overtook my face, so Inna paused her confusing answer again. "They sound a little intimidating from a foreigner's ear, but they are wise and kind—and very excited to meet you."

"Oh, okay..."

The more Inna talked about magic, the Guardians, Haim Gana, and this meeting, the more trepidatious my heart became. I know she said not to be nervous, but after describing them and seeing their realm and the sheer importance of it all, I felt... beneath them. I was just a normal human, and these cosmic beings were "excited to meet me?" None of it made sense—even with Inna explaining it perfectly.

Maybe a normal thirteen-year-old girl would feel more confident, knowing they are chosen to have this peculiar magic inside them, but I felt unsuitable for such a power. *Magic? For someone like me?* It sounded sweet and charming at first, but after seeing this place and magic in the hands of someone as angelic as Inna... magic was becoming more overbearing—more daunting than delightful. My body was small, had arms like uncooked spaghetti noodles and legs as straight as a stick—pale bleached loaves of narrow bread speckled with paprika—and my emotions were barely stable in times of fear. Yet, Inna told me I was chosen for magic when I did nothing to deserve it, and that its "protectors"—these Guardians and Elysians—are wanting to discuss it with me. It's like a powerful king being excited to see a lowly peasant, one who isn't even a part of his nation, and granting them a royal gift.

The only sliver of hope—the only tiny bit of confidence I could find—was in the fact that Inna said my heart was strong. Although, I am not sure what a strong heart entirely means in this situation. Mentally and physically, I was kind of a weakling, but this Agapéd Magic looked past that... at least, that is what I gathered from her.

We turned the corner of a pointed mountain in view of a majestic palace of white marble, covered in greenery with crystal rivers flowing around it. It didn't look real—more of a finely detailed painting if anything else—and stood tall upon a flowering hill with stairs leading to its entrance. The structure was open, unlike a castle built for protection, with large columns that closely resembled Greek and Roman craftsmanship to my eye, even from the distance we were standing at. Past its immaculate gardens of hyacinths, baby's breath, azaleas, and vines of wisteria were fountains and ponds of the clearest water I'd ever seen—reflecting the washed rainbows in the sky.

Small pavilions and very peculiar homes stood among the lush plains and not too far off from the majestic estate's entrance. There were only three of these large houses, and they all were sporadically placed, each having unique characteristics. Even in my daydreams, I could never have imagined a place this lavish: a place where beauty was invented.

"That is the Elysium up ahead," Inna said, placing her hands on her hips. "I apologize for making you walk so far at the beginning. The Elysium prevents any new humans from evanescing into its domain."

"Uh, *evanescing*?" I asked.

"Yes, what we did to get here, the teleportation. Evanescing is a way of traveling through the seams of our universe by means of magic. Luckily, we won't have to walk much further. Follow me, Lisa."

Inna led us both down the hill, where our tiled path expanded to form a broader one that branched into all directions. We stayed down the middle that curved and paved the way to the entrance, circling two marble fountains spouting frosted rainwater. More creatures started appearing in the purple-petaled trees and at the base of the plant partitions. Some were familiar, like the white rabbits and doves, while others resembled flower fays and dragonflies with the grand wings of a blue morpho butterfly. I could have stayed in that garden for hours and never gotten bored.

The entranceway to the Elysium was an incline of three stairways, each section separated by a platform that included chalkstone benches, a pond in the center, and two more curved pathways that led to golden and pearl-like plants. Once my feet reached the second platform, my nerves panicked. I turned my head and back around to get another glimpse of the scenery, kind of wanting to go back. Everything was serene, which felt odd for a place of this enormity. That is when I noticed—

"Where are all the Guardians that live here?" I asked.

"They are inside, waiting," Inna kindly responded.

My eyes widened. "*All* of them? In *there?*"

"I didn't think it to be that surprising—" At that point, Inna realized I was assuming that this was a civilization of Guardians—a legion of magical protectors, to be more precise.

I was shocked when she said they were all waiting because, from out here, a whole civilization could *not* fit inside the building.

"Lisa—please forgive me once again," she said, smiling and laughing quite ladylike with her words. "I'm afraid I've prioritized explaining the wrong matters. The Guardians aren't a civilization of people but a court of only seven: the Seven Guardians."

I would've liked to say that helped ease my anxiousness, but by now, Inna and I had already made it to the top, and my heart wouldn't stop pounding.

The design of the entrance to the Elysium was a belvedere of windowless walls with tall archways that led to more gardens and balconies. Strings of pearls and pothos plants dangled from the ceiling and sunroof, almost touching the displayed statues. Each statue was crafted from frosted crystal or pearled marble, resembling unusual flowers, water bursts, and some magical-looking stars. I had never seen gems or stones like that—shining like opals with more colors than a rainbow.

At the end of the anteroom stood a large double-handled door, the first we had encountered. It had embossed designs of spiraled vines with pearl-plated flowers and leaves along with the panels. I stood back, watching Inna extend her hand to grab the right handle.

Through the door was a great hall almost four stories in height. Its walls were not cornered but formed a sphere with doors along its perimeter that led to more rooms and another hallway... still no sign of the Guardians anywhere. A mosaic dome of glass was in the center of the ceiling, providing enough light for Inna and me as we walked further in. More of the giant white columns were aligned along the walls, but the huge stone statue in the center was the most amazing.

A heroic man was depicted in battle, fighting off a shadowy beast five times his size. The stone structures around the man formed waves and movements like water, empowering his body and forming a sword in his hand. The sword pierced the shadow titan; the man won the battle. I had never seen such craftsmanship as this before. So perfect—so enthralling that I wanted to know his story. I wished I could've looked longer, but Inna was already heading toward another door.

She opened the entryway to a long viaduct with only a single golden door at its end. I followed next to her as we both walked toward it.

"Through this door is the Elysium's courtroom," Inna told me. It had been a minute or two since we last spoke. She turned to me and subtly grinned. "Are you ready?"

I didn't answer. I just took a deep breath in and released it slowly.

"Just be as honest and kind as you have been toward me, okay? I will see you when you return."

"*What—*" I squeaked.

We had already made it to the end of the bridge and were now standing in front of the golden door when she decided to tell me she was *leaving!*

"This meeting is only for you and the Guardians," she continued. "I was just sent to lead you here."

"Please, don't leave me!" I insisted, turning my body away from the door and facing her with my pitiful blue eyes.

Inna grabbed my shoulders with her petite and perfect hands and knelt, her eyes now looking up at me.

"Lisa," she began, calm and serious, "there is nothing to fear. You have shown nothing but good nature toward me, and I know they will see that, too. I wish I could be there—I truly do—but this is above me. The magic that is in you…" Her words softened. "We have waited so long to finally see it choose a heart again. Do not let fear get the best of you, okay? Now," Inna started to say as she gently stood up and turned me back around to face the golden door, placing her hands on my shoulders again, "all you have to do is go through the door, and the rest of the journey awaits. I believe in you."

"Okay," I said as the weight of Inna's palms lifted off my hoodie, and she evanesced away.

Near the door were plated mirror walls and two benches. I saw my reflection and couldn't believe I was about to walk into a meeting in my pajamas. My sockless feet inside my black sneakers felt all pruny from the dewy grass I ran through back at my house, and my baggy sweatshirt and gray shorts did not coordinate at all. I used my fingers to try and brush my brown hair, but clammy hands could only do so much. The only thing that was permanent, unfixable even with time or a trip back to my house, was the petrified, glossy spheres of sapphire blue in my eye sockets ready to spurt tears if these Guardians even said the slightest unsettling remark.

I took a deep breath in my nose and out of my mouth. *Here we go...* and I opened the golden door.

The door didn't creak when I pushed it, revealing a royal meeting room. It was small compared to the vast rooms I had previously seen but was still just as ornate and regal. The furniture was minimal, consisting of white chaise lounge chairs in the corners, no windows along the walls, thin gold and marble columns, and a stairway that led to a small balcony looking over the large round table in the center. This table was a circular, perfectly carved marble with swivels of gold brushed throughout. A large hole was cut out from the ceiling—the only light source in the room—where a giant green and pink tree grew upside down, letting its penny-sized leaves fall onto the table. There were hundreds of other mysterious details about the room, but my attention could not stay stable.

Seven celestial figures were all standing in front of their seats at the round table... staring right at *me*.

They had to be some sort of paradisiacal human—no one could look *that* perfect. There were four men and three women, each having flawless skin and perfect stature. I thought they all were wearing gold jewelry, but as I drew closer, some of the gold was part of their skin—freckled dew from the golden sun. Small aureate strands wrapped and patterned along their ears, noses, and fingers, and more cosmic colors of gold decorated the stitching of the multitude of fabric each wore. Their eyes were vibrant shades of blue and green—emeralds and sapphires didn't even compare to their beauty—and all pointed at my face... but not with excitement as Inna promised.

Every adult stared at me as if they just received the most disappointing gift of all time... well, except for the masculine older man at the end of the table and the youngest girl in the room. Still, I wish all of them had faces like Inna. *I really wish one of them were actually Inna—*

"Ah! The Agapéd has finally arrived!" bellowed the lone man who looked happy about my presence. He was the one with the shoulder-length light gray hair—half of it gathered with a loose golden strand—and with a dark evenly trimmed black beard. Along his ears were bands of aurous metal, the same went for his fingers and nasal bridge. Gold, gold, and more gold. And yet, his clothing was simple—navy blue with only gold stitched on his low collar.

The lady dressed in a gown of white and blue started walking toward me while the rest stood at the fronts of their armchairs. Her facial features were very sharp and feminine. She was the only one with blonde hair, too, pulled back in an elegant, precise ponytail.

She softened her once solemn look and grinned her perfect lips. "Welcome, my dear," she said in a smooth and gentle voice. She grasped my hand, leading me to the empty chair next to hers and a man dressed in purple.

My hands were on my lap, nervously shaking as the meeting began. *What is happening right now? These—these people are way, way, way more intimidating than I was expecting—golden freckles, royal robes and dresses made of liquid gemstones, and the perfect definition of human anatomy! And they aren't even fully human—*

"Now, Miss, what is your name?" said the same blonde-haired lady.

"Lisa Robbie, ma'am," I softly answered, fiddling with my fingernails under the table's shadow.

"Surprisingly well-mannered for such a young age," said the man dressed in dark-colored cloaks. He had slicked-back black hair with a thin mustache, making it easy to see the disgruntlement in his smileless face. Like the man with the silver hair and black beard, he wore simple garb—gold stitching only on the lining of his shoulders and cloak.

"You don't have to say it like that, Dayasheel," said the blonde-haired lady.

"Agapéd, I suppose Inna had informed you of why you are here, correct?" said another man from the table, one with waist-long brown hair, ignoring Dayasheel's remark. He was seated far right of me, seemed to be about fifty years old, and was the one who looked least excited to see me.

Um... was he referring to me?

My new name threw me off, causing me to mutter my meek answer. "It is about the, uh… Agapéd Magic, right?"

I know they could sense my lack of knowledge of the subject due to the lack of confidence in my answer.

The same long-haired man sighed, which made me tense up. "Yes, that is the basis of the meeting. I am glad to see you at least know that part."

"Vilmad," the man with the silver hair and black beard remarked, "do not blame our guest for her lack of knowledge of magic."

"I did not mean it like that, Emunah," Vilmad rebuked, his long brown hair shifting along his back, "but it is obvious we are all a little surprised, and that is no secret. I won't pretend like we were not expecting to see someone a little more experienced and more… *aged*."

"Age and strength of muscles have little to do with the strength of one's magic," interjected a younger-looking man seated beside me, brunette and tan. He was cloaked in many layers of purple silken fabric—the only one in purple. He then looked down at me. "Though… a child being chosen is quite unexpected."

"I will *not* have my words twisted to seem like I am against The Light and his gifted Magic," Vilmad said, raising his voice slightly and crinkling his middle-aged face. "But I can speak for all of us when I say that having the next Chosen be from Earth was *already* foreboding enough, and then, in walks a small child—this is not what we waited 120 years for—"

"*Vilmad!*" Emunah upbraided, firmly placing his hand on the round stone table, his once smiling face now hidden beneath his black beard.

"I am glad to see you've arrived safely, dear Lisa," a voice spoke from behind me at the entrance, calming the entire room.

That voice—*her* voice—would be how I'd imagined the voice of the rising sun to sound on a perfect summer morning. It was the sweetest and most pleasant voice I had ever heard.

The demeanor of the Guardians changed as I looked up from my lap to see their faces. They all looked behind me with eyes of reverence and respect.

I turned my body and peered my head out from behind the back post of my chair to glimpse at the mysterious person who called my name.

She could captivate a room of ten thousand, even if only visible for a single second. She stood six feet tall, adorned in gold and amber gemstones that matched the glowing caramel skin color of her perfectly toned arms. A garment resembling a dress covered her legs but glistened and flowed like the sun's reflection in the water. No earthly fabric from any tree, plant, or human imagination could ever create a dress that alluring—that radiant.

What truly set her apart from the rest of the Guardians was her golden wings—having the appearance and movement of a betta fish's tail. The wings were aureate gradients, starting transparent at the spine, growing more golden and clearer to the eye when they reached their end and kissed the tiled floor. Her hair was thick and tightly curled, almost matching her golden, bronzed skin. The strands were adorned with golden hair bands and citrine gemstones, complementing the solid gold circlet that crowned her head.

And I thought no one could ever compare to Inna's beauty, but this lady... she was what every star in the sky wished to gleam like.

The Guardians stood up, so I quickly stood as well.

This place—this meeting—everything is beyond crazy—what is going on right now?

"Lady Ariela, we apologize for beginning the meeting so soon," Vilmad said, bowing in respect with the rest of the Guardians.

I also bowed, avoiding hitting the height of my chair with my forehead.

"There is no need for apologies," she said in a kind voice, warmer than a patch of green grass drinking in the sun's rays. "I spent some time with Inna before she left Haim Gana, ensuring that Miss Lisa was well."

Lady Ariela slowly walked right up next to me. Her eyes were orange and gold, and her cheeks were brushed with the colors of peaches and dotted with faint copper freckles. She had a perfect nose and the most welcoming smile. "Miss Lisa, would you mind sitting next to me?" Lady Ariela asked me.

I was both starstruck and at ease with her words, nodding as I followed her to the other side of the round table. The Guardians moved down to allow me an extra seat next to this Lady Ariela.

When she sat down, her wings disappeared.

I felt unworthy sitting next to her, my clothing, heart, being, and all.

Lady Ariela turned to face me as she talked, treating me more like a welcomed friend rather than a stranger. She began by introducing the Guardians in a well-respected, highly regarded manner.

Starting from the left of me was Bethesda. She had the darkest skin and wavy nut-brown hair and wore a form-fitting gown of aqua blues.

Next was the man with the waist-long hair, Vilmad. He looked much older than most of the court, with a pointed nose and clean-shaven face.

To his left was Dayasheel, who had skin as fair as mine but without a single brown freckle. He was the one with the slicked-back black hair and only a thin mustache.

The purple-silked man I was previously sitting next to was Micah. He was calm and looked to be the youngest of the men around the table.

The creamy blonde-haired lady was Alona, and next to her was the gray-haired, black-bearded man, Emunah.

Sitting on Emunah's right was Rayna, the only other person who grinned when I entered. She was the shortest and had an angelic baby face. Her black hair was tied in loose elaborate braids, by far the most unique hairstyle in the room.

Last, sitting on my right, was the Elysian, Lady Ariela.

"Please, address me as you would a friend: Ariela," she said as she finished up the introductions. "Inna informed me she had already told you about who we are, correct?"

Yeah, but forgot to mention how otherworldly celestial each and every one of you were—

I paused for a moment, unsure if I was supposed to answer, and low confidence washed each of my words. "That you... help protect the light magic... but I'm not sure exactly what that means."

"We do protect what is good, which is what light magic is at its core, but we also keep the balance of light and dark magic that roams through every living planet. For you see," Ariela said as she started moving her hands to create golden, shimmering illustrations from her magic to help tell her story, "all planets, but one, are star-crossed with the knowledge of magic due to the envious nature of my late brothers and late sister Elysians thousands of years ago. The Light, Ranemir, is pure goodness and the purest form of magic. Ranemir made us Elysians to guard Darkness, the purest form of dark magic, from entering the world. Ranemir loved mankind and knew magic was too powerful for a human's heart. Unbeknownst to us, we Elysians were ever so tempted by the knowledge of dark magic as well... and my three brethren could not resist and cast the knowledge of dark magic out to Man. They believed magic would help Man be happier—grow humankind closer to us if they, too, had magic. They could not be more wrong."

Suddenly, her illustrations changed from gold to crimson as she continued her story.

"This caused the chaos of titans and cosmic disasters to form across the universes. In response, I called out to Ranemir to release his knowledge of good magic to fight off the legions of Darkness. I regretted not intervening sooner but vowed to make sure Darkness would not take control over all creation."

The illustrations then shifted to rose gold dust.

"Light and dark magic has since evolved, diverging to create marvelous variations of magical powers. Most magic is drawn to a person based on their magical pulse; whether that be by blood or by how their soul was formed in the womb, magic will instantly connect to the vessel it has the strongest connection to."

"Like how lightning will strike the strongest conducting point?" I softly asked, trying to understand what she was saying.

"Precisely," Ariela said, smiling, not bothered by my comparison one bit. "This can be anything, from people to animals to trees in a field or gems in a cavern. There is one type of magic that is like no other, for it *possesses* the gift of choice. It can neither be born into the blood of a certain lineage nor drawn to one's similar magical pulse. It grants astounding magic based on the strength of goodness inside the heart of its choosing. It will wait as long as it needs and stay as long as it wishes. This magic that we call the Agapéd, dear Lisa... has chosen you."

I felt a painful sense of underachievement, knowing I had accomplished nothing amidst the vast history she was showing before me, fidgeting constantly with my skin and fingernails below the cover of the table.

"Now, I did mention that all but *one* planet was cursed with the knowledge of magic. Before this planet could be reached, I deemed to protect it, for Man does not need magic to survive or to be happy. Ranemir knew that, and I respected his original choice and vowed to protect this planet—to keep it free from the temptation magic brings. The Agapéd is powered by free will, and we all are unable to tamper with the gift of choice, so the location and heart the Agapéd chooses we cannot interfere with... You may have noticed the Guardian's apprehension when they discovered the Agapéd had chosen you, Lisa... that is because Earth *is* the lone planet without a magical pulse."

Ariela ended her magical illustrations and turned her amber eyes back to me.

"Lisa, you were born on Earth, and yet, the Agapéd still chose *you*—the only bearer from Earth to have been chosen since the Agapéd Magic was formed. Your knowledge of magic is as innocent as a babe's, and still, the Agapéd saw unmatched potential in you—wanting a relationship with your heart. If you choose to follow this path, we are here to help you learn magic and all about the other worlds. This is quite a lot to consider, so if it all seems like too much of a burden, you may also refuse. It is up to you."

Ariela ended her speech, and now, the entire room's focus was on me.

I looked down at my fingers, red and pink from all my fiddling, considering the options like Ariela told me to. *Me? It wants me?* Being wanted wasn't something I was used to. Around school, many classmates only wanted me next to them because I took good notes or to avoid sitting next to someone they didn't like. I never was picked by a teacher to do their errands or called out for outstanding work. Even my own friends... the only two I had... never once made me feel more important than the other: mundane, optional, a second choice. Hearing these golden-skinned beings tell me I was chosen made me feel inferior like this magic was made for someone other than me.

Having magic would be cool though... would I really be able to handle something this amazing... something this grand? Maybe this decision would have been hard for some, knowing they had been completely oblivious to the realization that magical beings had prevented them from learning more about their universe. A whole new reality and way of life would be scary as well. For others, they would see this *magic* as a tornado, whipping their comfort zone life out the window. I bet—even if it were a small portion—that even some would still believe this was all merely a dream.

"I accept."

After considering all the pros and cons, saying anything other than yes was *not* even a consideration. I was chosen to have magical powers—nothing in the world could be more exciting than that!

I looked up toward the Guardians and saw Emunah and Rayna grinning, but the rest either looked indifferent or concerned. I thought being forward with my answer would give them assurance in me, but it only worked for half the room.

"Straight forward and confident—*I like it!*" said Emunah, making me smile at the white table.

Vilmad rolled his eyes and hastily interfered, "Are you quite sure about this Lady Ariela—I mean, this isn't really what we were expecting—"

"Lisa has made her decision, and I stand by it," Ariela answered the Guardian in the same calm and demanding voice, causing Vilmad to slouch back down in his chair. She then changed the direction of the meeting. "With Lisa's acceptance, let us begin our course of action. The Agapéd Magic has yet to show us what powers it possesses because Miss Lisa is from Earth. Vilmad, Emunah," Ariela addressed. "I assume you both have accumulated various aims as to how to draw out the Agapéd's magic?"

Vilmad sighed. "Given the time restraint of only a *single* day, there are two options we have considered that have the most valuable promise. The first is that Miss Lisa would study under us until her magic aura is strong enough. This will prevent unnecessary time consumption of running around trying to discover what magic the Agapéd chooses, and we will be able to tell which powers she has been given. Personally, this is the more logical option and one I would highly advise for."

"The other option," Emunah announced, "is that she trains under trusted *human* instructors, ones who follow the path of Light and are familiar with the Agapéd. I believe she would do well, studying under some guidance here with us, but being able to learn with other humans would help expose her to the unfamiliar worlds and allow Miss Lisa a more hands-on experience."

Vilmad rebuked, "Having her stay here would be *much* more beneficial—"

"But less effective," Emunah interrupted.

"I side with Vilmad on this one," Alona interceded. Her elbows were on the table, her fingers intertwined in front of her chin. "Having her be with us would ensure proper teaching and constant..." Alona paused her sentence and looked at me and then back at Emunah. "Supervision."

Emunah started to become more animated, using his arms as he spoke. "How is having her train with us going to improve our chances of guessing which magic the Agapéd has chosen for Lisa to learn?"

"He does make a valid point," Dayasheel said.

Emunah continued, "Here in Haim Gana, we would be just as in the dark since she doesn't have a magical connection or lineage, but she would not have to be subjected to what only lies in our realm."

"So, you would rather the child *not* stay here in Haim Gana—the most guarded and protected realm—and instead throw her out into the world of *Man*?" Vilmad berated.

"*I* think," Bethesda interjected, "we should stay on course on how to effectively draw out the Agapéd's chosen magic for Lisa, and *then,* we can choose her place of stay."

Emunah and Vilmad relaxed in their seats before the latter spoke up again. "Micah," Vilmad said as he turned to face the man in purple, "in your studies of Magic Evolutions, have you come across any creature or human who has imparted some of their magic onto another who is without?"

Micah thought for a second before speaking up. "This may not apply to humans, but I have done studies on many plants and ore that seem promising. The one most similar to this situation would be the homogeneous method. I experimented with daisies—simple, ordinary weeds—to see if they could one day produce magic. I planted these non-magic daisy seeds in different soils, including soils that produce magic herbs and fruit-bearing trees. When the daisies bloomed into flowers, all were completely normal except for *one* batch. I studied the soil where this one batch grew, and it was revealed to match the nutrients of the soil of the parent plants. In my conclusion, the daisies were able to contain magic because the soil they grew in was similar to the habitat the seeds were produced in. The daisies, more or less, did not see the magic as a threat because of the comfort of familiar soil."

Micah looked back at Vilmad, who now looked just as perplexed as me and the other Guardians. With Vilmad's stare full of regret and doubt, Micah continued to explain further.

"So, I think if we train and expose Lisa to others who have something similar with Earth, maybe it will help her attract magic, like how the daisies had similar soil to help attract their magic."

"Micah—out of respect for your knowledge—I don't think comparing the Agapéd to daisies is of much help in our current situation—"

"Comfort brings trust, so if the heart can feel comforted, it will trust magic to come and make a home inside," Rayna said, the first I heard her voice. She had such a profound answer and one that made more sense to me than Micah's scientific method.

"Then what shall we do?" Alona asked rhetorically. "We cannot train her on Earth, where there is *no* magic."

"Being on a planet *would* feel more at home than a realm," Dayasheel interjected, continuously stating facts instead of picking sides.

Emunah smiled at him while Vilmad scoffed.

"Oh, you are all acting as if it has *feelings!*" Vilmad said, rather dissatisfied, his long thin hair flying off his shoulders. "It is *magic*. For magic to grow stronger, it just needs to be around more magic, and what better place than here, hm? It does not need to be treated as a spoiled child."

"Ah—because being around you is *far* more comforting than being around the soft hearts of Man," Emunah said, crossing his arms.

My shoulders tensed up. This was the first time I was in a meeting with arguing adults, and the fact they were all discussing *me* caused anxiety to fill my bloodstream. I did nothing wrong, but my heart kept saying otherwise with each pounding beat.

"Lisa..."

My eyes widened, and my throat dried up at the sound of my name being called by Ariela, ceasing the fidgeting of my fingers underneath the table.

The woman in gold continued, "What would you like to do? Learn with us strictly or test out Micah's theory and be around familiarities from Earth?"

Wait—what just happened?

I have never been asked by a group of adults what my opinion was, especially not for something as important and bizarre as *magic training—I don't even know what that entirely means!* Doing what adults say and never asking why is the whole point of growing up—in school that is. Students listen to their teachers, fill in the correct bubbles on their tests, don't question lifestyle choices, and casually move on to the next grade. When Ariela stopped the conversation to ask me something, I didn't know if any of my answers would be admirable enough... but I couldn't just not say anything. *Do I pick what sounds easiest, or what's the most fun?*

Then, I thought about Mom when she asked if we wanted to move to New

Jersey. She was the only adult in my life who put my opinion on the same level as hers, valuing it, and the decision turned out for the best. It wasn't easy to move, and going to a new school was tough, but it made Mom happy.

Before overthinking any longer, I replayed Ariela's question in my head. In complete honesty, visiting other worlds sounded like more fun than being stuck with a bunch of adults—especially since more than half of the Guardians seemed indifferent to the Agapéd Magic's choice with me. It would be hard, but nothing was scarier than being in that meeting. So, I made my decision.

"I like Micah's and Rayna's idea," I confirmed, still timid.

Vilmad, who was standing, sat back down, and Emunah smiled at my confident answer.

"Then, I agree, as well," Ariela said. "I think being around elements of Earth would be most beneficial for Lisa. Magic is an extension of one's strength. We do not want to build that power on a foundation of fear and hesitance of the unknown worlds..."

At that moment, Rayna broke the silence with a question.

"What if we have someone from Earth teach her magic?"

Everyone paused. *Wait—is that even possible?*

"There are only a handful of people from Earth that live across the universes, and none of them are qualified enough to be a teacher for the Agapéd—let alone know proper magic in the slightest!" Vilmad announced, disdain smothered on his agitated face.

Suddenly, the faces of the Guardians changed. Many of them grew wide-eyed, very taken aback. It seemed as if they all thought of the same solution at the same time.

"We *do* have three humans from Earth," Dayasheel said, almost like he had just surprised himself with the remembrance.

"The Keepers of Stars! Ah-*ha!*" Emunah reacted, smiling quite big. "Of course!"

"Inna would do quite well as a teacher," Rayna said, looking to Emunah on her right.

Inna? Like, the Inna that brought me here? She is from Earth? But I thought she said she lived on a planet called Kalm—

"I agree," Ariela said. "We shall have Inna be one of Lisa's teachers. What of the others?"

"Kamari would be the next choice," Alona started.

"*Excellent!*" Emunah concurred.

"*But*," continued Alona, "she could not possibly train a young student at this time. She is far too busy with the Wishing Stars. I vouch for one of us to be the other teacher."

"I agree," Vilmad quickly said, "and *I* would be honored—"

"*Declined!*" Emunah remarked. "Lisa needs to be around more than one teacher from Earth besides Inna. If Kamari is out of the question..."

Vilmad's face suddenly shifted from annoyed to appalled. Before Emunah could finish, Vilmad turned to Ariela. "We are *not* asking *him*!"

I looked around the room. *Who is this "him"?*

"What do you have against—" Emunah started saying.

"He is not professional enough to handle the responsibility of teaching the Agapéd—we all know that given prior circumstances—no matter how strong his magic may be!"

WHO?

"Isn't his settlement protected by an arboretum veil?" Rayna said, her index finger tapping her chin.

"Calendula—ah, in fact, it is," said Micah.

"*Perfect!*" Emunah exclaimed.

"He is far too busy with the Wishing Stars to spend time teaching," Vilmad burst, desperate to disrupt what was about to happen.

"Actually, the Wishing Star Migration was during Earth's last full moon, so he would have some free time before the next preparations," Dayasheel said. Vilmad turned to him with a look of slight disdain. "I was just stating a known fact, Vilmad."

"This is *absurd!* He is a brute and would *not* follow through with our teaching methods!" Vilmad announced, his true feelings laid bare.

"Lady Ariela, Vilmad is right about that," Alona said, taking Vilmad's side. "*He* has not visited us in almost a *century* and disagrees with our way of work and guidance ever since—" She cleared her throat and corrected her posture before starting a new explanation. "I just believe he would not treat or train Lisa correctly."

Vilmad gestured to the blonde Guardian. "Oh, thank goodness, *someone* is starting to see the situation for the way it is turning out to be—*him* teaching a *child*."

"He has refused many students in the past and, with the ones he has taken on, tends to do things in a more... intemperate way," Alona continued. "We can't afford his methods to hinder the Agapéd's success... I just think we should consider someone else."

Ariela pondered on the situation. The room stood silent again. I just wished that someone would have said this guy's name.

"I say," Ariela began, "we shall give *Gaius* a chance."

Gaius...

Vilmad slithered back onto his chair while Emunah, Rayna, and Micah looked rather pleased.

"Alona did mention that our relationship with Gaius has not been very strong. I believe having him help Lisa would allow that relationship to thrive once again. Calendula is *also* protected by the veil, as you mentioned Rayna, so the living situation would work perfectly as well. The obstacle that is Gaius' demeanor and teaching methods will have to be addressed, so we must enforce the importance of our teachings if he decides to train her."

"Having him teach is one thing, Lady Ariela, but asking to home a young girl for who knows how long? I cannot see him accepting that," Vilmad said.

"Oh!" Rayna began to say in her cheery, quiet voice. "The Balthiers live in Calendula! They follow the way of Light and are known throughout the town to be very kind-hearted and trustworthy! They also know Gaius and are such firm believers in us and the Agapéd. I am sure they would be more than thrilled to care for Lisa."

"*I like it!*" Emunah said, very content with yet another one of Rayna's perfectly timed solutions.

As Rayna finished, I hesitantly tapped on Ariela's golden shoulder. I was too nervous to even make eye contact with her, but I had a burning question that I needed to ask, one that was scraping at my heart and burning my throat. My heart thumped hard as I whispered, "Ariela, what about my mom and school? I am not leaving forever, am I?"

"Do not fret, dear Lisa," Ariela reassured me. "Inna made it very clear I not break her promise about returning you home before the sun rises."

Ariela then turned her attention back to the court and said, "Along with Gaius and Inna's teaching, Miss Lisa will also work alongside us as well. She will learn about magic and study the history and ways of our worlds. I will assign those jobs post-meeting. With Lisa being from Earth and still an adolescent, she cannot proceed as any normal chosen of the Agapéd. She would like to finish school and still be able to stay at home with her mother. It would be quite rude of us to strip that away from her."

"*School?*" Vilmad scoffed. "This could not *possibly* work. Every Agapéd prior has given up their former lives to train their power, for how can she expect to learn magic efficiently if she has a curfew we must return her by?"

"That would be quite difficult to handle, even for someone her age who already knew of magic," Bethesda said.

"Might I add?" Dayasheel asked, tilting his chin, asking for permission to speak even though no one seemed to acknowledge that common courtesy. Ariela nodded, and he said, "Though *most* of us"—his eyes drifted to Vilmad—"do not go against the Agapéd's choice, this idea of Lisa going through her Earthian studies is unconventional. We all know of the future ahead—"

"Dayasheel—" Bethesda hissed as if he was about to say something he shouldn't have.

The blacked-haired, thin-mustached Guardian rolled his eyes, continuing his explanation. "I am just saying that this will be tough enough as it is, as you—as *we*—all know. Not giving the Agapéd the full attention its magic deserves is wrong in my opinion."

Vilmad nodded a bit too haughtily. "I agree. We forget this Earthian life—let her grow her magic here—"

Emunah interrupted in a raspy voice, barring his forearms on the white table and staring down the long-haired Guardian, "She will be *fine*—"

Vilmad copied Emunah's posture. "*She* is a *child*—"

"Who was *chosen*—"

"With no idea what that even means!"

Alona rubbed her forehead. "Here we go again."

Vilmad heard the remark, as well as everyone else. He stood out of his chair and looked toward the golden Elysian next to me, pleading, "Lady Ariela, forgive

me and the ones who are *not* stating what is obvious here, but even if *she*"—
he darted his eyes of blue at me for a brief moment—"accepts this, that doesn't
mean she is ready or can do what she is called to—"

"I can do it."

*Oh my gosh—was that me? Did I really just say that? Why did I just say that
out loud?*

Everyone looked stunned after hearing my unprompted remark, not just
Vilmad with his baffled eyes.

I took a deep breath and continued with my subtle outburst, "It's—uh...
summer vacation at home right now, so I do not have school for another two
months... and I could focus on magic every day... for as long as you need me to..."

My reasoning was not thought out, but it was the only thing I could think of
at the time, no matter how pathetic it sounded.

"Agapéd," Vilmad said to me, filled with annoyance and bothersome
concern, scrunching every wrinkle on his forehead until his skin looked like
a row of udon noodles. "I understand your eagerness to learn something that
must feel so unbelievable to one of Earth, but won't your mother be suspicious
of where you are most of the day? I presume she doesn't leave you at home all by
yourself during summer."

"I can handle that part, too. I promise," I said with so much fake confidence
that I even surprised myself.

"You heard her, Vilmad," Emunah voiced. "The little lady said she can do it,
so let us not worry."

I looked at Ariela one more time and whispered another menial request,
"Would it be possible to return on some of the weekends so I can spend time
with my mom, ma'am—I mean, Ariela?"

"The weekends?" Vilmad gasped. "That is absurd—"

Ariela smiled at me again. "I see that as perfectly acceptable."

"Lady Ariela, I beg of you—"

With just a raise of her bronzed palm, the Elysian silenced the distressed
Vilmad. She then stood up one last time, saying, "With all that has been
considered and addressed, our path of the Agapéd Magic is as follows according
to Man's calendar: Monday through Friday, Lisa will spend time in Haim Gana
with us, as well as learning with Inna and Gaius. She will be evanesced here until

we can create portal potions for her to use. Lisa will return home Friday nights to be with her family over the weekend and continue her training Monday mornings. I know this is not conventional, but if Lisa is willing, then we will adjust as needed. We will need to prepare her accommodations and lessons, as well as visit Inna and Gaius and create a means by which Lisa can travel back and forth. Therefore, for the next seven days, that is what we will do."

Ariela turned to me. "You just get some rest this coming week. I will have Inna visit you once again on the eighth morning, the following Monday on Earth. Join her in the forest so she can bring you here to begin your training."

Alona veered her eyes toward Lady Ariela, worried and concerned. "Are you sure about this?" The blonde Guardian's tone was tense.

The golden Elysian didn't bat an eyelash, simply smiling at me before turning to her celestial court. "I will send Lisa back home, and we will resume our discussion when I return."

Everyone bowed as Ariela stepped up from her chair. Her golden wings returned as I followed behind, the shining reflection of the hem of her garment swaying back and forth.

Whispers and soft conversations began to emerge from Guardians, each still seated at the table, and they were obviously whispering about me. Though I did not know their voices well enough to tell who was talking, I did hear a female voice distinctly say, "Do you believe she will be strong enough?" to which a male's voice replied, "She will have to be..."

We walked through the golden door that led onto the arched bridge. The sky was bluer than before and filled with doves soaring high in the air. Ariela walked very slowly compared to Inna, soon stopping after only a few steps.

"I would like to thank you, dear Lisa," she said. "You acted most maturely despite many of the Guardians' poor demeanor. This life will be quite new and seem unusual at first, but I assure you that you are in good hands. Right now, it should be close to dawn at your home, so I will send you back to where Inna found you if that is alright?"

"It is," I responded timidly.

"The next time we meet, you will be on your journey of magical discovery. I am rather excited to see all the great things the Agapéd has in store for you."

Ariela sure had a way to make me feel safe and wanted, like how Inna did when I first met her.

"Alright then, are you ready?" she asked.

I nodded.

Ariela stepped back and made the same sign Inna did when she evanesced us to Haim Gana. The blue light appeared, and before I knew it, I was already back in the midst of the trees behind my house.

4

A GOLDEN PLAN

My flashlight remained where I had dropped it, its cone-shaped beam still stretching outward in the quiet woods. Suddenly, I found myself whisked back home, standing beside it as if nothing magical had ever happened.

Despite it being around 4:00 a.m., based on the darkness and silence of the neighborhood, I was not tired at all. Call it shock or excitement, but I could not believe what had happened. I had magic all inside me, waiting to be discovered! I ran through the grass blades underneath the shade of the trees as endless magical possibilities filled my head. *Will I be able to fly? What if I can use heat vision? Maybe I'll be some sort of superhero!*

Finally crawling up into my bed, I couldn't fall asleep, still smelling the scent of peonies and Haim Gana winds lingering in my hair. I was smiling constantly at all the ideas and wondering what the Keepers and Guardians would teach me— Inna and this *Gaius* guy too. Only a few hours ago, magic seemed to only exist in my daydreams and on movie screens, but now that it was *real...*

The more I pondered my new magic life, staring at the white paint on my ceiling, the more I questioned why this Agapéd Magic even existed. *Ariela said all magic is naturally drawn to creatures based on their magical pulse—whatever that means—but why can this magic choose?* Maybe I was thinking too much about it. I knew nothing of magic, so this could have been something completely normal that happened every couple of years. However, I did remember Vilmad saying something about "we've waited over 120 years." *Why did it wait so long?*

Did the Agapéd really not find another heart better than mine? I make mistakes all the time like any normal teen—I am nothing special.

It was weird to think I was this "chosen" one. I mean, I've harbored rude thoughts towards peers I didn't like all the time, procrastinated my chores, and lied to Mom about watching horror movies because I was dying to see them—though, after thinking the white noise on my TV would summon a ghost, I saw why she told me to wait until I was older. I definitely didn't deserve to be recognized as "good" or "strong-hearted," but now that I was expected to be, I wanted to give it all I had.

Laying on my bed as my digital alarm clock struck 4:32 a.m., I decided to be the strongest Agapéd Bearer there had ever been... even though that title and term still meant little to me. Still, I would shine with confidence and glow with kindness, emulating the same good aura Ariela did. Apparently, being from Earth was almost taboo. I knew I would be looked down on for that—all seven of those beings did, even the ones who smiled—not to mention my small size and young age, but I would not let that stop me. I would show Vilmad and the other Guardians just what I could do. I could do schoolwork *and* magic studies. I could *be* the Agapéd Bearer they were hoping for. I could do it, and I was going to do it!

Rays of sunlight were bursting through the window above my nightstand, and birds were singing familiar songs from their seats on the gutters of our roof, reminding me of how late I had slept in. It was nice to finally get a good night's sleep without waking up in a sweat. I happily jumped out of bed and rushed toward the shower, quickly brushing my teeth before preparing a late Saturday morning breakfast. I could hear the Reese's Puffs calling my name as I carefully ran down the stairs, hearing the sounds of the living room TV playing as I made it to the final step.

"Morning, Mom!" I said as I meandered my way through the kitchen, grabbing my favorite bowl and a gallon of milk from our fridge.

"Surprised to see you up so late," she replied, slouched on the couch while holding one of her many unique coffee mugs in her hands—this one a fat ceramic frog. "Did you stay up late playing video games again?"

Glug-splash—

I was so taken aback by Mom's question that I overpoured the milk in my cereal bowl, spilling it all over the counter and kitchen floor. She didn't yell, say anything out of the ordinary, or sound suspicious... but the moment she said it, my mind went into a frenzy.

... Oh, no...

I do not get surprised very easily. I had always been the level-headed one, never showing too much-crazed emotion. The only time I had ever been truly shocked was the day Mom hit a bird while driving, making us scream and swerve into someone's front yard... well, and the night the star fell from the sky. Those days were a mere hint of panic compared to the fear and startlement I felt when Mom asked that simple question.

"Uh—no, I was just, uh..." I started muttering while grabbing too many paper towels to clean up my mess without Mom noticing. "I couldn't fall asleep last night—lots of bad dreams—that's all."

"Oh, I'm sorry, sweetie," she responded as I wiped away the last bit of spilled milk. Thankfully, the sounds of the TV covered my clumsy mishap.

I had forgotten about Mom. I could not tell her—how could I? By *no* means did I have a way of producing evidence of magic, and it is not like she would ever let me leave Earth to learn how to master it... let alone believe any of this.

... oh, no, no, no, no, no....

My eyes widened, staring at my soggy cereal as an important piece of information scurried across my memory. Telling the Guardians I could handle the situation that was "convincing Mom to let me go off with strangers to learn magic" was something I had forgotten until now—*kind of important to the whole learning magic agenda, Lisa.* Sneaking around Mom to play video games during school nights was one thing, but sneaking off to a whole other world for days at a time seemed impossible.

What am I going to do?

I took a deep breath, trying to calm the hammering heart inside my chest, and poured out my soggy cereal before assembling a new one with just the right amount of milk and Reese's Puffs.

Mom asked what I wanted to watch the moment my bowl stood still on the coffee table. She passed by some animated movie, and we settled on that, though I did not care. There was one thing on my mind: I needed to create the most perfect plan I have ever imagined in my life, and I had less than seven days to do so.

⚬⚬⚬

The weekend passed by, and the last day of school soon approached. Still, I was drawing up little luck for a cunning solution to my predicament. Every scenario played out the same: me getting caught by Mom. I could not figure out a way to stay out all night without it being suspicious. The only plan that sounded sort of believable was telling Mom that Grandma wanted to spend more time with me, and in turn, let me stay at her house during the whole summer in Virginia. This was shot down quickly once I realized Grandma would probably call Mom one day and mention I was never there, to begin with. I thought about saying that Jenny Kim invited me to go to South Korea with her, but again, this would not work because I did not own a passport to fake an international-adventure-to-Seoul scenario. Saying I was going to camp came to mind, too, but most camps ended within a week or revolved around sports that Mom knew I did not play.

Camps... That's it!

The bell rang during my last seventh-grade biology class, and I shot out the door to find Lily. She was standing at her locker, dressed in blue and pink with her straight blonde hair tied high, and cleaning it all out before her second-period class.

"Hey, Lily," I said, out of breath, trying to act natural even though I had just sprinted down the hall, "do you have a flyer or form about that Arts Camp you're going to?"

"Yeah," she responded, turning her blue eyes toward me.

"Do you think I could have it?"

"Sure, but it's a little late to sign up." She rummaged through her backpack until a folded, partly crumpled piece of paper was in her hands. "You will have to pay an extra fee."

"Oh, that's fine! Thanks!" I said, ending the conversation before she asked more questions, and headed briskly to my last English class.

Mrs. Pelts—dressed in greens and in a shirt that was too small for her stomach—had the class pick a movie to watch (*Shrek 2* won by a landslide) and turned off the main lights in our classroom. Luckily, I sat near the windows so I could still see. Most students were either whispering or watching the movie, freeing me from unwanted stares. *Not being popular or in a class with my two friends actually came in handy today...*

I unfolded Lily's Camp of the Arts form and read through every sentence very carefully... and my perfect plan started to transpire. For the remainder of the class, I carefully assessed every possible situation and all the "what ifs" that could occur, but this plan was gold. Sure, the whole framework of my strategy *could* have been considered *lying*... but I had no choice. I had to do this—for the Guardians, for magic, and for the Agapéd inside me. If I said and timed everything perfectly, I would be a certified genius of problem-solving—*not lying*—and on my way to a world of magic.

That night during supper, Mom made us mashed potatoes, peas, and grilled chicken with a side of those little rolls you buy from the grocery store's frozen section. We sat at the dining room table since Mom had all the clean towels stacked on the couch waiting to be put away, her heart probably calm and mine running like a hamster on a wheel.

There was light small talk, mostly about Grandma and Grandpa wanting to see her and Mom ranting about all the reasons why she doesn't want to see them.

Mom wasn't very close with her parents, especially Grandma. When Mom had me during college, Grandma had a conniption and kept saying how Mom couldn't raise a baby at nineteen while still enrolled in school. To be honest, I think most parents would have acted the same, so that wasn't what broke their relationship; it was when she said the baby would be better off with them or never born, to begin with. Mom proved them wrong, bringing me up well *and* finishing college all by herself.

Now, Grandma calls Mom constantly, trying to mend things... but the conversation always ended up going down the "Lisa would be better off with us" road. I believe Mom would've wanted things fixed, but not at the cost of it hurting me in some way.

Mom then asked about summer after eating another roll, saying that she will be working normal hours but would want to do some fun stuff over the weekends. I honestly didn't remember everything she said. I had a plan I needed to carry out perfectly.

Mom was finishing her meal and knew I had to commence my golden operation.

"Hey, Mom," I said quietly, twirling my fork in my half-eaten glob of mashed potatoes, "can I ask you something?"

"Sure, sweetie. What is it?" she responded, sounding very intrigued.

So far, so good.

I revealed the folded Camp of the Arts form from my jeans pocket. The blanks that were placed around sentences with "location" and "time of pickup" I went ahead and filled out, even smudged a little bit of lip gloss on the phone number so she wouldn't want to call it anytime soon—something I learned from a TV show (and people say watching too much television would rot your brain—proved them wrong).

I got up from my chair, took a deep breath, and started unfolding the form in front of her. "So, Lily is going to this camp for the whole summer, and her mom asked if I would want to go with Lily so she would have a friend to be around. I asked Lily if I had to pay for anything, and she said I didn't. She also said her mom would cover the expenses and even drive me there if it meant Lily would have a friend to go with—they're pretty rich, I think I've mentioned before, which is why the money isn't a big deal. It's in Philadelphia, so Lily and I could still come back home during the weekends..."

I handed her the form, my heart sprinting miles and trying to force its way out of my ribcage, and watched her flip through it. Both of my palms were sweating—perspiring guilt no matter how much I tried to wipe them on my pants discreetly—and I could *not* look her in the eyes for longer than a second at a time. I didn't want to lie, con, fib, or whatever this magic cover-up truly was, *especially* for weeks on end, but magic—magic was at stake. And if she ever caught me... I wouldn't even know how to explain myself—to her *or* the Guardians.

Please, please, please, please let this go as planned.

Her eyes kept scanning the paper, so I continued, "I know I'm not the best at sports, and this sounds like a lot of fun. You get to be with some of the nation's best artists, designers, and musicians and learn all sorts of different stuff from them. I really wanna go, but I don't want you to think I don't wanna spend summer with you."

Mom paused for a second as she continued to look through the form.

"Wow... well, this is a little sudden," she said.

I fidgeted with my long hair as it hung off my shoulders. "I know, and I am sorry—but it doesn't start until next Monday. Her Mom offered to drive us there since you work."

She continued to glance over everything, so I added another "Please, can I go?" to the end of my speech.

"I never had a chance like this when I was your age—Grandma never letting me go anywhere if unfamiliar faces were involved and she was not..." Her words were slow, making my heart thump faster, "and I think it would be nice for you to learn something creative with professionals..."

I pulled my lip in between my teeth. *Come on. Please say you'll let me go.*

"... Alright, you can go—but I want you to give Lily's mom the money for the late fee, okay? And don't take advantage of this either. This is a very kind thing for Lily's mom to do."

I stood on my tiptoes from happiness. "Yes! Thank you, Mom! You're the best!"

Mom finished signing the form and stapled an envelope with twenty-five dollars to it for the late fee. I told her Lily's mom will come during the late mornings of Monday to pick me up each week and then drop me back off on Fridays, that way I could still be with Mom during the summer weekends. Getting a call from Lily's mom or vice versa didn't scare me because Mom had no way of getting her phone number and was only on a first-name basis with her. I also did not have a cellphone, so the fear of Mom checking up on me was not a problem, either. Flawless—the perfect plan was in full effect.

I went straight up to my room and released all the anxiousness from my body with a deep, long breath. There was a part of me that felt bad for telling such a small fib, but I had to keep reassuring myself it was all for good. The Guardians never said I should or shouldn't tell my mom, but I thought telling people on Earth about magic was not the right thing to do... so technically, me *not* telling Mom *was* the best choice to make.

I would admit that I didn't expect Mom to pay for the late fee. I didn't want to steal that and had no use for her money in the "magic world," so I waited until Mom went to the bathroom to slip the money back into her purse. The only thing I had left to do was wait until Monday, so my new adventure could begin.

5
EVERWAKE

The seven days were finally up, and it was just breaking dawn outside my window. I jumped out of bed and put on the clothing I had neatly laid out on my dresser the night before: pale blue jean shorts, my favorite green scoop-neck cotton shirt, and a heathered gray jacket. I was clueless about what I was supposed to wear since I didn't know exactly where I was going. I was just told that Inna would pick me up early on the eighth day—nothing about what to bring or what the weather would be like or if physical activity would be involved... Honestly, I should have asked more questions when I had the chance.

After eating breakfast, Mom asked me if I was all packed and ready to go, giving me hugs and kisses and making me feel almost guilty for planning my magical escape. I just kept saying to myself, *You're not lying... You're not lying... You're not lying...* and avoided eye contact as much as possible.

When 7:30 a.m. arrived, she went to the garage, started her car, and slowly left the driveway. When the white Corolla faded into the crowd of houses, I jumped out of the dining room seat, poured out the rest of my cereal in the sink, and laced up my sneakers. I grabbed my little blue backpack filled with extra clothes, travel-size shampoo and conditioner, a water bottle, and my plush cat—just in case I needed a little piece of comfort—and headed straight toward the woods.

I made sure our neighbors weren't outside before I jolted toward the bush of trees. Running through the forest, my heart started to race again from the jittery mixture of nervousness and excitement in my gut. Every time I entered our forest, a new adventure seemed to follow. I grew quite fond of the sounds of bugs and birds flying around, and the new grass stains on my shoes didn't bother me one bit. It signaled magical discoveries ahead, and I just could not wait!

Amid the flattened clearing surrounded by pine trees was Inna, already waiting for me with a pink smile on her face.

This is crazy! She's actually here! I knew I didn't dream up everything that had happened a week ago, but my naïve human mind kept pricking at my heart telling me "magic is make-believe." Seeing her—the blush blonde-haired lady wearing the fabric of the ocean in the middle of the forest—proved that this, in fact, *was* real.

"Oh, I am so glad you came!" she exclaimed. She wore similar attire to our first meeting, adding a lightweight cloak and sandals of ivory designs to her coordinating colors of teal and cerulean. "I was not sure what time to arrive and began to worry if you had changed your mind when an hour had passed."

"I am so sorry, Miss Inna—definitely not changing my mind on this," I said, feeling horrible for leaving her out here in the woods for so long.

Inna flashed her elegant, effortless smile. "Oh, that is alright! I am just so thrilled to be one of your mentors that I could not wait to see you again!"

Besides Mom, this was the first time I had someone tell me they were excited to see me and really meant it, causing my cheeks to turn pink and my eyes to dart to the ground.

"Well, let us be on our way! We have a couple of stops to make before you meet with the Guardians again." She held out her hand for me to grasp.

"Where are we going?" I asked, taking her hand in mine.

"To the city known as EverWake on planet Gadot—you are just going to love it!" Her positivity quickly rubbed off on me, making me smile more and more. Inna started to move her free hand as she did before, making a fist full of magic and punching it forward to evanesce us away.

I felt the same rush of wind and heard the bombing thunderous claps while being encapsulated by millions of lights. In a matter of three seconds, the air began to feel cooler, and the sounds of chimes started to be replaced with chattering crowds. Soon, my feet hit solid ground, and the light disappeared from all around us.

"Welcome to the city of EverWake!"

With the sound of Inna's voice, I slowly opened my eyes.

This... this can't be real...

I was standing in view of an empire of merchant's markets. Rooftops as high as four stories poked the clear blue sky, decorated with kaleidoscopic flags, plants, and banners rolling in the wind. The trails of colorful buildings lined the streets for miles, a sea of sturdy brick and polished concrete. Rigid cream-colored bridges of stone connected the buildings, creating archways for those to walk underneath as well as pathways for those above. All the architecture was bricked up, not chrome or alien-looking, and I even saw a couple of neon signs and other modern technology grabbing my attention with their blaring colors. Each structure was unique, clean—no cracks or signs of rust—and filled with an array of shops, carrying clothing, jewels, foreign plants, and delicious food. Water canals flowed along the tops of many buildings, providing nutrients to the vast greenery and produce that grew along the rooftops. I had never seen aqueducts in real life, so even that seemed magical to me.

My jaw dropped as I walked closer to the edge of the glossy concrete floor, placing my hands on the copper railway that protected me from falling below. A large shadow as big as a whale zoomed overhead, and when I looked up, I saw the underbelly of a pristine, white airship—a *real flying ship*—soaring with translucent wings like dragonflies. My eyes couldn't blink, in fear of missing even the smallest detail. After the flying ship passed, I saw a couple of small and large dirigible ships soaring behind like colossal metal birds. They didn't look like rocket ships or alien battleships; they were all colorful and ranged from simple sphere shapes to complex airships. Some even looked like ancient pirate vessels and winged sailboats with metallic chrome feathers and glass domes for doors.

I stood on the lower pipe of the copper railing to glance down below and saw no highways or interstate traffic. Alternatively, it was filled with men and women and children going to and from stores much like a downtown city. The crowds of people, vibrant buildings, intrusive smells, and foreign sounds—each and every bit of EverWake was not just new. It was literally *magical!*

"This is the most amazing place I have ever seen in my life!" I spoke, my eyes glistening in wonder with a never-fading glow.

"I just knew you would like it," Inna said as she walked beside me. "EverWake is the City of Cities. It never grows tired and is the trading heart for all merchants and buyers. It also contains the main hub and landing zone for all travelers called The Landing. There are terminals for airships, personal motorized vehicles like the galasi cars, bikes, public transportation like avelifts and citiships, and even for magic teleportation as well, which is where we landed."

I couldn't even focus on all the new words she spoke, staring at the dozens of families passing me by and entering the enticing shops.

"Follow me, Lisa. I will tell you more about EverWake as we make a few stops."

We walked down the curved flight of stairs that led to the exit of the terminals. Inna said The Landing went on for miles, carrying travelers from all over the universes. Apparently, space travel was as normal as taking an airplane across America. She even told me they use speed-enhancing magic fuel and the power of stars to travel at the speed of light! *So cool!*

Through the exit began the long street of markets and unique shop owners and civilians. Every man, woman, and child looked... normal. No one had fur like a wolf, pointed ears or tails, terrestrial bodies of green, wings of a bird—nothing strange in the slightest. Skin tones ranged from dark to light, bodies from fat to skinny, and voices were even a mix of foreign languages and English. If I hadn't just seen a man make green flames come out of his fist in a sidewalk performance, I would have thought these people were just normal humans like on Earth.

We had walked underneath an arch that led to an escalator-like stairway. Instead of the grooved metal revolving planks I was used to seeing in shopping malls, we stepped on moving white slates of a foreign metal. As it led us up to the second floor of the city's vendors, I mustered up the courage to ask Inna some personal questions.

"So, the Guardians said that you used to live on Earth. Is that true?" I asked, staying close to her creamy cloak that hooded her head.

"Yes, it is quite true."

"Really? Where from?"

"You might be surprised, but I am originally from an old town in the United Kingdom. It has since evolved into a rather bustling, colonized city in Europe—far different from what I remember it being when I grew up there."

After she mentioned that, I saw her accent peak through her words.

"How long ago was that?"

"According to your world's history books, you referred to my time period as the Late Middle Ages."

My eyes widened as a woman's shopping bag brushed by my leg. "You mean you are—"

"Just about to reach my 632nd year of being a Keeper of the Stars. I have changed much over the years, so I am not surprised if my origin caught you off guard."

"Wow, so you're like"—*Don't say old, Lisa!*—"immortal?"

Inna's long hair, intertwined in another loose braid of knots and swirls, draped off her shoulder as she leaned closer to me. "I have the gift of immortality, which I received the day Lady Ariela chose me to be a Keeper, but that doesn't mean I am immune to death. I am human, after all. I just have not physically aged since I was twenty-six years old."

I did not know that type of magic even existed or even that a normal human could possess it. Inna looked incredibly young, with no gray hairs or wrinkles to match, but she talked as if she mastered wisdom time and time again. If she was over six hundred years old, then that meant the Guardians and Ariela had to be over a *thousand!*

"Why were you chosen as a Keeper when you were from Earth?" I asked as we passed by another abnormal clothing store—windows displaying puffy pants and leather boots.

"There are a handful of Keepers across the universes to whom Lady Ariela and the Guardians gifted unique magic. There was a period of time when Man began to use magic for awful, greedy purposes, and Lady Ariela and her Guardians agreed that some power should be concealed to only a single person or trusted group of people. The Light gifted Ariela with the ability to disassemble magic and secrete it to good-hearted humans to perform specific tasks, calling the human vessels Keepers. I am one of the three Keepers of Stars, and our task is to grow and guide the Wishing Stars. When Man learned that magic hid within the Wishing Stars, they stole them from all across the universes, creating the Age of the Black Sky." Inna's face began to turn somber, losing her cheeriness I was growing quite fond of.

"That sounds pretty bad."

"It was disastrous... Humans used their own powers to steal, kill, and tamper with the growth of the stars, so Lady Ariela took that magic, redefined it, and placed it into only three people—three people she chose and trusted. Since Wishing Stars are in each galaxy, Lady Ariela decided to pick three from Earth."

Inna leaned in closer to me, fragranced with a pleasant ocean breeze. "You see, Lisa, no human outside of Earth can enter its galaxy unless their soul was birthed there—Lady Ariela made it that way to protect the planet from dark magic. So, she needed Keepers from Earth to watch over its Wishing Stars and collect its stardust, and I was chosen to inherit the gift of Magic Starseed Creation."

Before I could ask more about her mysterious magic, Inna strolled into an alleyway where a flamboyant shop lay at its end. The sign above the store was written in oddly curved scribbles, but after looking at it for a couple of seconds, my eyes seemed to adjust because it formed the words "Scarlet Gems."

"Did that sign just change to form English letters?" I asked Inna.

"Many merchants have a Reveal Charm cast upon their shops so that once you are near it, you will be able to read their prices and the name of their store," she said as she opened the glass door.

"That is so cool!"

A wave of floral redolence immediately rushed over my senses the moment my foot entered the jewelry shop. I was not used to jewelry stores having a green thumb, but roses and honeysuckles were placed near every display. The jewelry was not limited to glass cases as some were hung from the ceiling, hidden in glossy treasure chests, and scattered throughout small wooden boxes.

"What are we getting here?" I quietly asked Inna, keeping close to her white cloak.

"We are getting *you* an orbkit," Inna said to me, heading further back into the store.

We walked toward the counter and approached a short man dressed in scarlet red. He was pretty burly with bushy eyebrows and a well-kept mustache, not what I expected a jewelry shop owner to look like.

Inna unclipped one of the bejeweled bands on her belt, revealing a silver charm with a pink metallic flower on the end of its chain. She held it in front of her, showing the merchant. He looked at it, nodded, and went to the back of the store. *Did Inna know this man prior to coming here?*

"What was that keychain you showed him?" I asked, my voice even quieter than before.

"This particular version of identification is owned by a few—those who work with the Keepers and Guardians," Inna said. "Many shop owners believe in the good things we do and are always grateful for our work. In return, they will offer their services."

The burly shop owner soon returned with a small glossy jewelry box. Once unlocked, it presented four neatly organized charms atop a scarlet cushion. Each was a flawless, spherical gem encased in intricate metal or gold, and all of them were no bigger than the size of a dime.

"These are orbkits," Inna began to explain. "They are special lockets that can hold up to 50 kilos of, well, anything you wish to carry along with you. Each can hold an abundance of clothing, currency, provisions, medicine—taking the mass and weight of each object away, as it is all contained in each little charm. Go ahead and pick your favorite."

I was about to question why she said this little stone could hold my body weight and then some, but when she said it was a gift—

"What—are you sure?" I hesitated. The magic lockets sounded surreal and rather expensive, especially since they weren't even on display. Sure, I'm new to magic, but this type of power even sounded bizarre to me. I didn't think I deserved something that nice.

"Don't worry, Lisa. This is a gift from Lady Ariela and the shop owner," Inna sweetly insisted, putting her hand on my shoulder.

I looked back up at the shop owner. He didn't say anything; he just smiled pleasantly underneath his mustache.

This... she and Lady Ariela are really giving something this beautiful to me?

I closely examined each orbkit and pointed to the aqua-blue one that was wrapped in pearly, white vines. The shop owner selected that one from out of the box and grabbed a matching chain from underneath his counter. The strand was the same pearly white color as the orbkit's encasement, dainty and smooth. He then assembled the orbkit to the strand to form a short necklace, placing it into the palm of my hand.

"I... I have never received something like this before," I said in awe of the jewelry. I turned toward Inna and the shopkeeper. "Thank you, Inna. Thank you, kind sir."

We started to leave the store, and I felt like royalty wearing the iridescent orbkit around my neck. It was thin and shiny, adorning my collarbone and pulling all the attention away from my freckled, pale skin—the nicest gift I had ever received.

"Inna," I said to her as we slunk back into the crowd, "Thank you for this gift."

Her eyes partly furrowed as the corners of her lips rose.

"You already thanked me in the store, you know?"

"I know, but I just can't believe I get to wear something this pretty every day! Thank you so much!"

Her azure eyes grew wide before she made a soft smile. I wasn't sure why, but maybe she didn't expect to receive thanks for a gift like this. It could have been a normal piece of jewelry that most magic wearers had, but to me, it was the finest piece of jewelry I owned or probably would ever own. I could never thank her enough for that.

Our next stop wasn't too far ahead, according to Inna. We walked by one store that sold star-shaped sandwiches and puffed pastries, another that sold fuzzy cactus plants, another that sold fine jewelry, and even a second-hand bookstore called "Finder's Readers," which I thought to be rather witty.

We both made our way down the street, turned left, and came to a halt in front of a boutique with a large sign that read, "Adventure Tunics," and a singular long display window filled with expensive-looking outfits.

"Let's get you some new clothing, okay, Lisa!" she said to me, not as a question but as a statement of fact. She opened the shop door and led me into an array of wonderfully styled clothing. I was used to department stores, not boutiques, and felt a little out of place. All the clothing looked a little similar to daily wear but had more leather straps and an odd combination of fabric layering than I was used to. There were racks of modernized doublets for men, odd vests called jerkins, nicely styled blue jean-like pants, laced-up boots, and lots of thick, zipped-up skirts and dresses. Nothing was too bright or had a single logo of a company's brand painted on the chest, either. I had never worn more than just a jacket over a T-shirt, so the thought of wearing all of this made me smile.

A lady dressed in a style similar to Inna with fluffy brown hair came and greeted us, bowing toward Inna in respect, and took us back to a large changing room. She quickly took my measurements with a magic measuring tape that seemed to float all by itself, measuring my arms, legs, and torso—quite quickly, too! Once the lavish lady finished, she clapped her hands and said, *"Elbmessa,"* and the drawers behind her opened. Paper cards pictured with different outfits flew out of the case and into my hand—delicately so I wouldn't receive a single paper cut. *She just made all those cards move with her magic!*

"Tell me which styles you like best," the lady said to me, rather enthusiastically and with a boisterous tone.

I looked through the flashcards containing many articles of clothing. Each one—not a single pair of jeans or heather jacket to be found; the outfits were *far* prettier than I was expecting and yet still very breathable and athletic. *Expensive* for sure.

I picked three that looked most normal and comfortable for me.

"This one is my favorite," I timidly told her, giving her a fourth card. It showed a short off-white dress with brown biker-short spandex underneath. The garment was stitched with hues of peach and blue along the sides to add pops of color—girly but not *too* girly. It came with laced brown boots for shoes, a cute peach-cropped jacket to match the stitching in the dress, and a brown belt sewed with little pockets.

"A perfect choice!" the lady announced. She then clapped her hands again, and magic lit up all around me in the form of bubbles filled with glitter. Before I knew it, the off-white dress attire was already clothing my body! *How did that just happen?* Glancing at the mirror, I truly couldn't believe how different I looked. I was rather *pretty*.

"It suits you quite nicely!" the shop owner said.

"Do you like it?" Inna asked.

"... I love it so much," I exclaimed. I couldn't stop staring at myself in the mirror in the most adorned clothing I had ever tried on.

As if it couldn't get any more magical, the lady told Inna and me that all my original articles of clothing were packed into my orbkit *and* that I got to keep the other three outfits *plus* ten more—also inside my orbkit! I had never had someone buy me brand-new clothes before in this great amount. Normally, Mom and I shop together for school clothes and debate if paying full price was worth it or not. I did not think I deserved this many new pieces of fine apparel.

Leaving the store, I continually thanked Inna. Her response was always humble, saying to think nothing of it. I didn't care if she said it wasn't a big deal. She gave me so many wonderful gifts—how could I *not* thank her!

Continuing our small talk, I asked Inna, "How did that lady make all those items float like that?"

"She is a type of Mage who specializes in enchantment charms," Inna stated, "so she is able to cast her magic upon certain objects and make them float, work, move, and do other simple tasks, depending on what charm she is using."

"Is that type of magic rare?"

"No, actually." Inna giggled at my innocence. "It is quite common, and all who possess magic can learn skills like hers, even you. Those who can use charms, enchantments, glintz, galdurs, and alteration magic are what we call Mages and Mystics. Anyone with a magic pulse is a Mage or Mystic. Their skills can be powerful but not as coveted as other types of magic out there."

"Oh, I see..." *Wonder when I'll be able to do something like that...*

After touring more of the merchant town, eating new treats dipped in chocolate, and passing by an actual *potion* shop, Inna began to lead us back toward The Landing... only this time, we took a different route. I didn't realize how far we walked—the jungle of stone and merchandise had my mind all turned upside down—and going back the way we came on foot would take another hour at least.

There was a type of transportation system, sort of similar to a long tram ride, that went above many of the shop owner's buildings. *That* was where Inna led us to.

She said EverWake has a couple of underground subways, but many used the above transit to get to where they needed to go. There were purple signs all around the city to dictate "Flying Tram" stops—though it didn't really fly.

We went up the escalators to board the flying tram, going through its sliding glass doors to pick a spot to stand. Inna and I stood near the window as the tramway started to move. I noticed, past the town of merchants, there was a massive collection of buildings in the distance. Their structures were sturdy and less colorful than the vendors' shops. A type of wall enclosed the buildings, and many domes and terraces covered the areas, hiding away their secrets.

"What are those buildings for?" I asked Inna, who stood beside me holding onto the railing above our heads.

"That is the Magic Embassy," she said solemnly. "They govern and control much of the galaxies' highly populated settlements and even whole continents."

"That *whole* city of gray and white buildings controls *continents*?"

"They do not control them as a ruler or dictator would. If a new city, nation, or even country begins to flourish, the Magic Embassy will offer its aid in return for assistance. The country still has its choice of government style and how they wish to live their lives; they just will be a part of the Magic Embassy's alliance. The new settlement can refuse the Magic Embassy's help, but it is highly unlikely. The Magic Embassy offers protection, military, magic, provisions, and other necessities, only giving as much as the new civilization is willing to contribute. If the new nation asks for too much, the Magic Embassy will do whatever is necessary in order to receive payment."

"Whoa... what happens if you refuse their offer?"

"You can join one of the smaller federations or become independent. There are many nations that thrive just fine without the need of the Magic Embassy..." Inna turned away from the window to look down at me, her ivory cloak kissing my shoulder. "Still, I have seen many nations fall when against the Magic Embassy's military. Their forces are quite strong in magic and weaponry."

I glanced out the window, seeing a couple of flying ships disappear behind this Magic Embassy's massive gray walls. "Do you not like them, then?"

"Centuries ago, we used to cooperate with them. The Light was strong within the hearts of their governing officials, and they wanted to make sure magic was in balance all across the universes. During the election year a century ago, a new family inherited the Magic Embassy's seat of power and refused to follow the way of Light and the Guardians. They didn't like the idea of something more powerful than Man being in control of magic. We agreed to split from the Magic Embassy, for the greed and lust of magical power was not something The Light stood for."

"I see..." I said, watching as the merchant buildings below began to rise higher, covering the view of the unsaturated colors of the Magic Embassy.

Inna perked right back up again, seeing as my face was starting to turn as serious as her story. "Don't look at them too negatively, though, Lisa; it isn't all corrupt. Many kind-hearted people work with the Magic Embassy whom you can still trust, and many of their allies run strong, respectable nations."

I didn't think a magic world would have government problems, let alone a government at all...

The tram suddenly stopped, making me catch the railing before falling over, and flew open its doors in view of The Landing's gateway. We followed the signs and paths that led to the entrance of the teleportation terminals, going up more escalators and crossing another concrete bridge. Inna said that, unlike most worlds, you have to go to and from The Landing if you wished to teleport anywhere. EverWake had a magic veil covering their city, like how Haim Gana wouldn't let me evanesce straight to the Elysium on my first visit. It acted as a security clearance for travelers—rather efficient and less time-consuming than the procedures you would see at airports.

"The last thing you will need is a COIN," Inna told me, leading us both toward a tall, glass booth at the entrance of The Landing.

"What do I need a single coin for?"

She chuckled at my innocent question. "A COIN is not a currency you are thinking of. It is a form of identity and passport for traversing to planets. It stands for Certification of Identity Nexus. Since you were with me, I already had clearance to bring you along to EverWake without a COIN. One of the perks of being a Keeper."

Inna stopped at the glass booth labeled "Services" and showed the desk worker her pink and silver flower charm, which then led to that desk worker bringing in a *new* desk worker. I never thought a simple charm could be so powerful. The new desk worker had a name tag labeled "Gene," and he suddenly started asking me questions.

"Name?" he said, rather quickly, too.

"Lisa Rae Robbie."

"Date of birth?"

"April 29, 1997."

"Origin?"

I paused. I had never been asked what my "origin" was. I wasn't sure if he meant my species, place of birth, or—

"Earth," Inna quickly answered for me. Gene the Desk Worker raised his eyebrows and continued typing. *Guess it isn't every day he meets someone from Earth.*

After a few more clicks and dings from his computer—which looked very different from the computers I used at school—a noise arose from behind him on a clunky, domed machine. Gene the Desk Worker slid on a pair of black felt gloves, reached his hand inside the little compartment sticking out of the dome, and grabbed something out of the sphere. It must have been rather small because his entire hand hid the object from my view.

"Hold out your hand, please," he asked me.

I did so, and he dropped the COIN onto my palm. It was warm, slightly bigger than an American half-dollar coin, and shaped like a hexagon. It was made of tungsten metal with my information embossed on one side and a set of twenty numbers on the other. The most peculiar thing about the polygon was when it made contact with my skin: shimmering bright greens lit up the inner stroke of the COIN, similar to the glow of a neon sign.

"Is this thing magic too?" I stated, rotating the COIN between my fingers.

"It is. The moment it made contact with your skin, it activated. No one can claim to be you while traveling because your touch only activates the COIN. It glows green because you are still a minor and can only go to certain planets and landing stations without supervision."

Even something as simple as identification was magical here. I truly fell in love with the magic world with each new turn Inna led me toward.

"Now that we have gotten you new clothing and an orbkit, it is time you headed to Calendula," Inna said with her hands on her hips. "Vilmad will meet you there and have you introduce yourself to Gaius and the Balthiers."

My eyes opened wide. "Wait—you mean by *myself?*" I said, almost jumbling up my words from the sudden shock.

"You will be perfectly fine! I will be evanescing you, and it will be just like the last time." She acted like that was supposed to help, but it didn't.

"How come you can't go?" *And not leave me with the man that doesn't like me.*

We started walking toward The Landing when she sighed. "He insisted on doing this himself..." She paused, her hood covering her face, but I could see her pulling in her lower lip—thinking. "And Gaius didn't want to meet us here. He's not too fond of crowds."

My breathing stopped, but my legs kept walking. *Great. The only thing I know about my next mentor is that he didn't want to meet me... and now, I have to be escorted by a Guardian who didn't like me—the one who* really *didn't like me.*

Inna led me to an area filled with white open stalls. People would wait in line and, one by one, disappear into the stalls—even families as big as five. Inna informed me that not all people could evanesce and would use other means of magic to teleport. I saw so many different flashing lights and magic dust inside each stall as families would leave. We made our way up the line and waited our turn. I was still very nervous. *What if it doesn't work? What if I don't land in Calendula? How would I even know if I did land there—what does it look like? What if I fall down, or worse—some type of magic comes and cuts off my legs?*

My turn came. Inna lightly pushed me toward the white foreign stall, reassuring me I would be fine. I took a deep breath and clenched my hands together as I watched her summon the blue magic into her palm.

The moment she punched the air, I was instantly encased in light and heard the familiar chimes and thunder like before. When the three seconds of rushing wind stopped and the ground felt secure, I opened my eyes.

6
A BRUTE WITH A GREEN THUMB

Just trees.

A bush of oak and pine stood high and mighty toward the sky. Owls cooed, cicadas buzzed, and some other unfamiliar bug noises wheezed in the humid air. The forest was thick, going on for miles, and I was smack dab in the center... at least, I thought it was the center. I couldn't tell. The canopy of trees above veiled most of the sky, but I could tell one thing: it was sunset... and the night was coming. I was in the woods *alone*—

"Agapéd," a familiar voice sounded, making me jump from the abrupt change in silence.

Whipping my head away from the woodland labyrinth, I saw Vilmad walking quite briskly toward me. His long hair flowed with the warm air that swept in from the leaves above, and his golden-emerald cloak glided swiftly above weeds and roots. The soil beneath didn't even dare to taint his cloak as if it, too, was afraid of upsetting the celestial man. When his face came closer, I noticed his expression was the same as it was during our first meeting: unyielding and unimpressed.

If a Guardian wasn't in front of me, dripping in gold, I would've thought I was in a normal forest back in America.

"Would you mind following me?" he asked, the deep depths of the ocean swimming in his eyes, staring right at me. Not once did he mention the dense forest around us.

"Yes, sir"—I quickly shook my head— "I mean, 'yes' I don't mind following you." Even without any of his harsh opinions fired, Vilmad was still far too intimidating for a relaxed conversation.

He rolled his cosmic eyes and clicked his tongue as we walked forward, judgment whispering out of each breath. "Just... pay attention. I do not wish to repeat this more than once. We will promptly start your training and lessons tomorrow after you visit your mentors and the Balthiers, who have graciously allowed you to stay in their company. First, I wanted to discuss the arrangements and how your training with us will proceed. Listen carefully..."

He sighed, noticing I was flinching every time a bug buzzed by my ear. I couldn't help it. I was on edge, and his presence didn't help.

"I'm sorry... I'm listening, sir..." I said, though it didn't change his annoyed, squinted glare.

Never had an adult disliked me before, especially when I did nothing wrong.

He resumed, the wood's shadows not helping his joyless demeanor. "As you know, the Agapéd Magic has yet to reveal what power it has stored away in you—more or less, what form of power it is willing to give to you. In our meeting, if you remember, we decided you will have two Earth-born instructors for magic training, *but* seeing that your education of the other worlds is less than zero, this means you will need to improve your knowledge and mentality of the magic-bearing planets."

Glad he thinks so highly of me...

"We can't have you making mistakes because of a lack of common sense, so I, Bethesda, and Micah will teach you in Haim Gana. We will alternate days Monday through Thursday—starting with Bethesda's lessons tomorrow—going over the basics of magic, geography, history, and all things necessary to make you a dignified Mage and Agapéd Bearer. Your physical magic training will be during the afternoons, alternating between Inna and"—Vilmad rolled his eyes—"the brute, hoping to reveal what plethora of magic the Agapéd has set in your heart."

"What about Fridays?" I asked and immediately regretted it, seeing as Vilmad looked a little put-off.

He veered to the left. Nothing was there, but I didn't question his ability to see the invisible path. "Feel free to do as you like those days," he responded with little emotion, "unless your instructors feel your training could use a little extra time put in. No doubt you'll need it, and I recommend visiting Haim Gana when you do. Better to be there than here."

More crunching sounds were made as we walked, and I began to question whether or not Vilmad was taking me to Calendula or if I was about to be kidnapped and lost in the woods forever a trillion miles away from Earth.

"Um, Mr. Vilmad?" I began.

"Just Vilmad is fine," he said, keeping his eyes forward.

"So, uh, where are we exactly? Is this Calendula?"

He huffed—*huffed*—as if I asked a question when the answer was embedded in every strip of bark around me. "This is just the Outskirts. Not a part of the city—we are almost there, though. Better to get this over with soon." His eyes narrowed in on me, watching as I scanned the forest for creatures and being careful not to step in holes. "You know this will not be easy."

His words dinged my skin like winter storm sleet. I tensed, unable to answer... mostly because I didn't really understand what he meant.

He elaborated, taking note of my silence, "Learning how to use the Agapéd Magic, even for someone who knows the difference between a *charm* and a *potion*"—he scoffed—"is already a task in and of itself... and you're a child. Are you *sure* you're up for it?"

I fiddled with my fingernails. Sure, I didn't know the depth of my situation, and I didn't even know what magic felt like. But Lady Ariela seemed to believe in me—the lady who had to have magic swimming in her bloodstream, if she even *had* blood.

I mustered up a speck of courage and answered the Guardian. "This magic picked me, so... I'm willing to learn."

The man flecked with gold slid before me, abruptly stopping my steps. A couple of twigs broke beneath his shoes as he towered over me. "*Willing?* You have no idea what this magic—" He stopped his words. I saw each syllable bobbing in his thin throat, and I could tell he was holding back his tongue—holding back whatever he truly wished to say. After a rapid succession of blinking, he continued, his words calmer than before, "The Agapéd Magic needs *more* than just willingness. It will take days of mastering and will cause you aches and pain like you've not known before, seeing as how you could barely lift a stool without breaking a sweat."

He threw his head to the side, not caring that he ridiculed a kid for having the body of a *kid*. Though it was true that I was smaller than most girls my age, I wasn't *that* weak...

"It will already be hard for you as it is, and now, it will be even harder with that *brute* teaching you." His right eyebrow raised. "Gaius is not like Inna. Given that you took considerable time getting here, I can tell you enjoyed her company in EverWake. Gaius may be a decent gardener, even one *chosen* by Lady Ariela herself, but he knows nothing of delicacy. He will be brutal..."

My mouth started turning dry, and it hurt to swallow. *Brutal...?*

Vilmad inched closer. "And as you heard before, he hasn't visited us in a century... There is a reason for that. A reason a child couldn't wish to know..."

All sounds of the forest washed out from the rampage of thumps my heart blared through my ears. *Vilmad is exaggerating... right?*

"You can still turn back, you know—Lady Ariela would understand. Do not feel like you're obligated to do this. I can wave my hand, send you home, and you will be back to your normal life on Earth. After all, that is where you belong—where magic is simply a daydream and nothing more."

The scared, little girl in me wanted to say, *just take me home, please*, but... something anchored down my heart. Something in me refused to run... and refused to believe everything the Guardian, who *despised me,* was saying.

My feet stayed put, and my hands stopped fidgeting. "I know it'll be hard... but I can do it. I promise... nothing is too hard for me." That last part was a bit of a lie, but I didn't care.

It got the man in gold to sneer and back away from me in defeat.

And we didn't say another word for quite a while.

As the canopy of trees thickened and the grass below our feet faded into a clumsy dirt road, a small line of people appeared. They were dressed in similar clothing I saw at EverWake—muted-colored shirts, pants with lots of belts and pockets, and leather boots—and all were standing in front of an archway made of two oak trees guarded by two bulky guards. The man and woman at the front of the line were told to move forward, and when they did, they just disappeared! *Poof!* There was no light or magic dust—just pure *vanishment!*

When Vilmad approached the guards, they stood owl-eyed before bowing toward him. "Sir Vilmad," they said as they let us cut the line and step forward to the front.

Guardian perks...

Vilmad whipped his head toward me as the guards eyed my freckled cheeks, waiting. I stood still, waiting as well... for whatever was supposed to happen. My hands turned sweaty before Vilmad rolled his eyes and muttered, "Your COIN."

I didn't question the Guardian and fiddled around my body for the tungsten polygon. Stares of those behind me—those we *cut* in front of—were pelting my back like spit wads shot at lightning speed as I padded my thighs and waist for the celestial ID, finally finding it inside my jacket pocket. The stroke of the COIN turned green as I held it in front of my chest. Both guards examined it within one heartbeat, and then they nodded. *That was easy—Vilmad could've told me earlier instead of having me stand there like an idiot...*

The moment my foot stepped across the line of dirt, the scenery of trees disappeared, and I was at the entrance of a garden city.

It was a well-structured town filled with lavish greenery, cottages, and happy families. Everything was rather dated in an old centenarian kind of way the more I examined the scenery. Roads were cobble-stoned, leading to homes and small, sturdy buildings. Warm streetlamps lined the pathways to and from the homes, also lighting up the town brightly enough to see the happy faces of the citizens.

Most of the homes looked like cottages, but as we walked closer, I noticed the small houses had hints of biotech machinery along their roofs and walls—solar panels, glowing plants, and exposed copper pipes for their waterlines. The air smelled clean, with skies reminding me of rainbow sherbet, just like the colors I would see back in Keyport. I even heard music resembling the tunes of Irish and Scottish jigs coming from the middle of the town square. The hidden city was homely compared to EverWake and Haim Gana, and I liked that; it made me want to stay and explore even more.

"This is the arboretum-veiled town of Calendula. It is a village hidden and heavily guarded, so you mustn't go off and exploit its whereabouts or secret entrance," he said, sharp and stern, the first words he spoke as we entered the town.

I was truly hoping Vilmad would've given me a tour, but he seemed so dead set on his path that I just stayed silent. Mentally, I took pictures of all the laughing families and odd shops, enjoying the trip in silence as well as trying to remember where we passed since I would be living there. *Living here... actually living in a magical town...* My heart picked up pace again even at the thought of sleeping in a bed that wasn't mine or in a home without Mom.

I blinked rapidly as two kids rushed by me, swiveling away my nervous thoughts. *Lisa, don't you start getting homesick right now. You are fine and will be learning magic by this time tomorrow.*

The quaint, bricked shops and houses soon faded away as Vilmad and I approached a long, paved walkway leading to an enormous industrial greenhouse. This building looked very different and more magical than the rest of Calendula's architecture. The terrarium's walls were built using frosted or tempered glass that perfectly reflected the sunset sky, with occasional stone or wooden-paneled sections along the perimeter. Parts of the building that caught the light the easiest were covered with metallic solar panels, which seemed to be how the whole city obtained electricity. It truly was a greenhouse palace, and Vilmad was taking me right to the entrance.

"What is this place, Mr. Vilmad?" I asked, noticing not many people were going to and from the building.

He took a deep breath. "Just *Vilmad...* " he said, agitated, recollecting himself. "This is the Veradome, the largest conservatory that houses some of the galaxy's rarest and most magical species of the plant kingdom. Calendula thrives on the exports the Veradome produces. During daylight hours, you will see that many residents work here and go off to other nations to sell or trade the crops and herbs produced. The veil that covers Calendula protects the Veradome, for there are many plants and vegetation whose magic is too tempting and dangerous to be grown freely."

"This place sounds really cool," I quietly added as we approached the door.

Vilmad scoffed. "It is far more complex and valuable than the word 'cool' can describe it to be. This is where you will be honing your magic... as best you can from *him* anyways..."

This is where Gaius lives? This place is where the 'detested brute of a Keeper' lives?

Given everything I had just seen—the happy families, jubilant music, flourishing plants—I had a hard time believing Vilmad's opinions about my new teacher. I just couldn't see a harsh man having a green thumb.

There were no guards outside the Veradome like in the forest; Vilmad just opened the glass doors with ease, like in any normal building. Inside was a type of foyer, a "welcome center" made of white, glass, and plants—having two desks on each side, parting hallways, and... hardly any people. Everything was quiet. I assumed it was because nightfall approached, and most workers headed home. *So, even magical businesses work from 9 to 5...*

I had hoped to see some of the plants Vilmad talked about, but instead of heading straight for the twelve-foot-tall glass doors in the center of the foyer that were begging to be opened, we veered right. I was disappointed but not surprised; Vilmad was not the type of man to take detours.

The sunset protruded through the glass walls, painting the hallways with medleys of warm reds and yellows. Aromas of fresh herbs and cut grass wafted through the air further down as we passed by some night-shift workers dressed in dark greens and brown cloaks. They made no glances or abrupt stops, which I found odd because I was walking next to Vilmad, the man with gold growing on his ears and fingertips. He had on a cloak, but one glance at his face, and he could be easily recognized.

I thought the Guardians were well-known... Are there some who don't know who they are?

We approached a door that led us through a nursery of trees, most looking to be fruit-bearing or blossoming with white and pink petals. I thought we were outside, but the glass encasement was still above our heads. The Veradome's enormity kept surprising me the further along we went.

Vilmad turned another right down a flight of a well-hidden staircase. At its end, there was no boring or glass entryway like all the other doors we had been through. This door was wide, arched, and embellished with wood carvings of star-like plants. Besides the fact it didn't match any of the previous rooms or architecture of the Veradome—more archaic and woodland-ish, if anything— the door strangely had no handles, not even a metallic sheet nailed to the side to indicate it was meant to be pushed.

Vilmad went to the far-left side of the entrance and grazed his hand over one of the star carvings. A green, glowing dust emanated from that section of the door, making the wooden engravings light up and move! A chiming sound rang from the magic glitter, and the door unlocked before us.

"A *magic* door..." I said in amazement.

"Oh, yes," Vilmad reacted, "it is one of the few things *he* is fairly good at."

"Building magic doors?" I intriguingly asked.

"Keeping others out..." Vilmad sighed.

The door led us outside, but it oddly felt like Vilmad and I were still *inside* the Veradome. A large glass conservatory was to our right, surrounded by trees and overgrown vines. I couldn't see directly through the frosted glass, but I could tell something was glowing from the inside. *I wonder if there are magic plants in that greenhouse?*

On our left stood a strange cottage. Half of it was underground while the upper portion looked similar to the homes I saw in the city. The acreage was well-kept outside, and the broken tiled path below our feet glistened from the setting sun. Everything was full of life and quite mystical. *Is this really where Gaius lives?*

We went to the beautifully designed home on our left. There wasn't a door, just an archway that led down a curved stairway.

"As I said before," Vilmad spoke up as we descended the wooden steps, "Gaius is a *brute*. Do not expect much from your first meeting. It did take a lot of convincing from us Guardians to have *him* mentor you properly. He *will* teach you... no matter how much I may oppose it."

Vilmad sure knew how to make an introduction, just in the most indelicate way possible. My heart became nervous as we reached the end of the stairs. I didn't want to be taught by a person who didn't like me, but it sounded like it took all seven Guardians to convince this man to teach me magic. I would much rather Inna be my only teacher, but that was no longer an option. Ariela did say it would be good for this Gaius guy to instruct me, and he was also a Keeper of the Stars. *A man who works with magical Wishing Stars won't be all that bad... right?*

We set foot into a ligneous, open-floor planned room. It was quite big, cozy, and filled with walnut and cherry wood furniture. I wouldn't say it was messy, but Gaius sure did have *a lot* of books, plants, jars, and odd objects lying around. Planters were hanging from the ceiling above the living room where the large domed glass window stood, a dining area covered in books and a single place mat, a kitchen on the left that was more taken care of than the dining area, and a couple of wooden doors against the walls.

"Gaius," Vilmad announced, causing a shiver to crawl down my spine.

He paused for an answer, but we only heard the sound of the crackling wood from the fireplace. "Of course, he would not care to invite us in like a civilized human." Vilmad huffed.

We walked past the kitchen island.

"Gaius," Vilmad called, much louder than before.

Still, no answer.

My heart was racing so fast that my hands started to shake. If there were any good parts of this situation I could latch on to, it was the fact that Vilmad would make sure this meeting would be short, sweet, and to the point.

"In here."

Those were the first words I heard that weren't mine or Vilmad's. It was deep and somber sounding. Following the short phrase were sounds of tools hitting a wooden surface and steel cutting—all coming through a cracked door behind the green couch in the living room. I trailed behind Vilmad's cloak as we entered through the half-opened door, hoping the Guardian couldn't hear my heart about to jump out of my chest.

Inside was a type of workshop. One wall was covered with shelves containing the most peculiar instruments, scrap wood, plants, ore, and jars of paint. Displayed on another wall were foreign tools—weapons shaped like *swords*. Some, the smaller ones, were so ornate, carefully crafted from wood and crystal, that they couldn't have been used for combat—at least, that is what it looked like to me; I had never seen real swords before to tell the difference. Others, the bigger ones—one glowing green, one rusted and burnt, and one a giant piece of frosted glass—were worn and chipped at the tips.

My heart raced. *He has fought with those... but exactly against* what *and for* what reason?

I forced my eyes away from the weapons. Planters hung from the ceiling, and the drooping vines ran along many swords and daggers. Pipes trailed down toward the floor, and the lighting in the room was quite dim. The only bright light source came from the table lamp that hung above the crafting table... which *he* occupied.

"Gaius, I would like to introduce you to the new Agapéd Bearer," Vilmad declared.

Gaius was still turned toward his worktable, carving and burning designs into some type of wooden object. His shoulders were broad, and his back—though covered in a long trench coat—was muscly. He did not look at us and kept his fervid concentration at the table.

Vilmad instantly became impatient. "Would you mind showing a little courtesy toward your new pupil—honestly, Gaius?"

It was then that I saw Gaius for the first time. He was slow to turn toward Vilmad and me, not acting angry or too unbothered by us interrupting him. I expected a gritty, old, snarling beast of a man to be sitting in that chair, ready to demand that we leave... but all my expectations failed drastically.

Gaius had a placid yet kind look on his face, even without a smile. Short walnut brown hair trailed the top of his ears, growing thicker and wavy toward the top without a single gray strand. He had short, well-kept facial hair, bright green eyes, and a strong gaze (couldn't stare at them for more than a millisecond). I'm not great at guessing the age of men, but he didn't look too much older than Mom—the only wrinkles being near his eyes from squinting and possibly staying up too late at night. He was also very tan and surprisingly muscular for a gardener—not what I expected. A moss-colored shirt snuggly fit beneath his elaborate leather trench cloak, along with dark pants and off-white boots covered in grass stains. He was intimidating but definitely not this "brute" or "beast" the Guardians claimed him to be; he was a well-built, brawny, and handsome guy.

Is this truly the Gaius Vilmad hated? Is this what a brute really looks like?

Gaius looked at me, slightly grinned, and bowed his head, saying, "Nice to meet you," then turned right back to face his worktable.

I didn't necessarily see anything wrong with that encounter, but Vilmad sure did.

"Agapéd, would you mind stepping out for a moment?" Vilmad whispered to me, chafed.

"Okay," I replied and stepped out of the room... but I didn't close the door; only cracked it so I could still hear and see everything happening.

I had a bad trait called curiosity. Investigating was a friend I welcomed and loved to follow down its path, even if that meant greeting trouble along the way. Peering into Vilmad's conversation may have meant a lecture in my distant future, but I didn't care. The prize of magical information far outweighed any punishment.

Vilmad rushed toward the edge of Gaius's worktable. "You agreed to cooperate with us—least you can do is show a little more involvement and willingness to teach the Agapéd." Vilmad's tone was hushed and condescending.

Gaius continued to work on his wooden project. "And I will," he said very calmly, still not breaking his woodworking concentration.

There was a moment of silence. Vilmad paused, watching Gaius, looking for more than a simple "yes" answer. Their conversation reminded me of a teacher and an uncooperative student, where Gaius was not giving the correct response Vilmad had hoped for.

"You will not neglect your role in this, Gaius. Lady Ariela is giving you another chance and insists you guide the Agapéd, hoping to awaken its magic."

"And I said I would."

"I have a hard time believing that when you are careless enough to not even acknowledge its presence in your own household—"

"You didn't mention she would be so young."

"I hardly see that as an issue—"

"Then let me teach her *my* way."

Vilmad leaned his hand upon the table and glared right into Gaius' face. "You *will* teach her by the methods we discussed prior to this meeting to ensure the safety of the Agapéd."

Gaius rose up from his chair and stood facing Vilmad. They were both the same height, but Gaius was much bigger and stood with less etiquette—a thin golden twig trying to talk to a boulder holding a woodcarving knife. I thought he was about to get angry or yell in Vilmad's face, but instead, Gaius glanced toward the door, right at me!

Crap!

I jumped back and hid my appearance from the door's opening. All sounds froze. Nothing but random creaks from the Keeper's home settling sunk through the air. Soon, I heard squeaky boots break the silence, so I peeped back through the entryway.

"My 'yes' means yes, Vilmad," Gaius somberly said, now facing his wooden tool shelf. "I will instruct her as Lady Ariela directed."

Vilmad released a deep breath. "Good. I will have her begin lessons with you the day after tomorrow."

I instantly backed away from the door and stood up straight as Vilmad approached me, leading us both back outside the Keeper's domain.

"Well... that went a lot better than I had anticipated," Vilmad said as we exited the Veradome.

I didn't know how to comprehend what had just happened. The meeting was *supposed* to be an introduction, but I didn't even have a chance to talk, let alone say "hi." Gaius was rather calm, but Vilmad treated him like a rebellious teen. It could have been that Gaius covered up his true self since I was there, or maybe Vilmad knew he *had* to be harsh on Gaius for him to behave. My new instructor could be a horrible teacher for all I knew, and that is why Vilmad reinforced the importance of doing things Ariela's way. *Please don't let it be that...*

I didn't like the unexpected tension that built up in that room... It reminded me too much of Grandma yelling at Mom, and I did not want that to happen here. This new life was a dream come true, but it seemed that I couldn't escape strife and worry even in a world of magic.

I saw one strand of hope in Gaius' little workshop—a small but strong—that raised my spirits.

Gaius *wanted* to teach me. He saw me for me, not as this Agapéd Bearer the Guardians kept referring to me as. Gaius didn't call me an "it" or treat me as some "chosen one." When I met Vilmad and the others for the first time, no one seemed very thrilled I was chosen by the Agapéd Magic... but Gaius was different. When I—a small girl from Earth—walked into his room, he didn't scoff, sigh, or look down on me because I knew nothing of magic. Vilmad said they had to convince him to teach me, but that was not how I saw it. From the way it looked, it seemed like the Guardians had to convince Gaius to teach *not* using his *own* methods; meaning, he had already said yes, and the hard part was getting him to agree to follow someone else's method of "magic learning."

Knowing all that gave my heart a bit of relief.

7
VILMAD OBSESSORS

The streets of Calendula were very much alive even after the sun hid behind the trees. Many late-night eateries were open, filled with jubilant sounds and scents of grilled meats and vegetables.

Vilmad, his head hooded even though the night sky shadowed his golden features quite well, led us both through the town and up toward the public transportation system. Since most of the residential homes were uphill, a biotech mini railway was installed. It resembled the "flying" trams back at EverWake but was much smaller, a little rusty, and covered in greenery.

I was rather glad we took the trek instead of evanescing to the Balthiers, even though my legs were beginning to grow weary after so much walking. Vilmad didn't say much about the family I would stay with, which was either a good thing or bad. It could mean they were just like him—cold, argumentative, and unapproachable—or very kind people who wouldn't cause any problems. I was hoping for the latter.

While we were on the tram—seeing as no other people were in our compartment, I timidly asked Vilmad, "How come I'm staying with the Balthiers again, Mr.—um, Vilmad, sir?"

He let out a sigh. *Guess I was supposed to already know...*

"Calendula is protected, but that doesn't mean every citizen is a perfect example of Man. Seeing as staying with us was not practical and being with the brute would be catastrophic, the Balthiers were the best option—treat them kindly while you are here as well."

The tram system stopped, and my heart picked up pace in my chest as we continued up the neighborhood, making our way toward a two-story cottage with lights shining through every window. Unused flower pots were stacked in disarray next to the front door, which was wide open with a welcome mat underneath. *Okay, first sign of friendliness...* Through the open entrance, I could see a man, woman, and young girl pacing around inside. Each of them had black hair and cold skin tones, noticeable even from far away. When Vilmad and I finally approached their tiny front porch, the family instantly bent their waists and bowed toward Vilmad.

"It is such an honor, Sir Vilmad, to have you here with us in our home!" the man of the house said with much respect and enthusiasm, still in a bowed position. He was tall and thin, having short black hair.

"It truly is an honor!" their preteen daughter added, in the same tone as her father. My hair was pretty long, but not compared to the straight black locks on her head reaching down to her hip bones.

"Our family admires all that you and the Guardians do for our worlds, and we cannot express enough our many thanks," the wife swooped in with another adorning remark. She was shorter than her husband and curvy with a warm smile.

Wow—the Guardians are like celebrities here!

"We are the ones who would like to thank you for your charitable services in offering your home for the Agapéd Bearer," Vilmad responded, smiling— *actually smiling.* I was guessing he was the type who thrived from praise and adoration, seeing as he received none during all the time I had known him, not even from the Guardians.

The family of three straightened up as I began to say, "It is very nice to meet you."

"The pleasure is all ours, *truly!*" the wife quickly responded, shaking my hand quite fast and firmly. She had rosy cheeks and very warm palms. I felt bad she had to shake mine since I was so clammy from all the heightened nerves.

"Is there anything you need while you are here, for our daughter is happy to bring you—" the husband started saying, but Vilmad held up his hand and politely cut off his sentence.

"That will not be necessary, though I am much obliged. I have other engagements I must tend to this evening, so I will now leave Miss Lisa in your care..."

Vilmad then looked at me—his smile now gone—and whispered, "Be ready to depart at 8:00 a.m. *sharp!*" He then turned back toward the Balthiers, grinning again, "It has been a pleasure."

The cloaked Guardian walked out the door, gave another baffling smile, and evanesced away... leaving me all alone in the hands of his fervid enthusiasts.

The moment he disappeared, the family's energy and kindness surged on.

"Lisa, we are so blessed to have you here in our home," the husband told me, leading me to their living area to sit on their couch. "I am Roy Balthier, and this is my lovely wife, Emmeryn, and our daughter, Valhalla."

"Thank you for having me here, sir," I said, scanning the room wide-eyed. They seemed to treat me as a well-known guest, but I still could only see them as a foster family, so I stayed shy.

"Are you hungry or thirsty? I bet you've had such a long day and haven't eaten supper yet," Emmeryn said as I sat on the plump, yellow couch.

My kneecaps turned in and touched when my stomach then growled as if it heard Emmeryn's voice—signaling to her I was starving.

Blushing, I held my gut and answered, "I'm a little bit hungry, actually."

Emmeryn and Roy both shot toward the kitchen like bustling chefs, leaving me with their daughter. She looked my age, sitting on the same couch cushion as me, so being with her was a *little* more comfortable. The purple irises around her pupils were striking, making it hard not to stare. I didn't even know that trait could exist outside of colored contacts.

"I'm Valhalla, like my dad said when you came in," Valhalla greeted, eagerly smiling with a look of awe.

"I'm Lisa," I responded softly.

"I still can't believe you are staying with us, *here* in our *house!*" she exclaimed, turning her body toward me, staring at me as if she had never seen another human in her house before. "When the Guardian Rayna visited us last week, I thought my life couldn't get any better, but then, she asked us to let you stay here because she *trusted us*—I still can't believe you're sitting here on *our couch!*"

I truly didn't know how to respond and sat frozen on the lumpy cushion.

This girl fawned over me just because I knew the Guardians and was chosen by the Agapéd Magic. Heat rushed to my ears and cheeks, and I knew she had to see the red overlaying my freckles. Being talked to like that was weird—never in my whole life had someone looked at me the way she and her parents did as if I were as grand as the seven celestial beings of magic.

Valhalla then crisscrossed her legs, causing me to scoot over a bit; she didn't seem to notice my personal space was invaded. "Sorry if I seem a little excited. I just can't help it—you're like a magic legend, ya know?"

"I am?"

At that moment, Mr. and Mrs. Balthier said the food was done, and Valhalla led me to their dining room. It wasn't much different from the one back at my house, except that their chairs were stools and there was a mini buffet on the table. I didn't realize how hungry I was until I started eating Mrs. Balthiers' food; it was all *so good*! We each had a little bowl of broth and could grab the grilled veggies and meat from the table burner, making our own soup. I wasn't used to that type of family-style dinner, seeing as Mom would either prepare me a plate or I would scoop my own from the stovetop.

Averting the dinner topic of Calendula back to me and my purpose for being there, Mr. Balthier said, "Little is known of the Agapéd." He slurped up some of his soup. "Given that it's a one-of-a-kind magic spanning over all four galaxies. You won't find many books or articles mentioning it either—"

"Lisa's proved them wrong, though!" Valhalla interjected, still having a piece of potato in her mouth. "You sitting here is something I bet people would envy over."

"Really?" I quietly responded, stirring around my soup.

Mr. Balthier continued, "What's been given to you, Lisa, is something sacred—something beautiful and a beacon of hope."

I stopped the spoonful of vegetable soup from entering my mouth at Mr. Balthier's bold statement. "Hope?"

"Mhm—though we don't know as much about the Agapéd as the golden Guardians do—we are firm believers that the Agapéd is meant for something good. The last bearer was said to be a mighty protector and brought joy to many nations. He was not of our planet, though he *may* have visited as most grand Mystics do. Plus, that was over a hundred years ago. Hard to keep up with history in a town as small as ours."

What they said was strange. *Mighty protector...?* Those words definitely didn't describe me. Only time the word "mighty" was used to describe me would be if the word "small" or "pale" followed after, and "protector"... That was something I could never be. I had to have Mom come and kill the bugs in my room and couldn't even defend our home if it were robbed by the neighbor's grandkids— *they* weren't even in middle school yet.

The Guardians made my magic seem special but not as sacred or part of some myth, and they definitely did not speak about the last bearer before me. "Do you know anything else about the last bearer?" I asked Mr. Balthier as I stirred my soup.

"Sorry, but much has happened over the past one hundred years... and many nations run by the Magic Embassy try to push away any form of magic connected to the golden Guardians."

Valhalla voiced her opinions loudly into the conversation again. "But Calendula is independent and works with a Keeper, meaning we are kinda special—especially now that a Guardian even came to our door."

"Do they... not do that often?" Another question I added.

The Balthiers then stared at me as if I blurted out some shocking secret.

"You serious—" Valhalla began, but her mother cut her off.

"Valhalla—sorry, Lisa," Ms. Balthier apologized for her daughter. "Seeing a Keeper is already a rarity—even for Sir Gaius, who lives in our town. A Guardian—*My!* Being in their presence is considered a sign of good tidings— rarer than rare and as scarce as anything!"

Mr. Balthier chimed in, adding to his wife's adoration, "You'll learn in Calendula, Lisa, that we all believe in what the Guardians do—trusting The Light and using magic for good—but you'll not find many people in this town who have ever conversed with a Guardian. Being that we are one of the few, we are quite honored."

Valhalla then sat on her knees on her wooden stool, placing her hands on the table before loudly saying, "Dad's been approached by Miss Rayna *twice*—can you believe it? They really like us—telling us we were the most trustworthy and kind-hearted people in the whole city, wanting you to be our guest while you train with them and everything! The Guardians are so cool!"

It was quite odd to be on the other side of the situation because I thought seeing the Guardians was something as normal as seeing my neighbor mowing their grass. To this whole town, though, the Guardians are quite revered. Given that I had spent more time with magical beings than the humans on this planet, it was no surprise that my perception was all jumbled up. I didn't have the nerve to tell the Balthiers how the Guardians really acted around each other and how Vilmad couldn't stand to be near Emunah or Gaius. Timidness still reigned over my other emotions, so I wasn't able to ask more questions about their world and tales of the past Agapéd Bearer—I would have to save that for another time.

After dinner, Valhalla gave me a tour of their home. It was about the same size as mine and very cozy, though theirs had three bedrooms instead of two. There were stacks of books near their study room and randomly placed baskets and boxes through the upstairs hallways, which made the house seem smaller. Each room had two or three windows to provide light, but the house remained dimly lit since it was dark outside. Everything smelled like the essence of lilac and rose, not the fake kind poured into a spray bottle and then misted over furniture. Some family photos hung on the wall, none in coordinating frames, very rustic and old-looking. A part of me was surprised to see photographs. *Guess they have more technology than I was thinking... wonder if they have computers and cell phones as we do on Earth?* Overall, their home was inviting, calming my mind from the worries about spending the night there... for who knew how long.

Valhalla's room was not like mine. Drawings of men and women shooting fire and water out of their fists covered most of her walls, not glossy posters of boy bands or blurry pictures of friends. There were also bundles of magazines sticking out from underneath her bed, the word "magic" being in every single title. *Guess this explains why she was acting so weird—she's obsessed with magic.* She also had many plants in her room, which didn't surprise me given that Calendula was a plant paradise. Her bed was draped with a green quilt patterned with vines and berries, and she even had a section of the room where her clothes were piled (at least we had *something* in common). I told her how I had a television in my room, and she thought that was some form of luxury. I only ever knew that to be normal for a teenager.

It was strange seeing how similar their home and lifestyle were compared to mine—living in a neighborhood, having the same twenty-four-hour days, and eating dinner around a table. Earth enforced the idea that aliens and other lifeforms were scattered across the universe, never that other humans were building more civilizations—thinking just alike, too. In my mind, since my first impression was meeting the Guardians, I pictured magic to be... more special and ancient with castles and no indoor plumbing. Here and in EverWake, it was as normal as turning on the TV after a school day. People walking through invisible entrances to a hidden town was something casual, and teleporting was convenient and not an impossibility. As common as magic was turning out to be, I still found it fascinating and couldn't help but marvel at even the slightest glimpse of it.

The last room she showed me was the one I would be staying in. It was across from hers and even had a beautiful sunroof where all the stars could be seen in the night sky. She left me some of her clothes to wear for pajamas, too, and Mrs. Balthier even decorated the futon bed with many fluffy pillows.

"Oh, and you can use any of the soaps in our washroom as well. Mom also left you out some towels, too," Valhalla told me. She was standing outside my new bedroom door.

"That was nice of her," I added, now sitting on the futon.

"Well, I guess I will let you get ready for bed..."

"Thanks, I'll see you in the morning," I said, but she still didn't close the door and paused for a second or two.

"If you need anything and asking my parents makes you too nervous, just come to my room and wake me up. I don't mind..."

My words slowed. "I'll be sure to do that..."

Valhalla did not leave even after shutting down the conversation. I didn't know why she wanted to stay, but I did have one question that I felt was rather dumb to ask her parents. "Actually—"

Valhalla immediately swung the door all the way open.

I continued, "I was given an orbkit today, and I have no idea how to open it. Do you know how?"

Valhalla came right next to my new bed with stars in her eyes. "You actually have an *orbkit*? I have been begging my parents to get me one, but they cost so many credits and are pretty rare to find at most merchant shops—where did you get yours?"

"Um, at this jewelry shop in EverWake, but I forgot the name—"

"*Jacks*—you got to visit EverWake, Gaius the Keeper of Stars, *and* meet the Guardians all in one week?"

I nodded while taking the necklace off of my neck.

"Lisa, you are officially the coolest person I have ever met."

Valhalla stayed awake with me for another two hours after showing me how to work the orbkit. Turned out, with one swipe of my hand over the locket, a magical projection of the orbkit's empty pockets appeared right in front of me—just like a hologram! I then could "place" any objects in the magic slots by touching them with my hands, and they disappear inside. It felt like touching craft glitter that had been sitting inside the fridge for a couple of hours.

Both of us experimented with all sorts of different objects in the room, seeing how many we could fit into the necklace and how big they could be. We were able to fit the whole futon in the locket just by selecting an empty slot and then touching the bed. I told her about EverWake and Earth, and she told me about Calendula. We discovered we both had birthdays last month, were an only child, and had *never* owned a pet. Even from different worlds, it seemed we still experienced a lot of the same teenage things.

Even though she still thought I was this big-shot magical superstar, Valhalla had been more of a friend to me in those couple of hours than anyone had in my entire life. I thought I knew what a friend was—thought Lily and Jenny Kim were decent friends, at least—but seeing her enjoying my topics, thinking I was cool, and not just tolerating me, opened my eyes to reality. She was what a friend should be... maybe a little eccentric but completely heartfelt and kind.

Before Mrs. Balthier made her go to bed, Valhalla gave me a tiny alarm token—it was like a stopwatch but smaller—to make sure I woke up on time. She said I couldn't be late, or else I wouldn't be able to tell her all about my first day as the new Agapéd Bearer.

8
DAY ONE OF TRAINING

"... Do you think they will knock?" Valhalla asked, perched in the armchair and glancing out the living room window at the rising sun.

"I dunno..." I responded, my voice quiet, sitting in the chair's twin, though mine was further away from the window.

When the time struck 7:56 a.m. on the Balthier's analog clock on their dining table wall, we all waited in the living room with minimal talking. Vilmad said to be ready by 8 a.m. sharp, so I was, but so were Valhalla and her mom. I don't think he meant for the Balthiers to participate with me, but I didn't have the heart to tell them that.

Being at the Balthiers was different. Normally, sleeping in a new environment was impossible for me. My body knew it was in unfamiliar territory and stayed on high alert the entire night. This morning, however, I woke up refreshed and ready to start my first day of training with the Guardians and Keepers—not sleepy in the slightest. I took my shower and picked out the simple blue shirt and shorts outfit Inna bought me, throwing it on before heading downstairs. Mr. Balthier had left the house long before the sun even peeked over the horizon. Valhalla still had school, which was also called a "Tutor" according to one of our late conversations, so she was also awake. Mrs. Balthier made us cinnamon and honey pastries for breakfast—freshly baked with local honey, too!

7:59 a.m. arrived, and there was still no sign of Vilmad, Bethesda, or Micah. Mrs. Balthier was now standing near the door, trying not to seem eager to meet another Guardian.

"So... you sure he said 8:00?" Valhalla asked me, looking through the curtains of their living room.

"Valhalla—" Mrs. Balthier gasped.

"I'm just saying, what if he said *late* instead of *eight*, and we just missed what time to not be late for."

"The Guardians do not mumble, and Lisa and I were standing right next to him..." She glanced back out the door's small window. "Though, I do admit my hearing is not the best."

"Lisa, you sure you heard 8:00 a.m., right?"

"Well, actually—"

When the hour hand of the clock pointed to the number eight, the chair beneath me suddenly vanished, and I was surrounded by light and thunder. I was still in my seated position, and when the light faded away, I had no time to place my footing and fell right on my butt in the middle of an elaborate library in the Elysium. Floor-to-ceiling bookshelves of polished walnut wood decorated the walls, stuffed with thick books stitched in gold. Wisteria and pearled plants hung from the ceiling near the only wall without books—the wall with a spherical window that overlooked a majestic courtyard. A large desk of the same glossy wood sat against the window, which I landed in front of.

When Vilmad said, "Be ready by eight," he was not kidding. Why he didn't tell me he'd send me there by teleportation, I did not know.

"I see Vilmad didn't mention we can evanesce you here without warning," Bethesda said to me, sitting behind the elaborate wooden desk in the study room. "At least you were dressed."

I stood up as quickly as I could, trying to ignore the pain and embarrassment from the fall. Bethesda, dressed in a sunset orange robe and a pair of gold gladiator sandals, instructed me to come over to her desk and handed me a blank notebook. It wasn't spiral bound or in an industrial folder, just ivory pages in a sturdy leather-back cover without any printed type inside.

"This is Micah's study," she said as I walked over to the smaller desk adjacent to hers. "He, Vilmad, and I will primarily be working with you in this room, having a mix between lectures, hands-on study, and independent work. Now, shall we begin?"

I nodded, and right off the bat, Bethesda started class by explaining the most common types of magic.

"It all derives from the Light and Darkness—the purest forms of magic. When both collide, a world of cosmic color bursts into smaller pieces of power that gift nature unique abilities. After thousands of years, many different forms of magic have been seen all across the galaxies."

Bethesda shot up a large ball of green, orange, and blue dust—swirling around until rivers of emeralds, the essence of grass, and ribbons of magma formed—and floated it above our heads. She made it seem so effortless, not even flexing any of her muscles. "Elemental magic. It is the easiest to identify because it will resemble much of the plant kingdom's physical attributes and the sea's depths—anything you'd find on a planet. This also includes animals—being able to converse with or control them—and any tangible matter made by weather: lightning, frost, sunlight, and so forth. Elemental magic is powered either through one's connection with real-world elements or by the actual earth itself. It is strong, this magic. One of true beauty and ferocious strength."

The next ball of magic she cast above our heads was a pure orb of neon lights. When floating next to the elemental magic, this new power looked smooth and steady, with only subtle plumes of chromatic glitter circumnavigating the globe.

"Phantasmal magic is the polar opposite of elemental, for it takes what is imaginary and makes it reality. The Mystic or Mage with phantasmal magic creates their power with the magic in their soul. Illusions and ideas take the form of similar elements seen in nature. One can create phantasmal flames that rage red, blue, or green—yet it will burn just like fire. You could even create the illusion of invisibility and project that magic onto yourself. This magic thrives from one's magic strength, whereas elemental power grows stronger depending on one's environment."

The third orb Bethesda projected into the air was an illusion of colored liquids and lightning, bouncing around like raindrops breaking the water's surface.

"The last basic form of magic is that of potions and charms—base magic. Any Mystic or Mage can perform enchantments, create potions, and warp matter by using magic-based objects or following rules for a charm. This magic is not one someone is born with but is rather a skill that must be instructed or taught vigorously over the course of many months or years…"

Bethesda stopped her magical illusions and looked right at me. "Are you ready to move on?"

For the first time in my life, I wanted to learn for the pure *joy* of learning. My heart craved magic—wanting to touch it, to feel it, and to discover all of its wonderful qualities. Nothing in the world was more enthralling to me.

I looked at Bethesda, grinning ear to ear, and said like a little kid, "That was so cool!"

She smiled back at me. "I will take that as a 'yes' then. Let us continue."

A little over an hour later, I finished my first lesson with Bethesda and could honestly say—perhaps, for the first time in my life—that I loved learning! Magic was beyond fascinating… It was my newfound passion. Back at my public school, I never thought academic subjects were enticing: biology, poetry, geometry, or really any of them. I would study and learn only for a good grade in the end, but retaining the knowledge was never computed in my head. I made an A+ on my history test over the Civil War—the only 100 in my entire class—but a week later, I couldn't name a single general or even where the war started. Magic, though, poured itself into my heart and filled that empty slot labeled "fascination," and I couldn't wait to learn more.

"Thank you for my lesson today," I gleefully said to Bethesda, putting my leather notebook into my orbkit.

"Well, you had a surprisingly willing attitude to learn, and I am looking forward to our next lesson in the coming weeks," she said back, standing near my desk.

It was quite pleasing to hear that she appreciated me.

Bethesda then had me stand up and continued, "Now, it is time for your first true experience in magic training. I will send you back to planet Kalm to Mantene where Inna resides—hoping she can guide you in one of the three forms of magic—and she will greet you at the entrance of the Aquanaeum."

"How will I know what it looks like?" I responded worriedly, but Bethesda didn't seem to notice.

She smiled. "You will know it when you see it. Good luck to you, Miss Lisa."

Before I could ask for any form of directions, Bethesda teleported me to the seaside gulf town of Mantene.

The smell of saltwater hit my nose before my eyes had a chance to open. Squinting from the sunrays, I saw a blue ocean twenty feet in front of me. Being around water reminded me of home, but instead of rustic boat docks and parades of seagulls, there was a giant aquarium half a mile out in the middle of the inlet. Walls of chrome blue and white stone formed its intricate edges, and elegant marina slips rose along the right side of the massive structure, holding the most unique ships I had ever seen.

The humid breeze was coming in from the right, blowing my hair in my face and causing me to turn around. I expected to see dull, bricked buildings or a fish market. Instead, there were many small, pastel-colored homes surrounding the inlet. Looking at the colorfully painted buildings, Mantene seemed more like a little Italian town on the coast—the kind I had seen on postcards and in the movies. There weren't many people pacing the street, but the ones that were all stared at me. *Guess appearing out of nowhere isn't as common here as it is in EverWake.*

I immediately turned to my left. A long, wide bridge, less than half a mile in length, connected the aquarium's entrance to the tourist town. There hung a sign overhead that read "Aquanaeum." I walked up to the bridge, didn't see any type of toll or sign that required payment, and took a long stroll toward the entrance.

It felt weird to cross without an adult or someone standing near me so I could play follow-the-leader, and that moment was the first time I missed having Mom there, a smidge of homesickness beginning to fog my brain. She was always with me anytime we left the house, and being by myself to find my own way was a new, overwhelming feeling; I didn't like it. My independence was like a bear during winter, hibernating for months on end until nature decided it was time to awaken... or, in this circumstance, until a Guardian forced me to get up and walk.

I pushed aside my dependent attitude and walked to the end of the bridge, reaching a large glass and metal door. A tall, muscular lady stood at the door frame, and I froze. I thought she would tell me to leave or "state my business," but instead, she smiled and opened the door. *Did she know who I was?*

Inside—to my surprise—resembled a museum or gallery of the ocean and its sea life. I had only been to one aquarium back on Earth, and the inside of the

Aquanaeum looked extremely similar to that. I saw only a few people going in and out of the corridors, but none were Inna. Further ahead was a man at an info desk, dressed the same as the muscular lady. I perked up the courage to ask for help.

"Um, hello, sir?" I timidly said.

"Hello, is there anything I can help you with?" he responded, eager and alert.

"I'm here to see Miss Inna... for, uh, magic training?" It still felt silly to call it that, but I couldn't think of a better title.

"Oh... let me see if I can get her for you." He immediately grabbed a steel-plated phone and dialed some numbers.

That was way easier compared to visiting Gaius.

Minutes later, two Aquanaeum workers appeared down the hall. One was a man, and the other was a lady, though, with the woman's hair up in a bun, their tan skin, and blonde hair made it hard to tell them apart. Sunglasses concealed their eyes, and they were buttoned up with blues and turquoise. From a distance, they looked intimidating... until they saw me. They stood unnaturally straight, so stiff I thought they were about to snap in half, and refused to release the deep breaths each had lodged in their throat. *Are they nervous or something?*

When they approached me, they locked their knees and slapped their hands on the sides of their thighs like a soldier. I flinched as the man said with fervid, shaky attentiveness, "Please follow us, Miss!"

I swallowed and dipped my chin, doe-eyed and very surprised. *They are nervous... but why?*

Both Aquanaeum workers guided me down a large hall—never saying another word and refusing to look me in the eye behind their sunglasses—and onto another one of those escalators I rode back in EverWake. We approached an arching cylindrical room, almost the length of a middle school football field, and the walls were completely clear—the ocean in every curved corner of the room. *We are underwater!*

"Lisa!" Inna joyfully exclaimed from the middle of the room. She looked as radiant as the sea surrounding us, and I couldn't be happier to finally see a familiar face that didn't belong to an intimidating Guardian. "I am thrilled you are here! Are you liking Mantene and the Aquanaeum?"

"It's nothing like my port town back at home—are we under the ocean, or is this some type of fish tank?" I asked her, admiring the colorful fish swimming around us.

Inna turned her gaze out toward the sea walls and extended her arm like she was giving a demonstration. "This is one of the two viewing rooms that are, in fact, under Mantene's waters. We are about fifteen meters deep under the emerald coast in view of some of my home's most beautiful creatures... I come here quite often just to sit and listen to the water's tranquil sounds."

Schools of brightly colored orange and purple fish swam against the long seaweed that grazed the window. There were even spotted stingrays and grouper fish—I never knew how big sea creatures were until I stood inches from their faces.

When I touched the transparent wall, my body jerked away. It didn't feel like glass but almost like a rubber or plastic cling wrap. My fingers left ripples along its crystal-like projection, glistening against the sea, but no matter how much I pushed, it was impenetrable.

"I thought this was glass?" I inquired.

Inna stood beside me, her thick braid of strawberry blonde hair draping off her back and over her shoulder. "It is meant to appear so, but it's a magic mantle, and nothing can cross through it except for those wearing one of these."

She motioned for one of the twin Aquanaeum workers in the room to come near us. The girl worker tensed up and pulled out a blue wristband from her pocket as if her life depended on it. *Okay, so it isn't just me that makes them nervous but Inna, too.* Nothing seemed magical about the rubber band until I put it on. The moment my hand slipped through the large band, it instantly shrunk down to fit comfortably on my slim wrist. Inna's blue bracelet seemed to have done the same.

A magic bracelet for a magic room—so cool!

"Go ahead and touch the glass mantle again," Inna instructed.

I hesitantly reached out my hand toward the water, not entirely knowing what was going to happen. Suddenly, my fingers went through the veil—straight into the water! I reached further, and my whole hand was submerged in the ocean! My body on the outside was dry, and there was no hole from where my hand penetrated, yet I could move my arm around freely, making bubbles and currents in the sea. The most bewildering part was when I pulled my hand back in... it was *completely dry!*

"What—how did it do that?" I asked, utterly blown away at the magic of the wristband.

Inna giggled and answered, "Sometimes, the simplest answer is just purely *magic...* Now, come. We must first get you something to eat, and then, we will try and unlock that magic resting in your heart."

⁓

Happily satisfied after snacking on the Aquanaeum's concessions, which consisted of veggie sandwiches and assorted juices, Inna took me back to the upper level along with the two sunglasses-wearing twin Aquanaeum workers. We walked outside onto a large flat concrete surface that stood just above the water—the back of the Aquanaeum's main building—and trekked along the right side. A couple of workers rode on large water bikes, wearing wetsuits and carrying strange glowing containers. My curiosity piqued, wondering what made the heavily locked containers radiate, but I decided to ask questions later. Honestly, there were so many unusual, magical things around me that if I stopped and asked about each one, I would've been there until midnight.

"Alright, Lisa," Inna said as we both stopped at the edge of the concrete slate of land, "it's time for your first lesson in magic training. Lady Ariela and the Guardians informed me that the Agapéd has yet to reveal what magic it has chosen for you, so we will give your hand a try at the elemental magic of water. This does not mean you will innately become a Mage today or even inherit elemental magic at all, but since this is the magic I am gifted with, we will start with that... sound good?"

That sounded even better than good. "So, I could have any type of magic out there?" I asked, very excited about that being a possibility.

"In a sense, yes. The Agapéd Magic is... unpredictable regarding what magic it chooses for the human's heart. Normally, the user already has a magic pulse, and the Agapéd Magic will deem another power to compliment that said Mage or Mystic, but for us, we are starting from scratch. Kind of exciting, don't you agree?"

I nodded, grinning ear to ear.

"Okay, let's get started. There are two types of elemental water magic—"

"Creation and manipulation, right?" I interjected, remembering what Bethesda taught me earlier that day.

"Yes—I see you've been paying attention to the Guardians' lessons already. Those who can manipulate the forms of water, and those who can *create* one of the three states of water from thin air."

Inna then moved her hands in a rhythmic motion in front of her chest, and a bubble of water formed between her palms, crystal clear and with a blue tint. No mistaking it—that was *real* water she just made, and it was floating in mid-air!

She moved her arms in a fluid rhythm, creating more glistening water ripples around her head and body. "Whether you create water like I do or manipulate its waves surrounding you, water from magic should feel like dancing. It's elegant like a flowing stream but also as forceful as a waterfall—stronger when moving all at once. Water can create beauty and life—gifting peace and healing to all land—but should not be taken lightly either, for even a little rain can pile up and bring down mountains. It's a simple yet enchanting element of our world, and I want you to try and dance with it too, okay?"

What...? I had no idea what she truly meant besides the word "dancing." I had only ever danced in my room to the Jonas Brothers and when I played *Just Dance* on the Wii. Even thinking about it, I felt embarrassed and self-conscious, especially with the twin guards *still* watching us—both stiffer than a plank of wood. To make it worse, *more* workers were going in and out of the Aquanaeum building, too, and I *knew* they were staring at us—a kid being taught by an angelic woman in a leotard. Nothing about the situation was comfortable—not in the *slightest.*

However, my fear transformed into relief when Inna retrieved a blue five-foot staff from her orbkit (hers was a charm that latched onto her belt instead of a necklace like mine). The rod had a large blue gem at its end, the biggest jewel I had ever seen, heavy and sparkling in the sunlight.

"The gem on this staff contains the aura of elemental water magic," Inna stated, "and it will attract water like a magnet—but *only* for those with a strong magic pulse. I want you to practice moving with the staff as if it were an extension of your arm, and *you* are in control of the water, not the rod itself."

Inna handed it to me. The end with the blue stone was a little heavy, but I tried to act as if it didn't faze me. I felt... odd holding the staff. Never in my life was I given a weapon—or whatever you would call the rod—and I didn't want to look like an idiot in front of Inna. The only sources of reference I had were movies and video games, so I just mimicked what I'd seen.

I grasped the rod with two hands like I would hold a broom before sweeping. "Is this, uh, correct?" I timidly asked her.

She answered, "That is just fine—don't worry too much Lisa. Just give it a go."

I took a big gulp and went to the edge of the concrete floor where the water was free of boats and other vehicles. The ocean was only a foot or so lower than the man-made land we were on, so I didn't have to lean too far over.

"I want you to hold on tightly to the rod and graze the top of the water, making a figure-eight shape."

I did as she said, moving the rod around in a fluid motion, and I saw ripples in the water. The gem started flickering a bright blue as the current moved even more. *Was that the wind, or did I do that?*

"Good! Now, keep your wrists limber and move your arms in bigger motions—don't be afraid of trying, okay?"

I nodded and made my arms less stiff, going in bigger curved patterns. Suddenly, the gem started glowing more, and a small stream of water started rising from the sea. *It is me—I'm doing that right now!* It flowed with my motions, giving me more confidence in my movements. The water was moving like a snake, and I was the charmer!

"Superb, Lisa!" Inna praised. "Try bringing a small puddle over to the concrete, keeping your movement fluid, and flying it over to me."

"Got it!" I said, and I kept making circular motions in the air with my elbows and arms moving the staff. The water detached from the ocean molecules, and a large, boggy bubble flew above my head! I saw Inna smiling at me, and I got a surge of confidence to try and move it around my body.

I must have moved too quickly because the moment my staff made a 180° turn, the water jetted toward the twin workers twenty feet away from us. The blonde man and woman ducked, but unfortunately, two other workers were behind them. My ribbon of water bolted, knocking one of the unfamiliar workers into the ocean. The one next to him started belly laughing as my cheeks and ears turned red from embarrassment.

"Sorry, mister!" I yelled. Luckily, he was moving—*alive* and not bleeding—and started swimming back up to the concrete shore. *Thank goodness.*

Inna came closer and knelt just enough to make eye contact with me. "Lisa, you should be very proud of yourself."

"Even though I knocked that guy over into the sea?" I said, partially smiling, my ribcage rattling my heart as I held the staff upright.

Inna grinned and said, in heart-warming seriousness, "No, though that was quite amusing. It is because you were able to use your magic pulse to power the gem on your first day... it means, dear Lisa, that you can officially be called and considered a *Mage.*"

9

THE AVELIFT

Lisa the Mage.

Me—that was *me*. I used actual magic—making water move. Seeing myself lift strands of the sea with just a twist and twirl of the rod was amazing. I know the Guardians said I had magic, but finally, being able to use the celestial power solidified the realness of it all. *And* I didn't knock another Aquanaeum employee in the water or embarrass myself. Pretty impressive—pretty *Agapéd-like,* if I were being honest.

For the rest of the afternoon, Inna continued to help train me in using the magic staff and how to move the element of water effectively. She could show me ways of bending the water without losing control—all without using a staff herself. All her water movements with her hands were easy to mimic with the staff, and watching her feet and arms move with her waves was far easier and more enjoyable than reading it in class with Bethesda.

Between our lessons, Inna removed the staff and had me try to move with my hands. Every time I moved my arms in a rhythm and tensed up my muscles over the ocean, nothing happened. I felt silly at first, but that soon changed into frustration. The water was lifeless for me without the help of the magic rod. Inna would then tell me, "Don't worry, it's only the first day," before handing back the staff to practice more.

I would be lying if I said I wasn't a little discouraged, but having Inna praise me for the work I did accomplish brought my spirits back up. After all, I actually used magic—the stuff that used to only exist in my daydreams—so my good mood trumped any form of harsh self-criticism.

The sky began to show signs of reds and oranges, cueing the end of my first magic training lesson with Inna. She mentioned we had a couple of minutes before I needed to head back, so she led us to an outdoor patio on one of the higher levels of the Aquanaeum, not too far from the main entrance. There were benches and seating areas placed all around where we could enjoy the view of the seaside town.

Inna and I sat near the edge of the terrace while the two blonde Aquanaeum workers—who had been following us the entire day like guards—stood near the door. I was rather surprised Inna walked so freely through the large building since she was a Keeper. With her being immortal and acquainted with the Guardians, I figured she would be more like Gaius: excluded and mysterious.

"This view is just amazing!" I exclaimed, admiring the warming sun reflecting off the windows of the small town and the water ahead of us.

"Out of all the places I've seen, nothing beats the sunsets here in Mantene," Inna expressed, relaxing her posture on the white bench.

The opportunity to ask non-magic training questions finally arrived, so I indulged my curiosity. "Inna, do you live here at the Aquanaeum? Is it like your house or just where you work?"

"Well, I would say it is a bit of both. Lady Ariela gifted me this land and building when I accepted her gift of being a Keeper, but as you can tell, it is far too big for any one person. Years later, I decided to create the Aquanaeum, making my home into an organization that helps the creatures of the sea and develops aquatic-magic inventions—like the mantle and wristband you experienced in the viewing room. Now, it has blossomed into a tourist attraction where many can come and admire some of Mantene's most beautiful sea creatures."

"Oh, I see..." I looked back at the guards still standing by the door before asking another question, just to see if they were listening or not. "Inna," I softly asked, scooting closer to her on the bench, "you mentioned back in EverWake that, as a Keeper of Stars, you create starseeds. Is that secret, or am I allowed to know?"

She looked at me in shock and chuckled a bit. "Lisa, you will have to forgive me, for you being from Earth keeps slipping my mind. Me being a Keeper is no secret, though you will encounter those who will deny my existence or claim it is only but a mere title; however, Starseed Creation is one of the things that are sacred here, and only a trusted few know about it."

"So it *is* a secret then," I whispered, excited to learn more. "Are you like a creator or... harvester of magic or something like that, then?

"Remember when I mentioned the Age of the Black Sky?"

I nodded and reaffirmed, "You said that Ariela made you and other Keepers of the Wishing Stars so the humans wouldn't steal the magic, right?"

"Yes, and I and two others were gifted specific magic to prevent that from happening again. We each play a part in the life cycle of the Wishing Stars. There is Kamari, who watches over the stars that are already a part of the sky. She is the only one who can move the Wishing Stars and herd them in the correct direction once they are a part of our galaxies. No one can steal a star if they can't move it. Then, there is me, the one who creates the starseeds. When a Wishing Star falls and releases its magic, stardust will scatter across the earth, and when it falls into the water, we are able to harvest it—one of the most important jobs here at the Aquanaeum."

A salty breeze blew in, pushing my wavy brown hair off my shoulders. "As in *we*, you mean the workers here help, too?"

"Yes, you may have seen a couple returning from their excavation earlier today."

"So *that's* what was in those glowing boxes, but I thought only *you* could create the starseeds?"

Inna adjusted her seating position, fiddling with her sandals so they wouldn't scratch her extravagant wetsuit as she crossed her legs. "Oh, the bins you saw were just loose stardust. Anyone can collect it if given the correct equipment, but I am the only one who can transform it into starseeds. Without me, stardust is nothing less than sparkling soot. It takes a while to make the different seeds, depending on the location and magic essence the stardust contains, but once they are fully ready, I will bring them to the last of us three, *Gaius*. He is the one, in my opinion, with the most important role: growing and caring for the star saplings."

I turned my body to face her, and my jaw dropped. "You mean the Wishing Stars *actually* grow like plants—in soil and everything? I thought you were speaking... figuratively."

"Along with Gaius' magic, yes—like any normal plant. It sounds simple, but each seed is different and requires various types of care. When all the seeds have blossomed and produced fully grown Wishing Stars, Kamari then leads all the hundreds of stars into the galaxies. Then, the cycle repeats. It's pretty ingenious, huh?"

That's the coolest thing I have ever heard!

"Is that why you have your home in the ocean and why Gaius lives in the Veradome... because you both do your Keeper work beneath the name of your organizations?"

Inna smirked at me as blush-blonde wisps of her elaborate braid drifted from their hold. "You sure do catch on quite quickly, Lisa. The Aquanaeum and Veradome each have their own agendas, but like you so cleverly figured out, their main purpose is to offer protection for our Keeper agendas. Kamari works with the Stellarlegion—they guard the entrances to and from galaxies along with security control. I work here with the Aquanaeum, and Gaius helps with Calendula and the Veradome. Our work is very precious, so it must be protected at all costs. Since you also have special one-of-a-kind magic as well, I have no reason to hide any of this from you."

I was quite honored after she said that to me. It was not every day an adult would tell me secrets.

"Inna, you are definitely the coolest teacher I've ever had."

The Keeper of Stars started giggling. "Well, then, I am honored to be considered 'cool,' so thank you, Lisa."

After we recollected ourselves, Inna led the way toward the exit of the Aquanaeum with the same two guards tailing ten feet behind us. I was guessing they were her bodyguards, so I didn't bother to question why they followed us; she was important, and in my mind, it made sense to have protection. As we walked, one more question continued to pop up in my mind—one I wanted to know before I headed back to the Balthiers.

Fidgeting with my fingers and glancing at the planks of the entrance bridge, I quietly asked, "Inna, before I have to leave, can I ask you about Gaius? Since you know him pretty well, is he... a *good* guy? Vilmad just didn't seem to like him very much when he first introduced me, and I figured you would know him best since you deliver the starseeds to him."

Inna's pace down the long half-mile bridge back to shore didn't slow down, and her eyes didn't make contact with mine as she said, "I can assure you Gaius is good-hearted. He is just quiet and a more 'to himself' kind of man. You have nothing to fear about your lesson with him tomorrow."

"But, uh, what was with all those weapons in his workshop? I mean, you've seen them, right? Since you're friends?"

This time, Inna's shoulders tensed, and I saw her eyes look around the town as if the answer to my question was on the colorful siding of Mantene's homes. "He likes to craft weapons when he isn't working. It's kind of... his *hobby,* I guess you could say. He is rather good at it, and he won't deny that..." Her words softened as we made it to the end of the bridge, a bit rushed, too. "He's just an old man who likes weapons. Nothing more."

The strawberry-blonde Keeper ended the conversation with a vague answer, and it didn't seem like she wanted to talk more about Gaius... which left me even *more* nervous about lessons with him the next day. I already guessed he was a "good guy" because why else would the Guardians trust him to be a Keeper? The answer I truly hoped for was Inna telling me more about his quirks and personality—knowing his demeanor and what things I should avoid saying during lessons. I mean the man had *hordes* of weapons—*used* weapons—in his house... and I still didn't believe he simply had them all for fun. It would have been nice to know what I would be walking into.

We two and the guards walked through the seaside town, right in between the sweet-smelling homes and hotels lit up with warm orange and yellow lights. The restaurants weren't too full of people, but the noise from laughter and joyous conversations made it feel as if there was no vacancy. It reminded me of my home on summer nights, and I was glad, knowing I would be returning to Mantene more often as Inna's lessons continued.

A set of stairs approached ahead, leading us to a train stop of some sort. It was small, having a couple of awnings for shade and a few white benches. I didn't see any railways or steel tracks, just the same concrete and stone floor that we had been walking on all evening. A small booth stood near the edge of the stairs with a screen that read "7:25 PM NOW BOARDING..." in blue letters, and the name "Boolavogue Outskirts Station 1" popped up underneath.

Suddenly, a charming ring stirred up in the air, announcing the arrival of the vehicle for which this station was built. The empty railway began to glisten like liquid glass, and a track magically appeared. A second ring occurred in our ears, and a gust of wind burst through the air, brushing my hair off of my shoulders and onto my back. Before I could even blink, a long white and gritty golden train zoomed into the station. It flew out of the air—no wings or powerful jet engine attached! Glass windows covered the walls, and I could see rows of padded seating inside with a handful of people in them. The mystical vehicle's speed was like lightning, yet it made little noise, and I didn't see any form of smoke or smell of gasoline.

It's a magic monorail!

"Alright, Lisa, this is your stop," Inna said with her hands on her hips.

Completely taken aback, I blurted, "Wha—me?" My face suddenly lost all complexion, and I could feel my heart start to race again.

"It's just the avelift, a very common mode of transportation here on our planet. You'll be taking this to and from Mantene when you join me for lessons from now on unless the Guardians evanesce you here. I also won't see you again until after your first lesson with Gaius tomorrow," Inna said, still unfazed by my nervous reaction.

"But I thought I would be evanescing home?" I quickly interjected, fearing my first-ever magical train ride to an unknown location.

"I don't mind evanescing you, but Vilmad insisted for you to learn your way around our world without us 'holding your hand,' as he put it."

Of course, he would say that…

The avelift chimed a third time.

"Are you sure you can't ride along with me?" I kept turning my gaze back and forth from Inna to the train as some passengers trickled in. Public transportation wasn't something I was used to seeing in Keyport, New Jersey—*especially* without an adult.

A fourth chime rang through the air, and the sign on the booth and train glowed "DEPARTING IN 2 MINUTES…".

"You won't be going alone, that is why Asa and Ava are here," Inna rushed as the two Aquanaeum employees stepped up. It now made sense why they were stalking us the entire afternoon, but I didn't know why she waited so late to mention it.

"It would be our pleasure to escort you, Miss!" they both simultaneously said in a confident, loud tone.

A fifth chime rang—reminding me of my unavoidable trip to a foreign land—and this time, the avelift started making a humming noise. The magic track began to appear again.

"Wait—aren't we going to Calendula—"

"Boolavogue Outskirts is near the forest entrance!" Inna started to shout back as the guards began to lead me into the train. "Asa and Ava will show you where!"

"Boola-what?"

The avelift doors closed with a confused me standing inside amongst two Aquanaeum workers, who I thought were normal bodyguards for Inna up until now. I saw Inna waving at us before whipping her blush-blonde hair around and disappearing from the station, acting like she didn't just shove me into a magical box with two strangers. I wasn't angry or mad, just very flustered. Never in my life had I encountered a situation like this before, and I didn't know how to react.

As I stood watching out the window amid my bewilderment, a voice behind me said, "Miss Lisa, where would you like to sit?" It was Ava... or Asa... whichever one was the female Aquanaeum worker. Honestly, I couldn't remember who was who. They were still wearing their matching sunglasses and both of their names rhyming did not help my brain latch onto which was the girl and which was the boy.

"It doesn't matter... wherever you would like," I answered more timidly than I intended.

"Ava, I will find the very best seat for us three!" Asa interjected—letting me know that *Asa* was the *boy*—and quickly paced up and down the aisles. He moved with such urgency until he spotted the perfect spot... which looked like every other seat. We were the only ones in the compartment, so it wasn't like there was a limited group of three empty seats around.

Ava pushed me toward the row and had me sit directly in between them. I didn't find many things in life to be awkward or uncomfortable. I enjoyed the silence, trying strange foods, and exploring new places, but sitting in the middle of the two seemingly high-strung adults—who, by the way, were *still* wearing sunglasses even though the sun was almost done setting—won the trophy for

"Lisa's Most Awkward Situation Yet."

The last of the six chimes rang as the lights in the avelift began dimming, allowing the warm orange rays from the sunset to break through the windows. Suddenly, a jolt of acceleration overwhelmed me as the avelift left Mantene's station. The scenery changed from stationary to blurry trees and houses, and we were in the *sky!* The monorail was actually flying! I tried to glance out the window without it being obvious to the twins, but Asa quickly understood. He jumped up from his seat—train still in motion—quickly climbed over behind me and insisted I take his window seat. I found it rather funny seeing the two of them act so weirdly attentive toward me, which helped the awkwardness fade away.

From then on, my forehead was glued to the window as my eyes tried to take in all the new scenery down below. We weren't as high as an airplane because I could still see people below us, but it sure felt as if we were going as fast as one. I saw many rivers and valleys, all green and full of life. There were farms and towns scattered across the land, and I found it rather odd to not see any modern buildings or concrete jungles. Everything truly looked like a daydream world of mine. To think there were even more planets like this out there really lit a fire in my heart to continue working hard at magic.

———

Slam!

"Miss Lisa, we have arrived!" Asa shouted with as much energy as he had before we left Mantene.

My head hit the seat directly in front of me with quite a lot of force. It was a good thing the seats were padded on the back as well, or I would've had a purple bruise in the middle of my forehead.

I must have been so worn out from my first training day because I didn't even notice I had fallen asleep. I rubbed my forehead and adjusted my vision before standing back on my feet, a bit embarrassed I even fell asleep in front of Ava and Asa to begin with.

Both of the identical workers had already made their way to the door, standing perfectly straight waiting for me to exit the avelift.

Boolavogue Outskirts Station 1 was nothing like Mantene's terminal. The station was small, open, made of concrete with plants pushing through the cracks, and had basic, old benches made of black iron near the station's edge. I wouldn't say it was rundown, just more homely and made to fit its purpose. There was an old clock outside, showing the time of 7:30 p.m., which I thought was odd since we left around this exact time. I also noticed the sky was still full of sherbet orange, burnt reds, and purple clouds overlaying the forest scenery ahead of us.

"How come the sun hasn't set yet?" I inquired as I stepped out of the monorail.

With much enthusiasm, both workers apologetically bowed toward me, and Ava answered, "Asa and I apologize for not informing you of the time change and length of travel—"

"Which was exactly 55 minutes and 12 seconds!" Asa frantically interjected.

"Oh, that is okay—" I tried to apologize, bashfulness taking over me by the two bowing, but they cut me off again.

"*We are truly sorry, Miss Lisa!*" Asa and Ava both said in unison, not breaking their bowing position.

Stares of the only family around were daggers into my brain. I did not like drawing attention to myself, and it seemed like Ava and Asa truly did not mind it at all.

"No, no—it's okay, really! I was just curious, that's all. You don't have to bow."

The two workers recollected themselves, apologized again for apologizing too loudly, and then started leading the way down the graveled road. Once we left the avelift station, Ava and Asa informed me that the entrance to the forest was tricky to find and a thirty-minute walk from where we landed. According to Ava, both of them were acting so on edge because Inna had never asked for their help in all their days working at the Aquanaeum. They just happened to be the only two siblings who grew up in Calendula and, therefore, knew how to find the hidden entrance.

Soon, all three of us turned off the road and into the forest. There wasn't any form of the beaten path, so I *really* would have to pay attention to the trees around me if I wanted to walk there by myself. We passed many pine and oak trees, along with hordes of crickets and flies. After about fifteen minutes, we reached the familiar entrance I saw when I was guided by Vilmad. Ava and

Asa bowed toward me, saying their thanks simultaneously before heading back through the woods. For my first impression of the twins, I rather enjoyed their company; they made me feel special and not too much of a burden to guide around.

The moment I stepped over the line and into Calendula, someone instantly ran up and hugged me so hard I almost fell over. I didn't recognize her at first, so I just stood there and let the brute hug happen. It wasn't until she spoke that I realized it was Valhalla.

"Oh, I just *knew* you would show up here!" she said, very animated like normal. She released her arms and finished talking. "Lisa, you completely terrified Mom and left her rambling on even after I left for morning Tutor—it was the Guardians, wasn't it? They vanished you away, right—how *crazy!* One second, you were there, and the next, *voosh!*"

I tried to interject, but Valhalla was so persistent in getting out all her bottled-up excitement that I couldn't get any words out unless I yelled... so that is what I did. "*Valhalla!*"

"Oh, sorry! I am just so excited to hear about everything you did. Tell me all that happened on our way back! Mom is making traditional Calendulian Cooked Pies, and we do *not* want to be late for that..." Her words trailed off. "Though, you're probably tired, so we can walk your speed if you want?"

I stood stunned. In all my life, I never had a friend who cared about something as silly as my low stamina. Lily always made me do what looked best, and Jenny Kim didn't really have an opinion about my health. I was used to keeping up with people, never being the one they followed.

My heart was touched.

"Thanks, but I actually took a nap on the avelift, so we can go as fast as you want," I said, a bit embarrassed I had to admit my weariness on the monorail.

Valhalla giggled and locked arms with me. "Riding those always makes me tired, too," she said, and we briskly walked back to her home.

The moment my foot entered through the squeaky front door, I was greeted with yet another forceful hug but from Mrs. Balthier this time. Valhalla stripped me away from her Mom and sort of asked-told her we were eating upstairs, grabbing the individual pies from the kitchen counter. She ran up the narrow, rickety wooden steps like how a child would—very rambunctious and full of energy—and guided me toward her room. We sat down on her green carpet to eat dinner, but I could barely get in one bite of Mrs. Balthier's delicious pies— mini vegetable pot pies filled with soft, golden potatoes and carrots overlaid with fluffy puffed pastry—because Valhalla was so amazed by everything and kept asking me question after question.

When I mentioned using magic for the first time, Valhalla was *floored.*

"You got a training staff to work on your first try?" she said, stopping her bite of potato and pastry from entering her mouth.

"Yeah... is that not normal?" I asked, taking another bite of food.

"It took me *weeks* to even make a water gem glow, let alone make it actually move water!"

"Whoa, really? It seemed rather easy to me."

"That's only because the Agapéd Magic is so powerful," she said, stirring around the vegetables in her pot pie. "Lisa, you're gonna be the most powerful Mage this town has ever heard of."

"Pretty sure Gaius would be the most powerful person here, right?"

"You're joking—you *definitely* will surpass him!"

Her accusation seemed rather exaggerated. *Is she really serious?*

"I can't even use magic yet without some form of training wheels," I said.

"It's only your first day. Give it 'nuff time, and you will floor it with the most powerful magic this town has ever seen! Trust me."

I did not know whether or not Valhalla's logic was true or purely based on aspirations, but with what she told me... it sounded like the Agapéd Magic inside me was even more powerful than I thought. The Guardians and Inna didn't really explain much about it besides *why* it chose me. If moving water with a gem was actually something hard to do, and I could do it with ease, then it *had* to mean Valhalla was telling the truth.

Later that night, my heart became anxious after taking a shower and picking out my clothes for the next day. My first lesson with Gaius was hours away, and the fear of the unknown overtook me. I didn't know if he would be like Inna and use some sort of magic gem to help me learn or if he would force me to do manual labor in the Veradome. Vilmad hated him, Calendula revered him, and Inna admired his magic strength and care for the Wishing Stars. Yet, I didn't even get one sentence with the guy when we first met.

I rolled over on the fluffy floor futon in my room at the Balthiers, trying to sleep off my self-inflicted worry. Overthinking the situation would do nothing but prolong the night, so I decided to cling to the only good thought about the next day, and that was hopefully learning something new and fun in Micah's class.

10

THE ROCK AND THE WEED

My first lesson from Micah did not go as planned.

Even though I had my notebook opened with a page and a half of notes about the basic types of magic soil, I was not retaining any knowledge in my head. Micah was teaching his heart out, loving each second he got to express his wisdom to someone other than another Guardian. He would ask me a question, but I had to look down at my notes each time because I could not stop thinking about my upcoming lesson with Gaius. Micah would say the words "magic plant," and I would instantly think of the Veradome. *Will I get lost trying to find his house again*? Micah would say "powerful magic," and only thoughts of how powerful Gaius is would come to mind. *What if he expects me to pick up magic quickly and gets frustrated because I can't do anything? What if Inna was wrong about him being nice—what if he uses a sword or something!* I just wished someone would have told me to calm down so I wouldn't have had to be alone in my pit of worry—

"Oh, it seems our time is up for today!"

My troubling thoughts stopped at the sound of Micah ending class. *Did time fast forward or something?*

"I didn't even notice," I quietly added, packing away my notebook into my orbkit.

"Time just flies by when learning about magic, doesn't it?" Micah grinned as he repositioned the books on his desk.

"It sure does," I lied. Normally, I would have agreed with Micah, but not then—not when my mind was swimming with worry.

I gave him the textbook he used as a reference before readying myself to leave. Micah placed it on the shelf and stood a couple of feet in front of me. He held out his fist to evanesce me.

"Good luck today, Miss Lisa." He smiled. "Until we meet again next week, okay?"

His smile helped ease my self-inflicted worry, but only slightly. I was very glad to at least have him teach me and not Vilmad; my nerves would have been shot through the roof.

I nodded, softly smiled back, thanked him, and closed my eyes when his fist punched the air to teleport me to Calendula.

To my surprise, there were no old cottages, busy cobble-stoned streets, or even the Veradome in front of me. Only trees—trunks of bark for miles ahead and nothing but the smell of pine wafting around me.

Did Micah mess up—no, that's unlikely... then why am I not in Calendula?

When I turned around, two people stood before two familiar pine trees with families and merchants appearing out of thin air between them.

I put the pieces of the situation together and realized that no one could evanesce into Calendula, and that is why Micah teleported me near the secret entrance. People could evanesce *out*—hence why Vilmad could continuously take me away from the Balthiers without physically being there—but not back in. Now, knowing that really clarified the importance of the city's secrecy.

When I walked over to wait in line, I presented my COIN to the guards as before, happy they didn't ask any questions and vanished into the other side. Calendula—the city wasn't filled with boisterous music and laughter like last time. The main noise source came from the most unusual forms of mobile shops the citizens were driving. Each cart was a small camper-sized vehicle—like a carnival food truck—and either fueled by solar power, gasoline, or some type of blue magic fuel. They were mostly made of wood or steel and had an opening for the merchant to step inside and sell their goods. Each carried spices, potions, healing herbs, magic flowers, homemade trinkets, and barrels of colored dirt—I even saw a mobile shop manufactured to look like a cloud that sold something called "Cloudy Nightshades and Seeds."

Vilmad mentioned Calendula was made for exporting crops and produce—had no idea it would be in this fashion—and I guessed that many were returning from the early morning route. I didn't see any mobile shops near the forest entrance, which meant there must have been more ways to leave and return. *Wonder where they all go or where the entrances are?* It made sense because if all the merchants came and returned by the same road, then the secret of Calendula would be compromised. The culture of the town was truly intriguing, but I couldn't let my curiosity wander any longer. I, too, had my own agenda I needed to fulfill, and it was only a couple of blocks away.

I snacked on my almond butter and honey sandwich Mrs. Balthier made early that morning, unpacking it from my orbkit as I walked to the Veradome. A couple of workers were entering and exiting the main doors, definitely no wandering teenagers like me; I really stuck out from the crowd. Inside stood the giant twelve-foot glass doors Vilmad and I had passed during our first visit. They taunted me, and I so badly wanted to go through them—knowing there had to be a city of magical plants inside—but the fear of being late for Gaius overshadowed my curiosity. I abandoned my magical desire and briskly walked right past the doors.

After several wrong turns, I finally found the giant garden of trees where the hidden staircase to Gaius' home was. To my surprise, no one waited for me by the wooden door... and I had no way to get inside. *How did Vilmad get this thing open?* I remembered him waving his hand over the left side, so I tried that. My palm brushed the air right above the small wooden star with the leaf on its tip, but nothing happened. I tried again... and again and again and again. Still, no green mist or sound of chimes. I looked like a complete idiot waving to a handleless door.

Are you kidding me?

Since my plan failed me, I decided to go find a worker in hopes they could lead me to Gaius. I strode my way back up the stairs and planned on turning left. To my surprise, a tall employee dressed in brown and green stood at the top, but he did not look happy to see me.

"Where do you think you're going?" he questioned harshly, making my breathing stop. "Visitors are not permitted in this wing of the Veradome. What were you doing down those stairs?"

My body tensed up. Time to check off "be interrogated" from my list of "Situations I Never Want to Happen to Me."

"I'm just looking for Gaius, sir—" I started saying, but the worker didn't ease up.

"How did you know about that hallway and door?"

My eyes found it hard to stay locked on his intimidating face. "Mr. Vilmad showed me."

The worker furrowed his brows and scrunched up his nose, looking like he had never heard that name in his entire life. *Of course, I would be unlucky enough to run into the only worker here who didn't know who the Guardians were.*

"Who—never mind, you need to come with me immediately," he remarked, guiding me toward the opposite end of the stairway.

Normally, I avoided confrontation and just went with the flow. I would follow the guard out the door and try again later or just wait until another worker showed up at the door and asked for help. This man, however, obviously did not know Vilmad, but *I did,* and I was not about to discover what would happen if I skipped out on magic lessons because I couldn't get a stupid magic door open.

I stepped back and pleaded with the guard, "Sir, I promise I am supposed to be here. I am having magic lessons with Gaius, but I couldn't open the door."

"You can lie all you want, but I am not buying it. Now, come with me, or I will have to use force."

It was either choosing between dealing with the guard or suffering Vilmad's disappointed wrath back in Haim Gana.

The guard was much less scary.

"Sir, I am telling the truth—I came here two days ago with Vilmad the Guard—"

He then grabbed my wrist and pulled me away from the stairs.

Tears settled onto my eyelashes from the unfamiliar stress and accusation of a liar, and I knew I was one second away from a blotchy red face.

Out of nowhere, the guard lost all strength and let go of my arm.

I wobbled, whipped back my hand, and glanced up at him; it looked like he had just seen a ghost.

"She's with me," a deep voice bellowed from behind me.

"Sir Gaius—I promise I didn't know—I just thought she snuck inside and was lying. Please forgive me. I was only following protocol," the once fearsome guard began to plead, bowing his head toward Gaius, who was now standing inches behind me.

How did he get here so fast and unnoticed?

"I take full responsibility for the misunderstanding," he calmly said back to the guard. "You may continue your work, Laenit."

"Thank you, sir." Laenit tilted his head and hurried away while I still stood staring at the floor, fearing to turn toward the man who just saved my life. I was glad to have found Gaius, but I didn't think it would've been like this.

I didn't move from his shadow, waiting for him to say something, but there was only silence. His breathing hit the wisps of the top of my head as his bouldering shadow cast over me. Moving my feet was not an option. *Is he mad or frustrated because I went down to his home without permission? Am I going to get in trouble? I didn't do anything wrong—please don't yell at me!*

Suddenly, he broke the tense stillness with a deep sigh.

"... You sure do know how to make a first impression," Gaius said in a low, calm voice.

I slowly turned my body to face the six-foot-five stoic man.

He stood with his arms crossed, staring right at me, wearing a similar outfit from our first meeting. His brown hair was the same as before, slightly wavy and not going past his ears, with a couple of longer locks swooping over his forehead. I wouldn't say he looked mad, but he also wasn't giddy with smiles either. There was a softness to his eyes, though, and a small smirk peeked through his short facial hair. *Was he trying to make a joke?* Regardless, it did calm down my nerves.

He stood quiet for a second longer before saying, "Follow me," and headed down the stairs toward the wooden door.

I didn't hesitate and followed behind his leather coat that gave off scents of tonka beans and freshly cut wood.

"I see that Vilmad didn't teach you how to open the door," he stated as we made it to the bottom, his deep voice echoing off the hallway's walls.

"I tried waving my hand in front of the star on the left side, but, uh... I couldn't get it to open," I replied, my voice not even echoing past his shoulder, and I wasn't even sure if he heard my voice.

He never looked back or responded. The intimidating Keeper stopped at the entry point, looked at me for a moment—his extremely green eyes piercing my blue irises like a spotlight—and then back down toward the far-left side of the door frame. "Hold your hand out right here, palm facing the star, and push forth your magic."

Push forth my magic?

My mind was already processing his surprisingly slight brogue accent peeking through his words, and the magic question didn't help my focus.

Without any idea of what he meant and fearing to ask "why," I opened my hand with my fingers spread out and hovered it over the indicated spot. Like the many attempts before, nothing happened.

Gaius then extended his fingers and palm over mine, completely engulfing my hand with his calloused fingers and dirty knuckles. Instantly, the wood-carved crevices filled with green magical dust, making the door easily open.

"Give it time," he said, exiting the door and into his domain.

He's not very talkative... is that a good thing?

I had come down the stairway in hopes of opening the door by myself... but I left *not* knowing how to open it *and* feeling quite embarrassed. So far, nothing I had imagined about my first day with Gaius was going according to plan.

I followed next to the burly man as he guided me toward the center of his yard, right in between his home and the glowing greenhouse. The area was worn down with only a couple of rocks, shrubs, water pipes, and flowers around the perimeter. At the very edge, near a water pump, stood a three-foot-tall purple weed and a round rock that almost reached the height of my kneecaps. I guessed the circular patch of land was where I would be training, though it didn't look very big or magical.

Gaius crossed his arms again and stood beside me, his trench coat squeaking from his muscles creasing the leather. "Lisa," he began, the first time I had ever heard such a rugged voice utter my name, "I want you to make that rock or purple nettle weed move on your own."

That seemed pretty vague, and I was not too sure what he meant.

"Um, do you mean, like, with magic?" I implored.

"Go ahead."

I paused momentarily, my eyes going back and forth between the rock and weed. "I, uh, can't use magic yet without some sort of training staff or something like that. At least, that's what Inna had me do," I mentioned, feeling my timidness rising higher than all the trees touching the skies behind his home.

He let out a breathy scoff as if suggesting a magic staff was something silly to ask for. "You don't need training tools. I want you to move either that rock or pull out that weed and bring it over here. Just use your hands for now."

These short, vague responses I am growing less fond of each passing second...

I proceeded toward the rock and purple plant, deciding to pull out the plant since it seemed easier to carry. I grabbed near the stalk, but immediately, small hairy spikes pricked and punctured my fingers and palms. I looked back at Gaius to see if he noticed; honestly, I couldn't tell if he did or not because his emotions were more difficult to read than my attempts at writing in cursive.

Quickly, I moved toward the stone, but when I tried to pick it up, it was like carrying a stack of car tires. Even though it weighed more than the plant, no spikes damaged my hands.

Lifting it a couple of inches off the ground, I made it three steps in before I got tired. *Why am I so weak!* I saw Gaius glaring at me and knew I had to keep going down the thirty-yard stretch. My sorry excuse for a rock-carrying process went as follows: hold the rock a couple of inches off the ground, walk with it almost in between my legs, feel my arms about to rip off, drop it to catch my breath, repeat. This method continued for about three more minutes until I finally reached Gaius' cream-colored boots.

"I... made it," I said, catching my breath.

The Keeper looked down with arms still crossed, the sun making his brown hair shine like caramel. "Now, make it move with magic."

I know I had just told Gaius I couldn't use magic, but I wasn't about to disagree with him. He stood a whole foot-and-a-half taller than me, and he could easily lift me up with one arm.

So, I did as he said—or at least I tried to. I extended my arms toward the stone and opened my hands so my fingers and palms faced the rock. The muscles in my arms tensed and gave a hefty *push* to the air.

Just as I anticipated, nothing happened.

Shifting my face back toward the Keeper and hoping for guidance, he stood tall, having that same unreadable flat-lined mouth and crossed-armed pose. "Now, move it back over to the water pump and try again."

Is he serious?

I looked back at the pump. It seemed so much farther the second time around.

"You can still try pulling up the weed if the rock is too heavy."

He really is serious.

Moving the rock was not fun in the slightest, but since I started with it, I was determined to finish. Releasing a deep breath, I squatted back down and started the barbaric stone-carrying technique all over again.

My arms were experiencing tiredness I never knew existed. I was sweating from the heat and the galling exercise, and I knew my muscles down to the marrow of my bones would be sore the next day even after only one round-trip. Stopping was not an option, though. I was determined to show Gaius I was not a quitter. When I plopped the stone down next to the purple weed and old water pump, I tried even harder to make magic come out of my fingers. A *flick* to the hot air, and the rock still didn't flinch. I switched to punching the stagnant breeze, thinking that maybe a fist was the magic hand sign. Nope. Nothing. Just me looking like a total idiot in front of the few-for-words muscular Keeper.

"Until you can make the rock or weed move with magic, you will keep doing this exercise," I heard Gaius say from across the plain.

During my life, I had been asked to do many unfamiliar tasks and many unusual errands. In P.E. class, I was told that capturing a rubber chicken from the opposing team was a form of exercise and that standing on the sidelines was considered "poor participation." I actually thought the game was ridiculous and would have preferred learning a real sport, but I didn't question the teacher. Even though it seemed dumb, it still got me to run and walk, which I guess was better than no exercise at all. Instead of complaining, I normally tried to find even a small silver lining about how the situation could benefit me in the future.

Carrying this rock back and forth had to be the only thing in life I found *no* meaning for. I was here for magic, not pointless child labor. I had already carried it back and forth four more times, and the only thing my hands were producing was blisters. Gaius just kept standing there like a statue covered in calluses and grass stains, not giving a word of advice. By the time I reached the end of my sixth round-trip, he was gone. *Did he just go back inside his house?* All I wanted to do was to just stop and take a break, but I knew he had to be watching me.

He probably was staring at me through his little magic window, waiting for me to give up.

Not me. No way.

I carried the stone back to the pump. Tried all sorts of different dances and hand signs. Still nothing. I carried it back to the spot near Gaius's bootprints. Tried stomping on the ground to see if I could make the earth move the rock.

Nothing. The rock was now mocking me with its perpetual silence, and I began to lose count of how many times I brought it back and forth to the old watering pump. I even tried talking to the rock—pleading for it to just move so I could just take a break and learn *real* magic.

By the time the sun had peaked, I was done with the stone. I didn't care if Gaius was spying on me and decided to try moving the purple nettle weed. After rolling the menacing rock toward the plant, I removed the light blue shirt that clung to my black tank top and clasped it between my hands to protect myself from the thin spikes of the weed. From the size of the plant, I knew its roots had to be buried deep, so I grasped the stalk closest to the dirt and began to pull with all my might. I twisted my wrists to snap some of the roots. I heard some cracking. *It's working!* I kept pulling and tugging, ignoring a couple of spikes getting through the seams of my shirt and pinching my hands. More snapping and breaking noises came from the earth. The plant was getting higher off the ground. *Come on, Lisa! You can do this!*

The plant suddenly broke free from the soil, and I fell right down on the dirt. I felt so accomplished... for about five seconds when I realized that I now had *two* objects I needed to make move with magic instead of just *one*.

Crunching gravel crept closer as I got myself off the ground. It was Gaius with not even a speck of sweat on him.

"Your determination is quite impressive," he calmly said, green eyes brighter than normal even under the shadow of brow and hair, as I dusted the dirt off my back thighs.

I didn't do anything *impressive* from the look of it—just yanked out a weed and moved a rock back and forth. I didn't think I deserved praise for that. "I still couldn't get my magic to work though," I muttered, disappointment seeping through each word.

I thought my new teacher would've said something back, but we just stood in silence, listening to nothing but the trees moving in the breeze—which seemed odd because this place was technically still inside the Veradome... right?

"I would have been surprised if you did," he finally responded... with a very peculiar answer.

"Wasn't that the whole point of me carrying that rock around?" I asked, now questioning whether or not my punching and hitting the air actually helped my magic training at all.

"I was testing *you*, not your magic."

"I don't really understand... was I not even capable of moving the rock with magic?"

He gazed off toward his greenhouse. "The fact you kept going without any signs of improvement means you are fully capable."

I guess that makes me feel a little bit better—

"Lisa, you are weak."

—and right back to the bottom of my already dwindling low self-esteem.

He continued, arms crossed. "But you still kept going. You knew your limits, figured out a way to move the rock and weed without tiring yourself out, and didn't give up. Magic is the same way. It will be hard and brutal but rewarding. You can't rush into it. You must steadily push yourself to grow stronger."

Gaius released his arms from their crossed position and held up his right hand. In mere seconds, the purple weed sprang to life and dug itself back into the ground like a mole digging its maze of tunnels. It was moving fast, instantly growing to the height of a man. It wrapped up the round stone in its stem and leaves, crushing it into smaller pieces—*as if it were nothing but loose sand.*

My eyes were amazed, not by the plant—all by Gaius for he was the one who made it happen. He didn't move his body or even his whole arm—*just his hand*—but I could feel the ground vibrate when his magic overtook the plant.

That was magic—actual magic from Gaius—that destroyed a boulder! He's incredible!

Wonder filled my widened eyes, making my words hasten as I said, "I want to learn how to do that!"

He grinned and headed toward his house. "Follow me."

I looked at the crumbled rock for a couple more seconds—still bewildered about how Gaius could control the plant—and followed behind his footsteps.

He took me down the stairs into his home. The living room was brightly lit by the sun coming through the giant glass window, and all the plants that hung near the pane were even more vibrant with greens and yellows—more so than I remember. The fireplace wasn't burning, but the smell of cut wood still wafted through the air as he stopped by his small kitchen. For me, the kitchen was pretty normal-sized; for Gaius, who was taller than the fridge and most of his rustic cabinets, it looked a little snug. He grabbed a box from the bottom shelf, took something small out of it, and then placed it in front of me. It was a long, thick strip of cloth.

"For your hands," he said before heading straight for the fridge.

I looked down at my palms, both of which were pink, a little bloody, and covered in dirt. *When did he look down at my hands?* I didn't think he would be the type who cared about a couple of bloody blisters and scratches. His kindness was surprising but very much appreciated.

"Oh, thank you," I responded, pulling up the high bar stool to sit closer to the small kitchen island before wrapping up my palms with the adhesive bandage.

Out of the fridge, he grabbed a clear jug of water and poured a hefty amount into a jar. I thought I would receive a refreshing gift, but then, he added in this green powder before giving it a hardy stir. I'm one for trying new things but not when it comes to tainting perfectly good water. I scrunched up my nose at the thought of it tasting like spinach or seaweed. *I hope that isn't for me...*

He then took out a much larger jar and filled it with clear water, *not* adding any green stuff to it. *Phew—for a second I thought—*

"Drink this," Gaius said and handed me the green drink.

... I spoke too soon.

"What is this for?" I said, procrastinating from taking a sip.

He took the biggest gulp of the clear water I had ever seen before replying, "You said you wanted to learn how to do what I did."

He finished his drink before I even started and placed the empty cup back in the cupboard. With little context to go on, I figured the grassy tonic had to help me with magic. As his back was turned toward the cabinets, I took a huge sip of the drink and swallowed it swiftly. It was *not* good and tasted like bitter oolong tea leaves without any sugar—*nasty*. I didn't have to say anything about the bland taste because my face said it all.

"Vigor water. It will renew your energy and aid in healing your wounds before heading back out to practice," Gaius noted as he turned back around.

Did he just confirm this was a magic drink?

It being magical overpowered my distaste, and I began to swallow it down as if it were the sweetest drink in the world.

Gaius started to leave the kitchen and go through an unfamiliar door off to the right side of the fireplace.

"Finish the drink and head back out. You still have a rock and plant to move."

"Wait—didn't you..." I turned around in the stool to look through the large window because he destroyed my rock and weed, and I thought I had no way of training again. The moment my eyes lay in view of the yard, another rock and purple nettle weed were already there waiting for me.

But he was with me the whole time—when did he do that?

"Take a break when you need to" was the last thing he said before closing the wooden door by the fireplace, leaving me all alone in his kitchen to finish my drink.

If I were sitting in Gaius' kitchen hours before, I would have been thinking about why on earth I was drinking a horrible juice if only to go back outside and learn nothing. I would have wished to be with Inna and have nothing to do with the man who didn't seem to know how to teach at *all*—just following his rules to get training over with in order to hurry along the next day in hopes of learning Water Manipulation magic.

But I, Lisa, was not the same as I was an hour ago. I was told I could move a lifeless rock and rooted plant because of my determination *and* had just seen a muscly gardener crush a rock with a limp weed. Everything I needed was inside me to make magic happen. I just needed to keep trying harder. Gaius didn't seem like the kind of man who would waste his time or the time of others. He definitely wasn't the type to play games or joke around either. So, if he believed I could move that rock and that weed, then it had to be true.

I chugged the rest of the nasty magical juice, tightened my bandages around my palms, and went back up those wooden stairs to the training ground.

I am going to move that rock with magic if it is the last thing I do!

<hr />

My feet now created trenches in the dirt from my constant back-and-forth-ing. The rock seemed lighter than before—could have been the magic juice Gaius gave me—but that still didn't make my trek easier. I would bring the boulder to its now dignified spot in the dirt and attempt to enchant it. If nothing happened, I would do it all over again... which ended up being every time. I would then switch to the weed. Instead of ripping it out of the ground, I tried to make it move on its own with magic—moving my fingers and hands just like Gaius. Many times I did this and failed one hundred percent of those. I even pulled it out again, but within seconds, another one magically popped up across the perimeter of the training ground. *How is Gaius making another one grow without being outside with me?*

Throughout the session, Gaius was going in and out of his cottage. He wouldn't say anything—just casually pass by. One time, I saw him go down the hill that led to the lower level of his home, carrying a large white birchwood tree log on his shoulder. Another time, he went into the mysterious greenhouse, where he stayed for quite a while. Still, he remained silent, and I remained exhausted.

After another hour, I ended up taking a small break, sitting down on the rock to face the purple weed, just so I could rest my knees. It was as if Gaius had eyes in the trees because I didn't hear him when he walked up next to me. When he spoke, I easily got spooked by his voice.

"Lisa," he calmly announced.

I shot myself off of the rock. "I was just taking a break, I promise—"

"Are you trying to move the plant yourself, or are you trying to control its movements?" he asked me with his arms crossed.

The question was out of the blue, and I had to think about it for a moment.

I wiped the sweat off my forehead before answering, "Umm... I think, just trying to make it move?"

"This time, I want you to imagine you are a part of the plant and make it bend with you."

To me, that didn't make any sense, but I gave it a try anyway. I thought about the way the weed moved, how its roots were lodged deep, and how sturdy its stem was. I envisioned myself as part of the earth and reached out one arm. Whipping it forward, I made a right jab—sharp like the small thorns and strong like its roots.

It stood motionless.

Gaius didn't seem surprised and quickly moved on. "Do the same for the stone. Stand firm like its foundation and guide it forward."

I moved over and glared at the stone with more annoyance than perseverance. I really hated that rock and wanted nothing more than to show it who was boss. Unlike the nettle weed, the boulder was nonliving, but I could still envision myself as being a part of it. I put on its brawn, cast aside my frailty, and planted my feet firmly on the ground. Bending my knees, I gave a big punch forward.

The only thing that rock produced was more silent, motionless taunting, leaving me dejected yet again.

"From now on, I want you to practice with this in mind," he finished before walking back into his home.

He didn't say whether or not I was doing it right or if I looked like a lunatic flailing my arms around. Still, it was my first *real* piece of helpful advice, so I decided to act upon it. I started my cycle of rock lifting and plant picking all over again but changed the way I thought about magic. When I faced the weed, I pictured the leaves moving with me. When I faced the stone, I mimicked its sturdiness with my arms and hands. There still wasn't any magic happening, but that didn't stop me.

I did the same exercise until the clouds in the sky went from cotton fluffs to purple and orange paint strokes. My hair was now up in a frizzy ponytail, the ends matted with sweat, and my blue shirt was covered in dirt. No matter how badly I wanted to learn magic before heading to the Balthiers, my body disagreed. Gaius hadn't come out to tell me to stop... but then again, he never mentioned that he would. I took it upon myself to go and find him, hoping he would free me from my prison of rock and weed removal services.

Down the stairs in his half-buried home, the fireplace crackled, and the lights were dimmed. No Gaius to be found. When I walked further in, I noticed the tall walnut wooden door next to the fireplace was ajar—the same door I saw Gaius enter when he left me to finish off the green vigor water.

Maybe he's still inside...

I crept closer, taking an innocent, curious peek, and saw some sort of bookshelf with glimpses of metal, leather, and wooden books all shoved in rows. I inched even closer—thinking I saw one of them glowing. My curious heart wanted to know what was in there more than anything.

The moment my hand touched the bronze doorknob, my ears caught the noise of something from inside Gaius' workshop behind me. My conscience jolted my magic-yearning heart, tensing my shoulders and making me back away from the door.

Doubt sneaking in there is a good idea with Mr. Muscles around. Guess I'll find out what's behind this door another day...

Sounds of wood carving and steel scratching rang louder the closer I came to the workshop, making me reminisce about our first meeting. The floor was covered in white birch wood shavings, various types of leather strips, and snipped bits of silver metal. He sat at the desk, creating an elaborate white wooden dagger with a thick purple leather hilt entangled in vines of silver. It was very beautiful.

"Um, Gaius?" I added, a soft voice amid the wood carving. "It's getting pretty late, so I was wondering what time I should be going?"

He arose from his seat, found a spot on his wall of many weapons, and displayed the knife before responding to me. "You are finished, then?" he asked.

I couldn't tell if he was being rhetorical, so I answered anyway. "Yes...?"

He then sat right back down at his desk on the stumpy stool and solemnly told me, "Get some rest, and we will start again during your next lesson."

The relief I felt with those words he spoke was like no other. I could taste Mrs. Balthier's home-cooked dinner in my mouth already.

I thanked him and left the workshop but didn't quite make it to the exit of his home. The walnut-colored door was calling out to me again, begging for me to swing it open and reveal its Keeper of Star secrets in the form of magical books. I tip-toed closer to peer through the fissure of the archway and doorlock, seeing a short stairway and bookshelf that led toward a magic study.

Oh—I am so going in there—

"Lisa."

Without any warning, Gaius appeared behind me and scared me half to death. He didn't even say my name very loudly, but his deep voice breaking the room's silence was enough to make me jump. *How did I not hear his giant footsteps creep across the wooden floor?*

When I turned to face him, he didn't notice that I pried into his personal space. He held out his fist with something clasped inside.

"Use this to unlock the wooden egress next time you return," he requested of me, placing a green pointed gem into my hand. It produced a glow, matching the green hue of the door with the engraved star carvings when activated by magic.

"A magic gem..." I accidentally said out loud.

"Until your magic reveals itself, just hold this in your hand in the same spot I showed you earlier today. Be sure not to lose it."

"Oh, thank you."

As he began to walk away, he softly wished me a "Goodnight, Lisa" before reentering his workshop.

Out of all the words and phrases Gaius said to me that day—the few there were—that one was the most personal, and I found it rather sweet. I still didn't know much about my new teacher, so I couldn't call that "warming up to me" per se, but my heart felt pleased as I left his magic home.

When I left the Veradome, I was surprised to see Valhalla waiting for me. Her long hair dangled past her shoulders, and she smiled big when her purple eyes met my blue ones. It was nice having a friend waiting to see me for once.

"Okay, so tell me," she began, excitement pouring out of her mouth as the sunset turned the sky red and orange, "what was it like—your first day with Gaius and everything?"

I brushed my bandaged hands through my hair. "Well... it wasn't like Inna's I can tell you that... pushed a rock and pulled a weed all day."

The violet surrounding her pupils sparkled like an amethyst as we started the walk back to her home, which was odd; nothing I said was mystifying in the slightest.

"Whoa... the Keepers have such cool ways of showing you how to use magic," Valhalla said.

I couldn't help but giggle. *I literally did nothing magical.*

After getting to the tram that road to her neighborhood, we passed by a couple of kids our age. They were laughing and heading to the city, which got me thinking.

"Are there a lot of teenagers here?" I asked Valhalla.

She looked back at the group. "Oh, not really. Those are from the same Tutor as me though, seeing as there is only one in Calendula."

We stopped our steps at the tiny station for the old tramway.

"Guess that means you are pretty close with everybody?"

"Eh..." She looked down the street one more time. "I mean, I guess you could put it like that. I *know* them, but I'm more of the 'family' type—sticking to home with Mom and Dad."

The tram creaked its way to the station, causing the both of us to walk toward the front of the line.

"I'm the same way back home, too," I said.

She smiled big as the doors opened. "Glad you don't see that as a weird thing—another thing we have in common."

Finishing the tram ride and back at Valhalla's home, Mrs. Balthier came right up to me and saw my bandaged hands. "My *days*—Lisa, your hands! Are you okay?" she asked, not even bothering to take off her oven mitts before hugging me again.

I honestly had forgotten about my blisters and scratches until Mrs. Balthier brought it up. "Oh, yeah. My hands feel fine now, I promise. Just had a long day training," I replied. "Though... they do feel a bit better now."

I hadn't looked at my hands since after I drank the green water, so I was also quite curious. I unwrapped my bandages, and my scratches and blisters were almost nonexistent! There were no calluses formed and only small red lines from where the thorns hurt me—but no open cuts or tender spots. *It was magic juice after all!*

II

A HERO

"And do not get me started on human methods about how to preserve Vulvarin Sage Dust when we Guardians have more knowledge than a whole planet of your mortal minds," Vilmad spat as he blared on and on and on during our lesson. He was the one person—the one *being*—that could make magic boring. I didn't even know what Vulvarin Sage Dust was because he kept using so many archaic terms that flew over my head... and I think he knew that. He probably just wanted to intimidate me—scare me off from this magic way of life like he tried to do in the forest, even though he "promised" his lecture would be the best out of the other two Guardians.

Well, it wasn't. Bethesda's lesson was still at the top, and Micah's was a close second.

When he got off the topics of soil and boring geography, he briefly summarized the three galaxies Inna mentioned days before. That was when I started paying attention—enjoying my time in front of the long-haired Guardian. Luna Theta was the galaxy known for its high magic qualities and creatures on all its life-bearing planets. It also happened to be where planet Kalm is located—the planet where Calendula and Mantene reside.

Novatear contained planet Gadot, where EverWake was, though Vilmad mentioned Gadot was more of a "linking" planet. Apparently, it lay at the edge of Novatear and Luna Theta, making it a part of neither galaxy. The only comparison I could make of it was it was similar to Washington D.C. back in

America: more of a "district" for their Magic Embassy and merchants rather than a planet to call home. Novatear's planets also had high qualities of magic, but many continents were owned by the Magic Embassy.

Cassiopeia was the only one of the three galaxies where many planets had been destroyed. Only vagabonds and runaways lived there, claiming parts of the broken rocks for civilization. High levels of unbalanced magic also flow through its universe, so the Guardians were normally working there to maintain it. Vilmad didn't go into detail about how they did that... I wished he would have because it sounded really cool.

During the end of his synopsis, I raised my hand and quietly asked, "How come we on Earth have never seen these galaxies before and all the other planets?"

Almost in a haughty voice, Vilmad answered, "That is because we make it so. Lady Ariela wishes for the Milky Way to remain without the knowledge of magic, and with her guidance and our power, we can conceal all visual evidence of life outside of Earth. To be perfectly honest, your so-called 'astrophysicists' and 'Earthian astronomers' have seen our magic before, but they do not understand what it is, so it is invisible to their eyes. They merely see cosmic pinks and blues and assume it to be nothing but nebulas. Humans are quite simple to manipulate when they've no knowledge of something."

Suddenly, the doors to the study gaped open, creating a broad echoing sound in the room and interrupting Vilmad's lecture. The one pushing it open was Emunah, dressed in dark blues and turquoise, his gray hair gathered into a loose ponytail and black beard perfectly shaped. His tunic draped along his chest and showed off his middle-aged, muscular arms and the golden freckles on his tan shoulders. And, unlike Mr. Scoffy with his long hair, the black-bearded Guardian gave a gallant smile.

"I hope there is a good reason for your interruption?" Vilmad callously addressed Emunah.

"I come bearing good news!" Emunah announced, smiling quite big and looking directly at me. "Lessons will be cut short today on account of Lady Ariela."

"How is taking a pause to the Agapéd's training 'good' news to you?"

Emunah ignored him and walked toward me. "We have finished your Tvilling Draught, little lady—your way of traveling to and from your home to here—and I invite you to come with me."

There was a charm to the Guardian's words, a more welcoming persona compared to Vilmad. Picking to stay in a Vilmad lecture or following a charismatic Guardian was not a hard choice at all.

As I was packing away my notebook, Vilmad continued to plead. "I don't see how this couldn't have waited until after lessons were over—"

"I'm just following orders," Emunah said, half-smiling, half-serious. "I am sure you can make it up to Miss Lisa during her next visit."

"How vexing..." Vilmad mumbled to himself as Emunah and I left the study.

Once out of the long-haired Guardian's sight, Emunah smiled down at me. "Honestly, I just thought you would enjoy a break from books and like to see some *real* magic." He winked, a flicker of gold twinkling beneath his sapphire eyes.

For a company of celestial beings, I figured the Guardians would act more pompous, if anything. But yet, here they were—being annoyed by each other like a sibling rivalry. I guess that would happen when a family had been together for thousands of years.

I smiled down at the ground, surprised that a Guardian like himself would encourage ditching magical lectures; Emunah was now one of my favorite Guardians, though I was still intimidated by his powerful stature to talk as comfortably as I did with Inna.

The charming celestial man led me outside of the Elysium. We walked down the white-stoned pathways covered in purple flower petals toward one of the three buildings that occupied the surrounding fields. This building resembled the Elysium with its white, cream-colored siding and abundant greenery growing along the windows and roof, though it was as small as a house. Emunah said this was his quarters and where he would spend time creating potions and elixirs at Lady Ariela's request.

"Each Guardian has their own solitudes," he said to me, burly and as if we were close friends. "Vilmad, Alona, and Bethesda all stay in the Elysium with Ariela. The other two homes"—he pointed out beyond the flowers of his home—"are for Rayna and Dayasheel. We don't need these for sleep—we aren't human and rest our bodies by other means—but it's more for us to get away. We need space, too, kind of like you humans. It's not much, but it's better than being stuck inside the Elysium with stiff-necked Vilmad, am I right?"

I answered with a silent smile, even though I thought he couldn't have been more right.

"I do hope you enjoy it here, little lady," Emunah said as we approached the entrance to his celestial home. "I know your first encounter with us left you with an array of questions and maybe a little taken back. I was quite honored when Lady Ariela requested that I help the Agapéd—making potions and doing what I was made for. It has been quite some time since I've had this much fun."

I waited inside the anteroom as Emunah went upstairs to grab the so-called "Tvilling Draught." The room remained very open with minimal decoration. Thin trees grew along the inside, acting as columns to hold up the second floor. Blue and gold patterns of stars in the sky painted the ceiling, adding color to the white chamber. When I first walked in, I expected a comfy living room, but then I remembered that Guardians didn't sleep. *Wonder what the other homes look like...*

"Miss Lisa," Emunah began saying as he descended the winding stairwell, "I must thank you. It is not every day Lady Ariela comes to me with such a request. My workdays were growing stale as of late, and nothing is more rewarding than crafting new magic in the form of a liquid."

In his hands were two twin bottles, rather small and pointed at the end. Each one was sealed with a cork on top and tied with black string, filled with a dark blue serum that resembled a cloudy night.

My eyes lit up as I tried to contain my excitement—that was liquid *magic* in those bottles!

"The basis of this potion is called Tvilling, meaning they are birthed at the same time and to be used correspondingly. I call this Tvilling potion 'Ingress-Egress Draughts'—the first-ever twin elixir that can create a nexus from here to Earth," Emunah said as he admired his work, turning the bottles between his fingers. "Creating these was quite the challenge, one I handled perfectly, I might add." A gleam from his white teeth as he smiled. "The magic inside will only work for you, Lisa—neither I nor Lady Ariela can use its abilities."

He then handed me the pocket-sized bottle labeled "ingress."

"A *portal potion...*" I verbally said out loud, struck with awe and wonder.

"How this will work is quite simple. The magic in the bottle is connected, and wherever you release the liquid will release a portal to the other. I will place one portal here at the Elysium using the bottle labeled 'egress,' and when you return home, you will release the one labeled 'ingress.' Even though you are the only one who can see, touch, and pass through, the light from the portal is fairly bright. I suggest picking a spot in your home where it can be easily concealed."

"So, I just pour it out, and it will create a portal? To here?"

"Pour it, throw it, smash it—wherever the first drop touches is where the portal will be placed."

"That's so cool!" I said, looking at the potion in amazement. *I am holding pure magic in my hands!* "So, if this is how I leave *from* Earth, how do I get back home when I'm in Calendula?"

"Ariela has that all covered for you. She is having Gaius evanesce you back home each Friday and asked me to deliver you this." He pulled out an antique stopwatch that could be easily latched onto my belt. It was a light copper with a pink gem in the middle holding the hour and minute hands together. "The time is already set to match yours on Earth. Whenever you are ready to leave, you just tell Gaius and have him send you home. Easy, right?"

Our definitions of easy were on a whole other spectrum, and I took a big gulp even thinking about asking the stoic gardener to take me home.

He put his gold-freckled hand on my shoulder, careful not to pull my hair that draped over. "Lisa, if you require any other magic tools or potions, feel free to ask me. You are filling my days with quite enjoyable tasks."

Emunah is way more approachable than Vilmad... I wish he was my teacher instead.

He smiled at me one last time before sending me to Mantene, where I would begin my second magic training with Inna.

⁓

I still couldn't produce any *real* magic from my hands like Inna. Nothing happened whenever she had me try creating ripples in the sea without the rod. Still, no matter how much I failed, she never left me out in the hot sun with nothing but silence as Gaius did. She would say, "That's okay," or, "Let's keep going," and let me use the magic rod again. The only thing I was learning from Gaius was how to push a stone around.

On the monorail ride home, Ava and Asa still acted attentive and weird but not as overly protective. They let me sit in the seated row in front of them on the Avelift instead of being squished like last time, and I made sure to stay awake for the duration of the ride.

The beauty was unmatched out the window and down below—nothing like I had ever seen before. The rolling fields of green were occupied by fluffy bison and tan cattle, and the roads were filled with unusual vehicles that resembled tiny metal cars.

When the forest started to come into view, I was shocked by the radius of the trees—it stretched on for *miles*! Far, far north, I saw something poking the atmosphere. A mountain blocked most of my view, but it seemed to be the tip of a building... something pointed and elegant, a tall white tower.

I turned toward Ava and Asa, instantly grabbing their attention and causing their backs to stiffen up.

"What is that behind the forest? Is it just a mountain or another town?" I asked them both.

They glared out the window, still wearing their sunglasses, and squinted hard, wrinkling their tan foreheads.

"Ah—that would be the Kingdom of Boolavogue, Miss Lisa!" Ava shouted as if I weren't right in front of her.

"A *kingdom*—like with a castle and everything?"

Asa spoke up next, "Yes, Miss Lisa! A kingdom 'with a castle and everything' as you expected."

I was surprised that it was the first I had heard of a kingdom, making the name of the avelift's station more understandable.

"Have you both been there before?"

"Negative!" they said simultaneously.

"One must be invited by its residents to step foot into the Kingdom," Asa said.

"And we've not known the pleasure of being invited," Ava concluded.

"Oh, I see... how odd," I said, my voice trailing off, as the avelift made its stop, preventing me from asking more questions seeing as both my "bodyguards" had already left their seats.

I wonder if I'll be invited there someday...

Ava and Asa dropped me off at the secret forest entrance, and when I passed through the portal, I saw Valhalla and Mr. Balthier driving one of the mobile merchant carts. It was a wide tri-wheeled buggy with a roof and car windshield, run by solar energy and magic. On the driver's side were giant barrels filled with red and yellow spices and a large window that opened for the seller to transact with the buyer.

Valhalla saw me and made her dad stop the cart. I ran toward them as she started unbuckling her seatbelt.

"Is this your cart, Mr. Balthier?" I asked her dad.

"Well, good afternoon, Lisa—oh, this is one of the Veradome's trading carts that I am required to run this season," he responded, still seated at the driver's wheel. "We just returned from Raglan, a small town not too far from here—"

"Hey, Dad! Lisa should come with us one day—she'd *love* to visit Raglan!" Valhalla shouted as if I wasn't standing right outside the vehicle's door. "It's not as lively as Calendula, but they have the cutest wooly cattle, and the farmers normally let us pet them."

I smiled big, intrigued by the wooly cattle; I didn't know cows could be as fluffy as sheep. "It sounds like fun. I wouldn't mind going."

"If Emmeryn allows it and Lisa doesn't have her own lessons to attend to, I will be sure to let you kids know," he said.

Valhalla jumped fast out of the mobile shop and latched onto my arm. "We were about to drop off the cart and head toward Luca's—Dad, can Lisa come too?"

"Why don't you both go on without me? I still have to park the shop, sign off, and see if your mother has made it home yet. So, have fun you two!"

Mr. Balthier began to drive away as Valhalla led me toward their town's heart. I guess it was common for kids to go out after dark without their parents; it was a first for me, anyway.

We went down the brown cobblestone road, lit by warm orange street lamps, and toward the bustling village of Calendula. Even though the sky was growing dark, the small-town square was dazzled with lights from inside the buildings and a plethora of string lights—just as orange and bright as the streetlamps. Families were out and about, eating different foods or going to and from shops, and a couple of kids were running around without a care in the world. I couldn't help but smile and skip along to the fiddle and guitar music the street performers played.

Valhalla soon led me to Luca's. Anxiety swam up my body like a rushing river with just a quick glance. The building resembled pubs I had seen in movies—very crowded, with wooden flooring, loud music, and high-top seating from the outside view—making me internally freak out. *This is it. My first time at a late-night bar. Mom is going to kill me if she ever finds out.*

Once inside and through the chiming door, the smell of fruits and sugar denied any speculation of beer or bourbon.

"What is this place?" I asked Valhalla.

"This is Luca's—the best juice and candy bar in the world!" she replied. "They have drinks that change color according to the weather, some with sugar pearls and candy pops—my favorite is the Sugar Cloud Offie, which is colored like the sky with a giant cloud of candy floss on top of the star-shaped ice cubes! You are going to freak when you take your first sip!"

We ordered at the counter. The drinks' names were so bizarre that I couldn't tell if I was getting something fruity, sweet, or sour. I chose the one called Honey Beary, since it had the most familiar ingredients: honey, peach, vanilla, and cream. Valhalla paid the cashier, took our table number, and sat us both near the window of the restaurant... which was even crazier than the drink names and descriptions. I was used to seeing Valhalla act so jumpy, but she was operating like an adult leading her family to the best seats in the house.

"So, your dad just lets you go off by yourself at night?" I asked her while we waited for our drinks.

"As long as it isn't too late," she said as if it were completely normal.

"That's so weird—where I live, no one our age does that unless their parents are with them or if it's during the day."

"It's not like anything here is going to hurt me—all monsters and wild creatures are outside of the city and can't get through."

"Monsters and creatures?" I was thinking more along the lines of robbers and kidnappers and found it odd that she thought of animals first.

"Yeah, like vorrgs, Dawner hounds, bilefiends—"

"What are you even talking about? You mean magic creatures exist?"

Valhalla crisscrossed her legs in the booth, using her hands to help her explain almost every detail that came out of her mouth. "Yeah, but I have never seen them—just read about them during classes and from what Dad tells me. Creepy things for sure."

"We only have snakes and killer spiders to worry about back in New Jersey."

"Oh, we have those, too, but monsters made from dark magic are on a whole other level. They normally have giant claws or poisonous venom, and the big ones are filled with dark magic—sometimes able to fly or burn you with just a swipe of their paws. Some only come out at night—even heard of some that used to *be* human before becoming a creature. Now, *those* are mostly rumors, but rumors have to come from a smidge of a fact first. I'm just glad we don't have to worry about dark magic creatures in Calendula, but even if we did, we have lots of Hunters to take them down."

I hadn't thought about evil creatures living in this universe. The Guardians sure didn't bring it up. It also would explain all those weapons in Gaius' workshop, but why would he need swords to take down an animal? A hunter's rifle seemed more efficient, but then again, Valhalla said they were dark *magic* creatures. For all I knew, bullets couldn't hurt them.

Guess that's why the Guardians wanted me to live in Calendula, so I would be safe from creatures like that...

Before I could ask any more questions about these mysterious animals, the waiter came with our drinks... and my mind was blown away. They looked like pure forms of art in a glass bottle. My glass jar was shaped like a cute teddy bear and filled with peachy, honey iced tea, with the bottom of the drink having a strong honey syrup that tasted like caramel. A honeycombed sugar candy was balanced on top of the ice with a cloud of heavy cream dripping down the sides of the glass. Valhalla ordered the Sugar Cloud Offie, which looked even better than she described it—a mountain of blue and white cotton candy poked with a straw leading down to the bottom of her jar.

"Are you kidding? This is the craziest thing I have ever seen!" I exclaimed.

"I told you—you were going to freak," she said, not wasting a second and taking a sip.

The moment I, too, slurped up a big gulp of the liquid sugar, my cheeks perked up, and my eyes glistened like stars. "This is the best drink I've ever had in my whole life!"

Valhalla giggled. "They always add *tons* of sugar. Mom and Dad say it's a little excessive—"

"I think it's just right," I finished her sentence, licking the cream off the top of the ice cubes.

"Me too!" Valhalla smiled wide and took another gallant sip. "You know, Lisa, once you learn magic—without a training rod, I mean—you're gonna be the most amazing Hero this world has ever known."

"What do you mean *hero*?" I said, mixing the honey syrup at the bottom, making it stick to my straw. "I am just learning magic like you do every day."

She stopped mid-pluck from her blue cotton candy that sat perfectly on top of her drink. "What—you're *joking*?"

I stayed silent. I definitely was not joking.

"You're"—she silenced her voice the best she could—"the Agapéd Bearer."

"Why are we whispering?" I breathed back, leaning over the table.

Her purple eyes widened. "Because you and your magic are a secret… didn't you know that?"

My brows furrowed. "What do you mean?"

She took a sip of her drink as if it were the last sip she'd ever take in her life. "That's what the Guardians told my parents. I mean, you got the world's most powerful magic—isn't that why they are training you here? To become a legendary Hero or Saint, even a Lionheart?"

Again, nothing she said made any sense to me, and my sips began to get slower and slower the more new information was being added to our conversation. "I just thought I was learning magic because that's what people do? Like, how you go to school to learn how to read or play a sport or something."

Her loud voice returned. "*Everyone* goes to Tutor but just to learn basic magic stuff. People with magic like yours go off and learn how to master it in hopes of saving the world! You got the universe's most powerful magic, and you're tellin' me that the Guardians aren't training you at *all* to fight or how to become a legendary hero?"

I felt… rather dumb. I had never thought about why I was learning magic— just thought that powerful magic chose me, so I kind of *had* to learn. But a hero? That's all just from comic books… right? It would explain why the Agapéd was so powerful, to fight evil and "save the world" … but wouldn't the Guardians have told me that? Would they not have told me I would be kept a secret?

I pushed my hair over my ears and twirled my straw, making the peachy drink turn a creamy caramel. "So, when you say 'hero' or 'lionheart,' what do you mean exactly—like they fight crime and stop bad guys?"

"*Way* better than that! Hurry and finish!" Valhalla took the mightiest gulp of sugary tea in the entire world. "I'm about to *blow* your *mind* even more."

The excitement in my heart thumped with cheer, and I followed up with the same robust gulp of my own drink before we bolted out Luca's door.

After rushing back to her house, Valhalla went through her closet and drug out a large green bin, painted with stickers and colored marker streaks. Inside were mounds of magazines. They weren't glossy or covered with teen boys on the front page, most of which was matte and printed on thick linen paper. She had over twenty in the box, each thick and all from the same company, *Chevaliers*. She grabbed the one covered in green and with a large kingdom on its cover. She flipped through the pages until she landed on the photo of a chiseled man using some type of blue lightning magic.

"See this guy? He is a Hero, Gladius Snow. He devotes his life to protecting his country from sky beasts and dark Mystics and Mages. He is *super* powerful and handsome and has saved the lives of many, which is why he is in the *Chevaliers*," she said, pointing to the man. "A Hero protects people from dark magic, especially those who use magic to hurt others. They also fight monsters, too—whatever they need to do to save the lives of people. But the people who *really* know how to take down dark beasts are these—"

She then flipped through multiple pages until landing on a spread of burly men and women. "Monster Hunters. They train their whole lives on how to take down magic monsters that threaten their world... and these are called Warriors. Nations will have a select Hero who stands with them and fights in their battles—all while inciting fear into their foes. The difference between a Hero and a Warrior is their allegiance. A Hero kinda travels around and picks up random jobs or cold calls, while a Warrior pledges his life to a particular nation and normally fights in their wars."

Valhalla grabbed another book, knowing exactly what page to turn to next. "And these are Saints—recruited Mages and Mystics from all over the galaxies who fight for the Magic Embassy. This guy," Valhalla pointed to a tall blonde man whose hair was tied in a ponytail in the photo, "is Yusuf Cross, known for treasure hunting and weapon making, and he is from Raglan—can you believe it! The little town South of Calendula's forest birthed a famous Treasure Hunter! And the best of the best are known as Lionhearts—"

Valhalla then turned to the middle spread of the purple *Chevaliers* issue, where a man and a woman were printed in high-quality color, embossed with gold and silver. They looked intimidating, and both were heavily adorned in armor. "These two here were struck with Wishing Star magic years ago and recently saved a whole country on planet Bruin. Lionhearts are given that title by the Magic Embassy or by their nation after already being deemed a 'Hero,' and it's the *hardest* title in the world to get. They are the most powerful Mages and Mystics out there!"

My mind was going a mile a minute. I couldn't believe that real-life superheroes existed in this world and that they were the celebrities who took up the headlines. I continued to flip through all the pages and marveled over each Mage and Mystic.

"So, the people with the most powerful magic become actual superheroes?" I questioned.

"*Better* than super. They are majestic and written down in history. But Lisa, you will be the most legendary there ever was!"

Seeing all the elegant and strong Mages and Mystics in the books began to intimidate me. I didn't know why Valhalla could ever think I was going to be like them...

"I'm nothing like these guys, though—"

"But you have the most powerful magic of all time. You were *born* to be a Hero—the youngest Lionheart who ever lived!"

I looked down at her fuzzy green carpet without a smile. "But... I haven't even learned magic yet—*real* magic, without a training staff. I-I don't think I could ever be like those guys."

Valhalla scooted closer to me, her breath still smelling like molten sugar. "Lisa, you listen to me. You've just discovered magic exists, right?"

Kinda obvious but—

"Yeah."

"And you just made water move with a gem on your *first try*—not even

knowing what you were doing!"

I sat silent.

Valhalla grabbed the book she had on the floor and pointed to some random Mage. "I know you just started living here and learning of our world, but your magic is as strong as *all* these people in here. You may not see it yet, but that's why you're training with the best of the best—Mr. Gaius and Miss Inna. I bet by next week, you'll be throwing flames, making frost, or even flying in the sky in no time."

To be called a hero was never a thought that crossed my mind. I barely knew what classes I wanted to take in high school when it rolled around in a year, so thinking I could be a well-known saver of nations was impossible. Yet, it made sense when Valhalla said that was why I had the Agapéd.

Maybe this is what I am meant to do...

I wasn't very unique, talented at any sport, or even a wiz at academics, so having a grand goal of becoming something extraordinary was only *ever* a dream. Never reality in my world. But then magic slammed itself into the forest of my backyard in the form of a Wishing Star—giving me a desire and a yearning for something in life. Whenever I thought about learning more with Inna, the Guardians, and—though intimidating—even Gaius, I became more invested. A passion was growing in my heart. *Is this what it feels like to know what path to follow?*

I sat with my knees up, hugging my shins. "You really think I can do it?"

Valhalla smiled big. "One hundred percent *for sure*!"

Thinking about being as powerful as the ones in Valhalla's magazines, it would be pretty awesome—to see myself in one of the spreads someday. I was given powerful magic and hoarding it wouldn't make any sense. I wanted to become the greatest Agapéd Bearer there ever was, and becoming a Hero *had* to be the first step in that process.

Valhalla's gallant smile rubbed off on me. "Then, I'll do it."

She happily hugged my neck and swayed us both back and forth as we sat on her rug. "Then you *better* take me along to all the places you visit, especially if you get to meet more famous Heroes and Warriors!"

"Uh, *duh!*" I said back, and we continued the night, laughing and looking through all her magazines before I headed off to bed.

12
YOU'RE QUITE AN ODD ONE

Mr. Balthier gave me the best gift in the world: a you-don't-have-to-find-Gaius-all-by-yourself trip to the Veradome.

Emunah was nice enough to make me the potion to send me to Haim Gana from Earth, but I wished it didn't involve finding the daunting Keeper. Luckily, as I was going to bed the night before, Mr. Balthier offered to give me a tour of the Veradome while we searched for the Mystic. I had never been more thankful for a simple tour-guiding gesture in my whole life.

Valhalla's family was kind, and I honestly couldn't believe how nice they were to me—letting me stay at their house for free and eat meals with them. Jenny Kim and Lily's parents either didn't care to get to know me or were fine just knowing I was a "good kid" for their children to be around. I guess it wasn't a bad thing, but after being cared for and noticed by another who had no reason to be kind to me at all... it opened my eyes to wanting to be a more caring person.

Mr. Balthier was already waiting for me down the stairs just as giddy and excited as Valhalla normally was. His black mustache was extra puffy, and the sides of his charcoal hair were trimmed down, all complementing his wide-awake purple eyes. *I see where she gets her personality from.* The morning was still quite early, and many people headed toward the Veradome. We both had to stand shoulder to shoulder on the transport tram due to the number of people heading off to work. It was uncomfortable but allowed me to notice that Mr. Balthier was skinnier than most workers and had some circular glasses sticking out of his green shirt pocket (other workers had pens or name tags in theirs).

Down the road and through the morning mist, we reached the entrance of the giant greenhouse. Mr. Balthier led the way inside, right to the front of the giant glass doors—the twelve-foot-tall ones I had longed to walk through. He handed me a visitor's tag and said, "Our first stop, the Utopian Floor!"

We stepped inside the giant glass gateway into a room as large as a suburb, filled with an infinite phantasmagoria of every imaginable plant. Steel and glass pillars supported the ceiling at least ten stories high, and metal and concrete stairs along the walls led toward the upper balconies surrounding the Utopian Floor. A cornucopia of aromas filled the air, smelling of sweet mint and basil before changing into scents my nose couldn't recognize. Many workers—had to be almost 200—were going to and from different areas of the city-like garden. All the plants were specifically placed in habitats that best suited their growth; some were in large conveyor belts that moved by solar energy and magic, rotating from bright sunlight to rinsing in water; some were in gardens the length of soccer fields with cultivators in between the rows; others hung in a string of vines that drooped eight feet toward the ground. I saw a section with crossbreeding fruits near the west side of the Utopian Floor and another with vegetables— even saw smaller greenhouse rooms within the large space containing a variety of vegetation that needed specific types of weather and light to flourish.

"It's like a whole forest is in here!" I said, standing over the edge of the stairwell, feeling more like a child in a candy haven than a magic student in a plant conservatory.

"Sometimes, I forget just how big it truly is until I am standing from up here," Mr. Balthier chimed in, his purple eyes and black hair shining from the morning sun coming through the glass ceiling. "Given that it is still rather early, what would you like to see first as we search for the Keeper?"

"Honestly, anything would be fine with me, Mr. Balthier."

A large smile grew along his peachy face. "Then, let us start with the herbalists at the tropical sapling section. If we are lucky enough, we might even get to see them harvest Lilikoiram fruits. The fibers on their skin are what is used in many potions to make them taste sweet without affecting its intended outcome."

We passed by many workers actively doing an assortment of jobs. Technicians were fixing any problems with the heat and humidity, botanists were taking note of each plant's life cycle, and magi-ecologists were examining the magical properties of crops—not to mention all the traders and merchants gathering their exports. Mr. Balthier said he normally worked with root vegetables and spices, so he could show me that section of the Utopian Floor next.

For an hour, I saw plants with colors and scents I couldn't even dream of describing with words. Magic oozed from every inch of the Veradome—vines burned pink with glittering pollen, carrots glowed orange and healed opened wounds, and dogwood trees hummed songs that actually made me sleepy. Beauty flourished inside the glass castle of magical scientists and gardeners, and Mr. Balthier *worked* there every day. It was enchanting, and that was only the *first floor.*

With the tour of the Utopian Floor complete, we passed by a lawn of leafy green plants to get to the next section of the Veradome. Mr. Balthier was saying something pretty important about the lettuce herbage, but I saw someone familiar on the other side.

It was Gaius.

He was standing with a worker, listening and analyzing the leafy vegetation in front of us both. The herbalist next to him was doing all the talking while Gaius towered over. After seeing the method just to get into his home, I thought the Keeper was a hermit; I didn't expect him to be out amongst the rest of the Veradome's employees like a normal worker.

The burly Keeper did a slight double-take, probably curious as to why I followed one of his co-workers in the early hours of the day. We exchanged glances briefly until he acknowledged me by nodding in a "hello" fashion. Mr. Balthier didn't notice him, and I was having too much fun on the morning tour, so I didn't say anything—catching up to Roy's footsteps and continuing the greenhouse voyage.

After seeing the dessert fruits, rainforest sprouts, and the worst-smelling purple squash of all time—which was used in gardens to ward off feral creatures—we started to make our way toward the northern wing that had a waterfall at its end—an *actual* waterfall connected to a cliff that protruded into the glass wall of the Veradome! Mr. Balthier and I took a couple of steps toward the railing of the oasis when a dark shadow loomed over me.

"I didn't expect to see you here on your day off, Roy," a familiar voice said from behind us.

"Gaius, sir. Please forgive me, but I assure you it is for good reason," Mr. Balthier began to say toward my magic teacher. Valhalla's dad didn't sound scared, not like the security guard from my second encounter with Gaius, but more so startled for being caught back at work when he wasn't supposed to be there. "Lisa said she needed to see you today, and since she was quite curious about the Veradome's plant kingdom, I thought, 'Why not give her a tour as well?' So, here we are."

"I appreciate your work, Roy, so I can't afford one of your Uppers seeing you here on your day off. They might get the wrong impression, so enjoy today as intended." Gaius then looked down toward me before glancing back up to Mr. Balthier, continuing his conversation. "She does like to wander, so I thank you for taking her this far."

My muscles tensed. *Did that mean Gaius knew I was peeping into his room before he gave me that green gem?*

"She's been such a pleasure to have around. Thank you, sir. Hope to see you again—when I am working, of course." And off Roy Balthier went back to his home... without me.

There I was, standing alone with a Herculean gardener by my side. *No more comfortable tour for me.*

Gaius was dressed in similar clothing as the other workers but with a more embellished cloak and brown boots covered in grass stains. Like always, he didn't seem angry or bothered by my presence, but he sure did look rather amused with a thin smirk stretching underneath his boxed facial hair.

"I am more surprised to see *you* here," he said, arms crossed like normal. "It's your day off, too, if I'm not mistaken?"

I still couldn't look him in the eyes for very long, turning my gaze to the loose grass clippings on the floor as I timidly replied, "Vilmad said I can do whatever on Friday... so I figured visiting here would be fine since I already had to see you... and I thought I could work on my magic training a little more, too... if that's okay?"

I just threw in that last part sporadically. I wasn't planning on practicing my magic since "magic training" was technically me doing monotonous boulder-pushing work in the Keeper's yard. Though with Roy gone, I had more time to spare... and I couldn't go home just yet if I wanted my "camp" alibis to work. *If I'm lucky, maybe he will let me look around some more... or actually teach me magic if he isn't busy...*

He chortled at my reply. The burliest short laugh in the world. "You're quite an odd one, Lisa."

I felt more at ease, even though that wasn't necessarily a compliment. "What does that mean?"

"Normally, when a child is told to take the day off, they take the day off. Yet, you are here wanting to learn about magic-bearing plants and work on your training. Odd."

"I find it fun learning about magic, so it's not really 'work' for me." I fiddled with my fingernails, finally able to glance at his intimidating face for longer than a second.

His eyes were unnaturally green, matching the glow of the peridot moss near the waterfall. "It's your day off, so do what you want. Feel free to continue your training back at the Hearth. Just use the emerald I gave you to unlock the door."

My eyebrows raised. "Really? I can?"

He subtly nodded. "When you're ready for me to send you home, come and find me if I'm not back."

He sounded quite pleased when he left... could almost call it the "happy" version of Gaius.

With his free invitation to continue my magic training, I quickly returned to his home as he proceeded with his work route. When I reached the magic door, I took out the emerald gem from my pocket and held it toward the left side of the doorway. Instantly, green glowing dust filled in the cracks of the embossed star carvings, unlocking the wooden entry.

So cool!

I didn't know if it was just me, but I hated being in large places alone, and Gaius' domain was no different. It was quiet. No birds chirping or people chattering. Nothing. Just a light breeze blowing against the trees. I walked toward the training area, saw the rock and weed, and quickly searched for anything else that would be much more enjoyable to practice. Gaius was busy working, so I figured I had time to spare before continuing his senseless magic training.

Down below the hill was the backdoor entrance of the Keeper's house, looking to be the lowest level of the cottage. Off to the left at the forest's edge was a plant-like obstacle course: lots of giant roots and leaves, tall rocks perfect for jumping across, and miniature rocks just the right size for shot putting.

Not sure if this is meant for magic training, but it's better than pushing a rock and pulling a never-ending weed.

I did a couple of warm-up jumps to psyche myself up before starting Gaius' odd training course with some rigorous parkour.

<hr>

For a full hour, I did nothing but run, climb, and fall all across the earthy obstacle course. I noticed my balance getting better, my arm strength improving, and my stamina increasing... but no magic was seen from my hands. I tried making the surrounding trees and flowers move like how Gaius did but to no avail. I did as he said: "Be the rock" and "Be the plant." Still, nothing but magicless movements.

I took a break and wandered back toward the patio near the backdoor of his home. Upon closer examination, the rustic cottage was three stories high, and I had only been to the second and third floors... so naturally, I was curious about where the new door led. One peep through the door's tiny window... and my mind was blown away.

The room inside was *the* magic study—the one I saw through the cracked walnut door by his fireplace! Bookcases were overstuffed with thick and old books—magic-filled ones no doubt—and a table was topped with a strange chemistry set right next to a large glass case filled with potions; some liquids were even *glowing* inside the bottles.

Oh, I am so going in there—

I reached for the doorknob but hesitated. *Would this be considered a "breaking and entering"? Am I allowed to be inside his home... He never said I could... then again, he never said I couldn't.*

Gaius had not returned in quite a while and was rather busy when I last saw him, so I figured if the door was unlocked that going inside was meant to be.

Touching the dingy knob, it easily unlatched just like any normal door handle, proving to be destiny at work.

The study smelled like his workshop—hints of firewood and tonka beans—and the air was quite dry and cool. Cold stone flooring muffled any sound from my boots as I walked further in. The couch in the center was wide and soft like velvet, covered in books and scribbled-out pages that didn't make the final drafts. Unlike Micah's study, everything was sporadically placed and less elegant—very homely.

I looked closer at the chemistry set nestled against the left wall and beneath a thin window, seeing weird recipes for magic liquids and balms laid out flat on the counter. *He uses this to craft potions! This is amazing!* I didn't touch anything for fear of something happening to my hands; just admired the ingredients inside the desk drawers and amongst the cluttered shelves. The glass case next to it housed hundreds of otherworldly liquids inside several bottles. Some were thick and bubbly, while others were glowing like fireflies. *Did he make all these potions himself? How do you even catch magic to make potions like this?*

Toward the middle right side of the room was the stairway that led back to Gaius' living room. Books were encased in the hollowed-out steps, creating even more space to fit all of Gaius' magical novels.

There was one more door in the room right in between two bookshelves, but I didn't bother to proceed in there; figured sneaking into his house was already chancing my safety enough, and I didn't want to add anything else to my supposed "crime."

My spirit of inquiry brought me toward the shelf with the most colorful stack of books. One was perfectly placed in arm's reach, bounded by wood and green leather vines with red cherries on its cover. I opened it to see what was inside, and a field guide on magic fruits was on each page. The sketches looked hand-drawn with impeccable detail—explaining the growth, magic qualities, and potions you could make. I saw the author's name at the bottom of the page.

Gaius wrote this and drew the pictures, too!

Back home, I hated reading. I thought, "Why read when you can just watch it on screen?" So, I only ever read books when there was a grade involved. Many of my classmates found joy in reading and would finish books in less than a week. It baffled me, to say the least, and I knew I would never pick books over the choice of watching a movie.

Maybe it was the fact Gaius had written the book currently in my hand or my natural curiosity compelling me to read something about magic, but I was completely enthralled by every line and sketch as if it were the best hobby in the world. I just couldn't get enough of learning about this world.

I wouldn't say my break lasted too long, but I then knew everything there was to know about Cyrus Cherry's fire-resistant seeds, Morello Sweet Frenzies—how their glucose can turn one's hair red *permanently*—and the Rainier Cherry's ability to cause memory loss, only when dried and consumed during a full moon, of course. I grabbed another book after that, which was bound in metal with drawings of potions all inside, getting myself all comfy on the large lounge couch.

Out of nowhere, the backdoor swung open. I jumped and sprung up off the couch, dropping the book onto the floor, creating a loud metallic sound that rang through the room.

It was Gaius, his hulking figure outlined by the sunlight hitting his back at the door frame.

I mumbled like a frazzled creature, "I am sorry—I just was taking a break. I should have asked first if I could come in here, but I am done now, so I will go ahead and get back to work." I then began stacking the books on the floor and avoiding all eye contact with *him*.

My heart pounded hard and wouldn't stop, rattling my ribs like a tiger trapped in a cage. He *had* to be furious with me. It wasn't like I was caught sneaking through his bathroom cabinet—far worse. I was caught prowling through his books about secret magic and potions, not to mention sneaking into his house in general.

His boots clicked and clacked along the stone floor as he approached me. Feeling guilty, I looked up at him when his hand reached for the metallic book I had dropped.

My breathing stopped. *Why isn't he saying anything?*

He flipped through the first couple of pages, all in complete silence.

He is angry, for sure.

His head turned to face me with a rather pensive look in his green eyes, still holding the opened book in his hands. *He's gonna yell—he's gonna kick me out and yell and send me back to Earth right now—*

"Lisa..." His words were deep and calm, yet my lungs refused to breathe easily. "It has been many years... since I've had a student who genuinely enjoyed the learning of magic..."

Gaius walked toward the bookshelf, where I discovered the metal-bound book. He then returned it to its rightful spot and grabbed another one below.

"I've seen many come to me just to learn something flashy or powerful, whatever is the quickest way to fame or wealth. Yet, you..." He paused, placing a new book into my hand, "... came here today, persuaded by pure curiosity, just because you find it 'fun.' Am I right?"

I looked down at the book he gave me: *Beginner's Guide to Magic Vegetation: Growth and Habitat.*

My mouth opened slowly. "I just think... that magic is the coolest thing in the world..." I answered, the first time being completely genuine and open with Gaius.

There wasn't an ounce of anger or disappointment in his voice, and when I looked back up at him, his eyes were shining. It wasn't a grand emotion, as subtle as a blink, but a grin emerged beneath his chiseled nose.

"Lisa, you are welcome any time to come here and read as many books as you'd like."

"Really? You aren't mad at me for coming in here?"

"I could never be upset with someone who chooses to learn."

"Then..." I began, perking up the courage, "... can you show me your most favorite books you have?"

I must've said a magic word, because Gaius completely changed and opened up to me. He talked all about the books he had on his shelves; he had written just about every single one of them! He had whole sets based on location, creature types, plant life, potions, beginner and advanced charms, and even some about the different magic forms.

Gaius was not the kind of man I expected him to be. Even though he made me train for hours, doing the most repetitive routine I could have ever imagined, he did not come off as this brute Vilmad insisted he was. Before stepping into his home, I pictured him as the stereotypical angsty wise guy who took orders from no one. He was few with words at first, which was very frustrating but never showed signs of resentment. He didn't doubt my abilities or tune me out either. But what I appreciated most about him was his passion for magic. He truly loved it just like me. I knew then, that if I kept working hard, I could one day become as strong and wise as he was.

For the rest of the afternoon, I continued to read the stack of books my mentor put together for me as he went back to work in the greenhouse next to his home. I made it three-fourths of the way through the one about magical plants and their habitats before I noticed the time on my antique stopwatch said 4:01 p.m. Mom got off of work at five during the summer, so I knew I needed to be home before then.

When I exited the backdoor, the Keeper was picking up the round rocks I had thrown.

"I'm sorry!" I shouted. "I should have picked those back up when I was finished."

Gaius easily carried all fifteen stones in his arms. Each one had to weigh at least five pounds, and he was not even breaking a sweat. He then placed them back into the pile near the foot of his home.

"Were you using that area to practice?" he asked me.

I fidgeted with my fingers. "I thought that's what it was for...?"

He chuckled at me in his low voice. "Lisa, when you return next week, I promise to give you an actual training course with the intent of learning magic."

"Really? That would be amazing!" I exclaimed.

He rolled up his sleeves and guessed why I came to find him. "Well, I assume you are ready to leave for Earth?"

I nodded.

"Alright then," he began, placing his fist out toward me, swirling blue magic between his fingers. "Until next week. Stay safe until then."

I smiled and said thanks as the bright light of his evanescing magic whisked me away, back to the middle of the forest in my backyard.

My first week of magic training was nothing like I had expected it to be... and I loved every second of it.

13
HIDING A GIFT

The scent of summer rain instantly overtook me in the middle of my forest—the sunshine breaking through the storm clouds above me. It seemed as if forever had passed by since I was last on Earth, and I almost couldn't believe my new reality—enjoying myself so much in Mantene and Calendula that I forgot to miss Mom. Though I had been away from her before, it was never longer than two days. If it was not for Valhalla's family being so nice, I think homesickness would've consumed my heart.

As I was thinking about seeing Mom again, I remembered something very important that I had forgotten... I still had to convince her I had been at an art camp all week and *not* learning about magic, all the while concealing my excitement to tell her about everything.

Normally, hiding secrets would be gut-wrenching and quite difficult because of the fear of it getting out or getting caught. Besides a simple birthday or Christmas gift, I wasn't accustomed to keeping secrets from Mom either. With my current situation, I wasn't trying to hide something bad; it was the most amazing thing in the world. Given that it was so crazy and magical, it almost was like a dream.

That is what I decided to tell myself anyway, to make the secret easier to conceal. Whenever I would be back home on Earth—feeling the desire to blurt out to Mom I had seen actual magic—I'd just pretend like everything was another daydream. Mom would *never* ask me about my thoughts as I sat in the car or before going to bed, so keeping everything about my other life hidden away in fantasies seemed like the perfect solution. There would be no need for suspicion either because no one else would know about my magic life. Honestly, if I accidentally mentioned something of magic, it wasn't like she would believe me. It could work... I just had to believe that lie myself if I wanted Mom to buy into it.

I made it to the backdoor of my home, which thankfully was unlocked due to our habit of losing the key every few weeks. Seeing our microwave clock beam 4:10 p.m., I quickly ran up toward my room, took my backpack out of my orbkit, and began to change out of my EverWake clothes and into "camp clothes." I held my backpack in my arms but needed to find a safe place to stash my magical locket. One swipe of a hand... and my whole secret would be out.

Now, where to hide it...

Mom occasionally rummaged through my clothing, so my chest of drawers and closet were out of the question. Keeping it in a shoebox seemed efficient, though Mom liked to use them to wrap presents in, so that was out, too. I thought about burying it under my bed in an old jewelry box, but that was a disaster waiting to happen (so many things shoved under there, never to be seen again). I couldn't afford to lose *anything* Inna or the Guardians gave me.

Out of the corner of my eye, I saw my purple suitcase sticking out from the left side of my bed. Mom had no reason to use my suitcase, it was large enough to not be lost, my backpack could fit in there as well, and I could easily push it back under my bed.

Perfect!

I put my orbkit and backpack on the edge of my mattress as I opened the suitcase. After cleaning out the random assortment of clothing still left inside, I hurriedly grabbed my orbkit and backpack off the mattress when suddenly, something small fell out of its unzipped pocket. It hit the edge of my nightstand, breaking the glass and spilling right into the suitcase.

"No—" I shouted, but it was too late. The damage was done. A glowing purple and blue portal to Haim Gana was now inside my suitcase.

I stood wide-eyed at my new portal nightlight that would be shoved back under my bed. *Emunah wasn't kidding when he said it would be beaming.* I slapped my forehead hard. *Lisa—why didn't you put the potion in its own pocket in the orbkit and not in the crumby zipper of your backpack!*

The only good thing about my lapse in judgment was that I could still zip up the suitcase and block out most of its shine when I wasn't using it. The magic portal looked just like the moon's reflection on the sea if the moon was an interstellar purple and cerulean. It didn't produce any sort of noise, not even a chiming or faint ring. I was lucky enough for it to land inside, too. A couple of inches closer and I would have a giant blazing hole in my room.

Since finding a perfect spot led to a magical accident, I decided to just put my orbkit inside my nightstand drawer, close by me, and mixed amongst all the other knickknacks that would get thrown in there. A perfect disguise. The only thing I had left was to convince Mom of my simple alibis for the summer months before she came back home from work. My digital clock said 4:30 p.m., so there was no time to waste.

After watching TV in our living room for an hour, I heard the garage door begin to open, and my heart leaped. I was not sure whether excitement or fear drove me forward, but I quickly walked toward our kitchen. I was eager to see Mom again, and that was *all* she needed to know, too.

Mom was dressed in loose slacks with her wavy hair tied up in a ponytail. One look at her "summer camp" daughter and she came right over—not even taking off her shoes—giving me an energetic, loving hug.

"Sweetie! You don't understand how much I have missed coming home to you!" she said, dragging the hug along for quite a while. "I want to hear all about your first week! What all did you and Lily do? Were the counselors nice? Did you get to meet anybody famous?"

She let go of me and put down her purse on the kitchen table. The questions did not surprise me because I had already prepared some stories to spin.

"We did a little bit of everything," I began, trying to sound excited about it, but still, lying to Mom about something on this big of a scale was brand new to me. "They had us go to intro classes, and we got to see all the art options the mentors offered. I am not sure if anyone was famous or anything."

Keeping it vague is the tactic.

"So, did you get to paint or draw—maybe learn about music or play an instrument?"

Mom continuing to ask questions, *again*, did not surprise me. She did the same with our car rides home after school.

"Lily really liked fashion design, so I stuck with her a lot at first—but after classes, they had free time in the dorms. There were arcade games, a pool, and a movie room, so I was happy about that. Made a lot of friends the first day, too!"

Was that too random? Would an art camp even have arcade games and a pool? I hope it didn't sound too fake...

She smiled and grabbed a glass of water. "I am so happy you're enjoying it, sweetie."

My cheeks slightly perked up. *Is my cover-up actually going to be this flawless?*

As she took a sip, she casually said, "I can't wait to see all the things you'll be making! I'll hang up your best drawings—unless you pick music. Then, you can finally play me a song!"

Welp... there went my plan.

I did not even think about the aftermath. It is an *art camp,* so I should come out of it knowing at least one creative thing. *What do I say?* I did not have time to learn a musical instrument. Culinary arts was not my strong suit, and Mom would know if I were lying since she is such a good cook. Singing had no *physical* art form and could be an easy facade, but Mom and I loved karaoke, so she *definitely* would notice my same mediocre voice. Another cover-up was knocked out.

My words were slower as I tried to avoid stuttering, and I couldn't help but twirl the ends of my wavy brown hair. "Well, actually, we get to try out everything first before picking our favorite, and I wasn't the best at acting or musical instruments, and Lily didn't really like dancing or theater..."

Come on, Lisa! Think of something!

"You can't just stick around Lily the whole time—what was the most interesting thing you saw and thought, 'I want to be able to do that'?"

Dang it, Mom. Why can't you just be normal and not care so much about this?

My eyes rolled, glancing over the fake tile flooring in our kitchen. "You might think it's weird..."

"Sweetie, you can tell me. You don't have to be nervous around me."

If you only knew—

Suddenly, as Mom was leaning against the kitchen counter, I just blurted out something I thought I could go with: "I thought the illustrators were pretty cool—the ones who create little animal characters for cartoon movies and books... I wasn't *too* bad at drawing, and it seems I'm, uh, pretty creative when it comes to drawing magical creatures and stuff..."

Mom still stood stationary in the kitchen, refusing to ignore her daughter. "Really? I never knew you liked drawing that much?"

I remembered Gaius' books and how he drew so many illustrations, so I figured I could try and recreate some of them during my free time. It wasn't like Mom would ever ask me if they were real or not—plus, learning how to draw them myself seemed kind of fun.

"Me neither—but they made it seem so cool, so I figured I would give it a try."

She then smiled at me and started to get out the ingredients for dinner. "Well, I am glad you are having fun learning something new this summer. Be sure to thank Lily's mom for me next time she picks you up. It's so kind of her to do this for you. I'm making waffles tonight, by the way, so let me know how many you are wanting,"

With my mind at ease, I could finally relax and enjoy my time with Mom. Putting on a grin as she took out the eggs and milk, I asked, "Can I please have like two *huge* ones? I am *starving!*"

<div align="center">~~~</div>

I never thought I would have to keep such a big secret from Mom. If it wasn't for a good reason, I definitely would have told her. As the weekend went by, however, it seemed like I wasn't even hiding anything, concealing a gift just waiting for the day I could finally let her open it up. There was no guilt whenever I hid Mom's birthday present; sometimes, I even forgot I bought her anything until a week before. Not mentioning my magic seemed like that. Nothing terrible came from concealing its whereabouts since its intent was for good, so I could genuinely enjoy the weekend with Mom. Having a normal summer at home and a magical one just made it all the better.

14

BLOODBORNE, STARNATE, AND THE AGAPÉD

Do I just... jump in?

I stared at the rippled magic gateway inside my suitcase after Mom left for work, me supposedly at camp, and my nerves rattled. Emunah did not mention anything other than he would be placing the other portal in Haim Gana, so I had no clue where I would be transported to... and if it even was truly a working portal. After all, I've never seen one before to make a comparison.

I thought about sticking my face inside, just to see where it would lead... *but what if something happens and I lose my head in another meta-universe?* I decided to use something other than my body to see if it actually worked before risking my life. My backpack was on the floor—a perfect guinea pig for portal testing. I held it over the travel-sized glowing liquid and dropped it right inside.

It completely vanished!

When I dropped my bag into the magic realm, I heard an echoing thud, confirming the portal wasn't too high off the ground. Feeling more secure about where I would be landing, I decided to jump in all at once. I stood near the long edge with the zippers facing me and the flap against my bed.

It's just like jumping into a swimming pool, Lisa. You'll be fine.

I took a deep breath, wished for good luck, and jumped.

All gravity completely shifted. Apparently, Emunah had placed the portal against a vertical wall, and because my suitcase portal was facing toward the ceiling of my bedroom, I lost all sense of direction. My feet were not pulled down but backward, and I fell forward, hitting the marble ground hard and rolling across its cool surface. Bruises were going to show up the next day on my knees, but I was just lucky enough to have used my hands to catch myself, avoiding a broken nose.

My body slowly pushed away the ache of the fall as I stood up and grabbed my backpack that was shuffled toward the right side of the room. Looking around... I was *not* in Micah's study. The portal was placed in a small arched nook between two columns, right in the middle of a wall in a long hallway. I looked left and right. Nothing was familiar. I did notice the grass growing just steps away from the concrete hall, leading toward the green, flowering fields of the Elysium, which meant I was on the bottom floor. It then made sense why everything looked so foreign to me: the Guardians failed to give me their tour of the ground level.

Am I just bad at remembering to ask for directions, or is failing to give them a trait all Guardians have?

Going right, I started walking until I found a tall wide stairwell. Not a single Guardian was to be found, but I knew Micah's study was closer to the top floors. At the top of the staircase was an unfamiliar room: an enormous golden ballroom. The large, vaulted ceiling was the tallest out of all the rooms I had visited in the Elysium—bigger than my gymnasium at school—and was made for royalty with intricate details painted beneath the opal plants that hung above. Gold cocooned the beams and columns that climbed up the walls and ceiling, covered in green ivy and pearl flowers. When my shoes strolled across the gaping, shining floor—the most highly-detailed and tapestry-patterned flooring design I had ever seen—it created the sweetest-sounding clicking noise. *Why did the Guardians not show me this room? It's dripping with gold in here.*

Then began my unprompted Lisa party-of-one tour through the Elysium until I found Micah's study. Going down a columned hall, I entered a courtyard where the walls were lined with thousands of books—almost two stories high— and a giant tree grew near the far end, brushing up against one of the shelves. Layers of hand-crafted redwood separated the books and curved along the courtyard's perimeter. Along the top was a balcony that followed the length of the shelves, providing an excellent view of the garden below and Haim Gana's flowering fields beyond the Elysium's domain.

This is the prettiest library I have ever seen!

The courtyard was circular, except for its far-right side, where a pair of doors stood. I thought the library was covered by a glass dome, but after glancing upwards, I saw only clouds and a shimmering rainbowed veil that glistened every couple of seconds in the light—no glass to be seen. *Maybe it doesn't rain here, or maybe they have cast a magic shield over the library?*

Next to the two doors, I noticed a large domed window, the oval shape ringing a bell in my head. It was the same view from Micah's study, his short brown hair peeping through the base of the frame.

I hunched my back. *He could've waited for me by the portal, or at least one of the seven of them could.*

I walked inside his study—late. Micah was working on something at his desk, not seeming too bothered by my tardiness, dressed in more silky robes of purple and plum hues. I quietly sat down, pulled out my notebook from my orbkit, and waited for him to begin class.

"I was thinking..." Micah started, not grabbing a single book off the shelf. "How about we go for a different approach today, Lisa?"

My eyes widened. "Oh. Sure."

No textbook involved—like I was going to say no to that.

My back straightened in my chair as his fingertips began to make a stream of yellow and purple dust in the air. With his celestial magic, the brown-headed Guardian created multiple jars of different sizes. "In our worlds, the power of one's magic is limited based on its origin. There are four rankings magic can be placed in. The first, being the weakest, is Concealment."

Micah grabbed the smallest jar. "Concealment magic has a limit to its power based on the object it's concealed in." He then made rock illustrations from his magic dust and placed them into the small jar. "Pretend these rocks are the Concealment magic and the jar is the object it's bound to. The rocks can't bend to fit more inside this jar, and they can't grow like plants and flourish into something more powerful. Concealment magic is the same; it can't grow any stronger or any weaker, confined to the width and density of the object it's contained in. Therefore, this type of magic is mostly used for absorption stones, glintz, and training gear."

That must be the same type of magic inside Inna's training staff...

Next, Micah grabbed two blue glass jars for his next illustration. "The next and third strongest is Bloodborne. This magic is passed hereditarily and can only be as powerful as the mother and father before."

He filled one jar half-full and the other all the way full. "Pretend this is the amount of magic inside the heart of a man and a woman. Once they have a baby..." He then created another jar, purely made from magic, and poured magical water inside of it. He only poured enough water to match the same fill line as the blue glass jar with the most amount of water, "... that baby can only be as powerful as the strongest member of the family."

Raising my hand—as if I was in a class with more than one person—I asked, "So, will a baby *always* inherit magic if both parents have it in their blood, and will it be the same type of magic as their parents?"

"Excellent question. No, not every child will inherit their parents' magic. The ones that do can range from weak magic to as strong as their parents' magic. For your second question, yes. You can't inherit magic that has never passed through your family, and most humans will inherit only the magic from their immediate family members. Now, on rare occasions, one may inherit magic from one or two generations passed, but they still cannot be stronger than the strongest one in their family."

"Oh, I see..."

"The next type of magic, rarer and more powerful than Bloodborne, is Starnate magic," the Guardian announced, creating an elastic purple jar with his magic. "Starnate magic comes from the Wishing Stars. Whether a person is fully grown or still in the womb, a Wishing Star will be drawn to whichever heart it has a similar magic pulse to. What makes this magic more powerful is that it *can* grow stronger."

Micah then poured magical water into the elastic jar, and it expanded— *growing three times its size!*

"The vessel was small at first, but as the magic became stronger, it was able to expand. Those who are Starnate can also pass down their magic hereditarily, which in turn will create their offspring to be Bloodborne. However powerful the Starnate parent is during conception could be how powerful their child is. But the Starnate can continue to grow their magic while the child—now Bloodborne—has a set limit. Like with Bloodborne and Concealment, there is a maximum to how much magic the heart can hold. If one with Starnate magic becomes greedy with the lust of magic and allows Darkness to take control of their heart"—the jar popped like a balloon, making me jump in my seat—"their magic will consume them, and their heart will be destroyed... This is a rare occurrence but, still, one to watch out for."

Hearing magic could destroy a person's heart was pretty scary. *I never thought too much magic could be a bad thing...*

"Last, the most powerful magic Man can control is..." Micah then created another magic vase with his illustrations, "... the Agapéd Magic. There is only one of its kind, and it freely chooses its vessel, as you know. What makes it so powerful... is that it's limitless."

Micah then poured magical water into the vase... but it never overflowed. The water just kept disappearing as if a vacuum were sucking up the liquid. "The Agapéd Magic is still a mystery to us, for it always chooses a new elemental or phantasmal magic for its host. The strength of its magic varies as well, almost like it only grows as strong as it thinks the heart can handle... so for you, Lisa, the possibilities of magic are endless."

I won't deny it: after hearing everything about the Agapéd Magic, I did feel pretty cool. I now saw why Valhalla and her family treated me like a celebrity because, in a world based on magic, I innately had the most special kind... but that did leave me with a question.

I raised my hand again. "So, when you have powerful magic... you should use it to help people, right, and not just learn it for, uh, 'fun'?"

He didn't look startled by my question and answered casually, "Yes. Magic should always be used to better the lives and the planet it surrounds. Since humans now have it flowing in their hearts, they should tend to it as we do here, though most tend to use it for fleshly pleasures, fame, or wealth."

"Then... what's the point of mine being the most powerful? Am I supposed to be, like, a Hero or something?"

Unlike my first question, Micah seemed to be in deep thought over this one—pacing over to the bookshelf in silence and looking toward the floor.

After a couple of seconds of browsing over the books' spines, which he probably read a hundred times, he finally answered, "In the human world, magic should be used like an extra skill—a talent to improve the world you are living in. Right now... you should focus on growing your skill—learning magic and developing your mind about our worlds. Once you're old enough, you can use it how you like... that is all."

Micah's answer was... vague. Odd. And my heart couldn't accept it, especially with all Valhalla said to me last week.

My eyes shifted as I followed up with another yearning thought, "Then how come I'm being trained in secret? That's why I'm in Calendula, right, so the Agapéd stays hidden?"

He flicked the air, sending the pens and paper scraps into his desk drawer. His eyes never made eye contact with me as he rushed his words, sharp and casual, "You are simply training in Calendula because we trust that human family... and Gaius is there. That is all." He tossed in Gaius' name as if he had suddenly just thought of the Keeper. A *coincidence,* not an actual reason.

"Oh..." I trailed off as Micah began to grab a hefty novel off of the bookshelf; he was done answering my question.

He didn't really explain the point of my magic... I wonder why...

<hr />

"Might I have a word," an old, annoying voice said from behind me in Micah's study, "with the Agapéd, that is?"

I turned in my desk chair. Vilmad stood by the door frame, draped in an emerald robe different from the other green garb he wore last week. His gold-freckled, thin hands were intertwined, and the world's subtlest smirk rested beneath his nose. I only noticed the strange gesture on the Guardian because I didn't think he knew how to smile in the Elysium—only when offered praise by mortals.

Micah answered, "We were just finishing up, Vilmad, so that is fine—but Lisa has lessons with Gaius very soon—"

"I know of the prior engagements," he swiftly answered, hand raised like a stop sign in front of his fellow Guardian. "This won't take long. Plus, I believe Rayna or Bethesda requested your help with some dark matter."

Micah gave me a head nod, avoiding my please-don't-leave-me-in-here stare, and went out of the room. I did not want to be with Vilmad, especially when Gaius said he was building me an obstacle course. *If he makes me MISS my magic lesson, I will be angry... silently angry.*

The moment Micah evanesced out of the room to go who-knows-where, Vilmad strolled along in... the sly smirk still hinting on his face. I was beginning to miss the old Vilmad; the one that detested me. *What is going on right now?*

My hands remained on my desk, fiddling with the paper of my notebook, watching the long-haired Guardian waltz in front of me. His shadow stood tall, looming over me while I sat as still as possible.

"So," he began, his arms crossed, fingers drumming along the sleeve of his cloak, "it has been a week since you started your magic training." He eyed my hands. Most of the calluses and scratches from lugging Gaius' rock and weed were gone, but he was made of magic; he probably could still see them even with my hands beginning to retreat to my lap. "I've heard your lessons are going... decent. I didn't doubt Inna, a bit *too* nice in my opinion, but you survived the brute's boorish tactics."

Nothing about that was a compliment, but it wasn't offensive either... *maybe he is coming around to like—*

"You know this isn't some make-believe game, right?" Sharpness covered his words, biting at each letter. "The Agapéd isn't some little side-show act..." He palmed my desk, leaning closer and darting me with his ocean-blue eyes. I hated it. "They don't want me telling you this... but, as the *Agapéd*, you should know... This magic of yours brings along nothing but *death* in your future, Lisa."

My brows raised slightly, and Vilmad's smirk returned. "Not something you wished to hear? Come now, I know you're probably curious as to *why* we didn't want you to have this magic. The others want to keep this concealed, saying you weren't ready for it, but—you said so yourself in the forest last week—that nothing was too hard for you. Well, I'm here to tell you that being this Agapéd Bearer means the more you grow with it, the more you'll be inching closer to an early departure. Because"—he flared his index finger in the air as if he were conducting with the rhythm of his words—"every single bearer before you was murdered, slashed, slain, dismantled, and, in some cases, beheaded."

Breathing ceased as I sat in that chair. Half of my heart thought about each word of Vilmad's carefully, words I only heard in movies. *Murdered... beheaded...* I couldn't even comprehend what they truly meant—to feel or understand what it would be like to experience my body being *dismantled* or *slashed*.

But the *other* half of my heart knew the man in front of me... and he hated me. *Is he... being serious, or is he trying to scare me again?* Before, he said Gaius was a brute and made it out to seem like the Wishing Star gardener was going to be brutal in his teaching methods. Well, I was out there in his yard and the man gave me magic healing juice and promised me a jungle gym when I returned. And he never showed any hatred toward me... unlike Mr. Gold-Skinned here.

Still... Vilmad did bring up a point: there was something else about my magic the Guardians were hiding from me, even if he was exaggerating it.

So, I let a speck of courage mixed with curiosity slip from my thin lips. "What do you mean, exactly?"

He stood up straight again, flinging his fingers in the air, and green-dusted illusions formed. They weren't as pretty as Lady Ariela's magic, and not just because of the gruesome content he was showing, jagged and lacking the golden sheen. "I mean exactly what I said. The bearers before you were cut down"— an illustration of a man getting his legs snapped off by vines appeared—"blown up from the inside"—a woman exploded like a balloon, causing me to cringe and squint—"and hacked off from the shear power of the Agapéd Magic." More illustrations played, all ending in daunting deaths, stuff I had never even seen on television or in video games. Stuff that, according to Vilmad, would happen... to *me.*

His fingers twirled, rippling away his illustrations. "See, this magic in you is simply too much—too harsh on a feeble body as yourself, that is why we were all concerned. You've yet to produce magic, *real* magic, so you still have time to back out. Returning to Earth and saving yourself from this before you end up as nothing more than the next example in the line-up of the dead—"

"But why is it so important, though?" I interrupted, thinking back on Micah's lesson, the question he vaguely answered and Vilmad tried to avoid, too with his gross scaremongering. "Like, if this magic hurts me... why learn it anyway?" *What aren't you all telling me?*

Vilmad rolled his old eyes, swallowing back his agitation. "Were you not listening? This *magic* will *kill* you. It wasn't meant for a child of Earth—wasn't meant for a heart such as *yours*—"

"Then who was it meant for? A Hero or something?"

His haughty voice huffed. "A *Hero*—you think that is what you're meant to be? How simple-minded you truly are. You probably believe a Hero merely pops into existence and enjoys saving the world—a title full of glamor and wit. Well, it is not…" His tiny, vile smirk returned. "Being one—if that is what you wish to do—will kill you even faster. How would your mother feel then, hm? A child dying simply because she wanted a magical life as a Hero. It would be a shame, really—a *waste* for the Agapéd."

His pointed chin tilted down. "So, *Lisa*, forgo this magic. Give it over to us so we can try and find a *new* heart to home, and go and be with your mother—*away* from your soon-to-be death. It is the right thing to do."

My eyes went back and forth from his emerald-cloaked shoulders, watching his long hair slowly dangle over. All I wanted to know was the purpose of my powerful magic, and Micah gave me nothing while Vilmad foretold my gruesome death. And yet, not one of them told me a straightforward answer. Something was off—something about my magic worried them enough for Vilmad to come in here, trying to scare it away from me again. Maybe it would cause my death, but, according to Micah, that would only happen if I went crazy with it. I couldn't even trickle water without a rock; doubt I would be consumed with dark magic if I couldn't even lift a weed without tiring out.

But I definitely—one hundred percent for sure—was *not* giving away my magic to the likes of *him*. Lady Ariela trusted me. Valhalla did, too. Their opinions mattered most, because theirs seemed genuine.

"Like I said… nothing is too hard for me," I told Vilmad, severe but soft.

His jaw tightened while his nostrils flared. "You need to listen to me when I say—"

"Vilmad," a beautiful voice intruded on Vilmad's up-and-coming outburst. His back straightened up fast, stiff and still.

That voice was Lady Ariela, and she was standing right outside the door. Her silken dress, more beautiful than the last one she wore, kissed the tiled floor with golds and streams of liquid sunsets. When she intertwined her fingers, her slow-motioned curtain wings fluttered like a wedding veil in a buttery ocean along her back.

She glanced at me, gave a kind, elegant grin, and turned her eyes back to Vilmad. "I believe it is time for Miss Lisa to have lessons with Gaius. Wouldn't want her to be late, now would we?"

The Guardian took a deep breath, sucking in all his malice toward me and whatever I-hate-Gaius comment he had lodged in his throat. "Of course. My apologies, Lady Ariela." He then turned to me as I packed up my things. When he held out his fist, I saw the blue ribbons beginning to form, but suddenly, Ariela spoke again before the evanescing magic encapsulated me.

"Do well, dear Lisa," she said, and I returned to the forest entrance... still as confused about my purpose as before... and wondering if what Vilmad said was true or if he truly was trying to scare me out of my magic.

I stomped on the ground, my heel snapping a twig.

Vilmad hates I have this... so that means Valhalla was right: I'm meant for more than just magic learning. Maybe... Being a Hero is what I was meant to do... and Vilmad can't stand the fact I was chosen for it.

15
GAIUS' MAGIC

Using the gem to enter his hearth, I saw Gaius standing underneath the tall, dark green tree near his home. He wasn't wearing his usual dark leather jacket but still had his arms crossed, patiently waiting for me. Made me happy, especially after Vilmad's whole degrading spat.

When I approached him, he asked, serious like usual, "Did you rest this weekend?"

"Yes, sir," I said.

"Good. Then, follow me." His command was gentle, and he began leading me toward the back of his home.

Down the hill and past his patio, Gaius took me to the area where I first practiced my "magic parkour training," but it was completely gone! The once makeshift yard of giant roots and rocks was a flattened green grassland. *Did he do this with magic?*

"Lisa," he bellowed, "what are your strengths?"

"Um…" I honestly had never thought about it before. I knew he wasn't asking about my social or creative strengths, so I said the only thing I could think of.

"I guess my balance is pretty good. When I go roller skating with Mom, I don't fall over and can skate on one foot."

There was a pause. A *long* pause.

"… And?" Gaius continued to stare at the grassy field and trees ahead, assuming I had more physical strengths than that.

My eyes looked ahead, too, while I dug deep through my memories to pull out more positive Lisa Robbie qualities. "I guess I'm more flexible than most of my friends... I can *almost* do a perfect split."

Gaius made a short, breathy laugh, and I turned a little red; I really didn't need his reassurance of my lack of physical attributes.

"Lisa, you think too little of yourself."

My face instantly turned toward his green eyes. I truly didn't understand what he meant by that compliment.

"On your first day, you showed excellent endurance and discipline. Your strength lies in perseverance and desire to improve, which is what I'd hope you would say... but you didn't. So, Lisa, what are your strengths?"

"Um, my perseverance and desire for improvement?"

"And what are your weaknesses?"

That one is easy.

"Everything else."

"Do you wish to improve that then?"

"If it means learning magic, then I will do anything you tell me."

Gaius smiled and unfolded his arms. "Then, let us begin."

The ground rumbled and shook as if a large mass was burrowing under the dirt. The trees moved on their own, and leaves flew in all directions, creating unique paths and piles on the floor.

I looked at the Keeper next to me. *Is he... How is he doing this*? His hands were hardly moving, but nature still obeyed him. There was a strong force near his body, like how it felt to put my hand near the mouth of a vacuum. The air around him gravitated toward his hands, and with a sudden fling of his arm, a large green root as wide as a car came bursting through the dirt—breaching like a terrestrial whale!

This can't be real?

He kept moving his body and arms in rhythmic patterns, growing and guiding all the undergrowth, flowers, and weeds to create his desired shapes. I saw trees whose bark multiplied and their trunks twist and turn. Hibiscus and lilies from beside his house moved like snakes, creating inclines and platforms— big enough for someone like Gaius to sit comfortably on top of! Trenches and mazes of roots formed in the dirt before ascending back to the sky. He then used the roots underneath the ground as a spring and jumped over ten feet in the air, conducting the vines to act as rope and connect the vegetation platforms he created. Surfing—actually surfing—along the mossy elongated plants as if they were ocean waves, he formed high walls of sturdy shrubs, balance beams with thorned flowered pendulums, and rope swings from thick vines—ending his magical construction with intertwining ivy to form a towering climbing wall.

I stood stationary, glued to the grass with awe. *He made an entire obstacle course out of plants... the whole thing just formed in seconds because his magic told it to!*

Gaius then swooped down beside me, causing a rush of wind to blow back my hair. He was smiling the most I had ever seen him, sweat glistening off his chiseled brow and seeping into his beard. The magic, the forest, Gaius—everything looked like it came straight out of a movie! I couldn't wrap my head around what just happened. It was unbelievable.

"That was the coolest thing I have ever seen in my life!" I said loudly and on my tiptoes. "You were just surfing a giant root and then moving the trees like they were made of rubber! And when you jumped off the ground—*man,* your magic is just so cool!" I could not help myself from fangirling. "Will you be able to teach me how to do all that someday? It looked like the funnest thing in the world!"

"I will admit," Gaius began, admiring his craftsmanship, releasing a deep breath, "creating this was a first for me. I'm glad you mentioned it, Lisa."

"Then, what were all the torn down trees and rocks for—the stuff I practiced on before? Wasn't that a type of practice course?"

My magic mentor popped his fingers and elbows. "That was just a brush pile you mistook for something useful. Didn't expect you to use it for your training."

"You mean I was climbing on top of your *garbage*?"

He looked down at me with a smirk. "It was quite humorous."

I wasn't sure if Gaius was trying to be funny or if using his powers made him more comedic. Whatever the case, I was more comfortable around him and didn't mind the joke aimed at me.

"Alright, Lisa," Gaius explained. "This training ground is specifically designed for you. It will help improve your agility, balance, core strength, endurance, and—overall—draw out your magic strength. You will fall many times; that is a fact. I am telling you this now so you won't fear making mistakes—no doubt you will make *many.*"

He didn't have to emphasize that last part...

The muscly man lifted his chin, his eyes looking up toward the perfectly vertical tower of vines at the end of the course. "Your goal is to reach the top of the ivy watchtower and bring me the sunflower I grew at the top. Once you do... I will show you how to use your magic."

"Really?" I shouted, my eyes filled with stars of joy. "You will really teach me how to use magic?"

"You have to finish the course first."

"Then, let's *do this!*"

I was about to run up the first incline when Gaius extended his arm and stopped me. He then held up his hand, summoning a trio of maple leaves—plucked them right off a tree—like they were flying drones. He twirled his finger, and the leaves shot toward his home, opened the door, loudly rummaged inside, and burst back out carrying a brown potion the size of a teacup. *He can move plants not attached to the ground, too?* I would have guessed the leaves had a mind of their own by the way they zoomed through the air.

Gaius opened the potion and chugged it down. He wiped his mouth, standing with rugged confidence—arms crossed and chin held high—letting out a booming phrase.

"Tosaigh ag bogadh!"

The air changed, and the plants Gaius used to create the obstacle course started moving, but this time, they were working like machines. The thorny flower pendulums swayed back and forth, the mossy jumping platforms moved up and down, and Gaius stood motionless. That power I sensed before was not there.

Was he not doing this? What was in that potion, and what did that phrase mean?

All the plants rotated in a pattern, making the obstacle course a hundred times more difficult.

"Now, you may start," Gaius told me.

Not going to lie, fear bubbled up in my gut, but the thought of finally getting able to learn magic gave me the confidence to move forward.

After a deep breath, I ran up the first leafy incline. The rubber soles on my boots made it easy enough to complete.

Next were the rickety tree stumps covered in mushrooms, set up like swaying tire swings kids tried to jump on top of at the park; however, I was six feet off the ground and had nothing to grab onto.

"You're not gonna let me fall, right?" I shouted back at Gaius.

"There is a pad of moss and overwatered aloe vera leaves below you," he answered back.

I looked down below, and my voice cracked. "You used a *cactus* as my landing mat!"

"It's a succulent. You'll be fine."

Gaius said he made the course specifically for me and knew I would be falling a lot, so I decided to trust him... even though my mind could not comprehend a leaf saving my life.

Replaying reassuring thoughts to calm my nerves about the *succulent* as my safety net, I made my first leap toward the brown wobbly stumps. Instantly, my weight shifted the moment my foot made contact. I wasn't prepared for how slippery and unstable the obstacle was, and my body fell fast, right toward the ground. I screamed, fearing the worst as my nerves tensed up, bracing for a painful impact.

Suddenly... I hit something squishy. I looked around, noticing I landed perfectly on the mossy aloe leaves, as Gaius said.

After the fear of falling dissipated, I actually enjoyed the thrill and rush it gave me and got right back up to try again. I looked toward the Keeper as I made my way to the starting point again. He smiled, not even asking if I was okay, leaving me to question if he was holding back a laugh at my embarrassment.

"Keep your weight on your whole foot as you leap across," he instructed me. "If you balance on your toes or just your heels, you will fall again."

That was his first piece of advice that made sense.

I nodded and started again. When I reached the wobbling stumps, I made it past the first two easily using Gaius' advice, but I slipped on the third one having to use my arms to grab onto the platform, holding on for dear life. I could pull myself back up and crouch on top of it, so I started to crawl across instead, but the course just knocked me over!

"No cheating," I heard Gaius say as I hit the safety pad again. "Infants crawl.

You will run across with confidence."

Did he just make me fall over on purpose?

I then attempted the course again... and again and again and again. I made it farther each time, but I kept falling. Felt like I was training for the military! I was getting new bruises on my knees from hitting the grungy bark hip-hop bars, green stains on my hands from weaving through the gritty weaver, rope burns from slipping off the shrubbed vines, and even scratches along my face from just pure clumsiness. "You can take a break when you need it," he would tell me, but I told myself I wouldn't stop until I got that sunflower. The course wasn't going to kill me, just make me a little bruised and bloody.

The sunset approached, and my stamina was at an all-time low. I *know* I said I wouldn't stop... but a huge burger and a side of fries sounded like paradise by the time I finished my thirty-seventh attempt at the course. Gaius had given me tips and advice throughout my runs, which helped me improve by a landslide, but he returned to his home a little over an hour ago. The plants still moved on their own after he left, proving that the potion and chant triggered the machine-like movements.

I was about to start my next run when—right as I reached the taunting leafy incline—I collapsed to my knees, catching my body on my palms before completely toppling over. Being that weak, it was a first for me, and I thought it was normal to feel exhausted while running through a rigorous training course.

My body lay on the grass as my heart pounded hard.

Footsteps crept behind me, following a burly phrase. "I told you to take a break."

I turned around to see Gaius standing over me, not looking too surprised to see me lying on the ground, completely exhausted. Breathing heavily and sweating waterfalls, I hated to admit he was right.

"I just wanted... to get that flower... and finally learn magic..." My breaths were short as my palms supported my weight while I started sitting up on the warm grass.

Gaius joined me on the ground. "If that is your only goal, you won't reach it," he said, which didn't make much sense.

A drip of sweat swam down my freckled shoulder. I squinted at him. "I thought that was the point of the course?"

"Lisa, when you read through the books about magic, do you just skip to the last sentence?"

"... No."

"Why?"

I am not sure what this has to do with running through an obstacle course...

"Because most of what's important is in the middle, the cool details of magic. I wouldn't understand the creatures or potions if I only read the last sentence."

The green in his eyes matched the vibrancy of the grass beneath us as he turned to face me. "You could save yourself the time by skipping the details though, if you just make it to the end. Getting to the point faster."

I sat there and sighed. I now could see where he was going with this. "I wouldn't be learning anything if I just skipped to the end... just like I wouldn't grow any stronger if I tried to rush toward the end of this obstacle course, right?"

My teacher grinned. "The course isn't just an obstacle to get through. Each test is there for a purpose: to make you stronger. When you reach the end, you will feel more accomplished and satisfied with your result. You've got a strong passion for this... just don't forget that resting your body is a part of discipline just as much as endurance is." Gaius then stood up and gave me a hand getting back on my feet, yanking me up like I was a yo-yo. "You're finished for today. Get some proper rest and eat well."

I never thought resting was an important part of becoming stronger until Gaius explained why. I couldn't expect my magic to trust my body if I kept exhausting it to its limits, so I had to accept that learning magic would not happen very soon.

Gaius and I went back to his home, where he gave me more of the gross green vigor water. Chugging it down quickly like before was the best way to get the bitter grassy taste over with. I told Gaius bye as I left for Valhalla's home to rest... though I didn't want to wait until Wednesday to try the course again. Magic was just a flower away, and I made it a point that after lessons with Bethesda and Inna the next day, I was returning to Gaius' home. I would keep doing that course every day until that sunflower was in my grasp. *That flower will be mine in no time.*

16
MY BALL AND CHAIN

Oh, how wrong I was.

It was Thursday afternoon, and I still had not completed Gaius' soul-crushing obstacle course. During our lessons, that was all I practiced—even ventured to his home after my training with Inna and still never made it to the end. I would go farther down the course every hour and repeat the same dumb mistakes. It got to the point that embarrassment didn't even faze me anymore.

Gaius never yelled at me or put me down, though. He would advise "tighten your core when keeping balance" or "use all your arm muscles when swinging and not just the muscles in your hands." It did help, and my stamina stayed more consistent... but still, no *magic* was happening.

I stood at the edge of the incline as Gaius walked up toward me. My hair was tied back in a ponytail, curled locks swinging left and right as I did my warm-up bounces.

"Gaius, I'm gonna make it to the ivy tower today—just you watch!" I said to him, pumping myself up, feeling more comfortable with the Keeper of Stars.

"Let's see it," he said, grinning with his arms crossed again.

I started up the incline, passed the wobbly mushroom-covered stumps, weaved through the vined weaver, and landed perfectly on the balance beam below. *So far so good*. I walked across the wooden log and jumped down, then ran through the trench to get a running start on the hip-hop course. My feet weren't caught, enabling me to start the overhead incline climber. I grabbed the rough vines and swung across to the next running incline. *Keep it up, Lisa!* My endurance was steady, so I kept going and ran right toward the narrow walkway with the swinging pendulums. I already knew their timing and could run straight across; I only wobbled a little at the end. I jumped across the moving root platforms and *didn't fall—I have never made it this far before!*

All that was left between me and the ivy wall were the swinging vines. I had to summon my inner Tarzan if I wanted to swing across without any type of platform in between swings. I watched them sway, timed their speed, and jumped. I caught the first one, holding my weight with my arms and feet... but swinging to the next vine seemed impossible. My momentum was gone, and I couldn't get my body to move far enough forward.

"You'll have to try again," I heard Gaius say. "You need constant movement, so your arms aren't doing all the work."

"*I can do it!*" I yelled back. I truly did not want to run the course again.

"You need to fall and try again."

"*NO—I got this!*"

"Then grab the next vine."

Gravity loved me more than any person in the world, thanks to this obstacle course, and I could already feel its invisible arms pulling me in for a hug once again—straight down to the dirty floor of leaves and squishy moss. *I hate it when Gaius is right...*

I let go and slowly treaded toward the front of the leafy incline, not bothering to brush the dirt off my scratched-up knees.

"... How do I grab the next vine?" I begrudgingly asked Gaius, not making eye contact with him; I still knew he was beaming with that same smirk.

"Make a running start as the vine swings toward you and feel its rhythm as you go to grab the next one," he answered. "You will have to use all your strength to hold onto the vine while grabbing the next one. You can do it."

I took what he said and embedded it into my mind before making my way through the course again. *Not gonna fall this time...* I approached the vines, stepped back to get a running start, and sprinted forward. I grabbed the first ivy rope with my hands and feet, but I didn't have time to adjust before the next vine came into view. I reached out with my right arm but forgot to use my feet and fell.

"You need to use both your right arm and right leg," I heard him shout.

Got it.

I went back up and tried again, only this time, I moved with the rhythm of the vines with both arm and leg—it worked! I grabbed the next swinging plant easily but still didn't have time to hesitate. I used my momentum with my left arm and leg to grab the next vine—and then the next and the next. Before I knew it, I had made it to the bottom of the ivy climbing wall!

"Gaius! I made it!" I shouted, beams of sweat running down my forehead.

He didn't say anything, just nodded back at me and started walking toward the wall. *Guess I need to finish the whole course to get a "Job well done, Lisa" from him...*

I looked up toward the sky-scraping ivy wall. Some areas had indents and easier-to-grab vines, while others had a few gaping holes. No obstacles were falling or swinging from above to knock me over—thank goodness—so I only had to focus on climbing the thirty-foot green monster. There was one thing I didn't notice until my hand had already made its first ascent...

"Gaius... where's the safety harness thing?" I curiously asked.

My teacher stood near the bottom of the platform, near me and the ivy wall. "You don't need one."

My head shot toward him like a deer in headlights. "What do you mean I don't have one?" I shrieked. "Wha—what happens if I fall?"

"Then don't fall."

This cannot be the way Ariela and the Guardians wanted me to train by risking my life!

"Is there some type of safety mat or—or something to break my fall?"

"You do not need one. You will make it to the top."

You've got to be kidding me! I had fallen more times in the past four days than I had in my entire life—including my baby years of learning to walk. Gaius saw the many times I slipped up... yet he still believed I had the strength to do it.

I was petrified. *He really wouldn't let me fall to my death... right?* But I had to learn magic, which meant getting that dumb yellow sunflower at the top of the colossal ivy wall. I wiped the sweat off my forehead, dried my clammy hands with my shorts, and decided that I would have a better grip on my feet if my shoes were off. I plopped down and untied the laces on my brown boots, standing barefoot at the wall's base. *Let's do this.*

I made it up about a third of the way with little trouble. *Maybe this is easier than I thought.* I grabbed the next curved branch and went to reach for the one on the right, but it was much farther than the one before. Jumping was the only solution. *Just don't look down, Lisa...* I released my right arm, leaped with my toes, and grabbed it! I did the same with the next one on the left, but my feet couldn't find a spot in time—making me dangle for a moment. My heart raced 100 mph, and I couldn't help but look down to find a safe spot to hold my weight.

Oh, that is far...

I gripped that wall tightly, getting way too personal with the shoots and leaves. Fear of falling was overwhelming me. *Lisa, do not cry right now! You can do this, okay? You can DO THIS!*

With my furrowed brows, I slapped fear in the face, putting the desire to learn magic in command of my emotions. My attitude changed. I decided to not think about the crushing blow of the hard floor beneath me—only about getting to the top. I went for the thick branch above me, then the one on the left, the right, the far right, and stretched to get the one on the far left. Every pore in my body started sweating buckets, not because of fear but because I wasn't slowing down; I was using all I had to get to the top, and stopping was not an option.

The branches were harder to grab the farther I went, but I could now see the details of the sunflower. *Almost there!* I stopped caring about the blisters on the pads of my feet or the scratches on my hands from the spurred shoots. I leaped right and grabbed the next branch, wobbling a bit but recovering quickly. *You're almost there, Lisa!* Another reach with my left leg and another with my left arm. I kept going and going—the ground below didn't even frighten me anymore. I felt the strongest I ever had in my whole life, and before I knew it...

I reached the top.

I didn't hesitate for one second. I pulled my way up and plucked that sturdy sunflower out of its home and held it up high. I yelled out a mighty, *"YEAH! Wahoo!"* and jumped up and down on top of that leafy watchtower. That moment was the biggest accomplishment of my whole existence. I was proud. I was joyful. I was unstoppable. I beat Gaius' course. I got the yellow flower. Best of all, I was now one step closer to *finally* learning magic.

"Gaius!" I continued to celebrate, "I did it! I freaking won! I got the flower!" I looked down at him, and he was smiling pretty big, which was all the praise I could ever ask for.

"I told you—you could do it," he justified. I think he was proud as a teacher; at least, that is what his smiling face told me.

Soon, the watchtower I was on started to shake. The sides extended out, and the vines formed a bosky spiral surrounding the wall. Gaius used his arm to nudge the tower, and it instantly turned into a slide. I was quite happy he didn't let me walk down flights of stairs as a reward. I sat down, cradling the flower tightly, and slid down the organic slide. When I reached the bottom, my speed didn't decrease, and I zoomed off the slide and rolled right into a pile of leaves. I won't lie: it was pretty fun.

With green and yellow leaves all in my tied hair, I ran up to Gaius and proudly gifted him the sunflower.

"Here..." I started panting, very out of breath, "So... does that mean... I can learn magic now?"

He didn't take the yellow blossom. "Keep it as proof of your accomplishment today," he said, so I continued to hold the flower. "You showed me your determination and proved to yourself you had the strength to complete the course. So, yes, Lisa. I will now teach you magic."

I started jumping up and down. "Oh my gosh—*yes! I can't believe it! Thank you, thank you, thank you!*"

"Come. Follow me," Gaius directed, and I happily tagged along.

We headed for his home. I didn't bother to grab my shoes; magic was *far* more important.

I admired the flower in my hand, seeing as its aura somehow pushed aside my shy nature, and couldn't stop my questions toward the Keeper. "What are you gonna teach me first? How to make a flower grow or expand—no, even better—how to make leaves fly around as you did with the maple leaves?"

He didn't say anything, just smiled and tittered at my giddiness as we entered the clearing between his home and greenhouse. Gaius then stopped right in the middle of the circular dirt patch.

"So, what is first?" I continued. "Learning a new stance or how to make a tree grow or punch for me?"

Gaius then moved his right arm and used his magic on the ground below. Something sprung up from the soil about six feet in front of us. It was oddly familiar... the kind of familiar that made my excitement slowly morph into disbelief. Before I could grasp the situation, its leaves continued to move and dig their way back underground, dragging *it* up. The weed dropped *it* to the ground with a thud that seemed to echo for miles.

The sunflower trophy dropped out of my hand, as well as my heart.

There was no denying what my eyes saw. The weed was the *exact* same purple color, and that stone was the same one that dirtied and blistered my hands. My ball and chain were back.

He crossed his arms. "I want you to make that plant or that rock move with magic."

... You have got to be kidding me...

My eyes couldn't stop staring at the two ghosts from my past. I thought Gaius destroyed the rock—it was nothing but sand the week before. The purple weed still had all its mocking thorns and magenta leaves, and I just stood motionless.

"Go ahead," Gaius nonchalantly commanded. "Start with the nettle weed first."

He's not kidding. He's actually serious right now!

"Any... uh, advice on how to do that?" I pleaded, timid and still in shock.

"The same as last time: move with the plant, not against it."

"Anything else...?" I really wanted a hint as to what technique or stance to take as he did with me on the obstacle course.

"You completed my training course and proved your body and mind are strong enough to handle challenges—including magic. So, just force out your magic and make the plant move."

Just force—just force out my magic... Frustrated and annoyed, I held out my blistered hands toward the purple weed. I took a deep breath and pushed the air toward the plant, finding nothing but the same abominable silence I endured before. More times I tried—mimicking the same motions I saw Gaius use when he created the obstacle course. Failure once more.

I gritted my teeth. "It's not working."

"Try the stone this time," Gaius responded, ignoring my remark.

I reached out my hand but paused for a moment. "Can you at least tell me how to move this one?" I didn't mean to sound agitated, but I felt like I had every right to. I got myself all bloody and to the point of collapsing many times—I *deserved* to be properly taught how to force out my magic.

"I've already told you how. The next step is all up to you."

I took another deep breath and imagined myself as part of the earth, not just a force trying to move the rock. *This rock is sturdy, strong, and most of all... annoying, and I'd give anything to never see it again for the rest of my life. But it's just a rock... just a dumb, stupid rock that I can move—*

At that moment, I furrowed my brow and struck the air with a hard diagonal slice—one filled with power and force—and something amazing happened.

The stone moved an inch... a *whole inch!*

What just—

"Again," Gaius' calm voice commanded.

My hopes soared. I punched the air with the opposite hand. It moved a whole foot.

Is this really me?

"Now, try burying it into the ground."

I nodded, suppressing my excitement from my accomplishments. I thought about how hard it would be to move a rock into the ground, and instead of punching the air, I lifted my right barefoot and stomped the ground forward. The rock instantly dug itself a couple of inches into the dry dirt! *I'm... actually doing it!* I stepped forward with my other foot and stomped again—the stone went *deeper!* I threw myself out on a whim and decided to use both my hands to bury it completely. I tensed up my fingers and *slammed* my palms together as I stared down at the once beast of stone.

It. Was. Completely. Underground... and I did that. *I* did *that* with nothing but the magic inside me.

As my eyes filled with stars, Gaius said in the same cool tone, "Looks like you, Lisa, have just acquired terrain elemental magic."

"I did it... I actually did it!" I proclaimed because I couldn't contain my excitement anymore. "I... I can't believe it... I just moved the rock with magic! Me!" I started jumping in glee, feeling the reward of finally moving that dumb stone with magic.

I looked over to Gaius; he was also smiling at my accomplishment. "I just moved the rock all by myself! That was the most amazing experience of my life!"

Gaius let out a small huff as he was facing the rock. "Never have I seen a young Mage praise themselves so much just for moving a small stone."

"Please, teach me something else, Gaius! Gimme another rock or stone to bury!"

The Keeper then stretched his arms and popped his knuckles before facing me.

"Now that your magic has finally surfaced," he began with his confident stare, "we can finally begin your proper magic training."

"Oh, I am *so ready!*"

"It will be tough."

"Not a problem."

"And brutal."

"Of course."

"You sure you're ready?"

"Bring it on!"

"Then, let's start next week."

"Wait—what?" My shoulders dropped. "But I don't want to wait until next week. I feel completely fine and ready—"

Gaius stepped right in front of me and placed his hand on my shoulder. I almost fell back as if my knees couldn't handle the weight of his calloused hand.

"Lisa, I know you're excited, but look at you..." His voice was concerned and serious. "You are running on fumes—nothing but adrenaline and one step away from collapsing *again*."

Blinded by my newfound magic, I didn't realize how busted up my feet were from the ivy wall or the tenderness of my blistered palms. I was dizzy and wobbly and felt my body craving a hot shower. I wasn't used to putting forth so much energy, and the course had drained me dry. To top it off, that small bit of terrain magic I did use was a force I was not used to either. My body did need to rest... no matter how much I hated to admit it.

My head sunk to the floor. "Got it..."

His palm lifted off my shoulder. "You did well today, though, so you should go home feeling proud of that. When you return, I'll have a proper lesson in terrain magic ready for you."

He pointed two fingers at the sunflower I had dropped. The flower sprung to life, digging itself into the ground next to the stone I moved with magic.

"Do you think I could come over tomorrow just for one, *short* magic lesson?" I asked, staring at my trophy flower. "I know it's Friday, but I really, really wanna practice my magic some more."

He didn't look at me and started walking back toward his home. "You need rest—"

I ran in front of him and pulled out my sure-fire trick: the Lisa Robbie baby-doll eyes. *"Please,* Gaius? I'll go to bed early tonight and everything—getting plenty of rest and chugging gallons of that green juice—if you can just teach me one more thing before I have to go back to Earth?"

Gaius' face lost focus with my eyes, and he straightened up quite fast. I don't think he ever had a child beg to learn magic before, but then again, even Mom couldn't resist my baby-doll eyes. I had perfected the technique for years. It was how I convinced her to let me stay up late to play video games and receive second servings of dessert.

I didn't care if it was petty. I didn't care if it was a low move because it was working. Getting him to teach me magic was going to be a *whole* lot easier.

"... *One* lesson," he finally succumbed and continued his path toward his home. "Then, after tomorrow, you will get some proper rest this weekend, okay?"

"That is fine by me! Thank you!"

With my spirit lifted, I merrily skipped along beside him—smiling big on the way to the Keeper's home and ignoring my weariness. My mind was going a mile a minute. *I'm officially one step closer to becoming a Hero!*

Forgetting all the pain from my scratches and bruised knees, I asked the Keeper, "So, what's the plan next week now that I finally learned magic? Am I gonna learn how to fight with stones or throw rock punches?"

Gaius grinned with a light chuckle. "Rock punches? Didn't know fighting was high on your priority list."

"Well, if I'm going to be a Hero one day, I figured I would need to learn how to fight."

"A *Hero?*" He tittered. "Now, that is a pretty bold statement. When did you decide on that?"

"I thought that is why you were training me? The purpose of the Agapéd Magic?"

Gaius's smile became melancholic, and he just kept walking straight. "I am here to teach you how to use magic. That is all."

Something about the way he said that felt... off.

Magic gave me confidence and heightened my curiosity, causing me to blurt out my burning questions. "But, *why* though? I have the most powerful magic out there—according to you and the Guardians—so I can't just be learning it for the sake of learning magic. People with powerful magic go off and save the world, so I should be training for that, too, right?"

Gaius was just about to the backdoor of his home, and his voice was growing more serious by the second. "You aren't being trained to become a Hero and having powerful magic doesn't mean you have to go off and 'save the world.' If you do want to become one someday, that is up to you, but I was told to only teach you magic."

"But what if I asked you to train me to become a Hero *outside* of teaching the Agapéd Magic?"

His eyes refused to look at me no matter how much I glanced up at him, and his face remained stoic and smileless. "I can't."

"Can't"... Why did he say "can't"...

"So, it's not that you *won't* teach me... it's that you *can't*..."

We both stood on the tiled concrete patio in front of the back entrance. There was a pile of the wood he had cut that morning next to the door all neatly stacked, and it seemed his eyes couldn't help but stare at them instead of me.

"Yes."

I didn't know what to say. Gaius always seemed eager to teach me magic and said he would never stop me from wanting to learn more; however, he talked as if he wasn't allowed to teach me. *Does he think I'm not strong enough? Do the Guardians think I'm not strong enough? Is that why he can't teach me?* I didn't understand, and I couldn't stand it.

"Why aren't you allowed to teach me?" I asked once more, very solemn.

Gaius stopped for a moment and began to grab the wooden logs. It was hard to read his emotions in general, but I could tell he avoided eye contact. After he had about seven chunks of firewood cradled in his arms, he finally answered. "I'm sorry, Lisa. But I can't. For now, let's continue to work on your magic as planned," he responded, stern and glum. "Get some rest if you still wish to have another lesson tomorrow."

17

TO DO GOOD

"He said *no*?"

"He said no."

Returning that afternoon, Valhalla and I ate our potato soup in her room so I could confide all the details of Gaius' grueling answer to my question. I was confused and... just downright frustrated. I did not understand why Gaius said no and why I wasn't allowed to be taught how to fight. There was only one conclusion I could think of as to why: The Guardians didn't believe I could do it and told him no. After all, I was a thirteen-year-old girl from Earth, and they hated that fact. Especially Vilmad.

Valhalla cocked her eyebrow and gave a mischievous smirk. "Well, you know what you have to do now..."

My eyes widened as I stopped stirring my soup. "What?"

"You're gonna have to *make* Mr. Gaius teach you."

"But how?"

"You know—butter him up, compliment him, do everything he says without complaining. And when the timing is right, you quickly ask him again. I always do it to Dad when I want him to take me out of classes early. It takes a couple of days of asking, but it *always* works. Gaius *has* to be the same way. Probably will be easier for him than Dad."

Gaius did build a giant obstacle course for me, and begging for him to teach me magic on my day off did work before...

"Okay, I'll try it tomorrow," I confidently answered.

I was about to leave to shower, but more drawings of Heroes on Valhalla's bed caught my attention—poor drawings, but decent enough to see them with lightning powers like that Hero, Gladius Snow, from her magazines.

"Valhalla," I began, sitting on my knees, eyeing the artwork and *Chevaliers* copies she had in her bedroom corner, "how come you really want me to be a Hero—I mean, I know you said it's the reason for my magic, but I mean, wouldn't the Guardians have told me—even if they didn't think I was good enough for something like that?"

She shrugged, and for the first time, her words were soft—*quiet*. "I mean... I don't know much about the past Agapéd Bearers, or even about the last one, but I just think magic is so cool..." She played with the split ends of her long black hair. "I don't have any magic—not anything powerful. If I said a heat charm to spark a flame, I could only warm the matchstick; no fire would happen. And I'm stuck in this town, only able to visit places with Dad when he lets me. So, because I can never be a Hero or go off into the world to see them, I just dream of a world where I can—drawing and reading all about them."

She then smiled and flung her hand toward me. "But then suddenly Rayna and Vilmad show up, telling us about you—this Agapéd Magic girl who was my age—and I couldn't believe it. A Hero was staying in my house—well, a soon-to-be Hero. And when you didn't even know what they were or why you had powerful magic, I couldn't just sit back and watch you *not* use your new gift. You aren't from here, so"—she curled up in a ball, her arms wrapped around her shins—"I just got excited. Sorry if it was kinda pushy."

I didn't know what to say. Valhalla—a girl I just met last week—was more open with me than any friend I had ever had back on Earth. She saw me and thought I was worth something, even when the Guardians didn't think that—refusing to tell me the truth about my magic and pitying me the moment the Agapéd chose my heart. Valhalla loved the celestial power and didn't hate me for it, the power she longed for and drew pictures of, but instead pushed me to follow the dream of a Hero. She could've just sat around, never caring what I did with the Guardians, or even told me how unfair it was that I received magic when I was born on powerless Earth. But she didn't. She... showed me I had a purpose... and thought I was the coolest person alive.

I had never known a friendship like hers. I felt wanted for the first time by someone other than Mom.

"Well, I'm glad you told me about my magic and Heroes," I said, sitting beside her. "And you weren't pushy..." I playfully rolled my eyes. "Okay, maybe a *bit*—but the *good* kind of pushy. The kind that will make *me* make *Gaius* train me to be a Hero."

Valhalla giggled, hugging her legs. "Better tell me how it goes. My butter-up plan never fails. You'll be training to be a Hero in no time."

—~~—

I was up early the following day, ready to start my first magic lesson and commence my Gaius-will-make-me-a-Hero plan before I left for Earth. Through the Veradome and down the stairwell, my magic could finally open his enchanted wooden door, no more need for the green emerald. Walking into his half-buried home, I ran to tell him about my accomplishment, but he was gone. No sounds of woodworking or creaking footsteps came from inside the closed doors of his cottage. I checked the magic study. Still nothing. *Maybe he is outside...*

Out back on the stone patio, I heard tree bark breaking. I ran past the obstacle course toward the unknown territory of Gaius' domain. As the grass appeared greener, a small pond formed ahead. The sun had just risen, painting the still waters with warm yellows and blues. *How big is this property of his?* Gaius was at the water's mouth with two broken trees beside him. He wore a light linen shirt and the same muddy boots and dark brown pants.

When I came to his side, a formal greeting flew out of my brain as I looked down at the two logs. "Why did you cut down those trees?"

"They are dead," he said with his deep voice, "so I will use them for carving and firewood."

The Keeper used his magic and commanded thick roots from the ground to rise. Each one wrapped around in sections along the first fallen tree. He then closed his hand into a fist—hardly putting forth much energy—and the roots squeezed the trunk so hard that it cut through the tree! The slices weren't busted, almost perfectly clean-cut.

His magic is so cool!

"I didn't expect you here so early," he said, smiling with a few specks of sweat on his forehead.

"Well, I was excited about my first magic lesson, though I actually really like the mornings. It's always quiet, and you have more time to do stuff during the day," I answered. "Is that okay?"

He used the roots below as his personal butler—stacking the disks of wood one on top of the other—grinning at my response. "I am just surprised that is all, given that it is your day off. But I also prefer the mornings, so yes, it is fine. You *did* get rest, though?"

So far, buttering him up is working in my favor...

I nodded. "Mhm—I went to bed early and everything."

Three columns of robust timber were now neatly stacked near the water, Gaius not even needing to wipe his hands clean of dirt or wood chippings. "Good. Then, let's begin."

The Keeper took me a couple of feet away from the fallen trees, farther from the water, right in front of a dirt patch amid his forest. It still had a nice view of the pond through the thin pine trees, and I could see Gaius' house about thirty yards behind us.

"There are two types of elemental earth magic," Gaius began to speak, sounding more like a teacher than during our past lessons. "The type you have is Non-Living magic, specifically terrain elemental magic. You will be able to move and command the earth's minerals, including sand, ore, soil, and stone—anything deemed non-living that is of the Tellurian category. Other, smaller subtypes of Non-Living magic can manipulate metal, magma, dead plants, and gems, meaning you cannot control those elements."

Okay—my magic sounds so freaking awesome!

My mentor continued as we ventured under the high tree limbs. "The other type, and the one I possess, is Living-Earth magic. I can control and manipulate any living plant or vegetation, even ones that have just been plucked. As long as the plant is green or growing, I can do as I wish with it. Even though you and I have different forms, I have studied both types intently for centuries and will be able to teach you well."

My eyes widened. Centuries—*kinda forgot he is super old when he is rippling with muscles and doesn't have a strand of gray hair.*

We stopped at a random spot where the dirt was more moist due to the trees' shade. Gaius stood tall next to me and had me face the same direction as him. "The first thing you must learn is how to control your magic. Right now, your control is poor. When you stand, you need to be firm on the ground."

He bent his knees with one foot slightly forward, so I did the same. "Good balance, alertness, and a focused mind—that is what you must master first. You showed me you are capable of all three things during your run of the obstacle course, but now, you must do the same with magic."

"Got it."

"Now, for your first attempt at magic control, we will focus on training your mind. Magic is only as strong as the mind and heart that control it. What you think is what will come forth, understand?"

"Yes, sir."

"Good. So, your first goal is to make three perfectly rectangular blocks rise from the ground at three different heights. After that, I want you to create three domes of earth. Like this."

Gaius moved his right hand upward in a quick motion. The moment he did, the tree roots buried underground shot up and cross-stitched to form a perfect square. Next, he moved his hand again but in a sharp, small circle. A rooted dome formed. He did it all quickly, making it look rather easy; it was *amazing!*

I looked down at my fingers. "So, I just move my hands like you did, but imagine I am moving the dirt instead?" I asked.

"You are not imagining anything. You *are* moving it. When you run, you don't imagine it. You prepare yourself, tense up your body, and focus on what makes you run. When you make a fire, you don't imagine its flames; you create them with your skill. Even an artist can't rely fully on imagination; they must use their muscle memory for something to happen on the page. When you think of moving the earth, you are moving it as if it were part of your body."

Gaius looked down at me, right into my eyes. His were exceptionally greener than usual. "Lisa, magic *is* a part of you now. It's more than a trivial hobby. It's like a muscle that must constantly be trained and a skill that you can't afford to weaken. You understand?"

I didn't avert my gaze. "Yes, sir."

"Alright, then. Let's see it."

I liked it when Gaius would get serious about magic. It made it seem more real and a part of life than just some daydream. I took my stance and raised my hand... realizing he never answered my first question.

"... I just move it the same way you did and make the dirt into a rectangle statue?"

"There isn't a set move. You can use your hand. Your fingers..." Gaius pointed two fingers out and made a smaller rectangle form with roots. "Your foot..." He shifted his foot on the ground, almost making an "L" shape. Another entangled box formed. "Whatever works for you." He then cocked his head to the side, and all the organic shapes unraveled and ascended back into the ground—*all that just from that slight movement of his neck!* I hoped to be as powerful as him someday.

I decided to just use my hand since it seemed easiest. I raised it up to move the dirt below, but only a small mound of earth formed. I actually was impressed with myself but knew it was not my goal to make a pile of dirt, so I tried to act like I wasn't excited about it. I pressed the air back down with my hand, and the mound completely disappeared—it was like the earth was back to normal again. I tried again. A bigger pile was produced... but it was still a cornerless mound. *Gaius made this look so easy...*

"Keep working on this. I'll come back to check on your progress in a little while," he said and just left. I was used to him doing that, though, and honestly, I liked practicing alone; I didn't have to feel his bouldering presence around me, judging my imperfections.

As time passed, my mounds of dirt became more slender and sturdy, reaching about three feet off the ground. Little pieces of roots would be sticking out the sides along with worms and ants falling down the edges. I switched to using two hands, which helped tremendously with forming the edges of the mound. I would raise both simultaneously, parallel with palms facing each other, and focus on making the rectangular shape. With every new mucky shape I made, the more excited I became. I just couldn't get over the fact I was moving the earth with the magic in my heart.

Out of nowhere, it happened. My first rectangular block of dirt formed from the ground. It was perfect. I was so happy with my rock sandcastle and quickly attempted to make two smaller ones... and *it worked, again!* I was finally getting the hang of it, popping earth out of the ground with ease, and my smile wouldn't fade. I left the blocks up and moved to the left and took my stance to form a dome of dirt. Right on my first try... another cube of rock appeared. And then another and another. *Seems like... I only know how to make pointed dirt columns now...*

When the sun was high in the sky, I finally formed a dome of soil. My arms and hands were tense, and sweat dripped down my face. I barely took more than a few steps, but my body wobbled like it ran up and down a hill carrying heavy dumbbells. Magic made me tired—never would have guessed that—but I loved it still. I liked the heart race it gave, the languor that swept through my blood veins. The draining strength only clarified the realness of magic—how truly beautiful and intense it was—and I knew I needed to work hard at it, especially if I wanted to become a hero or warrior someday.

Strong footsteps came up from behind me, and I turned to see Gaius walking through the shade of trees.

"I did it!" I shouted as he made his way closer, sweat glistening on my forehead. "Look! Three different rectangle mounds and three different sized domes." I gestured to him to look toward my earthy shapes, in hopes to please him.

"Let me see you make one," he asked.

I was more than happy to. I nodded and faced the ground off to the right. I focused hard and used my hands to move the earth to form another small dome and tall miniature building of soil.

He stared at it momentarily before saying, "For your first go at magic... you did well."

I was bright and jubilant with his words of praise, feeling my heart flutter with butterflies. "Once I got the hang of it, forming the shapes became a lot easier! So, what's next?"

"I said *one* lesson," Gaius smirked, leading us back to his home.

I hoped he had forgotten that detail because I wanted to learn more. Suddenly, the Hero agenda resurfaced in my mind. My palms grew sweatier as I clenched them into fists even at the thought of asking him again. *Come on, Lisa. You can do this. He seems... happy. Maybe he will say yes...*

My feet kept up with the Keeper's pace as I fidgeted with my fingers. "So... do you think next week," I began to rush my words, "I could *maybe* learn a thing or two about fighting or some type of attack with magic?"

He didn't respond quickly, staring ahead as we turned the corner of his home. "You still have a lot to learn with magic, getting the basics down. We will focus on that and not any fighting styles."

Lisa—Valhalla would be disappointed in you! You have to try harder!

I took a deep breath and summoned Confident Lisa out from the pit of my soul. "When I'm done, can I just have *one* Hero lesson—"

"Lisa…" he calmly cut off my words, but his voice was surprisingly deep to the point I jumped in place. "I said I can't."

"Sorry…" I apologized, and even though I was disappointed, it was only the first day of trying.

He can't keep saying no to me forever.

Gaius continued to prove my assumption wrong. The entire next week was a failure when it came to convincing him to teach me how to fight or defend with magic. Monday, he taught me how to build rock walls and move floating pieces of earth. After succeeding, I kept thanking him for teaching me, doing as Valhalla said… but when I asked him about the Hero agenda, he said no.

I even tried asking Inna the following day, seeing as my water lessons still continued. Both she and Gaius said the possibility of me learning two types of magic was very likely, and even though that excited me, my heart was focused more on becoming a Hero—not a dual-wielding Mage. When I asked her, she sweetly smiled and said she wasn't qualified to teach me. I didn't even know what that meant; it sounded more like a fancy way of saying no to me.

Wednesday came, and I learned how to lift two rocks at a time—which was a *lot* harder than I thought it would be—and pressed him again. *Nothing.* I even came early again on Friday to see if my devotion to learning magic would inspire him to change his mind. It still was a no. Gaius was not budging. Not. One. Bit.

It wasn't that I was being stubborn and upset because I wasn't getting my way. I just didn't understand why wanting to learn something good was a bad thing. I wasn't learning magic because I loved being powerful, and I had no intention of being a Hero for fame. I was given a gift and told to not use it. *So why should I even have this gift in the first place?*

Mom had always taught me that not using the talents or skills you've been blessed with is just as bad as knowing to do good and not doing it. Our neighbors back home were quite old, and when their lawn mower was down, Mom went and helped because she knew how to fix it. When my fourth-grade teacher back in Virginia needed a last-minute babysitter for the week, Mom didn't hesitate to assist since she worked at home. I even helped the best I could with a toddler, though all I did at the time was play dolls with her.

So, I didn't care how long it would take. I would keep asking Gaius to teach me until he said yes.

"Did you finish?" he asked me as he sat at his workshop desk, carving a new wooden weapon out of a cherry maple tree stump. Seemed that, on Fridays, he worked in the evenings and had the mornings all to himself. An hour had passed since he told me to keep working on the rock-flying exercise and to keep practicing until I was able to lift more than five at a time *while* making them "dance" in the air.

I was standing at the edge of his workshop's entry, fiddling with my fingers behind my back. "Yes, sir. I was actually able to get six small stones in the air and make them float simultaneously."

"If you're done, just let me know when you need to go home. Good work today," he said, ending the conversation quickly, and returned to his whittling... setting up yet another perfect opportunity.

I walked further inside his workshop. "What are you working on?"

"A pocket cinquedea."

"Oh, I see."

I have no clue what that is...

I looked around at his wall of wooden and organic weapons. Gaius wasn't just good at magic but a crafting expert. "You're really good at making weapons. How come you use wood instead of steel or metal?"

"Been working with plants all my life, and wood is the most convenient resource."

"Well, you're definitely the best weaponsmith I've ever seen."

He smiled down at his work.

Guess my praise finally got to him.

He shaved another piece off the soon-to-be blade. "It's just something I've grown rather fond of over the years, but thank you."

Now is my chance...

I took a deep breath and stared down at his messy wooden worktable. "So, next week... I was wondering if you could teach me—"

"Lisa, I said I can't," Gaius interrupted, already knowing what I would say.

I persisted. "But I've been getting better—"

"It's still a no."

"What about next month—"

Gaius placed his tool down abruptly, causing me to jump as he interjected, "Lisa..." He didn't yell or raise his voice, but how he said my name made me uneasy, and I knew I upset him.

After a few seconds of nerve-racking silence, I couldn't handle it anymore and needed to say one last thing. "If you had the ability to save the world, wouldn't you go and do it?" I softly asked, breaking the room's quiet.

Gaius didn't respond, still facing his desk opposite me.

I continued. "I believe if you were given the abilities and power to do something good, you should do it. You've been given the power to grow the Wishing Stars and use it for good—doing what the Guardians and Ariela told you to do—and I've been given the most powerful magic of all, but I don't know why..."

I took another deep breath, feeling my stomach swirl around, not used to me being so forward with my opinions. "No one will tell me why I have it, but I'm not gonna hoard it around and waste it. I'm gonna train hard and use it to help people—to become someone they can believe in. I don't wanna be a Hero because I think it's cool or things like that... I truly believe it's what I'm meant to do, no matter how hard or challenging it may be."

I poured out my heart, hoping for a genuine response, but the unpleasant silence from before returned.

The Keeper didn't move, the table more enticing than the emotional girl behind him, telling me all I needed to know.

Accepting the reality of the situation, I whispered, "I'm sorry..." and left his woodworking room to go to his magic study, dispirited and dejected.

I couldn't let my feelings of defeat get to me, so I decided to work on more creature drawings for Mom, grabbing the same *Swamp Creatures* book I had last time and sitting on the couch. I knew if I sat within my own thoughts, I would overthink and get worked up over losing my battle. So, I took out my MP3 player and earbuds and listened to music as I began to find an animal to sketch.

———~~~———

While drawing on Gaius' couch in his small library, I had finished a good couple of illustrations and learned a lot about the guttate—a small lizard with armored scales that looked like a ladybug's shell. It would wait beneath the petals of red roses and eat the flies and mosquitoes that zipped by. *I have to say, I'm getting pretty good at this—*

"What are you drawing?"

I jerked on the couch cushion when I heard Gaius' voice intervene through the music in my ears. I didn't hear his footsteps walk in behind me or see his massive frame since his couch faced away from the door. A large scribble was made from my fright, giving the lizard a slight antenna on top of its head.

"You know I live here, right? No need to get so scared," he said, approaching the velvet sofa.

"Sorry," I replied, apologizing out of habit. "I am just drawing some of those creatures from your books—most aren't done, though. I still need to paint them."

Gaius, now standing before me, held out his hand, gesturing to see my drawings.

I wasn't embarrassed by them; I honestly thought they looked fine, so I lent him my watercolor sketchbook.

He flipped through the first ten pages before realizing that was *all* that was filled in, then flipped back and analyzed each one... in silence. Suddenly, he let out a breathy titter on the third page. "Is this supposed to be a swamplet?"

"Yeah..." I hesitantly answered.

"Why are there pupils in its nose?"

"I thought those were his eyes..."

"And it doesn't have talons."

"I was trying to draw webbed feet, but the pencil wouldn't cooperate."

He softly chuckled again. "If you're going to make a bestiary, you have to be accurate."

I was just showing them to Mom, so I didn't really see a point in being accurate. Just needed each one to be convincing. "It's not like I've seen any of them in real life before, so it's hard to know what is what."

The Keeper then sat down next to me on the couch, taking a moment to finish reading all the pages intently. I said nothing while he looked, folding my legs on the cushion. He smelled like freshly cut wood, his hair a little messy, and his beard was perfectly short, hiding a couple of scars along his jawline.

He snickered at the guttate, my last drawing, before handing me back the book, remaining seated beside me. His eyes focused on the stone floor, almost like he was contemplating something.

Is he going to say something about earlier? I wish I knew what he was thinking...

"'If you were given the abilities and power to do something good, you should do it'..." Gaius slowly began, quoting me as if I were some profound sage.

Why is he repeating what I said all of a sudden...

He continued in his deep voice, "I've lived through the lifetimes of many powerful Mages and Mystics who were unable to grasp such a simple concept as 'to do good.' Yet, you've barely lived a quarter of your life and already understand... Reminding me what I neglected to do when you first arrived here."

Gaius leaned forward, placing his forearms on his knees with his fingers loosely interlocked. "Lisa, I was instructed to only teach you the basics of magic and forgo any form of combative training; however, it seems a fighter's spirit has latched onto that heart of yours, and it's emitting a brooding atmosphere around my home until it gets what it wants. I've turned away many because of their pride and lust for powerful magic... and I shouldn't have done that to you. Your intentions for learning are selfless and not for the benefit of worldly desires. You deserve more than what I've offered so far... so, with all that said..." Gaius turned and looked right at me with a soft smile, "I will accept your request and teach you how to become a Hero."

My whole heart lit up like Christmas. I could not believe what all Gaius just said. He saw me wiser than I ever thought of myself before, treating my beliefs as a goal most didn't seem to reach. The compliments he gave me surpassed anything I had ever received, and I was overwhelmed with so much praise that I almost started crying from happiness.

"You—you really mean it?" I expressed, sitting on the couch with my knees bent. "You'll train me how to fight like a real Hero?"

"We will start next week, but you must do everything I say and follow my exact rules in order for this to work. I wouldn't have agreed to this if you weren't willing, so you must keep this hidden within our magic training lessons and not tell the others."

"Is it okay if I tell Valhalla, though?" As the words slipped out of my mouth, I realized what Gaius actually meant. "*Oh*—you meant the Guardians, didn't you?"

Gaius gave a glare of affirmation.

I followed up with another question. "How come they don't want me to learn how to fight?"

Looking at his intertwined, burly fingers, Gaius answered, "Being a Hero is more brutal and rigorous than you could imagine, and you're a child from Earth... they expected you to run from the idea of battle, so I agreed to their nescient methods, but that was before. They underestimated the heart the Agapéd chose, and it happened to choose one who thinks like me—which they won't be too thrilled about. So, now we will train the right way."

Having a friend trust me with a secret was one thing, but having an adult secret to keep was like buried treasure. I felt important and trustworthy. I was not going to let Gaius down.

"I promise to train hard, Gaius," I pledged, still smiling.

"I have no doubts about that," he grinned back.

For the first time, it seemed I was finally following the dream my heart willfully desired.

18
NEAR-DEATH EXPERIENCE

The next week approached, and a new fire burned in my heart.

After lessons with Micah, I rushed toward Gaius' home, almost running into several Veradome workers. He waited for me under the tree next to his home, immediately taking me aside and running through what I'd already learned—creating dirt blocks, levitating more than five rocks at a time, and forming sturdy stone columns. My terrain magic looked cleaner and more controlled as my earthy shapes were quicker to form than last week.

"I want you to try a new exercise with me," Gaius said, standing a couple of feet before me, the sun barreling down at his brown hair and tan skin. "Instead of just creating clay columns, I want you to try and use your magic to defend."

My first Hero lesson!

He reached down by his waist, to which I noticed his odd belt: it had flasks and test tubes strapped along the band with plants growing in each one. One flower was yellow—in the biggest jar, bound to the belt with a leather strap; another was blue and sparkling like the ocean; the one near his left hip had no petals and tainted brown—nothing but roots; the final three, in smaller bottles near his right hip, were thin strands of thorned ivy.

When Gaius moved his hand across the belt, the brown plant began to move out and extend like a rope. He sped up the herb's growing process, producing green leaves and thicker roots to form wadded-up throwing balls, floating them in the air as the plant still remained as lively as a snake.

If this is Gaius' form of weaponry, it is the coolest form of fighting I've ever seen!

"I will target you with these, and you will defend yourself using your terrain magic. Ready yourself as we've discussed: feet firm and mind focused."

I took my sturdy stance, but the moment Gaius fixed his posture, every part of me—even the marrow in my bones—started to quiver and shake. A beefy man was about to pummel me, a frail girl who only knew one move.

He used his magic to throw the wadded-up plants, but because they came so fast toward me, my first instinct was to run like a scared kid in the middle of a dodgeball tournament. I jumped out of the way—evading the first three vegetation spheres, but the fourth hit my shoulder.

It *hurt!* Gaius was not holding back at all.

"Ouch!" I yelped, my shoulder now throbbing and scratched. Luckily, there wasn't any blood, only thin pink marks.

"You are *defending* in this exercise, not retreating," he called. "You need to rely on your magic strength to avoid being hit rather than evading because of fear."

"I'm sorry…" I rubbed my shoulder and glanced around at the dry soil. "I just didn't feel strong enough to take on your attack, I guess, so I dodged."

"Lisa," Gaius began, walking right up to me, "to become a strong Mage, you can't avoid or ignore situations because it solidifies your weaknesses. Instead, you must use your strengths to overcome them. For example, right now, your weakness is every type of physical strength because you are a small, ten-year-old—"

"Thirteen."

"Sorry—thirteen-year-old girl. But *your* strength… lies in your magic."

I looked down at myself. *Do I really look like a ten-year-old?* "I just don't see how I could ever stand a chance against a guy like you…"

My burly mentor held out his hand, palm facing me. "Lisa, I want you to punch my hand as hard as possible with only your physical strength. No magic."

My eyes grew very wide, and my mouth turned small, blanketed with dumbfoundedness.

Gaius lifted one corner of his lips. "Don't worry, you won't hurt me."

While I knew that to be likely, it made me want to prove him wrong. I took a punching stance and gave it all I had. I cocked my right arm and swung it right into his large hand—powerful and with all my might.

The sound of impact was that of a toddler's high-five attempt. Pathetic.

Gaius didn't show any surprise. "Now, I want you to punch my hand again, but this time, I want you to add some magic behind it—all the magic you can muster up. Tense your muscles with that magic inside you when you clench your fist. Force it out like you do when you open the entrance door and use your terrain magic."

"What if I somehow hit you with a rock or something?"

"I want you to give me all you got. Just make it focused and controlled. I promise I will be fine," he assured, that subtle grin still plastered on his smug face.

He said to give it all I had, so that is what I did. I retook my fighting stance again and sucked in a deep breath. My right arm cocked as I squeezed my clenched fist tighter than before. I could feel a pulling force coming from my palm, heavy and powerful. I then focused everything right onto Gaius's palm and swung my arm with all my might.

It was as if I was a completely different person. I didn't just punch Gaius. I sent him back ten feet! When I released my magic punch, I was a hundred times more powerful and even caused loose pebbles from the soil to fly toward him. In doing so, my magic took about double my strength and stamina. I fell to my knees when my magic was released, winded and breathless.

Gaius caught himself and slid to his feet, using the plants from his belt to cushion his hand from impact.

I felt tired and worn out from just one punch, but I didn't care because the look of shock on Gaius' face was worth it.

No way I just did that...

"Are you... okay—" I asked in between my dry gasps. "I... didn't know I could do that..." My knees trembled on the ground, and my lungs felt shrunk, completely stunned by my own sudden strength.

"I knew you would hit hard with magic," Gaius began, smiling quite big, "I just didn't think it would be *that* hard." He came back and knelt before me so we were at eye level. "Lisa, your greatest strength will always be your magic, though right now, it may seem like it's taking more of your energy than you expected. No matter who you face, your magic will always be the strongest if you continue to train it. In most situations, you will only need magic, but when you encounter a situation where physical strength is required, use the strength of your magic to overcome that weakness. Let it power your muscles and core. Allow it to pulse the blood through your veins. If you can do that, you will never lose. You understand?"

"Yes, sir."

Gaius helped me back up and had me try the blocking exercise again. Even though that magic punch took a lot out of me, my confidence was stronger than ever. Gaius proved I was powerful and that my magic was strong enough to protect me, so when he started throwing the wadded-up plant orbs at me again, I was ready.

When the first object came flying, I immediately formed a jagged rock column out of the dirt to defend myself. It worked! Gaius' plant crumbled to the ground right after the moment of impact. *How hard did he throw that one?* The next one came, but my first column was too wide, and I forgot to return it to the earth. It blocked my view.

Gaius hit me *again*—the same shoulder, too! It hurt worse than the first time, but I didn't back down. Battling with magic was the most thrilling experience in my life—scrapes, mistakes, and all.

———

As I made my way to the tram toward the Balthier's neighborhood, I noticed a group of teenagers standing by the station. I had seen them a couple of times before, given that Calendula was so small, and remembered Valhalla telling me she knew them. The thing was, Valhalla was standing by herself to the left not saying a single word.

At that moment, it occurred to me that I had never seen Valhalla with other teenagers—never even mentioning them during our conversations. I told her about Lily and Jenny Kim on a few occasions, but not a single time did she tell me about her own friends. I figured Valhalla would have many of them for someone as kind and bubbly as her.

Kinda odd...

Valhalla's purple eyes found mine as I walked past the teens, and she smiled. "So..." she began, trying to whisper. Luckily, the group of five teenagers beside us was too enthralled with their own conversation to care. "Did he say yes?"

I nodded as my mouth stretched.

Valhalla squealed as we entered the tram, and I instantly placed my hand over her mouth before she alerted the passengers and group of teens.

"But it's super important that you don't let anyone know—not even your parents," I hurriedly whispered. "Gaius isn't supposed to teach me *anything* that has to do with fighting."

"He is training you in secret while training you in *secret?*" she whispered back quite loudly.

I nodded again, grabbing the pole near the tram's window to keep my balance.

"My method worked then, didn't it?" Valhalla said in a cocky tone.

I couldn't help but laugh. "No, it did absolutely nothing. *I* was the one who convinced him."

"I bet I helped a little."

"Yeah, if getting him frustrated with me counts."

"So," Valhalla said in another hushed tone, "do you know *why* he has to teach you Hero lessons in secret?"

"He only said that the Guardians figured I would run from the idea of fighting, so that's why they didn't tell me the point of all my magic training."

She looked surprised when I said that. "Jacks—that's crazy! Don't they want you to become a Hero?"

I glanced out the window to look over the cottage homes and trees, all painted with sunset colors. "I don't know—probably, just not yet. I tried asking Micah once, but he blew it off. *Ignored* it with a vague Guardian-esque answer. Even Vilmad tried to talk me into giving the magic back to him and the others to hold on to. Guess they want me to be older—"

"*Pfft*—Lisa, you gotta prove to them you are strong enough now!" Valhalla said louder, making the eyes of an older man look over at us. "You've barely had a month of magic training and can already make the earth pop out of the ground as tall as a person. Don't they know how strong you are?"

"Well, I mean, they know my magic is most powerful—"

"Then, you need to show them that! Look, I'm not gonna question their authority or anything, but if you keep training in secret, you'll never become as strong as you need to be."

I looked back at her purple eyes. "Then, what should I do?"

"... I don't know—but I will think of something. I promise."

"As long as it's better than your last plan," I joked.

"Fine, fine, fine. It *will* be better."

The group of teenagers started laughing, grabbing my attention.

"Hey," I said to Valhalla, "thanks for waiting for me by the way. I know you had Tutor today and probably lots of homework to do, but it means a lot to me. Never had a friend do that before."

It wasn't like I said a set of magic words or gave her a priceless gift, but Valhalla's eyes widened as her excited smile turned into a soft grin.

Her loud demeanor changed.

"It was nothing... I just know that all this is very new to you, and I wanna make sure you enjoy it as best you can," she said. "Thanks for calling me your friend, Lisa. Having you stay with me, Mom, and Dad has been really fun. It's nice not being so alone anymore."

The tram finally came to a rickety stop, and the doors opened with a couple of squeaks.

"Same goes for me."

Inna had taught me a new move with the training staff—Geyser Blast is what I called it. She made her own magic water, focused her energy, and made a horizontal blast of ocean waves that traveled twenty feet away from us! She told me to focus on creating a whirlpool of explosions while holding the staff over the sea, so I did. In seconds, a water geyser shot toward the sky right where the rod was pointing. It wasn't as strong as Inna's, but it was the most powerful magic I've ever been able to create with any training tool.

Could this be because of Gaius' Hero training? I didn't know for sure, but while working with Inna, a constant stream of confidence began flowing through me.

"You're growing quite strong," Inna said, and I couldn't help but smile. "I'm sure you'll create your own water in no time."

"Thank you," I responded. Suddenly, something behind Inna caught my eye. A large blue speed submarine resurfaced from the opposite side of the landing area. It had many compartments and a huge dome of glass near the front. I'd only seen bikes and small boats, so I couldn't help but stare. Many workers dressed in armored wetsuits began to emerge from the ocean craft, carrying large glowing boxes.

"Inna, what's that submarine for?" I asked.

"Ah, it seems the Harvesters have returned from their excursion. Would you like to take a closer look?"

I nodded yes rather quickly, and we walked toward the ship.

"Last night, in the city of Hyldavan, a good day's travel south of here, there was a shooting star phenomenon that was perfect for collecting stardust," Inna explained as we came toward the many workers in front of the submarine, all carrying the heavy glowing containers. "For the stardust not to lose its magical qualities, the Harvesters have to keep it submerged in the sea it fell in. That is why they are carrying those tubs of water."

"Then, they take it to you so you can create the starseeds, right?"

"Mhm. Nights of shooting stars are always a busy time for us, which is a good thing for me."

While I was admiring the glistening Aquanaeum boat, one of the female Harvesters struggled to carry one of the glowing glass containers. She and other workers were above me, close to the railing of the top level of the submarine.

"Look out!" a distressed voice shouted from atop the boat.

I looked up, and a giant glass container began hurtling toward me. I should have run, but my initial reaction was to hold up my arms to cover my face. I held my breath and closed my eyes, embracing for impact. *Please don't hit me—*

A loud crash rang through my ears... but I was fine.

Am I okay? I swear it was headed straight for me. I slowly opened my eyes as troubled voices came from the crowd, and right above my head was a glowing bubble of stardust. It was free-floating in the air, but that wasn't the crazy part. *I was the one doing it. I was making the water hover all on my own!*

"I am so sorry—is anyone hurt?" I heard the lady above say, the same one who dropped the container.

Out of shock, my fingers shielding my face flinched, and all the water came crashing down on me. Glittering sea foam drenched my clothes and wavy long hair before bouncing off the broken glass near my boots. Workers began to run toward us, but Inna didn't pay any mind to them; she hugged me tight, not caring about getting her clothes wet either.

"Lisa—you—you did it!" she proclaimed, worried but relieved, releasing the hug with her hands cupping my shoulders. "You just used your magic and stopped the water all on your own!"

"I just... thought about stopping the box from hitting me—you mean I really did it? It wasn't you?"

"I can only move the water I create. That was all *you*. You're a Water Manipulation Mage starting today!" Inna announced with such happiness that the workers around us began to cheer, too, though I think they didn't know how to react: a Keeper's student almost dying by a container of stardust.

"Please forgive me, Miss!" the female Harvester said, running down the stairs almost in tears.

Inna consoled her as many more workers gathered to see if I was okay, one bringing me a towel and another coming to clean the broken glass.

"Inna, what exactly happened?" I asked amid all the commotion, wrapping the towel around my shoulders.

"You pulled the water out of the glass container, causing it to shift to the left and fall to the ground. I was about to stop it myself, but you were one step ahead of me."

"So, this means I can start my actual magic training, right?" I expressed as if I didn't avoid death moments ago.

She elegantly laughed and helped dry off the rest of my hair, like Mom used to do for me back home when I was younger. "Not even a moment to rest, and you already want to learn more. You have a bold spirit, Lisa."

Inna had to dismiss the workers because many kept apologizing for the accident and couldn't help but ensure I was okay. They reminded me a lot of Ava and Asa. I guess it was a courtesy thing in Mantene, or they really didn't want to upset Inna. I felt bad for wasting the stardust because the glitter faded after a few seconds of exposure to the air. Inna said it was fine and that my safety was more important.

Most girls my age would've been shaken up from the almost-fatal event. Not me. I just saved my life—used celestial power to do it, too. Very *heroic,* and I couldn't help but smile. *This is going to help my Hero training so much more!*

Walking next to Inna on our way to the opposite side of the concrete boardwalk, away from other workers, my mind on Gaius' secret lessons, I had to ask, "So, did you think I'd learn Water Manipulation that fast—saving myself and all?" *Proving to be stronger than the Guardians expected,* I wanted to add on but opted out.

Inna tilted her head to the side. "I knew your magic to be strong, but it was rather surprising, given that you just learned terrain magic not but a week ago."

My eyes rolled to the gritty stone ground as my hands still clenched the towel around my shoulders. "Do you think it would impress the Guardians too?"

Her words were kind and confident. "I believe so."

I turned my head toward her. *If I can get Inna to say I'm strong enough, then the Guardians will* have *to believe I'm worthy to be trained like a Hero.* "Then, I could start using my new magic to learn how to be a Hero then, right—since I'm stronger than you thought?"

Her pace stopped—*completely* stopped, and not simply morphing to a slow stroll. I mimicked her abrupt pause. Inna then knelt to my eye level, gingerly placing her hand on my shoulder. "I believe your magic to be strong, but let's forgo this Hero idea, Lisa—for now, at least. Let's focus on training your magic, nothing with fighting—simply growing the bond in your heart with the Agapéd." She smiled. "Sound good?"

Sound good...?

Gaius was right—the Guardians really didn't believe in me, and now even Inna didn't... or maybe she simply followed the rules they laid out for her. She wasn't like Gaius; he didn't like the Guardians or revered their rules. Inna respected them and their decisions.

I wanted to say, "No, it does not sound good," but I refrained. Inna was doing her job: training me in magic. Even if she couldn't train me to fight with water, her teachings would still help.

"Sounds good," I replied, watching the blue in her eyes sparkle again—relief glossing over them.

———

With an hour left, the blush-blonde Keeper helped me get acquainted with using water manipulation magic. Moving water... I couldn't believe I was doing it. I watched myself scoop up bubbles and morph them into ocean ribbons, all with a wave of my arm and twirl of my fingers. I felt... powerful, strong without rippling muscles, and Valhalla's words continued to ring in my ears. *You will be the most legendary there ever was.*

Strength was a foreign word to my body. Never in a million years would I have ever dreamed I could save myself from a fatal accident, let alone with or without magic. I bruise more easily than an apple and freak out when I stub my pinky toe.

But I completed Gaius' obstacle course in a week covered in scratches, learned how to warp dirt in two days even though my body was aching, and just saved my life with a flick of my wrists. Inna and the Guardians didn't see my strength, but I did. Gaius did. And Valhalla did the most.

"You will be the most legendary there ever was"...

Maybe... maybe she is right...

———

Through the woodland entrance, the nightlife of Calendula was booming as usual, along with many of the Veradome's workers returning in the merchant vehicles. I grazed over the crowd to see if I could spot Mr. Balthier coming back as well, and sure enough, I saw his spice cart about a block away. I ran toward his vehicle and noticed Valhalla with him. Seemed she convinced Mr. Balthier to let her miss classes again.

"Valhalla! I did it!" I yelled, causing her to jump out of the magic cart, which *also* triggered Mr. Balthier to slam on the brakes. "I learned Water Manipulation!"

"No way! You're not joking? You really did it! You learned two types of magic?" she shouted, grabbing my hands and jumping up and down.

"Yes! It was the craziest thing ever—"

"Well, this causes for a celebration!" I heard Mr. Balthier say from the driver's seat. "Val, go and tell Emmeryn we are going out tonight! I will meet you all at The Forge! Congratulations, dear Lisa!"

Valhalla's family did not need to celebrate my accomplishments, yet they went all out on dinner for us. The Forge was a brick oven eatery in the town square—across from Luca's—that resembled Italian restaurants back home, but in Calendula, it was just normal cuisine. We ate Puffed Sauced Pies which looked like mini calzones—each one stuffed with cheese, olives, peppers, and tomato sauce. When we finished, Valhalla mentioned how much I loved Luca's, and her parents didn't hesitate one bit to take us there for dessert. I tried Thunder's Sky, a blueberry-plum juice mixed with other foreign fruits and drizzled with condensed coconut milk. Its glass was shaped like a tornado and topped with a white caramel halo. Valhalla got the same as last time, Sugar Cloud Offie, and her parents asked for a dry tea. It was just unsweetened tea mixed with heavy cream.

"You know," began Valhalla as we sat down to finish our drinks, "you're the first person I've ever met who has two types of magic."

"Really? I thought it would be kinda normal," I responded, siping my sweet drink.

"Far from it!" Mr. Balthier chimed in, sitting across from Valhalla and me in the booth near his wife. "It's quite rare, and only those with Starnate magic can possess two types. Even if both parents of a child have a strong magical lineage—from the stars or not—it usually evolves into a new form or a blend of both inside the child. Two distinct types are few and far between."

"I've only seen a handful of Mages and Mystics who've appeared in the *Chevaliers* with two kinds of magic, and that was many years ago," Mrs. Balthier said, nodding before she took a sip of her tea. "You're quite a special one, dear Lisa."

The rarity of retaining more than one type of magic was quite a shock to me. Again, the Guardians just made it seem so normal for me to learn more than one type of magic that I thought a lot of other Mages and Mystics did the same. *Is this another reason why the Agapéd is so powerful?*

"Lisa, if I remember correctly, you mentioned you were interested in visiting Raglan—the town not too far from here?" Mr. Balthier asked.

"Yes, sir," I said.

"Well, I'm scheduled to work the spice cart again at Raglan's trading market in three days. I'd love for you to come since that would be your day off. Correct me if I'm wrong there?"

"Yeah, that would be just fine! Thank you!"

Valhalla's eyes shot open as she pressed against the table. "Dad, can I *please* go, too? Lisa *needs* me to show her around the town and how to help you run the cart!" Buttery begging was in full effect.

"Well, that is up to your mother."

Valhalla gave her mom the baby-doll eyes and clasped her hands together. She looked like a prisoner pleading for mercy. *Is Raglan really that amazing?* "Mom, this would mean the *world* to me—Lisa, too!"

Her mom looked at me, and I quickly nodded a couple of times, agreeing with Valhalla. I didn't know about the town, but I really wanted her to be there with me.

"As long as you help out more than you goof off, you may go," her mom relented, making Valhalla smile very big.

"I will, I will," she said, taking another big gulp of her drink as we continued the night in glee, hyped up on sugar and laughter.

19

RAGLAN

Friday came fast, probably because I could hardly wait to finally visit somewhere new. Valhalla woke me up early and had us meet her dad at the Veradome. Dew dappled the grass when we left her front door, and I wished I'd brought a jacket. I didn't expect it to be so cool at 7:00 a.m.

Normally, when I went off to Gaius' home for lessons, I used the front entrance of the Veradome, but all the carts were down below in a huge parking garage. I definitely would've gotten lost if Valhalla weren't with me—had to be over a hundred people in that building supplying and emptying their exports. Many archways along the walls had different locations magically displayed across the top, and every couple of minutes, the location would change. I saw a couple of produce carts go through one of the gateways, and they completely vanished—just like how the hidden forest entrance reacted when people walked into Calendula!

"Those are other secret entrances," Valhalla told me while I clung close to her so I wouldn't get lost in the crowd of workers. "All carts exit through there and return at opposite entrances when their shift is done. Gotta keep everything super-secret here."

Suddenly, we spotted Mr. Balthier, all revved up and ready to depart. I shared the front couch seat with Valhalla and her dad; it was very soft, and the interior smelled heavily of mint and spicy chili peppers. Not going to lie, it wasn't the most pleasant scent compared to the Febreze car fresheners my mom used.

Mr. Balthier soon steered right, and we followed behind the trail of mobile shops going toward the archway displaying "Raglan Trading Post." We eased up behind the Roses and Rosemary cart, almost bumper to bumper, getting closer to the magic exit. Our turn came, and our cart teleported from a loud, musty garage to a dead-end road in a forest in the blink of an eye. The Roses and Rosemary cart feet before us had already made it a couple of miles ahead, and we followed its trail.

After about ten minutes of driving the backwoods road, the trees vanished, and the road became concrete as we turned toward a small city in the middle of a green and yellow valley. A large, poorly manufactured sign read "Raglan's Home, Raglan's Heart" and then had some smudged text underneath about its small population. The city reminded me of a small country town I'd find in the mountains with lots of farmland and knickknack shops.

I wasn't disappointed, but the way Valhalla begged to skip school to come to the town had me thinking it would be more like EverWake or Mantene. There was no magic—nothing was glowing except the sun in the distance and the antique row of street lamps patterned along the cracked paved path. *Should've known she exaggerated this place... those cattle better be super fluffy and worth the musty car smell.*

Soon, more and more carts started to travel down the roads, coming in all directions. Mr. Balthier took us to the main square where the Veradome merchants would park and set up shop. Seeing everyone unload and present their goods reminded me of food truck vendors at the county fair. They unfolded banners, staked yard signs near parked tires, and displayed free samples to attract soon-to-be customers.

"Not everyone here is from Calendula, by the way," Valhalla told me as we helped her dad set out the spices. "Some come from other cities or other planets, which is good for us. Would be quite suspicious if all the vendors just magically appeared and disappeared to and from the forest every week."

"Oh, I didn't even think of that..." I said, placing the golden cinnamon spice near the front of the display table.

"Well, thank you, girls, for helping me set up," Mr. Balthier said. "I won't need much help until after sunrise, so feel free to look around—oh, here are some credits for you two. If you see something, Lisa, feel free to get yourself a bite to eat or a souvenir."

He handed Valhalla a square card, about as thick as a cracker, that displayed "30" across the top, resembling the same type of magic my orbkit would emit. The card reminded me of a floppy disk Mom used before her work upgraded her to a laptop with USB ports.

"Is that some form of digital payment?" I asked Valhalla.

"*Digital?*" she chortled as if that idea was strange to suggest. "No, it's not, like, electric or anything, but it acts the same. It's a magic currency holder normally called an MC, a chip, or Magic Credit Case, but this is just a token—a small version of it—that Dad puts my credits in. If you don't have the town's form of money, you can pay with credits, which is a more universal payment. The only downside with credits is that it's not physical like coins and stuff. It's just like, 'hey, I have ten numbers that float around in space that have the same value as one Boolavogue dime.' It doesn't make much sense, but it's easier to carry around a chip than every type of money in the universe."

Ah, so it's like a credit card... but with magic money inside it.

"Come on! Let me show you around!" Valhalla yanked my arm, and we went to look around the town.

We passed by some shops and went down a good way to see some of the cows and goats near one of the farms. Never in my life would I have imagined seeing a cow with wool, but there it was—even let us pet her and her calf. *Okay, this is worth my dewy shoes and my hair stained with the smell of foreign spices.*

Most of the walkways were gravel or dirt, with the main road being concrete. People straggled in and out of shops, but most of them were farmers—gathering water, planting crops, or feeding their livestock. Many of the homes resembled Calendula, just more rustic and not covered with an abundance of plants. Every home and every person was peaceful.

I was surprised that Valhalla liked the town. She had the energy of a puppy and loved magic, and there wasn't a *hint* of the celestial power anywhere the entire time we wandered around. *Maybe she doesn't get out much—stuck in Calendula. She would really enjoy Mantene... Maybe she could visit with me someday...*

We walked by a small park—just grass and flowers with no swingset or pond—when Valhalla ran toward a giant notice board.

"Lisa, I just figured out how we can..." she said, her voice slowly softening, "convince the Guardians you're ready to become a Hero. By this!" She pointed up toward the notice board, which was stapled with many types of paper and linen flyers. All seemed to have "help" or "hunter wanted" written on them.

"What exactly is *this*?" I asked her.

"It's a request board. Just about every town I've been to has one of these. People who've lost something, need rare supplies, or need help slaying monsters will post their requests here in exchange for money or services. Raglan's small so they don't have Hunters, Saints, or Heroes on command to ask for help."

She gripped my arm, shaking me like an apple tree and trying to get every fruit to fall off. "Lisa, I bet if you do a couple of these that need a Mage to fight off monsters, the Guardians will finally see how strong you are. "

What—

The reality of helping people with real magic problems scared me, and she wanted me to fight *monsters*. I had never threatened, let alone killed, an animal before—only crickets and other creepy bugs, and *never* spiders; that was Mom's role in the house. I also had never had a job in my life besides whatever chores Mom needed me to do.

I wasn't mentally prepared for heroic work at the time... but the Agapéd Magic in my heart was growing stronger. Plus, Valhalla was right: stopping a monster with my magic *would* prove to the Guardians I was powerful and brave enough to be a Hero. I just needed to push away my fears and get Confident Lisa back out in the spotlight.

I scanned every single sign on the board, and I thought it was written in another language. Nope. Those were just some monster names I didn't know and never read about in Gaius' books.

"Maybe I should ask Gaius first before just picking a random job," I suggested after seeing one sign in particular painted with a red skull. "He could tell me which would be best to start with."

"I guess you're right. You think he will say yes to you?"

"If I explain *why*, then definitely."

———

"No."

Gaius didn't hesitate at all with his short and blunt answer. I had just returned from Raglan during the afternoon and ran straight toward the Keeper's home after helping Mr. Balthier and Valhalla unpack the cart. I saw him come out of the mysterious greenhouse next to his house, so I instantly asked him about doing a job from the request board... which was when he gave me the worst answer possible.

"Can I not even do a simple one?" I asked, following him back toward his home. "I saw some that looked easy." A lie. I couldn't understand a single one, but I was focused on proving a point, so it didn't matter in the given situation.

"You're not ready to do something like that, Lisa," he said, not even a hint of wavering in his voice.

"But you could *make* me ready. You can pick one out and prepare me—I don't even care about any rewards. During my training this week, you said I was improving, and I'm getting better at my water magic, too."

Gaius went down the stairs of his front entrance and into the kitchen, pouring himself a glass of water... not responding to my last statement. I watched him drink the whole thing in silence. I didn't want to pressure and upset him like last time, but I *had* to do a job from the board. Being a Hero and proving to the Guardians I was worthy of my Agapéd Magic was on the line.

He wiped his mouth with his sleeve and placed one hand on the kitchen island, facing me. His glare still intimidated me, even after knowing him for almost a month.

"Lisa..." he started.

Please say something good...

"... I'm not putting you out there at risk of being hurt."

My shoulders dropped, and my smile flatlined. I looked at the glossy wooden countertop of the kitchen island, searching for a convincing response. "What if you came with me then...?" There was no movement between us, which was a good sign, so I continued. "You could help me... and make sure I was fine."

"Why the sudden urge to take on a hunting job? I believe... I have never mentioned Hunters or Heroes. I doubt the Guardians or Inna have, either." His green gaze was stern and unyielding, cold with curious concern. "You just learned magic, so tell me: Why do you want to go out there and take on a hunt?"

I wasn't expecting that question, my fidgeting fingers returning. "I just... I just need to do this. I'm supposed to be strong—the 'Agapéd Bearer' you all wanted. If I can't even do a small hunt now..." I wanted to say *then how am I going to convince the Guardians I'm strong enough*, but those words were too scared to leave my mouth and swing into Gaius' ears. I took a deep breath: "... then how am I supposed to become a Hero someday?"

Gaius exhaled, also trying to find an answer between the wooden lines of the countertop. "If you really want to test your strength and magic training... and it's really that important to you..." his green eyes finally met mine, "... then *I* will find you a job to do, not you simply choosing something from a request board. You will accompany *me*, and *I* will prepare you for it as any Hero or Monster Hunter would, but it will still be tough. You sure you can handle it?"

My eyebrows raised. "My magic is strong enough, so I am—"

"I meant," he cut off my words, lifting his fingers off the countertop, "can *you* handle it, as in, is your mind and heart able to handle the killing of a magic creature if the job calls for it?"

I had to think about that for a moment. *Could I really stop a creature? Would I be able to stand up to a beast?* Hunting something was nothing like killing a bug, and I used my shoe to do that. Never in my whole life did killing a creature become a mindful choice and not just self-defense. *Can I really do this?*

When the fear of death came across my mind, something else stopped it from overtaking my thoughts. It was the thought of someone in distress... the thought of someone like Valhalla, magicless and a kid like me, needing help. If something were to hurt an innocent, defenseless person, and I had the power to stop it... then nothing would stop me from saving them.

Confidence poured into each word as I said, "I can do it."

The Keeper was talented at concealing his emotions, but I saw a tug on his lips—a grin from my bravery trying to force its way between his facial hair. "Well, then, I will keep a lookout for your first mission. Until then, we will keep practicing. Just promise me you won't accept any requests from Raglan or any other town—ever. Okay?"

"Yes, sir. I promise."

20
GLAINIES AND BÍROKAVARANS

I think Gaius lied to me.

The following week came and went, and my teacher hadn't mentioned anything about my first monster hunt. I didn't pester him about it; I only continued to work on my magic training, which went especially well. He taught me how to make spiked rocks come out of the ground, almost like a magic boobytrap. We continued the defending exercise, with him throwing the rooted ball of plants at me. During our lesson on Wednesday, I could block more than half of them using my terrain magic, even using a floating rock as my shield.

Though Inna didn't know of my Hero agenda, her skills still helped, primarily when she taught me how to manipulate the water's temperature, starting with freezing water waves. She used another training tool called freezing gloves, where she could freeze the water as she created it, but I could do it naturally. We continued our lessons of water freezing the entire week, and I quickly learned that making the water move with my magic *and* freezing it to form a tall icicle column was insanely tricky—like writing with both hands simultaneously. Still, the goal of being a Hero pushed me forward, and I didn't give up.

Heading back to the Hearth as usual, I went inside the muscly Keeper's home, surprised to find him inside his magic study, *not* in his greenhouse or raring to pelt me with wads of plants.

"Are we doing something in here today?" I asked as I came down the book-shelved staircase, my ponytail swaying side to side as I made it to the bottom.

"Yes," he said, grabbing a green and purple book off one of the top shelves near the potion-making table. "I am out of violvaran, which is used in potions to hide the magic scent surrounding many of my plants. Since obtaining this ingredient isn't too much of a hassle for me, I thought it would be a good first hunt for you."

Wait, what?

I did not expect to hear about my first real Hero job so early during the day. "*Really?* I get to help you fetch magic ingredients for my first job? That's so cool!" I said, smiling, and Gaius started flipping through the pages of the green and purple book. "Honestly, when I asked you the first time, I thought you were just saying 'yes' as a copout—getting me to stop asking."

"My 'yes' will always mean yes, Lisa," he said, continuing to flip through his book. "Though... it did cross my mind." There was a subtle smirk underneath his short facial hair.

"So, where do we get this, uh, potion ingredient from?"

"From this." Gaius found the page he was looking for and handed the book to me. He pointed to an illustration of a violet reptile creature with a rounded mouth and sharp teeth.

My heart fell into the depths of my stomach—

"A bírokavaran. Violvaran is its venom and can also be found in its bloodstream. You will accompany me to the Amaya Woodlands this Thursday night and take down that creature so I can extract the violvaran. Study this book during your breaks. I've written down all you need to know about the creature. I will also teach you the fighting methods that work well against bírokavarans. We have three days—plenty of time to get you prepped for your first hunt."

PLENTY?

I stared at the page with the creepy, *venomous* monster with *knives* for teeth, realizing what Gaius just asked me to do. "You mean... for my first mission... I have to *kill* this thing?" The creature in the book did not look cute or like a pet lizard. It had no eyes, two rows of razor-sharp fangs, and even had "venom can be fatal" written underneath its name in Gaius' handwriting. I did not see how three days were enough time to prepare me for a deadly monster hunt.

"All you need to do is knock it out. I will do the rest," he said calmly.

My eyes slowly peeled from the page as I hurriedly inquired, "But why kill it? I mean, sure it looks pretty scary, but what if it's not bothering anyone—"

"Bírokavarans are no animals." Gaius' eyes pierced mine as his voice turned even more serious. "They are dark magic creatures, formed when dark magic collides with other higher powers of Animalian and elemental magic. They were never meant to exist, and their only instinct is to grow their dark magic and kill anything that gets in their way. Monsters like these have no heart or bond, controlled by Darkness for eternity. Destroying them will release their magic back into the universe, hopefully turning into something used for good. So, when we arrive at the forest, you will fight the monster. I will kill it and extract the venom. Then, we will leave, and you will have completed your first monster hunt."

I had read through a couple of Gaius' books and drawn many creatures, but I had always figured they were animals with an instinct to protect and have offspring. I didn't think creatures could be made purely of magic with nothing but the lust for power, and I sure didn't expect to be fighting one so soon.

I stood frozen, anxious, and turning a ghostly shade of white, reading all the information about my new foe.

"Lisa." Gaius placed his hand on my shoulder. "I wouldn't make you do anything you couldn't handle. I will be with you the whole time, so there is nothing to fear."

I needed to hear that...

I took a deep breath. "Thanks, Gaius." Knowing he was there with me, half of the heavy burden of fear lifted off my shoulders.

"Alright, then. Let's start training."

"You ready?" Gaius asked me as I met him after sunset that Thursday evening. He waited for me outside the Veradome to return from dinner at the Balthiers, though I didn't eat much.

My nerves went crazy and suppressed my appetite for the past three days, but I couldn't even eat a single bite during dinner. Luckily, I had told Valhalla of my first mission, so she just covered for me by telling her mom I wasn't a fan of mushroom soup... but I actually was a big fan. I wished she would have told her something else, but it was too late. Now, I'll never be able to try that creamy delicacy.

"Let's do it," I responded, half-confident, half-anxious.

"Alright, then." Gaius held out his elbow for me to grab, and we evanesced away to the Amaya Woodlands.

In seconds, after the familiar chimes and bright lights vanished, we were in the middle of a dark forest. The air was much cooler than Calendula, and the floor was very damp, covered in dark shadows from the looming tree branches and thick roots. Even though the moon was very prominent and provided a slim light for us to see, Gaius still held out a small light stone to guide our path, shaking it like a bottle of soda to emit its glow.

"*Whoa*—how's it doing that—the stone?" I asked him, following close to his side.

"It's a glint," he responded, which didn't help answer my question.

"What's a glint? Is it different from the water gem Inna lets me use or that emerald to unlock your door?"

"Same thing, different names. Though, normally, with glintz, you attach them to weapons, unlike magic gems or that emerald. Put this on a sword, and you'll have light magic striking with each swing; stick a plain glowing gem on the hilt, and you'll just have a nice decoration. Both have magical properties they were formed with, unlike absorption stones—those Guardians not teaching you that?"

To be honest... they probably did. Sometimes, though, their lessons were quite boring if there were no visual aids involved, which is why I preferred to read Gaius' books or to be taught by the Keeper himself.

"Yes... just missed that part." I didn't let the quietness linger for too long, especially since dark forests on any planet were far scarier in silence. I looked up at Gaius. "I know in the book it said they live in damp, magic forests, but how do you know where to look?"

"Glainies," he answered.

"*Glainies?*"

"Memory sprites, as they are also called. Bírokavarans are known for eating small magic creatures, and it just so happens that glainies are their favorite, so we are headed to one of their habitats."

I hopped over a big tree root as Gaius started walking faster. "I never saw anything about memory sprites in your books."

"I only take note of creatures that benefit me and my work."

"So, are they like... good creatures or bad?"

"If, by 'good,' you mean gullible and simple-minded, then they are saints."

My legs finally caught up to him as he stopped to examine his surroundings with the light glint, and I asked, "When we defeat the bírokavaran, we will be saving the glainies then, right—from being eaten and killed?"

Gaius smirked at me. "I had a hunch you would see this venture for more than a simple ingredient extraction."

We continued to trek further through the forest, going down a hill and maneuvering through long, dangled tree limbs. We started to see blue fireflies, which, according to Gaius, meant we were getting closer.

"Why can't you just evanesce us directly to them?" I asked after getting my boots covered in mud, seeing as teleporting to the exact spot would have saved them from their filthy fate.

"You should only evanesce to places you've been to. Even then, if your accuracy is slightly off, you could be halfway in the dirt or falling from the sky," Gaius answered.

"Oh, I didn't think it was that dif—"

Gaius swung his arm in front of me, stopping my legs and speech in their tracks. "Listen."

My ears obeyed his command. A faint humming—no, whistling—was echoing in the distance. I couldn't tell if it was a plant, animal, or musical instrument. It was almost like a hoot from an owl but with the slow rhythm and daintiness of a wooden pan flute.

Across a small ravine, glowing lights of purple, orange, and green were bobbing up and down, right where the noise came from. They were too big to be fireflies...

I squinted my eyes. "Are those..."

Gaius squatted down beneath a tree. "Glainies."

"Then, what's that noise coming from?"

"They like to whistle."

I made a hushed giggle as I perched next to his hulky frame. "They sound kinda cute."

He huffed. "I think we have different definitions of that word."

"So... what now?"

"*Now*, we wait. When the lights go out, it means they've spotted a bírokavaran, which is when you go in and—"

"—take it down for you to finish it off." I was a little shaky as I finished his sentence. My heart was beating very quickly. I was physically and magically prepared, but the fear of the unknown wouldn't go away—eating away at my heart like a caterpillar on a leaf. I just had to sit and wait in anxiousness until the colored lights of the sprites disappeared.

Gaius and I sat in silence, carefully waiting and listening for the monster to arrive. I was thankful to have him with me. Doing something like this alone—even without a deadly creature involved—would have me shaking down to the soles of my boots and causing chill bumps to scatter all over my body. He, though, was a boulder—unfazed by anything. The perfect protection for a weak vine like me to grab onto if something went poorly.

After about ten minutes, all the lights in the forest vanished along with the soft whistling from the sprites, as quick and quiet as a huff to a candle's flame. My body tensed up, and I couldn't help but take deep breaths, trying to calm my stomach from sloshing around, knowing the time had come.

"Let's go," Gaius whispered, and we both made our way over the small ravine toward the sprites' home.

We came to the edge of their habitat, where tree branches snapped in the distance. The hairs on my arms stood up, and my hands shook. I had to clench them in fists so Gaius wouldn't notice. One small indication I was terrified would have him doubting my abilities—doubting I could knock the creature out—and forever *ending* my Hero lessons.

No way was I letting that happen. *Heroes do not show fear, so I, the Agapéd Bearer, can't show that either.*

Gaius slowly stopped and whispered, "Alright, Lisa. You know what you have to do. Just like we've practiced. I'll be waiting and watching you from here."

He handed me a stun potion—a fragile bottle of blue discombobulating liquid to throw at the creature—and his light glint to guide my way. The rest was up to me and my terrain magic.

I took another deep breath. *You've got this, Lisa. You've prepared for this. No backing down...*

I crept further along the undefined path into the glainies' habitat. Alone. Gaius was standing twenty feet behind me near a wide tree. There wasn't much besides tree stumps, a pond the size of a kid's plastic pool, giant blue tree roots, and mushrooms—*lots* of mushrooms. The only sounds were my scared breaths and the rustling of the trees blowing in the wind. *Where is it?* Gaius had told me bírokavarans were blind and rely on their hearing and smell, so I didn't have to worry about it sneaking up on me... at least, that was what I hoped. Unless it smelled fear. *Can they do that? His book didn't mention it—*

Snap!

Another tree branch broke, followed by a squelching growl.

My heart rate doubled, and my senses heightened. I turned toward the noise and put the light glint in my pocket. More crunching of twigs on the mucky floor rang in the air. In moments, a blue glow appeared from behind the trees... and it wasn't from the memory sprites.

Skulking forward with its bioluminescent scales and gaping circular jaw was the bírokavaran. Gaius' illustration didn't do the beast justice; it was *far* scarier. The dark creature stood as tall as a German Shepherd with a reptilian body and stubby legs, almost like a violet crocodile mixed with an alien nightmare. Its lips couldn't cover its huge, round mouth, and it constantly swung its tongue drooling green, glowing saliva.

I furrowed my brows and sucked in the forest air. *Okay... let's do this.*

The first thing Gaius told me to do was to throw the stun potion at the monster, causing it to stop in its tracks so I could get a clear shot of its head. Having the plan to go by helped calm my nerves, but my poor stance in the mud said otherwise. I took the potion firmly in my hand, threw it at the bírokavaran... and missed the beast entirely.

I missed! Lisa, you idiot!

The potion exploded beside the fluorescent killer, causing the beast to growl, screech, and run right toward me! Fervid panic took command of my body as if I had perfected the crazed emotion. *This was not a part of the plan!*

I sprinted left, and the creature instinctively followed. It was so dark, and the shadows from the moonlight and the daunting purple creature didn't help at all. I tried throwing rocks at the monster with my terrain magic, but I kept missing—mostly because I was looking forward and not behind me. Suddenly, the beast growled again—a horrid noise, worse than a metal fork scraping across a porcelain plate—and bolted right in front of me, cutting me off my path. Its spherical jaw was glowing from its slobber and, even though it was blind, was darting me down.

Hate this!

It pounced, so I made a terrain column to block its attack. Earth shot up from the ground, whacking the creature. I watched its body fall to the ground with a thud, but the bírokavaran recovered easily and jumped toward me again. I turned to run, however—

One of the many blue roots in the ground—right off a small three-foot incline—snagged my foot. I not only tripped. I *tumbled*—four times I rolled in the mud and mushy mushrooms, my tied hair catching every loose leaf in the world. When my brain stopped spinning, I glanced back up toward the sky.

Where did it—

The bírokavaran was already in the air—in pursuit of me and my magical blood.

I shrieked, crunching up my muddy body lying on the ground and reverting to my poor self-defense mechanism instead of using my magic. My whole being was quivering—anticipating a ravenous bite or worse: *death*. This was a mistake. Gaius was right. I couldn't do it—I *didn't* do it—and now, I was facing the horrid consequences of my pathetic excuse for heroism—

A gallant savior in the form of a purple tree root came jetting out of the ground and grabbed the gnarly beast by its right hind leg... with Gaius standing right next to it. The Keeper didn't even have to break a sweat and could still catch the monster, whereas I was on the floor, covered in dirt and scratches, sweating profusely.

Gaius' face wasn't concerned or worried about me crumbling on the floor. Both his eyes were solemn, and his mouth was flatlined. He expected this to happen.

"Lisa, you can't let fear overtake you," he said as the bírokavaran squelched and squirmed, dangling in the air. "I said I wouldn't let you get hurt. The worst thing that can happen won't, so you have nothing to fear. But you cannot retreat when your plans don't follow through. Get yourself back up, and try again. Remember your training. You are fully capable of doing this with and without the help of potions."

He was right, no matter how badly a part of me wished he had given up on me and slayed the beast himself. I let myself be consumed with fear even though I was fully capable of taking down the three-foot-tall monster. Gaius believed in me, and I couldn't let all his time training me go to waste.

I got up off the ground as Gaius backed away—releasing the monster from the root's grasp. My eyes glared hard at the purple beast, watching it return to its feet, ready to pounce. Only this time, I wasn't going to run. *The worst thing that can happen can't... so I don't have anything to fear.*

I stood firm and shot a spiked column of dirt toward the creature as it jumped at me. The attack landed perfectly, right underneath its tender stomach, but it wasn't sharp enough to cause severe damage.

I just need it to fall so I can get a clear shot of its head.

I needed leverage, so I quickly observed my surroundings, seeing a tall tree stump twenty feet ahead. Sprinting, the bírokavaran tailed behind me as I darted for the old stump. Its hot breath began hitting my calves, and I knew it was closing in on me. So, I retook action. I created a dirt wall between us, and it *slammed* right into it. This allowed me enough time to climb atop the tree stump and get a clear shot of the creature's glowing head.

I can do this!

With the help of the faint moonlight, I saw a gray rock sticking out of the ground beside a patch of mushrooms. *That will work!* With my muscles tense and my mind focused, my foot stomped hard on the tree stump as my magic plucked the rock out of the ground—floating it in the air. I then used my hands to rush the stone toward me so I could fully grasp my magic. Like a slingshot, I pulled back my right arm and launched the gray boulder straight toward the bírokavaran—fast and with incredible force.

It was a direct hit.

My rock demolished the dirt wall the creature ran into before, covering the beast in mud before striking the bírokavaran head-on! The purple creature tumbled and rolled into the ground, leaving glowing skid marks along the forest floor before striking the back of a tree.

I stood motionless—not even breathing—just waiting to see if the creature was still conscious. Beads of sweat dripped down my scratched chin. Heartbeats throbbed all the way up into my ears, pounding like a bass drum. One second. Two seconds. Three... nothing but the whispers of the forest. When there was no sign of movement, I quickly ran over to the beast. Its purple body was still glowing, faintly, but its legs and mouth were silent.

My shoulders dropped and my eyes widened.

I did it! I really did it!

"Good work," I heard Gaius say from behind me in a casual tone.

"I can't believe... I just did that," I said, panting heavily from my first fight. In all my *life,* I would have never guessed I'd be some form of a hunter, and there was the creature *I* took down. I did that—defeated Darkness in the form of the ugliest alien lizard known to Man. It could've poisoned me or torn me to shreds, and old Lisa would've run off, pleading for Gaius to kill it for me. But that Lisa was gone... and it felt good. Sure, the heart throbbing and almost dying portion wasn't the best feeling in the world—shaking my bones, begging for my body to retreat back into its uncourageous form: a little teenage girl who needed Mom to squash the hairy spiders. I was standing, though, feeling more accomplished than when I beat Gaius's obstacle course—feeling good about myself. Proud. Never in my life did that emotion encompass my mind. It was good to see my magic training pay off.

I watched Gaius go near the bírokavaran, grabbing a vial from his belt. "Sorry about your potion..."

"It all worked out in the end." Gaius knelt by the fallen beast, taking a small dagger from his pocket. A part of me didn't want to watch him kill it... but then again, I couldn't help but look.

He lifted the bírokavaran's head and slit a clean cut through its throat. An unsettling, squelching noise spurt from the creature, followed by trickling liquid.

I flinched and squinted my eyes, but after a moment, my body calmed down, and I could look without my stomach churning.

Gaius used the empty flask to catch the falling black blood and filled it to the brim. As the beast's body lay lifeless, dark particles began to emit from its scales, almost as if it was disintegrating away—right toward the ground and sky.

"What's happening to it?" I asked, standing behind the Keeper.

"As I said, they aren't animals. They do not decompose. The magic inside them is being released back into the earth and sky, and the Guardians will disperse it to one day be used for something else."

"Whoa... didn't know they did all that... How come its blood in your flask isn't disappearing?"

"I caught it before it could be rereleased—before the pull of magic stripped it away..." Gaius' head shot up, jerking to the right. "Oh, great..."

"What?"

He then turned to look behind me and started to hurry along his collection process. The soft whistling sounds steadily returned, and the forest began to glow.

"We have to go."

"Wait, why—"

"Before they start coming back out."

Soon, the lights began to get closer as the whistling and woodland hooting became more pleasant. From behind some mushrooms and tree stumps came my first view of the glainies. The initial ones I saw stood no taller than six inches and were orange, purple, and pink. One had a big head and small tummy; the others didn't have a neck or waist; another was just a squishy belly with a face on it. They looked soft but not fuzzy like a cat or dog, plumper if anything else. Each one had crystals—*real, hard, and glowing crystals*—embedded on their backs and on top of their heads, almost like permanent hats or backpacks. They had small black eyes with tiny mouths that reminded me of plushies I would see in toy stores, whistling away as if a giant monster hadn't even terrorized their village. Some were round, and some were ovular; others were lumpy like a rice ball, but each one had dainty little legs and arms to match.

In a nutshell, glainies were the most adorable things I had ever seen in my life.

"Aw, they are so *cute!*" I said, watching more and more appear from the woods, now in green and turquoise colors.

Gaius stood up fast, unfazed by the cuteness. "We are leaving now."

"But look—they want us to stay!" I pleaded, seeing a pink one come up to my muddy boot. It was hard not to pick it up and smother it in a magical hug.

"Lisa, we are not staying. We came for the violvaran, so now, we are leaving."

I turned to see a group of glowing glainies gather mushrooms, peaches, and tree nuts while others began to make a fire.

"Come on, Gaius. They just want to thank us—they are even cooking us dinner."

He then scoffed at me in disbelief, so I gave him my puppy-dog-begging eyes again as two more glainies came close to my ankles.

Gaius did a double-take, visibly annoyed I was even stooping that low to plead for a forest thank you present by the creatures he did not care for. "Begging will not work this time. We are leaving right now before they start to follow us back home. That is final."

21

AN IMMORTAL HEART

We ended up staying.

The glainies thanked us—not verbally since they could only whistle and hoot—by cooking us some of their favorite dishes... which happened to be whatever they found on the forest floor. I thought it was sweet and happily took part in the festivities. Gaius sat next to me on a large tree stump with his arms crossed, disgruntled that he succumbed to my begging eyes once again. The glainies were funny, putting on silly dances and whistling choir songs for us by the fire, making the forest glow with colors from the crystals on their heads and backs.

Since Gaius had no drawings of the glainies in his magic study, I decided to create my own entry. I swiped through my orbkit, popped out my sketchbook, and watched as they began to line up—curious and excited to see what the savior of their homeland was doing. Most were shy, but a couple approached me and sat on my knees, allowing me to draw their lumpy portraits for my bestiary.

Throughout the night, they kept handing us bonfire treats with their stubby toothpick arms. Gaius said they didn't know what cooking was, but I rather liked the simple fire-grilled peaches and mushrooms. A round blue glainie handed Gaius a leaf filled with roasted nuts, which he didn't ask for, and another gave him a kebob of roasted mushrooms. He refused the grilled fungi entirely.

"You don't like mushrooms?" I asked as a pink glainie came and rested on my knee, waiting for me to finish my meal so I could draw a portrait of her.

"They are not meant for consumption," Gaius said with his arms still crossed, his brogue accent peeking through again, trying to ignore the green sprite climbing on his shoulder, "and I don't see how you can eat them."

"But you're the 'plant guy.' You should like every type of plant out there."

He creased up with subtle smiles. "And you're the first child I've seen who willingly enjoys them. Suppose your mother likes them, too?"

"No way. She's like you—thinks they are slimy and squishy like she's eating a slug."

"A smart woman. Must be from your father, then."

"Don't have one to know," I said casually.

Gaius' smile faded, his words slow. "Sorry, I shouldn't have mentioned that."

"You're fine—I never knew my dad, so I don't mind talking about it. Always been just my mom and me... just the two of us."

There was a brief pause before Gaius spoke again. "She raised you by herself, I take it?"

I was finishing up the last glainie's portrait as I willingly answered, "Mhm, Grandma didn't think it was a good idea since Mom was still in college and all. Begged her to give me up, saying a girl as young as her couldn't raise a kid right, but Mom proved Grandma wrong: got a college degree and a good-paying job and everything. I wouldn't tell this to Mom's face—seeing as she would deny it—but she's the best there is..." I squinted and erased the sketchy lines on the paper as I continued. "She brought me up well... at least, I think so when compared to most of my friends' parents."

Gaius sat there, still, silent, and listening.

I didn't expect to spill my heart out like that, but it felt good. Talking about my personal life wasn't something I normally did. No one ever seemed to care, not even my friends at school. Not once did Jenny Kim or Lily ask about my single mom. They, like most kids and adults, just assumed that if a kid had one parent, something bad happened in their life and refused to pry—refused to get involved in something they guessed was an iffy subject.

For some, that was true, but that never meant kids like me didn't want to talk about their family life. Honestly, I bet they would love for someone to lean on and confide in... at least, that is what I wanted anyway.

"For your mother to raise you all by herself," the Keeper spoke amid the sprites' woody hums, "I couldn't imagine what that would be like. Though, if she is anything like you... having people doubt her abilities probably made her want to do her best to prove them wrong."

Suddenly, a glainie climbed on top of Gaius' head, whistling while playing with his hair. My mentor's face turned red from embarrassment, and I couldn't help but laugh.

"What about you then? Do you have a family or one from your old life on Earth?" I asked him as he shooed away the sprite before it tangled his hair even more.

"You wouldn't want to hear about that," he dismissed.

But I sure did want to know.

Many kids at my school didn't care to invest time in others if they didn't like the same TV shows or movies. I, on the other hand, loved hearing stories from other people's lives. It was what made a person who they are. It explained their personality, why they laughed and cried, and was always something unexpected and true. I also loved magic, so hearing about an immortal man's life *before* magic was the most intriguing topic in the world.

With my legs already crossed on the tree stump, I wiggled around to face him, along with a couple of glainies acting like they were just as interested in Gaius' personal life. "Can you please tell me?"

Gaius looked at all of us and made another chuckle: a nosy girl surrounded by dopey glowing creatures. "Seems I can't say no to you." He released a deep breath before saying, "I do not have a family to call my own."

"Not even before you became a Keeper? Not a wife or anything?"

"It wasn't meant for me. Back then, you needed wealth and a good name to indulge in the life of marriage; I had neither. By the time I became the man you see today, all families were already taken. Then, Lady Ariela showed up—scared me straight..." He tittered while staring at the fire. "Thought I finally met my end and was hallucinating... instead, she just talked with me. Explained that she needed me. Offered me immortality and whatnot, saying my heart was 'good' and the only one for the job she had."

I glanced down at my fingers in my lap, empathizing, "I kinda know what you mean..."

Gaius aimed a smile in my direction. "Suppose you do then... though you handled it far better than I did. Told her she was deranged, speaking about magic and delusions... She didn't like that. That's when she said, 'I'm not sure what is going to happen, but I can assure you it's a better life than the one you're living now.' I had nothing to lose, so I accepted her offer. Not a perfect life, but it's far better than the one I had."

I wasn't sure what made a heart yearn to know more or why it desired relationships... but at that moment, I wanted to learn all about my mentor more than ever before.

I cradled my knees as the glainies floated to the ground, sitting more comfortably. "So, you've never had kids, then?"

He slowly shook his head, unfolding his arms, leaning a forearm across his bent knee. "Wasn't meant for me either."

I prodded, "Did you *ever* want one though?"

He paused, staring at the fire. I noticed his grin fading as his memories wandered around in his green eyes. "Being a Keeper... I do not have the luxury or privilege to own something that precious."

I rolled my eyes—him speaking about a teen or child as if they did not cause more problems than he could ever know—seeing that he didn't really answer my question. *"Would* you want one, then—if you could have one?"

Gaius glanced over at me, staring at my freckled face as my cheeks absorbed the orange heat of the fire. His gaze softened, going back and forth from my blue eyes before he took a deep breath. He stared for a while, though I wasn't sure why.

"If one would have me... I would do all I could to protect them." He tittered. "Even if they were as stubborn as you—demanding to be made into a Hero without a care in the world."

The Keeper was quite open with me, and my curiosity was relentless. My words dipped as I asked the next question: "So... have you ever fallen in love then?"

He huffed. "I already told you I didn't have a family—"

"That doesn't mean you can't *love* someone," I interrupted.

"Lisa, I am not answering this question."

I rolled my eyes and threw back my head. I *was* getting this answer—no doubt about that. "Oh, come on—*please?*"

"What made you even curious enough to ask that?"

I raised my eyebrows. "You're a good guy, all bulky and muscular, so I just don't see how someone like you doesn't have a lady around."

Gaius laughed pretty hard at my remark, the first I had ever seen his full set of perfectly straight teeth. "Your questions have no filter, do they?"

My whole face stretched. "*What?* I thought it was an obvious thing to ask!" I pointed all my fingers at him, gesturing to his entire being. "You *have* a name and a home, you aren't some beat-up old guy or smell gross, and you have the coolest job in the world, so I just figured you'd have more luck finding that special someone."

"As I said before, family isn't meant for me."

He was still avoiding my question. "You've *never* been in love then?"

"Once, long ago, but when did you become so interested in the life of a Keeper?"

"I have my reasons." *Just pure nosiness.* "And, right now, I wanna know this more than anything else in the world—*pretty, pretty please,* tell me?" By that point, my arms barred around my bent legs as my palms slammed together, a perfect picture of a begging little girl.

My mentor let out a hefty sigh followed by a grin. "This is the last story you are getting. Then, we are leaving."

His facial expression changed as he was reminiscing. He looked serious—as he usually looked—but with a soft smile.

He leaned forward toward the fire. "It was during my first year or two of being a Keeper, and I was traveling through Raglan on my way back to the Forest—Boolavogue and Calendula had yet to come into fruition, so it had no ownership at the time besides me. I stopped by to ask about any new hunts when a maiden came running by, yelling about some beast. Jules was her name. She was a quare lass... but something of true beauty. Even though she came in with skin dirty from working on the grounds, she still was the fairest woman in the room. I took her request and slayed the monster. It was nothing too difficult really, but she couldn't stop thanking me, even offering her prized hen as a reward."

"She gave you a chicken as a gift?" I couldn't help but chuckle.

"If you would've seen the eggs it laid, you wouldn't be laughing... and she *offered* her gift, but I couldn't accept it. She wouldn't take no for an answer, so we compromised: one night's meal at her home. That was all it took."

"It was love at first sight, wasn't it?"

Gaius made a hushed laugh as he shooed away a glainie trying to climb up his boot. "I don't believe in such things as that, but after some time, we did become quite enamored with one another..." His eyes lowered, and his smile steadily began to fade away. "But, it wasn't meant to last, and we knew that. I knew my life would outlive hers, but I wanted her anyway. It sounds selfish... but all love is, really. We tried to ignore it, but once her skin began to wrinkle and her black hair filled with silver strands, we couldn't any longer."

My tone also lost cheeriness as my heart grew more invested in his past. "Why couldn't Lady Ariela take away your immortality?"

"Something as trivial as mortal love was not worth the risk of dismembering my soul, and I took an oath to be a Keeper—everything that came with it. But in truth, immortality was a gift Ranemir gave to Lady Ariela to give to us Keepers so we could protect Man from dark magic. It wasn't something you could just throw away. Even though I knew that... that didn't stop me from searching for a way to be with Jules. The twenty years we had together, I spent in search of a charm or magic that could cure my immortal heart..." A solemn sigh exited between his lips. "Twenty short years."

Gaius seemed to forget he was talking to a child by the way his story drew on. I didn't mind though... and began to feel sorry for him. I didn't know love besides the mother-daughter kind and whatever fake stuff I saw on TV, so hearing his experience of the emotion brought out a version that was foreign to me... and my heart only wanted to know more.

"I guess you didn't find a charm that worked then... since you're sitting here with me all these hundreds of years later?" I asked him quietly, still cradling my knees against my chest, resting my chin on my scuffed kneecaps.

"I did... but the price of failure was too high; not even my selfish desires could afford the risk."

"What was it?" Maybe I shouldn't have asked, but I don't think he would have mentioned it if he didn't want to tell.

Gaius stared at the fire as he continued to explain. "Immortality is just one's soul living as intended, unaffected by the human body; for it to become mortal again, the immortal heart must willingly give its abundance of life to another...

but a heart needs the essence of *death* to cancel out the abundance of *life*. My theory—canceling out death with the aura of immortality—would cause an eternal heart to become mortal and a fading heart to have one more chance at living... which meant taking the life of the one you are trying to save."

He waited a moment before responding again. Only sounds of the crackling fire and echoes from the glainie's *hoots* filled the forest air. "Performing the charm all based on a *theory* was inhuman to think of. I didn't even know the odds of success... we could end up losing both lives altogether—and I couldn't do that either. In the end, after I told Jules all this, she agreed that it wasn't meant to be. She didn't want to see sorrow consume me when death greeted her and passed me by... so, the next day... she was gone."

For a couple of heartbeats, we both sat there, the faint sounds of settling forest humming in our ears. Most of the glowing sprites had gone back into their burrows or fallen asleep on the floor, forgetting Gaius and I were still guests at their party. Maybe I should have said something, but I just couldn't. Gaius' story was the saddest thing I had ever heard, and it was real—he really lived through it. I didn't think love like that existed—to spend twenty years searching for a magical cure just to find out you can't even use it. My eyes became all glossy the more I lingered on his past life.

Due to the silence, Gaius turned to his right to find me almost in tears from his tragic love story and quickly took notice. "This was almost seven hundred years ago, so don't feel bad for me, Lisa. This old man's heart has healed since then—"

"Was it worth it though?" I interjected. "You know, to be with her, even though it broke your heart?"

"Doesn't matter. In the end, even gimpish love isn't meant for the life of a Keeper."

I straightened my back. "*Pfft*—well, I believe you deserve love and a family just as much as the next guy, with or without a mortal heart!" I said to him, very assertive and confident.

Gaius laughed softly. "Somedays, I envy that innocent spirit of yours. Now, come on. We need to get you back before the Balthiers begin to worry." He began to stand up and put out the glainies' tiny fire.

"But I wanna hear more—"

"Another time."

"Fine, fine, fine."

I closed my notebook—now filled with a complete entry about the glainies—jumped off the tree stump and was about to take hold of Gaius' arm so we could teleport away, but an orange glow began to run toward us. It jumped up onto the tree stump. A round glainie, with a single orange diamond on its back, stood tall and whistled confidently, strutting a brave pose. His little black eyes stared right at me as he just kept hooting away, almost with a sense of great urgency.

"I thought this might happen," Gaius sighed, standing beside me.

"What's it want?" I asked, walking close to the tangerine sprite.

"The reason why glainies are referred to as memory sprites is that they can protect and manifest memories with their magic into a physical projection—all the memories they've stored up in their crystals. They also have a fascination with humans and their memories, and if they muster up the courage, they will ask to form a bond with a human they admire."

The mighty hooting persisted, and Gaius crossed his arms. "This dote wants to be yours, hence the whistling."

"You mean..." I knelt in front of the brave glainie. He had his little arms bent on his tummy, almost like a superhero stance. "You want to make a bond with me?"

The orange glainie, glowing brightly from the giant jewel, nodded, which was his entire body. I was surprised he didn't fall over; the diamond on his back looked very heavy.

I whipped my head over to Gaius. "*Gaius, can I keep him?*"

"Normally, I wouldn't care what you do outside of our training, but a memory sprite's bond is quite rare and would benefit you."

"How so?"

"A bond with a glainie means your memories will be connected with it—right inside that diamond. If you ever want to replay an important part of your life, that little dote can use its magic to show you. They can also float around and hide within the atmosphere, but they are very loyal and won't leave your side no matter how much you may ask."

This little guy can do all that?

I looked back at the glainie—still standing in his superhero stance with his little stubs for legs. In all my life, I had never owned a pet and was about to be gifted a magical one. *This is the best day ever!*

"What's your name?" I asked the little sprite, even though I knew his only response would be a whistle; I just wanted to show common courtesy.

"You don't have to name it," Gaius interjected. I could tell by the tone of his voice he was ready to leave.

"I just can't *not* call him anything..." I squinted at the orange glainie, who appeared to be very tough—not running away at a curious girl and a six-foot giant beside her. Still, he was a little dopey but not as timid as his brethren. "Hmm... you look pretty brave... and rather tough... What if I called you Tuff? T-U-F-F. Would you like that?"

His little face blushed, and he let out the cutest hoot, so I assumed that meant yes.

"Well then, Tuff, I would love it if you joined me as my little orange sprite," I said to him with a quick nod.

Tuff stuck out his arm, and I extended my index finger toward him. The moment our hands touched—his just a fingerless stub—a small glow emitted, both on my skin and on Tuff's arm. Suddenly, I felt as if I could understand what he was thinking—like my brain was deciphering his woodland whistles into the English language—and I could tell Tuff was extremely happy to start a new adventure with me.

My orange sprite began to float around in the air, going from invisible to visible again like a plump firefly, before reappearing and sitting on my shoulder. His body wasn't too heavy, and he liked playing with my hair. He couldn't believe he found an adventurer to bond with so quickly. *It's so weird to know what he's thinking without actually hearing him speak... This is the coolest thing ever!*

"Alright, glad that's over," Gaius expressed with much relief. He *really* wanted to leave over an hour ago. "Let's get going."

I grabbed onto Gaius' leather jacket with Tuff on my shoulder as we evanesced away to the Boolavogue Outskirts Forest. We began our short trek back to the secret entrance of Calendula when I remembered—

"I should have mentioned this earlier, but thanks for teaching me how to fight," I said to Gaius with Tuff glowing on my shoulder. "Saving the glainies from the bírokavaran made me want to save even more creatures and, eventually, people from dark magic. So, just, uh, thanks for believing in me."

"You don't have to thank me for that. I am just glad to finally have a student worth teaching," Gaius began, "but if it means that much to you, then you are welcome... and Lisa..." He then slowed down his pace and spoke sternly. "You did extremely well for just learning magic not but a month ago, and with that said, you must not tell the others about this."

The secrecy of heroism came back up again, making my mind begin to wonder why that still was.

"Why not—"

"Promise me?" he uttered.

I did well... so why is Gaius still not wanting the Guardians to know how strong I've become? I wanted to ask why, but the mood of the current conversation was nothing like the heart-to-heart in the glainie's homeland. Gaius' eyes were sharp and focused, almost scary.

"I promise."

22

SHE TOLD ON ME

"You can breathe underwater?" I shouted, doe-eyed, standing on the edge of the concrete platform in Mantene—staring at the tan, blush-blonde Keeper swimming and sucking in the ocean waters.

Inna used her magic to create a powerful yet calming force of water to propel her out of the sea after staying submerged for minutes *without* drowning. Her turquoise wetsuit, the length of the right leg's fabric longer than the left, sparkled in the midday sun, glistening like refined diamonds as the water sluiced off her body. The thick, long braid in her hair was drenched and still looked as radiant as ever, her tangles and knots more beautiful than my hair on a good day.

Her bare feet hit the man-made ground near me as she said, "About one out of every one hundred Water Elemental Mages and Mystics can breathe in water—their magic pulling the oxygen out of it. Think of it as a magic perk, though the tang of sea salt takes a bit of getting used to."

"You mean, you can get another type of magic for 'free,' essentially?" My comparison was pretty poor, and it sounded lame coming out of my mouth.

Inna didn't seem to mind, grinning as she wrung out the water from her braid. "Think of it as your magic pulse wanting to be stronger, caring for itself by giving you another ability to keep it thriving—to keep you protected. Not everyone will receive a perk, only a select few; it all depends on the heart and blood the magic is bound to."

So cool!

She swiped at her waist, her fingers brushing the air above her keychain orbkit. Inna didn't even have to look at the magic pockets to know exactly where the freezing gloves were at. "Let's work more on your frost abilities—getting your mind and magic comfortable with freezing and unfreezing water at the flick of your fingers. Sound good?"

I nodded quickly and readied my stance.

⁓

After another hour of practice that Thursday afternoon, freezing waves and ocean bubbles, I wanted a magic perk. Seemed right as the Agapéd Bearer— seemed *essential* to have an arsenal of powers up my sleeve. And the one I wanted most was *hers*. The ability to breathe in water could help me save people, but there was a selfish part of me that just wanted it because I thought it was cool. I couldn't have been the only teenage girl who wanted the power to defy the laws of nature and be like the fish of the sea.

Oh, I am so getting a perk...

A couple of workers needed to talk with Inna about a stardust harvest or something-another, so while she was inside the foyer of the Aquanaeum, I slipped into the cylindrical viewing room where the ocean was on all sides of the dome. Emerald and cobalt waters painted the turtles and silverfish that swam around, and the sea hummed its ambient songs behind the magic-mantled glass.

And my heart had a crazy idea.

No one was in the room other than me and Tuff, who remained invisible by my side. Off to the right were the blue bracelets that allowed the wearer to penetrate through the magical dome. So, after double-checking the entranceway, I ran to the bracelets, snatched one, slapped it on, and faced the dome again.

"Tuff," I whispered. He hooted without revealing himself. "I'm gonna do it. I'm gonna press my face in and see if I can breathe in that water." I patted my heart. "Something in me tells me I can do it, so you stand by and watch, okay?"

I stood at the rim of the wall, my nose almost touching the rubber glass. The water didn't scare me, thanks to Mom, who sent me to a daycare with a pool when I was a toddler. There weren't any sharks or creepy fish with teeth lurking around, either. A perfect, serene painting of the sea.

I also was more confident in my magic skills. Defeating the bírokavaran last week really boosted my self-assurance. Plus, Valhalla helped with all her praises. I remember at first feeling odd, being celebrated as a powerful Mage, but after seeing all I had accomplished in just a month, I started to believe what she said.

I took a deep breath. *It's just water, Lisa. The worst thing that can happen is you choking... which is pretty bad, but breathing underwater will be worth it.*

My face went straight into the water while I stood in the room... but my body *refused* to choke on purpose.

I leaned back, taking my face out of the wall. Thanks to the bracelet, not a single drop of water remained on my lips or cheeks.

"Ugh," I said out loud, Tuff whistling a confused tune. I answered him, "My body just won't breathe in water on purpose..." I clenched my fists by my sides. "I'm gonna have to jump in."

He hooted again, bits of orange flickering from his invisible body, scared and telling me *no*.

I whipped my head toward him, knowing exactly where he was floating. "My magic perk won't happen if I'm scared. If I don't trust the Agapéd to save my life in the ocean, why would it give me a magic perk, Tuff?" He did not answer. "So, I will do it—clothes and all."

Another hefty breath of air filled my lungs, and I walked right through the shimmering veil as I heard Tuff tell me in my head to be careful. The water was cold, and the salt hurt my eyes, but I couldn't help but look all around—floating freely amid glittering emerald waters. I admired the fish and rays around me, stunned by the vast depths underneath the deep blue. My stomach dropped at the endless pit of darkness below.

Weird voices began talking to me in my mind. It wasn't Tuff; too squeaky sounding for a glainie. My head whipped around to see a small pod of rays swimming by, and I heard what they were saying... and my mind interpreted it as, "Look at that funny human."

Didn't know Mantene had magic-talking fish who judged you before getting to know you...

I could feel my lungs craving relief, and I knew... I had to try and breathe the water. Every nerve in my body said don't—every brain cell said I was stupid—but I ignored all the defensive signals my heart was blurting out.

And I took one small gulp. It was just a teensy, tiny one, but my body rejected it *completely!* I began to freak out, the fear of drowning overtaking my mind, and I grew terrified.

Abrupt splashing occurred behind me, and two sets of hands grabbed my arms and waist, pulling me out of the water and into the viewing room.

I plopped on the floor in the arms of Inna, coughing up salty water like a madman, my clothes completely dry due to the bracelet's magic.

"Lisa," she breathed, frantic and worried, her dry braided hair grazing the floor, "what—what were you doing out in the middle of the o... cean..."

Inna wasn't the type to mutter or stumble on her words, so when she did—forgetting about the teenage girl throwing up water on the pristine floor—I turned in the direction her eyes drifted off to.

Two sets of hands pulled me in, but no other workers were around. That second pair was tiny, almost like kitten paws, and that was when I saw Tuff. He was glowing and dripping with water. Completely *visible* and terrified he almost lost me.

Oh no, Tuff, why?

Last weekend, when I returned home with Tuff, I had to make sure he did *not* turn visible at all on Earth. Gaius was right about them being loyal... and I didn't think about Tuff being around me when I was with Mom. Before Mom got home, I sat him down in my room and explained how magic was a secret. Tuff took everything very seriously, even though his little naïve mind didn't understand why magic should be secret. He agreed to stay invisible unless it was just him and me alone, us and Gaius, or if I permitted him to appear. I also had to enforce that he not appear in front of the Guardians either... but I forgot to include Inna in the mix.

"I just—" I began, finally catching my breath. "I wanted to see... if I could breathe underwater... like you. But I guess it isn't meant for me."

She released a tight breath, cupping my face in her hands as we knelt on the floor. "Then next time, at least let me be there to watch you. You could've drowned." My stare went to her collarbone, unable to look into her worried eyes. "I'm just glad you're alright... but, uh..."

Tuff was still behind me, and Inna could not help but stare at him. There was no point in hiding my secret glainie anymore. After all, it was my fault he revealed himself; he just wanted to save my life.

"Thanks for saving me," I said to Inna before turning my face to Tuff, "and you too, Tuff."

My little sprite then floated on my shoulder, feeling proud for saving my life, though I really wished he would have stayed invisible.

"Tuff, is it?" Inna asked, standing back on her feet.

I hoped she ignored Tuff, but that was impossible; he was too adorable and contrasted with the blue in every corner of the room. I stood up, too, my eyes having difficulty focusing on her face. "Yeah, so, I, uh, got a memory sprite last week and named him Tuff."

Inna smiled at my sprite, making him blush and hide in my hair. "Rare to see one make a bond with a human, and even rarer to see one in Calendula or Mantene. Where did you find him?"

There was no use lying to her since Tuff already appeared, and Inna seemed trustworthy enough. As long as I didn't mention the monster hunt in the forest, I wouldn't be breaking Gaius' promise.

"Well, I actually found him in the woods with Gaius during one of our lessons... and Gaius let me keep him, so now, he's my sprite," I said, leaving out just some minor details.

Inna gently poked Tuff's noggin, making him blush even more before turning invisible.

I couldn't risk another half-truth, so I changed the subject. "I didn't know your ocean had talking fish. Kinda rude ones, too."

"If there were any talking sea creatures, I think I would have noticed that by now." Inna giggled.

"But it's true! The stingrays said—well, in my mind I heard them call me 'funny looking' while I was swimming around."

Inna let out a big chortle, trying to conceal her glossy smile with her hands. I did not understand what was so funny... unless... *Am I actually funny looking?*

Her eyes became crescent moons of sapphire. "I just can't believe it— you went in wanting to learn how to breathe underwater and come out with Animalian Insight magic. The fish were not magical; it was *you*, Lisa. You can understand them. How funny the Agapéd is, choosing such an odd power to gift to you."

"So, you're saying I can talk to animals now?" I asked, a smile growing along my face.

"Not quite. Animalian Insight just means your mind understands their instincts. I've never been acquainted with a glainie, but I assume the way you can understand its thoughts is the same feeling with animals."

I couldn't believe it. I now had three types of magic in my heart—one I wasn't even trying to learn! I had to admit, I felt pretty cool and more like the powerful Mage Valhalla made me out to be.

I was about to urge Inna into resuming our lessons and letting me listen to what more sea creatures were gossiping about when an Aquanaeum worker came up to her, taking her aside to tell her something. When she returned, she said seriously and calmly, "Lisa, I will have to cut our lessons short today. Something urgent just came up that I need to attend to. I hope it's okay with you if I go ahead and have Ava and Asa take you back to Calendula."

My magic-yearning spirit shrank at the new information. "Oh... that's fine. I guess I will see you Monday, then," I said as Ava and Asa suddenly marched through the giant viewing room's doors. *How did they already know to come?*

Inna thanked me for our lessons and quickly went to the opposite end of the Aquanaeum's entrance. I hated that everything ended so quickly; the sun hadn't even begun to set. Even though I still wanted to stay with her and practice more water magic, I was just glad she didn't get upset with me for having Tuff and with Gaius for letting me keep him.

Guess I can read some of Gaius' books before our afternoon Hero-training lessons start...

I made my way toward the Veradome, which was bustling with employees, and down to Gaius's wooden doorway. I noticed smoke coming from his chimney when I stepped through the magic entryway.

He's already done with work?

Gaius usually wouldn't return until after five or six, so seeing smoke when the sun was high in the sky was out of the ordinary. I thought he might have been busy making potions since he still hadn't used the violvaran we collected last week, so I went down the small hill to his back patio.

From Gaius' backyard, one could easily see the three levels of his home. The bottom level with the magic study's square windows was smaller than the giant domed window in his living room. Impossible to ignore, and easy to peer inside from the stone deck. When I glanced up at the eight-foot window, my eyes had to do a double-take.

A tall man with abnormally long hair paced inside Gaius' home.

Was that Vilmad in his living room?

I stayed close to the house to avoid being spotted. If that was Vilmad, something had to be wrong or very urgent, meaning I needed to find out the truth. I walked around Gaius' cottage and stood underneath the living room window, hearing muffled voices. There was no mistaking it: Vilmad was in Gaius' house, and he did *not* sound happy.

I have to know what's going on.

I looked down at Tuff, who had reappeared from his invisible state the moment we entered Gaius' domain, and a light bulb went off in my head.

"Tuff," I whispered, "can you go in there, turn yourself invisible, and, uh, 'memorize' what they are talking about? Then, come back and show it to me?"

Tuff was shaking from his nerves, causing orange dust to fall off his diamond, like spilled craft glitter, not liking the idea of leaving my side.

"I promise I'm not going anywhere, okay? This is just super important to me and you. That man in there could take you away, so I need to know *everything* they talk about. No one else can do this but you."

I probably overdramatized the situation, but glainies needed as much reassurance as possible... and it worked. My little sprite glanced back and forth from the window to my eyes before puffing out his chest like a mighty warrior; he couldn't bear to lose me, mustering up all the courage in his little plushie body. Tuff then disappeared into Gaius' home while I waited for his return at the pond's edge.

I sat near the shore, playing around with my water magic, feeling anxious about Tuff. I had never seen my glainie use his memory magic before, and I didn't know if he would be noticed or not. I didn't want to lose him. It was nice having someone around who looked out for me.

What could they be talking about in there? Does Vilmad know about last week—no way... unless he has some type of sixth Guardian sense that lets him know when I don't follow orders. I made frozen ripples in the pond as I shook off my overthinking. *It's fine—Tuff's fine. If the Guardians had some all-knowing magic, they would've stopped Gaius before we even went to that forest. Yeah—that makes more sense...*

After about ten minutes, I saw an orange light reflect off the water, and I turned my body around to see Tuff flying toward me. I hugged him and praised his good efforts, watching him blush from his heroism.

"Okay, Tuff, can you show me what you saw—or how does this work exactly?" I asked him.

Tuff stood on my freckled knee as I sat cross-legged, making his orange diamond glow. He whistled, held out his stubby hand, and caused a computer monitor-sized projection of magic to form in front of us—floating freely in the air. Its appearance looked similar to the orbkit's magic pockets but had an orange and yellow tint. Suddenly, the orange rectangle began to show the inside of Gaius' home. It was like watching a movie with a slight overlay of orange covering the magical screen! *This is so weird! I can't believe I'm watching Tuff's memories right now!*

It must have been not too long after their conversation had started. Vilmad was pacing the living room while Gaius stood against the wall closest to his workshop door. His arms were crossed, his glare at Vilmad was brooding, and his brows were furrowed. There was no essence of a smile on his face. Gaius was *angry*. I had never seen that side of him before... and it was scary.

"You *agreed*, Gaius," Vilmad hissed, "to not put the Agapéd Magic at risk of being seen or caught glimpse of, and of all things, you bring it in contact with a dark magic *beast*."

Gaius interjected, "She was safe—"

"*She* was not meant to be out there in the first place—I thought you would've learned by now. She wanted to keep this magic, so we sought to go about training in secret until she was ready and not a child any longer."

"I did as you said, but that was until I realized how ignorant it was. Plus, she asked *me* to teach her how to fight without knowing the Agapéd's true purpose."

Vilmad threw his head to the side. "Oh, so when a child heedlessly asks for you to make them a Hero, you take no mind to it and oblige—"

"When that child has more wisdom than her teachers, I do," Gaius bellowed, now away from the wall and directly in Vilmad's face.

"We are not repeating the past, Gaius. You will do your part as instructed—"

"Because that worked out so perfectly for you the last time, didn't it?"

Vilmad looked taken back and couldn't think of something quick to retort.

Gaius then spoke through gritted teeth. "She needs to be told."

"*Told?*" Vilmad scoffed. "You honestly believe if we told her what her fate entailed, she'd still be training with you—training at *all*, to be honest?"

Gaius didn't answer or move.

Vilmad continued his stark tone. "We will not have the risk of *fear* be what causes the Agapéd to leave that girl's heart and be lost for who knows how long. I am not for the idea of it picking the heart of a child, especially one as weak as her, but I am *not* risking it being lost—losing our only hope. You know as well as I do that because it has reawakened, Darkness is coming. Telling her now—what child from Earth would understand *that* unless they are fully trained in magic?"

"Lisa has proven her strength—"

"Strength? Whatever strength you think she has is nothing compared to what she will be up against... and *you* know that. You keep this up... and she will *die*, along with our first glimpse of hope we've seen in the last century."

Gaius stayed silent, and I am not sure how. His muscles were tense, and his eyes didn't blink, fueled with enmity and unrest.

Vilmad raised his golden finger, pointing at the Keeper. "You will teach her magic and *only* magic. This naïve 'heroism' dream you've implanted in her mind will cease to exist until the Agapéd Magic is strong enough and her heart isn't wavered by fear of what's to come." He straightened his back, stepping away from Gaius' unsettling stare. "The only reason you're still her instructor is because of Calendula's magic defense and secrecy. Though, if you take it upon yourself to indulge in this 'fighting off monsters' fantasy, we will find Lisa a new teacher— one who will do as told and not expose the existence of the Agapéd."

Gaius didn't say another word. He just stood there, bottled up with vexation as Vilmad evanesced away, concluding the end of Tuff's memory display.

And I sat there, frozen with my forehead crinkling. My mind was unable to find a steady spot to stare and think.

I... I didn't know what I should've been feeling after watching that; I barely could comprehend anything they said. I knew there was a bigger purpose for me other than learning magic, but I didn't think it was something so secretive that no one could find out about my magic. It all sounded wrong to me... like I was being lied to. I never had an adult lie to me other than Mom telling me Santa Claus was real. But this... this was different. This was my *life,* and these were Keepers and Guardians—immortal beings of the stars. They don't lie to kids... right?

"My fear can cause my magic to leave me? I can lose my magic?" I questioned Tuff, though I just needed a reason to express my thoughts out loud. "Vilmad... he was telling the truth about me dying... but how and why? And what did he mean by 'hope'? What do I need to be told? What happened last time? What aren't they telling me?"

Tuff shrugged as he floated in front of me.

"How did he even find out—I never mentioned anything, and you never did either," I stated to Tuff when I suddenly remembered that I *did* tell someone other than Valhalla.

Inna told on me? On Gaius? Because of me, Gaius got in trouble. *I... I broke his promise...*

My heart sank. I persuaded him to teach me how to fight, and I was the one who exposed Tuff's existence.

My eyes narrowed down to my hands in my lap. *But how is it all my fault? I* was the one left in the dark—the one from Earth who didn't know anything about the magic world. I did as they said, traveled trillions and trillions of miles away to learn about a world that wasn't mine, and lived with complete strangers without asking for a background check. *Why, then, should Gaius or I get in trouble for something that I didn't even know was wrong in the first place?*

I tried to piece together a hypothesis for why keeping my magic was a secret, and the only thing I came up with was that I *was* meant to be a Hero and the Guardians didn't think I was strong enough for it. It made sense. They thought I would get scared and run away—causing the Agapéd to leave my heart—and that I was only "strong" because Gaius was there to save me. There *was* something out there I was meant to fight, hence the reason Vilmad said I was the last hope, but they didn't believe in me. The moment I stepped foot in the Elysium's meeting room over a month ago, they all were scared and disappointed. Pity—they pitied me. And Vilmad *hated* me.

"Well, I am not helpless!" I proclaimed to Tuff, punching the dirt with my fist, causing some pebbles to shoot off the ground. "I will prove it to them. I am *not* losing my magic and will become something they can believe in."

Tuff gave a mighty whistle, telling me he was by my side to the end, which made me very happy.

I stood up quickly, glancing toward the Keeper's hearth. Smoke was still rising from the chimney. No way was I risking Gaius seeing me at his home and assuming I eavesdropped and heard everything, so I rushed out of the Veradome and straight to the Balthiers.

———

I let Tuff show Valhalla the memory of Gaius and Vilmad as we huddled in her bedroom.

"So, *they* think that *you* think you're strong enough because *Gaius* made you think that way, right?" Valhalla reiterated as we sat on her fluffy green rug.

I nodded.

She sat up on her knees as her long black hair fell over her shoulders. "Well... then that means you just need to prove to them they're wrong by doing something heroic by yourself."

"You mean—"

"Doing *actual* Hero or Monster Hunter work."

My eyes widened as my words sped up. "But Gaius said not to."

"That was before you defeated the bírokavaran. You saw what Tuff saw: Gaius said you're strong enough right in front of Mr. Vilmad. If he believes you can do it, then you can. I mean, I already knew you could from day one."

Valhalla scooted closer to me while Tuff sat on my shoulder. "Look, next time Dad and I go back to Raglan, I'll look for a job on the request board that is easy but still challenging enough to prove them wrong. You'll complete the job with no problem—obviously—and they will be like, 'Lisa, you're so strong! We should have never doubted you,' and you'll finally be on track for a Hero and Lionheart!"

I didn't like the idea of going behind Gaius' back. He always taught me what was best and never gave me a reason to not trust him... but then again, Valhalla's plan was about proving myself to the *Guardians*. Proving myself to Vilmad. If Valhalla found a job similar to defeating a bírokavaran-sized beast, then I could easily accomplish that.

"Okay, we will go with your plan," I agreed. "When do you think you'll be heading back out with your dad?"

"Sometime after next week."

"Then, let's do it."

Valhalla, Tuff, and I sat on her bedroom floor determined and raring for our heroic mission. I had never felt that confident in myself or that independent, but having them two by my side was all the reassurance I needed. I knew I could do it, and I was ready. I would train hard the following weeks and make sure my magic was strong enough. Nothing would stop me from becoming the hero I was meant to be.

23
THIS IS ALL WRONG...

During the next week of lessons, Gaius and Inna mentioned nothing of Vilmad or anything about me fighting the bírokavaran. When training with Gaius, I had to act like I knew nothing—as if everything was perfectly fine. Knowing a secret about me I was *never* supposed to know made my heart antsy, making my magic lessons feel different as well. I knew I wasn't just learning magic for Magic's sake; there was some other hidden meaning that Vilmad didn't want Gaius to tell me.

"We will focus on building up your terrain magic. No more hunts or combat training," Gaius told me at Monday morning's lessons. When I asked him why— as I thought would be an obvious question for someone who didn't know of the secret meeting—he flatly responded with, "Because it's what is most important right now."

Because it's what is most important... Another lie—another lie I *knew* he didn't want to tell me.

Even though he and I both were disappointed our Hero training had to stop, I still practiced diligently with him. When Gaius was busy in the greenhouse, I would practice my fighting skills with Tuff and use my sprite as my "Gaius Lookout." I also read more of his books, studying up on dark magic creatures to prepare for my future job Valhalla would be bringing me. I wished I could've asked for Gaius' help—hating to go train blindly—but I didn't want him to get in trouble again for something I made him do. I would rather take all the blame than for him to lose his position as my instructor. I liked being his student and did not want some other old dude teaching me—or worse: have Vilmad take his spot. I cringed at the thought.

It soon neared the end of July—the last Tuesday of the month—and I began to doubt whether Valhalla would ever be asked to go to Raglan again. One night at dinner, her dad mentioned he was going, but Mrs. Balthier quickly refused Valhalla to join him. I guess even she had a limit on how many school days she could miss. I told Valhalla to not push her parents so much, fearing they might catch on to our plans. I said we could wait until she finished school—which was in two weeks—but she turned that plan down. She was more dead-set on me proving my strength than I was, outwardly at least.

There was a part of me, every now and then, usually during a successful magic run with Inna or Gaius, where I thought to just learn magic and forget what Tuff saw. I wouldn't have my stomach in knots thinking about fighting a creature alone without Gaius protecting me. Magic training would have no added stress of becoming a Hero or whatever it is this "hope" was Vilmad mentioned. The Agapéd would grow strong. I would grow strong, and I would be safe. Safe...

From what?

The question of *why* would resurface like a piece of driftwood constantly bobbing back and forth in my mind. Why learn this? Why not tell me? What is so bad that the Guardians had to make Gaius and Inna lie to me—to train me in secret? Why is the Agapéd so important? Vilmad said I could die... shouldn't that be reason enough for me to train to be a Hero?

There was my reason—why I kept pushing. I may have only been thirteen and, *apparently*, looked like a ten-year-old, but my magic was meant to be something great. It was meant to be this mysterious hope—meant to be something worth living for. If they weren't going to tell me why, then *I* would decide what to do with it. And that was to become a Hero.

I made my usual route with Ava and Asa back toward the secret entrance to Calendula, and the moment I stepped through the woodland portal in the forest, it began pouring rain. All my clothing became drenched, along with my hair guiding water down to my back. *How big is this hidden town for the weather to change drastically with a simple step through two pine trees—*

I was about to book it to the Balthiers for dinner when an arm came out of nowhere and grabbed me.

It was Valhalla, soaking wet, waiting outside the entrance.

"Why are you out here in the rain?" I asked her incredulously.

"I couldn't risk being caught, and I needed to see you the first chance I got!" she said, her black hair *soaked*, trying to sound hushed, but she was horrible at whispering. "Right after you left for lessons with Mr. Micah this morning, Dad got an urgent call to cover for someone who normally runs the Sunseeds cart in Raglan. So, after a *lot* of begging, I convinced him to let me help him today, and look what I got!"

Valhalla took something out of her rain jacket pocket. It looked like paper, so I held my hand over my head and used my magic to make the rain stop hitting our heads like a water umbrella.

"Oh, thanks. I forgot you can do that. Look!" She then unfolded the crumby parchment to reveal its sloppy handwritten plea:

HUNTER WANTED!
Somethin's killin' my goats. Need it gone right array.
Can offer reward.
Claggan's Farm, East Raglan

"I saw this on the board today and just knew it was the job for you!"

"Well... isn't it kinda vague?" I questioned, rereading the horribly written request with my hand still holding the water. "Like, there isn't a description of the animal, and how am I supposed to know where Claggan's Farm is?"

"Look, most of the time, when farmers or cattle herders put up requests like this, it's usually due to a vorrg—dark magic hounds no bigger than your average wolf—which explains the lack of details. They are common animals and *way* less threatening than a bírokavaran; they are predictable and not poisonous, making it an easy job for your first solo mission."

"Okay, but I still have no clue where the farm is at—"

"That's why you have me!" Valhalla smiled widely. "I know exactly where that is! I'll come with you and be your guide, even witness your win just in case Mr. Vilmad and the other Guardians don't believe you."

It sounded perfect... but something inside me kept telling me it was a bad idea. *What if Valhalla is wrong? What if Gaius catches me or Vilmad does first?*

Valhalla saw the worry on my face. As I continued to move the water over our heads, hearing it fall around our shoes, Valhalla looked me dead-set in the eye. "Lisa, you can do this. You have been training hard—for what, like two months just about—and will have no problem doing this task. You're the strongest Mage I've ever met and my best friend. I wouldn't be surprised if you completed this job in less time than it would take for you to throw a rock across my front yard— that's how awesome you are. So, stop worrying and believe in yourself... just like I believe in you."

I never had a friend give me such kind and genuine praise. She was the reason I decided to become a Hero and the reason for my sudden increase in self-confidence. Every day—every *single* day—she looked forward to seeing me, and most of the time, she would wait for me and we'd walk back to her house together. Sometimes, her adoration for the Agapéd was a little excessive, but after getting to know her, I began to believe every word she said about me... and I felt special to be called her friend.

"Alright, we will do it," I said, grinning, full of determination, "but when do you think we should go? I can't leave during the day. Pretty sure you can't either..."

"Hmm... you have a point... guess we would have to leave tomorrow evening. It does take a good bit of walking to get there, even after using the closest hidden entrance."

My heart began to race at the idea of going out in less than twenty-four hours. "Isn't that a little soon?"

Valhalla started folding up the request as she explained, "If we wait any longer, the farmer might get some Hunter to do the job for him. So, it *has* to be tomorrow night—plus, both Mom and Dad work that afternoon; it will be easy for us both to slip out."

"Guess you're right..." I straightened up my back. "Okay, then we will go tomorrow after my lessons with Gaius."

———

Gaius had me practice forming dirt columns sturdy enough to jump onto the next day, all the while making each one escalate upward like stairs. My first run-through was slow, but after a while, I could make the columns increase in height without my hands. It was crazy to see myself create terrain staircases with only my legs and feet!

I looked back to see the Keeper sitting next to Tuff, who now was growing acquainted with him. Seeing Gaius smile at my progress made all the hard work pay off.

"Lisa," he called to me, the sun shining bright on his brown hair, causing me to descend off my tall column and run over to him. "Your control is getting much better, and I can see your terrain magic is growing stronger as well."

"Thank you, Gaius," I replied, my heart beaming.

"Feel free to keep practicing this afternoon. Inna dropped off the first batch of starseeds this morning, so I need to cultivate and plant their soil. Good work today."

Gaius got up off the broken brick bench near his home and began to walk toward the glowing greenhouse, and it finally hit me—

"You mean in *there* is where you grow the Wishing Star plants?" I said to him, making him stop to look back at me.

"It is."

Intertwining my fingers behind my back, trying not to seem too eager, I asked, "Then… would it be possible for me to see them someday?"

Gaius smirked at me before resuming his walk. "We'll see."

When he entered the giant glass terrarium, my magic training turned into Hero mode. I took Tuff back with me to Gaius' magic study and began to research vorrgs, grabbing *Basic Creatures: Volume Two* and finding their entry. They were long and skinny with muscular paws and hind legs but pretty bony—no magical powers either. Gaius noted their height was no taller than three feet, and they normally hunted alone or in packs of three, which was good for me. They could be easily spooked by loud noises and were weak against Gangdra Draught, so I searched through Gaius' potion shelf for that vial.

In the back were five different quart bottles of the potion. *I hope he doesn't notice one is missing.*

I grabbed one when a loud noise came from the bookshelf behind me, almost causing me to drop the bottle. I darted my head around to see Tuff, who was trying to help me research creatures, on the floor and covered in books.

"Tuff!" I whispered-yelled. "What are you doing? I thought you were

Gaius—you can't even read. Why are you over there?"

He gave me a whispered whistle, telling me he just wanted to help identify more creatures so he could protect me.

I thought that was sweet, so I forgave him for scaring me and walked over to my orange sprite to see many books open flat, revealing pages of terrifying, monstrous creatures.

I've never seen these before...

As Tuff started putting the thinner books back on the shelf, I picked up the one with the gruesome monsters and flipped through a couple of pages. Every single dark creature, all hand-drawn by Gaius, looked partially human, as if they once were human before dark magic overtook them. I read a couple of their descriptions, just to make sure they weren't from around the forest outskirts or in Raglan... and I didn't recognize any of the names, which meant I was safe from ever running into them.

My stomach churned, making butter in my gut. *These things exist in this world... and I bet Heroes have to fight them all the time...*

"Tuff... one day, I may have to fight these..." I glanced over at my sprite flying near my shoulder. "I'm just glad you'll be right there beside me if and when I do."

His little black mouth turned into a smile, letting me know he agreed.

I closed the book, and with uncertainty about its correct position, I placed it in an empty spot near the edge of the book about aquatic plants. "Alright, only a couple more hours until our first solo mission. You ready to help me practice some more?"

Tuff flew in the air and did his little superhero stance, making me giggle. "Good. Let's get to work."

The sun had yet to hue the sky with reds and oranges when I came to the Balthiers, and Valhalla was waiting for me on her front porch. Her black hair was a little tangled, and she wore boots similar to mine, a green shirt, and gray shorts. Down by her waist and attached to her belt was a holstered dagger; I didn't even know she had weapons in her house, let alone that she was allowed to use one.

"Do I get a weapon?" I asked her, trying to make a joke but also half-serious.

"Some of us don't have powerful rock-flying magic," she said, rolling her eyes. "Besides, it's *just* in case you need my help, though I highly doubt it. Now, let's hurry up and get going before it gets too late."

"What did you tell your parents we were doing?" I asked as we descended the hill of their grassy neighborhood.

"I just left a note saying I'm celebrating your Two-Month Magic Training Anniversary. I think we will make it home before they read it, but I still wanted a backup plan if we take too long."

"You didn't have to lie—"

"Says the one who lives in a secret town with secret powers and can't even tell her *own* mom." Valhalla laughed, and I couldn't help but agree.

We walked through the main downtown street of Calendula and passed the large fountain in its center. There was a secret entrance to Raglan down the northern neighborhood for residents only, so no Veradome carts were around for trading. We approached a wooden sign that said "Raglan" at the end of the sidewalk, pointing right in between two streetlights. Valhalla led me through, and just like the Boolavogue Outskirts Forest entrance, we instantly stepped foot into another town.

"Look, ahead," Valhalla said, pointing down the hillside mountain we were standing on. I squinted through the trees and saw a small rustic town lying in the valley's center. Farther ahead, even more so in the valley, was the center of Raglan—easily recognizable because of the wide-open fields for their wooly cattle. "Down this mountain is the Rura village, much more spread out, and where we will find Claggan's Farm."

"How exactly do you know so much about Raglan? It just seems to have a lot of forests and fewer streets—I dunno how you don't get lost," I said, amazed at Valhalla's adult-like sense of direction.

"When Mom and Dad are off work, we sometimes just like to explore here since it's so close, and I started remembering all the trails after a while. I've been here a lot during the day, but not at night... so I'm counting on you to finish this goat-attacking monster up quick."

"No pressure or anything," I joked as Valhalla led us down the mountain.

The pathways were all made of dirt with looming tree branches until we reached the bottom when small gravel trails formed. We walked a good bit before finally reaching the main hub of Rura, which was just a squad of eight homes and two goat farms—one of which was Claggan's Farm. I didn't see how kids went to school out here… or if there were even kids. Most of the residents and farmers looked middle-aged with no signs of smiles, all smelling like hay and wet goat fur.

Claggan's Farm was a small wooden house with a large goat stable and field built right up against it. We saw a similar hand-drawn "help wanted" sign nailed to their front porch. *Guess no one else wanted to take the job just yet. Glad Valhalla made us come early.* Valhalla knocked, and after a couple of seconds, a skinny, sunburnt, sad-looking man answered the door. His gray eyebrows almost covered his eyes, so I stared at his scraggly-bearded mouth as he talked.

"What yur want?" he said in a raspy voice.

Valhalla then unfolded the "helped wanted" poster she snagged from the request board. "We are here to stop the monster who is killing your goats, sir," she said, very assertive.

Mr. Claggan looked us both up and down before giving his honest thoughts. "Yur gon' stop 'at monster from killin' mah goats? Yur not ev'n tall 'nuff to reach the top a mah frige'ator." Whenever he articulated a "t," orbs of spit came flying out of his mouth.

"Mr. Claggan—" Valhalla grabbed my arm and pointed at my face. "You see this girl! She's got not one but *two* types of magic—powerful ones at that. Lisa can stop whatever it is that's killing your goats!"

My face started to blush from the embarrassment. "It's uh, true, sir. I promise I can save your goats and your farm."

"Well, if yur say so. Out back, pas' the fall'n oak trees is where mah goats star'ed disppearin'. Dunno what it is… missin' five goats and found two with claw marks down the sides. Prolly a wild dog, but I can't kill 'em like I used tuh. Come back with its limp body, an I'll give ya forty credits fer helpin' mah farm."

"Thank you, sir! Lisa will handle this no problem and before it gets too dark!"

The old man grunted and went back into his house. He didn't seem too surprised that two teenage girls offered to kill the monster attacking his farm. Still, I was glad he didn't turn us away.

Valhalla and I followed his home's makeshift path to the back of his farm. Most of the goats were outside, climbing on old benches and eating the grass, not very interested in us. I saw a couple of them near a fallen oak tree, and when we passed by, I heard them talking about not going near "The Cave."

"Valhalla, is there a cave nearby?" I asked her. "The goats were talking about it, saying it's not safe."

"I totally forgot you can hear what animals are thinking! And don't know for sure, but it's probably not too far from here. Man, your magic sure comes in handy!" Valhalla responded, more excited than I was about the whole mission.

Past the goats and the fallen oak tree led straight into the woods behind Mr. Claggan's farm. A mountain was nearby, so we made that our heading, hoping to find the cave the goats whispered about. Valhalla stayed close to me as the sky grew cloudy and our trail disappeared. Everything was quiet besides a couple of birds chirping. I was hoping to hear a goat in the distance or even the potential vorrg.

We passed by a large tree, and at its base, I saw a couple of flies zooming around some type of animal on the ground. Upon close examination, we realized it was one of Mr. Claggan's goats... dead. It had a large slash down its neck and side, but I couldn't make myself look for too long.

"If it was hurt this bad, it couldn't have run that far from its attacker," I hypothesized, turning my attention to Valhalla.

"I'm no monster expert either, but I don't see why a vorrg would let its prey go?" Valhalla questioned as we both tried not to stare too long at the dead goat. "I mean... it was a *goat* after all. I don't see it being too much of a hassle to chase down."

"Hmm... then why let it escape..." I wondered out loud.

"Lisa, look! You can see a trail of its blood! This must not be but a day old since this happened," Valhalla exclaimed, pointing farther ahead and toward the bottom of the woodland mountain.

The stream of blood wasn't very long and stopped near the shady side of another tree, right near the start of the mountainous incline. We were about to go up when Valhalla noticed the grass looked worn down just a few feet ahead. We shifted our course and saw that the newfound trodden path was imprinted with sporadic footprints. Some were goat-hooves prints, but one set was the most unfamiliar and smudged away. Neither of us knew what a vorrg paw print looked like (Gaius not noting that in his book), so we agreed that's what it had to be.

Out of nowhere, we heard the yelp of a goat coming from the side of the mountain—right where the trail was leading. Valhalla grabbed my arm from the sudden yell, as did Tuff—who decided to come out of his invisible hiding and help light our way. In moments, another goat cry came from beneath the cliff. I could feel my stomach growing nauseous as I heard the goat's yell in my mind turn into a plea for, *"Help me,"* before the scream died down.

If it weren't for Valhalla being there, I would've run—*booked* it back to Gaius and apologized to the old Mr. Claggan. But she believed in me. She believed I could do it, and I *needed* to do it if I wanted to be a Hero and prove to the Guardians I was strong enough for the Agapéd magic. *I defeated that bírokavaran on my own. I can defeat a simple vorrg... or two...*

We three, shaking and staying close together, ambled to the sound as all our senses were on high alert. I could feel Valhalla's heart race as she clung closely to my side, making me feel not as bad for being just as scared.

Like the goats said, a cave *was* hidden amongst dangled ivy and emerald moss. We could hear something inside, but it wasn't goat sounds... and the fact I couldn't hear another animal's thoughts meant it had to be a dark magic creature (Inna informed me that I could only hear *animals* and not magic creatures with my magic). *Please let there be only one monster...*

Tuff made his little gem glow as we entered the cave, shaking orange dust all over my shoulder. It was damp, dark, and cold... smelling of something putrid that could make one vomit. The walls were jagged with water trickling down the sides, creating slick puddles on the ground. We kept our composure and walked further down the rocky tunnel.

There was a small glow from a fire ahead. *Vorrgs can make fires, right?*

I was too nervous to ask Valhalla for fear of summoning the monster, and Tuff didn't know either, so we just kept walking.

At that moment, we turned a corner, the same direction as the dimly lit flame, and came upon the goat-attacker... and it was no vorrg. She stood tall and had patches of hairy skin the color of gangrene, all covered in mud and blood. Her hands were large with bloody claws, and her legs were muscular like a dog's but with large feet and claws like a bat's. Her hair was matted and black as charcoal, covering most of her face, which was eating the bloody meat of one of Mr. Claggan's goats.

Though her body was shaped like one, she was no human. She was a dark fiend—one I recognized from one of Gaius' creature books, one that used to be human before being consumed with dark magic. A *vezper*... and we three had trespassed into her domain.

This... this is all wrong...

24

THE CAVE

Valhalla and I froze as the vezper slowly geared her head toward us. With the fire flickering, it was easy to see the details of the female creature, and I couldn't help but look; I instantly regretted that decision. Her mouth leered, showing us her fanged canine teeth, dripping drops of blood down her face as she tossed the ravaged goat to the floor. My body flinched when the poor animal hit the ground and splashed on a puddle—as if it were nothing but a piece of trash.

No—no this can't be happening. Every nerve in my body stood on high alert—my heart not knowing whether to stop or speed. Blinking wasn't happening. Running was foreign to my legs—buckling with Valhalla clinging to me for dear life. No magic was coming from my fingers or hands either. Every single piece of me was cemented to the cave floor, even the magic pulse intertwined with my heart, and I could do nothing but stare at the horror in front of me. Utterly. Undeniably. Petrified.

Her eyes were black just like her hair, paralyzing us with their eerie glare. "Well, this is quite a pleasant surprise," the she-monster hissed.

I was not expecting the vezper to talk, especially not so articulately.

"Didn't even have to wait for the sun to go down to gather me some dinner… you're much better than some mangy shepherd's goats."

"W-we just got lost. We aren't looking for any trouble and will be going now—" I began to plead, trying to slowly back away, but the vezper did not like that.

She then glanced down at Valhalla's dagger latched onto her shorts, then at the potion I had in my jacket pocket. Her face changed, not falling for my lost-in-the-woods lie.

No—

"You've come to stop me from ravaging that farmer's goats, haven't you? A couple of pale, pathetic children like yourself think you're a match for me—I think *not*," she said to us, starting to climb away from the jagged rock she was sitting on by the fire.

At that moment, my shackles of fear fell, and Valhalla and I fully sprinted toward the cave entrance, but the vezper had superhuman speed. She blocked our path. Valhalla and I jerked back, screamed, and huddled together. The she-beast was six feet tall and fueled by dark magic as she towered over us. We both huffed and huffed, the panic in our chests rising with each passing second. We knew we were on the edge of a blade, one wrong slip away from being *killed*.

The vezper breathed her vile breath onto our faces. "Why leave so soon?" she toyed with us. "Didn't you come here to stop me?"

"A-and Lisa sure can!" Valhalla uttered, mustering up her courage, though I wish she didn't say my name. "Sh-she's got the most powerful magic out there and can easily take you down!"

The vezper's eyes shifted toward me, black holes the size of golf balls, lustful for both blood and magic. "*Magic*, you say? In you—in your blood? No, wait..." She stepped even closer, smelling me. "It's in your *heart*, isn't it?"

What do I do? What do I actually do! I'd been training for two months, but my body stood motionless before her. That heroism I thought I had was gone. I was a helpless child facing a heinous monster—a nightmare come to life—and I had no idea what to do. My arms couldn't throw rock. My hands couldn't swipe a spike of water. Fear and fright disabled all my magic, and I was nothing but a useless human. *Why is this happening? Come on, Lisa! Just do something!*

She prowled even closer, her hot breath sniping through her jagged teeth, leering at terrified little me. "I haven't had a good ounce of *pure* bloody magic in so long. So, why don't you just let me take yours—"

Out of nowhere, Valhalla released her grip from my arm, whipped out her dagger, and gunned for the monster—aimed to stab the beast— just as the vezper began to make an aim for my heart. Valhalla ran straight toward her gray and hairy chest, but the magic-blood eater was quicker. The vezper swung her razor-sharp claws right toward Valhalla, slashing her upper body and sending her flying across the opposite end of the cave. All in the span of three seconds—

"*Valhalla!*" I yelled as I saw her body hit the floor three times with an unsettling thud. *Smack! Smack... smack...* I couldn't see her face by the way she landed, just the back of her head... but I saw blood.

NO—

My breathing staggered—was I breathing? My heart throbbed, beating so loud it would have shaken the mountain we were under, but it, instead, rattled every bone in my body.

That's her—that's Valhalla right there. This can't be happening right now—she was trying to protect me! Please don't be... she is my best friend, and she has to come back home with me!

The vezper lurched for me next with her long, bloody claws, smiling at me as if she was enjoying every second of my pain. I backed up far—almost slipping on the damp cave floor—and took out the potion I had in my pocket. My mind was running on pure adrenaline and whatever instincts I had acquired over the past month, doing what it needed to survive.

Being a reasonable distance away before she ran toward me again, I threw the bottle at her—using the magic in my muscles to help with my momentum— hoping just for a couple of seconds of a diversion.

The Gangdra Draught smashed right up against her stomach and released a red smoke bomb. The scarlet mist began to swirl into her ears as if she were a vacuum before letting out an ear-piercing ring. To me, the activated potion only sounded like a car alarm; to her, it shook her brain like an earthquake. She yelled and fell to the ground momentarily. Plenty of time for me.

"Tuff!" I whispered in heavy breaths. "You have to go get help—someone from the town—anyone! Show them your memories and lead them here—*please hurry!*"

Tuff was as scared as I was and hated to leave my side, shaking like a flimsy tree in the wind. Seeing the situation and knowing my worry, he ignored his fear and nodded quickly before teleporting away.

It was just me and the vezper now.

I wanted to run straight for the exit—wanted to leave and never come back—but Valhalla was still there. I didn't know how badly she was hurt or if she... my thoughts stopped before fear cemented me to the floor again. No matter how much my legs trembled and my stomach turned into nauseous knots, I couldn't leave. I had to fight. I had to survive. There was no other choice, and I needed to either win or stall long enough for Tuff to get help.

"You vile, pathetic, little *maggot!*" the vezper yelled, rubbing her matted hair and scratching at her head. Her sinister smile turned into a snarl as she looked ready to attack.

Though I was afraid, I now had a plan. I had something to lean on— something to grasp instead of terror freezing me solid again—and needed to defend long enough for help to arrive.

I stood my ground, manipulated the stone floor below, and shot beefy bullets of rock at her, fast and with as much force as I could. She dodged those easier than I expected as I watched the baseball-sized stones crumble against the wall, and she came flying right toward me. My right hand flung forward, a rock column plunging from the ground next. It pushed her back against the cave wall, pinning her tight. I thought I had a little more time to run toward Valhalla to see if she was okay with the creature stuck, but the vezper broke my column with her bare hands—breaking the rock like a toothpick. She was strong—very, very strong.

I didn't even have time to make it one step before the angered monster lunged and grabbed my leg—swinging me across the wet cave floor.

Thud. Thud. Thud—I loosely counted three rolls on the hard cave floor before she was already back over me with her lengthy claws—mid-swing.

With just one clean sweep of her hand's bony talons, the vezper ripped four gashes across my stomach.

CRACK!

I *shrieked* from the intense pain—feeling nothing but an overpowering sting and burn in my stomach, not even letting my head recover from my thundering crash on the cave floor. Each gash was deep, breaking ribs and painting her claws red. My shirt turned wet fast, but I couldn't tell if it was blood or water from the cave's floor. There was no time to check because she was about to pin me down and finish collecting my magic heart.

My body was aching—screaming for me to stay down—but my heart was not giving up, not when Valhalla risked her own safety for mine. I didn't care about the pain at that moment—didn't care a single bit. *I am not going to die tonight!*

As the bloody vezper hung over me—just about to kill me, take out my heart, and suck out my magic blood—I switched my tactics and shot the cave water upward toward the beast—freezing it into a colossal beefy spike. The vezper couldn't react fast enough, and the toothed icicle penetrated the torso of the monster. She wailed in pain, sounding like the screeching of an angry bat, and dark black blood started dripping down the frozen spike.

I thought I won—bested the monster all by myself—but she whipped her muscled legs forward and crushed the ice!

How is she still moving!

I tried to get up, using my right arm to push me off the ground, but my vision blurred, and my head turned dizzy. I looked down at my tattered shirt as the vezper regained her balance. It was a sickening scarlet. *That's... that's a lot of blood.*

The demon-like vampire then slammed me on my back—whacked me like a fly on a wall—and pinned me by my wrists. I yelled hard—not even recognizing my own voice—from the pain of my frail skin hitting the rocky cave floor. Bones *snapped* in my wrists, and I screamed again, feeling a fear and misery that I didn't even know existed.

Her face was one from nightmares as it hung over the top of me, breathing bile-smelling breath onto my cheeks as I wallowed in pain. "You can't be dying on me right now—I need that magic heart of yours!" the vezper hissed.

Without warning, she then sunk her bloody teeth into the tender skin of my left forearm. I thought the pain from her slash and my broken wrists was bad, but it was nothing compared to her glowing venom infusing into my bloodstream. It *burned* like blue fire being injected into my veins. Even though my body was losing life, I still had enough energy to scream and let out bloody tears from the pain.

I wanted it to stop. I wanted—I wanted relief like no other. My body was breaking into pieces, being drained dry as if she was trying to get the last sip out of her favored drink. My face was stuck in pain, yelling and crying—*please just make it stop!*

I noticed that her poison began to slow down my bleeding, my body going numb, and, in turn, giving her enough time to carve out my heart.

This... this can't be how I die!

As the vezper's clawed hand began to make its way toward the left side of my chest, a huge emerald sword bolted like a lightning strike from behind me and stabbed the creature. My vision was growing blurrier, but I saw the sword move with so much force that when it punctured the vezper, it sent her flying and pinned her to the cave wall—the blade going right through rock!

An orange glow emerged and came toward me, a familiar tangerine color that gave my fading heart a glimmer of hope, followed by running footsteps and a glimpse of a brown leather jacket.

It was Gaius.

Tuff did it... He brought help in just in time...

I saw the fierce Keeper instantly take the green sword out from the vezper's chest and reach his hand down to his herbage weaponry belt. I didn't recognize any of the plants he kept in the bottles, but the one he moved with his magic blossomed with a yellow glow. The flower breathed a sharp, bright light onto the vezper—as bright as a flash bomb. In just seconds, the fiendish creature let out a blood-curdling yell as the flower's sun rays incinerated every last piece of her body. She was finished. Gaius slew the vezper, hardly even breaking a sweat.

He then rushed right over to me, frightened—a new emotion of his I never wanted to see.

I think I started crying, but the pain from my torn stomach and vezper's poison was killing me too fast for me to feel any form of tears running down my face.

"Gaius... I-I'm sorry," I whimpered as best I could. "Pl-please tell me... Valhalla's okay?"

Gaius looked back at her for just a moment but didn't go running. "It's you I'm worried about," he said, trying to sound calm, but his voice began to crack, and his eyes looked as glossy as the wet cave floor.

"Gaius... p-please... please don't let me die..." I softly cried, watching as the details of his face began to blur.

I needed to live. Valhalla needed to live. She would never see her parents again... all because of me... and I just stood there while the vezper ripped her apart. *I have to see her again... I have to see Mom again... I can't die here... not like this...*

The light from the vezper's fire pit and Tuff's glow began to fade away, as did the burning sensation from the poison... but it wasn't because Gaius was healing me. I knew he couldn't evanesce me away as badly injured as I was, and it's not like Tuff knew I would be bitten for Gaius to bring an antidote. As I felt my heart beating slower and slower, I began to see the final moments of my life slip away. The last image I saw before my eyes couldn't stay open any longer was Gaius producing a red aura with his chest and hands. It was warm... the last bit of warmth my body felt...

Then, I died.

25
THE AGAPÉD'S TRUE PURPOSE

Wh... why do I... feel... so... tired? Did I...? I did die... right? Then... why do I feel... like... I've been rudely woken up... from a summer's nap... and with a large crick down my spine?

Soft sounds of trickling water echoed. I couldn't tell if I was floating in a bath or lying across a bed, but I was warm... and slightly itchy in my stomach. My eyes slowly opened, feeling as if they were weighed down with lead fishing pole sinkers. I had a full view of the ceiling. Lush, vibrant pothos and pearled vines painted the columned rafters and filled the shimmering windows. A sherbet view of the sky was above me, right through the elegant sunroof, with purple flower petals wafting through the air. *This looks oddly familiar...*

My hands moved easily—no signs of broken wrists to be found—and I quickly realized I was lying on a lounge chair, feeling its feathered cushion with my clean palms. Once the muscles in my neck woke up, I turned over to look toward the sound of the flowing water. It was a hot spring trickling ripples a couple of feet from me. I had never seen that pool before, but everything else in the room made my memories shuffle around...

Either I'm in Haim Gana... or the afterlife has extremely similar interior designs as the Elysium.

An orange glow suddenly flew up next to my cheek, rubbing sparkling dust all over my face. It was Tuff, filled with happy tears in his eyes and thrilled that I was finally awake.

"I'm glad to see you're alright, Lisa," a lady's voice said from the other side of me, cold and calm.

I turned to see Lady Ariela glowing with golden light like normal, proving I was in the Elysium and not dead. She was sitting on a chair near me, her flowing dress almost brushing against my shoulders as she stared intently at my face.

Sitting right next to her was a man. At first, I didn't recognize him, seeing as my brain was still waking up. His back was hunched over as his forearms leaned on his kneecaps with fingers intertwined loosely. Then, his brown hair and muscly frame resurfaced memories. It was Gaius... but something about him was off. Never in my life had I seen his body language so dejected.

"How did I...?" I started to say to Ariela when I instantly remembered that I *clearly* died what felt like five minutes ago. "I thought I was—"

"Dead?" Ariela had anticipated the topic. "You were—or rather, you were caught in the liminal realm of life and death. Your body faded, but before your soul could leave you... you were saved by a miracle."

With the help of the golden Elysian, I slowly sat upright to face her properly as she talked, causing Tuff to snuggle up to me in my lap. That was when I noticed my stomach. Besides the fact I was wearing a rolled-up white tank top and elegant shorts to match—resembling the attire most of the Guardians wore—there were no deep gashes or stitched-up wounds! Only four large pink scars remained, extending from my lower right hip bone to right under my left armpit. I also noticed the bite mark was nothing but violet-red blemishes with no traces of poison to be found.

Ariela continued to look at me with more sorrow than joy in her eyes. "You're probably wondering how your injuries healed so fast. I can assure you that when Gaius brought you here, you were almost completely healed—little to do with me. However, you were in a deep sleep for quite a while."

Dizzy and groggy, I asked, "Really? How long was I, uh, out for?"

"As of now, it is early afternoon on Friday, so that makes it just about two days," Ariela said. "Gaius carried you in here not too long ago, saying he waited for you to wake up back at his home, but after a day, he brought you to me."

I was knocked out for two days? It only felt like a couple of minutes!

Lady Ariela's golden-leaf earrings chimed as she turned her head to look over at Gaius.

He couldn't look back.

She touched his knee on his grass-stained pants and warmly said, "He hasn't left your side and refused to sleep even though I assured him you would be just fine. However, the dark magic from the vezper's poison needed more attending to. This room, the Onsen, is meant for me and the Guardians to rid ourselves from Darkness, so you've been here with me as I've been using the Onsen's water to help cleanse its remnants. I do apologize for the scarring. Magic-inflicted scars are permanent, I'm afraid. No matter, a simple concealment charm will cover those right up."

I took a moment to process what she said, still feeling dazed from my post-death nap. "How did I heal then… if you didn't seal up my wounds?" My words were slow as my brain tried to comprehend everything.

Ariela lifted her hand and rubbed the wound on my arm one last time. Some of the purples faded, but it was still unseemly to look at.

She then looked over to the Keeper of Stars before turning her gaze back to me. "I will have you and Gaius talk amongst yourselves about that night and why you are still alive with us today, but first… there is something I think it's time for you to know. The Guardians and I had agreed to keep this suppressed from you until the time was right, in fear of the Agapéd leaving your heart. Though, in light of unwelcoming circumstances, I believe you need to hear it…"

Lady Ariela released a deep breath before continuing, a demeanor I thought only humans did. "The Agapéd Magic that came to you was created for a purpose, one of which demands the whole life of the person it's bestowed upon."

Ariela showed me her magical illustrations again as she continued, though they were notably black instead of her usual gold. "About 500 years ago, a little over a century after I chose the last of the Keepers, a dark power began to rise. It was Darkness in the form of my three fallen siblings' magic—Armaita, Saraqiel, and Gadreel. Their magic was most desirable by Man with hearts that were lustful for power, glory, and immoral magic. Fallen Elysian magic consumed these human hearts—gifting them unfathomable power and a darkened magic pulse. They began to rain terror over the planets, but my Guardians couldn't stop them."

"How come?" I asked, cuddling Tuff in the palms of my hands as he continued to rest in my lap.

"Because I didn't want to repeat the past, I made sure when I formed the Guardians that their magic could not harm me or each other, meaning their power was useless against the Fallen. I thought to intervene, but since dark magic overtook the hearts of Man, I could not harm them, for, you see, I cannot harm a human in fear of dark magic overtaking me as well."

The illustrations then turned from black to a warming shade of orange. "I came to Ranemir and asked him to gift us a magic strong enough to defend against the Fallen and also strong enough to destroy the magic pulse the Fallen had attached itself to. Lisa, you may not know this, but I can only create magic that already exists in our worlds, and no other magic on any planet was powerful enough to fight against the Fallen. It was then that The Light created a magic—stronger than any other—specifically designed and infused with Ranemir's light to fight against Darkness residing in the power of the Fallen."

Her gleaming ember eyes fixed on me as I began to put all the pieces together. I was breathy when I said, "And that's the Agapéd... isn't it?"

Ariela nodded and ended her illustrations. "The Agapéd is the only power in all existence that can destroy the magic pulse—the heart—the Fallen has bound itself to. It is meant to destroy the Fallen Elysian magic, making it release back into the galaxy to bring peace. For 500 years, this has been the cycle... but then, we saw no sign of the Agapéd for over a century. Lisa, I said before, during our first meeting, that the Agapéd comes when it's needed... which means it chooses a heart when it senses Darkness approaching. When it picked you, it was picking the symbol of hope and eradicator of Darkness."

Ariela grinned softly as she touched my freckled shoulder with her right hand, but her emotion was more of a solemn sympathy. "You were meant to be a warrior, so when a small little girl walked into our meeting, we all were overcome with worry and fear... To put the weight of the worlds on your shoulders... Lisa, it was something we thought you could not handle. That is why we sent you to train in secret with Inna and Gaius. We wanted you to learn magic because of pure *joy* and *curiosity*, not out of fear or the entitlement of becoming our freer of Darkness. If you were to fear the Agapéd... it would have never trusted your heart and left again for possibly another hundred years. We couldn't afford that risk... so we kept everything secret to keep you safe. But... it still seemed Darkness found a way to interfere, causing you grave anguish and a life almost cut short..."

The golden glow in her eyes dimmed with a sadness I didn't know she could emit. "I am truly sorry for not telling you this before... feeling as if this could have been prevented if I had not suggested that we all cloak you with the veil of innocence. I hope you do forgive me—all of us."

With all Ariela said to me... everything began to make sense. She didn't want me to expose my magic for fear of the Darkness finding out. The Guardians discouraged fighting because they didn't want to see me die and lose their one chance of destroying the Fallen Elysian magic. All of them were worried... and I couldn't be mad at Ariela for that. If she would have told me all that on the first day, I do believe my view on magic would have been different; I would've been terrified, probably never fully trusting the Agapéd to bond with my heart. They wanted a warrior, so I couldn't blame them for pitying me and wishing for another chosen heart, either.

But... now that I knew everything and what my true purpose was... Could I even do it? *Can I really be the warrior they are wanting?*

"So, I'm meant to vanquish the universe's most powerful dark magic..." I said, staring at the top of Tuff's head as my chin drooped down, doubting whether or not I could live up to their expectations.

My gaze couldn't help but look over to the Keeper sitting next to the lady in gold. Glancing up to see his face, now unshadowed by his unbent back, the green eyes that always seemed to shine like a peridot gem were scribbled with bloody veins as thin as hair. Dark rims of violet sagged under his eyes, and his smile was nonexistent. Gaius truly did stay awake all day and night... all because of me.

Ariela softly grabbed my hands with both of hers. Her fingers were comforting, like a warm blanket. "Do not worry about the future, dear Lisa. It has enough problems of its own. When the time comes, you'll be ready, but that choice is entirely up to you. Now, I must meet with the others and let them know you are alright..."

As she stood up, her gold wings appearing and extending high and low, she smiled down at Tuff as his little orange body sat on my lap. "Tuff, correct?"

I answered for my sprite. "Yes, ma'am."

"Would it be alright if he joined me? His memories of that evening of you and the vezper would prove useful for the Guardians to see."

Tuff was finally calm, though his little black eyes were still wide and glossy. I wasn't sure why she needed to show them the memories of the fight, but I didn't question her.

I held my little orange glainie in my palms and up to my nose. "It's okay, Tuff. I'll join you soon. I promise."

He nodded his body and floated to Ariela's side. The golden Elysian then smiled at Gaius and me. "I will return soon when we are ready to see you both."

As her sun-lit dress and wings trailed out the door with my glainie flying not too far behind, silence entered the Onsen. Gaius was sitting across from me with his back hunched over again. Looking in my direction seemed impossible for him to do. I didn't talk, either. How could I after everything I just heard? Comprehending the situation was a lot to take in, and the questions kept piling up about why my body was alive... but one ran across my mind that I needed to know the answer to most of all.

Before I had time to ask, Gaius said in a deep, hoarse voice, "You alright?"

I looked down at my freckled kneecaps as my legs hung off the cushioned bench. My voice cracked, and I ignored Gaius's question, asking, "Valhalla, is she... okay?"

Gaius let loose a deep breath, his eyes still on the floor. Not getting an answer quickly sent my mind into a frenzy. Fear punctured my heart, and tears started to gloss my eyes. *No... please don't be... she can't—*

"When I came to you," he began, somber with his gaze still on the floor, "you were minutes away from bleeding out and dying from the vezper's poison. There wasn't enough time for me to go and grab an antidote, and I didn't have the ability to heal your wounds with how deep they were. I couldn't..." Gaius bit his lip, even at the thought of continuing his explanation. "I couldn't let you die, so I took a risk—the only thing I could think of. I cast the Un-Immortal Heart charm upon you and me both."

My chin slowly lifted, staring at his thick, wavy hair as he looked toward the floor. *He—he what?*

Gaius continued, "It was a gamble, but I had no other choice. I had no clue what would happen to me or you." His green eyes finally met mine. Glossed and straining, needing sleep. "But I couldn't just sit there and watch you die."

I placed my hand over my heart, feeling its beats—feeling its life. "You mean... your charm to give up immortality in exchange... for life... worked... and you used it... on me?"

He slowly nodded. "After I performed the Un-Immortal Heart charm on us both, my body had to accommodate itself to a mortal heart. It caused me to pass out, and when I awoke, it was already morning..."

I clenched my fists that lay on my lap. *Please don't say it... please don't...*

"... and she had passed."

My heart plummeted like a meteor, and my eyes couldn't blink—frozen as terror took over every emotion in my body. *This can't be real—this can't be happening...* Everything turned murky as tears swelled, and my eyes returned to the ground.

"Her wounds were fatal, so even if I tended to her sooner, there still was nothing I could have done," Gaius said. "I was able to use vivaroots to seal up her wounds before letting her family see her..." He paused for a moment, maybe to look at me or to look away. I couldn't tell because my face was sunken to the floor. "I'm sorry, Lisa..."

Darkness overtook every part of me. And I sank. Tears fell fast down my cheeks, dripping onto my knuckles and thighs like pitiful, pathetic raindrops, as I let out not just the emotions of losing my best friend, but all from the bottled-up fear of my new life and feeling like Gaius wasted his immortal heart charm on me. I was utterly hopeless. I—I didn't deserve to live.

Everything... everything is just—just completely—

"It's all my fault," I sobbed hard, continuously using my hands to clean my face to no avail, my voice resembling a pitiful pig drowning in mud. "It's my fault she's—she's gone, and I just watched her die... She was my best friend. W-why did I even bring her with me into that stupid cave? And—and then I made you give up your eternal heart t-to save me... you could've saved Jules all those years ago—but now... but now, it's *wasted* on me..."

Ariela's words about my true purpose drowned my thoughts—everything about me being the Agapéd Bearer. I was sinking fast into a shadowing abyss of fear and guilt. I didn't deserve to be there. I didn't deserve the beating of Gaius' pulse in my chest. And I definitely didn't deserve to be called the Bearer of Hope—this chosen one they all waited so long for. *I failed to fight a vezper—how am I ever going to be able to save the world?*

I was weak, and I just let my best friend die and caused the man in front of me to give up his eternal heart. Her parents—*Roy and Emmeryn*—*w-what did they think?*

No—no. I just took their daughter away from them—I killed her. I ruined their family, their precious loving family, and slashed it to pieces. And I hated myself—hated everything about me—

The curled locks of my hair that dangled over my shoulders were now sprinkled with salty tears. "They were right." My palms pressed into my eyes, trying to barricade the ocean of tears from breaking through, but nothing was working. "I can't—I can't do this. I can't be this hero they are wanting." I started shaking, disgusted with myself. "The Agapéd was wrong. The Agapéd was *all wrong.* What kind of friend—" My voice quivered as my heart trembled, and my fingers curled up into fists on my eyes, scratching my cheeks, the tears never ceasing. "What kind of friend am *I* t-to just have stood there and done *nothing*? I did *nothing*, and she's gone. I'm sorry... It's all completely my fault... I'm so, so, sorry—"

Gaius rushed right over to me—facing me head-on—and clasped his hands on my shoulders quite forcefully. The jolt made me look right up at my mentor, watching his eyes fixate on my blotchy, pathetically red face as I continued to sob.

"Do not blame yourself for the evil that is in this world, Lisa," Gaius affirmed. "Darkness is what killed your friend, not you, so don't you dare let its dark power influence your mind into thinking it was your fault."

"But it was—"

"Bad things will always happen to those who follow Light, for Darkness can't stand to see it shine... and Lisa, your heart has the strongest light of all. I know right now you are hurting, but no matter what... you have to keep on living. Your life isn't precious because of some sheer luck of a charm; it's precious because *you're* worth living for."

"But—but you could have used the charm for that girl you loved—"

He gripped my shoulders tighter, careful not to pull my hair, as his voice breathed more raspy emotion. "*You* are far more worth saving than for something as selfish as young love, and I've already lived hundreds of lifetimes over. You deserve to at least finish out the only one you've got."

I tried to stop crying, but my tears of misery started to mix in with tears of happiness from the overwhelming love Gaius made me feel.

Why—why is he being so kind to me after what I did? I'm gonna fail—he saw that. I'm going to lose to Darkness and let everyone down—

"Lisa, you listen to me." His voice was stern, and his gaze was unfazed by my sappy face. "I promise I'm going to train you well so that one day, you'll be one class of a Hero and the best Agapéd Bearer there ever was—you understand? You aren't alone in this. No matter how tough it will be, keep your head held high and know I am here for you. I will *always* be here for you. So, please..." Gaius used his calloused thumb to wipe away one of the tears on my left cheek. Its subtle warmth, his caring fingerprinted touch, it was more than I deserved. "Don't shed any more tears."

I took a deep breath as my waterfall sobbing began to dry up, slowly regaining composure. Hearing Gaius' confidence in himself and in me was reviving my heart, and my emotions began to settle. He never spoke like that to me before... *no one* had ever spoken to me like that before... and I honestly didn't know he cared so much for me. *To give up his immortal life... for me? He... he really did that...* I never expected to be in a situation where the fate of the worlds was placed on my shoulders, but I knew if he was there, I could do anything.

"If you keep making me feel so good about myself"—I sniffled—"I won't be able to stop crying." A grin finally emerged amid my tears, followed by a light titter.

Gaius returned the small gesture, his cheeks returning to their peachy tan and green eyes glistening again. "I pour out my heart, all for you to just make a joke about it... suppose it's better than nothing at all."

I took a deep breath. "Thanks, Gaius," I said, making another big sniffle as I stared up at him.

As I was wiping my face, Tuff zoomed back into the room, knocking into my shoulder. His orange dust sprinkled all over me before I hugged him. "Thank you too, bud. If it wasn't for you, I wouldn't be here."

Tuff snuggled up to my cheek before perching himself on my shoulder.

"Care to join us?" a voice said from behind.

Near the entrance of the room was Lady Ariela. Gaius and I immediately stood up, though my eyes stayed on the floor. My face was an ugly red. Didn't need to look at myself in a mirror to prove that—embarrassed for Lady Ariela to see me.

The brawny Keeper walked next to Ariela as I followed behind with my glainie. We passed through the Elysium halls when Ariela said to Gaius, "I showed them the memories from Tuff of Lisa and the vezper and spoke of the charm you cast. Have to say, they were more appalled than impressed with your actions: exchanging your immortal heart for a mortal one."

"No surprise," Gaius said, his stoic emotions back to normal, though maybe a little more pensive than usual, "the lot caring more about magic than a human heart. It's my life and my soul. I have every right to do what I please with it. What did they say about Lisa and the Agapéd?"

My eyes widened, staring at my clean boots, as we entered the room with the stone statue of the man fighting the shadow creature.

"Though a few of them were impressed by her actions, it seemed they said what you would expect. They believe Lisa has already proven to them that she isn't ready for the weight of the Agapéd's magic, thinking it should seek out a new home... a new heart."

We began to cross the bridge that led to the golden meeting room door when my eyes couldn't help but droop even lower to the ground. My hair sagged over my shoulders as Tuff poked my face—attempting to cheer me up. Though I already knew their opinions of me, hearing them still confirm their uncertainty even after watching Tuff's memories pinched and probed my heart even more with doubt. *If they truly see me as weak and pathetic... then maybe it's true. They've been around for centuries, seen Darkness in all forms, and know how strong it can be... how strong I should be—*

Gaius' voice broke my self-torment, gritty and harsh. "Those heartless vorrgs—sorry, Lady Ariela."

"I see you believe otherwise?" Ariela questioned.

I peeled my eyes off the floor of the viaduct and looked over at her profile; she was grinning.

Gaius spoke as if I wasn't trailing behind him. "She's not expendable; she is human with a beating heart and genuine love for magic. Casting her aside like a useless puppet, using her when needed, and throwing her away when she wasn't enough for them... They don't see it, but the Agapéd made the right choice."

There wasn't much light left in my heart, but somehow, he rekindled the flame with mere rugged words when there seemed to be no more flint or tinder left to keep me from fading back into darkness. My face lit up, warm and still pink from crying, and when I lifted my chin to look at Gaius, he was already staring back at me over his shoulder. "Lisa can do it."

The Keeper of Stars had seen me fight, fall, and bleed until I died. He saw how weak I was against that bírokavaran, how hard it was for me to block his sparring attacks, and how feeble my emotions truly were. *And he still believes in me?* I couldn't see what he saw after everything that just happened. I couldn't see myself worthy enough for this... but he saw it. And Gaius wouldn't lie about that. Not a single bit.

"I see..." Ariela smiled as we approached the door. She then looked down at me, saying in a quieter tone as we stood at the foot of the golden entryway. "Now, Lisa, whatever happens in this meeting will be up to you, alright? I, the Guardians, and Gaius have our own opinions on the matter of the Agapéd, but when the time comes, it will be up to you whether or not you choose to have this life. I just want you to know that before stepping inside."

I took a deep breath and nodded, causing Ariela to reach for the door handle.

Inside were all seven Guardians. Most were sitting at the round table while Vilmad and Emunah were standing near the rim, seeming to be pacing the floor. All eyes peered right at me, even with Lady Ariela and her golden beauty by my side. My heart throbbed, but not from fear. I still wasn't sure about the answer I knew I needed to give.

Emunah spoke first as Ariela guided me to sit beside her, and Gaius stayed near the door. "I see that charm of yours worked perfectly, Gaius," the gray-haired, black-bearded Guardian said, acting as if the situation wasn't serious.

"One he had no right in casting," Vilmad muttered quite loudly under his breath. "Now, you walk amongst us mortal—taking the gift of immortality for granted like that."

Gaius stepped in front of Vilmad. His once tired, calm demeanor changed with the Guardian's remark as he snarled, "Without me, she would not be here... She'd still be lying on that cave floor."

"Without *you*, we wouldn't even *be* in this predicament in the first place!"

I sat and stared at my fiddling fingers in my lap, listening to the two argue and the other Guardians staying silent—seeming to forget I was even in the room. Seeing Gaius upset was a side of him I didn't like.

"If you never implanted in her mind that she was as powerful as a Lionheart, then she never would have run into the woods to begin with!" Vilmad continued.

"Put another lie in my mouth, Vilmad, and I'll—"

Ariela put her hand on my shoulder and held up the other, commanding the whole room's attention. "There is nothing to be done to change the past, and this meeting is to discuss what lies in the future. Lisa is alive and well now and knows what she must do." Ariela turned to face me. "We all here do care about your well-being and want what's best for you—please don't think otherwise, dear Lisa—and have come to the conclusion that offers you two choices."

Lady Ariela then tilted her head to Vilmad, motioning him to come over to me. His face wasn't pretty compared to Ariela's, and I knew his words wouldn't be as sweet. Still, I sat in solace as he glared down at me. "Assuming you now understand everything Lady Ariela has told you, most of us see fit that the Agapéd Magic may be more of a challenge than you had expected. So... we are offering you a choice once again."

My breathing felt heavy, and a lump of lead formed in my chest.

"One would be you returning the Agapéd Magic back to us—to keep hold of until it finds a new home," Vilmad said, his words smooth and silky, *wanting* me to listen... wanting me to *choose* whatever it was he had to say. "With the Magic not floating freely through the galaxy or inside of a Wishing Star, it may be able to find a more suitable heart to bear. With your full consent, we would then cast a memory charm over you, eliminating all memories of us, Haim Gana, and the Agapéd—everything about our magic worlds—and send you *home*. You won't have to worry or fear any longer... enjoying your life as normal."

Vilmad then crossed his arms and hurried his voice, biting each word. "The other option would be for you to continue your current path, now with all knowledge of what lies ahead. Most of us see it in your best interest to choose the path that leads you home... but we cannot force you; the choice is yours and yours alone."

So... I'll never remember that magic exists? I'll forget everything—all the friends and memories I've made... but that includes all the pain and sorrow as well...

I loved magic. I loved the feeling and purpose it gave me. I loved knowing the Guardians, Inna, Gaius, and the Balthiers... but I also knew I caused much doubt and heartache in those I loved, too. My body crumbled easily in front of that dark creature, and I had bigger monsters to face in the future, ones controlled by Darkness itself. They didn't like the uncertainty the Agapéd had made by picking me... and that didn't seem like it would ever change.

Maybe... I should just give it all up and go home...

Then, that small spark of light in my chest flickered again... and I looked right at the man who saved my life, those peridot green eyes still dry and worn.

And I remembered what Gaius said.

His opinion was the one I valued most because he was the one who knew me best. Out of everyone I had met... he taught me magic without my age or origin being an issue to complain about or to be concerned about. He guided me and showed me the reason why magic was meant to be loved, the purpose it had to save lives. Most of all, he believed in me—always had since the day I walked into his home.

If he thinks I can do it... then that is all the reason I need.

Looking at my fidgeting fingers—too nervous to face Vilmad's stare as I spoke—I slowly said in a quiet, confident voice, "You said that the Agapéd Magic waits and chooses a heart...and that it will wait as long as it takes until it finds the right one?"

"That is... presumed to be what we see as correct—" Vilmad reaffirmed, but I was already prepared for my follow-up question.

"And it chooses the heart, knowing all it will face, too, right?"

"I suppose one could put it that way—"

"So, even though the Agapéd knew I would struggle through learning magic with no experience beforehand, was weaker than any other of its predecessors—I assume anyway—and would constantly be facing death while knowing how physically weak I was... it still chose me."

Gaius turned to look at me and, along with the rest of the room, was too stunned to speak.

I honestly couldn't believe the wisdom coming out of my own mouth. "If it knew all that, then that must mean my heart is strong enough. So..." I looked directly up at Vilmad's stumped face, "I will keep it. I will keep the Agapéd and continue to follow its path for my life."

"Now *that's* a well-put answer," Emunah announced, grand and gallant, and

Vilmad stood speechless.

Ariela rose out of her seat, demanding the whole room's attention with just that simple movement. "With Lisa now knowing and accepting her true purpose, I believe we should have a change in our course of teaching, and I advocate *Gaius* be the sole instructor and for *him* to decide how Lisa should go about training."

What did she just say?

The utter incredulity and perplexity on everyone's face—including Gaius'— was unbelievable. No one would have guessed Ariela would say something like that, including me, but I was most thrilled about the new change.

Alona spoke, leaning onto the round table, her blonde hair falling on her shoulders, "Lady Ariela, are you sure about this? He's the one who *caused* all this—refused to listen to us, to *you!*"

Ariela calmly responded, "I'm more sure than I ever have been before."

Vilmad began to plead, "But it's not like Gaius will accept, and Wishing Star cultivation will start soon. He doesn't have enough time to—"

"I accept," Gaius said with his arms crossed, not letting Vilmad finish making excuses for him.

"Lady Ariela, I implore you to truly think about what you're doing," Vilmad whispered toward her. "Sure, he says yes, but don't we, too, get a say? And what about *her?* What if Lisa does not want this?"

"Lisa," Ariela said, ignoring that Vilmad was trying to whisper. "Do you wish for Gaius to guide all your training, including who you will see, what you'll practice, and how you will learn magic?"

Easiest question of the entire meeting.

"I do."

"Then, it's settled. From now on, Gaius will be the one who trains up the Agapéd and cares for Lisa. Whether he chooses to have her study here for academic studies or not is up to him..." Ariela walked toward Gaius, coming close to tell him something one-on-one. "Though, I do see it wise for Lisa to at least join us here once a week. Seems most of the Guardians have found a liking to her studious spirit. The Light be with you, Gaius... and it's good to see you with us all here again."

Ariela came back around to me and bent down so she was just below my eye level. "Lisa, you are in good hands, but I don't have to be the one to tell you that. Your body still needs rest, and I believe you could use some time away to just be with your mother, so I will have Gaius take you home. In a week's time, come back through the portal that leads you here. Then, we can discuss how your lessons will proceed as you incorporate your school life with your training. Does that sound good to you?"

I nodded.

Ariela then smiled and began to dismiss the room. Emunah winked, and Rayna hugged me before exiting through the golden door. Once everyone was gone, Gaius walked over to me. His face was back to normal, though it still looked like it needed a good nap.

Gaius stood beside me. "Thanks for what you said," he began. "Was surprising to know you still wanted to be taught by me."

My heart was still weathered by all the crazed emotions of the meeting and my new life to come, but a smile did peek, seeing Gaius happy again. "Well, you were the only one that believed I could do this whole Agapéd thing. If it wasn't for you... I probably would've said no."

"I doubt that. As I said, you have a spirit like mine; it's no quitter and loves magic too much to let it go. Can't be helped. You'll always be a part of magic now."

He then stepped in front of me and held out his fist. "And I meant it when I said you could do this. Believed it from day one."

Ribbons of blue magic started to fill his palm. "Now, when you return, we will be doing things *my way*. And I can assure you, it will be ten times better than what you've been doing so far."

I let out a gentle chuckle. "Can't wait."

"Get some rest before we meet again." A foot from my nose, he punched the air with his fist full of evanesce magic, smiling. Before I knew it, I was back home on Earth.

PART II

26
GIVING UP EARTH?

Despite the blissful ignorance of a magicless Earth, memories of the cave would not relent. During the day, I was fine because Mom didn't know anything about the nightmare I survived through. I contemplated telling her, just so I could have some comfort from someone other than Tuff; I love him, but nothing beats the sympathy from a human heart, especially from Mom.

But... I decided against it. When she came home in the afternoon after I returned from Haim Gana, she ran right up to me and gave me a big hug, promising me that we would spend the last week and a half of summer going shopping, eating out, and watching late-night movies—reminding me that "camp" was over as well.

Being with her... She made me forget the bad memories, at least for a while, and I liked that. The guilt of Valhalla's death would fade away when I saw her drinking coffee in the morning. When she would ramble about work gossip during our walks by the pier, it made me laugh—*real* laughter, too, and not just a facade to make her believe I was alright. When I saw my scars—which I covered up with oversized T-shirts anytime I left my room—the memories would resurface, but then, Mom would just say, "Hey, you wanna watch *Friends* and get take-out tonight?" and I would forget about everything for a while.

Earth was my escape. So, I pretended to be normal again... and I didn't tell her a thing.

Pretend. I never knew that simple action would be such a hard one to accomplish.

Nights—I hated them most of all. I would be curled up in my covers and force my thoughts to relive the good times, but it was like my memories had control over my brain, refusing to let me forget the vezper and Valhalla's death. Each time I shut my eyes, the black holes of the she-beast would be glaring right at me. My heart would then throb, beating my chest with a reminder of Gaius' selfless sacrifice... and that Valhalla did not have a pulse in hers anymore.

It was you, my pitiful conscience would say. *It is all your fault.* Gaius told me it wasn't, and I had to cling to his words like a life preserver, or I'd be drowning in an ocean of shame and guilt in the middle of my bedroom.

I cried horribly the first night, not knowing there was such a thing as mental anguish until then. My pillow was soaked with tears as my head burned—flashbacks of the beast towering over me as I stood frozen in fear. Burying myself in a cavern of my blankets and stuffed animals that night, I noticed a soft light—a tiny orange glow stick—peering between the crevices of my closed, bloodshot eyes.

It was Tuff. He cuddled up to me, and when his little warm body snuggled up against my face and shoulders, he began to import his own memories of the glainies into my mind. My little Sandman made sleep finally possible again, and he continued to do that for me each and every night. Nothing in the world I could give him could compare to the peace he gifted me.

"Sweetie, I was going to wait and give you this until Christmas... but you've seemed a little down the last week, so I decided to go ahead and give it to you now," Mom said as she came home from work late on Wednesday.

I thought I was doing well to hide my emotions, but I guess I couldn't hide everything from her.

"Let's just call this a back-to-school gift instead."

I was sitting on the couch, wearing an oversized hoodie, as she stood hiding her hands. From behind her back, she revealed one of the best gifts a teenager could ever receive from their parents. It was still in the box, but there was no mistaking it.

"You got me a cellphone?" I jumped off the couch and quickly grabbed the box. "Like, this is for real mine—and it's a Blackberry, too!"

"I know it's not one of those new touch screens that are starting to get popular, but they had a BOGO sale at the store, so I picked us both up one. I still hope you like it—"

"You kidding? I love it! Jenny Kim has the same one—*oh,* I can't wait to show her and Lily when school starts!" I hugged her tight before sitting back down to open up the box. "Thanks, Mom."

She always knows how to make me feel better...

———

The following day finally marked a week, which meant it was time to head back to Haim Gana through my suitcase portal. At first, the anxiety of returning pushed away any form of excitement. Luckily, I had Tuff remind me how great it actually was—seeing the magic plants, swimming in the ocean with Inna, and flying rocks with just a flick of my finger.

I pushed back my bad memories, my all-too-real nightmare, and covered them up with a blanket of magic-yearning and Gaius-training days. *Wonder what his teaching style is like without any Guardian input? Will he still have me study under them as Ariela asked?*

When Mom left for work that morning, I jumped right in the portal like normal. Fresh peony air hit my nose instantly, and the soft breeze of Haim Gana created a pleasant hum and echoed down the open-columned halls. But I didn't have time to enjoy the tranquility of Ariela's realm.

A familiar dismal face stood in front of me.

It was Vilmad with his arms crossed, wearing an elegant tunic stitched with gold to match the golden rings around his right hand, his thin brown hair perfectly straight... and we were completely alone at the bottom of the Elysium.

The blue and yellow sky warmed the walls through the colonnade; it didn't help make the long-haired Guardian's appearance any less intimidating. "Agapéd, a word," he said to me, not even with an ounce of care or "if you please" added to the end of his demand.

I took two small steps forward, mustering up the courage to stare at his leering, celestial eyes of blue. "Yes, sir?" I timidly said.

Vilmad didn't walk or waver, standing stoic and blocking my path, and I had no choice but to listen. "You are meant to meet with Lady Ariela and the brute, but something must be said before you make your way to the Grand Hall. Regarding your decision to remain the Agapéd Bearer, I must go along with what Lady Ariela sees is best..." He sighed and rolled his eyes. "Even if that means letting the buffoon take the reins on your growth, no matter how illogical that may be. So, given the circumstances, I cannot force you to give up the Agapéd, which leads me to my warning..."

The Guardian looked down at me as a breeze blew through that gently bounced off the marble walls. He was more agitated than serious as he spoke this time around.

"You've been chosen to be our freer of the Fallen, and when that time comes, we do not know. *But* I can assure you that wasting your time on Earth is irrational and will hinder your success. You need to be here, devoting all your time to training, and as far as education goes, you can learn more from us than you'd ever learn from the humans of the magicless world. This job you have agreed to is *not* one for a child, and you are *not* ready for it yet, seeing as you couldn't even stand up to a beast and save that Calendulian girl..."

There wasn't a minuscule drop of sympathy in his voice, and my heart sank, causing my eyes to stare at the floor. *He's right...*

I heard Vilmad move his arms, so I glanced up, seeing him touch his forehead with two fingers as if a throbbing headache entered his mind, furrowing his brows and squinting hard.

"And Lady Ariela has this inconsequential notion that you should be able to *enjoy* Earth..." Vilmad leered, the blue in his eyes sniping every freckle off my face. "But that option will not be apparent to you, which is why *I* am here, telling you this now.

Wait... what?

"You mean..." I quietly began, "I have to stop living on Earth?"

"We all agree, seeing as there is no reason why you need to stay. Every other Agapéd Bearer before you gave up their life to start their new one of gallant heroism. Isn't that what you wanted anyway? Begged the oaf to train you, and now, you want to live on Earth again? It is selfish, really."

Is that it... am I being selfish...

"So, Agapéd, you will *have* to give up your Earthian life and start the one you agreed to. If you don't, you'll get bogged down with petty things on the magicless planet and neglect your role here, in turn, failing to complete your purpose—which *cannot* happen. You understand?"

My eyes stared at the floor again. Nothing Vilmad said was wrong, and I did agree to be the slayer of Darkness... and that included everything that came with it.

That would mean... leaving Mom.

Her tan, smiling face popped into my mind, tugging at my heartstrings. Leaving my friends and even my extended family to go off and learn magic didn't bother me, but leaving *her*... now, *that* would be the selfish thing to do. Imagining Mom never seeing me again would break her heart—no, would burn it to ash, completely unrepairable. She had no one else in the world but me. Grandma didn't count, because Mom got annoyed by her, and her sister, Aunt Genn, couldn't care less about what Mom did with her life.

Mom also gave me something no one in Haim Gana, Mantene, or Calendula could ever give: an escape from my dark memories. Honestly, it probably was the only selfish thing I could think of, but I didn't care. My mind needed rest—Gaius even said rest was a part of growing stronger—and being on Earth with her was the only way I would ever get it.

I was a daughter before I ever was the Agapéd Bearer... and I have a duty to my Mom to keep her happy...

Vilmad watched me ponder in silence for who knows how long. I then released a deep breath with my eyes still on the floor. "I understand... and you're right about it being tough and that I do need a lot more training, but..." I then shot my eyes up to the joyless Guardian and said confidently, "I can't leave my mom."

Vilmad hissed with an eye roll. "You humans and your family ties... fine. Then, have her stay in Calendula with you—"

"No," I cut off Vilmad, to his dismay.

Appalled, he sniped at me, *"No?* I offer a human with *no* magic pulse a chance to live in the Hidden City, and you say—"

"I'm sorry, but I can't ask my mom to do that..."

I caused Valhalla's death... never would I forgive myself if I caused Mom's. She also had her life, her friends, and her job—I couldn't strip that away from her. And she would *never* be okay with letting me, her lone thirteen-year-old daughter, train and learn to fight dark creatures daily. She deserved a happier life—one without fear of me being at risk of death... and without *her* being at risk of death.

My fists were clenched by my sides as my mind tried to pull me down and think about mom dy... dying... because of dark magic. "She has her own life on Earth... The Agapéd is my job. So, taking her away would be selfish of me."

Vilmad bent toward me, peering hard into my blue eyes, voice deep and coarse. "I don't think I've made myself *clear*, Lisa," he said, hissing my name like a serpent. "You have *no* other option here. In a moment, you will meet with Lady Ariela, and she will inform you of the same decision. You either give up Earth and take your magicless mother to Calendula, completing the *role* you *agreed* to, or you hand over the Agapéd Magic to us. Being the Chosen is more grueling than you could *ever* imagine... and you obviously know I do not believe you're ready for it." He looked me up and down. "Or will *ever* be ready for it."

He straightened his back but kept his glare. "So, if you cannot handle your mother being *here*..." Coyness lifted the corner of his lip. "Cannot handle her being targeted by dark creatures, unable to defend her because you are nothing but a child with a magic meant for a worthy warrior, then I implore you to tell Lady Ariela 'no' when she asks if you wish to keep the Agapéd. Go on and keep you and your mother safe on Earth—*away* from magic, and away from Darkness."

My eyes grazed the ground floor of the Elysium. *Why... why are these my only choices?* Every part of me did not want to choose. I wanted all of it—I wanted Mom safe, I wanted my escape on Earth, and I wanted to be the Agapéd Bearer. Most of all... I wanted to prove Vilmad wrong, and I didn't care how selfish that was.

Vilmad huffed, my silence a pleasing answer to his ears. "Don't make this a burden on yourself, Lisa. Head to the Grand Hall and do what's right when Lady Ariela gives you the choice." He began to walk away, his voice trailing like a shadow. "I'd say 'farewell' but once you accept your Agapéd-less life on Earth, you won't remember a thing. No point in goodbyes after that."

I waited, both my fists still clenched until the clicking of his shoes stopped. The warm breeze whispered through the open-columned wall, brushing my hair, the only sound to be heard as my thoughts ran rampant. Every time I thought about giving up Earth and taking Mom to planet Kalm, images of her crying over my scratched-up body would appear… future images of *her* bloody body appeared. When I would think about giving up the Agapéd, Gaius' stubborn mug popped up next, telling me to *never* listen to Vilmad and to trust my heart instead.

My heart desired both. It had a duty to both, even if all of it was for the greediness of a teenage girl who wanted magic in her veins.

I made my way up the lofty staircase to the giant golden foyer—the Grand Hall—finding Lady Ariela. Her gilded dress matched the regal hues of the enormous columns and glossy tapestry flooring. To my surprise, Gaius and Dayasheel were also there, though the Guardian with the slick black hair and milky white face was most shocking. *Huh—wonder why he's here? Thought he didn't care about me being the Agapéd…*

A subtle smile grew across my face when Ariela turned toward me. Even in a room as elegant as the Grand Hall, she still was the center of attention with her golden-silked wings extended tall and glowing dress kissing the tapestry-tiled floor.

"Ah, there she is," Dayasheel said as I stepped over the last of the glossy steps. "Nice to see you again, Miss Lisa."

"Hi, Dayasheel," I said, feeling kind of odd saying his name for the first time, especially in such a casual way. Though, his kindness in calling me "Lisa" instead of "Agapéd" was appreciated.

"You doing well?" Gaius asked me. He was grinning without any tired eyes, wearing a different brown leather jacket—one without any grass stains or smelling of dirt—with the sleeves rolled up to his elbows.

Guess he's excited, too, seeing as he got all dressed up.

"Very," I answered, my soft voice contradicting all forms of excitement. I couldn't help my timidness. My heart knew it had to give an answer to Ariela's question… and the one I wanted to say involved me shoveling heaps of *heaps* of boldness into my chest.

Lady Ariela turned to me, her fingers interlocking. "Lisa, before you head off with Gaius, I have something to ask you—"

"I can do both," my heart gushed, that bravery stacking high in my throat, unable to contain itself anymore. Each one of the adults blinked rapidly as I continued, "I can live on Earth and still be the Agapéd Bearer. I promise I—I can make it work."

The men turned their gaze toward the Elysian as she faced me. Her sun-glittered eyes creased as her brows furrowed. "Lisa, what do you mean?"

"I know it'll be hard but…" I looked down at my hands as if I had written my answer between my knuckles. "Mom needs me, and I can't bear to bring her here, and I still have school and everything, but I don't wanna give up the Agapéd because it chose me and—"

"Lisa," she cut me off, gently cupping my shoulders. Her celestial eyes played tag with my stare as her cheeks rose from the smile emerging. "I would never ask you to give up your mother or life on Earth to learn magic."

"What—you mean… you never were going to make me choose?" I questioned.

She resumed her pristine posture. "Not even in the slightest. Actually, since the day you first met with us and told everyone you were willing to go forward with learning magic, Dayasheel and I have been working on something for you so you can continue life on both Earth *and* here. You have every right to complete your education and enjoy time with your mother like any Agapéd Bearer would, just like you have the right to give it all up and stay here." She made a hushed giggle. "But I appreciate your boldness in confirming your dedication to both your home and your new magic-filled life."

I wanted to *scoff*—wanted to draw a picture of that long-haired Guardian's face and crumple it up and smash it with a stone. Vilmad not only lied to me but tried to manipulate my thoughts, infecting my young mind with doubt and degradation. I knew he didn't like me and thought of me as more worthless than dust, but I didn't think he would stoop that low—going against Lady Ariela.

Though the bitterness grumbled my gut, puffing my chest, I kept calm, letting relief sweep me over. Whining about Vilmad would ruin the beautiful moment, and letting Gaius know the cosmic being did that to me would probably set off an alarm in his head… I didn't want to imagine what he'd do to the skinny, gold-sprinkled man.

A grin painted my face. "Thank you, Lady Ariela."

Her bronze lips glimmered. "Now, with that clarified, I have something to give you that will allow you to be both on Earth *and* training under Gaius. We all want you to accomplish magic and earn an education to the best of your abilities, and you can't go to school and expect to train only in the evenings. So, over the past two months, Dayasheel and I have been working with the Time Keepers, Sera and Idan, to craft you an object to allow you the ability to be on Earth while also being able to finish your training with us."

Dayasheel then handed Ariela a ring. The band was thin, made of shiny black metal, and had over fifty pen-point green and white crystals embellishing its perimeter. The material was loose like a fidget ring where each shard was embedded. When Ariela held it, the band jingled where the metal slackened. The ring looked as expensive as the orbkit around my neck.

She continued, "This is an Echo Ring and was designed specifically for you alone. Woven throughout the band and intertwined within each crystal is what we call The Sublimity Charm, a restricted magic that will allow you to create a duplicate of yourself, stretching your soul to exist in two places during the same lifetime. It took much convincing from Dayasheel and me to allow the Time Keepers to grant you this. For you see, Lisa, I took this magic away from Man because humans—just like I and my Guardians—are bound by time. Our life is precious because we only have one life to live. Pulling it apart to create multiple versions of one's self is nothing but greed and a lust for living. That is why I gave the magic to Sera and Idan.

"You mean, this ring lets me make... a *doppelganger* of myself?" I asked, the first time I think I ever said the peculiar word in a conversation.

"Earth's view of soul duplication is quite obscure," Dayasheel remarked with his cerulean eyes squinted, "so whatever it is that you're assuming this 'cloned-you' and its scientifically fictitious attributes to be, toss them. We all have *one* soul and *one* life, which makes time magic over one's soul even more of a risk—hence the reason for Sera and Idan. They only allow certain attributes of The Sublimity Charm to be gifted to others; for you, they are giving the ability to be in two places at once with a couple of restrictions added *only* because they know how important it is for the Agapéd to be properly trained."

Wait, what?

"I don't really understand how that works..." I voiced, feeling embarrassed I didn't comprehend Dayasheel's explanation.

Ariela retook the reins of the conversation. "The Echo Ring will gift you the ability to create another version of yourself—a perfect 'you' copy. The Sublimity Charm inside the ring will unbind your soul from the shackles of time to divide it in two for a split second. You'll notice another 'Lisa' manifesting in front of you the moment you activate the ring—activating the charm. It will seem like a perfect twin, but this isn't a different person. This *is* you. The shadowed-you will live on Earth, go about time at school, and live with your family for a *maximum* of seven days. During that time, you—the caster of The Sublimity Charm—will remain here, training with us and Gaius."

My eyes widened, and Ariela took notice.

"I know what you're thinking, and don't worry, Lisa. The moment you make physical contact with this doppelganger of yourself, all the memories of the copied-you will bind with you instantly. Innately what is happening is that your soul is becoming one again. Whatever you experienced on Earth will be embedded into your heart and mind. You won't miss out on a single detail of your life because it is still *your* soul, just in two places at once."

Whoa...

"So... if my, uh, duplicate soul has a bad day at school or enjoys a meal Mom made—"

"You'll know that same sorrow and savor the taste of that meal like it truly was you there—memories included. The moment you touch your duplicate's hand or the tip of her finger, she will disappear—glitter away in the blink of an eye back into your body, becoming one soul again. You understand?"

I took a big gulp, swallowing in all the intensive information. "Yes, ma'am."

"Now, Dayasheel did mention some restrictions on the ring. First off, it will only work for you—triggered by your DNA. The Sublimity Charm can copy every part of you—whatever clothing you are currently wearing as well—except the Agapéd. This simply means the copy will *not* have magic. Second, when you use the ring, be sure you are in a place where no others will see you, including when the duplicate days are up. I said before, the charm will only last a maximum of seven days. Once the seventh day is up, the duplicate of you will automatically bind with your soul, and we cannot have you magically disappearing in front of other Earthians. You—both on Earth and here with us—need to make sure you are always on time to bind with your soul's copy."

Lady Ariela put the ring in my hand. *Something so dainty and simple can split my soul... this is crazy...*

"Third, when your soul combines with itself again, it will cause a bit of discomfort to your body. When you contact your duplicate and retain all your memories, you'll most likely experience a mild pain in your mind—a headache or pressure near your forehead—from the oceans of recollections all entering at once. This also includes what your duplicate is currently feeling. If your copy is in physical or emotional pain *at that moment* and touches your other self, you will experience that same feeling, which can be painful when it's an emotion contradictory to your own."

I put the ring on my right index finger, sliding it down to my bottom knuckle.

All of a sudden, the band turned invisible!

"Oh, yes," Dayasheel started saying as my eyes widened at the phenomenon, "I added an invisibility attribute to the ring as well. Can't have Earthians getting a hold of this magic or even those on magical planets. To make it reappear, simply give it a good spin."

I spun the ring as he said, and the dark tungsten color and crystals reappeared again, making a satisfying rotation of clinging sounds. *This is so freaking awesome!*

He stepped closer to me and explained, "To activate the charm and create your perfect copy, simply hold out your hand, spin the ring fast, and press down hard for three seconds. In moments, you'll see another you appear, and your soul will now be in two places simultaneously. The rings will not work while your soul is already split in two and will need half a day to recharge the charm, so keep that in mind after the seven days are up."

It felt odd having so much power by my side. The Guardians put a lot of effort into getting me trained up well in magic and education back in New Jersey. But.. that meant they cared for "Lisa Robbie" just as much as they cared for the Agapéd growing stronger.

Ariela began to conclude. "That is all I have for you, Lisa. If you should need anything at all, feel free to ask us any time." She turned to Gaius. "The same goes for you, too."

"Appreciate it," Gaius said to her. He then held out his arm for me to latch onto. "Let's go, Lisa."

27

I'M ALWAYS INVITED

When Gaius and I evanesced, I first thought we were in the Boolavogue Outskirts Forest, but when I turned around, we were on the side of a cliff. Beyond, a perfect view of a large valley sat perfectly with roaming cattle, apple orchards, and rolling emerald fields that went on and on before the blue sky swallowed them up. Farmers were tiny ants from the distance we were standing, all working hard on their land early in the morning. Metal vehicles were going up and down the roads, too, similar to the mobile shops I had seen in Calendula, just without the magical inventory.

It was beautiful—a valley of sporadic brick homes, farms, and greenery everywhere. *Wonder where we are...?*

The cool summer morning brought in a breeze that brushed the hair off my shoulders, causing me to look to the right of the calming view. Misty clouds climbed along a mountainous city in the distance, thick, humid fog, but— even from our distance—giant stone walls were beginning to peek through the opaque overcast.

Standing beside me, Gaius took a deep breath of the fresh mountain air and let it out slowly. "I don't know how Dayasheel did it—getting those two to let him make that ring for you," he said, smiling and rather surprised.

"What do you mean?" I asked.

"Sera and Idan, some arrogant old gits of a brother and sister, never give up their magic to just anyone—especially The Sublimity Charm."

I squished a few flowers as I turned to face my brawny teacher. "The Time Keepers, right?"

"Mhm... They must've not known you were a kid; the day they see you with that ring is the day I want to be there. Nothing like seeing a Guardian argue with those two."

Gaius started chuckling at the idea of his—bizarre to see him laughing in the first place. Not sure if it had to do with us growing more used to the other or the fact he could finally teach like he's been wanting to from the start. Whatever it was, I liked this more casual side of him.

He paused for a moment, staring toward the unknown farms ahead of us with a simple grin between his beard. "Lisa, I want you to take a good look at your surroundings here. This is another entrance to Calendula that you'll be using—right behind us through those trees. Memorize the path as we walk."

I barely saw the wildberry bush and gateway of oak before the Keeper began striding down the beaten path to our right. "Where are we going?" I asked, keeping close to his side.

"There is more for you to learn when it comes to combat training and monster hunting... some of which I am unable to teach you. I'll be cultivating the Wishing Stars soon, and my time will be limited, so you'll be working with other instructors during then. You'll also still have your lessons with Inna like normal."

I shot my eyes toward his. "Really? I get to keep training with her?"

His green eyes glanced at mine as a canopy of trees hung over us. "She is the best water Mage I know. You and I will now practice in the mornings... except on Mondays. Lady Ariela suggested you work with the Guardians on more studies. I settled on one day. You'll find more knowledge in my magic study, but she insisted, saying they enjoyed having you."

"They really said that?"

"They just like showing off their knowledge—don't repeat that. The last thing you need is a good instructor for creature combat. Needed to be someone I trusted not to reveal your secret as the Agapéd and to teach you properly how to defend yourself, use an array of weapons, land perfect attacks, and take down beasts all on your own. I have the skills to teach you—I won't deny that—but I want to focus more on your terrain magic when we're together. You know your true purpose now, and it's time you begin your path of heroism properly. So, you'll be learning from the best there is, and that is in Boolavogue."

I smiled wide and ran right in front of Gaius, walking backward down the path. "You mean the *Kingdom* of Boolavogue? With the castle and everything?"

"It is the Kingdom of Monster Hunters and Creature Weaponry. We are headed there right now to ask the King and Queen for their hunters to teach you."

I noted his clean gardener wear again. *Ah, so that explains the dirtless shoes and spotless leather jacket. Could've at least told me sooner—I'm not dressed properly to meet a Queen!*

The reality of seeing royalty quickly overshadowed my middle-class EverWake clothing. "I'm gonna learn how to fight in a castle *and* meet an actual king and queen?" I skipped ahead a beat from the excitement. "Oh my gosh—I can't believe this is happening! But don't you have to be invited to get in?"

Gaius smirked as the sun pushed through the trees and into his wavy brown hair. "I'm always invited."

The trees of the pathway soon dissipated as did the low morning clouds, and the full view of Boolavogue's outer city became clear.

It. Was. *Massive.*

The outer grounds of the kingdom were covered in fields of vegetation and cattle that stretched for miles, patterned with brick homes and transportation vehicles. Many citizens were working hard, and I even saw a school—their Tutor—with kids playing outside. They weren't dressed much differently than the people in Calendula—well-put together and not as peasant-like as I expected (my concept of castle life is limited because I only thought they existed in medieval times).

Thinking back on what Gaius said, I asked him, "You said that the Agapéd is meant to be kept a secret, but I thought the world needed to know this magic returned?"

We began to hear more chatter than whistling birds the farther we walked, and my teacher answered without making eye contact with me, "Right now, you are still weak, and there are those who will only see that side of you, no matter how much you train. Your magic is also very powerful, and to prevent Darkness from finding you, it needs to be concealed until you're equipped with the right skills to protect it."

"I see... and Boolavogue is trustworthy enough to keep that secret?"

The gardener grinned. "You'll not find a stronger hand of candor and loyalty than you'll find here with King and Queen Sonon. You are perfectly safe, Lisa."

Further ahead was the entrance to the Inner Kingdom, surrounded by a vast, waterless ravine and white stone walls—fortifying everything inside. No one could cross over without being spotted, and no human could make the jump; the rocky pit was the length of an American football field, and the walls of the inner city were higher than a four-story building. It was *incredible!* Even with the white stone fortress guarding the inner city, I could get a good look at some of the brick buildings. The kingdom scaled up another mountain—creating a jungle of homes and shops that climbed toward the top.

But what I wanted to see most remained shrouded in the morning mist: the castle. *It has to be past the inner city and at the very top.* Gaius and I had a good bit of walking to do, but even from where we were standing on the mountain path... I could see something tall and made of white stone breaking through the clouds. *If that is the top of the castle—it has got to be bigger than the Aquanaeum and Elysium combined!*

The only way to enter inside the massive walls was by the three large viaducts that crossed over the deep barren gorge, each being crowded and heavily guarded. I saw a couple of small flying vessels—similar to the glass boats I saw soaring in EverWake—circling the perimeter of the Inner Kingdom high in the sky. I was guessing they had to be the security measures.

The dirt mountain path turned rough with gravel the further down we went. As I tailed behind Gaius—trying to keep up with his long strides—I asked him, "You said that Boolavogue is the place for Monster Hunters, but what does that really mean? I thought kingdoms were just fancy government buildings with many knights ready to fight wars?"

My teacher scoffed. "Whatever it is they are teaching you on Earth about how a 'magic world' would work, you need to forget. Boolavogue is an independent kingdom, not owned by the Magic Embassy or any other nation, and they rule with one goal in mind: creating Hunters worthy enough to fight off dark magic creatures. Many come from all over wanting to be trained by their Captains and Hunters, and the Kingdom has created a strong name for itself. You don't have to wield elemental or phantasmal magic to be a Hunter either, just strong enough to hold a blade and take down a foe when asked. To be given the title of Hunter from Boolavogue, let alone be asked to train with their Hunters, is one of the highest forms of honor and respect."

"Whoa... So, will I be learning how to use swords or something then?" I asked, a little skeptical.

"Yes," Gaius said as he ducked under a low, leafy branch. "Do you not want to learn?"

I walked under the branch, standing tall. "No, it's not that... just curious why I need swords since I have magic."

"Lisa, if you were taking down a Lava Behemoth, it would devour your terrain magic, turn your water into steam, and eat a bullet faster than its release from the gun's barrel. You would need a Frostbite Long Sword or a Gutter Batten infused with an ice glint, as well as knowledge of proper swordsmanship to even have a chance at taking it down. With all that said, knowing other resources besides the magic in your veins is crucial for a Hunter, a Hero, and the Agapéd."

"Oh... there are actual Lava Behemoths out there?"

Gaius tittered at my short attention span and continued to guide us both down the mountain.

We reached the bottom of the trail, which led us to a small patch of apple trees. *Easy enough for me to remember how to get back to the top.* There was another avelift station nearby, bigger than the one at Mantene and filled with many people going to and from the Kingdom. Gaius concealed his head with the hood of his leather jacket as we followed the crowd to the large viaduct entrance. There was a line of visitors near the front and two sections for those wishing to cross over—one for vehicles to enter and one for pedestrians.

"Name, please," said the Boolavogue guard at the entry, gazing down at his chart.

"Gaius," my instructor said.

"Last name?"

He crossed his arms. "The Keeper."

"Very funny." The guard chuckled, but his whole demeanor changed when he looked up and saw Gaius' face underneath his hood. "Oh, my apologies. Please continue in."

I couldn't help but smile, feeling pretty cool knowing I was with a guy who only needed a look at the face to enter into a magic kingdom.

The sidewalk of the broad viaduct was made of magic and moved like the travelators at the airports back on Earth. We just stood in place and zoomed straight toward Boolavogue's inner entryway, passing by the many vehicles and other magic carts that entered the traffic lane. Once we stepped off the moving walkway, it was nothing but music, chatter, and robust smells filling the air of the Inner Kingdom. Kids and adults alike were crowding the streets, either in a rush or having a leisurely summer stroll. Along the gate's walls and scaling up the mountain was shop after shop squeezed between long, skinny homes and apartment buildings. Everything was sturdy, made of red, white, or brown brick and concrete, resembling Calendula, just with less wood and more modern technology.

We were walking for what seemed like forever, which I usually didn't mind, but Gaius had magic in his veins that allowed him to teleport freely.

"Gaius, how come we can't just evanesce to the castle entrance?" I asked him as the incline of streets and shops seemed never-ending.

"You have to be invited, remember?" he calmly answered as we passed by a multitude of civilians crossing the stone street. "They have a forbidden entry charm cast along their borders, as most wealthy nations do. EverWake has one— bet you saw it with Inna; it had you land at The Landing when you evanesced there. You'd end up on their evanescing sigil stone if you teleported here. It's near where we first crossed the bridge."

"So, it's like how we can't evanesce straight into Calendula?"

"Completely different."

"How so?"

"You try and evanesce directly into my home, and you'll be ten feet into the ground. Always land outside the borders, Lisa."

I nodded, almost bumping into a couple of pedestrians. "I didn't expect there to be so many people here."

"It's a great nation to be invited to, and many don't want to leave once they've arrived," he responded. "Boolavogue is strong in both magic and skill. Besides training Hunters, they also create weapons for fighting beasts, and you'll not find a nation that doesn't have a dark magic fiend problem. As far as weapon craftsmanship goes, they are top class."

"Better than yours?"

"I dare say so... but only slightly," he joked.

Our long trek up toward the mountainous castle began to come to a close as the white stone outer gate of the royal structure was in plain sight. *That's a castle—that's a real-life castle! I can't believe I'm about to walk through it, too!*

The exterior walls of the King and Queen's home were like skyscrapers made of clean, cream stone, all adorned with windows and pale blue turrets at the top of each sub-building. Electric lights of warm yellows and oranges lit up many of the rooms inside, while some had large, opened canopies to allow the morning sun to peer through. Smaller arched bridges, similar to the one Gaius and I walked across to enter their land, connected many of the castle's towers; I even saw people with royal robes and elegant suits walking along them. Trees of vibrant, emerald greens peeked over the outer gate, crawling up the mountain Boolavogue's castle was built into, as well as a cloud of smoke coming up from behind the main keep's tower. *And I thought EverWake was the most magical man-made city I'd ever be able to see.*

Up ahead, the road split into many directions; some for carts and other magical vehicles; some for Hunters and guards; some for whoever needed to go down toward the backside of the mountain. We continued down the straight, broad path—right toward the main entrance.

There was no bolted gate crisscrossed with metal as I had imagined. Instead, a thirty-foot high white metal door infused with glossy stone and a faint emblem of a bear and sword embossed on the front. It was partially cracked, allowing guards to trickle in and out easily. The door also looked incredibly heavy, not made of that fake veneer stuff many homes in America used on their walls. *Wonder if they use magic to open it...*

A quartet of guards stood near and above the elaborate entrance. Their garment was not steel-plated or full of heavy chains. It was light, possibly due to the summer heat, and covered in white leather straps with a light-blue jerkin underneath. Each one also had cream-colored boots to match their leather arm braces—I noticed when I saw one walk across the front of the gate. Some of the men had swords while others had hefty belts similar to Gaius, just without all the plants attached.

"State your business," one ordered from the canopy near the top of the door, looking down on us.

"I need to speak with Head Captain Arond," Gaius answered, calm yet loud.

"And for what reason?"

Gaius crossed his arms. "Just tell him that Gaius needs to speak with him."

"Sir, I can't complete your request without any form of identification or letter of entry."

Gaius then removed a silver flower charm from inside his belt pockets. It was exactly like Inna's, only he had an emerald-green flower. When Gaius' hand touched the chain, it glowed a soft green color, like how my COIN lit up when my skin made contact with it.

The guard's face changed upon seeing the Keeper emblem. "I will send for him. Please wait here."

"There is no need, Tenen," a voice said behind the cracked doors. An older soldier walked through the main entrance, wearing a more decorative Boolavogian garment with a side-draped cape. His hairline receded, and parts of his ginger hue began to turn slate-white.

"Gaius, it has been quite a while since you've paid the Kingdom a visit," he said, giving the Keeper a firm handshake. It was weird seeing someone act so friendly to my burly magic instructor; he just always gave off the don't-talk-to-me vibe around other people that I didn't think he had friends outside of the Keepers and Guardians... if I could even call those his friends. "What can I do for you today?"

"I need to speak with the King or Queen and hoped you could take me to one of them."

"Straight to the point as usual with you. The King is away, and the Queen is currently meeting with the counselors and warriors of Midirei, and I am not sure what all the Royal Court has planned for their visit today."

"So she's here, then?"

"Yes, but even for you, Gaius, I can't intrude on the business of other nations."

Gaius let loose of his hood and grinned. "Arond, you're a class-of-a soldier, and I know the Queen trusts you wholeheartedly. If the meeting is important to her, it is to you, but what I have to discuss with the Queen is far more important than whatever is happening in that meeting. So, if you tell her I am here, she will understand."

The Boolavogue Captain raised his graying brows in silence, so Gaius put his hand on my shoulder and continued with a confident smirk. "*We are going to see her, and you're the only one that can make that happen.*"

Does Gaius normally do what he wants, or is asking for permission not a thing Keepers have to do?

Captain Arond sighed. "Seems saying no to you will not stop you from entering either way. Follow me, then."

We walked across the radiant courtyard of the castle, passing a large fountain encased in creamy marble and right through the glistening stone doors that led inside. There weren't many people strolling around the foyer or long white hallways, but the ones that were all stared at us, followed by soft whispering; everything was so quiet that it was easy to pick up the words "Keeper" and "little girl" from their gossip.

Arond led us down a long hallway adorned with oil paintings of past royal families and various landscapes. Like all the other corridors we walked through, everything was very clean; I could see my reflection from the floor, and no light bulb needed to be replaced. There were many balconies and rooms along the quiet hallway as well. Some were propped open and revealed clean guest rooms inside, while others looked to be some sort of study area. Each room had the same lush architecture as the last... and my curious nature wanted to see it all.

Please let the Queen like me...

A flight of stairs led us to a pair of giant white doors, guards stationed by each handle. Standing on the outside, all of us could hear faint, eloquent chatting from both men and women. Arond had us wait at the base of the stairs while he talked with the guards.

My fingers fiddled as my thoughts had a chance to wander... a chance to dive through memories I had pushed aside. Gaius was here to ask the Queen to let me train with their Hunters, but... *Where... where will I be staying after this?* My eyes narrowed on the unscuffed floor. The Balthiers. They were my other home, giving me food and clothing without asking for anything in return, but after what happened, would they have ever let me back in? Ariela didn't mention it, and Gaius didn't bring it up. *Did that mean I had to go back?* Thinking about seeing them again—I had ruined their lives, killed their—

I jerked my chin, facing the pristine castle wall. Teeth gritted. *Stop, don't think about it. Just ignore it—just focus on—*

"You alright?" Gaius whispered, his breath hitting the wisps of my long hair.

After blinking rapidly, my attempt at brushing away my emotions, I took a short glance at the Keeper. "Yeah," I whispered the quietest I ever had before, matching Gaius' tone. "Just nervous about meeting the Queen, that's all. Are you and her on a friendly basis or something?"

"As far as acquaintances go, yes."

"Then, how is it you're able to just waltz in and interrupt her meeting if you're just 'acquaintances'?"

A smirk slipped through his boxed beard. "Lisa, how long have I been a Keeper?"

I didn't ask for some sort of riddle.

"For like 700 years?"

"And Boolavogue has only been around for 600. They needed someone to help them get started, and I needed an ally I could trust."

"You mean, you're like a founder of the Kingdom?" I said almost too loud, causing one of the guards to look back at us.

Gaius leered at the guard; the husky Boolavogian turned around fast. "I helped them find their first king, giving them a strong leader from the start. So, let's just say... the Kingdom owes me."

"But, how do you know the Kingdom and its Hunters will say yes to training me?"

"Lisa, you never take a no from somebody who doesn't have the authority to give you a yes, which is why we're going to the Queen. We aren't taking no for an answer today."

I liked Gaius' confidence and his demanding attitude. I never would have guessed he had negotiating skills—a very loose definition of the word—but it was still surprising.

Arond walked back toward us with a not-so-happy look on his face. "Gaius, I talked with the Queen's guards, and I am sorry, but it seems this meeting is to remain in session for quite a while."

"We will wait," Gaius quickly responded.

"Then, you'll be waiting all day, my friend. Seems not even *you* can win their loyalty over the Queen's. You will have to wait until next week when she is free—"

As if he were king of the castle, Gaius crossed over to the Queen's guards and calmly demanded, "I need to speak with Queen Leonora Sonon."

The tall one answered back. "Sorry, sir. The Queen won't be stopping this meeting for anyone."

"She will for me. Just tell her, 'Gaius is here,' or I'll do it myself."

Both guards looked at each other in disbelief. Gaius wasn't budging, and it was not like they could just throw out a Keeper; it was quite the predicament. I knew if they didn't let him in, the giant gardener—who was armed with killer plants—would have his way no matter what.

Finally, after seconds that felt like hours of intense glaring from my stoic mentor, the bearded Queen's guard closest to Gaius caved in. He slowly reached for the door and took a deep breath. We couldn't see anything once he slipped inside, since he opened the wide doors just enough for his body to squeeze in. All of us waited as we heard all the muffled voices silence from inside the meeting room.

"Camden, what is the meaning of your intrusion?" a muffled lady's voice said from inside. She sounded very calm yet forceful and took time with her words. *Wonder if that's the Queen?*

"My Lady, um... *Gaius* is here," the guard responded.

The stillness of the room somehow picked up tension. *I do not wish for anyone to be in Camden the Guard's shoes right now.*

With no sudden movements or even a cough, clicks from heeled shoes began to trod toward the door, quite briskly, too. No talking was coming from the meeting room, so either the guard was turned away, or the Queen was coming right for us. I hid behind Gaius' muscly body, fearing what was about to happen.

The doors slowly opened, and a lovely tan lady dressed in navy blues of satin and cotton fabric stood between them. I didn't have to see the crown on her silky brunette head to know she was the Queen; her tall, confident stance and perfectly styled hair could have given away her identity instantly.

When Queen Leonora Sonon entered, everyone made a slight bow, even

Gaius, so I did, too.

"Gaius. My, it's been nearly two years since you've graced our halls. I apologize for not visiting Calendula in so long; my Hunters and kingdom traders have nothing but good tidings with each and every visit they make through the city," Queen Leonora said. She seemed to pay no attention to the fact she just left all those important people in the room behind her. *Is Gaius equivalent to royalty here or something?*

"Glad to hear that," Gaius answered, "but I must discuss an important matter with you. In private."

She then looked down at me.

I didn't know if eye contact was rude or expected, so I just glanced back and forth like a nervous wreck.

"I see. Then, if you don't mind, come and follow me—Arond?"

Captain Arond rushed over. "Yes, My Lady?"

"Please inform the court of Midirei that their tour of the Weaponry Forge will be pushed to now, and our meeting will resume when I return."

"Of course." Arond then made his way inside the meeting room along with the other guards.

She just stopped the whole meeting just to talk with Gaius and me. I can't believe I'm important enough for something like this!

Once we were far enough away from other Boolavogue guards and castle inhabitants—standing near an open archway not connected to any other door—the Queen began speaking to us more freely. Her stature was elegant and fit, and her eyes were pools of shimmering caramel with the morning sun rippling through the window.

"I do apologize for not introducing myself earlier, Miss..." the Queen suddenly began.

I wasn't expecting her to start the secret conversation by talking with me. "Oh, it's Lisa Robbie, Queen Leonora—or, uh, My Lady—Your Majesty? Sorry, you're just the first queen I've ever met, and I'm not sure what I'm supposed to say."

Wow, way to sound smart and not like a completely spaced-out idiot, Lisa...

She smiled gracefully, teeth perfect and lips peachy. "You're welcome to whichever feels more comfortable for you, Lisa. So, what do I have the pleasure to discuss with you and the Keeper of Stars today?"

Gaius casually told her, "I need a combat instructor to train Lisa, and I was hoping you'd allow her to work with the Hunters. There is no other kingdom I trust in proper skill training than yours."

The Queen raised her thin brows. "There must be more than asking to train for the sake of training itself that requires you to interrupt my meeting?"

"Yes." Gaius cupped my shoulder. "Lisa is the next Agapéd Bearer. I'm working with her on magic, but her understanding of battle and weaponry is below the starting level—that is why I am here."

What!

Gaius spilled my secret like it was nothing but loose talk of the weather! He must've really trusted the Queen to tell her the Agapéd had returned; he wouldn't have just blurted out my identity without a second thought, given the importance of my power.

He continued his explanation. "She needs to learn how to fight properly so she will be able to defend herself against creatures and the threat to come in later years."

The Queen's eyes widened as her facial expressions changed to match her sense of startlement. "This young lady has been chosen? My... quite a young age for such a task as this."

The Keeper's voice was hushed and very calm. "That is why I came to you. Her identity as the Agapéd must be kept secret, and your kingdom is the one I trust for honesty and proper Hunter training."

The Queen squinted, eyes wandering around the stone walls for answers. "Gaius, I understand the importance of this, but we do not train anyone under the age of seventeen, as you know. Sending out children to slay creatures is not a sport our kingdom takes part in. Even then, most children in our schools have already learned basic defensive skills by the time they are ready to apply to be a Hunter. Does she even know that much?"

"Leonora, I would not have come to you if I expected to be turned away. She needs to be taught here."

He just said her first name so casually! Is that even allowed?

Queen Leonora took a moment to think about Gaius' demands before she looked at me. I was used to the stare she gave me: the kind filled with sympathy and lack of trust in my skills.

I decided to say something, too.

"I promise to work hard and to become the best Hunter your kingdom has ever seen." My voice sounded incredibly girly, but I tried hard to seem as confident as Gaius was, even though my heart pounded hard knowing I was in the presence of a queen. "You don't have to worry about anyone wasting their time on me... because they won't. I know the job I need to be ready for in the future. Nothing is too hard for me to handle."

Speaking to the Queen was already scary enough, but to talk without first being asked was even more terrifying... but I did it. It felt good to stand my ground.

Gaius smiled back at the Queen, proud I showed her my willingness to be a Monster Hunter.

She turned to the Keeper, tilting her pointed chin upward. "A strong spirit, I see. Well... I could have Lisa train with my son for the time being; they look to be around the same age. Captain Ekron is currently working with him in basic weaponry combat as well as physical training. Having another student with him shouldn't be a problem; might even do him some good. This does mean she will be working with the Men's Hunter Troop. Is that alright with you?"

"Lisa can handle it." He took no time giving that answer.

The Queen turned to me to just make sure I truly was okay with it.

I nodded yes, even though I had no clue what I just agreed to.

"Then, all that is left is to ask Captain Ekron if he is fine with the sudden change—"

"He will be."

Queen Leonora couldn't help but smile in astonishment at Gaius' upfront and straight-to-the-point behavior. "Do all Keepers act as though 'yes' is the only possible answer to their demands?"

"I can assure you... I'm the only one," Gaius said with his usual smirking face.

A relieving sigh left her glossy lips. "Well, if you'd kindly follow me, we will go and speak to Ekron and have Lisa introduce herself to him."

As the Queen began to guide us ahead down a flight of stairs—grabbing the attention of two burly guards—Gaius leaned over to my left ear. There was a touch of smugness in his words. "As I said, never take a no when you can have a yes."

From entering the castle to demanding presence with a queen—not even letting Her Majesty have the option of saying no—Gaius was not one to be messed with. He truly was the best teacher an Agapéd Bearer could have ever asked for.

28
THE PRINCE

Gaius and I followed the Queen and her two guards to the training grounds. We came through the back of the castle—furniture and walls turning from pearly white to gray stone and red brick—where the air still was misty, and the sounds of silence were exchanged with steel clanking and burly chatter.

The Hunter training site came into view.

A chunk of the Kingdom's grand mountain was flattened on the right side, hidden behind the outer gate. The area had to be half a mile in diameter, covered in small hunts, forges, battle rinks, and fierce training equipment. Nothing was pristine like the castle was. Wooden planks formed paths, covered in mud and sprinkled with loose grass, with a couple of stone trails around the perimeter, and it was crowded with men and women dressed in brown and black leather. There were no trees either—completely flat to give plenty of room to the tents and small battle rinks. A couple of white daisies were sprouting near the entrance, but that was the only soft detail about the place. This truly was a warrior's ground, not meant for kids. Not one bit.

The center was most barren, with several guards and Hunters sparring. It was the first time I had seen weaponry as epic as theirs! One sword that a female Hunter was swinging would emit blue flames each time she made contact with the white steel of her opponent. I had never seen a frosted hammer that constantly gave off icy mist either, and a Hunter with rimy gloves was wielding it. *Okay—this is amazing!*

We veered to the right of the training grounds toward the Men's Troop—not the most pleasant of places. I would rather smell my own shoes after running a mile in gym class than sit next to a couple of the men we passed. Maybe it was my girly nature showing, but *man,* some of those Hunters needed a week-long shower and a pair of scissors to their beards.

Still, their barbaric appearance wasn't what caused me to glare at the ground; it was their eyes. Nothing but intense stares the whole way forward, and it wasn't just because the Queen was with us. I was the only kid around, and as far as being a female went, I looked nothing like the Amazonian warriors in the Women's Troop—all the while being escorted by a burly gardener and the Queen's royal guards. Some people loved drawing attention to themselves, but I was not one of them... another thing I would have to get used to since being the Agapéd Bearer.

We came toward a huddle of sturdy canopy tents, each decorated with Boolavogue colors—pale blues and ivories—and strange swords and spears. The one the Queen stopped at, however, was a sienna orange color. Both guards waited outside as the Queen, Gaius, and I entered.

"My Lady—" two hunters hurriedly said, at first lounging in chairs and now standing in attention, dropping their breakfast sandwiches onto the floor. *It must not be every day the Queen visits the training grounds.*

"Would you both mind giving Captain Ekron and me a moment?" she asked the two with great humility, seeing as another man was in the far-left corner of the tent. He was definitely Captain Ekron because he didn't squeal at the Queen's intrusion.

They did as commanded, cleaning up their soiled breakfast, and Captain Ekron approached us. He was much older than most of the others we had passed but not as old as Arond. His bald head contrasted with his long-braided beard of dark brown. Despite the wrinkles creased around his nose and eyes, muscles covered his arms and abdomen beneath his dirty garb. The man was almost as muscular as Gaius.

"My Queen, if I knew you were coming, I would've had the Hunters clean up the Laze," he said, lighthearted.

"It wouldn't be a Hunter's Laze without a little rummage of dirt and the strong scent of a warrior," she joked with the Captain.

Pretty cool to know she isn't afraid of dirt... I am liking her more and more.

"I guess that would be so—I see we have some unfamiliar faces?"

"This is Gaius, one of the Keepers of Stars—I'm presuming you two have not met before—and his pupil, Lisa Robbie, the new Agapéd Bearer."

Seems anyone is allowed to know my secret...

Captain Ekron's eyebrows raised, crinkling his forehead. "By the morn—would have not picked today to be one for such good fortune, especially to see a Keeper and a legend. I assume something other than a weekly check-in with Prince Caelum's training is amidst?"

"Yes. Gaius has requested the aid of our kingdom's training for Lisa, but as you know, we do not train minors to become monster-slaying pupils; however, given her role in our world, I believe this overshadows that rule. So, I thought it best for her to train with you and Caelum."

The Captain looked at me. He was as stoic as Gaius—warrior-esque in all word forms. Though he was smiling, my eyes were too nervous to stare back; the dirty Laze floor was my new best friend.

"I can't say no to you, my Queen, but... having her train with us would cause a stir amongst the other soldiers and Hunters, and I don't just mean about her magic."

"About her magic... if anyone asks, just say she's my student and nothing more," Gaius instructed. "Her identity as the Agapéd needs to stay hidden amongst us few until she is strong enough both in combat and in magic. The world will automatically label her as a Hero the moment she becomes known, and Lisa needs to be ready before that happens. Both I and the Guardians are not wanting this to be common knowledge just yet."

"Is that alright with you?" the Queen asked Ekron.

The Hunter Captain took a moment to think before grinning at his Queen. "Well, I have to say, this gives my days more meaning than ever. You've put a lot of faith into this old Hunter, My Lady. A Keeper's trainee and the Queen's blood—*heh*. I promise to not let you down—"

Out from the back entrance of the Laze, a boy came running inside, interrupting our private meeting. He had fluffy dark brown hair with subtle wavy locks and stood only a few inches taller than me. His shorts had belt straps down the side with a small dagger hooked to his left thigh, while his sleeveless shirt was simple and stained from the mountain's soil. The muscles on his arms weren't anything to rave about, but there were just enough where I could tell he must have been training daily... and in the sun, too. Overall, he just looked like a normal middle-school boy with hazel eyes, though when he smiled—teeth perfectly straight and creamy white—I couldn't help but return the gesture straight toward the ground.

"Mother, I thought you had a meeting with those people from Midirei—am I in trouble or something?"

My eyes shot all the way open. *He just called Queen Leonora his mom—he's the PRINCE?*

"Should be after your lackluster performance yesterday during parry lessons," the Captain joked with the Prince.

"Come on, Ekron. If I were perfect, then your job would be finished, and how boring would your life be then?" the young Prince said.

"*Caelum,* please take your Hunter training seriously," his mother quickly scolded, keeping her calm composure.

Prince Caelum shrugged. "It was only a joke. Ekron knows that." He grinned wide and casually shook some dirt out of his hair.

Whatever idea I had about the Prince being as eloquent and charming as the Queen just disappeared with that remark. Not even a title or a crown could fix the annoyance that was "teenage boy," even from all the way across the universe.

Queen Leonora shook off her son's behavior and continued with our meeting. "Caelum, I would like you to meet Gaius from Calendula—he's one of our world's Keeper of Stars—and Lisa, from..." the Queen trailed off, realizing she never knew where I was from.

"Earth, actually," I interjected for the Queen, my voice the shyest out of the group.

The Prince raised his eyebrows, showing off his hazel eyes. "*Earth?* Whoa, I've never met someone from Earth before."

I couldn't tell if he meant that in a good way or not.

The Queen told her son, "Well, you'll have plenty of time to become acquainted since she will also be working under Ekron's instruction alongside you. She is Gaius' pupil, so I expect you to treat her well and with as much respect as your fellow Hunters."

Ekron patted the Prince's shoulder with burly force; I was surprised he was so casual with the Queen's son. "Seems like you'll have some fierce competition, Young Prince." The bald Captain then turned to Gaius. "I wouldn't mind seeing what I'm working with. If it's alright with you, may I have Lisa spar with Prince Caelum just to get an idea of her skills and weak points?"

The what—

My heart fell faster than a boulder dropped from a mountainside. I've only ever practiced in private with Gaius, and it's not like the workers at the Aquanaeum paid much attention to me and Inna during lessons. Plus... I've never properly sparred before. *Is that even a type of battling with fists or does that involve swinging swords?* It would be different if I was showing off my skills in magic after training ahead of time, but now, I was going in blind *and* in front of royalty.

I couldn't let Gaius down, though. If I performed badly, it would reflect on him... and he's an *amazing* Mystic and fighter. *Maybe he will refuse—*

"That's fine with me," Gaius happily answered.

My eyebrows dropped. *Why did I ever think he would say no...*

Without ever asking the freckled girl who was standing petrified, we exited the tent and walked down to a small practice ground where the grass was heavily worn, and old benches surrounded the perimeter. Gaius, the Queen, her guards, and the two Hunters from the Laze all watched us as Ekron explained how sparring worked.

"Okay, you two," Captain Ekron told us, "this isn't an official sparring match, so we are just looking for the first person to pin the other down. Lisa, do you have experience with weaponry?"

"Uh, does magic count?" I asked, trying to avoid saying "no" and looking ignorant.

Ekron smiled at me. "For this match, that is more than perfect."

I was glad to hear that, even though it didn't settle my rattling heart.

He continued, looking back and forth between the Prince and me, "No headshots or cheap tricks—just a good clean match. Alright?"

Prince Caelum nodded confidently while I stood doe-eyed, tilting my chin while Ekron stepped back to stand with Gaius and the others—now with five more random Hunters sneaking in to watch. *An audience. Great. Do these men have anything better to do than watch a little girl get demolished by royalty?*

The Prince walked to the edge of the dirt ring, so I did the same but in the opposite direction. Every inch of me was terrified, wishing Gaius would have *asked* me first so I could have said *no*. As I did my best to hide my shaking knees, I turned to the Keeper in the stands. He stood tall with a subtle grin—complete self-assurance in his student on the field. Seeing him standing proud, I realized he wouldn't have let the match happen if he thought I had no chance against the Prince. Knowing that perked up my spirit.

"You know, I've never sparred against a Mage before," Prince Caelum shouted across the battleground, taking two dual wooden blades from the practice weaponry rack before returning to the ring. Though the weapons were fake and made of sleek wood, they were still swords, and plants *easily* hurt my skin daily.

"I've never sparred against anyone before," I responded honestly, which maybe wasn't the best idea, but knowing the Prince had never fought against magic was to my benefit. Then again, I also had no clue how to avoid blades—only wiry roots and whatever other plant life Gaius had up his sleeve.

As the Prince stood there, holding his wooden blades, my gut didn't swirl around in butterflies as much. I had practiced with *Gaius*—the beefiest gardener in history and the grower of Wishing Stars—so the more I looked at the Prince, the more I only saw a normal boy.

Maybe this won't be so bad...

With a bellowing force, Ekron shouted, "*Begin!*" and Caelum took no hesitation, charging right for me with both blades next to his sides, determined and with an intimidating glare.

I take it back!

My stance wavered for a moment as my first instinct was to run, but then, I remembered the crowd. Though the battle was now a piece of entertainment for the Queen and her Hunters, I knew Gaius was watching. Disappointing him was *far* scarier than wooden blades held by the hands of a teenage boy.

You got this Lisa. You cannot let Gaius down.

I pressed my hands down on the air next to me and grasped the cool breeze as if I were grasping the dirt below me. Six baseball-sized dirt wads rose from the ground and floated next to me. I looked straight at the Prince and ran off to the left, shooting each ball, one after another, toward him.

The Prince was almost hit by the first mound, but with the last couple, he knew my throwing pattern and evaded them with ease. *Dang, it—he's a quick learner.* He then regained his speed and swung his right blade toward my shoulders. *Is he crazy?* I instinctively shot up a dirt column, parrying the attack. He wobbled backward from the sudden contact, and I tried to make use of it by aiming another ball of dirt toward his chest. The Prince used his left sword to deflect it, which caused his sword to fly out of his hand.

With my burst of confidence, I pushed both palms forward and jolted a dirt column at his chest. The Prince shot a couple of inches off the ground and landed with a *thud!* Dusty dirt hovered around him. As he lay there, barely moving, a smile drew across my face. *I did it—I won!*

"*Pin him down, Mage!*" a gritty voice shouted from the audience.

"*He's gonna get up!*" another shout came, burlier than the first.

My fists lowered with my eyebrows. *Wait—I knocked him down! Isn't that what Ekron said?*

"Didn't I win?" I muttered to myself.

Prince Caelum then pushed himself from the ground, and an audible sigh came from the Hunters watching.

"Lucky hit," said the Prince, standing on his feet and walking over to get his lost practice blade, not caring about the scuff marks of dirt all over the back of his sleeveless shirt.

My body froze as my eyes looked toward Captain Ekron. I was too nervous to shout my confusion, but I had no clue why the spar was still happening.

The Captain understood my bewilderment from a simple look. "To win, you have to *pin* him down with a weapon or by force. Not just a good slagging will offer you victory, little lass," the bald man said loudly as my head whipped back to the Prince, who had already picked up both of his swords.

Embarrassment kicked in, causing my freckled cheeks to burn pink, and I hastily apologized, "Oh—I'm sorry! I forgot!"

"You're fine, Lisa," the Captain said with a smile. "Continue."

With the Prince back on his feet, he said with a smooth cockiness, "Nice magic, but it would help if you remembered the rules. Kinda important." A laugh followed as he gripped both his swords tightly. "No messin' around this time."

The Prince shot off toward me again. With the worst-case scenario going out the window—besides losing the entire match—my heart settled down a bit, forgetting the audience of scruffy men around me. I was ready to *pin* down Prince Caelum. My legs took off toward him, trying to match his speed. I didn't know what he was thinking, but I guessed he would swing his right arm again, so I shot up another dirt column to block the attack. He quickly spun away, swinging his sword around the earthy stone base, right for my arms.

He missed because I shot another dirt column up from the ground that leaped me into the air—out of his reach. I heard the crowd—now with two more Hunters joining—start clapping at my sudden burst of flight, making me feel pretty good about my abilities. As I was gliding above, I shot another column toward the Prince again.

Prince Caelum dodged and jumped on top of it, taking advantage of the new terrain. *Crap—wait—what's he—*

Right when I landed, I knelt down to soften gravity's pull, and the Queen's agile son jumped off the column and right on top of me with both swords in his hands. The rocks in the dirt scratched my shoulders as I rolled over to avoid his body hitting me.

Now, *I* was on the ground, completely terrified.

My hands skidded across the dirt one after the other, shooting baseballs of clay at the Prince, all the while my heels pushed me away. Caelum was no longer scared of my magic because he easily evaded the blows and even hit one with enough power to crumble it in mid-air.

His feet came right near my ankles, and using his right dual sword, he swatted my left wrist down hard, scraping my knuckles against the worn-down training grounds. *He's much stronger than he looks, or am I just stupidly weak?* With the sudden bind of my hand to the dirt, my magic stopped, and the Prince shoved his sword right up against my throat.

I closed my eyes tight as if a splinter from the wooden blade was as deadly as the tip of a steel one when Captain Ekron's voice suddenly called out.

"Battle decided: Prince Caelum Sonon wins!" The Captain's voice sounded pleased, making my royal opponent lower his guard.

I released a deep breath as the Prince's sword left my throat. The small audience of now ten Hunters was clapping loudly, proud of their Prince for not losing to a girl like me. The Queen beamed, along with Ekron, but I didn't care much about them. When my eyes shifted to Gaius, his arms were still crossed, and not a hint of a smirk or grin could be seen. *Bet he's upset with me losing...*

Sweat and dirt speckled the Prince's face, but I could still see him smiling beneath the grime on his lips and cheeks. To say I didn't feel my face blushing would be a lie—the boy was barring me between his feet! Quickly, I averted my gaze from his and noted his arms. Two scratches reddened on each of his elbows from where I knocked him down the first time, but it was nothing compared to the family of scrapes on both of mine. His dark hair remained fluffy, whereas mine had to be a wavy, knotted mess—not pretty in the slightest. *Looking hideous in front of a boy is now another thing to check off my "Situations I Never Want to Happen to Me" list.*

Prince Caelum threw down his wooden blades. He may have been a prince, but he was still a boy, and all boys hated losing to girls. *Here comes the sore-winner side of the Prince...*

The sun hid behind the clouds as the Prince reached his hand out toward me, and I could see his smile. It was genuine. "I didn't think you could use magic like that. Was pretty cool. Fair play, Lisa of Earth."

My eyes widened at his shocking kindness as I took his arm. He yanked me off the ground easily. "Thanks," I said timidly, trying to fix my hair and not freak out over the fact I just touched a prince's hand.

"Still, at least try to make it more of a challenge for me next time," he joked... At least, I hoped it was a joke.

My shyness kicked in as I said, "I promise to be better, Prince Caelum."

He made a breathy laugh through his teeth. "No need to be so formal with me. Just forget the 'prince' title and call me 'Cal' instead."

Most boys I knew back home loved to gloat about winning, even at the simplest competition, and *never* would they compliment a girl for being tough *or* think a fight was fair if put up against one. I was expecting a dramatic in-your-face-disgrace theatrical or even a "you are weak and don't deserve to be training with me" morbid attitude coming out of his mouth. When the opposite happened, I couldn't believe my own eyes; he even praised my magic. *Maybe there is some chivalry in him after all.* Plus, hearing the Prince—I mean Cal—say my first name made me feel noticed and not like I was just some random girl he would have to work with during training.

Back in the audience seats of the ring, Ekron gave me a hardy handshake while Gaius gave the Prince one.

"Gaius, your pupil will be a perfect match against the Prince—sharpening magic against steel," Captain Ekron said.

It made me happy to hear him acknowledge my strength despite losing quickly.

"Lisa, I look forward to training you in the upcoming weeks. We will have you wielding the finest Hunter weaponry in no time yet—a master of both magic and swordsmanship!"

"I, too, look forward to seeing your results, Ekron," the Queen said before looking back at her son. "I believe having Lisa will help your training as well, Caelum. It has been a pleasure with you all, but I must return to the Midirei court, and *you*," she gestured back at Cal, "I believe, still have lessons back at the castle. It was good to see you again, Gaius, and you, Lisa."

The Queen and her guards left, but before they disappeared behind the Laze, Cal turned back toward me and gave a subtle wave. Not once did he laugh at my messed-up hair or snicker at my scratches. It was strange... the good kind of strange, and a small part of me was excited to see him again.

"Didn't expect you to slag the Prince like you did—knocking him flat on his back in front of the Queen," Gaius stated as we left the Hunter grounds, heading back to the secret entrance. *Guess he still wants me to memorize this path... wish we could just evanesce because my face and legs are in pain.*

I sighed as the smell of sweaty warriors began to dwindle. "I was just trying to win... sorry I lost and made you look bad."

Gaius put his hood back over his head. "What made you think I was disappointed?"

I shot my gaze upwards. "Because I lost in front of everyone."

"You've not even had true training and held your own against Prince Caelum, who has been training—according to Queen Leonora—for only less than two months. You showed good tactics with your terrain magic, too. That Captain of the Queen's was quite impressed with you."

The blue in my eyes sparkled like the ocean. "Whoa... really?"

"Don't get too up in the stars about it. You still wavered and got scared toward the end, and in a real battle, you can't afford to lose..." Gaius then put his hand on my shoulder. "But that is why you are here: to grow stronger."

As Gaius dropped his hand and the incline down the castle grounds began, I grinned at the stone road. "To be honest... it did feel pretty cool fighting against him... and seeing the Prince fall flat on his back."

"Heh—nice seeing your hard work pay off?"

I couldn't help but snicker at my success. "Yeah."

⁓

After maneuvering back through the Kingdom, we made it to the secret mountain passage, which led us right into a flower garden in the Veradome, one I had never seen before. We walked through an indoor valley of pink and purple tulips before coming to a familiar corner near the stairway to Gaius' Hearth. Once through the magic door, he had me follow him down toward his home. I thought we would be going into his study, but instead, he stopped at the side of the kitchen, causing me to almost bump into him.

Off to the left and near the black refrigerator rested a door. I never noticed it before; it blended in with the wooden wall paneling, and I never saw Gaius go in there before.

"Lisa, I have something I'd like to show you," he said as he stood before the average-looking door. His voice was calm and serious. "It's through here."

Odd...

He twisted the doorknob to reveal... *his laundry room?* It was a narrow, windowless room like most people would have in their home, filled with plants that looked to be nocturnal. Further in, I realized they were the cause of the fabric softener scent that filled the room, and not some cheap air freshener like Mom would have placed on a shelf back home.

Everything about the space seemed normal besides the biotech washing machines and labeless cleaning supplies, so I wasn't sure why he had brought me there.

"It's actually through that door," Gaius jerked his chin toward the end of the room.

Like the last door, it, too, looked very average. I went for the bronze doorknob, and when the door opened, the sun immediately entered through—lighting up the earthy laundry room behind me. When my eyes adjusted, I saw that the sun's rays came through the glass walls. The spherical room was entirely made of frosted blue and green glass plates with a huge domed sunroof as the ceiling. Vines and other emerald leaves draped along the roof's exterior, crafting shadowy designs from the sunlight.

One corner had the most comfortable, queen-sized swinging bed, filled to the brim with magenta and cream feather pillows. The other side had a tiny wooden desk and matching cabinet with a large leafy monstera in between them. Some string lights were randomly hung and drooped across the wall above the desk, though it didn't seem like the room needed any extra light. A round, fluffy carpet of warm colors lay perfectly in the middle of the glass room, making the once greenhouse feel more like a lounge area.

It was the most enchanting bedroom I had ever seen.

"Wow... what is this room?" I asked Gaius, admiring all the unique pillows and gorgeous plants hanging from the ceiling.

"It's yours for when you're staying here to train."

I whipped my head back around to face him. "What? You're serious?"

"It used to be my personal greenhouse, but after I built the one you see outside, I had no more use for this one. It just stored a mess of things, but I rewired the air so it shouldn't be too humid, and the glass is True Blue Glass—meaning no one can see through it from the outside; it just reflects the blue sky instead. I, uh... had Inna come and help with the decorations, so if you aren't a fan, you can take it up with her."

Gaius' face looked almost nervous as I watched his eyes lose contact with mine, like how one would act when they aren't sure about the gift they had just given. He told me he had never had kids before, meaning he probably never had to buy a gift for a teenage girl either in all the 700 years he had been alive. For him to give me more than just a cot and a box for clothing was beyond kind. Everything was like a dream room in the forest, and it was all for me... I couldn't believe it.

"It's the prettiest room I've ever seen," I exclaimed, sitting on the swinging bed. It was surprisingly sturdy, using the branches from the protruding tree outside to hoist it up.

Gaius came and sat on the wooden chest that rested near the foot of my majestic bed. The pleased smile about me liking the room faded to a more serious expression.

"Lisa, with all that happened to you and your friend..." Gaius softly began, "I figured going back to the Balthier's would be hard for you—please feel free to stop me if I'm wrong—so, I thought it would be best for you to stay here... at my hearth... with me. You don't have to, but you'll have more privacy here than at the Elysium or in the Aquanaeum; no Guardians or gimpish swimmers to get in your way. It's your choice. Whatever makes you more comfortable."

The Balthiers and their warm, cozy cottage... I pushed back the memories of their home, in fear of crying or feeling that anguish again from all the sadness. Gaius was right about it being hard for me, and my staying with them would only worsen my guilt. Roy and Emmeryn made me feel like I was a part of their family... Replacing them was impossible.

Yet, for a reason I couldn't explain, my rugged magic mentor somehow gave off that same feeling. He wasn't "comforting" in the way most would interpret that word, and he encouraged fighting and getting his way. However, he built me a room so that I would have a home to go to when away from Earth. I didn't know what it was like to have a caring uncle, protective older brother, or someone to call dad, so I didn't know if this was normal for "father figures" to do for kids. Whatever the case was—Gaius made me feel cared for. He made me feel safe—protected. He already gave up his immortal heart for me; he didn't have to go and create the prettiest room a girl could dream of.

"You built me a room with an endless view of the sky, so how could I not say yes?" I softly joked with him, fiddling with my thumbs.

He let out a sigh of relief. "Glad you like it."

"Thank you, Gaius. Really—it's the best gift I've ever received."

"You don't have to exaggerate for me, but you're welcome. Now..." Gaius stood back up. "With all that's happened today, I want you to get some rest as you return home. The next time I see you will be after you've tried out that Echo Ring. We will properly start your training and have you take a crack at evanescing as well."

"I'm gonna get to learn *that*?" I exclaimed, imagining myself using the blue teleporting magic like a proper Mage.

He grinned. "If you think you can handle it."

I jumped off my bed. "Oh, I can handle that—no problem."

Gaius had me stand in the middle of my new room and began to commence the evanescing magic. "Stay safe" was the last thing he said before I landed back in the forest behind my house.

I didn't think anyone could make me feel safe and cared for like how Mom did, but Gaius was a close second.

29
THIS IS STRAIGHT-UP TRIPPY

"Was she still asleep?" I whispered to Tuff as he returned from the hall, peeping into Mom's room.

I sat on my bed in the early morning, having the only light in the room be the 6:02 a.m. beaming green on my clock, my purple lamp, and my glainie's orange glow. I couldn't sleep because today was the day I would make Earth's first doppelganger—right in the center of my bedroom in New Jersey.

Tuff's little body floated tall and saluted, followed by a hardy whistle.

I jumped out of the covers and stood in the center of my carpet. "Good—won't have to worry about her seeing two of me." I began to push the bean bag out of the way. "This is going to be weird…"

With the floor clear, despite a sock or two near the rug's edge, I straightened up my back and held out my fist toward the empty space—thumb grazing over the Echo Ring.

Tuff floated near my ear as I took a deep breath. "Okay… just a spin and a three-second press… is it really that easy?"

My glainie shrugged.

"Well… here goes nothing."

The loose metal of the Echo Ring jingled as my thumb gave it a hefty *swoosh*. When I stopped its speed—pressing down hard for three seconds—my knuckle began to feel cold as the band glowed white.

Instantly, a silhouette of luminous clouds formed in front of me—fast and as quick as steam rising—and my heart thrummed faster. The misty shadow didn't stay pearly white for long. Before I even had time to blink, the swirls of magic stood five feet tall and turned into flesh with messy brown hair, wearing the same outfit I was in: my black sleeveless EverWake top, thick pair of blue shorts, and white socks.

I was staring at me... staring at *me.*

Our eyes were wide, and given that she was me, our jaws dropped.

"Whoa..." I breathed, looking my double up and down. "This is straight-up trippy..."

"Definitely," my double said back. "I don't feel any different—do you?"

I shook my head slowly. "No..." My eyes couldn't help but examine myself, judging my outfit and how it fit my figure; the other me was doing the same. "Wow... I really do look kinda weak compared to all those Hunters."

My doppelganger grinned. "Yeah, but not a ten-year-old like Gaius thought."

We both giggled, sounding the same in fluctuation and length of laughter. It was bizarre but in a cool, non-creepy way.

My double moved her hair back, and that was when I noticed something around her neck that surprised me.

"Look—around your neck," I said to copy-me. "The Sublimity Charm also made a copy of my orbkit."

Other me touched the necklace and gave it a swipe. All my EverWake clothing was inside—a complete replica of what was in the orbkit around *my* neck.

"Ariela and Dayasheel did mention it would copy whatever I was wearing," double-me said, swiping the orbkit to make the projection disappear. "Guess this explains why this Sublimity Charm isn't meant to be roaming freely around the world."

"Yeah... this ring can copy anything I'm wearing... money and magic stones included..."

"But not for long, since we have those restrictions—"

The light in the hallway came on, cutting my conversation with myself short.

Crap—Mom's up early!

I whispered to my magicless doppelganger, "Okay, in six days, I'll come back here when you're out of school. Then, we, like, do the thing."

"Got it!" I told myself.

I unzipped my suitcase flap, making the room glow from the Haim Gana portal. "Have fun at school, me, and don't do anything I wouldn't do."

The other me nodded and rummaged to find a school outfit, starting with the pile of clean clothes near my closet. "This is so weird—don't embarrass yourself in front of the Prince!"

"I will try my best not to."

"I'll pick us up some pizza tonight, okay?" Mom shouted through the rolled-down car window as I left the passenger's seat at Keyport Middle School. "Love you! Have a great first day!"

"Love you, too," I called back before she drove to work.

It was the first day of eighth grade—finally at the top of the school—and it felt amazing. I had my new cellphone, a new pair of Converse that Mom found on sale, and another me all the way across the universe doing some type of cool magic. Kind of felt odd—being jealous that I was the one stuck at school—but then, I remembered that it was still me out there with Gaius. I could relax on Earth like a normal teen, and honestly, I liked that.

Starting school was always kind of exciting for me. I wasn't sure how everyone else felt, but I liked meeting all the new teachers and seeing who I would sit next to. I wasn't a fan of choosing seats in class; having the teacher pick was easy. Last year, no one sat with me during my first-period seventh-grade class, so I hoped to not repeat that sad experience.

I walked into Mr. Abernath's Science class—a tall, bald man trying to hide his giant red tattoo with his abnormally long, short-sleeved polo—and saw on the projector I was sitting next to Lily! *Thank you, new teacher!*

Lily hugged me and insisted I see all the design work she did during Art Camp. I glanced through her glittery notebook and tried my best not to hurt her feelings... but her drawings were pretty boring and rendered like a fifth grader's work on a good day.

"So, is this *all* you did during camp?" I asked, surprised she didn't improve during the two months she was there.

She flicked her blonde hair. "Well, I started doing design work, but I got bored and switched to theater and dance," Lily exclaimed, taking out all her new highlighters and pencils, exhibiting all the expensive supplies her Mom bought her. I didn't care, but I figured she was just trying to impress some of the other girls in class. "It's *way* more fun. Probably gonna try out for the school play this— hey, what happened to your arm?"

"Huh? What do you—"

As I was taking off my jacket (Mr. Abernath's room was unusually warm compared to the rest of the school hallways), I followed Lily's eyes to my left arm's lower bicep, right where the purple and pink circular scar was from the vezper's bite. My mind started going crazy, fearing Lily had discovered my magic secret. *Crap—not even a second of my bare skin showing and Lily noticed the kiwi-sized purple scar!*

I was so focused on my cool replica ring and talking with myself this morning that I didn't even think about my magic scar. The room was a bit stuffy—all I wanted was for my arms to stay cool so I wouldn't sweat; now, my jacket was off, and I was gushing salty water out from every pore on my body!

What do I do? What do I say? It even looks like a bite mark, so I can't say I fell! Lily isn't stupid enough to believe something like that.

Telling Lily and even Jenny Kim about my magic did cross my mind way before the start of school. It would be nice to finally be fawned over by my friends and have them request to hang out with me instead of the other way around. I never had anything to show off before, whereas Lily had her expensive clothes, and Jenny had her basketball skills. If I did tell them, I *knew* they would be over at my house every day wanting to see me move rocks and freeze water... but I couldn't do it. It was too big of a secret, and Lily didn't understand what that word meant. They were good friends and my only friends... but I didn't need their adoration to boost my confidence. It would've made it worse, making me question whether it was "Lisa Robbie" they liked being around or just the magic.

Think, Lisa—think!

"Oh, um, I got bitten... by uh, the neighbor's dog this summer. It's no big deal," I gave as my excuse, hoping she would just forget about it.

"*Gosh, Lisa!* I dunno how you weren't more careful," she began, taking out her new iPhone from her pocket. "You should put your jacket back on or cover it with makeup. It's kinda gross-looking, and you don't want any of the cute boys seeing you like that—but check it!" She wagged her black, glossy touchscreen in my face. "Dad got upset with Mom and bought me the new iPhone when I returned from art camp!"

Wow, the kindness is lacking today... but it doesn't look that bad, right?

The rest of the day, I wasn't thinking about anything except my magic scar, and I hated it. It was like I was the center of the universe, and everyone was staring right at me as if I had a huge sign over my head that read "Magic Girl Here." No one else said anything to me—that didn't mean they never saw it— but I tried my hardest not to let my left arm move, even with my jacket back on in the middle of August, keeping my bicep close to my side.

During lunch, I ate my food with my jacket still on so Jenny Kim, some new kid—too preoccupied with my eye-sore of an arm to remember his name—and Lily wouldn't see my purple bite mark. I hated it so much. *What am I gonna do? I can't wear long-sleeved shirts and jackets all my life!* Then, I remembered the enormous scar on my stomach. Though it wasn't as bad, since the vezper's claws weren't infused with dark magic venom, it still was another thing I had to worry about and probably for the rest of my life. *I will never be able to wear a two-piece bathing suit again!*

"Dude," Jenny Kim's voice said over the lunch table, half a chicken nugget in her mouth, "you sick or something?"

My eyelids shot back up, staring straight at my untouched food. *She knows, she knows, she knows—*

I was about to make my excuse before Jenny Kim's voice continued in my direction. "Cause if you're not gonna eat your food, can I have it?"

Half of my heart was relieved, glad she couldn't see through my gray jacket at my magic mark or that Lily spread rumors about my ugly wound. The other half was slightly offended and hurt, because the comment was about getting more food and not my well-being. I wasn't surprised, though... but after learning what having a real friend was like during summer...

I blinked fast, shook off the dark memories resurfacing, took my milk carton, and said, "You can have the rest."

My stomach growled as I drank the last drop of milk, and my legs wouldn't stop shaking under the table as I listened to my friends gossip. *I can't keep this up—can't keep living in fear of them noticing this, and I doubt this will be the last scar I'll ever receive. Other me, you better find some magical way to hide these scars before you get back!*

~

When reaching the glossy floor of the Elysium that early morning—seeing my doppelganger go off to the first day of eighth grade—I was immediately rushed into a forced hug. The abruptness made me stumble and almost fall over, my heart racing ten times faster. But after seeing the braided strawberry blonde hair that fell along her back, I knew it was Inna who scared me with the brute embrace, and my body grew less stiff.

"Lisa—Oh! I just had to come to see you and couldn't wait any longer," she said before releasing her grip, her eyes glistening with ocean waves. For the first time, I saw concern washing over her tan cheeks.

"I just want you to know that I am sorry for not being there for you during the Guardians' meeting. I'm so glad to see that you are alright. Goodness—after hearing what all happened to you, I admit I believed this might all be too much for you. But when Gaius came and told me what you said…" Her smile returned. "Lisa, I shouldn't have ever doubted the Agapéd's choice. I just couldn't bear to see anything else happen to you."

Inna's apology took me by surprise. I never knew she cared so much for me, and though I thought it was sweet, the way she reacted made me think of Mom—proving I could never tell her the truth about magic. *If this is the worry of a Keeper, then Mom's would be ten times worse…*

Still, the heartwarming smile she gave made me feel loved. Inna didn't have to worry about me, but I was glad to know she did.

"You don't have to apologize, I promise," I said to her, smiling. "I'm just glad Gaius is still letting me train with you."

"Speaking of that, you are welcome to train with me tomorrow as well; it's up to you and Gaius. I am dropping off a bundle of starseeds, so if you need someone to take you to Calendula—"

"You have them with you?" I interrupted with a sudden burst of energy. I couldn't resist; the urge to see the magic Wishing Starseeds was too overwhelming to remain calm.

Inna giggled, standing up straight. "I take it you would like to see them."

I nodded eagerly as she swiped the orbkit attached to her silver-chained belt. A long scepter with a basketball-sized orb on its end appeared in her hand. It stood almost six feet tall, wrapped in a shimmering ribbon. Glowing water filled the glass orb, sloshing around just like cosmic ocean waves. Inna shifted the staff so the glass ball faced me, and inside was hundreds of different-shaped glowing seeds: some pointed, some jelly-like, some even star-shaped!

"It's like looking at the ocean's reflection of the night sky!" I said, my nose almost touching the container of the seed galaxy. "So, Gaius is gonna take these and make them grow into the Wishing Stars?"

"Precisely. His Keeper magic is the only way they will thrive, blossom, and generate their celestial power."

"Whoa... How come they are in water?"

"It's not just ordinary water." Inna lifted the staff upright, causing the seeds to sway and hum inside the sphere. "It's Moon Water, straight from the pond of a minor planet called Zena. Kamari—the last of the Keeper of Stars, if you remember—lives there and gathers the water for me when nebula clouds form and produce their celestial rain. This is the only habitat that nourishes them after my magic helps create them out of stardust. Hopefully, you will have the chance to meet Kamari in the near future... might even let you take a drink from the pond."

My eyes widened as my curiosity sparked a brighter flame. "What happens if I do—will I get some type of new power, or will it make my eyes glow or something?"

"Heh—you'll just have to see to find out. Now, shall we be on our way?"

I grabbed Inna's arm as she evanesced us to Calendula's secret entrance, the one on the top of the cliff with a view of Boolavogue's farms. We headed toward Gaius' home, passing by many of the Veradome's busy morning workers. Many of them stared at us as we walked by, probably because I was standing next to a lady with fairer beauty than the bluest ocean.

Normally, the workers ignored me, or the ones I had grown to know just waved before continuing their task. Even though Inna had walked the Veradome halls more than a handful of times, everyone still couldn't help but be distracted by her beauty.

As I was, too, admired her perfection—wishing to someday be as beautiful and feminine as she—I compared her to my looks... and that's when my eyes noticed the ghastly giant purple mark on my left bicep.

The vezper's wounds on my skin were disgusting, even after being healed by Lady Ariela, and I became utterly embarrassed.

I instantly pressed my arm down by my side as I walked with Inna, hiding my burning face by staring at the ground. *I can't walk around with this on my arm all my life? It's one thing to hide it at home, but what about today? My first lesson with the Prince... and he will see this and think I'm gross. Dang, it! What do I do? It's blistering hot in Boolavogue—I can't wear long sleeves all my life!*

"Is something wrong, Lisa?"

Inna's voice disturbed my self-hatred toward my magic scar, and I quickly said a fib. "Oh, uh, no! Just a little tired... that's all..."

Please, please, please, tell me that my doppelganger wore a jacket today before someone at school saw this...

Gaius had just come out of his glowing greenhouse when Inna and I arrived. She gave him the seeds by taking the orb off of her staff, creating a cork-popping sound. He then went back into the greenhouse, and even though I asked nicely to see what was inside, he still refused to let me in. He said it wasn't ready for "curious eyes" yet, whatever that was supposed to mean.

The muscular gardener returned quickly. "We still need to work on training your body for evanescing," he said with a grunt. "That is all you need to worry about for today before heading off to Boolavogue."

"Really? Then, let's get to it!" I said, making Inna giggle by my side.

"I wouldn't mind staying a bit longer to watch this," she said. "First-time evanescers are always a little spontaneous with their teleporting."

Gaius led us three to his small training ground and removed a handful of flaky flower petals from one of the vials he had attached to his belt. They were thin indigo petals and hard like sugar from a lollipop, quite an odd texture for a floral leaf.

"This is a petal from an Evanesce," Gaius explained. "It will allow you to obtain the magic to evanesce but only for a short period of time."

"You mean the magic you use to teleport... comes from a *flower*?" I questioned, astonished that all that power was in a small leaf. I honestly thought it would be something a bit more grand.

"Yes. It will gift you the power to teleport to other locations until its magic in your body dissipates. However, if you take more of these daily, your body will naturally absorb its magic—like a vitamin or mineral—and adapt to your magic pulse. You won't need any more petals once that happens. Due to their rarity, they are highly expensive, and many people can't evanesce naturally. Luckily for you, Lisa, I have more than enough, so learning this magic will cost you nothing but time."

So cool!

I took the petal in my hand... assuming the only way to make it work was by... eating it.

"Do I just...?"

"Yep." Gaius stood with his arms crossed, waiting for me to eat the crystal leaf.

I popped it in my mouth like a mint and hesitantly crunched down. The petal crushed easily into smaller pieces and melted away as I swallowed. I was happy it tasted more like almonds and grapes than an actual flower petal.

My mentor straightened his back and explained, "Now, to evanesce, you have to think about where you want to go and where you want to land. If you just imagine your home, you could end up falling from the sky and crash-landing onto your roof. You need to know the exact spot you want to teleport to—*always* staying focused. Understand?"

"Yes, sir."

"The motion you need to make is holding out your fist and forming the Evanesce's magic into your palm." Gaius then showed me the motion I'd seen him make many times before. "As the magic is forming, envision yourself at the location you want to go to. Then, give the air a nice punch. Go ahead and try teleporting from here over to the bank of the pond."

I looked toward the pond and did as he asked, envisioning the shoreline right before me. I held out my hand and tensed up my palm like I would do when opening the magic wooden entrance to Gaius' hearth. Suddenly, flowing blue dust filled my fist. It was warm and ticklish the more the magic began to form. *To the pond, Lisa. Just go to the pond.* With a hardy punch, I struck the air and teleported to the pond... just not exactly where I was hoping.

My body evanesced *above* the pond's waters—*six feet* above at that! I began falling straight to the depths below until I hit the water. I gasped for air as I broke through the pond's surface, covered in cold, dingy water and utter embarrassment.

Okay... this may be a little harder than I thought.

I dragged my soaking-wet self back over to Gaius and Inna, who both giggled at me. I now knew why Inna wanted to stay and watch; from her side of the shore, it must be pretty funny though my red face said otherwise.

"Why didn't it work?" I muttered to Gaius, using my magic to jet off all the unwanted water from my clothing and hair.

"Did you envision yourself on the shoreline of the pond... or just the pond itself?"

I scrunched up my nose and stood speechless because it was the latter of his two guesses.

Gaius smirked at me. "It will take time, but if you keep practicing, you'll learn it soon enough. Just make sure you never evanesce to an unknown location or change your destination mid-teleporting."

"Why's that?" I asked, forcing the water out of my sneakers this time.

"If you aren't focused properly, the flower's magic will lose control and backlash, causing the evanescer deep wounds or, in rare cases, internal bleeding."

"Happened to you once, didn't it?" Inna chimed in.

Gaius nodded. "Was like getting sliced with spiked fishing wire."

I took a big gulp. *Okay, maybe he should have told me all this BEFORE I casually teleported without a second thought...*

He smiled down at me, noticing my widened eyes. "Don't worry, Lisa. That will not happen to you if you keep practicing with me."

By lunch, I could finally evanesce at the shoreline without plopping in the middle of the pond. My knees received a couple of bruises from my earlier crash landings in the dirt, but it wasn't anything too noteworthy and well worth it.

As I happily succeeded three times in a row, I walked back over to Inna and Gaius, both of them coming out of the glowing greenhouse.

"Finally did it," I said, a bit out of breath due to my magic usage and hunger.

"You catch on quite quickly, Lisa," Inna complimented, putting one hand on her hip.

Gaius reached inside the pocket of his leather jacket. "Here are more petals." He then dropped sixteen mint-sized sugar petals into my palm. "Eat these for the next week, and we will see if your body needs more before it can evanesce freely. Your lessons with that Captain are soon. Don't be late."

While thanking my burly Keeper and putting the petals away in my orbkit, I saw the eye sore on my left arm as I swiped through the magical pocket projections. My gaze shifted to the wound, causing me to scrunch up my nose.

"Gaius," I timidly began, my thumb attempting to smudge away the mark to no avail, "is there, like, a concealment charm or something that can cover up my magic scars?"

He and Inna were about to go their separate ways, but my question stopped them.

"Why cover them?" he responded far too casually to my question. "Proves you've survived harsh battles."

My eyes sagged. *I shouldn't have expected him to understand—he walks around with dirt-covered shoes and wears the same jacket almost every day...*

Inna released a pitiful sigh. "Maybe for you, but I believe Lisa doesn't want others to know of her struggles from merely a look," she continued, walking in between me and her fellow Keeper. "Sometimes, that part of a Mage's life should be by word of mouth only. Lisa, care to lend me your hand?"

I extended my left wrist.

Inna also stretched her arm out toward me. Her wrist was perfectly tan, her fingers decorated with dainty jewelry, a glossy polish veiling her clean-cut nails. A small thread hung around her wrist, too, glistening like opals. The threads too thin to be considered a bracelet. Nothing about it said magical or special, and I wouldn't have noticed it until she used her left hand to lift it up. It looked like two hair-thin pieces of silver twine and didn't compare in beauty next to the rose-gold jewelry she had everywhere else.

"This is my concealment band, though it is simply two fibers of an Eternling—a rare tree that contains elements of the Concealment Charm," she said, gesturing to the tiny duo of strings around her wrist. "This conceals all my magical scars whenever I wear it, allowing me to live more comfortably at the Aquanaeum. It's more efficient than casting the Concealment Charm, seeing as the Eternling fibers power will not fade as long as you wear it, so"—Inna took off the dainty band and put it through my hand—"I believe it will also benefit you."

The moment it clung to my arm loosely, my vezper wound swooshed away like ink floating in water until only my pale, freckly skin remained. I lifted my shirt slightly; the claw marks had also disappeared.

"Whoa, how did it—" My words cut off once I looked back at Inna.

A large blue scar spun around her neck as if something strangled her badly enough to leave a permanent bruise. Her hair was styled back to reveal her ears, and the entire right side of her forehead down to her right earlobe was laced with paper-thin scratches. It looked like she landed in feathered glass, and my heart sank.

She never talked about her battles... never knew she was even in battles...

Inna wasn't embarrassed like I was with magic scars, seeing as she didn't mind me staring. "It's the Eternling's work, and as you can tell, it's pretty effective. All magic scars and fresh magic wounds will be concealed when you put it on. If you wear the band when injured again, that scar or wound will remain on you until you do these two steps: First, remove the band and hold it between your fingers. Second, simply say '*hylja*'. This word is part of the Concealment Charm and 'resets' the magic veil."

My eyes couldn't stop looking at the beauty behind her scars. "Are you sure you don't want this back—"

"You keep this Lisa," she said, stopping me from removing the bracelet. "I will use the Concealment Charm until my workers find another Eternling. With you being home on Earth, I believe this may be more useful to you than to me now, so please, see this as a gift."

Inna was kind by all definitions of the word, and I couldn't believe she cared about something as silly as my appearance.

"Thank you, Inna," I said, feeling my anxiousness die down.

～～～

Gaius gave me some Boolavogue money for lunch before I left to train with Captain Ekron; it was just blue and yellow paper with an elegant castle on the front. He told me to "snag a bite" from one of the town's shops, though forgetting to mention which one to visit or when to return. I had never gone by myself to buy food… or to the Kingdom alone… or to a city without an adult in general, but I was getting used to the independence of being the Agapéd Bearer and quite enjoyed doing what I wanted.

I went through the entrance that led to the hilltop of Boolavogue's farmlands and made my way down the trail. When my stomach growled, I saw a farmer selling fresh fruit and fried potatoes on a stick; obviously, I chose the potatoes and ate them as I walked to the Kingdom's entrance gates. The same guard from before—the one who knew Gaius just by the look of his face—stood tall as I approached him.

"Name—oh, I remember you," he said. "You're the freckled girl with the Keeper, right?"

Didn't think my freckles stuck out that much.

"Yes, sir. Lisa Robbie."

The guard checked his list and found my name.

They already have me on the list—so fast!

He looked back down at me. "Well, I still need a form of identification to prove it's you." I then showed him my COIN as the edges of the stone glowed green, proving it was me and not an imposter. He nodded at the confirmation and let me through. It felt pretty cool to enter a Kingdom with nothing but my name and glow from a metal chip.

It took me a good while to find my way through the city, even with the pale blue street signs pointing which way was to the King and Queen's home. When I finally reached the huge entrance gate to the castle, bald Captain Ekron was waiting for me. He was like Gaius with his robust stare and muscly arms, and I'm sure most people would agree him to be intimidating. Not me. I had been with a burly, stubborn teacher for two months, so Ekron was just another friendly face.

"What does Gaius have you teaching me, Captain?" I asked as he led me to the training grounds.

"Today, we will be seeing your skill at weaponry," he said in his deep masculine voice, his braided goatee going up and down as he talked. "Gaius says your magic is strong—saw all the proof I needed yesterday—and wants you to channel that through other means of fighting." We passed by the garden fountain as Captain Ekron continued. "When fighting beasts, sometimes using magic isn't enough. You will need a proper weapon infused with specific types of ore and material to take down the tricky fiends. That also means knowing the right fighting tactics for each as well. We will train you with the fiercest of Hunters, making you stronger than you've ever imagined."

"I'll get to fight with a sword today?" I asked him, feeling a mixture of excitement and anxiousness.

"Wouldn't be a proper training day without one!" he happily bellowed.

I smiled as we entered the Hunter grounds. *Alright—this shouldn't be as hard as learning magic. Let's do it!*

30
YOUR SUN-PUNISHED GIRLFRIEND

Why am I so weak!

It was mid-afternoon, and not only was I worn out, but I looked like a complete *fool* battling with swords. The full-length weapons were *so heavy*—even the practice ones made of wood. Prince Caelum made it look easy when he practiced sparring with Ekron. I, on the other hand, could barely get two swings in before Ekron tagged me with a practice sword. I couldn't even swing fast enough—stupid muscles for not being stronger—and wasn't used to such close combat. Normally, I used my terrain magic and kept my distance when training with Gaius, so adding that on top of never wielding a weapon before made my first lesson nothing but frustrating.

"Can I try something shorter or lighter, please?" I asked Captain Ekron as I lay on the dirty ground.

He said, helping me up, "Well, I suppose for now... until your strength and stamina improve."

"She could try the cutlass," the Prince interjected into our conversation as he stood off to the side of the training rink. He and I were taking turns sparring with Ekron, though I was pretty sure he was just taking notes on what not to do during a spar every time I stepped in front of our Captain. "It's shorter with a slight curve. Plus, the training sword is about the same weight as the original."

"Hmm... I think that could work." Captain Ekron then went to the training table and pulled out a sturdy wooden sword, much shorter and thinner than my current one. The blade curved at the tip, reminded me of a pirate's weapon. "What do you say, Lisa? Want to give it a try?"

I picked it up, and it felt much better in my grasp.

"I like it," I said, giving it a couple of swings.

"Alright, let's continue our practice, then!"

Captain Ekron had us work on our footing and sword stance. It reminded me a lot of Gaius' magic training: making sure my feet were sturdy yet ready to move at a moment's notice, moving with my opponent, and backing away in the right direction when an attack came. We even practiced guarding with a sword, learning how to block an attack without the use of a shield—just using the blade and proper hand position on the hilt. I still wasn't the best at it compared to the Prince, but I did see improvement as the day went on.

During Cal's training, when I was off on the sidelines supposedly taking notes, I couldn't help but watch him... He was... rather cute. Could have just been the reality of him being a prince, but when he swung the sword and defended against Ekron perfectly, I couldn't look away. Especially when he smiled. Somehow, that gesture of his sent my heart strumming like a harp, and I had to keep eyeing the ground when he sent that grin my way or my face would blossom with pink embarrassment.

As Captain Ekron finished up our lessons, I went to return my practice sword and take a rest at the Laze when sparks of fire and sounds of ice cracking zoomed past my ear. Out past the Laze were some Hunters training with *magic*. My curious heart wanted to see more than my body wanted to rest, and I saw two male Hunters sparring.

One had magic that made his arms turn as hot as lava, using them as boiling boulder swords to fight against his opponent, who could create frost out of thin air. *He must have Frost Creation magic, like how Inna can create water.* He was making frost shards, working on long-range attacks as the lava Mystic used close-range combat. I had never seen people fight with magic before... and it was one of the most thrilling experiences of my life—

"That's Elio and Nole."

I was in such deep concentration that I didn't even notice the Prince come up from behind me, making me jump like a startled rabbit.

"Wow, you scare easy," he said, smiling at my embarrassed self.

"I don't—you just came up out of nowhere," I refuted, even though that was a lie. I would jump at the slightest sounds, even when concentrating on the most menial task. I looked back at the two Mystics fighting. "Are they like Heroes or something?"

"Those two? No, they are purely Hunters—only fighting dark creatures and beasts; no fighting real humans or saving towns from gangs of enemies, and no treasure hunting either. Everyone knows them here, and they like to show off a lot. They always have the most requests from across our continent and bring in quite a lot of glory to the Kingdom."

"*Oh,* so people here can be hired to do hunting jobs?"

"Yeah, of course. Would be kind of pointless if the Kingdom of Hunters and Monster Weaponry didn't have actual monster hunters—you didn't know that?"

I lowered my voice. "Sorry, no."

Cal then looked at me differently, putting away his jokester and blunt remarks. He stood next to me and leaned closer to my right ear. "So, my mother told me you're something called the 'Agapéd Bearer' and that's why you're out here training with me... but what exactly is that?"

I guess anyone can know without my permission, can't they...

With a straight face, I answered him. "Honestly, I don't really know for sure, just that I'm supposed to get stronger and defeat the universe's most dangerous dark magic one day."

Cal stared at me as if I just said the most unbelievable news he had ever heard.

Noting his bewilderment, I hurriedly added, "Okay, it sounded a *whole* lot scarier once I said it out loud."

"*A bit!*" Cal guffawed in amazement. "Well, guess you'll be here a while, then, training with me."

"What is that supposed to mean?"

"I didn't mean it as 'you're weak,' I promise! However, lifting a long sword is usually a requirement for basic 'save-the-world' work."

"*Hey—*"

Cal laughed. "I'm just joking... mostly—I just meant that you have a long time before that happens to get as strong as you need to be, and I have to keep practicing myself before I can take the role of King someday... I just meant it will be nice having someone else working toward something bigger—that's all."

I wasn't too sure about working with the Prince at first... but it seemed we had more in common than I thought; he didn't make me feel so alone.

Admiring the Hunters still sparring, watching as fire clashed with ice, I asked him, "So, do you have magic like them as well, seeing as you're a prince and all?"

Cal turned away from me, looking at some random Hunter in the audience. "Not really," he answered, rubbing his hand through his fluffy hair.

That was the first time the Prince's confidence—in the short time I knew him—went away... but my question was not strange. Magic was normal. We watched two strong men use it well in front of us, and I used it during practice.

I thought a prince would love to talk about magic...

"What do you mean by—" I began, but the crowd's *oohing* made me shift my gaze back toward the battle.

Nole smashed Elio's lava sword with a huge snowball of pure frost, freezing the fiery opponent in his place and winning their match. Each side cheered for both men—including Cal and me—and we watched as Nole unfrozen Elio's feet, giving a hardy forearm handshake.

"That was so cool!" I said with a huge smile, making Cal's grin reappear. As the Hunters dismissed to continue on with their training, I looked up toward the castle. Lessons were over, and my curiosity finally had a chance to breathe. *I really, really want to go exploring in there...*

I must have been a pretty obvious daydreamer or looked flat-out ridiculous when staring off into space because Cal nudged my arm and started walking toward the exit of the training grounds.

"Hey, follow me. I'll give you a tour around the castle if you don't have to go home yet?"

My hair was in a messy ponytail, my shoes were covered in dirt, and bruises speckled my elbows and shoulders—definitely not fit for a royal tour. *"Really?* Do I need to, like, change into something nicer?"

He huffed. "It's my house, and I say a Hunters' wear is always appropriate... unless Mother catches us, so just stay close to me."

Cal was also covered in dirt and looked as filthy as I did, so having him be confident in his appearance made me feel less embarrassed about mine. I ran up next to him and smiled as he led me up into the castle's domain.

"This is the Grand Hall," Cal said as we walked by a pair of colossal, opened doors, peering into a giant ballroom with an arched ceiling and elongated windows that ran along each side of the walls. Some workers went in and out, clearing away tables and chairs, dusting every nook and cranny. "If the Kingdom hosts a party or needs to gather a lot of Hunters in one place—clean and free of dirt, of course—it will be here."

"So cool!" I said as some maids and chefs worked diligently, putting away dishes from a table in the corner.

"And this is the kitchen!" he said as we walked through the Grand Hall and into a smaller room off to the right. The smell of grilled chicken and cinnamon apples instantly hit my nose as we entered.

I assumed he and his family would have a private chef... but not twenty of them! They all were busy cleaning dishes from lunch and preparing meals for the Hunters who had long journeys ahead. Neither of them were bothered by our intrusion, smiling and bowing at Prince Caelum as he went around their busy bodies.

"Everything looks so *good*!" I said, trailing Cal.

A chef was making something resembling chicken alfredo, flipping the creamy pasta into the air and easily catching it. Another was cooking apple cider or possibly apple jelly—the smell of sweet citrus and cinnamon wafting through the warm kitchen air.

"Here." Cal held out his arm and passed me a sandwich in the shape of a flower—crusts cut off and pinched on the edges—right out from inside one of the *seven* refrigerators. It was a pillow of delicious beauty. "It's almond butter and apple jelly—bet you don't have this on Earth."

I grabbed it and awed. "We do, but not like this! So cool!"

Back through the doors and down a flight of stairs were the familiar duo doors to—

"The Throne Room, which you've seen before, right?" Cal whispered as some guards were near the familiar double doors.

Walking by the guards, I whispered back, "Haven't seen inside, but I did pass by when the Queen came out of it."

Cal hushedly giggled. "Only an Earthian could make Mother drop a meeting as you did. If you ever get to see the room, let's just hope it's for something good. It's used for knighting Hunters, royal weddings, confidential meetings, and whatever else is too important to discuss in the open."

So cool!

"And if you gotta go, you gotta go here," Cal said with his arms on his hips as we stared at two glossy wooden doors. "It's the Royal Bathroom—mainly for guests and not for Hunters, but you're a guest of the Keeper, so you can use these—oh, but, uh, one is for—"

"I know how bathrooms work," I interrupted as I went toward the one that had "women" etched in silver on the door frame.

This is a bathroom?

Inside was a couch, changing rooms, and individual cubicles with their own toilet, shower, and sink—all pristine white and adorned with pothos plants that hung over the doors. There was a mirror the span of the wall right next to the complimentary robes, reminding me of how dirty I looked. I know Cal said not to worry about the grime, but being in a bathroom nicer than my whole neighborhood made me want to use the amenities. So, I quickly washed my hands and face before returning to continue my tour with the Prince.

Upstairs, after seeing the guests' rooms, library, and study areas, Cal showed me his room, but I only got to see the door that led into it.

"Is your room dirty or something?" I joked, noticing him blocking the handle with his body.

He chuckled. "No—maids clean it every day. I just, well… you'll get to see it sometime. But I can assure you, you'll be impressed when that time comes. Oh—I saved the best for last! Come on!"

The Prince ran down the halls with me tagging along, slowing down his speed anytime we turned a corner in fear of bumping into his mom. It was fun sneaking around with Cal, being close to him—our hearts racing when he thought he saw his mom on two occasions. We ended up outside and behind the castle, away from the Hunter training ground and where the mountain was nothing but a field of lush green grass with a forest in the distance. The sun was just beginning to set, making the scenery look picture-perfect with sherbet clouds.

Through the woods and on our right was the rockface of a mountain, where huge caves resided. From our distance, the entrance to each cave was as tall as a two-story building, with lights strung around the openings. Boolavogue workers were coming in and out, wearing different garments than those in the castle. Their chests were padded with thick leather while their armbands and gloves were dusted with dirt and small loose patches of brown fur—odd.

"Besides the Kingdom's weaponry forge, which I'm not allowed to see without Mother's permission, this is by *far* the best thing about my home," Cal said, walking by my side, straight toward the huge caves. "Most kingdoms have armies of men, horses, and even wild dogs; what we have slags all of them. Just wait and see."

Suddenly, meaty roars bellowed from the cave, each one sounding louder and grizzlier than the last. My heart dropped in my chest. After what happened to Valhalla... the unknown of a cave filled with yells terrified me, human, beast, or animal. I stepped behind Cal to take cover, thinking something had to be wrong, my shoulders tensing.

"What's the matter?" he said with a grin. "You need to stop being so scared if you're gonna be a Hunter, you know?"

Two guards passed me; their faces looked unfazed by the monstrous yells. Another ran past us and entered the cave with a sack of apples in his hands. He was *smiling*.

I straightened up but still stayed a few inches behind him. "Sorry, just a habit." *What is it Cal is about to show me? Do they catch monsters or something— hiding them away in this cave? Why is everyone so calm right now!*

We stepped inside, and Cal announced, "Here it is—Boolavogue's finest warriors and a Hunter's best friend-of-a beast!"

With just one glance, my eyes took in the sight of a cave filled with giant, furry, minivan-sized *bears*—all ranging from black, brown, and speckled caramel-colored fur. Two roars came from a duo of brown bears to my right, making my heart rattle hard in my chest as I continued to use Cal as my shield; he either didn't mind or didn't notice, continuing the casual walk forward.

I thought the bears were fighting because they jumped on each other, rumbling the floor and causing dust to fall from the cave's ceiling, but the two workers next to them were *giggling!* Upon closer examination, the animals were tugging and fighting over a giant ball resembling a rubber tire.

Are they... playing?

But all the others—every single bear farther inside the tunnel—were surprisingly... calm, almost like tired dogs after a long day of running outside. Most of the bears were in their cubbies—large sectioned-off pins made of wood and stone—sleeping on leaves and old blankets, while a few had elaborate saddles strapped around their backs like horses.

What in the world—

"You have domesticated grizzly bears?" I uttered in shock as we walked further inside, noticing some fur-covered Boolavogians bowing at the Prince.

"These aren't *grizzly* bears; they are *Gora* bears—the mighty 'Mountain Wardens' they are also called," Cal said as we walked by a bear keeper feeding the beasts' meat as if they were harmless critters. "Gora bears are kind of like oversized dogs. They love to play, be petted, and go for walks... and kill the occasional vorrg or bilefiend when their Hunter allows it."

We walked closer to one of the Gora bears that was eating a plate of fish and berries. I noticed its fur wasn't grizzly but shaggy, shedding like crazy. Its face was pointed like a polar bear's snout, had happy, tired eyes, and had a long wagging tail that looked to be the length of my leg. Some war paint streaked its forehead, and strands of long fur were braided with beads and string. As it finished its food, I heard it say in my mind, "I wish they brought me more apples," before dozing off to sleep.

My nerves finally calmed down with the threat of being eaten alive completely gone. *Wow, they are just like giant pampered dogs.*

"Which one is yours?" I asked Cal, watching the bear snuggle up in a corner to sleep. "I'm assuming, as 'The Prince,' you would have your own."

"She must be out with the other bears running through the forest—you'll love her. Actually, wait by the entrance of the cave, and I'll go get her for you!" Cal then took off running, very excited for me to meet his bear. Never thought I would see a day when a boy would be bringing me a monster-killing beast as his welcoming gift.

I sat on a stone bench by the entrance of the roaring cave, listening to the bears wishing they had more apples and thinking about what they would do tomorrow. The atmosphere of the Kingdom was boisterous... yet inviting. Everyone was so kind to me, and using swords was thrilling even though I was very bad at it. Cal said the best part was the bears, and if he asked, I would agree... but that would be a coverup, a lie. Being with him... *that has been the best part—*

"*Who* are *you?*"

I jerked, tensing my shoulders, at the sound of a young girl's voice yelling in my ear. I quickly turned to see a little brown-headed girl inches from my face, breathing on my neck as if my personal space didn't matter to her. She had hazel eyes, wide and very glossy, and didn't have a speck of dirt on her elegant garment. She squatted on the bench, but even then, she was still short—probably six or seven years old. *What the heck is a little girl doing out in the woods and not running away from the sight of bears?*

"Uh, Lisa," I answered the little girl.

She looked my body up and down before squinting toward my shoulders. "What's wrong with your arms?"

I glanced at my arms, but nothing seemed out of the ordinary. My vezper bite was hidden with the concealment band Inna gave me, and I had a couple of new bruises. That was it.

The little girl grew impatient with me for not answering instantly. "Are those moles or millions of birthmarks, or are you just dirty?"

I squinted. "You mean my... *freckles?*"

She widened her eyes before squatting farther down beside me on the bench. "Oh, I didn't know people had hordes of them like that. Dad's got only one on his ear. How'd you get them?"

Who IS this kid... to know the word "hordes" and act as if freckles are a rarity?

"From the sun."

"What do you mean?"

"Instead of getting tan, I just get freckles—kinda like getting kissed by the sun as some people say."

"So, it's like a punishment for not wearing sun lotion when it's hot outside?"

By this time, I couldn't help but laugh. This little girl was the bluntest kid I ever encountered and had no problem making fun of a stranger. "I guess so—what's your name, by the way?"

Suddenly, a booming vibration rustled through the forest, fast and swift. Twigs broke, and leaves crunched just yards ahead of me. I looked up to find Cal riding on the back of a Gora bear, only this one had oat-colored fur with ears and feet the shade of caramel. I thought only polar bears could be white; she was truly a beautiful, mighty creature.

He jumped off the leather saddle, giving the giant pet a cookie-shaped treat he took from the side satchel. "Celine, what are you doing here?" Cal said to the little girl.

She hopped off the stone bench, her boots crushing the daisies below. "I got bored after dinner and came to find you. Mother didn't know where you were, but I saw you through my bedroom window going to the bear caves, so I followed."

"This is your sister?" I asked, now seeing the resemblance in both hair color and confident attitude.

"Yeah, Celine. She's seven and *not* supposed to be out of the castle without the royal guard," Cal said, glaring down at his little sister.

"I wasn't alone. I was with your sun-punished girlfriend."

"What—"

I interjected, "She means my freckles," though, slightly offended by the Princess' remark.

"Celine, you can't call people names like that. Now, go back to the castle—"

"But I wanna stay with *you.*"

I approached Cal's fluffy white bear as the royal siblings bickered. The beast had brown eyes and well-kept fur as soft as a Pomeranian dog. Her face was as tall as my head down to my navel, but she wasn't threatening at all once I got up close. She told me her name was Honey as I went to pet her. I extended my hand and scratched right underneath her chin, making her tail wag hard against the forest floor. *I can't believe I am petting a bear right now!*

"How come you named her Honey?" I asked Cal, my fingers brushing through the Gora bear's fur.

He and his little sister stopped fighting, and neither one was breaking their stare. "How did you know her name was Honey?" Cal asked with curious eyes.

"She told me—I kinda can understand what animals think." I smiled. "And she said she wants more apples tomorrow. Actually, all the bears said they do."

Cal's face was lost for words.

On the other hand, the Princess was utterly impressed and awestruck with me, about to burst with excitement and questions. "You have magic that lets you *talk* to *animals?* Oo—what else is she thinking? Does she like it when I brush her fur—I didn't know Cal had a friend like you!" She kept blurting out, running right up next to me.

Cal was beaming, letting out a huff. "*Two* kinds of magic? You actually have *two kinds of magic?*"

"*Well...*" I started blushing, not used to impressing someone like the Prince and Princess of the Kingdom.

"You mean you have *more* than two?"

"For now—it's kinda why I'm training secretly with you."

"And I thought being from Earth was the strangest thing about you." He walked over and started scratching behind Honey's ear. "Sometime, you'll have to show me what all your magic can do—after training, of course."

"So... you call her Honey because..." I reminded him.

"Oh, right—it's because her ears and paws look like they've been honey-dipped. I knew her as a cub, and the name 'Honey' just stuck with her ever since. She's one of the best Gora bears in the pack when it comes to endurance and loves it when we take her out for rides."

As Cal was talking about his furry friend, I thought it would interest him to meet my less fuzzy one.

"I also have a companion who joins me on adventures. Tuff, you can come out if you want."

My little orange sprite appeared on the side of my left shoulder, where he had sat the whole time invisibly. He was nervous about meeting new people but gave them each a bow out of courtesy.

"*Whoa*—what is that thing?" Cal asked, bewildered, inching closer to look at Tuff's adorable face.

I was surprised the Prince didn't know of memory sprites. "Tuff is a glainie, a good magic creature that helps me remember things I might have forgotten. I saved his life, and he wanted to repay me by being mine. He normally stays invisible and floats around me during the day—has been here the whole time, a bit scared of the bears, if being honest."

Celine started standing on her tiptoes and raised her voice with excitement. "*He's so cute! Can I hold him, please?*"

Tuff then floated to the top of my head at the sight of Celine's grabby hands.

He didn't like being held by anyone else except me. "Sorry, but glainies are pretty shy around... well, everyone except the person they are bonded with."

Celine started pouting but quickly got over it when Tuff whistled at her, showing off his glowing gem. Out from behind Cal, Honey came over and sniffed Tuff, scaring him half to death. My little sprite went flying right behind me and turned invisible again. We all started laughing; Honey just wanted to say 'hello,' but Tuff didn't understand that.

Cal petted Honey's head with a charming smirk on his face. "So... would you like to take a ride with her?" he asked me.

Though I could read Honey's mind and knew she was kind to humans, she still was a massive animal. Her paws were the size of my ribcage, and one fall off of her back would knock me unconscious. "Um, are you sure?" I said with hesitation as I examined the furry beast from head to toe.

"Don't worry," Cal said, giving Honey a bear biscuit from inside the pouch on her saddle. "I'm a top-class rider, so you have nothing to fear." He then cocked a smile. "You saying you don't trust me?"

My cheeks turned red as my heart put up a defense. "What—no! It's not that. It's just..."

"Then, come on," the Prince said with his hand held out. "You'll be fine— you really think I would risk a lashing from my mother if I got the Keeper's pupil slagged off a bear on the first day?"

My eyes widened as I looked at his hand. *I mean he has a point... but do I really need to hold his hand—mine are so sweaty from the sudden embarrassment—*

"I wanna ride with Lisa, too!" Celine shouted, jumping in front of Cal and making his hand fall back down to his side; I was relieved.

Well, if Celine isn't scared...

I smiled back at Cal. "Then, I would love to."

The saddle on Honey's back had two seats, but it looked like Celine and I could easily fit in one. I was no expert on riding gear, but I could tell this was nothing like a horse's saddle. Instead of a bridle wrapped around its head, Honey had two straps that crisscrossed, going from the shoulders to underneath her tummy and back up to the saddle. It reminded me of an oversized dog harness. To control the bear, the saddle had two large leather handles near the front with the horn in between. It seemed that if one were to pull hard, it would pull the restraints on the bear's shoulders.

Cal hoisted Celine up first toward the front and then helped me next, using his clasped hands as my footstool as I grasped the saddle with my arms. We two girls fit perfectly together in the front seat. Cal hopped onto the back of the saddle and sat behind me, the closest I had ever sat with a boy before, and I felt my heartbeat quicken.

"Make sure you hold onto the saddle horn or use the leather grips with me," Cal said right up against my ear, reaching forward to grip Honey's handlebar reins. "Riding a bear is nothing like riding a horse."

"Well, I have never ridden either to be able to tell the difference," I said, partially joking but *very* much serious.

Cal leaned forward, extended his arms with Celine and me in between, and grasped the leather reins. He shouted *fara* as he used his heels to hit the sides of Honey's stomach. Honey then jolted forward and ran full speed across the grassy mountain plain.

I had to get used to the bumpy ride, but after a few seconds of readjusting, I began to enjoy every second. I held on tight as the mountain breeze zoomed across my face and through my tied hair. We were going so fast, passing by roaming Boolavogue groundsmen and guards, seeing all of the castle in just a matter of seconds. *"This is amazing!"* I shouted through sheer excitement.

"Told you—better than a horse any day of the year!" Cal said from behind me, making me very happy he invited me on a tour of his castle.

⁓

Stars and night began to paint the sky, and the castle lights flickered warm yellows simultaneously. We could see the Inner Kingdom in the far distance as Cal's pet bear rushed across the castle's mountain—streets still lively with music and late-night partiers. Many Boolavogue guards started following the lit stone pathways back towards the castle and exit gates, either to go back home or start the night shift.

Spending the day with Cal was the most fun I had in such a long time—the most thrilling thing I had ever experienced, honestly. Even though he was a prince, he didn't act like it. My only concept of one was through movies I saw on Earth, which probably were not the best comparison. I thought he would be stuck up and selfish, hate dirt, and wear a crown, but he was fun and enjoyed learning how to fight just like me.

Back home, I didn't have many friends who were boys. It wasn't because I was awkward—at least, from my point of view anyway. Life always just kept putting me in groups or next to tables with girls whenever a new school year came around. I also wasn't too obsessed with boys to care enough about them noticing me like Lily was. She intentionally wore short sleeves when it was cold in hopes of getting a basketball player's hoodie to wear during class. She would even walk around the lunch room with some of her cheerleader friends just so the athletes would notice her. I didn't understand it at all. Though with Cal, I kind of liked the attention from him... but that could just be because he was royalty.

Cal went ahead and dropped off Celine before his mom started to worry, and he and I rode Honey back to the Gora bear cave. The two of us began our trek to the castle along the lit stone pathway in the fields, making light small talk.

"Sorry about Celine calling you names," Cal said as the blues of the skies turned dark. "She doesn't get out of the castle very often and learns a lot of talk from the guards."

"Don't worry about it. I thought she was adorable," I responded. "Takes a lot for someone to hurt my feelings... I take it she doesn't have many friends her age either?"

"Not really. We both take our studies in the castle while everyone else has Tutor outside, so being around other kids isn't something we grew up with. When she turns fourteen like me, she'll be able to visit the town and make all the girl friends she wants—hopefully learning more manners than hunter-talk as a real princess should..." The Prince leaned forward to look at my freckled face. "By the way... the way you fought with magic during our sparring match yesterday was *insane*."

I couldn't help but smile at his compliment. "I'm not that good yet, nothing compared to those two Hunters we saw sparring—Elio and Nole—but thanks for saying that." I fiddled with my fingers behind my back when I asked, "So... before when I asked you about having magic... is it that you don't have any or something—I just noticed you weren't too excited to talk about it earlier today... and I was just wondering?"

I pulled back my lip in between my teeth. *I hope that wasn't too pushy. What if I embarrassed him? Maybe I shouldn't have said anything...*

Ruffling from his shorts interrupted the silence as his hands stuffed into the pockets. "Well... I mean... I do. I just don't really talk about it."

My eyes widened and curiosity made me forget anything about personal boundaries. "Why's that? I figured being a prince would make you want to talk about it."

He tittered out of the innocence of my answer. "Yeah... but my magic isn't the kind I should have."

"I didn't think there was a type of magic that future kings shouldn't have."

"Well... everyone thought I would inherit Dad's magic. He has some of the most powerful Crystallian magic most people have ever seen, but I turned out to have Illusionary magic a couple of years ago. No one in our lineage was born with that power, so it had to be Starnate. Heh—didn't even get a chance to see it fall from the sky when it landed in my heart. Even though that means it could be more powerful someday, it's not the kind of magic I could ever use as a Sonon."

I was a little confused and didn't understand how having certain magic was bad. "What's wrong with Illusionary magic?"

"Oh, right, you're not from here. See, my father isn't from Boolavogue, and he had to work hard to earn the people's trust when he married Mother... at least, that is what she tells me. No way would Father ever talk to me like that. Since his magic is so powerful and uses it to slay many beasts, it would look wrong of me to go around with a different power—one that can turn you invisible and is known for sneakery. We are Hunters... and my magic can't fight. It's only good for running away or winning dishonestly."

The words "turn invisible" rang in my ears and intrigued me, and I couldn't stop my nosiness from wanting to know more. "Well... I would never judge you... do you think I could see it, then?"

He raised his eyebrows. "Well... since I know your Agapéd secret, guess it's only fair. Promise not to tell, though?"

I nodded. "I promise."

Cal then held out his hand and made sure no one was looking around. In seconds, his fingertips down to his wrist vanished—completely invisible!

"This is about as much as I can do, seeing as I only practice when I'm alone..."

A guard, twenty feet away, started to approach us.

Cal quickly reappeared his hand but still hid it behind his back. "Well, now you see why magic like this is wrong for someone like me."

I waited for the guard to pass—him bowing at the Prince and continuing his route—before whispering excitedly, "Are you kidding? You just made your whole hand disappear—coolest magic I've ever seen!"

"Thanks, but I can't let others know about it—not even my own family. No matter how grand I think it is, I can't even use it and expect the Kingdom to trust me as they do with the King. I will take the throne someday, and I can't have Boolavogue see me as weak—turning invisible to manipulate my foes. I need to win my battles because of skill and might..." Cal looked down at the ground. "I'm supposed to be like him—to *be* King one day. I can't afford to slip up and be different. They wouldn't trust me if I weren't like my father."

"Have you ever talked to him about it?" I asked. I could never see anyone being disappointed with the power to turn invisible.

His chin jerked and he let out a smile. "*Talk* to him—you're funny, Lisa. I could never do something like that."

My eyes surveyed the dimming sky. "Then, how will you know he and the Kingdom won't like it if you never show them?"

Cal shrugged, his hands back in his pockets. "It's just the way it is. Not sure what Earth is like, but here, it's easier to trust a new King if they are *exactly* like their predecessor, and in a land of Hunters, the strongest and most powerful sit on the throne. So"—he kicked a stone laid perfectly on our path—"I'll just have to never use this sneaky magic—can't fight with it anyway. Kinda useless for a Sonon."

His face drooped with doubt, and I could tell he truly believed that his magic was bad—that he could never become a great Mystic *and* King at the same time. Even though I had no idea what royalty life was like for him, I couldn't let him believe that lie.

"I may not be from here, but I do know that isn't true," I began. "What I learned in this world is that there are only two types of magic that are purely good and bad: light and darkness. Everything in between is just a combination of them both. We all have a little bit of each in us, but that doesn't make our magic bad; it's what you *do* with the magic that determines if it's good or evil." I smiled up at him. "So, if you use your magic for good things, I doubt the Kingdom would ever see you as weak. If you wanted..." My eyes found the stone pathway to be more intriguing again as my face blushed. "I could, uh, help you with it sometime, though I would probably be just as clueless as you."

"Huh... I've never heard it put like that before. You sure you're from Earth? You sound more like a Magic Guardian if anything else." Cal chuckled, seeming a little more impressed with me than before.

"Well, I'm not surprised after being around them for so long."

Cal then laughed harder. "Of course, you've met them—I should've guessed after seeing you so calm around the Keeper of Stars."

"He's about as scary as Ekron, and you seem to act just fine around our Captain."

We soon made it to the back entrance of the castle, where we saw Queen Leonora looking down at us from the upper window; it was the classic mom stare, saying "It's late, and you shouldn't be out this late," with just a glance.

"Guess I'll see you tomorrow then—and about helping me with my magic... I'll take you up on that offer some time," the Prince told me.

"Sounds good," I said, smiling as I watched him pass by the entrance guards and up the castle stairs.

My heart wouldn't stop beating the entire way back to Gaius' home, thrumming with a new happiness I never felt before. And I couldn't wait to see Prince Caelum again.

31
LIVING WITH A GARDENER

Last night was the first time I slept in my new enchanted bedroom at Gaius'
home.

I had returned from Boolavogue and hadn't seen him at all before I went to
bed. Figured he would've waited up for me, standing by his door with a worried
look because I stayed out past dark. He was not like Mom; one difference about
the Keeper I enjoyed. I used his odd rainforest shower, found an assortment of
thick, luscious towels under the sink, and drew a new entry of Gora bears in my
book—all without him returning from work. Being the morning person that
he was, I figured he would be in bed, but it seemed to me that he worked all
morning *and* all night, taking breaks during the afternoon. *How does he run on
such little sleep?*

An abrupt commotion from outside my bedroom door woke me up. It
sounded like pots and pans being rummaged through, along with a scent of
sizzling pork coming through the door crevice. The sun hadn't even finished
rising, but with the unknown sounds from Gaius' cottage stirring up, I couldn't
go back to sleep. *Guess this is my new alarm clock: early morning Gaius cooking
breakfast.*

Never before did the Keeper of Stars make me nervous, but the fact that I
had never lived alone with the male species before made leaving my room quite
challenging. *Does he get grumpy in the mornings? Is this his 'me time' and doesn't
want to be disturbed? What if he's, like, indecent and doesn't think I'm awake? Or*

what if he DOES think I'm awake and cooks me breakfast and I never show up to eat it—making him upset during our lessons and I have to suffer the consequences!

Tuff woke up from his sleep as my overthinking started to take over his thoughts as well, lazily rolling over the throw pillow next to my feathered one.

"Sorry, bud," I apologized to my little orange sprite.

He then flew up next to me, wiped his sleepy eyes, and gave me a reassuring hoot.

I pushed back all the needless worries and finally reached the door. *It's just Gaius, Lisa. Nothing to be scared of.* I slowly twisted the knob as if I was sneaking through a stranger's home and walked through the laundry room. The door on the other side was wide open, allowing the smell of skillet vegetables and smoky meat to overpower the scent of plants—making my stomach growl. Luckily, whatever Gaius was doing in the kitchen covered up its rumble.

Peering past the black fridge—there was my burly magic teacher, transformed into a chef. He wore a sleeveless shirt and the same old work pants, wearing house shoes instead of walking barefoot like I was. The brown waves in his hair were extra curled, but his short boxed beard looked to be freshly trimmed. His eyes were wide awake and rather happy as if cooking was just as fun as woodworking to him; it was shocking. I didn't think manly men like him would ever find cooking enjoyable—it always seemed like a mother's job.

"I didn't know you cooked," I said, feeling comfortable enough to enter his cooking domain.

"That surprises you?" he questioned in his deep morning voice, frying up some skillet potatoes with green and red chilies.

"You just seem like you'd order in a lot or eat around town."

Gaius chuckled at my remark. "Why call someone else to do a job I'm better at? Take a seat. I'll get you a plate ready."

Getting served breakfast that isn't from a cereal box or the snack cabinet—I could get used to mornings here.

Gaius grabbed some eggs from his fridge and an assortment of fresh herbs from the plants hanging near the kitchen cabinets. He chopped, minced, and julienned a rainbow of spices and threw them all into the hearty breakfast skillet with the pork and potatoes—giving them all a nice flip or two in the air before landing back into the pan again. Next, he grabbed a smaller pan that hung above the gas-powered stove and cracked four eggs inside it. I normally would have my eggs scrambled with minimal spice, but I wasn't about to tell Gaius that. He then took out three plates and served me up a small portion on one, his on another—twice the size with three eggs on top of the meat-potato mountain—and an even smaller one of just potatoes for Tuff.

We sat down at his small dining room table and began eating one of the best breakfasts I had ever had—sunny-side-up eggs included! I know some teens out there find it hard to start conversations with adults or even find being alone at a dinner table and eating with someone awkward. Not me. I was weird and found talking to Gaius to be as easy as talking to myself.

Mixing my runny egg with my mountain of oily breakfast, I asked Gaius, "How come planet Kalm and the city of EverWake are a lot like Earth?"

After swallowing the biggest bite of pork I had ever seen, he answered, "We're humans, not aliens, Lisa. We grow and think just the same—even in different galaxies and planets."

"Hm... guess that makes sense..." I stabbed a potato with my fork. "But, like, *why* are so many things called the same—like, *why* are potatoes also called 'potatoes' here? Why not... 'starchies' or something?"

He took a gulp of water, completely unfazed by my odd question. "How do you know Earth didn't get that name from us?"

I was about to bite the glistening tuber but could only hover it over my mouth as I pondered that question. *Wait... could that be true?*

As I lowered my fork, Gaius smirked as he glanced down at his plate and stirred his food. *Ah... another Gaius joke... I think...*

In mid-chew of potato and pepper, I took notice of the Keeper's bare, muscly arms, shoulders, and chest covered in white and pink wounds. He always wore a jacket or cloak with a cotton shirt underneath, only ever showing his elbows and neck. He was well-built and probably would have no trouble getting a lady if he desired, and it did make me question how he stayed in shape. Not once did I see any trace of workout equipment or see him lift weights, but then again, he was a *Keeper*. The man had the power of plants by his side. *Maybe he uses trees as dumbbells, or maybe it's just his magic perk: muscles galore.*

I scanned his tan-scarred shoulders and chest beneath the manly tank top. Gaius was knowledgeable in combat, and I never saw him struggle with magic.

The multitude of wounds was a surprise to me. "How come you have all those scars?" I asked.

He took a drink from his giant glass of water. "Battles."

I pointed my fork toward him. "What's the white one under your collarbone—the biggest one?"

Gaius didn't look up at me. "From a ferna vorrg. First time I ever fought one."

"Couldn't you just heal it with one of your plants?"

He grinned before making eye contact with me. "At the time, I didn't know how. It was about 500 years ago."

"*Whoa*... sometimes, I forget you've lived forever..." I said, making Gaius chuckle. "So, since I'll be staying here, I wanna help out some if that's okay?"

"I won't refuse help if you insist," he said, taking another bite of pork and vegetables, still unbothered by my random questions.

"Can I help *wherever,* then? Like, with the Veradome, too?"

"As long as you don't mess with any of the pollinations or wander where you aren't allowed."

I smiled big. "Then, can I also help you with the Wishing Stars?"

Gaius stared at his almost empty plate. "Ah—no."

"*Please?*"

"I know what you're doing... and it won't work this time."

He didn't look up, already knowing I gave him the baby-doll eyes again. *Dang, it...*

After breakfast, Gaius and I sparred with magic, and I noticed my reflexes and agility suddenly enhanced. It surprised me because I hadn't practiced fighting but only for two days... and with swords, nonetheless.

"Am I getting a magic perk of agility or something?" I asked him, the morning sun peeking through the clouds as I used the soil below to bar his plant strikes. "I just haven't blocked this many of your attacks before."

Gaius raised an eyebrow as he spiked another root in my direction, which I parried rather easily, probably *too* easily; he was going easy on me for that one. "Magic *perk*?"

"You know—a magic perk—like how Inna can breathe underwater," I reaffirmed to him.

My instructor tittered and stopped his plants from attacking me. "Lisa, you're just growing stronger. The Agapéd gifts you magic but not skill. Seems that Captain of the Queens is doing his job well already. As far as your strength of magic goes, that just means the Agapéd trusts your heart more."

As Gaius talked, I used the soil below his arms to grab his hand—the one throwing the plant whips toward me. With his attack disrupted I was able to *nail* him in the stomach with a rock, causing him to bend over in pain. It was the first time I had landed a hit on him! *Did he mean for me to hit him, or was that a legit win by me?*

"Sorry! I didn't mean to hit you so hard!" I shouted, but he was simply smiling away—proud.

"I'm fine... nice hit," he said, straightening up and dusting off the debris from his shirt. "Let's just hope you can put that strength into that weapon training with Ekron."

"I'm trying, but using a sword is way harder than using magic."

"You will get the hang of it soon enough. I've already noticed your fighting style growing more organized... like a true Hunter."

"Really?"

"You slagged me just then, didn't you?" His brogue accent slipped through his assertiveness.

I stopped clenching my fists, dropping my guard. "You mean... you didn't let that happen on purpose?"

He came up to me and put his hand on my shoulder. "You need to start thinking of yourself as a grand Mage already, Lisa. Don't let your physical appearance and lack of experience tell you that you aren't strong enough. You hear me?"

The compliment was a bit blunt, but it was true. Genuine. I couldn't help but smile. "I hear you. Thanks, Gaius."

"Good... and just in case you seem outmatched with a sword, don't forget you have that magic inside you. You could pull a nice punch on some of those gimpish Hunters out there."

He winked and patted my shoulder—one that almost knocked me over. Since he took the reins of my Agapéd training, the Keeper of Stars seemed happier and more comfortable with me. I enjoyed it. This was my first time having someone other than Mom who made me feel protected and cherished. He built me a room, made me breakfast, and trained me to keep me alive. Not sure if dads or uncles did this with their kids and nieces, but I liked it. It was nice to have someone like him in my life... I just hoped he felt the same and was not simply obligated to teach me because he gave up his immortality to keep the Agapéd safe.

Those memories gnawed at my brain, knowing I had changed his entire way of life. Gaius now had a normal heart because of me—a heart that would fade like any human. Because of my mistake, he had to keep me instead of the Balthiers. He had to give me food, become my magical guardian because Mom wasn't there, and focus on training me *while* tending to the Wishing Stars. The man said the family life wasn't for him... and I just invaded his hearth like a lost mouse. A pest—Vilmad would definitely agree on that.

What if Gaius does, too?

But then, as I watched the Keeper straighten his back, stepping ten feet across from me, there was a smile. "Alright, Lisa," he said, throwing up four wads of plants. "Let's see some magic." Happiness beamed and glistened with the sweat on his forehead.

And at that moment, I knew he enjoyed me being his student as much as I loved him being my guiding mentor.

I bolted two dirt rods out of the ground, sparring with the smirking gardener until it was time to leave for my training with Ekron.

32

SOUL-COMBINING CONFUSION

A week of living with Gaius and training with the Prince had ended, and it was time to return home... and try out this soul-combining thing with my double. Never thought that action or phrase would ever cross my mind. Gaius evanesced me back to New Jersey in the middle of my woodland backyard. Though I had the magical ability of the blue crystal flowers, teleporting trillions of miles away through space was not the same as teleporting from one Boolavogue mount to another. Gaius didn't mind, and he was the one who suggested it—*enforced* and *demanded* it if I were being honest.

But, there was a problem when I landed in the hot forest behind my home, and it wasn't the fact I smelled like a Hunter.

My look-alike was not in the woods.

Tuff joined me on my shoulder as I released an agitated sigh. "Dang, it... I never told myself *where* to meet... knowing me, I'm probably in my room waiting by the suitcase or eating dinner."

As I ran through the flourishing trees, crunching branches and stepping on bugs, I abruptly stopped at the forest's edge.

Right through the backdoor window, I saw the silhouette of me *and Mom*— both grabbing some food and making their way to the living room to eat.

My inner sleuth activated as my heart throbbed. *Okay, just need to get my attention without alerting Mom... while in the same room... I can do this... hopefully.*

When Mom's figure walked past the door and toward the couch, I ran up the hill, staying low to the grass. My head dipped down and slowly peeked through the bottom of the back door window, just enough to see past the dining table and through to the living room.

Double-me and Mom were sitting—watching *Friends...* impossible to interrupt.

I ducked back down. "Tuff," I whispered, squatting on the concrete slab.

My orange sprite appeared, using my long locks of hair as a shield from any peeping neighbors.

I continued quietly, peering through the glass pane again. "I need you to go in there—invisible, obviously—and tug on my hair or something, but you *cannot* let Mom see, okay?"

Orange dust shook off his body and onto my bent knees as his little eyes turned glossy.

He was terrified.

I pursed my lips and rushed my words. "Tuff, just grab my attention, please— you have to do this. I promise to not let this happen again."

His little black eyes peeked through the window. After another moment of watching the two of us on the couch, Tuff narrowed his eyes and gave a confident *hoot* before turning invisible.

I watched from the outside, seeing me and Mom lounging on the couch eating potato soup. *Kind of odd for her to make soup in summer... bet they had a sale on potatoes or some—*

Suddenly, the brunette locks on my doppelganger lifted up from behind the couch, causing the other me to grip her head. Two more pulls came before my doppelganger turned her head around and peered past the dining table—right at the back door.

When my doppelganger's eyes saw me, she acted exactly how I would expect: nervous and agitated that we both didn't discuss our plan in more detail.

Double-me put down her soup bowl and said something to Mom before walking over to the kitchen. She didn't go to the backdoor. It would have been odd if she did because Lisa Robbie doesn't go outside mid-meal. Her eyes stayed fixated on me, and a chin tilt gestured for me to follow her toward the laundry room.

We each kept up the same pace until I heard her enter the garage. I ran over to the door on the side of the building near the trash cans, seeing as pushing the button to unlatch the huge garage door would be loud—cueing Mom to leave the living room and ask what was going on.

"Psst—just use this door," I said, standing outside, quiet enough so only my replica could hear.

Her footsteps shuffled inside, scooting past Mom's car, and to the other side of the door. "We don't use this door—spider webs are all over it."

"It's only *webs*—"

"As far as you know... why can't *you* just turn the knob?"

I jiggled the handle. "Because it's locked, and you better hurry before Mom wonders why you left dinner. Come on, me—just do it."

My replica sighed as I heard her scurry around the garage, probably looking for something to whack away the webs. "Oh—our *scar*, by the way, is *very* noticeable. Lily saw it, and I had to wear a jacket all week!"

"Don't worry. Inna gave us something that will work—why did you let Lily see it—"

"I wasn't trying to," my doppelganger hushedly yelled through gritted teeth, finally back to the other side of the garage's back door.

After a couple of hardy twirls with an old mop, the webs were gone, and she opened the door for me.

My perfect twin looked rather nice and comfy in a purple hoodie, though a bit agitated that she had to go up against some spiders.

"Inna gave me this," I continued, gesturing to the silver string around my wrist. "Covers magic scars and other cuts and bruises. Since the Echo Ring copied my orbkit, I bet it will copy this—"

"Lisa, don't leave the door open to the garage—"

Mom's voice was a tornado warning coming through the laundry room, and both of me could see her shadow approaching.

Quickly, I looked at my replica and high-fived her hand fast. I wasn't thinking much about what would happen—only avoiding Mom seeing two of me—but as soon as our skin touched, duplicate me vanished like a puff of smoke... causing her to drop the mop of nasty spider habitats to the floor along with the clothes she was wearing.

My head began to throb. Ariela wasn't kidding about the ache. My brain pulsed hard from all the memories rushing back into my mind, but I had to act like everything was fine because the shadow of Mom was now her full body.

The mop landed on top of my shorts, purple sweatshirt, and undergarments with a *whack* when Mom took her curious stance at the laundry room entrance to the garage... staring past our white car and right at me.

"Huh... did you change clothes or something?" Mom asked.

I was thankful for her noticing my *blue* sweatshirt, helping my lie not be as unprompted. "Oh, yeah. Left my sweatshirt in the car, that's all."

She shrugged. "Well, just be sure to close the door, even if it's for a moment. Don't want spiders in the house."

I released a deep breath and gathered my doppelganger's clothing, noticing everything except my duplicated orbkit was there. *Guess that means the clothes I duplicated seven days ago must have "glittered away" as well...*

After putting my purple hoodie and shorts in the hamper on the way out, I followed Mom back to the kitchen with my hand pressed against my forehead.

So... it seems I had a pop quiz on Wednesday and stepped in gum... honestly, not such a bad first week of doppelganger magic in the eighth grade.

33
OTRERA AND THE KING

Not gonna lie, I was growing quite popular in the Men's Troop after training with Ekron and Cal for the past month. The most obvious reason why was because I was the *only* girl in the troop and also happened to be the youngest beginner Hunter the Kingdom had ever trained—no pressure or anything. The fact that I was from Earth also added to my unwanted attention and spread like weeds throughout the camp. At first, it didn't bother me until I realized being from Earth was like someone saying they were from the Moon—complete nonsense. Those who knew me—Ekron's pupils mostly—didn't treat me differently, but occasionally, I'd earn weird looks from Hunters across the grounds, followed by short whispers with "Earthian" sprinkled throughout.

Honestly, it fueled my desire to train harder—to prove to them I was as strong as they were—and our bald, burly Captain helped me out with that tremendously. When he finished training the ranked Hunters from both the Men's and Women's Troops in the morning, he would teach the Prince and me during the afternoon, which meant we started to acquire an audience.

Luckily, today, it was just Cal, Amos—a burly Hunter in his mid-twenties, red-headed and red-bearded—and Erin—a shaggy-haired brunette Hunter-in-training who was as thin as a pine tree.

"Alright, Lisa," Captain Ekron said as I was at my ready stance in his training ground, "I'm going to send out some jackjaws. Use your cutlass and aim for their feet first and then their necks. *No magic* this round—focus only on your strength and skill in swordsmanship. Ready?"

"Yes, sir!" I shouted back, steel cutlass sword in hand.

"Let's go, Lisa!" Cal chanted on the side. He finished training against the dark panthers and sat with the other Hunters on the sidelines.

"*Begin!*" Ekron commenced my training. He extended his arms, creating a pattern of hand motions that shot out magic from his fingers. Violet waves of glowing dust zoomed forward onto the dirt battleground, forming into two large jackjaws. Each resembled black panthers but had talons like hawks and scaly skin along its jagged spine. Though it was just phantasmal magic of beasts that Ekron had defeated in the past—Beast Duplication, I soon learned, was the name of the Mystic Hunter's power—and no blood and guts were involved, they still landed with a heavy pound on the dry dirt... with teeth as sharp as a lion's.

The purple-dusted jackjaw on my right sprinted straight for me. I knew they could jump high, so I slid on the dirt right near its belly and sliced its left hind leg, causing it to fall hard onto the ground. *One down, one to go.*

Some male Hunters cheered for me on the sidelines at my quick thinking, boosting my confidence.

The next jackjaw jumped off the side of the battle rink, gunning for my left side and leaving purple glitter in its path. I spun around and swung my sword but only cut through the air. The panther arched its back and hissed at me, showing off its unnatural, grizzly amethyst teeth. Even though Ekron's magic beasts wouldn't hurt us—he made sure to manifest them without the ability to kill—it still felt as if the giant feline was planning on mauling me to death.

Suddenly, the jackjaw sprinted forward without jumping high like the first one. I wasn't expecting that and ended up rolling to get out of the way. The panther then aimed for my neck as I was on the ground, but I stuck out my sword and used a blocking stance, holding the weapon horizontally as the panther's mouth went straight for it like a dog with a bone.

My heart throbbed—my breathing tightening and growing hoarse. *Ekron— why did you have to manifest these to be so powerful and cunning!*

The blade cut the mouth of the jackjaw, causing it to back off in pain and jolt away from me, but it also sliced a three-inch gash on my left palm—a clean shear, at least, so the blood didn't gush. I could still grip my sword, and that was all that mattered.

Now is my chance!

I forced my mind to ignore the pain in my hand as I swung my sword at the purple panther's muscular front legs, slicing Ekron's magic beast at the knees. When it knelt forward, I spun around and then cut at the nape of its neck. No magical blood splattered, only glowing purple liquid splashing onto the ground, light and soft like melted craft glitter. I'm pretty sure Ekron could make the jackjaws' "blood" more realistic, but that would result in violet puddles tainting his practice ring and painting all our bodies with it, too.

Once that one was defeated, I did the same to the next one I took down earlier—completing Ekron's jackjaw training.

Cal, Amos, and Erin cheered for my victory, but Ekron only looked partially satisfied. He came down onto the battleground, made his jackjaw duplicates disappear with a swipe of his hand, and graded my work as I caught my breath.

"You did well at the beginning, but you let your known pattern of the jackjaw's hunting style get into your head—causing the second one to catch you by surprise," he said very seriously. "However, blocking instead of running away was the smart move, which allowed you to defeat both beasts. Overall, good work..." His hazel eyes darted toward my hand, which I was trying to hide behind my back. "That'll be enough from you today. Come on, let's get that wrapped up for you."

I followed Ekron back to the Laze as Cal, Amos, and Erin trailed behind. I grabbed a bandage from the infirmary box I was all too familiar with and wrapped up my left hand as best I could. It hurt pretty bad, stinging worse than a slice from a kitchen knife, but I didn't want the boys to know as they came barging in.

"Put up a nasty battle with good ole Ekron's frilly magic—gotta be more careful with the real swords, Earthian," Erin joked with me, a smile cocked upon his beardless face. His shaggy brown hair ran past his ears and hit his jawline, making him look less like one of Ekron's students and more like a high school graduate I'd find in New Jersey. He wasn't an official Hunter yet, just a Restricted Licensed one until Ekron deemed him ready. When he wasn't complaining about Ekron's "cruel" methods, he was sleeping in the Laze or trying to talk to the female Hunters.

"It doesn't hurt that bad," I responded jokingly, lying through my soft breaths.

Amos, with red hair and a scruffy beard fierier than usual—not by choice, just genetics—that made him look much older than his actual age, said, "Still not as fast as the Prince, though." He, too, was a Restricted Licensed Hunter, but only for a couple more months.

"I dunno—she slagged that first one out with no problem. I bet she could've beaten his time," Erin countered.

Captain Ekron jumped in. "And she would have."

"*Naff it*—you hear that, Prince? Not even good ole Ecky believes you could beat Lisa now!" Erin joked.

Cal came around the tent's corner, smiling at me as I sat on the lounge chair and tightened my bandage. "We will see soon."

"That's right! You have your first official Spar right around the end of the season. Gonna be a crowd, that one," Amos voiced, grabbing an apple off the table.

"Though," began Erin, "if Lisa gets to use her magic, you'll need a Blessing from The Light above to even have a chance at winning."

"Maybe something even stronger," Ekron said, making us all laugh except for Cal.

The Prince's face couldn't believe our Captain would agree with the two Hunters, shouting back, "*Vorrgs*—I could have you banished for that!" He then gave a hard, playful punch to Erin's stomach, causing them both to wrestle like longtime brothers—acting as if Cal wasn't even a prince to the royal family.

As Amos and I watched the two, we heard a small battle start on the middle training grounds. It wasn't unusual to hear unofficial spars forming periodically, but due to how large the crowd was becoming, we knew it had to be both the Women's and Men's Troops brawling it off.

Amongst the hunting troops, there was an unofficial tournament always at play—all day and night—and it was "Men's Troop vs. Women's Troop: Who Reigns Supreme." Every couple of weeks, after training or when off duty, someone from the Women's Troop would challenge a man from our troop or vice versa. These challenges would range from as serious as a sword battle to something as simple as "who can drink the most sour-sap-cider without their tongue giving out." Sometimes, they would make bets with credits or acts of service if the

Captains weren't watching. Usually, it was all about the glory of proving to be the best in all of Boolavogue. Each side had strong Hunters, but according to Cal, the Men's Troop won last month due to Elio returning early from his hunt. The Women's Troop had been training harder ever since.

I followed close to Cal as we snuck toward the front of the male audience, seeing that most of the women were on the other side. Battling for the Men's Troop was a male Hunter I didn't know, using a long dark metal sword with a gloop glint on its hilt. I learned that many registered Hunters could purchase and wield magic weapons. The glintz attached to the weapon could make a normal sword fiery, acidic, venomous, or—in this male Hunter's case—slippery.

On the other side was the young female Hunter whom everyone knew: Otrera. In every sense of the word, Otrera was vicious. She acted tough and talked tougher as if she was *the* Hunter, and she hated losing. I had only seen her fight a couple of times, and she was good with a Dao—a blade similar to a longsword but with a slightly curved tip. Erin and Amos said she was the youngest female Hunter-in-training here until I arrived... and she was not happy about it. I didn't know why; I never spoke to her or gave her a reason to hate me. I honestly thought she was pretty and an amazing swordsman.

The two Hunters began their battle, and the male Hunter swung his sword first, but Otrera evaded it rather easily. He wasn't the best Hunter, and I felt for his pain. She hit him in his spine with the hilt of her sword so hard that he tensed up and toppled over, not even getting a chance to finish his attack. She wasn't rippling with muscles or anything—fairly lean to be honest; the male Hunter was just a twig without good evasion skills.

The Women's Troop cheered for Otrera's win while the losing Hunter's friends came and dramatically carried him away like a poor, hurt puppy.

Otrera looked out toward the crowd and said, "Is that the best you have, Men's Troop? I would at least like a challenge or one worthy of my victory." Her voice was snarky and obnoxious, and many of the older Hunters from both sides didn't even bother to participate in continuing the show.

The younger crowd, fueled with the urge to show off and dive right into danger, all stayed to watch to see the next chosen battler. *Wonder if it'll be Amos or Erin—doubt he could even fight against her—*

"You."

The tip of Otrera's silver sword pointed right at me, and the crowd became full of whispers.

I didn't have to look around to know she wasn't pointing to some man behind me; her eyes were darts, and I was the bullseye.

"The little girl who fights for the Men's Troop. Why is that actually, huh?" she snickered as she slowly strutted toward my position in the crowd, her long caramel hair tied in a high ponytail swaying as she taunted. "You're from Earth, right... yet there's been talk about your magic—saying you're a Keeper's student. That must mean you're pretty strong, though, I don't see that. *I* only see a little girl being pitied by a bunch of men."

Am I... being bullied right now?

All my life, voicing my opinions was not something I did, so kids at school never had a reason to go up against me or push me around. Being invisible was easy for me before magic got involved and was probably the reason why I only had two friends. Experiencing threats, being told off by punk teenagers, or even being physically harassed didn't happen to me—until this moment. I wasn't sure if I was supposed to feel self-conscious or frightened. A sword pointed at me with a full-grown teenager at its end, making an entire crowd of other young adults stop and stare.

But I wasn't scared; I was annoyed. Something in me was put off to the point that courage was beginning to bubble up inside my gut.

My heart was beating quickly... only because I just really wanted to prove to her that I was strong. In my usual, quiet voice, I replied, "Yeah."

Otrera lowered her sword and stepped closer to me. "You think you could win for the Men, then?"

Cal nudged me on my arm and gave me a look of confidence. I answered Otrera, "Let me use magic, and I'll show you."

The crowd *oohed* and instantly grew louder with chants.

I didn't mean for that to come off as prideful; I just knew I had zero chance of winning without my magic.

Ekron's male Hunters backed me up, since many had seen me use magic before. On the other hand, the ladies and some other unfamiliar male Hunters were doubtful—which is why they all stayed to watch. This was going to be my first battle with a Restricted Hunter... and she would not go easy on me.

Otrera smiled slyly as I walked onto the battleground. Since I wasn't an official Hunter or a Restricted Licensed one, I wasn't allowed to battle with an unsheathed weapon unless under Captain's orders, so we switched to wooden swords. *Thank goodness.*

"This isn't a royal battle, Earthian," she sniped, "so feel free to give me all you got. First one to knock the other out of the rink or on the ground longer than seven seconds wins. Let's see if the freckled girl can win for the men, huh?"

I pursed my lips. *Oh, this freckled girl will win—just watch.*

We stood at opposite ends of the rink, gripping our practice swords tightly. The crowd around us doubled in size, and some even placed bets on who would win, adding pressure to the battle. Like a gunshot, our unofficial referee shouted *"begin,"* and Otrera sprinted right toward me, which I expected to happen. She was just like the jackjaw—fast and conniving—which meant quick and slick movements would allow me to win.

Otrera swung her practice sword.

I blocked and parried back, but because her physical strength was more overpowering, she began to push me closer to the edge of the rink. I gave a hard swing to match hers—Ekron's training shining brightly— but her sword still flew at me. I ducked and rolled away from her to try and get some space between us.

"Come on, Earthian," she chanted at me, running full speed with her long-tied hair whipping around like a horse's tail. "Is this all you got?"

I gripped my sword tighter, not caring that my sliced hand was still thundering behind the bandage. *No, it's not!*

I saw Otrera's feet darting for me, making a perfect patterned line in the dirt. I guessed her next step and shot a dirt column out from the ground right as her leg made contact with the soil.

She went straight into the air.

The crowd went crazy as she landed with a thud and rolled onto the ground. Hearing their cheering energized my aching muscles and throbbing left palm, and I planned on jolting toward her. I tried to step forward, but my feet wouldn't move, as if they were stuck in glue.

Yellow sap covered my boots, causing me to wobble and fall backward.

What the—

I looked over to Otrera, who was still on the dirty ground, and her hands were now covered in the same sticky substance. Yet, she could still move freely. *Is this her magic? I can't move my feet at all!*

"You're not the only one with tricks up her sleeve!" Otrera said, smiling with a busted lip as if falling over was all a part of her plan.

The huntress quickly got back on her feet and came straight for me, gripping her wooden sword with the intent to keep me down. Her legs sprinted off the ground—aiming to nail me with an air attack.

Thinking as the clever Mage Gaius taught me to be, I pushed the soil beneath me, causing my stuck body to travel on a rocky wave across the battleground. To the eyes watching, they had never seen someone surf on the dirt like water, and they cheered even louder.

What I wouldn't give for some water to freeze this—wait, a second—

Otrera landed without hitting me, which gave me another idea. I gathered more soil and rocks to attach with the sap on my feet until all of Otrera's sticky magic goop was covered in dirt. My terrain magic forced all the rocks off my ankles and feet, which ripped the sap off my boots, freeing me to continue with the battle.

Annoyance took over the young female Hunter's face while determination brightened mine. We bolted right for the other, shooting back balls of sap and rock like a deadly snowball fight. Many Hunters in the crowd had to dodge our fast throws, though I remember hearing Erin getting hit in the chest with one of Otrera's sap balls because Amos made a boisterous laugh. I then shot up a staircase of rock to land an aerial strike.

Out of nowhere, Otrera whipped out a rope of sap and pulled me hard to the ground.

Thud—rocks scratched my elbows and face as my body bounced hard off the dirt. The crowd reacted to my pain as I came to a complete stop after skidding on the crackling dirt floor. *Come on, Lisa. You need to get up, or you'll lose!*

I didn't have time to catch my breath. I turned around as quickly as I could to swing at the glaring female Hunter, but she struck my sword with her yellow goo, sending it flying across the battleground.

NO—

Another bracing hit from her wooden weapon began to approach me, sending my heart into thunderous beats, but I instinctively used my legs to magically whip the soil underneath her body. It wasn't a pretty move, but it was a Lisa Robbie tactic.

Dirt whipped beneath her as if someone had pulled a rug out from under her feet. She slipped, flipped, and fumbled—clumsiness at its finest. The men in the crowd laughed, causing my opponent to get very embarrassed and angry.

"You will pay for that," she snarled at me slowly so only I could hear. "Cheap tricks don't make you a fighter." *Says her, Miss Sticky-Sap.* "Come on, let's finish this, huh?"

Otrera then tossed her sword away and held up her fists.

What's she doing?

She spat a mixture of blood and saliva into the dirt due to her busted lip from her fall. "Just magic and fists, Earthian," she muttered before coming full force at me.

What—this wasn't a part of the rules!

I couldn't grab my sticky sword, so I shot more earth columns at her.

She evaded them easily, and her speed wasn't slowing. All the blood in my veins seemed to heat up while my sweat dripped cold down my arms and neck. She looked crazier than before, and I could tell this wouldn't end well for me... so I did what I had to do.

I held up my good hand, balled it into a hardy fist, and piled up my magic in my palm, tricep, and bicep—all the way to my shoulder blade. My arm quaked and felt as if it were as strong as a roaring landslide, the magic growing more unstable.

Otrera came, aiming for my face, but I ducked under her swing and released my arm right in the middle of her abdomen.

I struck her... and she went *flying*.

With my one punch fueled with all the magic I could muster, making my muscles triple in strength, I slung Otrera across the battleground and into the flimsy wooden wall around the rink. Paneling broke the moment her body collided with the fence, sending wooden confetti into the air and her out of the perimeter of the rink—out of bounds. Every voice and grumble fell silent, even the squawks of the birds circling the castle. Not a single Hunter was guffawing, coughing, or gossiping either. They all watched intently as the once snarky Hunter fell to her demise.

My stance was shaky, my arm and legs about to crumble like a crisp granola bar, and I knew I, too, was about to join Otrera on the ground. It took all I had to continue standing. But I refused to move until I knew the result—refused to let the Hunters see how weak I was after landing only one punch.

The unofficial referee came around to Otrera, saw her slowly move along the floor—had to make sure she wasn't dead—and said, *"Match set: Lisa is the winner!"*

It was as if it were Christmas morning on the Hunter grounds. The Men's Troop jumped into a frenzy—ecstatic they proved to still be the best Troop of Hunters, even with a little girl like me on their team. Amos, Erin, and their rambunctious gang of Hunters came across the battleground and picked me up in the air, showing me off as one would a trophy or champion. *I did it—I can't believe I won a spar—Gaius is going to be so proud of...*

Not an ounce of strength was left in my body, and when the Men's Troop put me down, my legs gave out. And I fell right to my knees. I tried to stand but wobbled over and over—drained dry of all my stamina. The last time I was that weak was when I pushed myself too hard on Gaius' obstacle course, but even then, I had grass to fall on. My whole body was about to face-plant onto the gritty ground—embarrassing myself in front of everyone.

Familiar arms and hands shot out from beside me. It was Cal, coming like a chivalrous savior through the commotion and catching me before my head hit the floor.

"Lisa, are you okay?" he asked me, cradling my head, his eyes and a plethora of other men staring right at my weakened face.

Though I probably should have been freaking out over the fact a prince caught me mid-fall, I was so thrilled about winning that all I could do was smile up at him. "You kidding?" I huffed, sweat gleaming on my forehead, grinning my freckled cheeks. "I've never felt better... just may have used a little too much magic."

There was a hefty sigh of relief from the men seeing me crack a lie and a smirk, and the sense of urgency left, leaving nothing but joy to surround us.

Amongst the roaring and cheering, the horde of Hunters began to part as Captain Ekron walked through their midst. Cal hurriedly helped me off the ground, letting me use his shoulder for leverage as our Captain approached us—

solemn and squinting from the sun. *Was what I just did allowed, or am I about to get a tongue-lashing from my Viking of an instructor?*

Ekron stared down at Cal and me, his bald head reflecting the afternoon sun, blinding the birds that soared above. We were now the only ones on the battleground; the Men's Troop knew better than to stick around a Captain when he was about to give a lecture.

"Now *that*..." he began in his rustic voice, "was a right show of true magic. Gaius sure knew what he was doing when he had you join our Troop."

My instructor utterly flattered me, his words giving me some of my strength back. "Oh, well, uh, thank you, Captain."

"How about you head off to the Caregiver's Wing and take a rest? Have them look at your hand, too; I could tell it hurt you during battle. The Prince and I will finish the lessons. You're quite the Mage, Lisa. Will be a class of a Hunter in no time."

As I stood on my feet again, wobble-free, Cal said, "I'll come to see you in a bit, okay? I got something I wanna show you." He then smiled and hurried off to catch up with Ekron. "Way to win one for the Troop, Lisa!"

Never knew winning a battle would hydrate my body with so much refreshing invigoration. In all my life, a crowd cheering my name was not a reality I envisioned for myself or one where I would be wielding a sword, nonetheless. It felt good—more than good—to know I could win against someone I thought was stronger than me. I stood my ground and fought well despite being tossed around several times, and I wished Gaius was there to see it. He would've been proud but would have definitely scolded me about letting my guard down and overdoing it with my magic.

Up the stairs from the ground level of the castle and to the left were the Guard's Quarters and Caregiver's Wing. It wasn't my first time traveling to get bandaged up; I knew exactly what halls to go down and where to turn. As I admired the castle's artwork on the walls, a guard in front of me suddenly stopped and bowed in place. I accidentally walked into his shoulder, getting his creamy-white garb dirty, but he didn't look fazed.

What caused him to—

Like a commander demanding the attention of his army, a warrior waterfalled in gold and blues came marching through the royal hallway. Every castle maid, guard, and fancy, unfamiliar guest stopped and bowed, but I didn't. I couldn't. He was extravagant and scary, very stoic with not a laugh line on his face. The mightiest man I had ever seen.

That man... was the King.

He had wavy black hair brushing the top of his shoulders, eloquently styled with a couple of strands braided with beads of gold. His beard was thick to match his eyebrows, yet the crown above his head stole my attention first. I had never seen so many blue gems in my whole life, and he had an ocean of them sunken into his golden diadem. His garb was thick with a shoulder cape on his right, which had the Boolavogue crest stitched into it—a Gora bear roaring with a sword behind it, matching the emblem on the front gate. One of the last things I noticed, still not bowing like the rest of those in the hallway, was the buckle holding the royal weapon on his side. It was only the hilt of a sword. Empty—as if the craftsman forgot to construct and attach a blade.

I was so busy admiring the King that I made direct eye contact with him as he walked past me. Immediately, my body bowed, and my heart rate tripled.

How can one man's stare be that intimidating?

Then, the sound of his clicked boots stopped... as well as my breathing. The footsteps started again... only this time, coming straight for me—straight to the strange little girl who didn't bow at the appropriate moment.

This is it. This is how I meet my end. I'm grimy, covered in dirt, and a complete stranger to this man. I knew I should've bowed and not stared for so long at his fancy clothes and weird incomplete sword!

Thick, strapped boots appeared, standing in front of me as my head faced straight toward the glossy floor. One of those boots had to cost a week of Mom's paycheck—that leather glistened with gold stitched along the rubber edges.

If storm clouds could talk, they would sound like the King's voice. "Gaius' pupil... Lisa, am I correct?" King Sonon asked, calm, serious, and deeper than the echoing of Ekron and Gaius combined.

I slowly faced upward. "Yes, sir," I said, staring at his hazel eyes.

Whoa... he is very tall... and not as smiley as the Queen...

"Leonora tells me that you've been training alongside Caelum... Seems he is improving faster with you around."

There was a pause, so I figured he was waiting for me to say something.

I swallowed. "I don't think it has much to do with me, Your Majesty. He was already a great fighter before I arrived."

"Hmm," he breathed. Still no smile. "I look forward to seeing a spar between the both of you in the coming months... Until we meet again."

The King then continued his walk down the quiet hallway, and once he was out of the line of sight, everyone in the hallway stopped and stared at me. My face was the palest it had ever been before. *I just met the King... and he wants to see me fight his son... No pressure or anything...*

34
FYSIKS

The Caregiver's Wing had two areas: one for guards, Hunters, and other warriors and another for royalty and guests. Since I was technically a guest of the Kingdom before becoming a pupil with Ekron, I was able to get all cleaned up in the cozier wing. The Hunters' was cold, crowded, and always loud, so I was glad when Cal told me about the one he and his family used.

The nurse I always came to see was Lila, an old semi-sweet, not-much-of-a-talker kind of lady. But when she did speak, I could tell just by the snippets that she had spent a lot of time with the Boolavogue Hunters: lots of strange phrases with little etiquette sprinkled throughout her sentences.

She quickly used her healing magic on my hand, making the cells in my wound replenish their strength twice as quickly, wrapping it back up in a clean cloth to finish healing. Her magic was strong enough to completely remove non-magical scars like ones made from normal swords, which was nice for me; I would have quite a collection of careless marks if that wasn't the case.

Lila also gave me some hot green apple tea with lots of honey and a side of plain crackers, telling me I should rest up and not "brawl it off" with the Hunters *again*. There was no sympathy in her tone either. Even she was fed up with me always getting hurt... mostly because it involved the Prince telling me to practice sparring with him. And I always came away with bruises and bloody knees—never a win.

"Thanks for healing me, Lila," I said, putting my concealment band back on my wrist, covering up all my magic scars.

At that moment, the door to the Caregiver's Wing flew open, and Cal came running through. He was very sweaty—probably had sprinted straight from Ekron's lessons.

The Prince walked over to me slowly, catching his breath and staring at my healed-up body. "Lisa, are you doing better?" he said calmly, seeing that Lila was still in the room.

Her wrinkly eyes leered at him. "As long as she rests, she will be," the old nurse interjected, fearing the Prince was about to take me on some silly adventure... which did happen quite often. She finished washing her hands and made her way toward the exit. "I better find Miss Lisa still in that same spot when I return, Young Prince. Her wounds are healed, but she used quite a lot of magic. She needs sleep and food—you peely little thing."

The moment Lila left the room, Cal jumped into excitement. "Alright, so I've been practicing my magic, and look what I finally learned to do!"

Cal stood back from me and clenched both of his fists by his side. Right as he smirked, he vanished! His clothes, shoes, body—everything disappeared as if he was never in the room. "See! I've finally learned to make my whole body invisible!" his voice uttered in the empty room.

"No way! I didn't know you could make your clothes invisible, too?" I said, trying to remember where his eyes were.

"It's not completely perfect. Watch," his voice spoke, and I heard his boots stride beside the window by my cot. The sun rays beamed through the glass hard, but I still couldn't see Cal standing beside it—not even a shadow.

I squinted hard and leaned closer, hearing him twirl in a circle. That was when I noticed a crystal veil as clear as water surrounding his body. It was very faint, and I would have never noticed from far away.

"I think you've really mastered it—no one would think twice if you walked by them," I reassured him.

The Prince suddenly turned visible again and sat on the cot next to me, looking happy with his results. "I'm glad you told me to keep practicing my magic... I never really thought about perfecting it before, but I want to be able to do what you do and use it during training and spars." He sighed, looking down at his fingers. "I just can't figure out anything else I can do with Illusionary magic besides making me and other objects invisible—and I know what you're gonna say, but I already checked our library, and they didn't have anything on my magic."

He guessed what I was thinking pretty quickly...

I then struck up an idea. "You know... I bet Gaius has something about your magic in his study. If you wanted, we could go there right now and see."

"What? You mean in Calendula?"

"Yeah... wait, have you never been there?"

The Prince sat silent, which I took for a yes.

"Well, then, you have to go! Come on, let's go right now!"

I jumped off the cot as Cal reminded me, "Aren't you supposed to be resting?"

"*Pfft*—did you really think I would just sit here the whole day knowing you have never been to the Hidden City?"

"Just to make sure—*you're* the one telling Lila it was *your* idea to leave and that I didn't drag you out of here to practice with the Hunters," Cal joked, following me out of the room.

"Don't let her catch us sneaking out, and I will gladly take the blame."

I wasn't confident enough in my evanescing skills to just whisk the two of us right in front of the secret entrance, so we walked instead. Cal knew all the secret ways of getting out of the Kingdom that didn't involve the front gate due to many late-night conversations with Hunters. Once we got to the apple orchard, I took control and led him straight to the entrance. He was shocked to see it not heavily guarded, but it wasn't like many people would know a magic world on the opposite side of a broken tree and wildberry bush decorated with spiderwebs.

We walked right into the Veradome. I wanted to give Cal a tour, but after one worker seemed to recognize his royal face, we had to abort any tourist ideas. Ducking and tiptoeing became our only goal on our way to Gaius' house.

When we walked into his half-buried home, Gaius was nowhere to be found. I didn't think about whether I was allowed to bring guests into his domain; my only thought was to find a book to help the Prince. So, I invited starstruck, wide-eyed Cal to the bottom of Gaius' home and through the back door. As we entered, I went straight for the magic books as Cal stood in the center of the stone floor. He stared at everything.

"So, *this* is a Keeper's home? Are we allowed to be in here?" he asked cautiously.

"Yeah. I come in here just about every day. Gaius lets me read as much as I want and whatever I want," I replied, skimming through the titles of the *Magic Forms* volumes. "Hey, come and help see if you can find anything about your magic over here."

"Wait—did Gaius write *all* these?" Cal wondered aloud as he picked up *Magic Forms: Aeon*, seeing Gaius' name on the front title page.

"Most of them."

"And he fought all these beasts to learn about their magic? Kinda just thought he grew those stars. No wonder you pick up Ekron's fighting styles so well."

"Gaius is a pretty great instructor."

We looked through about one-fourth of the *Magic Forms* bookshelf before I decided to try and search around through the others. Amongst our flipping of linen and brittle paper pages, I heard Cal say something about books on the top of the bookshelf.

"Hey, do you know what these are?" he asked as I was on the opposite side of the room reading through a red book called *Elemental and Phantasmal: Beginning Forms.*

Without looking up at him, I said, "If they are on the top shelf, I probably have never seen them."

Cal wasn't that much taller than me, but enough to tip-toe himself closer to reaching the books. I heard him lean against the bookshelf, the silver on his belt scraping against the ebony wood, trying to reach for the mysterious books when, all of a sudden, the back door flung open. Warm air rushed in fast, smelling of bergamot and freshly cut grass. Cal immediately jumped back and couldn't help but stare at the doorway.

Everything went still except for the quiet sound coming from me continuing to flip through the pages of the scarlet-bound book. When I decided to see why Cal stopped searching for a guide on his magic, I saw the beefy Keeper of Stars looking very surprised to see the Prince in his home. Cal was utterly terrified as if he was caught committing a crime. I, on the other hand, didn't know why he was freaking out; it was just Gaius.

"Your Highness...?" Gaius muttered, still standing at the door frame.

"Hey, Gaius, do you have any books on Illusionary magic?" I asked, sitting on the stone floor near his old couch, not paying attention to the awkwardness between him and the Prince.

Gaius, clearly noticing the Prince in the room, ignored him and answered me. "Why are you interested in that?"

I didn't have the right to give away Cal's secret about his magic, so I looked up at the Prince, hoping he would answer; he continued to be as still as a statue. *Why is he so scared of Gaius?*

"Cal, you can tell Gaius if you want," I reassured him.

The Keeper stood with his arms crossed, staring at Cal, waiting for him to respond.

"It's uh, for me, sir," the Prince said to Gaius, the first time I had ever heard him speak as shyly as me.

Gaius released an exhale through his nose. "You aren't in trouble, Young Prince, though judging by your secrecy and book choice, I assume you have Illusionary magic, then?"

The Prince stood in silence for a moment, seeing someone other than me and himself knowing of his magic for the first time. Ashamed, Cal didn't look Gaius in the eye and nodded at the Keeper's grass-stained shoes.

Seeing the Prince sad about his awesome magic, I shot up off the floor and quickly asserted, "Caelum wants to learn more about his magic so he can use it during battles. He already can make himself invisible, but—"

"I can't use that during matches with other Hunters," Cal finished my sentence. "It... wouldn't look good for a prince to win by sneaking around... if you know what I mean?"

I chimed in again. "And I thought you might have something about his magic in your study."

Gaius tilted his chin—could almost call it a nod. "I see..." He then strolled toward the middle of the bookshelf and grabbed the dirtied book with the glowing trio of diamonds on its cover. He quickly flipped towards the middle and stopped at the section labeled *Illusionary*. "Is your magic physical illusions or those of the mind?"

"Uh... I guess physical since I can still touch things I make invisible," the

Prince responded.

The Keeper's burly hands flipped to the section labeled *Fysiks Illusion* and handed the book to Cal. "The magic you possess, Prince, is known as Fysiks magic—one of the two types of Illusion magic. It lets you create or remove the illusion of something physical in the real world. As far as your goals are in battling as a Mystic, this will help exceedingly. Feel free to take this with you when you head home."

Caelum gave a grand smile. "You mean it?"

I dropped my jaw to the floor. "*What?* You never let me take magic books back home. How come Caelum gets to?"

"You live here, and the Prince can't be seen sneaking out of the Kingdom, so I don't mind him taking a book back with him until he tells his mother to find him a proper teacher."

Gaius was about to walk up the book-shelved staircase and to the kitchen when I stopped him. "Can you at least show Caelum maybe just one move? That way, he has a starting point to work from."

"It's not a big deal if you can't, sir," Cal said, trying not to pressure the Keeper or further test his generosity.

I thought otherwise.

"*Please, Gaius?* You helped me learn magic... and I know you could at least show him just one thing."

Gaius turned around; my baby-doll eyes were in full effect.

His green eyes stared at me—defenseless. "*One* thing... then, you're back to the castle before I get in trouble with the Queen."

Gaius had Cal face him outside, like how I would during our Keeper versus Agapéd training sessions. I sat with Tuff on the sidelines, excited to experience magic I'd never seen before.

"One of the basic elements of your magic," Gaius began directing, the sun glistening against both his and the Prince's tan skin, "is its ability to reflect light and air, taking its invisible touch and making it tangible. You can manipulate a small space of your atmosphere around you to create shields, walls, and barriers—making something untouchable... touchable—just like how you said you can make your visible body invisible. It's still there, but your magic can trick our eyes into not seeing it. I want you to hold out your hand like this."

Gaius then held out his palm in front of Cal, fingers extended wide and arm nice and straight.

Cal duplicated the same motion.

"Now, envision the air around your hand becoming hard like stone. Use the same magic you use to create your invisible cloak—that same tension and feeling—appear in the air, creating a circular shield."

Tuff and I watched as the Prince furrowed his brows and tensed up his magic. When he flexed his fingers, a sound like knocking on glass protruded from where he stood. And Cal smiled.

Right up against his hand—floating, barely touching his palm—was that same opaline veil I saw when Cal made himself invisible. Only this time, the veil was thicker and glistened more in the daylight—a transparent sheet of flattened diamonds. It was amazing.

Gaius smiled and began to back up. "Let's test it out. Use that Fysiks shield to guard yourself as I throw objects your way."

Just like he did with me, Gaius sucked up some roots from the dirt and created four thick throwing balls. He then faced Caelum and shot them fast right toward his chest, not giving the Prince more than a second in between each pitch. Caelum lifted his invisible shield to block the incoming shots. When the plant wads came zooming at high speeds right toward it, crashing into Cal's magic, they all burst into nothing but diced root pieces!

He did it!

It wasn't just because of the impact but because of the shield's magic—Cal's magic! The impact on the shield caused it to crackle with light, turning visible for just a split second before returning to its glassy state. The same thing happened with the next few throws to the magic surface. It really did look like Caelum was battling with invisible yet glistening weaponry!

The happiness on the Prince's face was like nothing I had ever seen before. His teeth were showing, and his cheeks grew rosy-pink; he truly loved learning magic as much as I did.

"I can't believe I just did that! I can use this as a shield or even a weapon— could probably make one as big as me!" Caelum rejoiced, experimenting more with his magic, creating smaller magic shields of translucent diamond slates with his hands all around him. He then turned toward Gaius and shook the Keeper's hand. "Thank you, sir. This… this means a lot to me—the book, too."

I walked up toward the two of them. "Why can't he train with you and me here?" I asked Gaius.

"Seeing as the Prince has yet to tell others of his magic, it would be oddly suspicious for him to be sneaking off with my pupil every day. It is not wise to learn magic secretly."

I crossed my arms. "Isn't that basically what I'm doing?"

Gaius mimicked my stance. "You're the exception. Prince Caelum wants his magic to be veered as honest and worthy of adoration, which starts with him being confident in his skills… and telling his parents. I'm sure they can find him a dignified teacher who can teach him far more than I ever could." Gaius then directed his attention to Caelum. "Be proud of your magic, Prince. It *is* worthy to be used by you and your Kingdom."

The Keeper of Stars left us outside on his practice grounds as he walked back inside his home. Seeing Cal delighted made me happy—my friend starting to believe in his own abilities.

"Lisa, I want to thank you," Cal began. "If it wasn't for you, I don't think I ever would have guessed I could do something like that. It felt incredible! And Gaius—*man,* I thought he would slag me when he walked through that door. How does he not scare you?"

I giggled at his remark, rolling my eyes and letting all my memories of the Keeper and me resurface. "I saw the man eat nuts from a leaf given to him by a glowing pink glainie after we saved their woodland village. After that, he just became another familiar face I enjoy being taught by. I was surprised to see *you* all freaked out—your dad is *way* more intimidating."

Cal's eyes grew wider. "When did you meet *him*? I haven't even seen him since Mother said he returned from his venture."

"He passed me down the hallway on my way to get my hand fixed. Said he was happy I was training with you."

The Prince was even more shocked. "And you *talked* with him?"

"Why do you keep sounding as if seeing the King walking and talking in his own home is something so unusual and scary? I mean, he *was* scary but not in a bad way; just like a 'Hey, do as I say, and no one gets hurt' kinda way. You know, like a bodyguard type deal."

Cal started to chuckle at my statement. "Lisa, your innocence of our Kingdom sometimes is amazing." His words didn't sound like a fourteen-year-old's—reminding me of his royalty.

"What do you mean by that?"

"You just act like people with power are no different than your average Hunter. If my father caught us sneaking into his magic study, he would have my stock. I would not happily ask for more help looking for a secret magic book and then proceed to follow it up by begging for a demonstration. Instead, I would be begging for forgiveness."

I leaned my head toward him as Tuff circled around us. "Well, that's what living with a Keeper who doesn't take no for an answer—even from the Guardians themselves—does to ya, I guess."

Gaius wanted to spar a bit before dinner. After I told him about my win against Otrera, he wanted nothing more than to see my tactics for winning. I didn't mind showing him, though he wasn't *too* impressed with my overuse of magic, and then demanded I not do it again during our pre-supper spar... or any spar after that. Still, he smiled at my cleverness in using the soil to surf. Even gave me some tips on evading and feinting while we sweated in the setting sun of his backyard.

Suddenly, crunching gravel appeared behind me as one of Gaius' plant wads zoomed straight past my head—nowhere near my body. Chimes and hums of falling sand *wooshed* through the air, no sound of the wadded plant crumbling or even hitting the ground. Both of Gaius' eyes sagged. "Did you need something?" he asked bluntly to whoever was behind me.

Dressed in a sage robe with gold stitching was Vilmad. Fingers were in mid-air, turning Gaius' attack to gold dust, and his long brown hair was flowing with the summer breeze. And yet, he still was not pleasing to look at, especially with that smileless face. "I just came to check if the Agapéd was still alive, being in your care, and if she is being trained and growing stronger," he answered, his brows arched.

Gaius huffed, running a hand through his thick head of hair. He began to walk toward me and Vilmad. "She's fine, and since you insist on prodding, she won her first match today down at the castle."

Vilmad snorted through his nose. "Against that childish prince?"

"No," I said as Gaius put his hand on my shoulder. I crossed my arms, standing proud. "Against a real Hunter, one who was *twice* my age," I answered, half-truth, half-lie. The Guardian had lied to me before; didn't see it as a problem to return the favor.

Vilmad fixated on Gaius. The Keeper of Stars merely smirked, giving my shoulder a shake and pat before saying, "See. Doing just fine. So, you may go... unless you need something else besides wasting our training time?" Gaius' rugged grin was beaming bright, shining with pride in his student. Shining like a star because of me.

Vilmad opened and closed his mouth with gritted teeth. I swear the gold on the Guardian's face lost some of its luster as he jerked his chin and clicked his tongue. Fabric ruffled from his cloak as he turned to leave. Amid his celestial grumbling, I heard him mutter, "A mere buffoon teaching a child... Utter nonsense..."

Nothing but mimicking and snickering proceeded after the pompous Guardian left.

35
HE WAS ECURAS

No.... Please, no.... Lisa, get up! Get up and move! You have to do something—
"*Valhalla!*"

My eyes jolted open. Sweat dripped down my neck, soaking my shirt and pillow, at the sight and sound of Valhalla's death. Her body smacking on the floor, the smell of her warm coppery blood mixing in with the cave water, it ran cold chills up my spine... and I did nothing but watch her die again.

My heart rampaged inside my chest as I looked around the darkened room. The night sky showed through the glass ceiling, and an array of hanging plants dangled over my head. Tuff made the True Blue Glass panes gleam orange on my right side, his body curled up on a pillow—away from me, unable to soothe my mind.

Breathing—my heartbeat grew steadier as my mind realized it was just another bad dream in the Keeper's home.

Rampant pounds still pulsed from my heart, along with a throbbing headache, causing me to wake up in a sweat in the middle of the night. Again.

I truly hated the cave. It made me remember the guilt and sadness I had been trying to forget. A month ago was when I finally stopped crying after seeing the horrific dreams, though my doppelganger on Earth struggled the most since she didn't have Tuff there—*I* struggled, I should say. Now, the tears were replaced with sweat, but the nightmares were still unrelenting, still gnawing at my brain like a dog on a bone. I'd trained myself to just say *it's only a dream,* but sometimes,

I couldn't force my mind to believe that lie. It really happened… the vezper killed her… and she was gone. Forever.

Tuff would sleep right next to me in Gaius' home, trying his best to fill my head with happy thoughts, but some nights, like tonight, not even the best of his illusions could stop the penetrating dark memories from resurfacing.

I wasn't sure what triggered the memories to stain my peaceful sleep, but returning to slumberland was impossible, especially with my head pounding.

I hope Gaius is still awake… Maybe he has some medicine or some magic migraine plant to dust me with healing pollen.

Tuff woke up after sensing my bad dream, sleepy with droopy eyes but ready to comfort me. He accompanied me with his little orange body perched on my shoulder as I walked toward the living room. The fireplace still had a slight ember, meaning Gaius had planned to return to put it out. I walked into his workshop. Not there. Under the bathroom door, I checked to see if the light was on. Dark as dark could get. I strolled down to his magic study next. Still, nothing.

I walked by his potions desk and noticed out the window that his giant greenhouse was glowing brighter than ever. Its frosted windows danced with warm blues, pinks, and yellows, causing me to forget my throbbing headache as curiosity overtook me.

He's definitely in there.

I threw on my oversized sweatshirt but didn't bother with my sandals or fixing my hair, having Tuff join me before wandering toward Gaius' magical greenhouse. He mentioned a couple of times that I couldn't go inside… However, since I didn't get a chance to ask him recently, he could have changed his mind and planned on letting me in if I ever asked again.

That was what I told myself as I stepped up to the glass door. I reached for the cold handle and pushed down, releasing a loud latch that I was positive Gaius heard, yet there was no sound of shouting or footsteps.

I continued opening the door, and all along the glass walls were rows and rows of the most extraordinary magical plants. Mushrooms, translucent like bubbles, hid in the damp corners while bouquets of peonies and lilies flickered like pink flames to lighten up the room. Not even the Veradome had flowers like that. Moss dripping with flowing water from the indoor pond ran across a huge horizontal tree with blooming red flowers. The petals were red clouds during a sunset—*actual* lumps of clouds. I went up to touch one, and *all* the other red flowers immediately *poofed* like a puff of smoke.

Tuff and I traded dumbfounded glances.

Okay, no more touching anything until I find Gaius.

Ahead, the way was split in two. I was about to head right when I heard a singing man's voice.

No way is that Gaius singing. Has to be someone else.

Tuff and I followed the voice down a dark hallway—the moonlit glass wall on my left and the thick concrete wall on my right. The singing became clearer and sounded fairly decent. I passed by a couple more interior magic plants until I reached an open room—lit up with blue flowers—where the voice was coming from. I tiptoed closer, listening to the deep, soothing voice sing an old folk song.

> *Take me to your clouds, my dear.*
> *Ones in mist, with views so clear.*
> *Give me rest, give me warmth.*
> *You're the home my heart yearns for.*
>
> *Send me down your paths again,*
> *Where weeds and roots have sunken in.*
> *Give me love like rain for leaves.*
> *Feed my soul with heartwood trees.*
>
> *Oh! How I've missed my mountain home.*
> *Though your pathways leave me weary and torn.*
> *I'll keep forward, for your love's worth every storm.*
> *Oh, my soul, how I've missed my mountain home.*
>
> *Spring adorns you with its grace*
> *And winter snow, laid white in lace.*
> *Show me how you stand so tall*
> *Sorrow, pain—you've seen it all*
>
> *Let me lay upon your chest*

Where flowers bloom and give me rest
Dream of me when skies are dim
I'm coming, dear—my home, again.

Oh! How I've missed my mountain home
Though your pathways leave me weary and torn
I'll keep forward, for your love's worth every storm
Oh, my soul, how I've missed my mountain home

Would you wait for my return?
Keep your trees, don't let them burn
Don't let man tread while I am gone
I promise, Love, to be yours before too long
Dreaming of you and singing your mountain song.

My mind couldn't resist seeing who the cantor was, causing my legs to walk involuntarily toward the door's entrance. Gaius was right before me—singing like a brawny, baritone bard. I stared in amazement.

The man can SING?

The Keeper of Stars must have had some sort of sixth sense because he noticed me without ever looking toward the door. "I thought you were asleep?" his voice echoed.

Even though I was the one sneaking up on him, he scared *me*—making me jump in place and snap out of my bewilderment. "Sorry, I just uh... had another nightmare." My eyebrows raised along with a curious smirk. "I didn't know you could sing?"

"I don't," he said far too seriously, probably embarrassed I caught him in the act. He was tending some type of plant that had flower petals like the ones I ate to evanesce, wearing his comfy tank top, sweatpants, and gardening boots.

I rolled my eyes. "What*ever* you say... but I think you sound great." I padded closer to him and the crystalized plants. My hands fidgeted behind my back as Tuff sat on my head, soil dusting my toes. "Are these Evanesce flowers?"

"Yes. They grow during the night. Most of the plants here do. They absorb starlight and moonlight rather than sun rays to photosynthesize."

"*Whoa...* that's so cool." I stuck my face right up to the blue crystal flower, smelling its grapy aroma.

"So, back to why you are here..." Gaius glared at me, noting my bare feet.

"Oh, yeah..." My face was still inches away from the crystal plants. "I had another dream about the cave... and it woke me up all sweaty and with a headache. I was going to ask you for medicine, but, uh..." I trailed off since my reason for coming into the greenhouse to find medicine for a puny headache made no sense. "Sorry... am I still not allowed in here?"

My teacher looked down at me and Tuff—still perched on my head and leaving orange glitter down my tangled locks—and smiled, maybe out of pity for my nightmares or just because he couldn't believe I thought walking into his forbidden glass house was a good idea. He then took off his dirty gardening gloves. "Seeing as I haven't kicked you out yet—"

"You mean I can see the Wishing Stars, then?" I interrupted, smiling quite big.

"Most are still saplings, but I suppose you'll still enjoy it. It's down this way."

Gaius led me back down the hallway I came through and continued forward. We came to a hazy double-glassed door leading into the greenhouse's middle. Standing near its window, I could see blue and soft white lights flickering inside like fireflies—soft and gentle glimmers. Gaius hovered his hand over the metal door handles, releasing a chiming noise into the air as the entrance unlocked with his magic. *He really has a thing for magic doors.*

He pushed open the entrance to reveal what was inside... and my eyes stared into a celestial dreamworld.

A spherical auditorium filled with floating stardust created an atmosphere of peaceful lights and nebulous hummings. Down the center and taking up almost every inch of the room were hundreds of newly planted starseeds, lining the rows and rows of metal tables. Some sprouts were like sapphires, beginning to produce glowing buds of blue, while others were immaculate vines floating in the air as their roots stayed stationary in hanging planters.

But the plants that stole my attention the longest—the ones in the middle of the room right under the nebula glass dome—were the Wishing Star plants, dazzling as warm and bright as the ones in space. There weren't many, seeing as Gaius was right about most being saplings, but the ones that shone bright like neon glow sticks all had five appendages growing right out of a stem!

Star plants that look like stars—is this for real?

Stardust stuck to the bottom of my bare feet as I ran closer to get a better view of the Wishing Star plants. Tuff trailed behind, our faces getting dusted with the rainbows of the glowing soot that wisped around. One of the Wishing Stars was a soft yellow, twinkling brightly and still attached to its leafy stalk. *I can't believe it's actually growing—even has leaves growing out of its glowing body.* Islands of stardust floated around its plush exterior, spinning in the air as my breath hit the magic fruit. The more I stared at the star, the better my mind felt— celestial emotions blanketing my body—as if happiness and tranquility were the effects of the plant's aroma. I couldn't believe I was looking right at pure magic— right at the thing that fell from the sky and landed in my backyard months ago.

"You can touch one if you want," Gaius offered, standing next to me, grinning at my gawping of his magical plants. "Just don't pluck it from its stem."

"You mean it?" I truly couldn't believe he allowed me to hold one of his precious Wishing Stars.

He nodded, so I gently placed my hands around the star fruit. It was a bit bigger than Tuff and just as plump. The texture was like a warm blanket that had just been removed from a dryer, and I could've snuggled with it all night. When I carefully pressed its center with my thumbs, painting my fingers a celestial yellow, it was squishy like a waterbed. *I can't believe I'm touching a star right now! This is insane!*

"It feels so comforting and... happy," I said in awe of the glowing fruit. "How come this one looks different than the one I saw fall in my backyard?"

"When any Wishing Star finds its connecting magic pulse, it will 'burst'— transforming from a fruit state to a purely magic one—and shoot down to wherever the connection is. The speed and heat from traveling also change the star's appearance, which is why you probably saw a more ethereal aura of magic instead of a tangible one."

"Whoa..." I squished the star again. "Do you know what kind of magic is inside this one?"

The gardener smiled. "That's the wonder of it. We never know until it finds the heart it's drawn to."

"How do you know when they are ready to be picked or, uh, harvested, I guess?"

"See up there?"

I followed Gaius' eyes as they went toward the ceiling. Floating at the top like lost balloons were about ten yellow, pink, and orange Wishing Stars, bumping into each other and releasing more stardust to the floor and in our hair. "When fully ripe, they float to the top of the greenhouse. Right now, a handful from the last harvest is still there, but it's not time for them to be released yet. Kamari is the only one who can guide them into space where they can fully grow into the powerful Wishing Stars you look at during the night. In about eight months, the whole ceiling will be covered in stars; it'll be just like a galaxy in here."

When I turned to see Gaius' face, he was smiling brightly, standing proud in his tank top and sweatpants—both of us in our pajamas underneath the stars. I had never seen him look like that—blissful. He didn't have to say anything; I could tell by the twinkling in his eyes that he truly loved being a Keeper and caring for the Wishing Stars, staring at the ditsy star-fruits on his ceiling. On the outside, no one would ever guess he had a heart for plants, yet his muscles and stocky physique still were gentle enough to care for the delicate flowers. Ariela did a good job picking Gaius as her Keeper of Stars. I couldn't think of anyone else better for the job.

The excitement of the Wishing Stars left me wide awake, and since Gaius wasn't making me go back to sleep, I decided to take a seat at the perimeter of the galactic garden just to stare up at the ceiling. Stargazing at its finest. It was perfect—watching the aura of colors and listening to their peaceful humming while Tuff zoomed around; he liked the feeling of the falling stardust hitting his cheeks.

Gaius soon joined me, sitting on the stone step as we watched my glainie float happily around. I don't know what it was about nighttime, but it always brought about deep thoughts and yearning questions... and I still had a couple I wanted to ask Gaius. I couldn't think of a better time than in his magical greenhouse to ask.

"Gaius..." I began, staring up above, watching Tuff paint himself with the colors of the cosmos, "what do the Guardians actually *do?*"

He chuckled with a huff. "What do you mean?"

"I *know* you said they disperse dark magic or something like that, but whenever I see them, they just are reading or at the Elysium writing stuff down in their books. Like, do they just... *roam* around or something."

A rugged laugh left his lungs, hefty and showing the whites of his straight teeth. "What I wouldn't give to hear you say that in front of them, Vilmad most of all. Would knock that git flat on his back. It may not seem like much to you, but they play a big part in controlling all magic. We would have legions of dark creatures roaming our galaxies if they didn't go out and contain the dark magic and disperse it evenly across the planets. They also create charms and new potions. Anything you see down here had to be created by them first. Then, there is Lady Ariela. She watches over the light magic and can create variations of magic."

"Whoa, I didn't know she could do that..." I then thought about a question I'd been delaying asking the whole summer. Fidgeting began with my fingers as I mustered up courage, looking at my mentor. "Can I ask you... another question?"

"Go ahead."

My voice became earnest and tranquil as I focused in on the Keeper, noting the thin wrinkles by his peridot eyes. "So, is there a reason why the Guardians weren't super thrilled about you teaching me? Like, the day I met them, only Ariela seemed to be for the idea while the rest were indifferent or against it—especially Vilmad. Did you do something to make them upset?"

There were only the gentle sounds of wind brushing against the glass windows and the theremin humming of the magic plants for a brief moment. The Keeper sat deep in thought.

A warm breath whispered out, his chest depuffing. "Let's just say I was right, and they were wrong about the last Agapéd Bearer, and they can't seem to apologize for it."

"*Really?*" I asked, not believing that to be the whole truth; holding a grudge didn't seem like something Lady Ariela would do... or *could* do. "You sure it's not just Vilmad who doesn't like you?"

"It is true. Though, with Vilmad, we disagree on more than just on how to train you."

"Then, what happened? I don't know much about the last bearer... or any of them for that matter."

Gaius released another deep breath, extending his arm over his kneecap to sit more comfortably on the stone steps. "Before you, there was Ecuras. He was decent with a sword, mighty with magic, did more listening than talking—a perfect pupil, which is why I accepted him as mine."

My eyes widened. "You taught the Agapéd before me?"

"Mhm. I used to have at least one Mage or Mystic a season who would work under me to learn a thing or two about monster hunting or living earth magic. Having Ecuras inquiring about being my pupil wasn't something surprising. He wanted to become a grand Hero and was well on his way—even before the Agapéd chose him. The Guardians thought he would do well under my guidance when it came to fighting against dark magic, so I accepted the role and taught him many things."

His green eyes went to the floor, memories wisping by just like the stardust wafting around us. "I hate to admit it, but I saw a piece of myself in him at the beginning. It was nice having someone around who enjoyed learning magic and could give a good brawl."

Tuff silently floated down to my side and rested by my hip, slowly dozing off to sleep.

I mimicked the Keeper and looked toward the stone floor dusted with sparkly soot and crumbs of soil. "He sounded pretty perfect... but I guess something bad must have happened, seeing as Ariela and the rest of the Guardians were being extra careful this time around with me?"

He sighed. "With the magic you have, it chooses a good heart, but that doesn't mean a heart will remain good; it was like that for Ecuras..." The Keeper rubbed his jawline, scratching his boxed beard. "Before the glory of being the Agapéd Bearer got to his head, I believe his heart was in the right place. I even showed him the Wishing Stars... trusted him that much.

My blue eyes were now glued to his green ones, unable to look away from his lingering, solemn stare down at the stone flooring. *Whoa... guess being in this room is a bigger deal than I thought...*

"Then, one day, while I was tending to the peony blizzard sprouts in the Veradome, he asked me a series of questions that involved my magic and what makes a heart eternal. He ended by asking me, 'Wishing Stars can live for thousands of years, am I right? Until they find the being or organism they are drawn to?' I told him yes. Then, he asked, 'Have you ever considered experimenting with them? Seeing what all you could do with a power like theirs?' The question wasn't too shocking. Been around Man long enough, and they never seem to stop looking for eternal youth. It was when he asked to sacrifice a couple of the plants—sacrifice a gift meant for the heart of another—so he could live forever to 'save the worlds.' Lisa…" The Keeper's face was serious, without any tiredness in his eyes. "A question like that should never be entertained or further indulged by one's heart and mind."

My tone matched his as I asked, "It was then you knew… that his heart had changed?"

Gaius slowly dipped his chin. "I knew then that Ecuras' love for magic was becoming a lust for power. It was never about saving those in need. He loved being the all-powerful Agapéd Bearer; living longer would be the ultimate way to grow in magical strength and fame. So, after he asked me that, I quickly dismissed it and told the Guardians to remove the Agapéd from him. They said my opinion was not sound and that Ecuras was a great hero; taking him out of the galaxy would cause many people to die because he couldn't save them…" His green eyes glimmered at the floating Wishing Stars hovering on the glass ceiling's surface. "That is when I decided to take things into my own hands."

I pulled my legs close to my chest and wrapped my hands around my shins.

Gaius continued to speak to me not as if I weren't a student or pupil of his—as if I meant something more to him. His heart laid bare with each word he spoke. "When Ecuras returned for training, I confronted him about my suspicions. He had a way with words, saying everything was just for the sake of learning. Then, I mentioned that he was forbidden to enter the staritorium. He became put off—almost irate that his gimpish self wasn't allowed to see the plants before their release. In a fit of anger, he said, 'Immortality would be better suited for a man like me. You have magic unseen in that glass dome. It should be explored.' So with that, I banished him from the Veradome and Calendula. The veil that conceals the land and prevents those evanescing in also exiles him."

I wasn't necessarily shocked at Gaius' statement, believing he truly would banish someone he didn't like, even for a simpler reason than hurting his Wishing Stars. "And that's why the Guardians were upset? Couldn't they just overrule your decision?"

His chin tilted as his eyes swung to the ceiling. "I also erased his memories— every single one that had to do with the Wishing Stars location, Calendula, and the secret entrances. He would only see a Keeper and nothing more when he thought of me." Gaius then looked right at me. "That was the tipping point."

My eyes became frozen as my jaw dropped to the floor. "You *erased his memories?* But how?"

"Forget-Me pollen from a Blackout Bouvardia mixed with a trance charm to specify which memories would be permanently erased. It's a rare and tricky charm to conjure and is impossible to reverse. Memory magic without consent was... and still is... illegal—hence why the Guardians were so upset. But years later, it turned out I was right. Ecuras began to only save cities and nations that gave him profit and stopped listening to the Guardians' guidance. When the time came for him to stop the Fallen Elysian magic, he did so quite easily, but months later, Ariela informed us that the Agapéd had returned to the stars. Whether he died in battle or because his heart became too dampened with Darkness, no one knows—just that the Agapéd stayed dormant for over a century... until it found you."

"So *that's* why you were so hesitant to let me see the Wishing Stars... you didn't want to repeat what happened in the past?"

Gaius softly smiled before turning his head toward me. "No, it wasn't because of that. I just knew you would be disappointed if I didn't have any Wishing Stars ready."

My back straightened, my chin lifting away from my bent, cradled knees. "Wait... Does that mean you trusted me from the beginning?"

Gaius nodded slowly, that grin of his showing through his facial hair.

Warmth filled my chest, and the heart Gaius gifted life back to beamed behind my ribcage with happiness. He trusted me the entire time, even after all I had done: taking the request from Raglan, begging him to break the Guardians' rules about teaching me to fight and failing to stay safe when the vezper attacked. I was clumsy and careless, loved snooping more than a girl should, and I was a teenager. A privilege as precious as this—seeing magic in its purest form—was something I didn't deserve or could ever earn.

And he just said he didn't let me see them because he was afraid of disappointing me.

I grinned at him before looking back to the ceiling, gazing at the sky through the glass roof. "Nothing about this place could ever disappoint me. But I am glad

I waited. Getting to touch one of the magic fruits was pretty cool…"

The happiness in my chest should have stayed, but after hearing about Ecuras and how his heart was good at the beginning… I began to question if that would ever happen to me. A heart can be so easily persuaded and tempted. *What if I follow his same path by accident? Is that even possible?*

I turned my face to the greenhouse floor, my hands still wrapped around my knees. "Do you think… I will end up like Ecuras?"

Without any hesitation, Gaius answered, "No. You have nothing to fear when it comes to your heart turning evil. The Light may have chosen Ecuras for the time being, but Ecuras never chose to follow The Light. You have. When you told me your reasoning for becoming a Hero, I knew you were the right choice, even though you didn't know what you were getting yourself into."

A smile drew along my face, filled with relief and releasing all doubt in my heart. "So, why did you choose to take me in, since teaching the Agapéd last time got you into trouble with the Guardians?"

His answer wasn't as quick, taking a moment to go through his memories. "They said you were from Earth, and the fact they came to me meant they desperately needed someone they could trust to do the job right. Plus, I wasn't about to let them make the same mistake again."

"Well, I'm glad you did. Being here in Calendula is the coolest thing that's ever happened to me."

We sat for a while longer, just staring at the sky above the greenhouse. Stardust from the Wishing Stars made ambient sounds in our ears, creating the perfect lullaby for me, and I could feel my eyes droop. I tried to stay awake so Gaius wouldn't know I was tired; I hated people seeing me sleepy. Without me knowing, however, I dozed off on Gaius' shoulder.

I didn't know how long I was asleep—maybe a minute or two—but he tenderly nudged me awake, saying, "Let's go," and he gave me a piggyback ride back to the Hearth. He even carried Tuff in the palm of his callused left hand, supporting me with his right arm to not wake him up. His brawn and kindness came in handy for sleepy nights like this.

Gaius dropped me off in his living room and placed Tuff in my hands—warm and completely knocked out, daydreaming about the star plants. Before the Keeper left to put out the fire in the living room, he stopped me in my tracks with his deep voice.

"Lisa, I know it may be hard for you right now, but if you want the nightmares to stop, I believe visiting Valhalla's family will give your head and heart the peace it desires... when you're ready, that's all."

I didn't know what to say and stared silently at the door handle to the laundry room. I knew he was right.... I knew I should go and see her family... but I didn't think I could look at them after what I had done. Most of all, as selfish as it sounds, I just hated saying goodbye. It meant the end of something good. I couldn't even let songs play through when I listened to them on my MP3 player, and I had a hard time finishing TV shows because I liked the idea that the story kept going.

Saying goodbye to my friend... I didn't want to think about it. Valhalla wasn't someone I wished to be gone. I wanted her with me every day because she is—*was*—the truest friend I ever—

My eyes glossed over. *Don't think about it, Lisa.*

Since I remained silent with my hand on the laundry room door, Gaius continued speaking to my sleepy, pitiful self. "If you wake up again, feel free to visit the staritorium or come and find me. You aren't alone here. Get some good rest."

I watched him return to his magic study before entering my room and quickly collapsing onto my giant swinging bed. Tuff cradled up close to my chest, putting images of the Wishing Stars in my head in hopes I wouldn't have to think about the cave.

At least, for that night, I slept well.

36
WHERE'S THE PORTAL?

It wasn't merely a typical day in the middle of October. It was the Spar—the exam Cal and I had been training for.

If passed, examinees would receive beginner Hunter licenses, allowing us to do small jobs for the kingdom as Restricted Hunters. We couldn't do any solo hunts, but it gave us a chance to finally fight real monsters alongside other Hunters. I had already taken down quite a few with Gaius, but Cal hadn't. For him, this was a much bigger deal.

For me, I saw it as a stepping stone to becoming a stronger Mage and future Hero, but for Cal... it was his reputation on the line. Not passing would mean the King and Queen would be dishonored, as well as Ekron and his teachings. He had more to worry about than me, so I hoped he would do well during the exams.

My doppelganger and I had developed a good system: She goes off to school while I sleep an extra hour. Then, when the sixth day comes, while Mom is in the shower or changing clothes after work, duplicate-me will wait by the back door for me to arrive—making a quick recombining of souls and shuffling of loose clothing before resuming the evening at home. *And Vilmad thought I wouldn't be able to handle this—sure showed him, the long-haired stiff neck.*

I saw my other self go off to school, and I quickly changed into my Boolavogue garb—consisting of pale blues and cream-colored patterns—and pulled my hair up in a ponytail. Tuff was on my shoulder, ready to go, so I lugged out my portal suitcase and opened it right up—

All the whites in my eyes shone once I unzipped the outer shell.

Pure devastation.

Under the flap, there was no light. No ripples of magic. No portal. It was just an old, purple, completely non-magic suitcase straight off of the sale rack... and my heart burned hot before falling to the pit of my stomach.

"Wha—where's the portal?" I said out loud, my words turning raspy.

Tuff had no idea either, shrugging and standing on my bed.

I hit the bottom and zipper pouches on the inside over and over like a maniac, but no magic popped out or triggered an abundance of bright lights. Nothing but a mocking fabric noise from my nubby fingernails scratching the surface.

"This *cannot* be happening right now. Not today—any other day but today!"

I paced my room as my brain was counting the seconds going by. Emunah said nothing about portals disappearing—kind of seemed like an important factoid to mention—and I had no way of contacting anyone. I thought of asking Tuff to go, but the moment it crossed my mind, Tuff refused to leave my side with a hardy *hoot*. I admired his worry for me, but I sure wish teleporting millions of miles away wasn't a big deal for him.

Ah... teleporting! But...

I bit my lower lip and froze in the middle of my purple rug.

My evanescing was... good. I didn't need the petals anymore, seeing as their magic was now a part of me. I had never messed up to the point I needed healing from the burly Keeper and always landed in the right place... except for maybe a foot or two off from my desired point. *I traveled from Calendula to Boolavogue, so how different can traveling trillions of miles from here to Boolavogue actually be?*

Looking down at the stopwatch Ariela gave me a while ago, I saw time ticking away. *There is no other option here.*

I took a deep breath. "Okay, Tuff... we can do this. It's just like normal, only that I will be going through space at the speed of starlight. No big deal, right?"

Tuff gave me a confident pose, stubby orange hands firmly against his sides, even though he didn't understand the depth of our situation.

I stood in the middle of my room and placed my hand out. *Hidden entrance Boolavogue... hidden entrance Boolavogue... please, please, please go to the hidden entrance in Boolavogue...* I curled in my fingers to form a fist and let the blue rivers of magic fill my palm—focusing my thoughts harder than ever before—and punched the air.

An instant rush of ice-cold air picked at my skin when I landed. When I opened my eyes, hoping to see trees and just a random chill of mountain air around me, I saw the night sky... and not just above me. It was below me, behind me, beside me, and in front of me. Everything was as quiet as quiet could be and nothing but blue, black, and purple nebulas for miles out.

There was no mistaking it. I. Was. In. Space.

Oh no... no, no, no, no, no, no, no, this can't be happening. WHAT DID I DO?

Glancing down at my feet, I stood in the middle of a stone circle with a magic emblem in the center. I had seen the sign before in Bethesda's magic books; it was used as a portal beacon for evanescers or teleporters—an evanesce sigil. Gaius mentioned that Boolavogue and EverWake had these so that anyone who visits their city by magic would be automatically beamed to that specific spot. The question was *why I was transported to one on top of an asteroid!*

The rock beneath the symbol was a dark purple with strange lavender shades of grass growing out beneath it.

When I turned around to look behind me, up at the top of a bigger asteroid was a house—not a space station or alien planet—with an asteroid bridge leading down to the teleporting sigil. The home had a glowing cotton candy pink tree at the top of the roof with white and gray brick walls and even a back porch and second level. Two windows on the second floor illuminated orange and yellow, and a large glass dome on the bottom level was similar to Gaius' huge window in his living room.

What is this place? And how is it I'm not suffocating to death?

Tuff whistled as he sat on my shoulder, telling me he sensed more magic creatures around—the *good* kind that wouldn't kill us.

Without the idea of a threat nearby or inside the fantasy-space home, I decided to tread toward its front door. The frigid space air caused me to rub my shoulders to try and get warm; it didn't help much going up the purple-rock steps. I could even see mine and Tuff's breaths when we exhaled. Space was freezing—should be even chillier than this, right? Unless those science books lied to me in school...

The front door was thick and durable with a small viewing glass on its frame, allowing the orange lights inside to beam through. Too bad I was so short; I couldn't peep inside the window—stranded to knock and hope for a kind, gentle, non-threatening magical stranger to be on the other side.

I knocked, and it opened after a second or two, but no human was there. Instead, it was a purple creature—resembling a small anteater, like a tamandua— standing on its hind legs and pulling back the door handle. Sharp white eyes like shiny pearls beamed on its little head, and he had a belly glowing as if stardust was floating inside. We stared at each other for a couple of seconds. Never in my life had I seen a creature like that—neither had Tuff.

"Um... hello there," I said to the creature. "Can I come in?"

It didn't blink or answer my question... just continued to stand straight up.

How can something so cute be this ominous?

Clatter erupted from up on the staircase and trickled down the steps. Following it was an old woman's voice with a thick accent—very melodic. "Yami—why you answa'in da doh, lettin' all da cold breeze in?"

The galaxy-purple anteater backed from the door slowly, crawling away into the home. As it turned around, glowing pink petals were visible on the creature, tracing across its spine and matching the leaves from the cotton candy tree on top of the roof.

With one foot inside, I looked toward the spiraling staircase that hid behind a cluttered wall and saw a wrinkly woman descend from it. She had dark umber skin and even darker hair—half of it being gathered into a bun. Most of the strands were thick dreadlocks with silver-haired braids mixed in between, but all were as long as a yardstick—ending with frilly plum puff balls at the tips. She wore a mauve cardigan that had extremely loose arms with plum boots to fight off the cold. The only thing about her clothing that wasn't of the purple family was the sky-blue shirt underneath and about twenty different tribal necklaces around her neck.

She gazed at the door to where I was and walked briskly toward me. For an old woman, she sure had the strength and spirit of someone half her age.

When she saw my face, it was like she knew exactly who I was. Her bright hazel eyes smiled with her lips, giving her wrinkly wings near her eyelashes. And then she proceeded to hug me.

409

I wasn't about to stop her, so I just stood there and let it happen. She smelled like cinnamon.

"*Na so—da Agapéd!*" the woman said, releasing me from her hug. Now, I smelled like cinnamon. "My, when yo'r sta fell from da sky and cross da Milky Galaxy, I was sho as sho itself I was dreamin', but even my dreams aunt *dat* crazy... look atchu—you must be freezin' cold! *Yami!* Grab da good glassas fo me and my gues." Her speech was deep and bold, adding many "da" and "ah" sounds to words that I wasn't used to hearing. She was quite endearing, but given the abruptness of the situation, I didn't really have time to stay and chat with a stranger... *or* take part in whatever drink she was about to prepare for me. However, I was shy and stranded in space. My only option was to follow along until I could kindly interject.

The purple anteater came crawling back down the stairs and entered the crazy lady's kitchen, climbing on top of the counter and knocking over a couple of spices. Seemed the old woman was more preoccupied with me than caring about a wild animal playing chef in her kitchen.

What is going on right now?

"Um, I'm sorry," I began as she pulled my arm to sit on the armchair across from her, "but how is it you know who I am without me having to tell you—"

"I know every sta dat has fallen," she began, moving her hands in a very animated motion, "and I been watchin' yo'r sta fo' quite some time."

More rackets came from the kitchen, but I felt rude to turn around and look. "So, uh, who are you... exactly?"

The old woman started belly laughing as if she had just heard the funniest joke of all time. "You must be pullin' my leg—you tellin' me dose Guardians have yet to speak of me? I know I been busy, but dat does not mean I be too busy fo da Chosen, *abi?*"

Even though I struggled to understand her clearly, I began to catch on to who she was. The stars, the Guardian talk, the house in space—it all pointed to one hypothesis.

"You're Kamari, aren't you? The last of the Keeper of Stars?"

"*Da FIRST*—whaddya mean *LAST*? Ariela came down like a beacon to my village, plucked me right up first brink of daylight 740 years ago, and I not been da same since... while da odda two were not even souls yet."

"Oh, I just meant the last of the three I met. That's all."

Out of the corner of my eye, I saw the anteater creature she called "Yami" come carrying a tray of two frosted glasses and a pot of tea. Its little eyes gave no emotion and continued to look bright and ditsy as its body wobbled over to the coffee table like a little butler. Yami put down the tray, stared at me *again* for no particular reason, and crawled away after Kamari said thank you.

Does she train them to serve us—didn't know magic creatures could be so attentive—

"Now, tell me you and da orange glainie's names," Miss Kamari said to me and Tuff—who had been hovering around on my shoulder the entire time.

Wonder how she knew I'd named him...

"Lisa, ma'am, and this is Tuff," I answered.

She then began to pour some hot water into the frosted glasses, adding two tea bag packets to our drinks. Once the water began to diffuse with the tea leaves, it changed from clear to strawberry pink. She then finished it off by pouring a lot of honey into both cups. Was glad to see she had a sweet tooth like me, unlike a certain muscly Keeper I knew.

"Now, dat be a fine name. Here. Drink." She handed me the glass. "It will warm yo'r veins down to yo'r bones."

"Thank you, but, uh..."

"You muz be wonderin' how you showed up here instead of somewhere else."

I nodded, and she continued.

"Dat is because of da rules. No one can enta anodda galaxy without pamission from da Stellarlegion. If you try to teleport or portal away, you will be transported to one of us instead. Dere are many ports and sigil stones around the odda galaxies—but only *one* connected to da Milky Way, and dat is mine."

That explains why I've never been here before... since I go through a portal straight to Haim Gana...

"Then, how is it that I have never met you before when Inna or Gaius had evanesced me back home?"

"Da Keepas of Stas need no pamission. Deir magic is good and always welcome."

I took a sip of my tea. It tasted *good*—the best tea I had ever had in my whole life—making my heart all cozy.

I must have been smiling quite big because Kamari turned to me and said, "I see you have a taste for Verisweet. Its leaves are best grown here, where da nebula wata runs deep through da tree's roots. Its breath covas my home, which allows you and I to breathe da arctic air with ease. We would be frozen pods of flesh widout da tree's warmin' aura."

Warm? It was freezing outside! But, now that I think about it, if I were on a normal rock in space, I would've been frozen solid with my first step.

"Does that happen to be the tree that's on top of your house?" I asked.

"Seein' it from da ground below do not do it justice. Come—dis is a chance you cannot afford to miss, Lisa."

Maybe Gaius won't mind if I am a little late for morning lessons before the Spar...

I followed behind Miss Kamari as she led me and Tuff up her old staircase. She grabbed her tan coat with fluffy fur inside and gave me a dark purple one. It also smelled like cinnamon, which meant she probably wore it recently. I didn't care; anything was better than nothing when stepping back into the arctic space.

Walking up her stairs, all her flooring and siding was made of white brick or stone, with many mementos hung without pattern against the walls. Seeing space outside her windows rather than green grass or a city was strange. I honestly wouldn't mind her view; it would be quite peaceful.

Something fuzzy rubbed up against my leg, causing me to flinch and jerk my shoulders. Yami and another purple anteater had come crawling on all fours up the stairs with us, bellies glowing pink and blue and spines still sprouting magenta leaves.

"What are those?" I asked Kamari, watching her violet boots stride up the stairs in front of me.

"Yami and Nuru. Dey are known as yaminurus, magic creatures who clean da skies of stardust. Dough, deese two seem to do a lot more loungin' dan cleanin'."

"Do they live here with you? Seems you would get quite lonely out here."

"Da stas are my home—never a time where I find myself pityin' da life of oddas. When visitas do come, I enjoy deir time; when dey leave, I enjoy my time. I visit the odda planets for necessities, but Man sometimes gets too loud for me. I would radda stay here with Yami and her friends... even when dey sometimes do not clean up after demselves."

"Well, I'll come to visit you more if you'd like. I love the sky and the stars."

She smiled at me, eyes shining bright like the galaxy outside her windows. "Den, my home is always welcome to you, Lisa."

Kamari then opened the top door of her home that led to her roof. Amid the cold, the Verisweet tree blossomed strong, emitting a pink light from its foliage. Seemed as if gravity was not as strong the higher up we went, given that the tree's loose leaves were swirling up, down, and in circles despite there being no sign of wind. In the middle of her roof, where the tree's roots were dug into, sat a rippling pond of glowing blue. The pink leaves danced along its surface, making it radiate and glisten like the ink from an indigo glowstick.

Yami and Nuru went over to the pond and stuck out their long tongues to drink the water. With the sound of space silence and the radiance of the stars around us, it truly felt like I stepped into a cosmic dreamworld.

"Wow..." I said out loud.

"*Na so*—a gleam of beauty each and every time," Miss Kamari concurred.

"Your home reminds me of a dream I had... well, the scenery around your house anyway."

"*A dream?* Was dis da night da sta came to you?"

I looked up at her after touching the magic water, which was quite warm. "Yes, actually, but it was just a dream—"

"For a normal girl, yes, but for you, dey mean more dan just a mere night fantasy. Did somethin' in yo'r dream come true in da real world?"

"I mean... it told me to go to the woods, and when I did, Inna was there, waiting for me."

Kamari came right up to my face, her hazel eyes turning blue and pink from the luminance of the Verisweet and the pond. "See. Dat is da Agapéd—its sta burnin' bright wid magic, guidin' you to your purpose. Lisa, a dream from da heart—yo'r heart—will always be most powaful, and what yo'r heart feels is what yo'r mind makes inta dreams. Never ignore dem, no matta how good or dark dey may seem."

Miss Kamari wasn't like Inna or Gaius... or anyone I had ever met in my entire life: going with the flow, content with her lifestyle, and speaking in odd proverbs... a little bit like a crazy grandma. What she said about dreams, though, I had never really questioned before. I had the two visions after the Agapéd flew into my chest, but that was it. My heart was filled with magic, so it would make sense for it to influence my unprovoked dreaming world.

I also had painful dreams about Valhalla. Nightmares, for anyone, weren't unusual after something like that... something that skin-shredding and heart-shattering. For it to mean something more than bad memories resurfacing during sleep—I didn't want to think about it. Though... Gaius' words rang in my head, *Go and see her family.*

I blinked with my eyes facing down—batted away the fear of doing the impossible.

I looked into the water of the glowing pond and remembered something Inna had mentioned. "Miss Kamari, does this happen to be planet Zena?"

"It does, dough it is not much of a planet anymo. Been dinged and crashed a bit by da cosmos, and a part of it was crackin', so I pushed it off before it caused any mo trouble."

Okay, I will get back to the fact she just said she pushed an asteroid later...

"So, does that mean this pond is filled with something called Moon Water?"

"Ah—I see Inna has told you about her staseeds and da wata dey need to survive. Dis is in fact such wata; da magic in the nebulas creates weepin' clouds across da galaxies dat rain down dis miracle liquid. It allows da Verisweet to prospa, givin' it da immaculate glow you see now."

"Just wondering, but what happens if a person drinks it?" I couldn't help but ask, given that Inna never told me.

Kamari lifted her hand, and droplets of water rose from the pond. Like a string of glowing pearls, the water drifted toward the Keeper's fingers as if she were its magnetic pull. She then pointed her other hand to the staircase, and two new empty tea glasses flew up and out of her house. I thought she had water magic like me or Inna, but enchanting kitchenware was very unexpected. Using her strange floating magic, the old Keeper made the glowing water pour into the two glasses and flew one right into my hands.

"How did you make the water and cups fly like that?" I asked her, hugging the mug in between my palms.

"Da powa of da planet's unforeseen force is also one I share. See, I can change da push and pull of gravity, makin' myself da axis point if I desire—

causin' whateva objects I want to follow me. It is quite fun. Now, go ahead—take a sip and tell me what you feel."

She sat squatted on the pond's edge with me, waiting like a giddy little girl for her friend to try her weird concoction. I cradled the cup of Moon Water and took a small gulp. I blinked—blinked twice. Other than it glowing, it tasted just like normal hot water—kind of a letdown after drinking the Verisweet tea.

"It's refreshing in this cold weather," I said to her, trying to make it as positive as possible.

She smacked her right hand on her kneecap while grasping her mug in her left. "Dat it is! It also replenishes da magic inside you. Evanescen' cross planets drains yo'r magic dry, and dis will keep you fit and ready to go. Givin' yo'r attire, I assume you had odda plans dan stoppin' for a drink of da Verisweet?"

I took another sip immediately, knowing it *was* magical and not just glistening, boring water. "I do, but I'm glad I stayed. I don't think Gaius will be too upset, but I know if I'm any later he will probably hand it to me during lessons."

Kamari gave another hardy chortle. "*Na so*—he be dat way sometimes, but I am glad he be da one teachin' you instead of me. He is a good man. Good heart. Strong like da Wishing Stas he grows." She chugged the entire glass and made her empty jar float back down the hallway, presumably to the kitchen. "Now, you best be off. Just go back down da stairs to da sigil stone, and to da left is an Aura Beacon—da blue crystal glowin' like a lampshade. Touch it wid yo'r hand, and when it glows green, you are clear to evanesce back to planet Kalm."

Kamari gave me another smile with her wrinkly eyes and laugh lines as I returned her cinnamon-smelling coat and Moon Water mug. The only old lady I was close to was Grandma, and she was nothing like Kamari. I always just assumed that when it came to age, the older you got the more naggy and stubborn you became. At least that was what Grandma was like, hence why she and Mom didn't get along. Kamari was different. She saw life in a bigger way and made me feel important. She invited me in, hugged me without warning, made me tea—okay, Yami did that, but it was still *her* tea—and didn't say one negative thing about Gaius. She made me feel like I was doing everything right... I didn't know how else to explain it. I just knew I definitely would be coming back to visit her again.

I thanked her for the water and tea, making my way back down to the sigil stone. I saw her wave at me outside of her front door, along with Yami climbing on her back. I smiled at them both before turning around to walk down the asteroid stairs. The Aura Beacon Kamari mentioned really did look like a lampshade—which is what I thought it was when I first arrived. I touched its cool surface, and it turned a peridot green the moment it recognized my fingerprints. *What a cool type of magic...*

I stood on the sigil and thought hard about the Veradome's secret entrance again. I punched the air with my hand full of magic and whisked away from the asteroid planet Zena.

37
THE SPAR

Like I had expected earlier, I teleported right to the top of the mountain entrance in Boolavogue, the weather perfect and the blue sky clear—not a single star twinkling above. *Thank goodness*—

"You're late," an agitated, brogue voice bellowed behind me.

My shoulders jerked at the sound of *his* tone. I slowly turned, fear trickling down my spine, and found Gaius standing right behind me with his arms crossed a bit too tight. His being there was not a part of the plan, clearly stating to meet inside his house, which only meant one thing: I was *beyond* late.

He did not bother to wait for an explanation. He eyed me down like a hawk, assuming I'd follow, and dug his grass-stained heels into the mountain trail toward the Kingdom.

I had never seen that look on his face—mid-morning Keeper vexation. I quickly followed behind, explaining myself as if my life depended on it. "I'm sorry! My portal back home just went up and disappeared out of my suitcase—"

"Your *suitcase*?"

"—and I had to evanesce instead, which was all good and fine until I ended up in space—*literal space, Gaius*. You never told me about 'da rules' *or* that portals have expiration dates."

"So you met Kamari then…" He made a guttural sigh. "That explains why you are so late."

I threw my chin to the side. "Don't blame her. It was all me. I was freezing cold, and she offered me tea. Not like I was gonna refuse."

Gaius cocked an eyebrow as he looked over at me, showing off his green eyes. "As long as it was tea and not Moon Water, you should be fine for today."

All the whites of my eyes shone as my head gunned upward at the Keeper's face. "What do you mean—Kamari said it was okay."

My mentor steadily turned his head away from my direction. There was something smug about his gaze as it drifted toward the trail ahead. "Well… there's nothing more we can do now."

I ran out in front of him and started walking backward, freaking out a little more. "Gaius, what do you *mean*? What's gonna happen to me? Am I alright? Is there something wrong with my magic now?"

No response from the Keeper.

"Gaius, say something!"

When the sun poked through the tree canopy above, Gaius broke into a coy smile, trying to fight back a chuckle.

"Wait a second—you're joking with me right now," I said, smiling, though still slightly unsure.

He still said nothing—those green eyes of his stabbing me with worry.

"You are joking with me, right…? Gaius?"

Nothing but the sound of crunching gravel beneath his hefty boots came from him. Even the *birds* pestered me with their loud songs.

Whatever amusement he found in this situation, I did *not!* "Gaius, I don't know if you are just trying to be funny or if you're laughing about some future event involving me and that water. Please, just tell me!"

After more anxiety-stricken seconds of Gaius hiding behind his mischievous smile, he finally responded. "You're fine, Lisa. Just don't let your excuse for being late be because of something as gimpish as Moon Water."

I couldn't believe it. The brazenness of the man—trying to get back at me for making him late by pulling such a mean joke. *Him*—late. As if he was the one about to fight in the Hunter rink. "I truly thought something was wrong with me!" I snapped back, trying to not laugh at my own gullibility.

With Kamari still on my mind as we made it to the trail's end, following the civilians toward the castle entrance, I couldn't help but ask Gaius for something.

Confidence shone through each syllable as I asked, "Gaius, I want to learn how to fly."

The burly gardener kept his eyes facing forward over the heads of Boolavogians. "You can't fly."

Not even a glimmer of hope in his words!

My shoulders dropped. "But when the Agapéd came down from the sky, I had a dream I could fly—flying *with* it actually, and Kamari said—"

"You shouldn't take everything so seriously from her, Lisa. She lives with those oversized rodents and talks with the stars as if they were people."

"That still doesn't mean I *can't* learn it. You and Inna taught me your magic, and I ended up with my own, so why can't I learn how to fly?"

Gaius scoffed at my idea as we turned a street corner. "Well, for starters, you shouldn't just assume the Agapéd will willingly gift whatever power you desire. Flight magic is considerably rare, and not one the Agapéd would merely give away to a child because she *wants* it. Second, your head should be on the ground focusing on the Spar—not crackin' on about something that bags of a woman told you." His answer kept getting worse and worse, given the funny slang coming out of his mouth.

Still, I refused to believe anything he said. He was just upset I was behind on being *early*. I crossed my arms, muttering, "I still think there is a chance..."

"Just like you thought there was a chance you could breathe underwater?" Gaius toyed, making that same smirk beneath his finely trimmed facial hair.

My cheeks turned into two red tomatoes. "Inna told you?"

His eyes squinted, and both rows of teeth shone pearly white as he laughed— the biggest laugh he had ever made before me. "And I can't believe you thought choking on water was the smart way to figure out if you could breathe it or not."

I bunched up with my arms still crossed. "It's not *that* funny..."

He calmed his laughter and patted me on my head like I was a six-year-old, messing up my ponytail. "Seems days are never dull with you around."

<hr />

"You ready?" Cal asked as we both stood in the Laze of the main battleground. We wore similar pale blue and white apparel, though he looked way more like a real Hunter than I did. It was tradition to dress in Boolavogue colors for any Hunter exam, even for a beginner one the Prince and I were about to take.

I gave Cal a determined face. "Yeah. You?"

"Mhm. Just so you know... I won't be going easy on you during our third challenge," he said, grinning.

I returned the gesture. "I wasn't expecting you to."

Both of us peeked through the tent and out toward the crowd. It seemed like all the Hunters had no other jobs or prior engagements other than to watch us take the Spar! It wasn't a big deal or anything overtly special; all soon-to-be Hunters had to take this exam.

My heart played a horridly loud song as I saw the sea of rustic men and women, but when I looked over at Cal, I noticed his breathing growing heavy. He was nervous, something he *never* showed outwardly—at least, not during lessons with Ekron. Making mistakes at school is one thing, seeing as there is an expiration date for the embarrassment after four years; for a prince like him, whatever mistakes he made would stay with him and the Kingdom forever. I know Cal said he was ready, but I could tell a part of him was overflowing with anxiety like any normal boy about to step up on stage for all to judge.

Looking upward over the crowd, I saw standing at the top balcony Gaius, Ekron, the Queen, and *the King!* My heart began to play double-time in my chest at the thought of His Majesty watching me battle.

"Your dad is going to watch us?" I asked Cal in disbelief.

"Seems like it," he responded, sounding just as surprised.

"Wait, you're saying you didn't know?"

"Not like he is much of a talker. Going to be quite a surprise for him when he sees me use magic."

I glared right at Cal, my words turning sharp and swift. "You mean you haven't told him you've been practicing magic with Ekron during your private lessons... or with me in the forest with Honey? You're just gonna let him find out like this?"

"Mother, too."

"*Cal!*"

"*Lisa!*" he mocked me as the tent flap swung open.

Captain Clover—the middle-aged, bronzed female huntress in charge of refereeing during our Spar—came bursting into the Laze. "Lisa, Your Highness. Please acquire your weapons of choice for the first challenge and meet me out here in five minutes."

We both went over to the weapon table and rack, but our conversation was not done. I couldn't believe he was about to reveal his magic in front of the whole Kingdom during the Spar.

"You've been practicing your Fysiks magic for over a month... Won't it be a little shocking for them to see you—"

"Lisa, Lisa, Lisa..." he interrupted me with a roguish look on his face, shaking his head as he examined the spread of steel blades. "I don't know why you are so surprised. You know as well as I do that doing what is conventional is not who I am. Plus, what better way to show the Kingdom my magic than when I'm using it to beat you? You did the same thing the day you first arrived here. You're the one who told me to practice and helped me realize that my magic is good for battle. And now that I've learned more than invisibility, creating shields and other surprises," he toyed with his eyebrows lifting, "it's time for my magic to be the talk of the Hunters."

His hazel eyes shone confident in his plan as he fastened his dual swords on his belt, so I just had to believe he was making the right decision.

I grabbed the steel cutlass with the blue ribboned handle and attached the scabbard to my side, feeling his surety radiate outward to me as we headed toward the battleground.

Hardy chatter swam through the air as we followed Captain Clover around the perimeter of the dirt arena. We passed many cheering Hunters from the Men's and Women's Troops. Cal smiled at them, keeping up his princely image. On the other hand, my stare was cemented to the mountain soil. This was the biggest test of my life, and even though I was prepared, my boots wouldn't stop shaking. I could practically hear the throbbing of my heart over the crowd's chants, pounding like a hundred kettledrums in unison. I honestly couldn't believe what was about to happen; never in my life would I have guessed that I would be wielding a sword next to a prince and taking an exam to fight dark magic creatures—all the while being watched by an entire fleet of barbaric hunters and a king.

I took in one final deep breath before we teens entered the center of the dirt arena. Normally, there would be more than just two beginner Hunters taking their exam, according to Captain Ekron, but Cal and I were a special case.

I also wasn't even in line to take the Spar, given that I had only been training for a little over two months. With a little convincing from the Queen, due to Gaius' you-will-have-her-complete-the-exam-because-I-say-so attitude, Captain Ekron taught me only the essentials for the exam to take place with the Prince. I was glad; being next to Cal helped ease my heart, even with all the tension surrounding it.

Captain Clover went over to the elevated stage and bellowed out in her demanding voice, "*Commencement of the End of Season Spar for students Lisa Robbie and Prince Caelum Sonon will now transpire. Passing the first two challenges will gift said Hunters their Restricted Hunter's Licensure. The prize for winning the third challenge lies in the hands of Captain Ekron.*"

Captain Clover then made a snicker at her fellow Captain's request and looked straight at the two of us teens with her brown eyes. "Guess you will have to win to discover what it is. *Now—let us begin the first test starting with Prince Caelum Sonon.*"

"Good luck," I told Cal as I left the dirty rink, making my way to the waiting area near the edge of the arena, which was solely a simple bench away from the crowd.

Placing my sword by my side, I sat nervously with my hands pinned under my thighs as Captain Ekron stepped forward from the balcony. He held out his right hand and created three violet vorrgs with his magic. He informed Cal and me of what to expect and that he was not holding back with his purple, glittery beasts. Before, when he would conjure up his creatures, he would make sure they couldn't kill. For the Spar, they were as real as real could get, killer instinct and all. My throat turned dry just thinking about it.

The three purple vorrgs—mangy, ravenous wild dogs—all thudded to the ground, fierce and craving the magic running through Cal's blood. As one began to move forward, the other two followed its trail. *Looks like Ekron made one the alpha... Cal should take that one out first...* They weren't too fast, but three-versus-one did make it a challenge, especially with their teeth looking longer than usual.

Cal whipped out his dual swords and stayed light on his feet.

The one with the boniest tail charged first, jumping toward him, hoping to knock him down with its beefy paws. Cal dodged it easily and struck the monster with his sword, a clean slice along its body. *One down!*

Cal took no time to rest and immediately went for the smaller vorrg, but the alpha had other plans. It leaped toward the Prince, leaving a faint trail of amethyst dust, and tried to bite his knee. Cal used the hilt of his blade to punch its nose straight down to the ground, discombobulating the dark beast.

I smiled as my legs kept bouncing up and down with my hands still underneath my thighs, hearing the crowd of Hunters clap and cheer. *Quick thinking, Cal.*

The smaller vorrg took its chance and pounced toward Cal next. Like the smart Hunter he was becoming, Cal ducked down and stabbed the dog's belly with his sword, throwing its body across the arena. Splatters of purple blood painted Cal's hands and steel sword before fading away like glitter in the wind. *Adding magical blood, too—Ekron is keeping this as real as possible.*

"*Nice one, Caelum!*" I heard Amos shout rows behind me.

"*Good one, Princey!*" Erin bellowed along.

The Hunters around gave him a good cheer. Even I was impressed to see him lift such a heavy beast.

In no time, the alpha regained its composure and charged its slobbery fangs toward Cal—angry and riled up.

The Prince took turns dodging its pounces, calculating when it would be the best time to strike under its neck. After a few more rolls on the dirt and sprints in circles with the dog, Cal finally ran straight for it. He veered right and left to confuse the beast, and when it least expected it, Cal sliced the monster's front left leg. It knelt in pain, making an eerie whimper, which gave Cal time to finish the kill at its neck. With one strong slash of his sword, being careful to dart away from the vorrg's hyperactive mouth, Cal struck the underside of the neck, defeating all three of Ekron's violet vorrgs.

At the end of Cal's first test, more cheers and booming claps came from the crowd. I was included in the mix.

Looking pleased with his work and very out of breath, Cal jogged over to me. He always smiled best after winning against Ekron's beasts, showing off all his incredibly perfect teeth. Today was no different.

"You were amazing!" I congratulated him, placing my sword in my lap. "But I thought you were going to use your magic?"

He continued to smile as he sat next to me, sweat dripping sparkly down his forehead, coating his fluffy dark hair that ran along his eyebrows. "Oh, you thought I would ruin the surprise on some vorrg battle? No way—I'm saving that for our one-on-one."

"Lisa Robbie, please make your way to your first challenge," Captain Clover announced, making my nerves strum like a gallant harp across my bones.

"Slag 'em hard, Lisa," Cal said as I gripped my sword and walked into the center of the dirt-filled attention circle.

My mouth turned dry as my hands grew sweaty, and I dared not look up at the balcony in fear of my sword grip growing as limp as a soggy noodle. They were watching—Gaius and Cal's scary dad were watching. I didn't want to disappoint those two the most, fearing a Keeper's hulking silence for months on end and the King possibly kicking me out of Hunter training. *Could he even do that—I would never hear the end of it from Gaius or the Guardians, especially Vilmad.*

I took a deep breath, smudging my worries with the soles of my boots, facing toward the spot I figured Ekron would summon his violet vorrgs. *You got this, Lisa.*

Just like with Cal, Ekron summoned three vorrgs as my opponents. Watching Cal battle them first was an advantage, though that also meant I wouldn't have a chance to rest before our cooperative match. I clenched my sword tight and took one final deep breath before Captain Clover shouted, *"Begin!"*

You. Got. This. Lisa.

Each of the vorrgs snarled at me with their banged-up mouths and beady purple eyes, waiting for the alpha to make the first move.

I wasn't about to wait for them all to strike at once, so I decided to use a ranged attack with my magic. I was *very* happy that Ekron said all magic was approved weeks before today, just as long as I made *one* kill with my sword.

On the left side of my belt, I, with the help of my crafty Keeper, made a leather sling for a thin flask meant to hold drinking water. Only, for me, it was a weapon. Using my sword as if it were my hand, I summoned a stream of water out of the bottle—quick as lightning—straight toward the furriest vorrg. Ice bolted fast and stabbed the vorrg hard in the chest.

Purple magic dripped to the ground where the vorrg was impaled by my ice spear, and then, it fell, releasing a howl before disappearing away. Not the most elegant attack, but it got the job done. And I was pretty proud of myself.

The Hunters in the crowd went crazy, loving that magic was now used in the battle.

"That's our Mage!"

"Let's go, Earthian!"

The other two vorrgs immediately gunned for me.

I paid attention to their demeanor, noticing the bigger one getting ready to make its hefty jump. I shot a dirt shard out of the ground—one as high as six feet—and pushed the vorrg's gruesome body out of the air and way off to the side of the rink. The Prince had strength and could lift the carcass with his hands, whereas I needed the dirt to be my muscles.

More chants roared from the audience.

I'll come back to you later—just me and the small one now. I pointed my cutlass at the third vorrg and dodged off to the left, barely missing its gaping mouth. The beast's body was as big as me, and I knew one *smack* of its paws would pin me to the ground like a thumbtack.

I furrowed my brows and approached the magic wolf from behind.

Slit—slice!

I scored its leg, making it wobble, and then gashed its neck, causing Ekron's magic to paint my sword with glowing plum blood before dissipating away.

Now, back to the big guy...

I whipped around and went head first. My heartbeat was steady—confident in my skills as I sprinted right toward the biggest vorrg. Before it could regain its center of gravity from my first terrain magic knockdown, I used the dirt underneath me as a spring, like how I saw Gaius do many times with his plants—jolting myself forward.

With my speed doubled, the foul monster stood no chance. My sword swung swiftly and slashed a giant blow down its side and through its neck, slaying it instantly.

The Hunters began to roar and clap again—much more for me than for the Prince... probably because my fighting style was a little more unpredictable. Cal clearly killed the vorrgs with much more refinement, proving to be the better Hunter out of the two of us, in my opinion. Nonetheless, it was amazing to see myself take down three beasts all on my own. Little me, who could barely kill a spider the size of a quarter just three months ago.

Captain Clover announced the end of our first test, cueing Cal and me to rest and prepare for the second challenge. He changed his weapon to a straight sword while I stuck with my easy-to-handle cutlass before following him out to the rink again. Though my nerves should have been on edge from my rising fatigue, sending worry all down my spine and to the tips of my toes, I remained calm because I wasn't alone this time. I was with Cal. Whatever Ekron would make us fight, I knew I'd be fine with the Prince by my side.

Cal and I waited patiently, guessing which monster Ekron was about to summon. And the more I thought, the more anxiety started to churn up in my gut like acidic ice cream. *Is it going to be an alpha jackjaw? A Gilliath Warner? A pack of bilefiends, maybe? I hope it's not some type of giant fire spider or snake... or both... or a hybrid that can also fly and sting—gosh, please don't be that.*

Forming from the magic of Ekron's fingers, a giant purple creature began to take form. Boulders for feet plopped hard on the ground, and a bright purple light continued to swirl around, painting the colossal beast's silhouette. More magical rocks formed its body and hands, but no head was to be seen. Instead, there was only a big gaping hole, as if the monster was incomplete. When the purple ball of light finished creating the beast, it stopped where its face should be.

Looking at it all together, I recognized it from Gaius' books. It wasn't an animal with blood and bones but a pith, specifically a Terrabody. They were dark magic essence monsters that formed in places where even the grass was filled with dark magic. This one just had a boulder for its body with more rocks for its arms and legs. Pure dark magic held the Terrabody together like glittering glue, the being standing at least fifteen feet tall, and its boulder belly a diameter of eight feet. It had no fur, bones, blood, or neck—just pure rocks and a giant glowing light atop its round body.

It is so like Ekron to give Cal and me a creature that we've never fought before...

Cal leaned over to me, his eyes as wide as mine. "Uh, Lisa, any idea what that is?"

"Yep, and I suggest not using your sword on the rocky parts," I responded.

"That's *all* its parts!"

Suddenly, the Terrabody swung its five-foot arm right at me and Cal.

We both jumped out of the way, me going right and him going left. The creature wasn't swift, but one hit and we would paint the battleground red.

I shouted at Cal, ignoring the audience cheering behind us, "You need to hit the glowing light where its face should be!"

The Terrabody swung toward the Prince in moments, but its fist disconnected itself from the body. Purple magic extended from the stony punch like a rubber string attached to a paddle, and the fist was a ping-pong ball, only made of rock the size of a tractor tire.

It has long-range attacks, too?

Cal rolled underneath its wide, stubby legs to avoid the attack, and when the boulder-for-a-hand hit the ground, *everything* shook. The crowd gasped, catching their balance, while I wobbled to my knees. The impact was like an earthquake, swelling the soil with thunderous tremors, and that was just from one punch!

The Terrabody's fist bounced back in place like a yo-yo, causing the being to shake and sprinkle off violet soot—some of which fell into Cal's hair as he escaped the personal space of the pith.

The Prince shouted back at me—finally able to answer my demand, "Okay, but I will need some help reaching that high!"

Even though this creature was scary, it was my perfect opponent. I would not stand much of a chance if it was made of blood and bone, but this cyclops was made out of rock. It may have been covered in dark magic, but rock is earth—*terrain*. I had to try to do something to knock it down to allow Cal a chance to strike.

As Cal distracted the beast—not really by choice—I took a firm stance in the dirt. I put my sword back in its sheath and held out both hands toward the Terrabody. My magic helped me latch on to the pith even twenty feet away, trying to move its body as I would with the rubble I practiced with. The moment I grasped it, I could feel its strength as it tried to resist my terrain magic pulling it down. It was like trying to stop a car from rolling down a hill. My nerves strained, my muscles throbbed, and sweat gushed down my body. *Guess dark magic-infused stones are a bit trickier to move.*

The crowd cheered as the Terrabody slowed down due to my terrain magic. I knew my strength couldn't hold the monster for long, so I looked over to Cal and gave him a nod.

As the colossal beast was encumbered by my magic, the Prince ran around to its back. That was when I used all the strength I had in my arms and pulled the monster down—right *smack* on its boulder knees. I let out a grunt, clenching my jaw, as my shoulders had the magical weight of the Terrabody on them. *Please let this work for you, Cal!*

With the Terrabody kneeling, Cal sprinted up the rocky incline of the monster's back. When he came to the glowing orb it had for a face, the Prince jumped high into the sky and pointed his sword straight down toward the dark magic light. At the same time, my arms gave out and my grasp on the Terrabody, but it didn't matter.

Cal pierced the glowing orb in the air and straight into the dirt surface of the battle rink—landing in a very superhero fashion with the light shish-kabobed to the ground. When the purple orb was stabbed and disconnected from the pith, the rocks of the Terrabody ceased to stick together, and all collapsed. Loud, thundering booms echoed against the soil and throughout the entire training grounds.

"*Challenge two complete! Excellent work!*" Captain Clover announced, and the Hunters all raved for us.

When the words were uttered from her mouth, I took a moment to relax, falling to my knees, smiling quite big. *I can't believe I was able to stop a Terrabody with my magic!* I looked up toward the balcony and saw Gaius. A burly smile was across his face, making my heart insanely happy. At that moment, I felt as if I could accomplish anything in the world.

Cal, who slowly started to walk over to me, had the same expression. He reached his arm out, offering me a boost off the ground.

"I truly couldn't have done that without you," he said, sweat dripping down his jawline. "Guess we make a pretty good team, huh?"

I took his arm. "Guess we do," I said, breathing heavily but very relieved.

We had about five minutes to prepare for the last challenge, the one I was most looking forward to. Cal and I were doing a traditional spar: each opponent battles the other to obtain a tied cloth around their opponent's neck. In our case, we used bandanas—his red and mine blue—around our necks. When Ekron first introduced me to this type of battling style, I thought it would be quite easy... That was until I saw some higher-ranking Hunters spar using the same rules. It was easy to hit someone with a sword or magic; being able to grab something off their body, however, meant you would need to put your guard down at that moment so you could have a free hand for grabbing.

Regarding who had the best advantage over the other, it was definitely Cal. I had little hands and shorter arms compared to him, *and* fighting close range was my weak point. Luckily, we were using practice swords again, and all magic was cleared to go.

Captain Clover stood back up on the podium again, giving us her same booming announcer voice. *"The final challenge will now commence. Please make your way to the opposite ends of the ring."*

This is it.

I, with my blue bandana around my neck, stood twelve feet from the Prince. For the first time, he wasn't staring back at me. His eyes went straight to the balcony where his parents stood. No doubt about it: He was just as anxious as he was confident about using his magic.

I had only helped him with his Fysiks power a few times, so I didn't quite know what he learned outside of our time together. I tried convincing him to show me more of his transparent glass shields, but he kept saying, "It's not ready." I think he was either embarrassed that he wasn't perfect at it yet or just wanted to wait until the Spar unveiled it. For all I knew, he could have mastered new techniques that work perfectly against my water or terrain magic. I just hoped his parents accepted his magic and saw it as worthy of having.

"First one to successfully take possession of their opponent's bandana wins the match. Now... begin!"

Like he usually did, Cal sprinted toward me first. He was quick, grasping his practice longsword tightly, raring for a blow to my side.

I parried his attack and the few more that followed, feeling his powerful hits along the wooden blade of my cutlass.

Suddenly, Cal made a grab for my bandana after successfully making a strong parry against me. I instinctively jolted my arm high and shot a wall of dirt right where his hand was. I'm pretty sure I gave him a nasty scrape on his left palm; the battleground's soil was really dry and filled with a lot of rough pebbles.

As I ran around to the other side of him, I saw him stand tall—lifting his chin and giving a crooked grin. *What's he thinking?* The Prince then quickly sheathed his longsword on the baldric strapped along his back and grabbed one of the dual swords he had hooked to his belt.

Cal came running at me again, and when I went to hit him, he blocked my attack... but not with his single, dual blade. He used his forearm, though I hit something hard when my cutlass made contact.

It was his magic! A frosted glass shield appeared the moment my weapon made an impact, which also caused my sword to ricochet back.

The crowd's cheering turned into gasps, seeing the Prince use nothing but the air to block my attack.

Cal didn't hesitate. With me in mid-wobble and his sword in hand, he swung at me *hard* on my side. I was too distracted by his magic to block it in time, and he *knew* that would happen; I loved magic too much to focus on anything else—

I stumbled down in the pain—knowing I would have a bruise the size of a baseball on my stomach the next day. His rosy cheeks perked up at his successful magic attempt in battle, complementing the coyness in his hazel eyes. Enjoyment brightened his face. *The crap! Why did he have to hit me so hard? And why is he smiling so much about it?*

I then used the rest of the water in my flask and splashed it in his face with my magic, just to give me enough time to evade.

His glare changed when he wiped his eyes, and I knew exactly what he was thinking without a single word coming out of his mouth: *it's a magic battle.*

Golf ball-sized rubbled darted out of the ground—one, two, three—with a twinge of my fist, and I began to fire them toward His Highness. *If I can just wear him out or hit him a couple of times, I'll be able to grab his red bandana in no time.*

Cal darted off the ground, blocking each shot with an array of invisible force fields. Bright circular pieces of crystal filled the battleground air, creating reverberations of cosmic cracking glass each time the stones hit Cal's magic. No matter how many more wads of hardened soil I threw, I could not break through his barriers. His magic was strong—something he had worked on, no doubt.

The crowd was going crazy. Jaws dropped to the floor at the Prince's magic, and many Hunters didn't even want to waste a second to blink. They saw their Prince using a skill they'd never seen before, all completely immersed in our battle.

One of my rocks finally hit him in the shoulder, knocking him off his game.

I ran toward the Prince, the rocks below becoming my organic springs. *Let's see him get out of ice.* I magically grabbed the water I spilled on the ground, separating it from the rocky soil and spinning it around in circles. More stones sprung me forward, speed coming to me easily. I was ready to freeze his arms to the ground when suddenly—

"The Prince can fly!" I heard a man shout from the audience, though he was way off with his assumption.

Using his ability to create Fysiks shields, Cal created invisible floating platforms to step across the sky, and the Prince ran on air. Each one emitted a crackling glow every time he took a step, and he wasn't even using his hands to form them—just the magic in his feet! It truly looked like he was walking on a staircase made of flickering glass.

I was so proud of him, which probably wasn't what I should've been thinking about mid-battle. *Lisa, focus!*

Cal bolted through the sky on his floating glass stones right up behind me.

I quickly shot pellets of ice toward him, but he deflected it with more of his magic. *So, he thinks he can get me from an air attack? Clever, but not enough to win.* I decided to join him in magical staircase-making. I ran right on his tail and started creating my dirt staircases with my own feet as well.

Back and forth we went, creating our own magical terrain, balancing while trying to aim hits at one another. When I slung a dirt rope near his royal feet, Cal made a graceful turnaround and started running straight for me, making it almost too easy to grab his bandana. *This game is all mine!* I was just about arm's length from the Prince when—

SLAM!

My body nailed an invisible wall made by Cal's magic, making me lose my concentration on my terrain magic. And I fell—fell a hard five feet from the air straight to the ground—causing a big *ooh* from the crowd.

Everything went fuzzy as I rolled onto my back. I tried to get back up, but I couldn't; all the wind was completely knocked out of my lungs. My mind was boggled, and pain slithered with spikes throughout my body. *Where is he—*

When I looked up above me, I saw nothing but the shadow of a sweaty boy pinning me down with his sword on my neck. As a cloud drifted in front of the sun—mocking me with its shade—it revealed Cal smiling all too eagerly as he ripped the damp bandana off my neck.

"Prince Caelum is the winner of the third and final challenge!" Captain Clover announced, sounding rather happy to see that her Prince won.

The Hunters gave exhilarating cheers as Cal continued to stare at me with a mischievous, smug grin. Sweat soaked the wavy ends of his hair, somehow making human perspiration look decently attractive... until he lowered his chin. "Told you I wasn't going easy on you, *Earthian*," he uttered. His tone was too bold and cheeky that whatever "royal handsomeness" I may have found in him was gone.

I already knew I lost; he didn't have to rub it in. I was in pain, still feeling the hard ground using my spine as a punching bag, and he just continued to pin me down, absorbing the crowd's cheers as a plant does with sunlight.

I did not care if he was a prince or if his parents were watching. In the *friendliest* way possible, I lifted my right hand and punched the ground, causing a small dirt pillar to shoot Cal off me. He rolled backward on the beige soil as I leaned on my elbows to get a good look at his cocky face.

"No need to be a sore winner," I muttered, half-joking, half-dead-serious.

The Prince was too happy to care about me hitting him, and he quickly got to his feet and came back over, helping me off the ground. Some chivalry had returned. "Sorry, but I knew I had to fight with all I had to beat you."

"I'll take that as a compliment, then," I said just as Captain Clover approached us.

"You both did exceptionally well today," she said in her normal voice. "Meet up with Captain Ekron at the bottom of the castle's back entrance. He has your licenses and, I assume, your prize as well, Young Prince. Congratulations to you both."

Cal and I thanked her with a bow and made our way toward our Captain. I made Cal walk slowly, using his shoulder as a crutch, given that I was still recovering from his blow and fall. He thankfully didn't mind.

When we came to the broad staircase, Ekron brought Gaius, the Queen, and the mighty King. I shot off Cal's shoulder, not wanting to look weak before the mighty four. All of them standing together—it was like staring at a golden painting: Ekron with his white and blue armor and Hunter gear, Gaius with his burly crossed arms and glowing magic plants along his waist, the Queen with her frosty blue summer dress and tiara, and the King with his adorned chest plate and shoulder cape.

I couldn't believe I knew these people—heck, I couldn't believe they knew *me!* Back home, I was happy if Lily's popular friends remembered my name or even the teacher when handing back our homework. I was really glad to be Lisa Robbie at that moment... even with the back and stomach pain from Cal's attacks that caused my pathetic fall.

Gaius came over to me and patted me quite hard on my shoulder. "Good use of magic and swordsmanship out there."

I held back a cry as his muscular hand felt like a giant's hammer nailing my already hurt shoulder. *Did he not just watch me fall over in battle?*

I ignored it the best I could, forcing a smile through the pain, though my tone was sarcastic as I said, "Thank you, Gaius."

The Queen hugged her son, not caring if her garment got dirtied from Cal's battle-worn clothes. "My Prince, you performed beautifully. You looked like a true Hunter out there, and it seems that your magic has gotten much stronger."

Cal's face turned from glee to surprise. "Wait—you knew about my magic this whole time?"

Had to admit, I was just as shocked as him.

Queen Leonora grinned with her glossed lips. "Ekron told me of your private lessons with him."

"*Ekron*—I told you not to tell them," Cal muttered to our Captain.

Ekron smiled back, his braided goatee wagging. "I'm sorry, Young Prince, but even the Queen has rule over your demands, and I couldn't lie to her when she started getting suspicious of our late evening sessions."

Cal's eyes couldn't focus on his mother's gaze, and his voice lowered. "Well... I just wanted it to be a surprise. That's all."

Suddenly, the King spoke forth in his mountainous voice. "I say you still accomplished that. You did well, son."

The Prince's eyes immediately started sparkling like stars. Hearing that from his dad—those few words—meant the world to him I'm sure.

"Thank you, sir," he said, reserved, holding a subtle grin on his glistening face.

The King then leaned in closer to Cal, his shoulder-length black hair falling over his ears. He rumbled with the hushed tone of a bear, "But I do not condone your lying... We will discuss this later."

Bolthor's whisper sent chills down my spine and probably an avalanche of goosebumps down Caelum. *Cal did well... Is he being secretive about his magic really that bad?*

The Queen was unfazed by her husband's stoicism or simply ignored it and persisted to grab my hand. Her skin was exceptionally soft; I hated she had to touch mine, covered in dirt and bloody scratches. "Lisa, your performance was excellent. A fine Mage and grand Hunter you were. It truly didn't seem as if you had only been training for half a season."

"Thank you," I began, tilting my chin, "but it wasn't all me. I had Captain Ekron and Gaius help me out—oh, and Prince Caelum, too."

Captain Ekron gave a hardy grin and also a pat on my back—causing even more pain I had to smile through. "I promise, my Queen, I can only take credit for her sword skills. The magic—now, that was all the Keeper of Stars' doing. Even with the Prince, I only did so much; it was the book Gaius gave him that turned his knowledge into skill."

Gaius wasn't the kind of man who liked to be praised, so when everyone came after his teaching abilities, he quickly rebutted, "It was Lisa who gave the Prince the confidence he needed. I did no such thing."

"But she had to have learned it from you first," the Queen said, adding to the who-deserves-the-praise chain, "which is why I would like to ask a favor of you. Would you mind taking Caelum along with you and Lisa on any forthcoming monster-hunting quests? Seeing as Lisa's knowledge and skill in magic has improved much under your leadership, I believe Caelum would also benefit from the experiences."

What—is she serious?

Cal and I turned our faces toward each other, surprised at the Queen's request. *I hope Gaius says yes!*

Gaius unfolded his crossed arms and was about to speak when the King answered, low and serious, "Leonora..."

She turned to her husband and quickly replied casually to his one-word sentence, "Our son showed his skill by the sword and by magic, and I would like to thank the two who inspired him by asking for their aid."

"He should be taught by *our* instructors... not a Keeper," he stated, eyes fixated on his wife.

That gaze could break boulders, but Leonora was a diamond with hazel eyes. "And he will, but until we find a suitable teacher, Gaius should train him—as a Keeper *and* a resident of our Kingdom."

There was an unsettling pause as we four watched the King and Queen almost talk like a normal husband and wife discussing their son's future. Even Cal seemed uncomfortable. *Guess this doesn't happen often.*

King Sonon's eyes hardened on the Queen, but she was not wavering—winning the staring contest. Leonora was not afraid of her husband one bit... which left me wondering what *did* scare her. If the King spoke to me like that, I'd be immobilized with just a second of his shark eyes darting me down.

As if he heard my thoughts, the King's hazel eyes looked at *me*—my knees could've buckled and toppled straight to the floor. Then, after what seemed like an eternity, he backed away from Leonora, releasing a deep breath of defeat, and looked toward Gaius. "Train him well," he said like a thick wind knocking down a pine tree.

And then, he left, with a swoosh of his shoulder cape, up the stairs of the castle's back entrance. *Didn't know the Queen had His Majesty wrapped around her finger like that... or that he didn't care for Gaius training his son... odd.*

Gaius' stance was rigid, and I could tell he was not fond of the idea that he now had two kids to babysit, and I couldn't help myself. I leaned over to Gaius—knowing he now had no choice in the matter—and whispered, "You can't refuse the command of the King."

My mentor sighed, gave me another hard pat on my back, one I think I didn't deserve, and said to the Queen almost through gritted teeth, "Guess we will be seeing the Young Prince bright and early tomorrow morning."

"We are most grateful for you and your work, Gaius. Thank you," Queen Leonora responded, bringing back up the mood of our huddle.

"Well, I think it's about time we give these two what they came here for..." Captain Ekron then took out two tungsten badges. Each reminded me of a hefty, fortified keychain. The sturdy clip and chain together extended about four inches long, and the flattened piece of metal was attached to the end. The Boolavogue crest was embossed on its thin slate, along with our names and "Restricted

Hunter" printed on the back. I didn't expect our licenses to be a keychain or made of heavy material. Way better than a piece of plastic to carry around in my pocket all day.

"These are your Restricted Hunter licenses," Ekron continued to explain. "You've proven to me and the rest of the Hunters you are ready to serve our Kingdom well. Wear them proudly; you've rightly earned them and shall be treated as equals amongst other Hunters of the same rank."

I saw Cal clip his to his belt, so I mimicked him. *Wow, I feel so empowered right now! Lisa Robbie, newest beginner Hunter for Boolavogue!*

"So..." Cal finally said with a cocky smile. "What about the prize for the winner?"

Ekron smirked at him, reaching for the sword he had sheathed on his side. "The reward was determined based on who won. For you, My Prince, your first glinted sword."

Ekron unveiled the short sword from his side, and it was a work of art. Its blade was white like the moon and thinned at the tip. The guard and grip of the sword were a combination of navy and pale blues, having a few pieces of glistening stone embedded near the blade. At the center of the pummel was a gem: a bright opal-like ore that shimmered when reflected in the sunlight. There was no denying that Cal's prize was far better than either of us had expected.

"It's infused with the magic of a Moon Dusk glint," our Captain said, putting the sword in Cal's hands. "During nightfall, the blade's edges glow and gift you more power with each swing. It will perform best during the nights of a full moon, seeing as it will inflict moonlight magic on dark creatures. A grand gift for a grand Hunter like yourself."

I stood close to Cal as he held the sword's grip, admiring its craftsmanship. It was hard not to be jealous.

"Thank you, Captain. I promise to use it well," the Prince said, beaming from ear to ear.

"I have no doubt about that. Now, I must be off to finish lessons with the slaggers back at the Troop." Ekron turned toward the Queen and gave a slight bow. "My Queen." Then, he headed back to the Hunter Grounds.

Cal and his mother dismissed themselves soon after, following the same trail the King left moments before. *He didn't even stay to watch Ekron give Cal and me our licenses...*

Even though I had lost, I was actually glad to see the Prince win. I don't know what it's like to be part of a family where if one person does something wrong, it reflects on everyone. It could have ruined our friendship, too, for all I knew. Ultimately, I still came out with my license, meaning I had grown closer to becoming a mighty hero for the Agapéd in my heart.

Standing under the shade of the castle was now just Gaius and me.

"So," the Keeper said, "you think you did well?"

Is this a trick question?

The fact he asked me meant I messed up. I thought about my answer before responding. "I did well against the monsters, but I should have stayed more alert during my match with Caelum."

"If you were given real swords, you would be dead..."

I let out a sigh because I knew it was true. He didn't need to be so blunt about it, though.

I was about to respond with a habitual "I'm sorry," but he continued. "However, if it weren't for you, the Prince would have never been able to take down the Terrabody. Seems all that time in my study drawing pictures has proven useful for you. You were the reason for the triumph in that round. Makes a teacher proud. In light of today, I made something I'd like to show you."

Gaius reached inside his leather trench coat pocket and pulled out a sheathed dagger. The scabbard was deep purples and nebula blues, reminding me of the starlit sky. Embossed into the thick material of the dagger's grip were designs of Wishing Star plants and swirling vines just like the door to his magical home.

"This is for you," he said to me, handing me the elegant, surprisingly lightweight blade.

"What? This... this is really for me?" I was utterly shocked. I hadn't even unsheathed the blade to know how beautiful and perfectly designed it was.

I popped the button open to reveal the weapon, beholding a mystical masterpiece crafted by the Keeper of Stars. The blade was entirely made of wood but unlike any tree I had seen before. It was a cold walnut color with a deadly sharp edge that faded to a glowing purple. It was infused with *magic!* There were subtle star carvings near the rain guard where the magic shone through, adding more violet hues. The cherry on top was the magenta gem in the center, the heartwood of the blade—glowing a beautiful pink color. The grip, blade, scabbard—every single part was crafted with so much detail, and I could see Gaius' heart poured into it. To me, that blade was priceless.

I gripped the dagger in my hand; it was perfect. *He really did make this specifically for me. I truly don't deserve something of this value.*

"Gaius... I don't know what to say," I said, flipping the blade around to view both sides. "You really made this for me?"

"Of course. You need a proper weapon that compliments you as a Mage and Hunter. It's crafted with wood from a Khooni Neelam Pine—a deep-rooted tree that thrives in magic-filled caves. Cutting even a piece of its bark takes a good amount of work, so you'll not find many weapons forged with this material, but it's worth it. Wood infused with durability magic—it won't break easily or burn and can pierce through most metals, but I advise you not to go smashing it against rocks; it's still a blade and needs to be treated properly."

He crossed his arms again. "What makes it perfect for you is that it is not one of ore or steel, so it shouldn't burden your muscle strain. The Prince's gift was great, but this is better. I hope you find it useful... and please don't start weeping over something as gimpish as a blade."

I couldn't help it. My eyes filled with happy tears after hearing what he did for me. No one had ever made me anything to that extent in my whole life. I think the only time I was given a handmade gift was from Grandma, and it was an incredibly itchy toboggan the color of dirt. Pretty sure she was making it for herself when it turned out to be too small for her head. So, the fact that Gaius crafted a blade using his perfected woodworking skills during his busy schedule overwhelmed my heart.

I gazed up at his happy green eyes. "Thank you so much, Gaius. It's perfect." I twisted the blade in my hand, noting its flawless Keeper-esque details. And I thought hard and didn't care if Gaius was giving me a confused look or not. "I'm gonna name it... Valor. Suits it, I believe."

With his crossed arms, Gaius huffed. "You don't have to name a weapon."

"Isn't that what you're supposed to do?" All those medieval movies I watched and video games I played had their characters' weapons named. I figured it was something required, especially for a Hunter.

"For those who like to label their possessions as they would pets," he answered, "but you don't need to, Lisa." My head slumped, but before I could attach the dagger to my belt, Gaius' hand gently cupped my shoulder—*not* patting me ruggedly on the back. A smile emerged. "Though, if you must name it... Valor seems like the most heroic name. Glad you like it."

38
OOGLEYEAR IN FLADDEN

"So, *we* are the bait—that's what you're saying?" I asked, holding a box of magic-smelling salts Gaius had handed me while standing in front of a swampy pond.

Cal wondered the same thing but didn't bother to ask, accepting whatever fate lay beyond the meaning of "bait" as he stood silent next to me.

Despite the frigid winter weather, our teacher then removed his leather jacket and his plant weaponry belt, letting his muscles shine. "You're only bait if you let yourself get bitten," he said, putting his belt on the branch of a barren tree so his magical plants didn't get ruined. "So, just don't let that happen." And he took one step into the murky water.

It was the end of fall in the land of Boolavogue—the middle of November back home in New Jersey—and Gaius had me and Caelum working hard on magic quests together. Ever since the Queen told Gaius he was to bring the Prince along with the two of us, our magic quests had been getting much more rigorous... and flat-out bizarre. We fought many strange creatures in the mountains and across the Kingdom, all for Gaius to obtain his odd array of potion ingredients for the Veradome. At first, he helped us learn to fight off creatures, teaching us how to use our magic effectively in peculiar situations.

As of recently, however, it seemed he was just using us for the dirty work.

Today, for example, Gaius was using me and Cal to fight off some dark creatures called swamp mites while he harvested magic algae. In his books, the illustrations of the dark magic pests resembled a half-spider, half-octopus amphibian with pincers like a tarantula and eight suction cup legs. I thought it was no big deal until he said they live in hordes and *jump* out of the water like flying fish. Nothing could be worse than a giant flying spider, and Gaius was making us fight them while he played farmer.

"Why can't Cal and I do the algae harvesting and *you* fight the swamp mites?" I asked as he grazed over the pond, looking for the magic weed.

"Because..." Gaius started, stepping another foot into the water to get a closer look at the swamp's depth, being careful not to splash or ripple the current, "this algae is delicate and must be treated properly... and it will be a good monster hunting lesson for you both."

The Keeper then took something out of his pants pocket. It looked like a rubbery ribbon with a small blue gem at the end, but to my surprise, he latched it around his neck. The band was snug but didn't choke him... the question was why Gaius was adorning himself with it.

"What's that do?" I asked him, standing on the shoreline with Cal, gripping the wooden box of smelly swamp-mite bait.

"It's a breethur," he replied, wading in the water. "A neckband that surrounds your body in a film of air so you can swim underwater for thirty minutes at a time. It's an Aquanaeum invention."

I gasped. "*What*—Inna never told me about those?"

His back was turned away from us, but I swear he was giving me a smug look. "Suppose she doesn't think you need it. Would rather see you try and breathe underwater yourself."

Cal peered his head over to me. "What's he talking about—"

I pursed my lips. "Nothing—irrelevant and *unimportant*."

He just has to keep bringing that up, doesn't he...

"Mr. Gaius," Cal, thankfully ignoring me and Gaius' un-funny inside joke, began, "how exactly does this stuff work?" He, too, was holding a smelling salts box.

The Keeper slowly stepped further into the swamp, not even caring that his boots and pants were getting mucky from the dirtied water. His head stopped moving when his eyes met something green and mushy sticking out of the pond. He then reached under the water with his hand—being extra careful not to disturb the tranquility of the swamp—and grabbed a football-sized stone.

While keeping his body stationary in the water, Gaius said, "What I need is over here. You both walk to the shore of the swamp near the broken tree we passed, about twenty feet from where you are now. I will throw this stone in your direction into the water. That is when you open the frog-egg-smelling salts. The moment you do so, the swamp mites will swarm. Just keep them occupied while I harvest the algae."

"You mean kill them, right?" I wanted to confirm.

"Unless you enjoy blood-numbing wounds all over your skin, then yes."

Cal leaned over to me and whispered, "I'm not the only one who thinks his humor is a little on the morbid side?"

My eyes thinned. "Pretty sure he wasn't even joking in the first place, Cal."

We trekked to the shoreline with the rotted fallen tree, not even attempting to avoid stepping in mud puddles. Everything around us was tranquil, and I began to question if any of these so-called swamp mites were around.

"Step further into the water without splashing—they can sense your movement," Gaius told us.

Even though I wore thick boots, I still could feel the sharp pinch of the cold water seeping through the seams. *How is Gaius halfway in this stuff—it's freezing!*

"Ready?" our teacher asked, causing my heart to pound hard at the thought of unknown creatures about to attack us.

We—the live bait—nodded and placed our hands over the lids of our smelling salts boxes.

Gaius pulled back on his arm and threw the stone right toward us.

As it soared through the air, we released the boxes' lid. It took no time for the smell to release, and my *gosh,* it was putrid! Smelled just like a fish gutting station back home at the harbor—*pure rotten!*

The intensity of the smell caused both of us to drop the boxes and start coughing immediately. Just as we dropped the smelling salts into the shallow end we were wading in, Gaius' stone broke through the water, and that was when we saw *them* cascade. Both slimy and hairy, twenty to thirty swamp mites jumped forth out of the shadows of the swampland's water toward us—heading for the crash of the stone that disturbed their slumber. They were green and had four eyes on their mushy faces with giant pincers sticking out of their mouths. To top off their creepiness were the eight suction-cupped legs propelling them out of the water that could easily latch onto our bodies. *Why can't we ever fight normal-looking dark magic creatures?*

Cal immediately took out his sword and sliced the three aiming for his right arm. *Squelch—squirt!* The clean sound of them slicing into two was unsettling—their dismembered bodies swirling in the air before fading away into dark particles—but I knew there was no escaping it for a long, long while.

I joined the Prince in fighting, using the water around me to make sharp icicles that shot upward at the dark creatures, creating unsettling swamp mite kabobs all around us.

Out of the corner of my eye, I saw Gaius break through the chilling water's surface. He was dripping wet, holding a container filled with algae. I was already impressed enough that he could withstand the arctic swamp but more so that he was so melancholic by his students fighting for their lives.

"Gaius!" I shouted as Cal blocked one of the swamp mites from hitting me. "Are we good to go?"

"Almost," he said calmly, not the slightest bit fazed by the hordes of spider amphibians swarming us. He then submerged himself back into the swamp water to gather more algae.

Cal gave another hard swing with his sword and another bash with his Fysiks shield at the gross creatures. "It's like they are spawning from thin air! How many more are there?"

One landed on my leg and started climbing up my pants. *So slimy!* I quickly grabbed Valor, my purple dagger, and stabbed the ugly thing before it reached any higher up my body. "I don't know, but this algae better be some kind of miracle plant for all we are doing for it!"

Gaius emerged from the pond a second time, carrying another jar of algae, right when a swarm of fifteen swamp mites started chasing Cal. While the burly gardener casually walked to the edge, we bait started booking it—splashing frantically in the water.

"Keep up the good work," our teacher nonchalantly said before returning to the water.

More swats and swings we gave toward the arachnid octopi, chopping up at least fifty of them. Our clothes were soaking wet, covered in loose swamp grass and mud from all our evading and attacking. I was just lucky they were dark magic creatures and not actual animals; I'd have goopy, amphibian blood stains all over my winter gear.

My arms and my patience with Gaius were starting to give way. *How much algae can one man need?*

When we thought the marshland nightmare would never end, fewer swamp mites began to attack.

"Lisa, I think we almost have them all!" Cal said, catching his breath after killing two more in mid-air. He then grabbed the soaking wet box of empty frog-egg-smelling salts. "I'll get the rest to chase me, and when they are all together, slag the lot of them in one go!"

I nodded, and Cal shot off, causing a hoard of twelve more jumpy swamp mites to follow him. I ran to the shoreline as he distracted them and shouted, "Lead them over here!"

Cal then made his invisible stepping stones in the air, making it easier for him to outrun the octo-slime creatures. I watched him closely, standing firmly in the mud. The moment he sprinted right past me out of the line of fire, I extended my arms. In an instant, two rows of frozen mud stakes shot out from the water, stabbing the swamp mites—toothpicks puncturing into twelve slimy amphibian olives as they leaped into the air. Their impaled bodies squelched for a final time before each one faded into magic soot, back into the Earth and sky.

Silence followed.

I bent my hips and placed my hands on my knees, catching my breath after completing the hunt. "Oh, thank goodness that is *over*!"

Cal rested his back on a tree, panting hard and rubbing his neck. "I swear one almost got me—right in the face, too. I'll be happy to never see another one of those things for the rest of my life."

Once the adrenaline wore off, the cold seeped in, causing my body to shiver. I immediately manipulated the water soaking my clothes and pushed it all out with my magic, including my hair. Cal nudged me on the shoulder and held his arms in a "t" pose, an inaudible request for the same relief.

Our burly, swamp-covered teacher came out of the pond with his fourth jar of green algae. His soaked shirt hugged his body and all the muscles underneath, the cold water continuously flooding down his back as he came closer, and still, he wasn't shivering. *Does he have a magic perk of stone skin or something?*

"Good work, you two," he said to me and Cal. "If it weren't for you, this could've taken me all day."

"So, why can't you just use your magic and make the algae come out of the water and save yourself the time and effort?" I asked Gaius, even though I was really meaning, *Why can't you just use your magic and save us the trouble of fighting off that nation of slimy bugs?*

Gaius clicked the latch on the back of his breethur and put the choker back in his pocket. He then began to seal up the giant glass jars with his magic by using the roots from the earth to create sturdy lids. Mid-lid-making, he answered my question. "One, using magic on these makes the plant feel threatened. It will wither up and die before I ever have a chance to take hold of it. Two, manipulating magic-filled plants of any species is extremely tough or near impossible if they are predominately magic-based. Remember back at your Spar last month, when you tried to move the boulders connecting Terrabody?"

I nodded.

"You couldn't do anything but stop it in its tracks. If it were a normal rock, you would've been able to slag it across the rink. The same thing applies to living organisms as well. And three: seemed you both needed a challenge as of late."

As Gaius finished up his explanation and tightened the lids, I noticed his pruned fingers were a lifeless purple. *So, he is freezing. Guess he really did give Cal and me the easier part of the job.*

Though I had no reason to feel bad for his cold hands, seeing as this was all his idea, I couldn't just stand back and watch the man freeze to death. Without his permission, I swiped my hands over the air and caused the water to leave his drenched shirt, pants, and thick hair.

His eyebrows raised, and his work stopped for a moment. "Thanks," he said, gently smiling before tightening the last lid.

Cal, watching closely as Gaius finished sealing the last jar, chimed in, "Mr. Gaius, how come you need so much of this algae? Is it super powerful or a good export for the Veradome?"

The Keeper of Stars opened up his orbkit, a long dog tag necklace he always kept hidden away under his shirt, and magically stored the green jars inside. Most of the magic pockets were empty, but the ones that weren't happened to be filled with an assortment of tools, plants, and potion flasks. Very cluttered.

"Enkurious algae is one of the very few organisms the Veradome can't grow due to the plant's delicate nature," he said, putting on his leather jacket. "They have a team of willing Mages and Mystics they send out to harvest the magic scum, and occasionally, I will offer my aid. It is very valuable because it is used in magic anesthetics."

"So, it helps stop the pain of magic-related injuries?" I asked.

"Normal medicine for normal pain, and magic algae for magic pain," my teacher reiterated to me.

It's like the ibuprofen of the magic world—cool.

Gaius latched on his plant weaponry belt he had placed on the tree prior to the escapade before looking back at us two. "I acquired a good lot of Enkurious algae, so no need for us to continue further down the swamp to look for more." He looked at me. "Feel free to return to the Hearth or to the castle with Caelum. I will be busy making potions for the next couple of hours."

"Mr. Gaius," Cal politely interrupted, "is it alright if I show Lisa the town nearby? It's Oogleyear here in Fladden, and many merchants sell gear for Hunters during the festival."

I had to admit I was quite surprised the Prince asked Gaius for permission to take me out on the town. He's the Prince, so he technically has rule over Gaius. Plus, it wasn't like Gaius was my dad and Cal was asking me to go on a date—it was Fladden for crying out loud. We passed the rural outskirts of the town on our way here; nothing much to rave about except for the herds of black sheep, which were all pretty cute with their little dopey faces. The main part of the town could have been interesting, though, but definitely not as beautiful as the Inner Kingdom. Still, Gaius probably would think nothing of it.

Gaius held out his fist, creating the blue evanesce magic inside it. "It's just Fladden, Prince. You don't have to ask for permission as long as you watch her— she likes to wander." He winked.

I hissed. *"Hey—"*

"Do as you wish." Then, he evanesced away.

We made it two steps from the shoreline before I asked, "What's 'Oogleyear'?" trying not to giggle at the sound of the funny word coming out of my mouth.

"It's something a lot of towns outside of the Inner Kingdom do to celebrate Hunters from Boolavogue during this time of the year," Cal explained as we walked toward the exit of the swamp.

"Why did you ask for me to go?"

The Prince kicked a stone placed perfectly in his path as his eyes stared toward the ground, his hands shoved in his pants pockets. "Because I knew you'd like it. You talk about Earthian festivals as if they are the epitome of true fun, but you've yet to experience the ones on planet Kalm. So, I figured it's time you go to one for yourself."

I paused on our dirt path, but not for too long, and my heart throbbed. *Lisa—it's not like he complimented you on your appearance or anything!* Then, my face warmed up, and I knew it was turning pink. My eyes shot to the ground. *Why am I getting so flustered right now at him remembering such a small detail about me?*

He was right, though. I loved holidays and festivals—mostly because back home, it was a time when the whole state or even the country was in a happy spirit. Spring was my favorite season because of the flower festivals, October was my favorite month because of Halloween and all things "cheesy horror movies," and Christmas was my favorite day—even more so than my birthday— because Mom would save up all her vacation days to get two weeks off with me. Everything down to the food and random traditions with Mom during every new celebration was pure fun.

I didn't think I talked about my love for festivals that much for Cal to notice, though. It was sweet of him to remember that. *Doubt even Jenny Kim or Lily know that about me...*

Cal started running out in front of me. "Come on, you don't want to miss a single second!"

He gestured for me to follow, and we both ran through the mucky woods straight toward the bustling town of Fladden.

We had not even entered the town's main strip when music and laughter filled the air. Fladden was much like the older parts of Boolavogue's inner city, with aged brick, cottage-style shops and houses lining the walkways. Thick gray stones paved the roads up and down with accents of tall street lights on each corner—decorated with blue and cream-colored tassels and flags in celebration of Oogleyear.

Fladden's center road was closed off for the festival to prevent vehicles from going through. Instead, vendors, Hunters, and citizens alike took up all the space. Everyone around us seemed jubilant, and I had to admit that Cal was right... because I couldn't help but smile and stop at every little thing we passed by.

Every once in a while, as we wormed through the happy horde of festival-goers, my heart would start throbbing hard. One second, I was walking past a merchant selling vibrant-colored Hunter jewelry—completely fine in the chest—and the next, my whole nervous system started to go crazy. The thing was, it would go away just as fast as it took over my body.

My only hypothesis as to why my heart grew uneasy was that I was enjoying a day with a boy—*not a date, though*—who happened to be a Prince. Any girl would grow nervous or turn giddy if royalty asked them to be by their side at a celebration. I wished it would stop because, sometimes, I wouldn't even be looking at him, and the nerves in my chest would malfunction with rapid beats, distracting me from the festivities.

Heart, would you just calm down, please!

As we walked to and from the Hunter-themed booths and tents, I was surprised that a lot of the citizens of Fladden didn't recognize Cal; he *was* the son of King Bolthor, after all, practically a celebrity in my mind. There were a couple here and there, and one even insisted we take their gift of frankincense home with us. I wasn't sure what I would need a smelly rock for, but I just stuck mine in my jacket pocket to keep as a souvenir.

Staying close to Cal as we passed by a booth selling candles, I accidentally bumped into his arm, trying to avoid the human traffic. My heart instantly clung to the back of my ribcage—the blood in my veins thrumming against every nerve in my body. I had sat close to him before—in the Laze, on Honey's saddle, and during lunch with the other Hunters—so I had no clue why I was freaking out.

He turned to look at me, and I *knew* my face was blooming with heat—bet he could've seen my pounding heart through my chest. I quickly said the first thing I could think of before he noticed my girly, nervous self: "I figured, with you being a Prince and all, that everyone in town would recognize you. Isn't Fladden a part of Boolavogue?"

A family of five walked us by without giving the Prince a second glance. He turned to me, not even noticing my pink-cheeked face, replying, "Yeah, it is, but my mother and father are the faces of the Kingdom, not me. Once I'm seventeen or a full-fledged Hunter, I believe more people will take notice. For now, it's nice to just enjoy the town as normal."

We walked up to a vendor selling savory breaded cones filled with fried chicken and potatoes, but as we waited in line, my heart started racing again the moment Cal offered to pay. I tried to shake it, but the throbbing in my ears was so loud I couldn't even tell what was going on. *Lisa—he didn't even do anything flirty—what in the world is going—*

"Uh, little lady?" a man's voice said.

Rapidly blinking, I found myself gawping at the salty treat in the vendor's hand; Cal wasn't even standing near me anymore.

"Oh—sorry, sir," I hurriedly said while taking the festival food, hiding the rubescent glow overheating my face. "Thank you."

Cal tittered while he held a similar cone filled with meat and potatoes. "What was that about?" he asked as we left the vendor's outdoor shop. My eyes stayed on the treat in my hand. "You were staring at the food as if it were a vorrg."

No way was I about to let him think I was nervous around his presence. He would treat me differently, probably turn cocky and prick and prod me until I told him the reason for my blushing face.

I blinked fast, pursing my lips, fake toughness covered every syllable of my words. "I just zoned out for a second—you don't have to make fun of me for it." And I began to eat my food, walking in no particular direction.

Cal followed behind, explaining he wasn't making fun of me. A smile emerged from my face. And just like that, my heart settled down, making the stroll with the Prince easier again. *Stupid teenage emotions...*

The center of the town was boisterous in all the best ways. Showmen offered free musical performances consisting of fiddles, handheld harps, vertical drums, and strange wooden flutes. Face painters decorated the cheerful cheeks and foreheads of children who wanted to embrace the "Hunter" inside them. Watching them "battle" in the small park was fun—rolling around and defeating imaginary beasts. At least five merchants were selling cute plushies of farm animals, and Cal offered to buy me one of each. I had to refuse, even though I knew money was not an issue with him; I just didn't want to take advantage of that.

We also passed by some festival games, like the ones I would see at the county fair, except all of the ones for Oogleyear were Hunter-themed. One, in particular, caught my attention called "Hunter's Rings" because the prize was a large plush of a Gora bear dressed in battle gear with a tiny, stitched smile under its nose.

It was too cute to pass up.

I stopped at a vendor's game and asked Cal, "Can we play this?"

Caelum looked up at the grand prize of his Kingdom's furry friend. "So, you won't buy a gift that you know you will get to take back home and instead will pay for a *chance* at winning one?"

"Yep—now, pay the man and tell me how to win," I said to Cal, my chin jerking toward the game merchant in charge.

"Look, you're going to need some help winning that all on your own"—Cal cocked his grin and lifted his chin high—"so *I* will assist you." Cal smugly giggled at me while he took out a silver MC Chip. He gave the food vendor actual Boolavogue money, yellow and blue paper, so I was shocked. The boy was only *fourteen,* and he had a *credit card.*

"What—you have an MC Chip?" I said, watching the game merchant tapping his not-so-shiny MC Chip to Cal's. A faint glow flickered once on the glass corner of Cal's, and four credits magically transferred over to the vendor.

That same smug smile drew across his face. "Lisa…" He leaned close so no one could hear; my heart fluttered again. "I'm the *Prince*, remember. Royal perks—you'll have to get used to it."

I rolled my eyes as the old merchant plopped a bucket of twenty steel rings on the table. Each piece was flat like a cracker and as heavy as a small rock.

Cal explained, as if he was the game master, "You take these rings and try to skip them across the platforms to land in the buckets ahead. The farthest one—happening to be the smallest—will get you that big prize at the top."

"Seems easy enough." I then grabbed one and tossed it like a pond-skipping stone. It immediately hit the floor, avoiding the gaming platforms altogether.

The Prince chuckled at me before grabbing the bucket and pulling himself out a couple of rings. "Not as easy as you thought, huh? Let me show you how it's done."

We then took turns skipping the steel rings, aiming for the grand prize. It was trickier than I thought; I couldn't even get one ring to hop into the smaller prized buckets! Cal landed one in the container near the grand prized one, but it bounced right out, causing the Prince to invest more money into the merchant's business. He couldn't bear to lose when he was so close to winning—

Thud—thud—thud—thud—my heart started stinging, blaring in my chest and roaring through my ears. My fingers held the game piece in my hand, my body on pause. This—it was different than all the other times before. The throbbing wasn't sweet or fluttery. It hurt and continued to cascade with billowing thrums. Chills ran up and down my spine. Blood wasn't rushing to my face; it was pooling away.

What—

Then—without warning or sound, as quiet as a thief in the night—fear punctured my entire body with an army of needles. The steel ring in my hand dropped, and my mind focused on nothing but the horror in my bones. All the sounds of the festival ceased and became nothing more than murmuring noise in my ears. Something was behind me... something bad, what nightmares were made of.

This isn't like before... this is far worse...

A chilling presence as I had never known before shook my bones like a car swerving down a slippery road, boiling my heart while my body froze in fear. My ears burned red. My eyes couldn't focus in front of me. My chest was clanking with crescendoing beats. All my senses were turned off, and I only knew fear— the same bone-chilling, ominous fear a child feels when they think a monster is hiding under their bed in the dead of night, ready to attack them.

W-why am I so utterly terrified right now?

That was when I turned my head away from the game to face behind me. I didn't know where I was looking or what I should have been looking for, but the moment my eyes glazed over a man in a blue velvet cloak, that rattling rhythm behind my ribcage stopped—dropping down into my stomach like a stone being thrown into a lake. I had never seen that man before, but something inside me did... and I stood petrified.

As if he could feel my gaze pelting him, the hooded man changed his casual walking course and turned straight in my direction. Wherever he was headed— whether enjoying the festivities like the others or simply on his way to his home—didn't matter anymore.

In that one second glance, I knew that man was bad. I wasn't judging him by his hollowed eyes and smileless face; it was my magic pulse inside me that could sense the grim magic inside him, and it was also telling me to run, but my feet wouldn't move. I was cemented to the floor—cemented by a foreign, unrelenting horror.

He started walking toward me, bumping the people around him without much care. The closer he came, the more wrinkles I saw in the shadows of his face surrounding his gray eyes.

Lisa, just move! He's coming right over!

Half of me wanted to book it, but the other half was curious to know why his figure sparked true dread in my body with just a walk by. Without me knowing, he had already come right up beside me. He didn't have a scent and stood the height of an average fifty-year-old man, but still, I couldn't move or even remember to breathe. *What is he about to do?*

He reached into his pocket and plopped out four coins, giving them to the game merchant. I wish I could've said that made me feel better, but his attention was still fixated on me.

Then, he spoke.

"It's quite a chill afternoon," the man said. His voice was raspy and without much emotion. He sounded like he was grinning, but I was too scared to look— my eyes watching steel pellets all bounce off the platforms and fall to the floor.

The merchant placed the bucket of steel rings in front of the hooded man, and he fiddled around in the tub, looking for the perfect playing piece.

Is he wanting me to respond... I don't even want to look at him.

I took a big gulp, seeing as the mysterious man wasn't leaving my side. "I guess so," I muttered. The throbbing in my chest continued.

"This town is rather small and not filled with many powerful Mages... how is it I've never known you?" he asked, his voice turning eerier by the second. He still was rummaging through the bucket, not having thrown a single game piece.

So, he can sense the magic in me as well... I didn't know that was a thing people could do...

I pretended not to be interested in his conversation and quietly muttered, "I'm just here for the festival."

Cal had almost emptied the bucket with his determination to win the Gora bear prize, not even noticing I was talking to a stranger.

The man in his blue cloak leaned down toward me. His breath was *cold*. "Listen, I've been searching for something for quite a while—two things actually..." he continued to speak so casually to me as I faced the festival game.

I still avoided all eye contact, feeling his icy breath whisper through my hair and tainting the skin of my jawline and ear.

"And I believe... you have one of them."

Like before, I tried to dismiss it. "I'm sorry, but I don't know what you are talking about, sir. You must have me confused with someone else."

"You see, I don't believe I do... and you know that as well. It called to you the moment you saw me... and I need it back."

My eyes widened, and chills crawled up and down all over my body like a swarm of ants.

He's... talking about the Agapéd... no mistaking it... I don't like this... I really don't like this...

As he slowly grabbed a steel ring from his bucket, call it courage or fear-stricken curiosity, I inched my head around to see his side profile beneath his velvet hood. The shadow veiling his face was dense, but I could see his skin color: it was a ghostly pale—a sour-blue milk pigment that my eyes could only linger on for a second.

"I came here in search of something... forgotten..." he continued, "and to my luck... I found something even better and in the form of a little girl... I'm sorry about this—truly, I am—but I can't afford to let this divine moment slip away from me."

Just then, the sound of cheers came from the audience near Cal. *"Finally— Lisa, I did it!"* the Prince shouted, but when he looked toward me, he noticed something I didn't.

The man, who knew exactly who I was, wasn't just playing around with the merchant's game piece; he was using magic on it. As the grimacing man pulled back his arm and released whatever magic he bound to the steel ring, Cal sprang into action.

Like a bomb, the steel ring combusted right in front of my chest.

Thankfully, Cal used his Fysiks magic to create a shield in front of me, and the steel ring bounced off—blowing up the merchant's game and knocking steel rings and prizes into the air. The combustion of the blast left no flames, piles of wooden debris everywhere, and all the surrounding people—including me and Cal—on the stone road.

The music and joy of Oogleyear vanished when the sound of dynamite blasted, and all eyes were on us and the chilling man. Many people ran while others stood to watch, selfishly curious to see what disaster or magic caused the explosion.

When my ears stopped ringing, I felt Cal grab my shoulder. "Lisa, are you okay?"

Before I could respond, my attacker stood ten feet before me—hood off revealing his evil glare—and lifted his hands back up to strike again with his magic. Normally, I would have jumped back or used my magic to stop him, but hundreds of people were around. *What if they get hurt? The Agapéd is a secret as well, so should I not fight this guy?* I still didn't know enough about the man to engage, and by the look of it, I was very, *very* outmatched.

The Prince did not seem to care, sprinting forward like a panther as the attacker threw another steel explosive ring toward me. Cal jumped in front of me and deflected the combustive object in the air, causing it to expel its explosion upward to the sky.

The crowd grew frantic at the deathly firework, running all over to avoid the battle.

With the magic smoke in the air as a distraction, Cal swung his arm, covered in a boxing glove of Fysiks magic, and aimed right for the vile Mystic. The Prince *nailed* him—hard enough to bloody his nose and give us time to escape.

Cal ran toward me and grabbed my arm tightly. "Let's go!" he shouted as we started running away through the crowd.

We didn't make it but ten feet away when we heard another combustion behind us, throwing stones from the ground into the sky like gray confetti, hitting vendors and people alike. Today was supposed to be a fun celebration, but it became a perilous venture because of me and this guy.

I turned to look back at the man and saw a magic symbol on the ground where the explosion was. The sigil was an intricate design of black and blue, oozing with dark magic before fading away into nothingness. *What type of power is that?* With not even a second to spare, the man created another magic symbol underneath his feet. He blew up more of the road, propelling himself right toward us.

I had fought monsters and Hunters but never a true dark magic Mystic. I was scared, petrified, and worried about everyone around me. *This is my fault. My being here is causing him to fight, and I don't want any more people to be put in danger!*

"Cal! Whatever you do, don't let go, okay?" I shouted, trying not to get trampled by wild civilians as the attacker came barreling down on us.

Cal's grip tightened on my wrist as he nodded, and we sprinted through the sea of people. In a matter of seconds, the shadow of the evil Mystic came right over us, but I had already started gathering my evanesce magic in my hand that Cal wasn't latched onto. I punched the air hard, almost tripping over some loose stones in the road, and evanesced from the town.

A second too slow, and we would have been killed.

The blue light, chimes, and surge of thunder rang around us as we were still running, but when we teleported away, we didn't land on our feet. My mind was stressed, and I couldn't focus properly. I thought about Gaius' home, but right when I punched the air, I remembered I couldn't teleport directly to Calendula. On a whim, I changed our location to the hidden entrance I normally took—the one on top of the cliff—which caused the charm to be ninety percent successful, an important ten percent missing.

Cal and I fell three feet from the sky and began rolling down the forest trail. Leaves and twigs crunched beneath us with each tumble—trying to help us slow down, but it was useless. My eyes were shut, but my brain said I rolled at least ten times before the ground leveled out, causing me to stop.

After seconds of forest silence and darkness clouding my eyes, the rustling of leaves began to fill my ears again.

"Lisa? *Lisa*?" Cal's muffled voice surged through my ears, but my brain didn't know if it was in my head or actually happening, so I didn't answer.

Tuff suddenly appeared out of his invisible state and started whistling over me. I wasn't sure why, but he was scared. His frantic hoots must have been loud because I heard Cal's shoes rush through the leaves over to me. The moment I heard him running was the moment my nerves decided to start working again.

And, *man,* I wish they hadn't.

Razor-sharp pain all across my stomach and lower back poured over me in blasting waves filled with barbed wire. It woke me up from my discombobulated state, and all I wanted to do was cry. I didn't know how badly I was hurt curled up in the fallen leaves, but I could feel long scratches on my torso and along my ribcage scraping me like deadly paper cuts.

When I saw Cal's boots approach me through my squinted eyes, I bit my lip hard so I wouldn't scream in pain, but that didn't stop my eyes from watering. Everything hurt—my body crying from the inside out, and I had no clue why.

"Lisa—what happened? *Naff it*—you're bleeding!" he said, looking down at my stomach where my jacket was unzipped.

My face rubbed against the cold grass as I finally glanced down.

Small stains of blood were seeping through my shirt from my torso, but not a tear or burn was made on the fabric. Even though I was bleeding a decent amount, feeling strands of steel slicing my tender skin, I didn't have time to care. My whole body could be scratched up and painted purple with bruises, and I still would be focused on the more pressing problem at hand.

"Cal, you—you have to get me to Gaius," I said, voice crackling, pushing through the pain.

"You need to see Nurse Lila first—"

"NO—Gaius first. He can heal me—I need to see him," I sobbed back.

Cal's eyes stared right at me, looking like a pitiful puppy; I hated to have seen him that way. Hated he had to see *me* this way.

"I just messed up my magic. I-I'm not gonna die, okay? The entrance is up the hill to the Veradome. Sorry, but"—I cringed from the pain—"you're gonna have to carry me."

He sighed, knowing I was getting my way no matter what. "Okay." Cautiously, he picked me up. My skin along my ribs stretched, releasing more blood and spiking my nerves with lightning.

I let out a saddening whimper, biting back my scream as I gripped his neck when he adjusted his strength to hold me properly.

"Sorry!" Cal said, feeling bad for the unintentional ache.

"It's okay. It's my fault anyway. Better me than you," I pathetically joked, trying to stay strong, but I couldn't cover it up anymore. As he carried me in his arms and up toward the secret entrance, I just silently cried, lying near his shoulder.

Because it was late afternoon, most of the workers of the Veradome had gone home, making it easy to not draw attention to ourselves. The couple we did pass, Cal turned us invisible until they walked out of our vantage point. I knew that must have used much of his magic strength, and I bet it made his muscles quake. As we went down the stairs toward Gaius' home, I told him I was okay to walk. That was a lie, but he had already carried me far enough and saved me from that eerie man, and I didn't want him to attempt to go downstairs. He let me use his shoulder to lean on as my other arm pressed onto my stomach. *Yep, that's definitely blood and not sweat. Going to have a couple of new magic scars to add to the collection.*

I opened the magic door to Gaius' home, wincing and weak, and saw his chimney smoking. *He must still be making those potions—thank goodness.* We went through his front entrance to his cottage and down his stairs to the living room.

The moment we entered the open floor plan, Cal shouted in a panic, "Mr. Gaius!"

I wobbled over to the Keeper's couch and lay on my side in a fetal position. Both my back and stomach were in fiery pain, as if my body was refusing to heal itself.

As my eyes leaked silent salty tears, I heard heavy footsteps briskly walk up from the magic study to the living room.

Cal caught up to the squeaky shoes and said, "Sir, it's Lisa—I don't know what happened, but she's hurt and bleeding badly."

Gaius' steps never paused as he walked over to me, staying calm and serious as his eyes met mine; I hated him seeing me cry again. "What happened?"

Before Cal could say anything, my quiet sobbing ceased. I whimpered loudly to Gaius like a scared animal as he knelt beside me, "It's him, Gaius. That magic—that dark magic. He's alive and—and here looking for me. I didn't... I didn't know what to do and—"

"Lisa, I need you to calm down," Gaius said. He then lifted my hands from my stomach. I watched as his eyebrows furrowed down, his chest rising with a hot breath.

My navy shirt beneath my coat was now dark violet as if it were never blue, to begin with.

"I messed up evanescing and—*gah, it hurts really bad!*" I cried to him.

Cal stepped in. "It wasn't her fault, sir. Someone attacked us, and Lisa used her magic to get us away from him."

Gaius then stepped into doctor mode. "I see. Caelum, I have a small jar of Enkurious algae on the table and a blue potion labeled 'Evanesce Serum' in the cupboard—bottom row. Grab both of them for me."

"Got it!" Cal rushed toward the study room in search of Gaius' ingredients.

The Keeper lifted my shirt above my navel to see how bad my wounds were. When he did, about twenty lashes the width of a ruler and as slim as thread tore on my stomach. Each one was a couple of centimeters deep and bloody, but that wasn't what concerned Gaius the most. It wasn't just normal scratches.

Inside each wound were strands of glowing blue magic—thin as hair—which was causing me twice the amount of pain.

"There's more on my back," I said in tears as Cal ran into the living room, giving Gaius the serum and algae.

"Before I start healing, you need to eat this," Gaius told me as he slithered a strand of algae from his jar. It was slimy and dark green—most unappetizing.

"Can't I drink a potion or something?" I asked him, wincing from my pain.

He placed the small jar of the wet weed in my hands anyway. "Potions need time to ferment. I would suggest you just swallow it whole to avoid its fusty taste."

Okay, if Gaius thinks it tastes gross, then this has to be pure rotten... but anything was better than feeling the pain in my stomach.

I didn't think about it long and just slurped the swamp weed fast into my mouth. *Oh my gosh, I hated it!*

I made a sour face and scrunched my eyes as I swallowed, releasing more tears down my overheated face. "Gah—why does it taste like how that swamp-mite bait smelled?"

"The pain is going away, though, isn't it?" Gaius asked.

He was right. All my wounds were still there, but my nerves were growing more numb to the magic pain.

"A little, yeah," I responded, though my words were still weak and shaky.

"Good. Now, the Enkurious helps numb the evanesce magic pain but not the physical pain. You said there were more on your back?"

"Mhm."

"Okay, go ahead and take your jacket off and let me look."

"But…" I hesitated, looking into his green eyes, "I don't want to get blood all over your couch."

Gaius made a breathy chuckle, his calm nature helping ease my worry. "Then, I'll just buy a new one. Now, hurry… before your wounds get any worse."

As I sat upright, I pulled one arm out of my thick jacket. Each time I moved any part of my muscles or the skin near my ribs, my body freaked out, and I could feel the cuts opening more. I tried to hold back my screams, clenching my jaw tight, but girlish squeals were unpreventable with my wounds. If I hadn't taken that algae, I knew the pain would've been ten times worse, so I just bit my lip and suffered through it. Never would have thought removing a winter coat would be so painful.

I held up my shirt to reveal all twenty-seven twelve-inch lashes around my torso, ribs, and lower back. Gaius didn't seem too nervous about it, but when I looked at Cal, I only saw pure worrisome unease. He had never seen me like this. Maybe he had never seen *anyone* like this, given that wide-eyed gaze and thinned frown. I didn't like causing him strife or concern, and I truly wished he didn't have to see me look so pathetic and covered in blood.

Gaius opened the evanesce serum. It was bright blue and thick, like hair oil.

"Lisa," he said to me, "this will hurt but only briefly because of the anesthetic. I have to clean out the magic in your wounds with this serum. Then, I can finish healing the tears like normal."

"I've been through worse. No need to be patient with it. I can take it," I said before biting my finger to suppress the pain I was about to feel.

Gaius took a piece of cloth and put the serum on top of it. He gently pressed it down on my stomach, cleaning my wounds.

It hurt so much worse than rubbing alcohol being poured on open sores or hand sanitizer seeping through paper cuts at school. I gripped the top of the couch and bit my finger hard, leaving indents of my teeth in between the knuckles of my index finger.

"Mr. Gaius," Cal started asking, serious with furrowed brows, "what exactly happened to Lisa?"

Our teacher continued to rub the oil over my tattered tummy, and after a couple of seconds, I stopped feeling as much pain. "When evanescing, if you aren't focused on your exact location, you can cause the magic to lose control. It backlashes and diverts back to the user, hence why it only hurt Lisa and not you. She will be fine, though."

My magic healer whipped his hand up in the air and summoned a pale green vine to extend out of a pot he had hanging from the ceiling. He charmed it like a snake and made it blossom before me. When the pollen came off the stamen of the yellow flower, it began to glow with a warm magic light. I had seen the flower before in Gaius' books: it was called an Aeson Spurge and was known to aid in sealing up wounds. I never noticed it here before... given he kept it high off the ground near his giant glass window. When Gaius aimed it toward my injuries, they suddenly began to heal faster, and my nerves began to loosen up. I finally could relax on the couch as the flower did the rest of the work.

"Now, you said someone attacked you?" Gaius noted, getting up off the floor to sit on the coffee table (I say coffee table, but it really was a giant, glossed wooden block with four stubs for legs—sturdy enough to hold anything, which is why it didn't break when Gaius used it as a chair).

Cal answered first. "We were just playing a game at the festival when I looked and saw Lisa about to be struck with magic by this cloaked old man. I didn't know him—*we* didn't know him, actually, but he seemed to know Lisa by how he looked at her."

Gaius turned to me. "You said, 'He is back,' but you never met this man?"

I looked at Gaius with no more tears, remembering the menacing feeling that man's magic aura gave me. "I felt it, Gaius... I didn't know that man... but I knew his magic, and he knew mine."

The Keeper continued to stare at me, and his words grew deeper in tone. "When you sensed his magic aura... was there a name that came to your head?"

I never heard the dark Mystic say his name or hear one play in my mind, but when Gaius' words made me question it... my heart pumped its warm blood faster and made my brain recall something it never knew.

"Saraqiel."

Cal stepped forward. "Wait, you did know that gu—"

"Your Highness, I think it is best you now leave." Gaius didn't break eye contact with me as he interrupted Cal's words. I came in with blue and scarlet lacerations, and there wasn't an ounce of fear in his eyes. But anxiousness coated every tan pore on his face when I said that name, an emotion I didn't think the Keeper of Stars even had. "Lisa and I have somewhere we need to go."

"What's going on? Does this have to do with Lisa's magic—the, uh, 'Agapéd' thing?" Cal continued to ask, but Gaius was already up off the coffee table, using his magic to put the Aeson Spurge back to its normal length.

"Until we return, do not speak of this encounter to anyone or mention anything we've discussed. This is outside of your realm, Young Prince. Let's hope it stays that way."

"But sir—"

"Do you understand me?" Gaius came right up to his face. He didn't get angry or upset with Cal; he just was in a rush.

"... Yes, sir," Cal answered. He glanced back at me before he walked up the stairs toward the exit of Gaius' home.

I wish I could have explained everything to Cal, but how do you tell someone Ariela's fallen brother Saraqiel is back, and I just know because his vessel looked at me funny at the festival without it sounding like you're crazy? It even sounded weird when trying to explain it to myself.

Gaius gave me back my jacket and held out his arm toward me. "You well enough to evanesce again?"

My stomach stopped bleeding, and I could move easily, with only minor twinges happening when I twisted my waist.

I took his arm and nodded. "Yeah... we're going to Haim Gana, aren't we?"

"That we are."

39
INEVITABLE INTERVENTION

Gaius and I hustled through the halls of the Elysium in search of Lady Ariela. I hadn't been in Haim Gana in quite a while, given the fact my portal had faded away and I didn't know how to evanesce there yet—kind of hard to teleport to a place that only exists in the realm of magic—and my burly instructor didn't pressure me to go. Hopefully, Emunah would pass us by, and I could ask him to make me more of the Ingress-Egress Draughts before I went back home. But that all depended on what Gaius needed to talk to Ariela about. I knew it had to do with Saraqiel, but I didn't think it would be something Gaius would grow anxious over. Being scared wasn't an emotion I thought he had until now.

Was something else wrong? The Keepers and Guardians should've been used to this by now: the Fallen showing up; they've experienced this for hundreds of years. *Maybe I overreacted—probably shouldn't have said the name the Agapéd made me remember...*

Soon, we walked past Micah's study to find him and Vilmad.

Gaius visibly sighed at the sight of them but continued with his hastened question as we stood outside the room. "Where's Lady Ariela?"

Both brown-headed Guardians looked rather shocked to see him in their home without an invitation. "She is preoccupied at the moment," Vilmad advised, "with Alona and Emunah discussing something much more important than whatever it is you—"

"Why the hurry?" Micah interjected. "Wait, is that *blood* on—"

"Just tell me where she is," Gaius demanded in his low voice.

"In the Courtyard Library," Rayna's voice emerged from the opposite end of the hallway. She was looking rather happy as usual.

"You can't just go barging in—Gaius!" Vilmad tried to command, but Gaius didn't care about a Guardian's authority and immediately went toward the Courtyard Library.

I followed right next to Gaius as Vilmad and Micah came rushing behind, my stomach still aching but not to the point of tears anymore.

We went straight through the doors that led to the domed garden filled with circular bookshelves. Vilmad and Micah were pestering Gaius with "hows" and "whys," but my mentor didn't care to answer. He grabbed my arm at one point, ensuring the two nosy-robed Guardians didn't snag me for an interrogation.

Saying I wasn't nervous would be a lie. I had known Gaius for almost half a year, and not once had he ever rushed into something. Not a single time did he ever worry... besides the night of the vezper attack. When he gripped my arm, preventing me from talking to Micah and Vilmad, it was the first time he used any type of force. The Keeper... He was distressed, and for some reason, my heart started nicking me with guilt... as if everything was my fault.

Ariela was talking with Alona and Emunah when we came in, her golden wings ebbing like silk fabric in the water. The sun shone brightly over the lush courtyard and illuminated the curved bookshelf that lined the perimeter, a beautiful sight about to be infected with my bloody self led by a riled-up Keeper and two agitated gold-dusted men not too far behind.

Alona, her blonde hair wavy like fields of wheat and her dress sewn with satiny blues, stared at us with a dazed look. "What is the meaning of this?"

"Didn't know we were having a party?" Emunah joked, stretching his black beard wide, but no one laughed.

Vilmad made an excuse first, quite loudly, too. "My apologies, Lady Ariela, but *he* came barging in like a behemoth demanding to see you, refusing to tell us his reasons as to why—"

Gaius didn't slow until he reached the winged Elysian amid the Guardian's outdoor library. "Saraqiel revealed himself to Lisa in the middle of the town, just west of Boolavogue."

Everyone fixed their eyes on me and fell utterly silent, except for Vilmad, who bickered, "That's impossible! Zephan would have notified us if he sensed the Fallen Elysian Magic."

Zephan... Who is that?

Lady Ariela looked at me with a serious yet calm gaze. My shirt was bloody, and my hair was a complete mess, but because I was well enough to return to her home and barrel down the halls, she continued with Gaius' pressing matter. "Is this true, Lisa?"

There was a pause as everyone waited for my answer—for *me* to speak. I stared up at her aureate eyes. "Yes, ma'am," I whispered, my mouth no bigger than a black olive.

Vilmad scoffed. "Preposterous! I'm not accusing the Agapéd of lying to us, but it is not like we have proof other than her word—"

"I can prove it," I said in the same quiet tone, though with a bit of unintentional abrasiveness, interrupting Vilmad's argument; probably wasn't the best idea to cut off a Guardian while in mid-explanation.

My little orange sprite popped out of thin air and floated behind my head, hiding from the stares of the Guardians.

"This little guy just keeps coming in handy, doesn't he, Vilmad?" Emunah chortled with a hardy *pat* on Vilmad's back, reminding the Guardian of Tuff's memories of me fighting the vezper—proving I was stronger than they had expected.

Vilmad did not find it pleasing.

"Tuff, you can show them. It's alright," I said to my companion.

With my word and a shaky nod, he floated onto my shoulder and projected his memories into the air. An orange film of the past began to play, starting with me and Cal at the festival. Everything was different watching it from outside of my mind. I remember feeling scared and as if the whole universe stopped, but through the eyes of Tuff, it just seemed like a young girl and an old man randomly made eye contact.

After the man made his threats and blew up the game with his strange form of combustion magic, his hood came off, revealing his face. He didn't look as old as I thought with his rough beard and gritty black hair, but something felt off. His eyes were definitely an old man's while his body said the late forties from the neck down.

When I turned to see the Guardians and Gaius' reactions after the clip ended, all of their faces were flushed—*stunned. Can they just tell by looking at the guy he is evil, or is this something much more serious?*

Micah spoke up first, saying in a bewildered tone, "Is it just me, or was that—"

"*Impossible!*" Vilmad declared as he started to pace back and forth, his long, brown hair catching the courtyard's draft. "It's been over a century! He would have to be a living corpse walking around like that!"

Who are they talking about?

Alona spoke with concern as well. "There are ways... dark ways for Man to find a way to outlive the human heart. Even with those cursed eyes of his, there is no mistaking that to be—"

"Ecuras." Gaius finished her sentence.

Wait, what?

I whipped my head toward Gaius. "But—but how?"

"I don't know," he responded. Gaius had never *not* known something before; he always knew everything. For him and the rest of the Guardians to be that shocked meant that serious dark magic was involved... the kind only the Fallen Elysian magic could produce.

Ariela knelt down to me and held my shoulders with her clean hands, rubbing the slick fabric of my winter jacket. "Lisa, when you saw that man, did you know it was Saraqiel inside him?" Her golden eyes... they were concerned. Ariela had been alive for thousands of years, so for her to be nervous—

My heart started to pick up pace in my chest. "I... didn't know at first. Everything just felt dark... I had never been that scared in my life... but when Gaius asked me if I knew a name, it was like my heart told me that was who was inside that man... I promise it's true. I just didn't know it was Ecuras at the time."

Ariela let out a sorrowful sigh, and the stares from all the Guardians didn't cease, pegged with silence.

Worry started to swirl around in my gut, causing more hasty questions. "What does this all mean for me? Isn't his showing up supposed to happen eventually—the reason for me getting this power?"

"We just thought there would be more time," Micah said, taking a deep breath and exhaling through his nose.

I furrowed my brows as my tone became more muddled. "I'm training right now in order to fight him in the *future*, right? He didn't seem that strong yet—letting us escape, Caelum punching him and all." It was an excuse, but it seemed logical. Darkness should be more powerful... right?

Emunah looked toward Ariela. "She is right about that. If he was fully consumed with Saraqiel's power, Zephan would have noticed, and Ecuras wouldn't have let her escape so easily. We've seen what the Fallen can do. That wasn't but mere child's play—a speck of dust in a sandstorm."

My throat tightened at Emunah's words—so solemnly serious, an emotion he *never* showed, and for what it entailed. *That was a crumb of the Fallen's magic...*

"But the fact he is here *and* already made contact with Lisa means she has no choice in what is to come," Alona said. Her sapphire eyes glued to mine, pitying me. "She will have to fight him... soon."

Wait... w-what did she just say?

I knew I would have to fight the Fallen eventually, but I thought that would be years down the road and with the help of others—when I was an adult or a Hero. When I was as strong as Gaius—*stronger* than the Wishing Star Mystic, if I was being honest. I was nowhere near ready to take on Saraqiel's magic alone, and fighting him implies stopping him... killing him.

A panic alarm went off in my head. *I can't—I can't fight him. Not yet—old man or not. He almost killed me with one hit if it weren't for Cal. Emunah just said that wasn't even a speck of the Fallen's true power. What I am gonna—*

"Lisa." Gaius' serious voice stopped me from going over the edge of a waterfall of worry. I didn't even notice his hand replacing Ariela's on my shoulder. "Did he know your name?"

I shook my head, quick and sharp. "No, sir. I-it didn't seem like it."

The Keeper looked back to Ariela. "He has no means of locating Lisa," he said, relieved, "so for now, I think it would be best to continue things as normal. We know of his strength, but he doesn't know Lisa's. If we can keep it that way, he may stay dormant for a while longer—aiming to get stronger before... before he comes."

"B-but what if he tells others?" I nervously asked Ariela. My fear of the unknown was driving my mind crazy, bringing about distressed courage, and I just wanted as many questions answered as possible to give me some form of solace. "What if he somehow finds me too soon?"

Ariela smiled down at me, trying to ease my distress. "Lisa, when a thief finds treasure but cannot yet obtain it, does he go and tell others of the prize, or does he keep it hidden for himself?"

An odd time for a riddle, but I took a moment, paused, and answered. "He keeps it for himself."

"Precisely. It applies to Ecuras as well. Only he knows of you and won't dare go spill his secret to others... in fear of them finding you first. As long as your identity and your low strength of magic and skill stay hidden, you are safe."

With Ariela's affirmation of my safety, the rapid beating of my heart began to settle, and my breathing steadied, knowing I was safe—*safe. I still have time to prepare and grow stronger...*

Lady Ariela straightened back up and made eye contact with each Guardian in the room. "For now, we do as Gaius says."

Vilmad jerked his chin, and I swear I saw Emunah grit a smile.

Ariela ignored her two eldest court members and continued. "If this is the strength of the Fallen, there isn't much of a threat to be seen. Ecuras most likely still has the same heart he did years ago, and he will gather more power before he intends to set out on his goal—whatever that may be. He will not attack again—not at this stage. To him, Lisa could be as powerful as he was when he first received the Agapéd Magic. Let's have him continue believing that and resume training Lisa under the leadership of Gaius, Inna, and the Kingdom of Boolavogue. As for discussing this with Zephan," Lady Ariela put her relaxed fingers up against her lips, pondering her next thoughts, "I will take it upon myself to talk with him tomorrow morning and see why he hasn't felt the presence of the Fallen. You all may be dismissed."

She turned toward me one last time, coppery glitter painting her thin smile. A smile that took on a new form: hopeful pity. "Remember what I said, Lisa. Don't linger on the future. Continue your training as normal and grow strong with the Agapéd with each passing day. Okay?"

As the Guardians began to disperse, I nodded at her, my mind going a mile a minute. "Yes, ma'am," I muttered, unable to say anything else.

Gaius wrapped his fingers around my shoulder with a fist full of blue rivers in his other hand, quickly evanescing us away without a word.

We landed on the hillside of Boolavogue, where the sunset burned with reds and oranges against the castle, my face tinged with a brush of cold mountain air. I finally had a second to breathe—a second to grasp the attack, the Fallen, Ecuras, and every new hastened bit of information about my purpose in being the Agapéd. *Ariela smiled... a facade for my young, innocent self.*

Everything was just—just so overwhelming. Too much food on my small, child-sized plate, all piled and slopped on at once, and it was hard to keep it all from toppling over. Hard to keep myself from overthinking the situation. And still, there was something else at play they either didn't notice or simply just ignored, not even Gaius bothering to see.

I let out a deep sigh, no stinging across my stomach to be felt as my chest puffed out and in. My face was glued to the yellowing grass below my feet when I saw Gaius' boots turn in my direction. "You okay?" he asked.

I paused, staring at my muddy shoes to avoid looking at the Keeper. "Yeah... I just forgot to ask Emunah for more portal potions..." I muttered to my teacher, but that was only partially true, and it definitely wasn't the reason for my gloomy face.

What caused my shaking hands and deep, fragile breaths was not because of Ecuras. It was something else—something they didn't notice... though I didn't expect them to. Something that caused my nerves to summon tears to perch at the ends of my eyelashes and crack my already tattered heart. Something I absolutely hated.

It was the fact I was attacked and dragged *Caelum* into this that unsettled my stomach and sent my mind into a silent fright. Again—because of me—another friend was in danger, and dumbbells of guilt and heartache pressed down hard on my chest. The pain of Valhalla... her death... the death that was my fault... I suppressed those memories for the past couple of months. All the nightmares were finally dying down—replaced and covered up under the thrill of learning magic and how to battle with Hunters. Losing another friend was not something I wanted again, something I could not handle... and I thought I had escaped that unwanted experience for the rest of my life.

I fidgeted with my fingers until hangnails formed, masquerading my trembling hands so Gaius didn't see my fear. *I can't go through that again... not ever...*

40
IT'S A SECRET

The next day was cold, especially inside the Arctic Wing of the Veradome. The night before, Gaius and I didn't talk about the conversation in Haim Gana... mostly because the Keeper demanded that I rested until morning—physically and mentally, though he didn't mention the latter. I ate some leftover dinner as he worked in the staritorium, and I didn't see him again until this morning when he told me that our magic-training lessons were canceled. He wanted more time for my wounds to heal... at least, that is what he told me.

I thought he, like Mom and most other adults, would've asked about my gloomy face. I was just told that the Fallen had arrived, that the Agapéd Magic's purpose was coming to fruition...

But then again, maybe that was why he didn't pester me. He knew what was coming and didn't want to bring it up in his home, or maybe he wasn't worried. He trusted Lady Ariela, never once putting her notions down as he did with the Guardians' tactics, possibly expecting me to do the same.

So, I stood by him and helped the man cultivate the glacieranthus flowers, pushing away the fear as Ariela told me to. I enjoyed working in the Veradome and didn't mind my terrain magic break. Weed plucking and plant potting weren't something I would deem as exciting, but they helped take my mind off of Ecuras and everything the Guardians had told me the day before.

As I held the ice box for Gaius, who was chipping away the frozen pollen from the glacieranthus flowers to put inside it, loud chatter came from the opposite end of the room. It normally remained quiet in the Arctic Wing, as no more than seven workers were allowed in at a time. Visitors arriving were *very* unusual.

When I turned to look, two Boolavogue guards were talking with one of the biologists.

I whispered to Gaius, "Is it normal for the King's guards to come inside the Veradome?"

His green eyes veered at the entrance. "No. They are probably looking for someone." He then proceeded to harvest the flowers' icicle nectar.

Suddenly, the Veradome worker announced, "She's over there."

My eyes looked up from the frosted flowers again. The worker's finger pointed directly at me, and both guards started walking in my direction.

My body became stiff like the plants in the room. I didn't know what was happening—could be something good or terribly bad. But, given that it was early in the morning and they took the time to track me down, it likely meant something bad.

Gaius set down his little ice ax as the two Boolavogians marched toward us. "Is there a problem?" the Keeper asked.

"We have a message for Miss Lisa Robbie," the shorter one of the two men answered in a rather loud voice. He quickly unfolded a letter that had a light blue waxed emblem on the front and read it out loud.

"'To Miss Lisa Robbie, under the watch of Gaius the Keeper of Stars, resident of both Earth and Boolavogue: Lisa Robbie, you are hereby summoned to the court of the King this day in the privacy of the audience of the Royal Court. As such, the contents of the meeting will not be disclosed until the summoned is present and accounted for. This is not a request but a command upon which the summoned must immediately attend. Any further resistance or...'" The guard furrowed his brows, focusing on the paper. His lips moved slowly and with confusion, all in silence.

"'... recalcitrance will not be tolerated...,'" Gaius said perfectly and without even looking at the document *or* the guard miming of syllables. We all stared at the Keeper; he merely shrugged with crossed arms. *Seems this isn't the first time he has heard a court summons before...*

The shorter guard blinked fast and continued. "'Any further resistance or *recalcitrance* will not be tolerated and treated as defiance against the King and the Kingdom itself. Signed, King Bolthor Argoth Sonon of Boolavogue.'"

Wait... Did I just get called to court with Cal's dad?

When I say the room went silent, I meant everything down to the breathing of the plants. I thought the men would ask me about my Hunter's license or something to do with Ekron needing me for a hunt with another Hunter. Never would I have guessed I would be summoned like a prisoner to court! *What the heck did I do to make the King upset me!*

"Do you know why the King wants to meet with me, sir?" I timidly asked the guard.

"That is between you and the Royal Court, for we are only here to escort you to the castle, ma'am."

My mind wasn't settling. It wasn't like I was summoned to see a principal or called downstairs from my room to have a lecture with Mom; the ruler of a country was officially calling me out to have a private conversation... and I didn't even know what about.

I thought Gaius would have said something, anything to question why I would be demanded in the King's presence, but the Keeper simply proceeded to go back to work! *How is he acting as if this isn't a big deal right now!*

"We will be leaving now," the taller guard said. "Please relinquish whatever tasks you were given and accompany us to the castle."

I looked to Gaius, hoping he would say, "Let me join you," or, "I demand you tell me why you need Lisa to go," but he just glanced back at me with his little ice chipper in hand and quietly said, "You can't refuse the command of a King, *Lisa.*"

The *nerve*—the *irony* of that statement made my stomach sink down to the floor. *He did not just use the same words I told him weeks ago after the Spar!*

"Let us go, now," the guard urged me, placing his hand on the shoulder of my jacket.

"But Gaius—" I pleaded, but the Keeper simply kept working, unfazed and almost idyllic.

"I'll see you in a bit," he calmly replied, leaving me completely baffled and *not* royally dressed for the occasion.

I can't believe him—is this truly not a big deal to him? I am literally being taken away right now!

Before I knew it, the soldiers and I had already left the Arctic Wing and headed toward the Kingdom. We went through a secret entrance I didn't know of, which began near the left side of Calendula's main city. When the guards, who didn't speak a word to me after we exited the greenhouse, and I went through the new secret entrance, it led us inside a cave where the roars of the Gora bears could be heard. Strings of lights hung above our heads, attached to the rocky, damp ceiling, and many boxes and barrels of supplies filled the perimeter of the walls. *Must be an entrance solely for the Kingdom's guards since Cal never mentioned it before.*

We exited the narrow cave, and far down the mountain was the white towering castle. I followed closely behind the guards, scaling down the cliff's stone steps still covered in the cold morning mist; silence continued to trail us like shadows. I normally didn't mind the quiet, but I didn't like being left on hold to wonder why the King wanted to see me. *Please, please, please let this be some type of formal invitation to a ball or something—anything that doesn't involve me getting into trouble with Gaius afterward.*

Through the crunchy grass of the castle grounds, the guards led me up to the main floor's hallway—the one with all the oil paintings framed in gold decorated the walls. The moment we turned a corner, my eyes saw Prince Caelum. He, too, was being escorted by a Boolavogue guard, patiently waiting for me to arrive. Judging by the wide-eyed look on his face, he had no clue I would be joining him in the meeting with the King.

My party walked up to Cal and his guard. The guards exchanged their greetings—a large handshake that was just a grab of the forearm with both their right hands—and the short one said, "Miss Lisa, Young Prince... if you would care to follow me."

We let the guard walk in front of us, but Cal nudged me... just far back enough to whisper without being heard. "Are you okay?" he quietly asked, standing right against my ear. His breath was warm, swimming through my tangled, wavy brown hair. If this was a normal situation, I'd be freaking out over my appearance since I truly just got out of bed and threw on some winter clothes, only thinking Veradome workers would be seeing me for the entirety of the day.

"Huh—oh, yeah. Gaius healed me up pretty well, so I'm fine." I had almost forgotten that the last time he saw me, I was scratched bloody on Gaius' couch. "Do you know what this is all about?" My eyes stayed focused on the heel of the guard's boots.

"No idea, but I do have a hunch it has something to do with Fladden. I promise I didn't tell anyone about what happened yesterday, though."

"Even if this was about yesterday, why would we be in trouble?"

"I don't know, but given the fact we were both called in means it's a pretty big deal and not just a wigging..."

There was a short pause as we descended another flight of stairs toward the Throne Room—the same place Gaius and I first met the Queen—and my heart blared a horribly fast rhythm.

We are going in there—crap! I didn't want to see the fancy chamber like this!

Cal continued our hushed conversation. "Am I allowed to ask what that was all about... with you and Gaius?"

Suddenly, two guards told us to wait outside of the giant marble doors.

I hurriedly whispered back, "I'll tell you when this is all over. It's kinda a long story."

When the Boolavogue soldiers pulled back the doors for us to enter, we were greeted by the thick silence and tension of the room. The walls were tall and brightly lit, and the windows brought in all the dawn from the morning sky. Ceilings rose high like the ones in the Elysium, chestnut beams patterning the top and creating a beautifully arched roof of stone and glass. There were no chairs, benches, or tables along the glistening gold and marble floor, but up on the dais were two thrones... each occupied by Cal's parents, and they did not look pleased.

Our subtle strides across the Throne Room's floor sounded like bombs dropping from the sky. My hands started to sweat as my breathing grew heavy, and I swear I could hear both my and Cal's heartbeats racing inside our chests. To make matters even worse, we weren't alone in our secret meeting. On the side of the room, close to the dais where the King and Queen sat, was bald Captain Ekron, dark-haired Captain Clover, a man in a guard's uniform I didn't recognize, and a very regal lady unfamiliar to me as well.

The Royal Court is more *than just the King and Queen—this is way, way, way worse than I thought...*

Then, right behind Ekron, emerged a familiar man, the only person in the room that wasn't a part of the Court. It was the game merchant from Fladden, the one whose game blew up during the Ecuras attack. Frizzy brown hair covered his head as he arched his back and stood with sour lips beside our Captain. Seeing his once cheerful game master's face turn scornful only confirmed Cal's suspicions to be true. We were in *serious* trouble—the kind of trouble where a lecture from Grandma on a bad day would seem like a walk in the park.

Cal stopped walking as we were about ten yards from the King and Queen on the dais, so I did the same. Even though it was his parents up there, nothing about this meeting indicated they were related. They were truly treating their son and me just like any other civilians of the Kingdom. It was a whole new type of terrifying I never wished to know.

"Lisa Robbie... Prince Caelum..." the King began, sitting up straight on his throne with both feet locked and planted on the cold, glossy floor. His dark brown hair, almost slate black, hit the shoulders of his navy and cobalt trench coat. The cloak was elegant beyond belief, stitched with silver threads and strapped with buckles—a celestial Viking's garb. Upon his head was no crown, but all those sapphires I saw before could be found on four of his ten fingers, embedded in bands of pure gold.

He didn't move a muscle in his chair as he continued. "Late last night, I was approached by two Hunters stationed in Fladden. They both said that the town was savagely attacked during their Oogleyear celebration, and it wasn't due to any type of dark magic monster. Normally, this would be a concern of their Thane and dealt with promptly... but when it was relayed back to me that it was my *son*..." His voice raised with a deeper echo. "It then became *my* problem... Do you deny this to be true?"

Cal lowered his gaze to the floor and answered. "No, sir."

My face wanted to change expressions to reflect what I just heard come out of the Prince's mouth, but I resisted. Cal didn't do anything wrong, and yet, he didn't dare correct his dad. *He saved me, so why is he not telling the King the truth?*

The Queen looked over to the merchant. Her Majesty wore an emerald robe, hugging the pistachio dress underneath, sleeves snuggling around her slender arms. Thin ivory fabric draped across the front of her chest, creating a V-neck shape stitched with silver to match the silver boots she wore underneath. Upon her head, adorning her silky, smooth brown hair, was a dainty circlet speckled with blue gems—not a crown either, but still made with pure silver and real sapphires, no doubt. "Would you mind recalling what happened... both before and after the attack on your business?"

The merchant seemed frazzled, his coarse brown hair frizzy and his eyes unable to focus solely on the Queen's face. "Of course, My Lady. I was busy tending to my customers when the Young Prince and his friend came to my booth. I didn't recognize him at the time—there were many faces in the crowd, so I didn't see it fit to remember who came up to me. As long as they brought coin, I didn't pay no mind. Then—oh, when was it..." The man started snapping his fingers to spark a memory. "Yes, I had just finished gathering the loose game pieces when I turned my head to see the Prince whip his hand toward my venue, blasting the walls with his explosion. When I came to, I saw them both start running away and that girl evanesce them to safety—no apology or care in the world about their actions. I put good money into that business. Every year, I make enough profit that one holiday to afford two weeks off of work, and *he* goes and—"

The Queen held up her hand. "Thank you, sir. I can assure you your business will be taken care of immediately. We will have the Thane of Fladden give you enough supplies and materials to replace that which was destroyed."

My muscles tensed as I stood still. *What—are they really just gonna believe that man? Did no one else see Ecuras attack and believe Cal and I were innocent?*

With a smile on his face, the merchant bowed his head forward. "Thank you, My Lady. Thank you very much."

That was when both King and Queen Sonon turned the attention back on me and Cal. Everything from the merchant's eyes said we were to blame, but it was misunderstood. I couldn't see how Cal was standing there letting his own parents believe we would vandalize someone's property like that. *This isn't right...*

The King's twice-braided, bearded chin dipped down as his glare pierced Cal's petrified face. A royal gaze that could melt steel. His voice grew stronger with his raised shoulders as he scolded, "You are not just a boy... but my *son*." The walls rumbled with his bellow.

The Prince avoided all forms of eye contact.

"The way you behave reflects more than just your reputation... it is a direct reflection on me and your mother..." He then looked at me.

My breathing stopped as my eyes bolted to the foot of the throne.

"Both of you are well known throughout our kingdom... you need to know your place and be aware of who you represent... I don't need to tell you what you did was wrong... but this behavior cannot go unpunished, do you understand?"

But we didn't do anything wrong—why is Cal not saying anything?

The Prince gave the same solemn response, "Yes, sir."

I just kept my head down. *I don't care if I get in trouble, but Cal... this is not right!*

The King's voice grew louder as if he wasn't satisfied with Cal's answer. "Then, why did you act so carelessly?"

"I don't know, sir."

I can't stand this...

"You are not a child—your actions have more consequences than gold could ever repair. Do you understand?"

"Yes, sir."

This is wrong!

"And explain to us why you—"

"*It wasn't his fault.*"

Those four words that came out of my mouth rang through the room louder than any siren or alarm and could be heard for miles.

I did not just say that—I just interrupted the King... I am dead. So. Incredibly. Dead.

As Cal slowly turned his bowed head in my direction, every single eye fixated on me... and I just kept my gaping gaze on the floor. I was not about to look Death in the face unless compelled to.

Thankfully, the Queen responded to my unprompted remark first, though her voice was anything but sweet. "What do you mean, Lisa?"

I lifted my eyes toward her and quickly began to plead my case, my arms stiff-straight by my thighs. "I was about to be attacked with magic when Caelum stepped in and blocked it. I know, from the merchant's point of view, it seemed like Caelum threw the explosive toward the booth, but that's only because Caelum deflected it..." I started fidgeting with my fingernails beneath the cover of my long sleeves and jacket. "If it wasn't for him... I would be dead." Courage mustered up in my chest just enough so my eyes could shift toward the King. "He saved me, sir," my soft voice continued, "and I know if he knew that the magic was explosive, he wouldn't have deflected it toward the merchant's stand... and we ran away because the guy who attacked us started following us... that's all."

There was a brief pause... though it felt like months of silence. I wasn't the type of girl who spoke up when things were going wrong—I wasn't even the type who *spoke up*—but then again, this was the first time I had ever been in a situation like this. I couldn't let Cal get in trouble, even if that meant telling the King he was wrong, even if that meant shackles in a dungeon with bland food and zero desserts for the rest of my life.

The Queen shifted her attention to the merchant, causing the Fladden man to unbend his back. "Did you happen to see the man Lisa speaks of?"

The merchant began, "Well, it is quite possible. As I said, there were many faces in the crowd..." His old eyes shifted around as if staring at the room's decor helped him remember details of yesterday. "Actually, I do recall seeing a cloaked man standing near the girl. I didn't see a face, but his clothing was nothing like I had seen before. Velvet and dark blue, something worth remembering. Definitely not a Boolavogian garb—a traveler for sure."

"That's him!" I interrupted again since I didn't get in trouble for doing it the first time.

King Bolthor stared me down with his cold, hazel eyes. "Who was this man?"

My mind stopped. I slowly examined around the room: five guards near the doors, two familiar Captains and two unfamiliar ones, the flustered merchant, and a lady taking note of the entire summons. Out of everyone there besides me and Cal, only three people knew about the Agapéd in my heart... and there was *no* way I was about to reveal that surprise during a royal scolding.

With only the thought of keeping my identity hidden, I took a deep breath, one that scratched my dry throat, and casually answered, "It's a secret."

Instant regret followed as quickly as I spurt those words. *WHAT—why did I just say that? A secret—really? I should've just LIED! Lisa, you are BEYOND dead this time!*

The King clenched his fists on the armrest of his throne—only a flex from snapping off the ends of the golden wood—and glared me down as a vorrg does with its prey, bellowing, "And by *whose* authority do you stand under that overrules mine?"

My waist bowed fast, tilted toward the floor, and my eyes shut tight. I said the first thing that came to my mind. "Lady Ariela's authority, sir!"

That same deafening silence swallowed up the room once more, and all the previous stares from before were now piercing my skin like needles. I hated this—hated this so much—and could hear my heart pound in my ear, about to jolt out of my chest. I had no clue if Lady Ariela's word was better than a king's, but I was under pressure. Given the fact that she was kind of like a golden star in human form that watched over the world's magic, I assumed her say in the matter was far superior. *Please, please, please, believe me.*

The King took a moment to collect himself, a mighty exhale swelling in his chest. And another, and another.

Thud, thud, thud—my heart was not letting up. *Please say something. I hate this agonizing waiting. Hate this so much.*

"Everyone is dismissed..." King Bolthor's voice finally echoed, calm but stoic. His eyes leered in my direction again. "Except for Lisa and my son."

Why is his calm tone still as intimidating as his normal voice?

The Prince and I stood motionless with our heads facing the floor as we listened to the scuffing of shoes leaving the room. Once everyone—even the guards and Captain Ekron—had left the Throne Room, the Prince and I looked up toward his parents. Their unpleasant looks from before were now nothing but pure startlement, and I could not tell if the situation went from bad to worse... or from bad to partially worse.

King Bolthor changed his posture and placed his elbow on his throne, still keeping his attention on me. "You may speak freely now."

Though I had no reason to be hushed about seeing Ecuras, I still didn't want to shout at the King anymore, so I took it upon myself to walk up the dais and to the throne. It was no more than a couple of strides, but across that glossy floor with royalty watching me made it seem like I was walking the span of a soccer field.

Upon reaching the throne of Cal's father, I was able to notice the wrinkles near the King's eyes and the freckle on his ear that Celine mentioned. It was odd to be that close to someone so revered and feared at the same time. *Cal's dad is definitely the scariest man I have ever had to talk to one-on-one before... I hope I don't sound stupid when he hears me speak.*

I took a deep breath and told the King and Queen everything. I told them of Ecuras and about the Fallen Elysian Magic in his heart, explaining that to be the reason for him attacking me. I explained Cal's heroic behavior—how he saved me and carried me all the way to Gaius' home with my wounds and made it clear that Gaius told him not to speak of anything until we further discussed it with Ariela, which was why it was Hunters who revealed the crime and not Cal himself.

The last thing I told the King and Queen was Ecuras' goals. "He said he was searching for two things: one is the Agapéd, but the other is unclear. I, uh, the Guardians and Lady Ariela don't believe it has anything to do with your Kingdom, seeing as he was passive at the festival until I arrived." I fidgeted with my hands. More hangnails formed beneath the hem of my coat sleeves. "It's just my magic he wants, but Lady Ariela said not to worry for now, given that it seems he isn't very strong yet... though I understand if my being with the Prince only causes trouble... I am sorry," I explained, staring back down to the floor and at the King's glossy boots.

Queen Leonora stared at her husband, waiting for him to respond. He scratched his bearded chin. For a long while, he sat in complete silence. *Was that believable? I mean, they don't think I'm crazy, right? Crap—what if they don't even know about Ariela? I would have sounded like a complete nut job if that's the case!*

His Majesty averted his hazel eyes back to his son. "Is it true... that you saved the life of Lisa?"

In a calm yet nervous tone, Cal responded, "Yes, sir."

"I see..." The King then looked back at me, his voice serious but without his previous anger. "Lisa... your actions today were... quite unbridled... but brave and honest. I understand you have been given a heavy burden to bear... A mighty power to hold in such a small body. This strife between this so-called Ecuras hasn't made a fight with the Kingdom as of yet... but if he is spotted again in our land... I can assure you it will be handled promptly." King Bolthor softened his gaze underneath his thick eyebrows. "And you being with Caelum has nothing to do with the dark actions that fell upon you. You are a fine Hunter prodigy... and you may still train with my son."

I was sure he would kick me out of the castle, forbid me from being friends with Cal, and banish me from his kingdom. When he instead praised my courage, my eyes became teary. "Thank you, sir!" I said to him, grinning, giving him a slight bow before walking back toward Cal.

The latches and silver chains on His Majesty's belt jingled as King Bolthor stood up from his throne. He still wasn't happy. "There is still damage that must be undone by you, Prince... Once your morning lessons are complete, we will head off to Fladden to address the Thane. We will explain the true crime and assign two soldiers there to keep watch for this man Lisa speaks of. Until then... you are free to leave and escort Lisa out."

We both nodded and took the uncomfortable walk toward the giant marble exit doors. Cal pushed them open before the guards finished pulling them for us to leave, and I followed him down the hallway in silence.

We ended up outdoors on one of the high viaducts that connected the North Tower to the main building, sitting on a cold stone bench. It was chilly, but I was sweating so badly that my heightened nerves kept me warm. There, the Prince released a deep breath as though he had been holding it throughout the entirety of the summons.

"You shouldn't have had to do that for me..." he said, hands gripping the edge of the bench and clenching hard. "I'm sorry."

"You don't have to apologize..." I scooted closer to him, seeing his eyes looking as glum as ever. "But... why couldn't you tell your dad the truth?"

"I don't know... he's just—I'm just scared to say the wrong thing. I'm supposed to be him—a strong leader everyone can trust. If I make a mistake, it makes him look bad." He shook his head as if trying to rattle off the fear in his heart. "I mentioned before that my father isn't from Boolavogue. My mother was royalty here, and she was the one who married him. He was no king and had to earn the trust of the Kingdom... so I have to do the same. In situations like this, it's easier to agree with him than to try and prove the truth."

I didn't understand what Cal was saying, nor did I know what it was like to have parents like his, but saying the truth should not be something worth fearing.

The cold breeze whisked by as my hands rested in my lap and my shoulders hunched forward. "I won't lie, speaking to the King was one of the scariest things I have ever done, but you shouldn't be that afraid of him, you know...

Even though he's King, he's still your father. If you're honest with him, I'm sure he would believe you over some guard or merchant."

Cal huffed before looking up at the view of the Kingdom out in front of us. "The life of an Earthian must be nice..." He turned to look at me. "But thanks for doing what I couldn't."

"Well, you owe me, then," I joked, though I was partially serious.

"Fine..." Glum was beginning to leave Cal's body, allowing him to sit more comfortably. "So, what all you said—about Lady Ariela and that man... Was all that true?"

My eyes found my fingers more interesting than staring at the Prince. "Yeah."

"And you're not scared?"

I swirled around my Echo Ring, toying with it as if it were a true fidget band. "Of course, I am..." Suddenly, my self-consciousness appeared, refusing to let Cal see Lisa Robbie as a weak Agapéd Bearer and causing him to worry. Quickly, I continued, "But she told me not to worry, so... I'm not gonna."

"That's it? The Elysian of Magic told you not to worry, and you just... don't?"

"Well... yeah," I lied.

Cal tittered, believing my fib. "You're something else, you know that?"

The entrance to the opened bridge swung outward, and the Queen walked toward Cal and me. Her strut was brisk, her stare cold in that emerald dress.

Cal stood up, so I mimicked him.

"Are you still in trouble?" I whispered before the Queen could hear our voices.

Another sigh exited his lungs. "Ah... yeah, it seems so. Still gotta go fix everything in Fladden with Father—but it'll be fine. Probably won't see you at lessons with Ekron for a couple of days, though."

Queen Leonora arrived and said in a serious tone, "Come, Caelum. Lessons are starting early today."

I waved goodbye to the Prince as he walked away with his mom. The moment he turned from my gaze, my hand lowered, and my smile faded. Remorse began to tug at my emotions quickly.

The whole thing was my fault. Ecuras was after *me*, Cal brought us to the festival because of *me*, the attack was aimed at *me*, and still, Cal took all the blame. Everything that happened to him was supposed to happen to *me*—and the worst part was... he could've died. I could've killed the Prince... just because I was careless and not strong enough to defend myself.

A guard brushed by me, so I quickly turned my body to face the edge of the bridge.

"Lisa."

I hadn't paid attention to the faces of those around me, just figuring everyone to be Boolavogue workers, but that echo of my name was all too familiar.

It was Gaius, coming from the opposite end of the bridge.

My eyes couldn't look up at his face—fearing he would see my eyes start to water—so I stared down at his weathered boots. "Hey, Gaius..."

Why did he have to show up right now...

"What did the King want?" he asked, not forcing me to look at him.

My tone was weak. "It was about Fladden... I, uh, told him everything... about Ecuras and the Fallen... he said he understood, but... was it okay for me to do that?"

The leather in his trench cloak creased, meaning he crossed his arms. "That is fine. Glad he knows actually... Was that all?"

I gave two quick nods, still staring at the stone floor of the bridge. "Yeah— let's just, uh, get back to the Veradome—I wanna finish helping you with the, uh, glacieranthus flowers... if that's okay?"

Waiting for Gaius to respond was not happening. Before he decided to get nosy and see my face slowly becoming blotchy red, I held out my hand, cueing I was ready to evanesce away.

Standing there in the cold morning of Boolavogue was the first time a miserable heartache took over my body in the Kingdom... and all I wanted to do was go to Luca's and grab a Sugar Cloud Offie with Valhalla, but I knew that would never happen again.

I ended up feeling down and pitiful the rest of the afternoon.

After I helped Gaius, I stayed in my room to rest, only making occasional trips to the Keeper's magic study to grab more books, but not even drawing creatures for my bestiary while listening to music could ease my thoughts.

My burly mentor didn't help either... though, he tried—*really* tried, too—but I wanted nothing more than to be alone. He cooked dinner, but I wasn't hungry. He made me a plate anyway, but I said, "I'll eat it later," and went back to my room.

I'm pretty sure I made him worried or upset because he stayed in the living room for a *long* time "working." Been with him long enough to know he doesn't do anything but eat and pass through that room—*not* study plants, craft weapons, or practice magic on the sofa.

The moon rose, and the stars peeked through my glass walls as I sat at my desk drawing portraits of Tuff; he was kind enough to give me some funny poses for my inspiration. After faking the whole art camp scenario, I actually grew to love drawing magical creatures, especially my orange glainie. No doubt, in a year, I'd have a whole diary entry labeled *Tuff and His Many Faces* completed—

Breaking the silence of the night was a knock on my bedroom door. I knew it was Gaius but didn't bother to get up, figuring him to say something about lessons or the dinner I hadn't eaten.

Well... neither of those things happened.

Soft scratching sounds came from the ground at the base of my door. I looked away from my desk to find a large scrap of paper on the floor, the string lights above spotlighting the note perfectly. I squatted near my door, seeing the sheet to have a tiny phrase in Gaius' small handwriting reading:

You alright?

Is this... his way of consoling me?

I couldn't help but smile; Gaius probably had never in his life had to comfort a teenage girl.

Back home, Mom kind of did the same thing when I was upset. Instead of running straight into my room after a bad test grade or some kid making fun of my freckles or wearing the wrong kind of shoes, she would sit outside my bedroom door. We wouldn't be face to face, but we still talked... talked until the emotions were stable again.

Anytime things were tense, I would cry—even a hug during an emotional time would cause my speech to go blubbery and my tears to pour waterfalls.

Mom was the same way, though I never saw her cry very much. The "door method" was easier for us both. We said what we wanted to say without uncontrollable feelings getting in the way, and once it was over, that was when Mom would open the door and give me a hug... and I loved it.

For Gaius to do the same thing but with paper made me happy. It was nice knowing he cared that much. I knew the laundry room hallway was cramped for him even just standing—all to pass that torn paper to me.

I slid the note back:

Yeah... just felt bad for what happened today and yesterday, getting the Prince involved and everything. Sorry for not eating dinner.

A couple of scribbly sounds later, the paper came shifting back.

Don't feel bad for what was not in your control.

I wrote back:

Thanks, Gaius. I mean it.

I thought we were done with our childish note-passing, but Gaius slid the paper back under the door again.

I made you dessert. At least eat something. Can't have you training on an empty stomach tomorrow morning.

Gaius didn't know it, but he just said the most beautiful thing in the world. Never in all my time living with the gardener, did he make me dessert, claiming the meal to be pointless. He only cooked Hero-training food, consisting of many vegetables cultivated from the Calendulian farms and pounds of chicken and beef from the butcher in Boolavogue. Dessert to him was a handful of dates with a side of milk. Well—no way could anyone convince me a giant raisin was on the same level as cake, ice cream, or Oreos.

I jumped off the floor and cracked open the door just enough so my left eye could peer through.

The Keeper was squatting on the floor, far too big for the narrow laundry room. He was in his boots, sweatpants, and gray tank top—the one that showed all the scars on his shoulders and chest.

I took no time with my words as I muttered, "What *kind* of dessert?"

Gaius' knees popped as he stood up, grinning with his eyes. "Something filled with sugar I'm sure you'll like."

I squinted. "You mean... *real* sugar... not just fruit?"

He started walking toward the kitchen. "With chocolate, too."

Though he couldn't see my face, I was beaming at his simple gesture and happily followed him back to the kitchen.

Out from the oven were golden pastries spiraled with chocolate ribbons, and I was shocked. They were huge fluffy rolls with chocolate perfectly oozing out the cracks. I knew Gaius could cook... but not bake; they looked like he just snagged them off a shelf at an up-scale patisserie shop!

While he grabbed a glass of milk and dates—not even eating his own masterpiece of buttery, flaky goodness—I sat at the kitchen island, scarfing away the most perfect-looking strudel.

After saying my thanks to the Keeper, I asked with my mouth full, watching the steam rise from the crackled treat, "Gaius, who was that Zephan guy Lady Ariela mentioned?"

Given all the unwelcoming circumstances, we still hadn't talked about the day before, but now, I was curious and wanted answers.

The Keeper placed his glass down. "He's many things. None of which I care for. But..." He sighed. "He is a Keeper, nonetheless."

"Really? What kind of Keeper is he—like his magic and stuff?"

"He's the Keeper of Knowledge... though, this century, he prefers to go by 'Game Keeper.' Lady Ariela concealed the Magic of Insight in him: the magic that allows one to know the heart of another without their consent. He can sense the most powerful magic across all the galaxies and tell the strength of magic from just a look. There is a limit: he can't sense *all* magic... only the *strongest* in a given land or planet, so he isn't *all-knowing*..." Gaius gave an annoyed look at his glass. "Though, he likes to think he is." He then took a huge gulp of his milk.

"I take it you don't like him?" I asked, suppressing my smile.

He wiped his mouth. "Can't stand the git."

I picked up another pastry, holding it delicately with both hands as my elbows perched on the counter. Staring at the golden layers mixed with chocolate, I thought about Saraqiel. "So… he would be able to sense if the Fallen Magic was strong in Ecuras, right? That's why Lady Ariela went to talk with him?"

"Yes, seeing as Saraqiel *is* here, and he didn't tell us. But, she met with him today while you were with the King, and he informed her that Ecuras isn't as powerful as he once was. Still, the Fallen has homed its magic pulse in his heart and will grow stronger in the distant future."

Fear began to squash my appetite again, causing me to put the pastry back down on the counter.

The Keeper took note. "Lisa," Gaius said in a deep voice, forcing me to stare back at him. Surprisingly, his green eyes were soft and without a worrying gaze. "You are safe. Though I do not care for the pompous Keeper, I know he wouldn't lie to Lady Ariela. If Ecuras truly had the full power of the Fallen in his heart, Zephan would have told her. We have time to train and get you stronger before the day comes when you have to…"

Gaius' words trailed off, so I quietly finished his phrase. "To destroy the Fallen Magic in his heart, right?"

He nodded slowly. "That time is far from now, and I promise to prepare you for when that day comes, okay?"

I took a deep breath, faintly grinning at my mentor. "I know… thanks for saying that."

Clanking sounds of glass hitting hollow metal broke the quietness of the kitchen as Gaius put his empty jar in the sink.

"So, will I ever get to meet this Zephan guy, then?" I asked.

He scoffed. "You wouldn't want to, but—seeing how you keep getting yourself involved in all the Keepers' lives—you'll end up meeting him one way or another." He turned back around and popped the pitted date in his mouth like a piece of chocolate. "Now, tell me about this 'portal potion' you mentioned yesterday before you head back to bed."

His words were deep, loud, and happily serious. It was comforting in the strangest way; I loved it.

41
SHOULD I?

Landing back in the cold woods of New Jersey, that week was the first time I was alone—away from the magic world—but Ecuras' face kept reappearing in my thoughts. His hallowing voice invaded my ears, even with the winter birds chirping about the cold weather and wishing for more worms to pop out of the ground. The dark magic explosions—how quick they were and the fear that followed—still shook my bones.

I was constantly surrounded by Hunters, Keepers, and Guardians all week—keeping my thoughts easily distracted from my first-ever assault by a dark Mystic. Even sleeping that night was easier knowing Gaius was there, and Tuff stayed snug to my chest the entire time, inserting memories of him and the glainies singing and dancing. But after taking my first step through my backyard forest... my calm vanished.

Every little sound scared me, and I quickly picked up my pace to the backdoor.

After touching my doppelganger, I gathered the clothes she left behind and made my way upstairs. I didn't have to worry about Mom making a run-in with my magic since she was in the shower, so I took my time and changed out of my Gaius-home-smelling clothes, giving a good brush to my hair as well.

My head was throbbing more than usual as I sat on the edge of my bed, the memories of school piling in. Apparently, Lily made fun of girls wearing Converse with skinny jeans, leaving my doppelganger—leaving *me*—feeling bad about my appearance. Jenny Kim ignored me in the hall when I waved to her *again*. And to top it off, I stepped in gum. Great week, doppel-me.

Tuff floated near my nose as I sat on the edge of my bed, giving a warming glow and whistle to my nervous face. He also received my memories, just without the emotions behind them, but he could sense my current unstable heart.

"I know..." I began, still hearing the pipes throughout our house swirling with lukewarm water as Mom's shower lingered. "There's no reason for me to be scared—Gaius and Ariela said so—but..." I blinked, feeling Ecuras' hooded face breathing down my neck. All muscles in my body cringed. "It's hard to shake off something like that..."

Taking on the role of my therapist, Tuff swiped on my orbkit without my permission.

"Hey—"

Using his little orange nubs, he swiftly popped out my refilled portal potion that Gaius asked Emunah for after my poor explanation of the draught. His little black mouth smiled as his stubby hands held it high in the air, whistling away, happy to see a grin stretch across my thin lips.

I giggled at his request. "You want it *back* in the suitcase?"

He nodded his entire plump body.

"Well... it did work quite well before..."

I followed my glainie's demand and pulled out my purple luggage. The moment I flipped it open, the water shut off... and Tuff flinched.

He dropped the vial in the suitcase, *barely* missing the corner.

We each released a deep breath, glad that the potion landed perfectly in the suitcase and not on the corner of my bed.

As I shoved the suitcase back under and picked up the loose clothing around my room—my mind needing something to do other than worry—Mom came to the door. Her long hair was soaking wet, dripping down her oversized hoodie, slowly leaving a raindrop trail from the bathroom to my room. Because my door was open, she didn't knock to invite herself in. *And* because my door was open, she saw me cleaning unprompted by her.

But she said nothing about that.

"You alright, sweetie?" Her voice was soft, and yet, it made my heart warm up and start throbbing.

I was cleaning and didn't care if my anxiety was showing through on my face, leaving my eyes wide and the corners of my lips sagged, and I didn't expect her to notice with all my pacing. But Mom simply had a knack for being nosy like me, taking note of every detail that was not the norm in our home.

When she said that, I hesitated before picking up my pair of jeans beside my beanbag. I wanted to say, *No—I was almost blown up, I got scolded by the King, I got the Prince in trouble, I've had weekly throbbing headaches lately, I have twenty-seven new scars across my stomach, and the Fallen has returned—*

"I'm fine. Just a long day at school," I said, half-lie, half-truth.

Mom had her towel in her hands and scrunched her caramel locks with it, drying them off with her head tilted. After she finished, not speaking at all or moving from the entryway, she crossed her arms with her towel squished against her chest.

Then, she stared at me. "You sure... you know, you can tell me if something is wrong, right?"

Am I that readable?

At that moment—the time it took for two heartbeats in my chest to pulse—I wanted to tell her everything. The lie before wasn't too hard to choke down, but now... I was looking at her... looking at the mom I love and who would do anything for her little girl. Lying had never been so hard. *I can make the earth move, Mom,* I wanted to say. *I've seen magic—real magic,* I almost yelled. *I have a little glowing sprite as my companion who is floating right next to you and have seen stars grow from plants, too. I even touched a star and got stardust all over my hair. Did you know they felt like little waterbeds and hummed in the air? It's real, Mom...*

But then, she'd see my scars. She'd know I fight. She'd know I got hurt. She'd know I have nearly died... and how does a girl ask her mother to let her go back to something like that? *How can I explain to her I'm fine when I am clearly not?*

Magic was the most beautiful thing in the world, and I couldn't tell her. At least, not yet. Not while Ecuras was out there.

The two heartbeats were up, and I blinked away the anxiety, followed by a slight smile. "I promise. Everything is just fine."

We continued with our night, watching a rerun of *Friends.* Mom still didn't know of magic, and because of that, I was able to enjoy at least one night without worrying about the future ahead.

42
FORTUITOUS

The fear of Ecuras returning finally eased by winter. Both Gaius and the Guardians weren't worried, seeing as Ecuras never made a recurrence again or was sensed by Zephan's magical radar, so I stayed calm as well. He couldn't find me, and I wasn't looking for him, and to be honest, everything just kind of went back to normal.

One thing that did change was monster hunting. Cal and I weren't just training anymore; we were doing actual missions with other Hunters. Our first one was with Ekron, and it was to stop some vorrgs on a small farm. We eliminated them rather easily, and even though we technically worked for the Kingdom, Ekron still gave us payment. Not sure if he was allowed to, but I wasn't complaining. It felt good to receive money for a job well done.

It was now early December, which meant snowy days in New Jersey and, surprisingly, in Boolavogue as well. Soft flurries were swimming freely through the air as Cal, Nole, and I returned from a hunt. Our senior Hunter was very quiet, only speaking when needed, but also courteous to both of us kids. We were sent to check out a tundrabeau sighting—a dark magic serpent-like wolf that comes out during the winter—up the far north mountain. It was also the first time we rode the Gora bears on our journey. Cal and I rode Honey, and Nole rode a brown one called Yune, our party making the trek up the incline twice as fast.

Once we found the tundrabeau—and the three others with it—Nole took charge. He was able to freeze their bodies, slowing down their speed, giving us enough time to kill them and release their magic back into the sky. Honestly, he could have done the whole thing by himself, but that was only because there were three.

"There's usually a whole pack of those things," he told Cal and me, riding Yune next to us as we entered back into the outskirts of the Kingdom, "which is why you were requested to join me. I don't mind, though. Made today quite easy."

We came to a crossroads where Nole stopped. "I have another hunt to take care of, so this is where I leave you both. Mind telling Captain our hunt was a success?"

"Sure thing," Cal responded, sitting behind me on Honey's back.

Nole smiled beneath his thin mustache. "Stay warm, you two." He grabbed the bear's saddle handles and headed right, riding Yune quickly down the trail.

I gave Honey a big rub on her head, hearing her tell me she was hungry. "Think we can stop for lunch or something?" I asked Cal. "Honey's starving."

"You don't have to use the bear as an excuse," he said, and I could feel his eyes rolling without taking a second glance behind me.

"I'm serious!" I laughed, turning around to face him before rubbing Honey's head again. "And make it somewhere warm."

"Did Honey say that, too?"

I tilted my head. "In a way..."

Cal's arm extended beside me, grabbing the front of Honey's saddle, and began steering her toward the left, straight for the Kingdom's main entrance. "Then, I'll be sure to grant her request."

We both rode our way toward the Inner City. Winter meant most of the streets were empty while the homes and shops were full of civilians. I was growing comfortable with the royal town; everything was squished together and always had something new on each corner.

After crossing the bridge, we dismounted Honey, and Cal walked her like a big dog going for a stroll. Boolavogue was so used to giant bears that Honey was nothing more than an oversized pet, welcomed through the streets with smiles, not screams.

The Prince soon stopped us at a large two-story restaurant. It was rustic with no visible sign or company slogan, and it had a large den in the back for bears—a legit area just for Gora bears when Hunters would stop by. It was rather kind of the eatery to think of the Kingdom's pets, even though the smell of the bears wasn't the most pleasant.

Inside was warm and cozy, bustling with families and sizzling entrees. Being that Cal was the Prince, he was offered a free meal the moment the friendly hostess recognized him. He refused politely and, instead, showed his Restricted Hunter license, requesting to be treated like one of the monster slayers. I, too, took my embedded tungsten tag off my belt and presented it to the hostess. She smiled and offered us free apple cider, the "Hunter's Drink," she called it.

Cal and I stayed for a long while, sitting at a table bar facing a large window. We could easily see Honey as she scarfed down a pot of mashed fruits and vegetables from the second-story seating.

Normally, the two of us spent time at the castle after training or hunts, talking with the other Hunters during breaks—which I didn't mind at all—but it was nice sitting alone with Cal—*again,* not a date; just two friends hanging out. He was very interested in "The Middle School" as he kept calling it, and why we hung up Christmas trees almost a month before the holiday even started. I never had a friend who was a boy and was so intrigued in my daily life before; I liked it.

"So, you really believed a big fat man with a red suit came down your skinny chimney to deliver you presents... with cookies as payment?" Cal asked, mid-laughter.

"Cal, you don't understand—*presents* were on the line!" I explained after taking a sip of the cinnamon-spiced cider. "I would've given a whole rack of cookies to anyone if they promised me a new game or toy—*even* to someone I didn't even know existed."

"He broke into your house from your *roof*—"

"I sent him a *letter.* It's not breaking in if it's welcomed, *Cal.*"

"Okay, fine. Guess, for four-year-old Lisa, that would be pretty convincing."

I slurped my drink, knowing I was *well* over the preschool age before I discovered Saint Nick's true identity.

Cal stared me down due to my silence. "Five years old?"

I just kept looking around.

"Six... Lisa, don't tell me you were *seven* and still believed a man from Earth had magical flying livestock?"

I muttered into my cup, "... Nine."

Cal shot into a dying laughter. "*Nine*—Lisa, you aren't serious!"

I turned away from him and stared out the window. "When the whole country is in on the act, it's hard not to be convinced... "

When I took another sip of my apple cider, nerves tightened around my heart. I became alert, tense, and nervous—the same scary feeling I would get before fighting a dark creature. Looking behind me, I saw only happy customers. To my right was only Cal. *Why am I so—*

That was when I turned to the window again and saw someone outside standing a block away. I stared for a moment, hoping my brain just mistook his blue velvet cloak for someone else's, but when I saw him turn around to talk with a shop owner across the street, chills pricked up my body and my breathing grew thicker.

No mistaking that face... It was him. It was Ecuras, right in the middle of the Kingdom.

I abruptly ducked down, almost knocking over my hot cider, so only my forehead and eyes were visible from the window. *This... this can't be happening right now.*

"Lisa, what are—"

I yanked Cal down with me. "I just saw Ecuras. Right across from that clothing store."

We both peered out the window together, slowly inching our foreheads above the high-top table. Cal squinted his eyes until the blue velvet-cloaked man turned toward us.

Ecuras was smiling away, chit-chatting it up with a couple of Boolavogue residents.

"How did he know to come here?" I whispered worryingly as if Saraqiel's vessel could hear me from across the street.

Cal exhaled and clenched his fists. "He probably figured out I was the King's son and came here... I'm sorry, Lisa. It's my fault."

"It's no one's fault," I told him.

Suddenly, Ecuras started to leave our view from the window. Though I was utterly terrified, the Fallen being in the Kingdom was not an opportunity to pass up. But... I was with Cal. *I can't let him get hurt because of me.*

The Prince suddenly jumped from his seat, threw some money on the table, and put on his coat. "Come on—we have to see where he goes!"

I grabbed the cuff of his jacket. Before blush bloomed on my face, I retreated quickly and whispered-yelled, "But Cal, what if he sees you—"

"Then we will be sneaky," he said in the same tone. "I'm not letting you do this alone."

I sucked in a deep breath, not arguing with the Prince or his burst of chivalry, and followed him out the door. We headed toward the street where we last saw the cloaked man and kept near the walls of the buildings.

Off to the right, there he was, walking casually and not drawing attention to himself. *Is he asking about me? He has to be, right?*

"He's going down Sorglan Street," Cal said, exiting our hiding spot. Right as he stepped one foot out from the corner, I grabbed his arm—yanking him back into the shadows with me.

"Wait," I exclaimed in a brisk whisper. "If I'm near him... he will sense my magic and start attacking again, and if you get too close, he might recognize you."

Cal looked toward Ecuras, who was almost out of sight, and then back to me. His hazel eyes were serious, staring right into mine without any wavering. That fourteen-year-old boy wrapped in a royal winter jacket was gone. "I'll go," he said like a warrior. "I'll turn myself invisible and follow behind him—"

"*No way!*" I quickly interjected. "What if he catches you and you get hurt—"

"My magic is getting better, and he's in *my* kingdom. If something were to happen, there are enough Hunters on every corner that he would be slagged and pinned to the ground before he had time to blink."

My mind didn't like the idea one bit... but knowing why Ecuras was in Boolavogue was something we, the Guardians, Ariela, Gaius, and I, couldn't afford to miss.

Cal gave me a grin. "Don't worry, Lisa. I'll be back here as soon as I get enough information. No way am I letting this man hurt my people or you again."

Ecuras then turned a corner.

I nodded at Cal. "Okay. I'll try and talk to those shop owners and get more information, too. Be safe."

The last thing I saw from the Prince was his confident stare before he turned his whole body and clothing invisible, running off to do what I could not.

He's gonna be fine... Now, just gotta go talk to some strangers and not seem suspicious asking about a random man in a blue cloak. No big deal, right?

I tucked my hands into my coat pockets and my long hair into my toboggan, not wanting anyone to recognize me just in case Ecuras retraced his steps. I walked into the clothing store where I saw Ecuras exit earlier. Burly winter jackets and trousers for men and women filled the display window, and a shoe polishing station was near the back. *Pretty up-scale shop... does he think the Prince shops here or something?*

"Welcome," said the man at the counter. "Looking for anything in particular?"

No one else was in the store as I scoped the place one last time. *Well, since you asked...*

I strolled to the counter, acting as sweet as possible and avoiding any wary behavior. The man wore the same fancy dress as the store mannequins, painted with sun-kissed skin and dark wrinkles around his happy eyes. "Actually, I am looking for my, uh... uncle—yes, that's right. He's wearing a blue cloak with a kind of velvet material. Do you know if he came by here?"

The cashier believed my lie wholeheartedly. "Ah—you were the one he mentioned. Well, I'm happy to tell you he is also trying to find you! Though, he believed you to be with the Prince of Boolavogue—how funny! He just went around the corner not two minutes ago."

So... he is looking for me... and he knows I was with the Prince...

I continued my act, even though my heart was banging a barbaric beat. "That's great. Did he happen to mention anything else—uh, just in case he isn't around the corner?"

"He only asked if the Prince had a girl he normally trains with up at the castle, saying he was looking for her—" His chin tilted as his eyes surveyed my face. "Wait, could that be you?"

My chest throbbed even heavier. "N-no, no, no, of course not. He—my uncle—must have gotten one of my friends confused with the Prince. He doesn't get out much..."

"My apologies, then. Wouldn't that be something, though—to see the Keeper's trainee right here in my shop? That's what they are saying about that girl anyways, but it could be all hogwash. Not seen either to know for sure... oh, you were looking for your uncle—right, just head off to the left, and he should be up the road."

"Thank you, sir," I concluded and rushed out the door.

I went left at first, just to make sure the cashier saw me, but once out of view, I immediately returned to Honey at the restaurant. My mind was building up worry quickly as I walked toward Cal's Gora bear. *If that cashier heard rumors about me being a Keeper's student... then, that means more people probably know. What if Ecuras discovers it's Gaius?*

At that moment, I crouched down near Honey's warm tummy as she napped, remembering what Gaius told me about his century-old pupil. I knew Gaius said he wiped Ecuras' memory about the Wishing Stars and Calendula... but that didn't mean he couldn't have rediscovered it again.

I shook my head. *No way—Gaius is way too powerful for Ecuras to recover his memories. But him being here...* I sucked on my lower lip, pressing hard with my teeth. *Why is this happening—Ariela said I had more time...*

Out of thin air, Tuff appeared and cradled up to my chest. He sensed my worry and wanted to give me company, reminding me I wasn't alone. There wasn't much he could do since he was startled by even the Prince, but I did appreciate my little sprite's comfort. I hugged him tightly, waiting for Cal to return, hoping to receive some useful information.

He's fine. Cal is just fine... if something happened, the Kingdom would be in a frenzy right now... yeah—no way Ecuras hurt him... right?

After about twenty minutes, footprints barreled down the alley, straight toward me. My face shot up from the ground, staring into the hazel eyes of the Prince. I instantly jumped up, still holding Tuff in my arms, feeling a weight lifted off my shoulders. *He's alive. Thank goodness...*

"What did you find out?" I asked.

The Prince came close to me and Honey, very out of breath, probably due to the amount of magic he had to use to stay invisible for so long. "So, I... followed him, right—store after store—and every conversation was about... trying to find the 'girl who trains with the Prince,' which is obviously you... Then, he ran into some Hunters—Lisa, I do not blame these guys, for this Ecuras man has a way with words—and they told him... told him you were Gaius' trainee. But that is a good thing—"

"What—how in the world is that a good thing?" I exclaimed, causing Honey's chin to jerk up from her nap at the abrupt change in tone.

Cal looked at me without a speck of worry on his face. "Ecuras' look changed—he looked scared. Lisa... he thinks because you're Gaius' student, you're powerful, especially by the way the Hunters talked about you. I don't know much about the Agapéd Magic, but in his eyes, you are *invincible*. After that, he stopped asking questions about you and started going around the city... almost like he was looking for something. He went near some of the mobile traders—the ones from Calendula near the main square—and followed a couple out of the city. I'm not sure why though... that is when I came back here."

I took a second to think about the new information, pacing back and forth... putting together the pieces I knew of century-old Ecuras and new-evil-doer Ecuras. He followed those Calendulian carts, which most people don't even know are from Calendula. *What would he need that they sell... Not like they sell glints or other magical stones, only plants.*

My eyes widened, pretty sure the Prince of Boolavogue was giving me a blank stare. *Wait... he is looking for plants. Magical ones—*

"He's not just here looking for me..." I rubbed my face as the puzzle pieces slowly fit together. "I don't think he was ever looking for me in Boolavogue; I was just in the wrong place at the right time. He wants the Wishing Stars. That's what he meant back at the festival when he said he was searching for two things. It wasn't just me... but the stars, too."

Cal furrowed his brows. "Lisa, what are you talking about?"

"Look, besides Ecuras being the Agapéd Bearer before me, he was also Gaius' student. He wanted those Wishing Stars before, and now, he still wants them, and to make things worse, he also wants the Agapéd back—*his* magic back—or wants to destroy it, because he *also* knows that's my purpose: to defeat him. 'I'm searching for something forgotten,' is what he said right before he attacked me. Gaius wiped his memory about the stars years ago, but it seems he figured it out again, makes sense why he was in Fladden, to begin with."

"And him following those carts must mean—"

"He found out they are from Calendula, but he was banished from there, so there's no possible way for him to enter again."

Cal squinted his eyes. "When you say banished..."

I blinked rapidly, throwing my hands up as if to help explain my point. "Banished as in his being cannot physically cross over to Calendula. That's what Gaius told me. That hidden veil can stop anyone from entering, just like it can conceal an entire civilization and nullify evanescing."

"Then, why go looking for a hidden city he knows he will never find?"

"I don't know..." I stared at the dirt and rubble as I retraced my pacing steps. "But we gotta go tell Gaius, and you will have to tell him what you heard." I was about to evanesce us when I remembered there was a 1,000-pound member in our party. "Um, I don't know if evanescing works too well with bears, so—"

"You go, then. I'll take Honey back home. Plus, Tuff saw the whole thing, so he can, like, do his 'memory thing' if Gaius doesn't believe you, right?"

Tuff whistled to the Prince, agreeing with his statement.

"Guess you're right," I said, watching Cal mount his pet.

He grabbed the saddle's sturdy reigns. "I'll tell Captain you got called in for magic training so he won't get mad at you for leaving early. Lemme know what happens, okay?"

"Sure thing."

"See you later, then. *Fara!*" the Prince called, commencing Honey to escort him back to the castle while I began to evanesce myself back to Calendula.

———

Gaius slid back into his chair at his woodworking desk, facing me, not his whittled weapon. Tuff's memory concluded, and the Keeper stayed silent, breathing deeply throughout its entirety. His eyes kept to the floorboards below when the glainie returned to my shoulder.

"Your actions were reckless and could've gotten the Prince killed, you know that?" he asked in a deep tone, still looking toward the ground.

"Yes, sir... I know," I responded, fiddling with my fingernails.

"But..." He let out a sigh. "It was clever. We now know his agenda."

I perked up. "So, what does this mean, then? He can't get me or the stars if he can't find Calendula. I'm still safe, right?"

The sun from the only window in his workshop beamed through coldly, illuminating the dust that wandered around the room... but Gaius stayed quiet.

He scratched his nose, rubbed his face, moved his hand on his knee, and glanced at every single sword in the workshop—all the habitual thought-provoking gestures he normally showed when he was thinking hard.

Suddenly, he rolled his shoulders and neck as if an answer he had come to caused him discomfort. "The night of the Wishing Star release... he's planning to come then."

Blood began to pool away from my face, my nerves growing anxious. "Why then?"

"It's the only day during the year when the veil that covers Calendula is lifted in order for Kamari to guide the stars into the sky. It's when I'll be preoccupied and... most importantly... when you'll be vulnerable."

Gaius stood up, crossing his arms and pacing the room. I trailed alongside him.

"He knows if I'm with you, the stars are exposed... and if I'm with the stars, then you'll be unguarded... but we have the upper hand. He doesn't know we know any of this. He's going to prepare until then, but so will we."

"So... that means I'm gonna have to... fight him... right?" I said, my breathing growing unsteady. A cold sweat started to trickle down my back in rivulets, followed by clammy, rattling hands.

"Beginning of spring here—end of April back on Earth." Gaius' words were a sharp blade and pierced straight through my heart.

I couldn't hide my nervousness anymore, my thumbs permanently red from all my nicking. "But—but that's only five months away! I thought I had more time—like years. I thought he wasn't strong enough. Can't the Guardians fight him or something?"

"Their magic is powerless against the Fallen Elysian magic. Lady Ariela made it that way before she knew the Fallen could reincarnate into the hearts of Man."

She told me that before, but—*Please tell me that isn't true... please tell me there is another way...*

"What about you or Inna or—or someone else?"

Gaius pivoted, focusing on my petrified face. His stare was not the same serious look I'd grown used to seeing. It was different as if something was aching behind his pensive eyes. He bit back his bottom lip as I saw his throat bob up and down. Aching words were dying to spill out, but he did not want them to. This demeanor of his was strange, as if—

Is Gaius nervous? Or is he upset—conflicted maybe?

He uncrossed his arms with that same solemn stare toward my face. "Why your magic is so special Lisa... why it is our only hope... is because the Agapéd is the *only* power that can destroy the magic pulse of the Fallen. And Ecuras knows that—he knows you're the only thing that can stop him, and he will do everything in his power to prevent that from happening."

My eyes kept switching between the green peridots on Gaius' face, and I could feel the tears begin to emerge—beginning to linger on my eyelashes.

The fear in my heart was evident, but Gaius continued, though it was hard for him to look at me. "I will be there, but I cannot kill him without you first destroying his magic pulse, for there, Saraqiel is bound—intertwining with Ecuras' heart and soul... You're his only weakness—the only thing that can shatter Saraqiel's magic, reducing it into nothing more than dark powder. Anyone else who tries to kill him will just destroy the body, allowing his magic to escape into another, continuing to grow stronger and stronger with each new heart it homes, or—given Ecuras' endurance for life—could keep him immortal even if someone tries to fight him..."

"B-but I can't—I can't fight him—I'm not ready... what if I fail and—and he not only gets me but also the Wishing—"

My teacher knelt on my level, grasped my shoulders hard, and stopped my trembling. His eyes were steady—a crisp, sharp green—and completely immersed on me. He spoke slowly and with grave solace, not a tone meant for a child but for a warrior. "When we are in battle... most likely, Ecuras will let Darkness consume him—discarding his body in exchange for a sinister dark magic vessel. He won't be human after that, but he will become incredibly dangerous. That is when you take your hand..."

Gaius moved his right hand and placed his palm on the front of my winter jacket, right where my heart was.

Its thumps were fast, and I knew he could feel my anxiety with each pulsing beat.

"And you grab his heart." He curled in his fingers, a swishing sound coming from the scratched fabric. "You release all the magic you can, right there into his chest, as powerful and as strong as you can make it. You do *not* stop, not even if your arms and legs are begging you to. You give it all you have... every last bit of yourself until the magic pulse in his heart is nothing but ash... The moment you do is when I'll take my sword and finish the job... this is what you were made for. I need you there, because without you..." His tone changed, softening. "Darkness will destroy everything. And Lisa, you cannot fail. We are relying on you."

I stood there in Gaius' workshop, though... I didn't even feel as if I were there. My mind was so consumed with the future; it was as if it was already that night of the battle... and I was scared. I was *really, really* scared. I knew I had agreed to this, but... there was no way I could destroy his pulse—get that close to him and destroy his heart without dying myself. I was weak and barely a novice at magic—*how on Earth am I supposed to destroy the heart of a dark-infested man in just five months?*

I had no words to say, in fear of having tears of doubt start pooling from my eyes like waterfalls. My face was burning up, and my knees could barely support my body weight, even with both of Gaius' hands back around my shoulders. I knew he could feel it—could see it on my doe-eyed, freckled face—but I couldn't hide my fear. *I can't do this...*

Before panic completely overtook me, Gaius clutched my shoulders, pulled me toward him, and embraced me.

I had never hugged him before... and his chest was so warm. His hair smelled like cedar wood, and his arms were strong around me, refusing to let me go. It was the most comforting hug I had ever received... and it was given right when I needed it most. I never felt more protected in my whole life than I did right there in his arms, and it was hard not to start crying.

As he hugged me tight, he said in a calm, rescuing tone through my brunette locks—lassoing my heart before it fell into a pit of despair, "You can do this... and I will be right there with you, fighting alongside you. I'm not letting you go. You will destroy his heart... and Lisa, you will win. You and I will live to see the stars, I promise you that."

He released his arms and gave me a soft smile beneath his tan cheeks and boxed facial hair. Green sparkled in his eyes, glistening with the confidence he had put in me. "Until then, we will train hard. He won't know we're coming... but we will be ready. No worrying, okay?"

I took a deep breath, able to push back my tears, and faintly returned the grin. "Okay."

But still... deep in my heart... It was hard to believe the words he said because it was hard to believe in myself. *Can I really do it...?*

43
MY FAULT

"And what's *your* sweater supposed to be?" Lily asked John Peters as he came and sat across from us in Mr. Abernath's class, flicking her blonde hair off her shoulder, eyes halfway opened and appalled. He was wearing an ugly Christmas sweater covered in smaller ugly Christmas sweaters. It was truly the most unattractive piece of clothing I had ever seen, making it the perfect one for class.

"Uh, it's called *The Winner*—I don't know what you're talking about. You didn't even try!" he said back to Lily, looking down at the minimal snowman print on her Mom's oversized sweater.

I wasn't surprised, though; Lily would never attempt to wear anything ugly, even if that was the theme of Mr. Abernath's Science Christmas Party.

She rolled her eyes. "I don't care if I win. I'm passing the class already with an A, so I don't need any extra credit for wearing the ugliest Christmas sweater."

"It's part of the *fun*. See, even Lisa tried: Santa with some sunglasses while drinking Coca-Cola. Perfect," John Peters said, admiring my sweater.

I was scared about wearing it to school, but I didn't feel as silly since everyone was doing it. John Peters taking notice made me a bit happier, the first time he talked to me the entire semester. I was surprised he even knew my name, and it should've lightened my spirits... but that was impossible. "Oh, thanks," I said to him, nicking the sleeve hem of my sweater underneath the cover of my desk.

Even though it was the last day of school before Christmas break, I could not bring myself to be as hyped up on the holiday cheer as the rest of my class. Every day since Gaius told me about Ecuras' plans, I'd been living in fear. I thought Christmas would release me of its grasp, but not even a class party filled with hot chocolate, pizza, and ice cream could cheer me up one hundred percent. I wasn't moping around or throwing some pity party. I was still able to grin and be happy... but not the kind of happiness that was genuine. That emotion was walking a tightrope in my mind, and with just a subtle breeze of worry or nudge from a self-induced nightmare, it would slip and fall to the floor. And it would take a while before it was well enough for it to fully walk freely in my heart again—before it could cast true bliss and joy across my face.

Right then, even, it was struggling to balance.

Smiling was nothing but a facade as I sat hunched over in that wobbly school desk knowing I would have to fight Darkness in just four months, despite having a Keeper by my side.

"Hey, my mom is still picking you up from school today, right?" Lily asked, taking a drink of her mildly warm hot chocolate.

"Yeah," I responded, my words growing quieter with each new syllable. "Thanks, by the way... since Mom had extra hours this week and couldn't make it."

"You know my mom doesn't care to—you're like her favorite of all my friends. You could sleep over on a school night, and Mom wouldn't care. Oh, by the way..." Lily took a bite of one of the Christmas cookies she had stuck into her vanilla sundae. "I'm thinking of taking gymnastics starting in January. I wanna be on the cheer team when high school starts next year, and I kinda have to know how to do a backflip. Are you gonna join a sports team or something? I mean, you could try out for cheer, though I really don't think you'll be able to make it if you can't do a backflip."

I was surprised she was already thinking about high school, but then again, that was something normal to be worried about. We, the eighth-grade class, were halfway through our final year of middle school, and it wasn't like we had anything better to do than to daydream of being out of this confinement filled with little pre-teens. At least, that is what ninety-nine percent of the students— and even the teachers—were thinking.

Me, I had more pressing things on my mind other than something as trivial as cheerleading. "I don't know yet... I think I'll just wait until then before I decide."

"Hm—suit yourself."

———————

The end of school came quickly due to the two Christmas parties and movie marathons in the other classes, celebrating the end of our first semester of eighth grade, and I was riding back to my home with Lily before I knew it. Her mom was kind enough to drop me off at my house last minute since my mom wanted two weeks off for Christmas just like me, which meant staying later than normal at the office.

Once their pristine silver car drove away, I didn't jump into pajamas, grab a snack, or watch TV like normal. I slugged my backpack on the couch, almost knocking off a Christmas tree ornament, and shuffled my way to the kitchen. Anxiety was sagging on my face due to the silence in our house. Normally, Mom perked me up, but with her gone and just me—

My back slid down the wall near our backdoor until I squatted on the fake-tiled floor, waiting for my magic self to arrive with Tuff. I didn't bother to change out of my Christmas sweater—the cotton getting snagged on the specks of unsmooth paint on the wall—hugging my knees as I felt my heart pounding against my thin legs.

Why am I so scared about this? Gaius has been training me well, and he will be there when I fight Ecuras... I hugged my legs tighter. *But what if... what if things go wrong? What if I don't—*

My fingernails scraped along my jeans as my hands curled into fists. *Stop it, Lisa—it's not for another four months. You have plenty of time to—*

The backdoor swung open, early—way before it should have. Cold winter wind blew in without warning, waking up the quietness of the house.

It was me, smelling like vorrg drool and covered in muck. Nothing about that was unusual. Until I saw magical me's face. When she looked down at me squatting on the floor, only did I realize something was off. It was her eyes and freckled cheeks that shocked me, blotchy red and covered in fear.

I had been crying, and I wasn't finished.

Magic-me didn't say anything, so neither did I. About to burst into tears again, she simply touched the shoulder of my Christmas sweater, and that was when everything began to make sense.

———— ᘒᘒ ————

The ferna vorrg was the worst creature I had ever fought, being a hybrid of a vorrg and some other dark beast. It looked more goblin-esque in the face, with black human eyes and double rows of protruding teeth in its jaw. To make things worse, I wasn't doing well the whole week with my beast battles. Gaius had me fight an array of dark creatures outside of my hunts assigned by Ekron, most of which were just for pure practice, and I felt as if I wasn't improving. Beast after beast, I was almost scratched, bitten, and poisoned to death on multiple occasions. I couldn't even be proud of my wins—how could I when Gaius was always there to help me? Some Hunter I was turning out to be...

I slammed the snow in front of the ferna vorrg, hardening the frost into a wall of ice, but the panther-sized monster used its sharp claws to shred right through it. I looked back at its nightmare-ish face as its moldy green body ran faster toward me. Quickly, I shot up spiked pieces of Earth toward the monster. Bullets of rock pelted its skin, causing it to slow. *Time to strike its neck and send its magic back into the earth.* I swiped the snow along the ground and froze it around my hand, swirling it until a sharp sword formed. I ran toward the monster when all of a sudden it lunged toward me—black magic blood pouring from its wounds and all!

Not part of the plan!

I instantly evaded to the left, but because the ground was slick, I went up and *slipped*—fell flat on my back. *Lisa, you idiot!*

That was when the ferna vorrg jumped on me.

I instinctively swung my ice sword right toward its grimacing mouth, watching its teeth grab the thick icicle—hovering inches away from my face. Its breath was horrid, like a musty attic scattered with mildew spores, and my arms could only hold its body above me for so long.

"*Gaius!*" I shouted, sensing my strength giving way.

Cracks began to form on the icicle from the beast's strong jaw gnawing down.

"*Gaius, please help me!*"

I then tried to move my foot to use magic, but the ferna vorrg stepped right on it, causing me new pain in my leg.

I stared at the ghoulish creature's face as its sticky drool fell on my chest. *Gosh—it smells like rotten meat!* I had both arms holding up my icicle weapon when all of a sudden—

Crunch!

My magic weapon broke as the ferna vorrg's teeth punctured its surface.

NO!

I had not even a second to think as fear began to control me. My head sharply whipped to the right, and I attempted to swing my arm forward, but like lightning, the monster bit the hood of my coat and slung me out of the way— straight for a sturdy tree. I was a loose skipping stone, sliding on the mucky snow until I hit a wall of scratchy bark.

My head flailed back hard on a root stuck in the ground as my spine took most of the impact from the birchwood tree trunk—bruising too much of me even with my winter jacket on. Everything went black for a moment, my mind barely able to remember what had just happened. When I opened my eyes, I only saw a menacing monster hurtling toward me. I had no time to think of a plan or escape, only enough time to cover my face with my hands. Utterly petrified and defeated.

A loud skin-shredding sound burst in front of me, and it was not from my body. I removed my shaking hands to see Gaius, his giant green sword inside the beast's body. The Keeper, wearing his walnut winter coat and leather gloves, removed his weapon from the body of the ferna vorrg, We both watched as the creature became black magic dust—dissipating into nothingness.

I was happy to be alive, slowly sitting back up on my knees... but I couldn't express it outwardly seeing as Gaius had a solemn look on his face.

He was upset, saving me yet again.

My mentor put his sword back in its sheath along his back. He didn't help me up, just went for the magic eggs he hurriedly placed on the ground, and muttered, "You know you can't let it get on top of you like that. Be glad it slagged you against the tree instead of ripping you apart." His tone wasn't too sharp but still nicked at my heart like a dull blade.

Frustrated, I got up slowly and took off my slobbery jacket, trying to hide the ache going down my spine. My coat was soaked since the ferna vorrg's spit wasn't attached to its body before Gaius annihilated it. Unpleasant in all forms of the word.

"It's cold," Gaius said, obviously advising me to keep my jacket on while checking his basket to make sure no eggs were cracked. Luckily, they were all a golden color, the size of cherries, and unblemished.

Ignoring his concern, I put the jacket in an empty slot in my orbkit. Being cold was better than being sticky with monster slobber, though some spit was still dampening the ringlets of my hair.

Normally, I would ask why he needed the strange eggs, but I didn't really care. I failed the mission. Gaius killed the monster I was supposed to hunt *and* still got his magic eggs. He didn't even need me there...

Can we just leave already... I didn't want to be there any longer.

Gaius stood still. "What's wrong?"

I sucked in the frigid air. "You had to save me again," I answered, feeling bad I had to even admit that to him.

"Just stay on your feet next time. Keep the high ground."

I muttered quietly to myself, "... I'm never going to be strong enough..."

Gaius handed me his basket of golden eggs. "Strong enough for what?"

Is elephant ears a part of his magical powers, too?

I couldn't just stand there without saying anything, so I dropped my shoulders, gripped the basket, and spoke up. "I couldn't fight a stupid monster, needing you to save me... Cal had to save me back in Fladden..." I bit back my lip, my words growing angrier and softer, "... and I couldn't even save Valhalla... so how am I supposed to save the whole world?"

A heavy jacket fell on my shoulders as my watery eyes looked down at the eggs. It smelled like tonka beans and wood, warming me up instantly; Gaius' scent never seemed to change.

"I told you that night with the vezper wasn't your fault—"

"But it was—"

Instantly, tears started filling my eyes as I unintentionally let my emotions take over. I hid from Gaius' stare and avoided making any more noise. *Gosh, pull yourself together, Lisa.*

Gaius didn't preach at me or pressure me to talk, only continued to walk forward in the cold with only a thin long sleeved shirt to warm up his arms.

I think he knew it was the frustration talking... or he truly was upset with me as well. Or he just didn't want to deal with me sulking. His emotions, though, remained hard to read as always, even after knowing him for half a year. *Why am I still so pathetic...*

The muscular gardener looked through a couple more trees for the golden eggs, finding only a dozen more to add to the collection. The tip of his nose burned red, bitten hard from the cold as he put the last magic oval on top of the rest I held. *He really needs his jacket back... he wouldn't have had to give it to me if I wasn't so careless.*

While I stared at the glistening blonde eggs and the dirty snow floor, Gaius held his arm toward me. I thought we were evanescing away, so I pressed the basket against my chest and used my free hand to grab his forearm.

Nothing happened. White trees and sloshy snow still surrounded us.

"Lisa," he said, my hand tucked loosely through his arm, "why do you still blame yourself for that day?"

Not a question I thought he was going to ask... and not a question I wanted to hear.

"I don't know," I said, but I did know. *It's because I wasn't strong enough.*

"You should go and visit her family."

Please stop telling me things that are impossible to do...

I took a deep breath. "I don't know how..."

His words were not weary like mine, sincere and deep. "You need to say goodbye and stop letting this self-inflicted fear burden your heart any longer. You won't be able to battle well if you see failure and weakness as the result before you've even swung a sword."

I didn't respond for fear of crying again. *Am I really fearing failure because I think I'm too weak? Is that what this is? How will saying goodbye to my best friend heal this gut-wrenching, guilt-festering pain in my chest?*

Gaius said one last thing as he began to muster up his evanesce magic. "When we get back... take the berdabee's seeds back to the incubation wing of the Veradome... Once you're ready to start practice again, come and find me. I'll be waiting."

I took a long walk through the Veradome trying to find the incubator wing, carrying the large basket of berdabee's seeds. I was surprised to know they weren't eggs—seeds don't usually have something jiggling inside them like gelatin—but I guess it would be weird for a greenhouse to store tiny animals. I walked up to the second floor after an herbalist gave me directions, which I didn't ask for; my face must have looked really, *really* lost.

Inside the room were many unusual seeds behind glass chambers. Some were watered with snow, while others were heated with boiling brown liquid. I even saw a couple being licked by butterflies. Not sure what butterfly spit did to a magic seed, but watching it raised the corners of my lips—only slightly. I continued my way inside the yellow-lit room until a worker stopped me and took the basket away, giving me a hardy "thank you" before taking it to the back.

I decided to take a stroll around the Utopian Floor. My heart needed a break from the Keeper and anything that brought up memories of my poor magic and Hunter skills. The way he told me to find him when I was ready made me think he wanted me to "think about my actions" or something before seeing him again.

So, while I walked through the indoor forest and magical gardens, I did what he said... which only lasted a few minutes before my mind found other more interesting things to think about. When in the Veradome, it was hard to think of anything else besides all the hidden magical qualities of—

"Lisa?"

I heard a startled man's voice say across the row of red cabbage. I was so deep in thought, wondering if the crop was magical or just a normal head of cabbage, that I didn't recognize his voice.

When I glanced up, Mr. Balthier stood on the opposite side of the produce row. He looked the same as I remembered, except a little thinner—which could have been because of his mustacheless face and trimmed black hair—and without a smile. He was utterly stunned, gawping at me with his purple eyes, and flushed from all colors of pink.

My heart became stone and thudded to the floor, and my eyes were now one blink away from letting loose salty rivers. Emotions bubbled up inside my stomach—feelings I couldn't even describe. Feelings I never, ever, wished to know. I wanted to hug him and escape his gaze all at the same time, tell him how I've missed him and yet how sorry I was for everything I did.

The Veradome was so big, and I hadn't seen him since summer—not since I last saw Valhalla. I didn't want to see him, not after everything I did to their family, no matter how much I knew I should.

So... I ran. I pretended I never heard him say my name in his worried voice or that his eyes ever met mine. I backed away quickly, almost knocking over a botanist in the process.

"Lisa, wait!" I heard him shout, but I dared not look back, and my steps became wobbly as I sped up.

I can't face him. I can't. Not after all I did to him and Emmeryn. Their broken family—it's—it's all my fault.

I brushed through the crowd of workers, maneuvering through them fast as if my life depended on it. I didn't know if Mr. Balthier was behind me or not—I didn't have the guts to check—letting fear be my driving force forward. I ran faster and faster, feeling a blinding spotlight on my back with each new stride. They all were staring—all seeing me cry. I hated it but deserved all the shame I was getting. *I need to get out of here!*

As soon as my hands reached the giant glass entrance doors, I pushed them open and ran for the town. I didn't care where I was going—anywhere was better than facing my guilt inside that greenhouse, pathetic as it was. When I made it across the concrete bridge, I tried to find a corner to hide in—a place where I could just sit down and cry—but I had no such chance.

Remorse refused to let me get away until I saw *her*.

Dressed in a warm winter jacket and loose slacks, carrying a boxed dinner for her beloved husband—Mrs. Balthier was coming up the road straight toward me.

My breathing was not human—not consistent or deemed healthy.

No. Not her... I—I can't do this! I can't—

"Lisa, is that truly—" Mrs. Balthier began to say, her purple eyes glowing, shaking with her words.

The time for running was gone.

I had only one choice, and I didn't care who saw.

I turned my blotchy red face away from the kindest woman in the world and toward the empty face of panic. Blue magic filled my fist while I turned around, and I ran, punching the sky with my hand. *Send me home, please!*

When the lights and chimes faded, I was in space on Kamari's planet, almost tripping over my shoes.

I hate these stupid magic rules—just send me home!

I immediately reached for the Aura Beacon when I heard the old Keeper's voice call from up on her front door. *"Na so—Lisa, what be da rush?"*

I didn't look. I was tired of the stares—tired of everything. I hated it *all* and just wanted to be alone.

When the light turned green, I scurried toward the middle of the sigil and evanesced away one last time. *Please—just please, send me home!*

Snow was beneath me, freezing my fingers and knees as I hit the ground on all fours—struggling to regain my balance. I never loved the icy winter of New Jersey more than I did at that moment. I was in the forest of my yard, officially and utterly alone.

My heart, though, still wasn't sure about it, hearing the winter birds and squirrels all around. Whispering. Darting me with stares. *Sometimes, I hate having the ability to understand what they are thinking—*

Seeing the snow, the trees, my Boolavogue boots—I could have sworn a ferna vorrg was right around the corner. Anxiety was billowing in my gut. I was on Earth, but my mind was playing tricks—toying with me—not letting me forget my mistakes. *I need to get home—to my room—to anywhere but here—*

I pathetically ran toward the back of my home, saw no lights on, and slung open the door.

To the right, there I was, wearing the tackiest Christmas sweater with my legs pulled up to my chest. My doppelganger looked sad, but nothing compared to the torment swirling around in my heart.

She didn't say anything to me, staying confused as to why my face was red. So, I simply touched her shoulder, and she disappeared.

Now, I not only had the pain of Valhalla's death in my heart but also the fear of fighting Ecuras. To top it all off, my head pounded hard—reminding me of the price I had to pay for wanting both a magic life and a normal one—as I walked up the steps to my room.

The moment I shut my bedroom door, it was like I shut out everything around me. No one was coming in. Not a single person could see me—judge the self-induced guilt splattered on my face. My heart and mind were finally free.

That was when I melted into a small ball on the floor, squatting on my feet and hugging my knees. The emotions from that day in the cave—that day Valhalla's life slipped away—finally fully resurfaced.

I wish—I wish they never, ever did.

Barriers were down. My overheated face quivered.

And I *cried*. Shameful, guilt-stricken tears gushed and gushed and gushed.

Two of the sweetest people in the world became nightmares in my mind that wouldn't leave. I could only see the shadow of regret every time their loving faces reappeared, causing me to make water stains all over my pants and pitiful moans croaking through the room.

Tuff soon came out to comfort me, but not even his good-hearted touch could make me stop hating myself. Still, I embraced my little sprite as I sobbed in the corner of my bedroom... releasing every bit of heartache in the form of salty tears.

———

Thirty minutes had passed before my crying subsided and my chest stopped rattling. I wasn't better by any means, but I was okay enough to get up and change into something comfy—not smelling of vorrg—before returning to the same spot on the floor. The tears had stopped, and my heart had finally settled down. My emotions were worn out, leaving my throat scratchy and dry, so I was able to relax as best as I could.

Tuff was sitting on my lap as I played with his little hands—watching him glow, spin, and whistle; it was nice having him with me. Even though my soul was feeling better, I knew it wouldn't last very long. I had to go back to Calendula eventually... and I knew I had to confront my fears.

Rickety ticks of the garage emerged from downstairs, along with the sound of the laundry door opening to the kitchen.

"Lisa!" I heard Mom shout. "You home?"

Tuff then turned himself invisible, leaving me alone in the room to answer Mom's call... but I didn't. I couldn't in fear of my voice cracking and her coming up the stairs.

Like the nosey mom she was, she came strolling up the wooden steps anyway. I listened to her movements. She didn't go toward the bathroom. She didn't go into her room, not even to change. Instead, she approached my door, which my back pressed against.

I should have known she would do that, but I hoped she wouldn't have cared about her daughter's silence today.

Her shadow breathed beneath the crevice, her feet at a standstill. She definitely saw my silhouette at the base of the door.

Mom knocked twice, using one knuckle on her finger. "Lisa... are you okay, sweetie?"

I gave a sniffle as my answer since words would only produce more crying.

Mom slid her back against my door frame. She sat on the floor behind me and waited... waited until I was ready to answer her question.

I thought intently. *Very* intently.

I wanted her advice and company, but I couldn't tell her about magic, especially not in a circumstance like this. Lying seemed the easiest, but for some reason, I couldn't do it. Not in my unstable state. And something was tugging at my heart telling me not to lie to her again.

I gripped my knees, pulling them in tighter. *What do I do?*

I thought... and thought and thought. At that moment, sitting in my room, I wasn't crying because of Gaius getting agitated with me or because of my failure at killing a dark creature. I also wasn't utterly tormented by the thought of Ecuras and needed to be told "it will be okay" to feel better.

What upset my heart the most—what had been eating away at my soul for five months—was the fact my best friend was gone, and I refused to believe it until I saw her parents today. They solidified that she *did* exist and that I tore her away from them. Ripped apart their family.

All I wanted from Mom was comfort for that.

My knees cradled against my chest, so when I spoke, my voice hit the tear-soaked material and muffled my speech. "So, uh... during summer... one of the friends I made... She died... and today, I saw her parents... but I couldn't go see them and just... ran away from them."

Normally, Mom would sit outside until all the emotions were gone. Not this time. She cracked open the door, cueing me to shuffle to the wall. When she walked over and looked down... I started crying again, and her face was just as sad as mine. She immediately met me on the ground and hugged me—my arms, legs, and everything else. She didn't preach to me or ask what happened. She simply hugged me and let me cry.

I didn't expect so much sobbing to happen in my bedroom that day. I would've grabbed the tissues from downstairs instead of using my knees and hands.

"I'm so sorry, sweetie," Mom said on repeat, holding me tightly, her voice sounding as sad as mine. "You don't deserve to know that pain yet. I'm so sorry."

Mom sat there for who knows how long, waiting for my tears to stop. She was nice like that and didn't say a word. I had no pressure to talk or explain my reasoning for why seeing Valhalla's parents made me so sad. I didn't even have to explain what happened—why it took five months for it to finally sink in.

I could just cry until I was finished.

When I was finally able to speak, my voice crackled—hoarse and broken. "I'm just sad and—and I don't know what to do... like what if—what if I could've saved her?"

Mom didn't question my choice of words. She squeezed me firmly, brushing away my damp hair from my heartsick face. "I know that it's hard to lose a friend, and I hate that there is evil in our world, but you can't let it consume you, sweetie." She paused again, still hugging me tightly. "Was your friend nice?"

Another sobby sniffle came... but so did a subtle grin. "Yeah. The best, actually. She really liked being around me and could make me laugh." I couldn't see Mom's face, but I felt her smile as her cheeks perked up and pressed against my wavy hair.

"Then, that's how you will remember her, okay? I know now... it may seem hard to only think of the bad things. But from now on, when you think of your friend, only think of the happy times. After a while, that's all you will remember. Your friend would like that, knowing you're happy... I know I would."

"I think she would like that, too," I mumbled, finally letting a true smile escape at the thought of Valhalla being happy. "Sometimes, though... it's hard not to think about it, especially when I go to bed... been having nightmares about it lately..."

At the sound of her daughter's plea, Mom sprang into action. She got off the floor and extended her arm out to me. "Come on. I will show you what always works for me when I'm sad—bring your MP3 player, too."

Mom started walking downstairs as I rapidly grabbed my MP3 player from my backpack, not bothering to question her strange behavior. When I caught up to her, she had already opened her work laptop on the table with both our music libraries pulled up. Normally, when I asked Mom for music, she would put my songs on my playlist labeled "Lisa's Tunes." This time, however, she had everything opened. *What is Mom doing right now? Kind of a weird time to be downloading new songs.*

She held out her hand. "Let me see your MP3 player."

I gave it to her, and she quickly plugged it in. Without my permission, she just dropped bucketloads of songs onto it—I didn't even have time to see what they were as she was scrolling through the music library at lightning speed.

Everything happened so fast—so abruptly. But it distracted me from all the tears minutes before, leaving me to guess if that was her goal or if there was a reason behind this...

"Uh, Mom... why the random song downloads?" I asked her, watching as my MP3 player tried to keep up with the oceans of new tracks being added to it each second.

"You want to stop your nightmares, and the best way to do that is through music—good music, at that."

I couldn't help but chuckle, feeling the dryness of my tear-stained face crinkle. "But I have music already—"

"But for days like this... you need *real* music. The kind of music that makes you feel good, picks your heart back up, brings that smile back on your face, and gets you through the night—as you were requesting."

I softly laughed. "So, 'Mom Music' is your answer, then?"

She huffed, her long caramel hair falling off her shoulder. "Uh, your 'Mom Music' is the best music of all time. And now..." She then handed me back my black MP3 player, still warm from all the sudden songs added to it. "It's going to be *your* music. Before you go to sleep, just give a couple of these songs a play, and you'll have good dreams, I promise."

I opened up my music library. At the very top were bands I only ever heard of but never listened to because they were old. Like, older-than-the-internet old.

"'Aerosmith, Air Supply, Bonnie Taylor, Chicago...'—Mom, I thought you said this was supposed to calm my mind. How are Rock n' Roll and 80s pop music supposed to do that?" I said, continuing to scroll alphabetically down the list.

"What do you mean—this stuff will 'soothe the soul,' just like you were wanting."

I rolled my eyes playfully. "Okay, I will listen to them as long as you stop talking like that."

She turned in her chair. "Like what?"

"Trying to sound 'cool'—half this music is older than me, by the way!"

"Some are older than me, too!" She shrugged. "Think about all the people who've listened to them to ease their sadness. That's what makes them so good— finally, you'll be able to jam with me in the car—"

"Mom, *please stop!* You sound ridiculous!" I laughed, feeling already a hundred times better. I knew Mom said the music would help, but honestly, I just needed her.

As she closed her computer, she noticed the time on the microwave. "Shoot—I forgot about the Christmas party tonight for work." She turned her head to face me. "Sweetie, I can miss it if you want me here. I'll just tell them to save my bonus check until after vacation, and we can stay up late and watch whatever Christmas movie you want."

I was about to say yes, seeing as watching *Elf* or *Christmas with the Kranks* sounded more fun with her there to laugh along with me, but then, I remembered there was something I needed to do. I now had the strength and courage to finally face my fears.

"Actually, you should go. I kinda want to be alone for a bit longer and listen to some of your music if that's okay?" I said.

She pressed off the chair, creating crescent blue moons with her eyes. "Well, I won't stay long—in and out fast, I promise—grabbing the check and some food, possibly some Christmas karaoke if Jamie brings the discs this year, and then, I'm home with you."

As Mom rushed upstairs to throw on her cheesy Christmas sweater— the same one as mine but in green instead of red—I sat patiently on my bed. When I heard the garage door close, I jumped, threw on a clean Earthian coat, and laced up my sneakers.

Tuff came swirling up next to me as I zipped up my jacket and held out my fist of blue magic.

Time I finally did what Gaius told me to do.

44
SHE WAS HAPPY

I landed atop the cliff like normal, only with a different view of the farmlands of Boolavogue. It was dark and snowy, and beams of orange lights flickered in the town. The Kingdom's nightlife was not something I got to see very often. Cold shadows loomed over the homes and sleeping cattle from all the trees, and cosmic metal hums of the avelift stirred even from a far distance. No yelling or sounds of beasts, not even a Gora bear roar.

The land was quite peaceful, with faint trickles of moonlight, barely making the hills visible in the distance. Maybe I just didn't notice it before, or maybe it was because my heart was starting to feel the same way.

When I turned around toward the hidden Veradome entrance, I saw a man sitting on an old stump. My heart jumped at his presence.

A light glint in his palm, I could see his stoic, manly face. Even in the dark, his bright green eyes could not be missed.

"Gaius... why are you waiting outside in the cold?" I asked my teacher.

He slowly got up off the stump and examined me in my non-Boolavogue attire, noting my face wasn't as glum as before. "Said I would be waiting... So here I am."

He truly was the best teacher an Agapéd Bearer could ask for.

I made a slight giggle. "You didn't have to wait outside in the cold though—how did you even know I would come through this entrance?"

"Because..." He walked right up to me, the light glint radiating lemony beams in his hand. "You still need Ava and Asa to help you find the other one, and you don't know where the other two are in the Veradome. Hence the clifftop."

"There are two more inside the Veradome!"

Gaius smirked. "Neither of which are meant for wanderers like yourself."

"Well, thanks for waiting for me... but I can't stay very long. Mom's expecting me soon, and there's something I have to do."

He raised an eyebrow. "Does it have to do with the commotion earlier on the Utopian Floor?"

I took a deep breath through my nose and exhaled. *Figures he already knows—everyone probably does. Who wouldn't gossip about a girl running rampant in the middle of a workday?*

"Yeah..."

"You alright?" he asked, genuinely, fiddling with the light stone.

I nodded. I think he knew what I was feeling, too. "Mhm... finally ready to talk to them. I shouldn't have waited so long."

Gaius began to lead the way inside the Veradome. "They will be happy to see you. Here. Take this." He then gave me his light glint, still warm from being cradled in his palm, glowing as bright as a flame. "It gets pretty dark during the winters when farther from the town square. If you need anything, send Tuff or evanesce to the Veradome. I'll be here."

I glanced up at him, care brightening my teacher's once concerned face. "Thanks, Gaius. I'll see you in the morning, ready for more training."

With his warm smile and a nod goodbye, I parted ways with the Keeper and began my venture toward the Balthiers.

The tram stop that took me up to their neighborhood was the same as always, though it was something I hadn't done in over four months. It felt weird going back up the incline. The scrapes of the steel railing had me do a double take behind me, cueing memories of me and Valhalla waiting inside and gripping the metal poles to keep our balance—I almost thought she would be there. All the brick houses covered in light snow and less greenery were the only things new to me. Winter was pretty in the neighborhood, and I regretted missing the chance to see what Autumn was like.

Had to admit, my heart was racing with each step down the road, but it was the good kind of beating; it meant it cared for the people I was about to see again.

When I approached their front door, I noticed their welcome mat and assortment of empty planters were missing. Before I knocked, Tuff joined me, sitting on my shoulder and letting his orange glow reveal all the paint specks on the door. He gave a little hoot of encouragement, sensing my nervous thoughts swimming through my mind.

I knocked three times, and in about ten seconds, the door creaked open.

It was a complete stranger.

My heart dropped—sunk beneath the cracks of the wooden patio—as I stared at the unfamiliar middle-aged man dressed in jeans and a gray T-shirt.

We exchanged glances for a second, his going back and forth between my eyes and Tuff's and mine going back and forth between his thick mustache to his not purple pupils. *Who is this man?*

The stranger spoke first. "Can I help you?" He sounded very confused as to why a teenage girl was at his front door in the middle of the night with a glowing tangerine on her shoulder.

"Um... I just uh..." I started talking, but I was so confused. "Isn't this—I thought this was the Balthier's home? Do you know if they live here or..."

His brown brows rose. "Oh, Roy and Emmeryn? Yes, they just moved about a month ago and sold their house to me and my wife. Sorry, they didn't tell you. They aren't too far, just up the road a good ways. House number 17, I believe—whichever one has the stone fence covered in lunavines. You can't miss it."

They moved?

I thanked the kind man and followed his directions, using my light stone and Tuff as my glowing guides.

With each new step on the road, I thought about why they moved. *Did they plan to the whole year? Was it a last-minute decision? Was it because of Valhalla?* I let out a shaky sigh, causing Tuff to start whistling a comforting tune. I had to stop the guilt from eating me alive again. Their moving had nothing to do with me, probably just wanted a newer house—possibly with more storage like any normal family. That's what I kept telling myself, at least.

A few minutes into the dark winter night, I saw the stone fence with the lunavines. The blue leaves grew quite well in the cold, emitting a faint azure color.

This is it.

Acidic jitters churned in my stomach, and my hands became horribly sweaty, stuffed into my coat pockets. A string was tugging my heart, bobbing it between my throat, one jerk away from releasing the dam of tears. *Lisa, do not start crying. You've done enough crying today to last you a lifetime.*

I walked up to their porch, which was much bigger than the one at their last house. There, the empty planters near the door and the same welcome mat sat. I could hear my heart beating through my ears as I knocked on their new door. *Wait—what do I say? Should I like... I don't know. What if they are busy or in bed or—*

The door opened swiftly, and it was Mrs. Balthier, wearing her oven mitts with her black hair tied in a messy bun; she looked as kind as ever. Not a word came out of her mouth. When her purple eyes saw me—not even taking a second to comprehend her long-lost foster daughter from Earth standing at her new home—Emmeryn threw off her kitchen gloves and hugged me tightly.

The moment I heard her sniffle through the waves of my hair was when I started tearing up, too. I couldn't help it; when I heard someone cry, I had to join in the sea of emotions.

My voice cracked first, seeing I could no longer contain myself, sniffles and all. And what came out was from the depths of my soul, simple but painfully heartfelt. "I'm sorry... I'm *so* sorry..."

I wanted to get more words out, but nothing but sobs, sniffs, and apologies pushed through every time I tried.

Mrs. Balthier squeezed me tight and softly spoke, her voice breaking yet sweet, "You have nothing to be sorry for, Lisa. *My*—we have missed you so terribly. I am just so glad to see you alright."

It was like my mind couldn't control my heart, and I just started spilling out what I had been bottling up since summer. "But—but it's all my fault... I couldn't save her and—and because of me, she's gone. I'm just—I'm just so sorry."

Mrs. Balthier looked at me, brushing away the rivulets of water from my cheeks, and she was smiling with tears still smudged around her eye wrinkles. *How can she be smiling right now? I'm the reason for her heartache—her sorrow—her broken family—*

"Don't you dare think that," she said to me. "Because of you, she was happy."

I stared up at her all glossy-eyed, more confused than before. "But if it wasn't for me—"

She hugged me again, probably to stop me from saying something that wasn't true. "Lisa, I know it's hard... gosh, we miss her so much..." Her arms clutched me tighter, getting her fingers caught in my long hair. "I'm just glad I didn't lose two daughters that day."

A daughter? They... they really saw me that way?

"How—how can you say that after all I did to your family?"

Emmeryn released the hug and cupped my face, her shaky hands grew steady the moment I felt their warm touch. The purple in her irises glistened with the moonlight as I sniffled too many times staring up at them. "Lisa, we could never be upset with you. Both of you were simply trying to help the farmer... trying to do what was right... even trying to prove to those Guardians you were strong enough."

I stood owl-eyed. "You... you knew?"

A gentle, breathy laugh seeped through her lips as a tear fell down her cheek. "Valhalla always did have a horrible time keeping secrets and could never seem to grasp what a whisper truly meant... But most of all, you made her life one filled with happiness. You made her feel so incredibly wanted. And there isn't anything in the world a parent could want more than to see their daughter find a friend like you..." She hugged me again, saying through my hair. "What befell... dear, it never was your fault. So, please, stop blaming yourself. You are alright here, Lisa."

The kind of love Mrs. Balthier was showing me... I didn't even know it existed, and I didn't deserve a single crumb of it. It was pure and true, making my heart react with nothing but tears and rapid beats. *How can she still smile at me when I am the reason for her daughter being attacked in that cave? I am the reason they can never be a whole family again... so how can she still love me?*

I didn't hear his footsteps, but Mr. Balthier's tall, skinny frame stood still at the door, probably wondering why his wife was letting in the icy air. He didn't bother to shut the door or ask why it was left open; once he saw me in between his wife's arms, he immediately embraced us both.

The family I had feared was now hugging me as if I never left... as if I didn't cause death to take their only child... and my heart couldn't fathom their overwhelming compassion. *They... really love me... even after all I have done to them.*

After all our tears had dried and our hugging stopped, the Balthiers invited me inside their new home. Their furniture was all the same but in different places; everything seemed eerily familiar. Still, it was cozy and had the same smell of freshly baked bread running through the air.

"We had planned to move a little over a year ago," Mr. Balthier explained. "Valhalla liked the view from the hillside, and when this house came up for sale, we immediately took the offer."

"But we held off moving once you arrived," Mrs. Balthier chimed in, "and the Clements—the ones who owned the house before—didn't mind us waiting. Was well worth it, though—being able to have you stay with us in the home before it was sold."

The boxes in the old home—all the clutter pushed against their walls—that was because they were planning to move... way before I even arrived. It wasn't because of Valhalla's death. It was because she wanted it—they wanted it. Not because of me...

"I enjoyed being with you..." I said, peering into all the hallways and rooms as they passed me by.

Just then, a small table caught my attention in a little corner at the end of a hallway with a perfect window view of the town below. Next to a potted plant with a little green sprout was a picture of Valhalla. Her black hair was still crazily long, blurry at the ends from her bad habit of not being able to sit still even for a picture.

Missing someone that was never coming back was a surreal feeling, and seeing her smiling almost made me start crying again. Though my heart ached, I did as Mom had told me: "Think of the happy times together."

Mr. Balthier noticed I had stopped. "That is her corner—has the best view of the town." His words washed with gentleness as he spoke.

I followed him as he went to the little memorial. Upon closer examination, I noticed that the plant growing in the pink ceramic pot was starting to bud into a yellow flower.

"Normally, there would be two burials for someone who deceased outside of town: one in a proper cemetery and one at the place of passing," Mr. Balthier began to explain as he looked at the plant, "but in Calendula, since our town is so small, we honor those who are gone by using their ashes to grow a seed… Yellow chrysanthemums were her favorite… We do this because, even when their time with us may seem finished, there can still be a life that blossoms forth into something beautiful again."

I then noticed next to Valhalla's photo was the note she gave her parents… the note that was a lie. Chills ran up my body just looking at it. They had it stuck in the frame, a small piece of loose paper with her bubbly handwriting smudged on it:

Taking Lisa out tonight to celebrate her two-month "I Finally Learned Magic" anniversary!
Be back later!
Love, Valhalla

I picked up the picture when Mr. Balthier said calmly, speaking from the heart, "Even though she wrote that for a different reason… we still believe she planned on celebrating with you afterward…" He put his hand on my shoulder, causing me to look back up at his becoming-red face. "Lisa, she really loved having you as a friend. You might be surprised, but she struggled to make friends in her classes. It hurt us to see her unhappy, cooped up in her room, wishing for a better life—reading all those excerpts about Heroes and Hunters all day long."

"Really? I never knew that…" I knew she didn't spend time with other kids, but I didn't figure it was because she struggled with it. Thought it was just her choice…

Mrs. Balthier nodded. "When she found out you were coming, she perked right up and was thrilled to find out you had so much in common. You made her happy, and we were glad to see her that way." She breathed deeply, calming her emotions from the memories flooding in. "And I know if she would've known the dangers of that night, she still would've gone because… well, she just loved being around you… She wanted nothing more than to see the Hero you'd become." Emmeryn wrapped one arm around Roy's waist as he hovered his chin over her silky black hair. "And we are so thankful to know that her last days with us… were joyous ones because you gave her the happiness she so well deserved. Lisa, we love having you here, and you are always welcome, just want you to know that."

All the pain… all the guilt, regret, sorrow, and the boatload of other emotions I didn't know the names of vanished in that little hallway of the Balthier's home. I didn't think Gaius would be right… which was silly of me in the first place. I thought they would hate me or resent me… but that was just my mind feeding into fear. Seeing them happy… seeing life still go on—love still growing—made my mind at peace again, and I knew I would be just fine.

"I just made some honey scones minutes before you arrived—would you like to stay for tea or something to eat?" Mrs. Balthier happily asked, but I knew I couldn't stay no matter how tempting the offer of her freshly baked pastries was.

"I would love to, but I have to get back to my mom—but I promise to come by and visit more," I answered.

"You are welcome anytime, dear."

They watched from their front door as I stood out in the cold, beginning to evanesce away. My heart was happier and *definitely* done with tears. Their peace latched on to me, and I knew I could fight better, sleep more soundly, and think of Valhalla with calmer thoughts after that night.

<hr />

Like always, I had to stop on Kamari's planet before teleporting through the Milky Way, only, this time, she wasn't at her house. When my feet hit the glowing sigil below, I heard her quick voice from behind me.

"Never seen a Mage move through da galaxies so much in one night."

I jumped in place and turned around, looking at the Keeper of Stars with her arms crossed and standing near the Aura Beacon. Her dark braids and dreadlocks were all bundled up on her head, and vast amounts of purple cloth hugged her old small body.

My shoulders dropped. "Sorry, tonight just was a little—"

"Crazy?"

I nodded. "Yeah."

"But yo'r all betta now?"

I smiled—a true, genuine smile, finally content. "Mhm."

"Then, dat is good to hear. Just take it slow wid da magic, abi? It needs rest just like da bones in yo'r legs afta a run."

"Yes, ma'am. I promise."

She then backed away from the beacon still with her warming smile on her face.

When I touched the stone lamp to make it glow green, I arrived back home in the forest, immediately going to my room.

To my surprise—after changing into my oversized sweatshirt and Christmas pajama shorts—the laundry room swung open. I walked down the stairs, expecting to see Mom in just her cheesy Christmas sweater, but instead, a whole party was in her arms. Grocery bags full of candy, cookie dough, frozen chicken wings, pizza rolls, and a gallon of chocolate milk were all being carried in one trip.

"Sorry I am late, but I couldn't bear being out having fun when you were here by yourself," she began, wobbling toward the kitchen counter.

I helped her grab the milk before she dropped it.

"So, I stopped by the store and grabbed everything for a perfect Christmas movie night—even scored the last copies of *Home Alone* 1 and 2! No one is being sad before Christmas, okay? I'll put the food in if you start the movie—oh, care to close the garage door for me? I couldn't reach the button."

I was never the person who would initiate a hug, but in that kitchen, my heart was consumed with so much love for having a Mom like her that I had to give one.

She dropped her purse on the table, and I wrapped my arms around her. "Mom, you know you're the best, right?"

A breathy huff left her lips as she squeezed me tight. "Well, obviously— you deserve the very best, and *I* deserve this junk food. The party had *terrible* 'hors d'oeuvres', no one could beat my high score on karaoke, and that new punk accountant with the big ears would *not* stop staring at me—and do not even get me started—"

Mom continued to ramble while we enjoyed our party of two that night, the first time I had belly-laughed and felt at peace in such a long time.

45
STRENGTH OF LIGHT

"You mean, it's like a festival?" I asked Gaius as we walked down the Kingdom's lively streets, heading toward the castle.

"The biggest one here," he answered, trying to avoid bumping into the people on the sidewalk.

It was now only two weeks before the Wishing Star release. Boolavogue was blossoming into spring and, to my surprise, was also getting ready for the magical migration as well. Citizens were building parade floats, costumes, stage props, games, merchandise—anything and everything to celebrate the stars. From inside the Kingdom, it didn't seem like a battle would happen in just a week. That was a good thing, according to Gaius. The fewer people knew, the less likely Ecuras suspected anything, and it would give us a better chance at fighting.

Many vendors displayed star-shaped plushies in their windows, and my eyes widened. It just hit me, and I felt pretty stupid for not thinking about it before—

"Wait, so you mean all those stars in your greenhouse—all the ones Kamari is going to guide toward the sky—will be flying *over* the Kingdom?"

"Like they do every year," he said, gesturing for me to veer toward the alley on the right.

"Do they shoot up, or is it more, like, 'swim' to get to space?"

He huffed, raising the corners of his lips slightly. "A bit of both. Slow enough for us to admire them but swift enough to challenge a hawk's speed."

The alley we walked down was free of ears, and I looked down at the crackled stone path. "So... you think when we are done fighting Ecuras... we can come to the Kingdom's festival?"

Gaius didn't respond quickly or give his usual smirk. His eyes were bothered, given the pause in the conversation. "When the battle is over... you may go. I'm sure the Prince will be there as well."

Thought he would be happier talking about the magic he spent months growing...

I didn't look away from his face, though he refused to look at mine. "But, it's your big night. Don't you wanna celebrate, too?"

He swallowed as his eyes surveyed the crowd ahead. Whatever was on his mind ate at him like worms on a farmer's crops, causing that confidence he always had to waver with softened eyes.

Then, he reached out his hand to touch my shoulder but retreated, curling his fingers before his palm hit the side of his pants. "We'll see."

There were more words he wanted to say, I could see them clogging his throat. Maybe he was nervous, too—given what would happen in two weeks. I know I was, no matter how much I prepared.

Over the past four months, I trained—each day being as brutal as the last, but I was improving. I worked with Inna, getting the hang of freezing and unfreezing water so I could make ice whips and surf on beams made from the dew of the morning mist. Even though she wasn't a fighter, she helped me understand my surroundings, and I saw my agility increase drastically. Her compliments were always encouraging, which also contributed to my self-praise.

During the days with Ekron, he didn't hold back on me or the Prince. He sent out beast after beast, ensuring we could adjust to whatever situation might be thrown at us. I worked less with a true sword, using my terrain magic and the purple dagger that Gaius gave me instead. Ekron didn't mind, just as long as I came out of a battle without too many scars, which my body grew less of a collection of.

Gaius—every morning, no matter how late he stayed up—would work with my offensive training when it came to using magic in battle. His lessons were the most important. My terrain magic wasn't puny columns rising from the ground anymore. I was lifting boulders and slicing rocks in half without breaking too much of a sweat. We sparred, and he never allowed me to breathe, always surprising me with new attacks. I didn't complain, though, because I knew, in a true fight, the enemy would not go easier on me simply because I was a kid.

Throughout winter and the beginning of spring, I saw my magic grow. I didn't tire as easily, my magic replenishing quicker and holding out for longer. My body didn't look as muscular, but I could see a bit more definition in my arms and calves; nothing to boast about, though. Still small, pale, and freckly.

I could feel in my heart, too, that the Agapéd was finally doing what it was meant to do. The bond we had—not too sure how to explain it—was sturdy like a mountain. Magic was a part of me, and I felt myself becoming a Hero.

Along with all our training, the Guardians were keeping up with Ecuras—at least, they were trying to find him. He was never spotted in Boolavogue again, and according to Gaius, Zephan couldn't sense Ecuras' presence, which meant he still wasn't very strong. Gaius said his disappearance in the Kingdom was a good thing; it meant he still had no clue that I or Cal knew of his plan.

And today, we were to finalize our plan with the King and Queen.

Gaius and I finally reached the front gate of the castle. The walls of the immaculate building were also decorated with Wishing Star decor. Yellow flowers replaced the white ones, resembling the star's shine, and gold and sapphire banners embroidered with celestial designs dangled along the white wall's edges. Knowing the King and his... personality—this had to be Leonora's idea. I very much liked it.

Captain Arond and two other guards greeted us at the large front entrance. We were supposed to be on a royal waiting list to see the Sonons for today... but Gaius either didn't know what a waiting list was or refused to acknowledge the existence of one. The Keeper showed up two days before—right in the middle of my practice with Ekron and Caelum—and said, "We're meeting with the King in two days. Be ready," and went on his merry way. Then, five minutes later, Ekron received notice that *his* meeting with the King and the Royal Court was postponed to the following week.

I don't know what he said or did, but here we were: walking through the marble halls, passing by the galleria of oil paintings with Captain Arond as our guide.

As my eyes wandered, they naturally turned to Gaius, and I noticed something different about the Keeper. It had nothing to do with his grass-stainless shoes or his new sage-green garment; it was his hair—a small, thin strip of it on the locks above his ear.

On my tiptoes, I whispered to him, "Gaius... are you dying parts of your hair white or something?"

The Keeper chortled at my remark and whispered back, "It's called mortality, Lisa."

I knew his heart was mortal, but I forgot that also meant he would now be aging, too. I felt bad for pointing out his oldness... which raised another question. "So, if you're not stuck at 700 years old now, how exactly old are you?"

"We've got a battle coming up, and you're more concerned with my appearance?"

"Well... at this moment, yes."

He paused, making sure no other guards or Arond could hear. "Then, let's just say... I'm still young enough to be considered a wise fool."

The one time I want a blunt answer, he goes all "Kamari" on me...

I ignored his statement. "So, what? Like the forties?"

"I'm not Ekron old just yet."

"Mid-*thirties,* then—"

"Lisa..."

I couldn't help but chuckle at Gaius getting upset over being called old—*he's outlived millions*! "Okay, okay—sorry I asked. But, for what it's worth, you look good with little strands of silver mortality in your hair."

He didn't say anything back, only subtly grinned after rolling his eyes.

The door to the Throne Room was then opened for us, and right in the middle of the room—not on their thrones—were the King, Queen, and Cal. I was not expecting the Prince to be there. He wore clothes similar to his father's, a simple blue and white garment with no dirt stains or weapons attached.

Gaius and I walked toward the center of the room, him taking long strides while I had to fast-walk to keep up. Like always, the Keeper spent no time talking of the weather—straight to the point—as did the King, and he brought up our plan.

"The night of the release," Gaius began, "Ecuras will make his way to one of the far ends of the forest. He's no fool and knows not to enter your kingdom during that day, and I don't believe he has any intentions with your land—only with Lisa and me and the stars. He knows if he were to involve himself with you, he'd be taken down quickly by the hand of your Hunters. We don't know which end he will enter, so I request that you invite the neighboring towns to attend the festival. Decreasing the number of civilians in town will decrease any casualties that could possibly occur. I'll keep everything as close to the Forest Outskirts as possible, but the fewer eyes watching would allow the battle to proceed unnoticed—as if there was never one to begin with."

King Bolthor scratched his bearded chin, deep in thought, as his wife responded in haste. "All neighboring towns? All the way toward Fladden and past Raglan, too?"

The Keeper's arms were crossed. "Hire more guards and keep the Hunters out around the Kingdom's border if you must make room," Gaius answered.

Bolthor Sonon simply nodded. "I will have a notice sent out immediately... The Hunters from Captain Clover's team will see the borders stay safe and the Forest remains empty."

The King didn't go against Gaius' request or ask questions—it *amazed* me, given how he didn't care for the Keeper taking his son out monster hunting with us. Though Bolthor seemed very particular about how his Kingdom worked, he wasn't naïve. He knew who Gaius was—knew he had battled more wars and animals than he ever could in his entire life. If anyone knew what was best for the Kingdom, it was the muscular gardener on my left side.

I figured he would agree, but not that easily. *Seems he and Gaius think a lot alike: quick and to the point...*

Before the Queen could say anything in response to her husband's rushed agenda, *Cal* interrupted the balmy agreement. "What—you mean we aren't going to help them?"

Speaking without being asked was not in Cal's nature, especially to his father. Bolthor was a bear dressed in royal blues and whites and terrified the Prince, a grimace from his eyes could rattle a mountain.

The King was also surprised, his hazel eyes looking down toward his son. He let him finish.

"Shouldn't we be the ones protecting our kingdom and fighting Ecuras, not sending Lisa to do it instead?"

Wait, me? He's worried about me? I didn't think even Lily or Jenny Kim would have ever said something like that. They cared for me but not on the level of distress from Cal's voice.

"This is not our battle, son," the King responded solemnly.

"But he's been in our kingdom and—"

"A war over a single man who wants nothing from our kingdom's people would be a fool's play." The King glared at his son, his voice, surprisingly, not as loud as it was during our summons about Fladden. He was merely informing Cal of something he didn't seem to grasp. "It is Gaius and Lisa's battle... not ours... Calendula may be under our name in secret, but they are their own people. Most importantly... the work of the Keepers and Guardians is out of my control... and that includes Lisa. We are to remain independent, out of the way of the Protectors of Light and Healers of Darkness, revered only as Hunters. They were chosen to protect magic; we were chosen to protect our people. This is why they are here..." He looked to Gaius, only this time, with a fire in his eyes—a demand. "And they will succeed. "

Cal went silent, shutting his mouth, and looked right at me before staring toward the floor.

I was given this magic because Darkness was coming in two weeks, and Gaius was given the role of a Keeper to protect the stars. We were just doing our job, essentially. If others didn't need to get involved, then the King was right. Putting his people in danger of something that we were meant to control was ignorant... even if that meant a two-versus-one battle with a little girl on one side.

"You're right... I'm sorry, Father," Cal breathed out, uneased.

I appreciated his care, so I spoke up, grinning. "Don't worry. Gaius and I can handle it."

Gaius concluded the meeting. "Everything should go as planned, and I'll have the release the moment night falls. Once the stars are high," he looked down at me for some reason before staring into the hazel eyes of His Majesty, "Ecuras will be gone, and the neighboring towns may be returned. A sky full of stars will be your signal of our job's completion."

"Then, we will await their shine... may The Light be with you both."

Time seemed to speed up, along with my anxiousness—feeling the emotion move back into my nervous system like a virus as it hit the one-week mark before

The Battle. No matter how much preparing Gaius and I were doing, I knew there would never be enough time to teach me everything. The Guardians even were growing troubled—they weren't even the ones going into battle!

Gaius evanesced me to Haim Gana, where I was on my way to visit Micah per the Keeper's request. Gaius said the Guardian wanted to teach me something "new," but I could tell by the way the Keeper's words softened that he just wanted to get my mind on something else... or maybe *his* mind.

Gaius... He had been acting odd as time inched closer to the day of the Wishing Star release—the day of our battle. We had grown a strong bond over the past year—training and living in the same house—and I finally could read *most* of his emotions, but during the past couple of weeks, he stayed distant from any talk about future plans with me. If I asked about the festival, he still said he wouldn't go. If I asked about new hunts after the battle, he would never say anything except, "We'll see." And during dinners or time not training, he kept our personal talks short, sweet, and to the point—a very *Vilmad* thing to do.

Maybe the thought of seeing Ecuras scared him... or maybe *me* being in battle and having to fight the Fallen did. I didn't ask for fear of pushing the wrong button on his stoic emotions. Whatever the case, it wasn't just me who was nervous about my first fight.

I was headed to the purple-silked Guardian's study when muffled voices of Alona, Bethesda, and Vilmad emerged from the room next to it. Those three together, I learned, was a rare occurrence, one that meant whatever they were talking about was indispensable information, cueing my essential eavesdropping. Though Micah was expecting me, he didn't know *when* I was coming... and this was more important: I heard the three mention my name.

Their voices were louder than the subtle squeaks of my shoes, so they didn't hear as I tiptoed next to the door.

Bethesda was rambling about something, but I only caught the end of it. "... Lady Ariela is thinking about this lightly, though the odds don't seem very favorable."

Alona talked next in her slow voice. "Well, he has been alive for years... Dayasheel believes his body is weak physically... but with Saraqiel's magic invested in his heart, it is allowing him more life and a strength thriving off Darkness."

"*Life*—if that is what you call it." Vilmad scoffed. "But I agree with you,

Bethesda."

"That's a first," Bethesda remarked, and I could feel her dark lips smirking at the long-haired Guardian even from my hiding spot.

"I see a fifty-fifty chance of this going well in the end, given the time restraint on the Agapéd, especially with Gaius involved," Vilmad said.

"Of success?" Alona questioned.

"No, no, no, no—she will *have* to succeed, even if the brute forces her hand into the chest cavity of Ecuras to destroy the pulse. I will not even place odds on the idea of failure seeing as no one has ever failed before—can't have that. I am meaning her *life*. We've seen strong human warriors battle vessels of the Fallen Elysian and succeed at the cost of their vitality. Now, Lisa will have to win, but to do that—I just don't see her heart being able to still gift life after giving all her strength to destroy Ecuras."

All breathing and blinking ceased, my eyes growing wide. *What did he just say... that I might die even after succeeding? But... but that can't be true—wouldn't they have told me something that important—something as important as my life?*

Bethesda's voice crept closer as she continued in conversation. "You are lacking all compassion today, Vilmad—"

"Truth and feelings don't belong in the same realm. I am just stating the obvious. I said there was *half* a chance of her being strong enough. Would be less if the brute wasn't with her."

Alona spoke again, her voice trailing nearer and nearer to the door, but I could not move. "Did no one tell her the cost of destroying his pulse?"

"Lady Ariela said it was best not to," Bethesda said. "She didn't want to scare Lisa, hence the whole reason for her training to be veiled in 'magic lessons' and not strengthening her magic for the death of the Fallen. Though, Gaius may have told her, since he has been training her fervidly since the discovery of Ecuras' plan."

I began to see the shadow of Vilmad. "Pity she is so young. Barely lived her life, and now, she will most likely lose it even *after* saving the worlds that aren't even hers—"

Bethesda huffed. "Look who is acting more human now?"

Vilmad clicked his tongue loudly, the shadow of his hair swishing with the silhouette of his body. "A *fact*, Bethesda. But there is nothing we can do but wait and hope they succeed without too much collateral damage around the Kingdom."

With Vilmad's voice approaching the door, I immediately tiptoed away, going into a corner to hide. They turned right as I continued left, feeling an unsettling emotion in my stomach. It wasn't anger or sadness billowing about; it was like... an irritation that made me want to cry and fight at the same time. Any battle with a beast or human meant risking my life; I just didn't know that winning would still be a gamble on my heart.

I furrowed my brows, leaning against the cold gilded wall. *Is this why they wanted a different bearer for the Agapéd... because they knew I probably wouldn't survive in the end?* No wonder they couldn't tell me the truth when I first walked into that gold meeting room. I was basically a sacrifice for a land and planet that I didn't even know existed until last year. *Beacon of hope,* the Balthiers said I was all those months ago... even they didn't know the true consequences of the Agapéd.

Memories from last summer kept sweeping in. My first day, Inna bought me all those nice things, the clothing, the orbkit—giving me gifts because she, too, knew of this. Ariela even let me stay on Earth with my mom—let me finish something as trivial as the eighth grade and use the Echo Ring to do it. They all wanted me to enjoy my last moments of life. I wasn't learning magic to be a Hero who stopped the Fallen; I was fattening up my heart with magic strength so I could destroy something they didn't have the power to.

Vilmad didn't even say whether or not I would fail either. He just said I couldn't, and the thought of Gaius forcing me to destroy Ecuras was bizarre— something I quickly shot out of my mind.

Gaius never mentioned anything either... Was this why he was acting so odd? He said I could go to the festival when it was over. Did that mean he thought I'd be fine? *"Don't worry," he says, but now... how can I not?*

I tilted my chin. Yes, I was upset, but I didn't cower away or have a desire to quit. That piece of information changed nothing. I still had to fight him and destroy his magic pulse, whether knowing death was a part of winning or not. All those stars—all the magic would shatter if I didn't stop it, another Age of the Black Sky reborn. Ecuras would win... and Gaius, Cal, the Balthiers—they would fall prey to Darkness. Ecuras would then use that power for evil. And they could all perish. Could all die.

I was their hope.

And their lives and the lives of others were worth it—all of it—no matter how scary it was. My life had a purpose, and it was for this. I would save them, even if that meant dying.

A deep sigh left my chest. *More pressure added to the lead weights already strapped to my back.*

Tuff came out from hiding once we made it clear down to the second floor. He floated before me, affirming that I was growing much stronger and would be fine. I let him stand in the palms of my hands.

"Thanks, bud," I whispered to my sprite. "You know... I don't feel like lessons today... Do you think Micah would mind if we skipped?"

Tuff gave a happy whistle.

I laughed. "If I just say, 'Gaius needed me,' then you're right. He won't even bother to question that."

I grasped the evanesce magic in my hands and began to head home, stopping by Kamari's house first. I figured I could talk with her with the extra time I had; she knew how to lift my spirits, even if it was just with a cup of pink tea.

When we landed on the teleporting sigil, the same purple and black nebula space surrounded Tuff and me. I saw Kamari gathering loose stardust from off her back porch. She still wore an absurd amount of necklaces, draped in violets, catching the star soot with her gravity axis magic.

Once we made eye contact as I approached the asteroid staircase, she quickly stuffed the rest of the stardust in her jar, shouting, "*Yami!* Hurry and get us some tea—make it quick or no stardust for you! Lisa is here!"

Kamari's excitement for my arrival—no matter how short-lived the visit would sometimes be—always made me feel happier. She knew how to make me smile and feel wanted, even though some of her phrases took a little more time to process in my head. Still, I loved being in her weird space home.

We both sat in her viewing room with the giant glass dome that looked out toward space. The orange loveseat was perfectly plump and squishy, way softer than Gaius' couch, and I happily took a seat as Yami brought me my cup of Verisweet. I had my warm mug of tea cradled in my hands, letting whatever thoughts and worries in my memories float to the top of my mind.

Kamari, with Yami in her lap—purple stardust swirling around in its belly—

looked over at me. "Ah, now, what be yo'r worry, Lisa?"

How did she know I was—

I accepted the fact I needed to work on controlling my facial emotions, but at that moment, it was too late. I responded to her with a simple slump of my shoulders and a blank stare into my cup.

Kamari continued to talk in her curiously kind voice. "It will make yo'r heart feel betta once da burden of your worry is spoken. Come now—tell me why yo'r face be as pale as da moon?"

I normally didn't tell people about my problems... I just didn't want to load a bunch of sad cargo on them like a freight train when they already had their own boatload. But, since Kamari asked, I decided it was alright.

I tapped on the side of my teacup and stared down at the loose leaves floating inside. "I have to fight Ecuras next week, which I guess you probably know about, and... I'm just scared. Like, what if I mess up or, you know, *die*—I don't know. Gaius said not to worry, but... I don't know how not to..."

Kamari shooed Yami off her lap, the purple anteater crawling away in silence, and sat beside me on the orange double sofa. "Ah... it be a mighty task you have, but Lisa, you have a mighti'a hand and heart by yo'r side. I know dat da Darkness be a scary ding—as it should be—but you have noddin' to fear. No matta how black da dark may be, da light will always be stronga. A single flame..." She put her arm around me, giving me a little squeeze on my shoulder, "... even one from Earth who may dink she is not bright enough... can still light up a whole room."

She put her other hand on mine, causing my glistening eyes to meet hers. "You want to save da world, right?"

I softly answered as genuinely as I could, "More than anything."

Kamari smiled at me. "Den you, Lisa, have noddin' to fear... for what power does darkness have ova da radiance of light? And what powa does darkness have ova you? Fear be but a pebble in yo'r shoe; it will only ache you for as long as you let it rest inside. You tell it to bug off—*ha!* You are strong, Lisa. You have a light—a heart—dat can make even da darkest day seem as bright as da sun as long as you keep lettin' it shine. Do not let da worry be yo'r weakness. Do you hear me, child?"

I nodded.

"Good. And when Gaius says not to worry, you best be not worryin'. He will protect you—but you don't need me to tell you dat, abi?"

I giggled. "You're right. I can do it... thanks, Kamari."

She then gave me a hug, one that smelled like cinnamon—no surprise there. Hearing what she said... I never heard words as wise as hers, and they hit my heart hard. My biggest enemy was myself... and I should've believed it when Gaius said not to worry. I have the greatest power in the universe in my heart and one of the galaxy's most powerful Mystics on my side. I knew all that... I just needed a star-loving lady from space to reaffirm it to me while drinking space tea on her couch.

I'm going to stop Ecuras, and I'm going to live to see the stars flying over Boolavogue. That's a promise to myself.

46
THE BATTLE

It was sunny and warm—the end of April. *The Day*... and surprisingly enough, my birthday, April 29th.

I was so consumed with the upcoming battle that I forgot until the day before... when Mom asked me what I wanted to do for "The Big One-Four." I haven't been a birthday party person since I was nine, and the idea of celebrating this year just didn't cross my mind. I had already planned a "sleepover" at Jenny Kim's as my cover for not coming home, so it worked out perfectly. I told Mom I was having a slumber party and would see her Sunday. I *was* going to see her... I wasn't going to die; didn't even want that possibility running through my mind. Normally, I would use my Echo Ring, but for this day... I wanted there to only be one of me.

Once I finished Fourth Period, I ran to the family restroom down the school hall and changed into my new garment: The Battle Uniform, I called it (it was just something new I specifically saved to wear for that day). Inna was nice enough to buy me new clothing during one of our lesson days, taking me into the town of Mantene to go shopping. The outfit consisted of a lavender hem cape cloak that buttoned at the neck, a darker pastel purple shirt underneath, navy blue shorts, and dark brown boots with sturdy soles. To top it off, she got me a side holster for Valor, one that matched the plum hues of Gaius' magical dagger. With a zip of my boots, I evanesced myself away to Calendula. *Lisa, you got this.*

The view from the hilltop was utterly breathtaking. Underneath the magentas and sherbet oranges of the setting sun were animals, cars, bikes, carts, and even riders on top of Gora bears scattered across the fields and stone roads. I had never seen so many people going into the Kingdom before. More flying ships hovered above the outer gates, keeping security tight as the King promised. Civilians in the hundreds—possibly thousands—were also entering the Grand Kingdom, covered in colors that matched the soon-to-be sky full of stars.

My stomach churned at the thought of my future reality soon becoming my present. Gaius and I had practiced our battle plan to the point I was muttering it in my sleep flawlessly, but my nerves were still shaking my bones like a small earthquake. I knew our strategy, and I knew plans *A* through *Z*, and yet... I still couldn't stop the anxiety. *Is this normal? Do all people get nervous before going into battle, or is it just me?*

"You ready?"

I jumped, turning around to see Gaius standing near the secret entrance. He wore dark green pants and a sage trench coat with rolled sleeves. Cream-colored boots strapped to his feet, and his array of vegetation bottles of weaponry wrapped around his belt. A stoic vigilance blanketed his tan chiseled face as he stood tall, no usual Gaius-y smirk to be found. It was my first time seeing him like this—like a dauntless warrior. He had used swords and plant artillery before during our hunts... but today he embodied a Hero ready to slay Darkness. Guess the preeminence of the day made me notice every little detail about the Keeper of Stars.

He looked me up and down, taking note of my emotions. I couldn't let him know I was scared, especially after I just jumped at the sound of his voice, so I squared my shoulders. Warm light of the setting sun swam through my tied-up hair, highlighting the freckles along my cheeks and the tops of my ears. "Mhm," I answered, my lips pulled in.

A subtle breath left his lungs. "Let's get going, then."

Gaius led me into the forest to begin our plan, which started with none other than Tuff. My little orange sprite visualized himself and floated between us. His job was the most important—and all my idea. He was to be our "Ecuras Lookout" along with the other glainies we rescued from the bírokavaran months ago. Gaius and I didn't know where Ecuras would appear in the forest, and we had to get to him before he passed through the opened veil of Calendula. The glainies would hide invisibly and come to us if they spotted him—it was a perfect plan.

"You got this, Tuff," I said to my little friend.

He then saluted me and disappeared.

A minute later, the forest began to glow with a rainbow of little floating orbs. Faces with black dots for eyes appeared on the glowing colors until a river of lumpy crystal sprites were marching across the overgrown forest; the glainies were all ready to help us, returning the favor for Gaius and me saving them.

Tuff made some powerful whistles, giving his speech on the battle plan. Didn't know he had such a way with words—assertive and quite demanding like a sergeant presenting orders. His demeanor made me smile and giggle; pretty sure I saw Gaius make a smirk or two at the little soldier.

My orange glainie commanded his friends to go to the forest's perimeter, which spanned *miles*, and to return to Gaius and me once they spotted Ecuras. Tuff then pulled up a memory of the villain's face.

My stomach sank again, sloshing around, and I had to fight back nausea. *Can't believe it's happening all so fast.*

Not wasting a second, the glainies vanished, leaving Gaius and me to wait.

Trying to calm my heart down as twenty minutes passed, I asked questions to distract myself. "Will the stars be okay?" I quietly inquired of Gaius as we both walked around the dimming forest.

"No one is getting into Calendula tonight," he guaranteed. "Inna and the others are there right now. Even Kamari."

"Really?"

He nodded, stepping over a root in the ground.

I let out a deep, shaky breath, which caused my teacher to look down at my anxious face.

"It's okay to be nervous."

I fiddled with my dagger strapped to my thigh. "Do you ever get scared, then?"

"Am right now, but it's not because I fear we will lose..." He put his hand on my shoulder, staring at me intently. His eyes were striking with peridot green hues. "We will win, Lisa."

A rough breeze slung through the treetops, sending leaves and dead twigs to coat the forest and causing Gaius and I to look up. We figured it to be a flock of birds or even a winged dark magic creature. No. Pinks and greens and blues and oranges—the little glainie army appeared overhead, flying away. They were hooting a song that sent cold chills down my spine. Every single one of them was fleeing, and there was only one conclusion—

"He's here," Gaius muttered deeply, "at the southern end." He clasped my shoulder and filled his palm with blue evanesce dust. "Let's go."

We reached more trees, and I wouldn't have known we evanesced miles away if it weren't for the sun setting on the opposite end. My hands down to my toes were trembling like a crumbling sandcastle in the wind, and my heart was pounding hard with every step—so loud I thought Gaius could hear each and every deep, quivering *pulse, pulse, pulse.* Fear was morphing into a new emotion, one shadowed by worry and trepidation, causing all parts of my stomach to bubble up. If it weren't for Gaius being by my side, my knees would buckle, colliding my body with the soil. He was my rock, the earth I needed. He made me powerful, no matter how strong the Agapéd was in my heart, because he was the one thing I knew wouldn't fail me.

"Lisa, when we fight Ecuras," Gaius said in a robust, austere voice as we walked forward, "you are not to back down. With each strike, you intend to land a brutal blow, just like you would with a beast. He won't tread lightly on you either. He will try and kill you, so you don't hold back for him, you understand?"

I took a big gulp. "Yes, sir."

"Saraqiel's magic didn't possess him either or take his heart by surprise. Ecuras willingly chose this path and is fully aware of the consequences that will befall him. So, do not think we are stopping some misunderstood man. His heart is nothing but Darkness now. We are here to protect what is good, and I am here to protect you. We fight with all we have, and we will win."

We came to the edge of the trees. Everything around us was painted with peacefulness, but even a tornado whipping through the lands of Boolavogue would be calmer than my heart. I was terrified but confident in Gaius' words. *We are going to win... I am going to win.*

The forest's edge came into sight, and down below, a solemn man began walking up the hill.

It was time.

Sunset red was the sky as Ecuras made the incline. We were far from the city, and the small country houses below sat silent. The only sound in the air was the trees brushing in the spring breeze.

I stood behind the shadow of a tree, my chest pounding thumps of rolling thunder and reverberating all the way up into my brain. I wanted to cover my ears to make its beating stop... but I knew I couldn't. I had a job to do, no matter how scared I was.

Gaius stood farther out from the edge, and I couldn't help but peer behind the bark—being sure to keep myself hidden until it was time.

Ecuras was tall and unnaturally skinny, yet with muscles protruding from his forearms, almost as if his body wanted to die, but the magic inside him refused it. No hood covered his hollowed eyes, unveiling his graying, soured-milk skin and veiny neck. He looked worse than I remember. The only thing about him that still seemed human—like the Ecuras Gaius once knew—was his smile... though it was unpleasantly disarming. Ghostly and haunting. He was the scariest man I had ever seen... and what made him even fouler was what was in his hand.

All blood left my face when I saw Tuff squeezed between Ecuras' fist, struggling, unable to free himself from the long fingernails of the evil man. My glainie was whistling—crying horribly—unable to vanish and fly away due to the dark magic poking his orange body. I wanted nothing more than to tell Ecuras to give him back. *He's—he's gonna kill Tuff—*

Grass rustled from where my foot hesitated, but I quickly retreated when I saw Gaius jerk his eyes toward me. Those burning green irises silently said to *stay hidden*. So, I listened... trusting the Keeper to save my little friend.

"Of all those little pests," Ecuras called, raspy yet somehow charming, even with Tuff hooting and squirming in his palm, "this is the only one that didn't flee at the sight of me. He froze in place like a stone." His grimace cracked like a whip toward Gaius. "A clever plan, one I did not expect someone like *you* to come up with. After all, you're not one to make bonds with creatures, are you, *Gaius*?"

"Release the sprite," Gaius bellowed on the forest's edge. "We both know why you're here."

Ecuras raised a brow and flicked Tuff away as if he were a crumb agitating his skin. My eyes turned glossy as Tuff vanished and flew toward me in the tree's shadow. I cupped his plump body from behind the trunk, kissed his little head, and nodded with a mental message: *Thank you for being so brave.*

Tuff then vanished away—off to check if the other glainies were okay.

"Ah... that may be so, but why not catch up?" Ecuras croaked. "After all, it has been a century since we've last seen each other; at least, I *believe* it has been. But then again... what would I know? That is what you were hoping for, wasn't it? Tried to rid me from exploring the power of your Wishing Stars, but it seems not even a memory charm can stop destiny at work—"

"Destiny doesn't serve you," Gaius bolted in a low tone, "and you're not entering my home tonight."

My muscles tensed. Never had I heard Gaius' voice so guttural before. So... merciless.

Ecuras snickered, his teeth yellowed and sharp—not human. "Whether or not you stand in my way doesn't matter... because you've failed to realize that with the magic I have now, you can't even hope to stop me."

Before the battle, and according to our plan, Gaius told me to reveal myself when Ecuras claims himself to be "unstoppable"... which I felt was at that very moment.

I stepped out from behind the tree's shadow and into the perfect view of the grimacing foe.

The cocky smile from Ecuras' face faded once he saw me, the Agapéd Bearer, standing next to his former teacher. I could tell he still didn't know my true strength because no one fears a child when they have the power of Darkness by their side.

It didn't take him long to scan me up and down, his eyes pelting me like an army of thumbtacks. Then, he *huffed*—an abnormal, grated rasp. "You believe I will back down simply because you brought the Agapéd—is that what this is?" My eyes turned wide, and Ecuras took note, figuring out our plan to avoid a battle.

"You know how this will end, Ecuras," Gaius uttered from my left, standing tall and alert. "Light will always win against Darkness. So, leave now and never return."

"I will say..." No movement came from him—only from his throat and eyes. "Leaving the Wishing Stars unguarded was a bold move I, for one, wasn't expecting. And—Lisa, was it? I apologize for before, but even so"—he sniped those black and blue eyes toward Gaius—"you are still *weak*, and I will not be leaving empty-handed tonight."

Plants began to sprout in Gaius' glass vials girded to his waist as I stood next to him. "You can bluff, but we know you are not as strong as you once were," the Keeper said, staying wary of the cloaked man's muscle tension and hollowed eyes.

Ecuras crowed with a dark-infected leer. "Oh, that *is* what you think…" Blue shadows swirled around his bony hands beneath the hem of his sleeve. A stone with a pointed end appeared, his eyes admiring it between his fingers.

Nothing seemed exceptional about the stone to me, but to Gaius, it was as if it were a live grenade, the safety pin released. *It's just a rock… so why is Gaius staring at it like that?*

"Your new pupil looks confused, Gaius," Ecuras uttered, his voice crescendoing, turning cynical. "Did she not learn there are ways to conceal magic—did *you* not tell her? Or is it, you simply doubted my power?" He turned his eyes to me. "That day in the festival, you only saw a glimpse of my power because I willed it so. This mere stone contains half my magic because I knew there were those watching me—Zephan, that heart-reading Keeper. So, it isn't that I was too *weak*—"

Ecuras pressed hard on the stone as if it were a button. In an instant, sharp flames of dark fire burned the stone, the heat being felt even from where I was standing. Plumes of magic burst out of the rock and flew straight into the chest of Ecuras—his body sucking it up like water to a sponge.

And that was when my heart burned with nightmares, worse than it did during the festival in Fladden. Dark magic from the Fallen was in that stone, and Ecuras absorbed it all like a black hole.

As the magic swirled into Ecuras' chest, Gaius held his hand out in front of me as the other hovered over the glinted pummel of his sheathed sword—a thick, blocky shard with a glowing green gem attached to the rooted hilt. He commanded me: "Lisa—stay out and hidden until I'm finished—"

"But—" My breath sawed through my throat.

"He's at his full strength—I am *not* sending you out there until I have him bound and bleeding."

Nothing was going right. Fear trembled my hands and bones, sending whatever courage I thought I had down the edge of the cliffside. Gaius was nervous—*Gaius, the most stoic man I knew.* That stone containing bits of Saraqiel's magic pulse had to have been so rare and uncommon for it not to have crossed the Keeper's mind or even the mind of the Guardians.

Ecuras began rippling coarse shadows and sparks of blue around his hands, the muscles in his neck throbbing—thrumming with dark magic. "I was merely half-alive until now, so it is *you* who will fail, old friend. And I will *gladly* make use of those precious stars of yours..." He turned his fiery beryl eyes toward me. "And I will be taking the Agapéd, too—"

In seconds, the eerie Mystic formed an iridescent weapon out of thin air composed of pure darkness. A longsword, but its steel blade was replaced with blue beams of shadows.

He then pressed off the ground with the force of a landslide—bolting straight toward me.

Gaius pushed me out of the way with his hand and used the roots below to hold him steady as he blocked Ecuras' attack with his green shard sword.

The Fallen hissed, "You should've wiped every last memory of me while you had the chance!"

The Keeper gritted his teeth, green and blue sparks slicing the space between their swords. "I let you go many years ago..." Thorned ropes began to snake around Ecuras' legs as indigo mist leaked from the dark Mystic's pores. "A mistake I will not make again."

Thorns and vines cracked like thunder, and shadows became an army of flying tungsten spikes.

And the magic battle began, but everything was so different compared to the imaginary battle I had run through in my mind over the past five months.

Gaius made trees move to his will, blocking Ecuras' large combustion sigil magic. The first hit—the *true* first magic hit—sounded like a shotgun going off right next to me: loud, powerful, and lightning-fast. I had never felt or seen magic like theirs; it was the most incredible, frightening experience in my life, and I was sure to stay on my toes the entire time.

The Keeper of Stars used the cliffside roots to propel him upward, and Ecuras combusted the air around him—both Mystics flying in the sky, wailing blows against the other. Gaius slammed his sword against Ecuras, who then parried each attack with dark magic.

My eyes tried to follow them as I stayed planted on the ground, but their speed was unmatched.

My teacher swatted Ecuras farther down the plain, using nothing but the rustic roots beneath the earth. I didn't stay hidden at the forest's edge for long and followed behind, surfing along the dirt with my guard up, watching Gaius closely. He was a warrior, grimacing and swift. My burly teacher would switch between swinging his sword and whipping a fiery plant from his vegetation weaponry belt. Ecuras would try and make a hit or two with his bombs of dark magic, but Gaius was agile—only letting debris hit his body.

Suddenly, Gaius landed a *hit* on Ecuras' chest—sending his skeletal body flying hard to the ground! I didn't see how the bony Mystic didn't break into a million pieces. Gaius slung out his chains of thorned ivy from his side and shot it toward Ecuras' arms and wrists before he could recover, pinning him hard to the banged-up soil.

That's my cue!

Gaius didn't have to call my name; my body moved on instinct.

I propelled myself forward with the dirt below, seeing Ecuras bound to the soil. I balled strength in my hand as if I were about to give a death punch to the man on the ground. *Aim for the heart, Lisa. Fast, quick, and full of power!*

In his fit of rage from being tied down, Ecuras grinned at me as I came toward him. His eyes were dark, glowing blue, and his mouth stretched far like a clown's face paint. *Now that's a scary smile...*

"*That's your plan?*" Ecuras roared as if he was happy about it.

As I was still barreling toward him, he made a sigil underneath his body and blew himself into the sky. The explosion was loud and powerful, but it didn't even phase him! *Can his magic not hurt himself—*

The large blast threw me off course, but I didn't fall over; something caught me.

Around my waist were squishy vines. I looked toward Gaius and saw him rushing near, his hand reaching out toward me.

I let out a deep breath—thankful he saved me from a brutal fall.

Ecuras came crashing back down, using his magic to suppress his landing. The thorns from Gaius' grasp tore our opponent's arms like a butcher's meat grinder, releasing blood down his body but still, he was standing.

His face began to look more like a skeleton, and the veins on his neck were like purple snakes. *Is his magic hurting him? Does his "eternal life" depend on his usage of magic? Whatever it is—something is making his body change.*

Running next to me, Gaius swung his arm out in front of my chest.

Ecuras took notice. He studied both of us and stopped in the dirt, giving a smug smile. "You're... *protecting* her..." he said mischievously as if he enjoyed it. "I must say, you had me fooled. To believe the Agapéd was powerful like me—even a kingdom of Hunters was in on the sham! Do you believe you will win? Your magic can't even destroy me now, and the one thing that can *isn't even strong enough*—needing your useless protection like the child she truly is. You will lose, old man!"

My heart sank.

I looked up toward Gaius, but he remained focused on his former student. His confidence was still strong—sturdy like the mountain we were on. The Keeper was sweating and breathing hard. I saw a couple of bloody scratches on his hands and red seeping through the seams near his knees, but he wasn't backing down. Hurt—he was hurt because he was protecting me. *I have to help—*

Ecuras stopped staring at Gaius; his evil eyes were now on me. He knew Gaius was guarding me, and he knew I was the only thing that could defeat him. All he needed was me out of the way if he wanted to win... and to him, stopping a novice kid was easier than stopping his former teacher.

Shadows of darkness pushed Ecuras toward me, but Gaius blocked him with his sword. After a successful parry, the same happened again. Gaius continued to shield me, trying to make Ecuras strike him first. I would've attacked, but earlier, Gaius said, "Fight back if it's our *only* choice." I didn't want to mess up, and dodging was a lot easier at the moment... but now, Gaius was trying to fight *and* defend.

Ecuras suddenly made a sigil above my head—one as big as a car. The moment it blew up, a dome of trees covered me as well as stone from my magic. Rays of the setting sun shot through the crevices of the warped trees as specks of dirt hit my face.

In seconds, another explosion burst six feet to my left, right where Gaius was, toppling the tree barricade. When the smog of dirt cleared—in that split moment—I saw Ecuras coming toward the Keeper... and Gaius looked banged up with blood and soot covering his forearms and chest.

Seeing him in pain—it gutted me. I was about to run toward him to help when my teacher's green eyes met mine. That stare was serious and one I hadn't seen before; his eyes screamed at me to stay back.

I obeyed, no matter how much I did not want to.

Gaius swooped down and immediately grabbed the leg of Ecuras with his vines, whipping him fifty yards away.

He's... trying to get him away from me... so I don't get hurt.

As Gaius threw the fearsome Mystic, Ecuras was ready to fire back. Before landing across the plain, he sent a rainstorm of blue sigils toward Gaius, each one going off like fireworks—*boom, boom, boom*—

My eyes were wide and afraid as I saw my instructor run on roots, trying to avoid all fifty missiles of magic.

I clenched my fists. *Sorry, Gaius, but I'm not standing around watching you get hurt for me any longer!*

I rushed toward him on the waves of dirt the moment I saw him take a hit, leading to another. His back was charred, his cloak torn, and his face covered in blood and soot; still, he kept running.

When I sprung forward into the battle, another sigil appeared behind Gaius. *"Gaius, behind you!"* I shrieked, but Ecuras changed his course when he looked at me.

Saraqiel's vessel dismissed the sigil in the blink of an eye and shot himself toward *me* like a spider springing toward a fly in its web.

Gaius tried to catch up, but a sigil appeared in front and behind him. They exploded—sending a shock to his body. And I watched as he fell to the ground, right on his bloody knees.

Darkness in human form hurtled like a train toward my body. I shot two hefty boulders made of the soil beneath me toward him, but Ecuras easily evaded them. I was so scared—so petrified—that I couldn't focus on what to do. I shot more and more, but—

I need Gaius!

Ecuras was gaining on me—fast.

I formed a wall of stone in front of me, but Ecuras put a sigil on it. The moment I saw the glowing emblem, I shot the earth back down into the ground, causing it to blow up beneath me, sending me rolling onto the soil. I scraped my back, my knees, and my face. My cloak was getting ripped by the sharp stones below, parts even seared from the heat of the combustion. When the last roll on the ground came, I slapped my hand down hard and grabbed the soil, giving me a chance to regain my surroundings.

I wish I never did that.

Ecuras swooped down and grabbed me by the front of my cloak, right where it buttoned on my chest. He breathed inches from his face, a horrid man—something not even my worst nightmares could have ever imagined. His cheekbones were harsh, his eyes were blue craters of shadows, and his smile was too grimacing to be considered happy.

He grasped my cloak tight, scratching my chest with his bony fingernails—peeling off skin and freckles beneath. I bit my lip from the pain, wiggling like a fish on a hook in his grip. My first instinct was to get his hand off of me, so I began grating his wrists and forearm bloody to try and free myself; it was to no avail. I tried to whip rocks from below to maybe hit him, but he suddenly used his free hand to squeeze my arm and stop me. I yelled in pain; his grip was infused with dark magic—darkness burning me like a hot iron.

A deep rumbling shook the ground, and my glossy eyes veered to the left.

Gaius came zooming toward us, using the grass as springs for his feet, blood dripping from his ears.

Ecuras didn't look too upset. "This isn't just about your stars—I'm here for you, old man!" he yelled with vengeful angst. "You took *everything* from me!" Saraqiel's vessel leered back toward me with a dark snarl, and his eyes lost all signs of humanity. Disgust tightened his face as he uttered to me, "And you're just in my way."

"*Lisa!*" Gaius shouted, shooting his bloody thorned spears toward the enemy.

Ecuras made a sigil right next to Gaius and one right in the palm of his gray-dying hand—the one holding *me*.

Both sigils combusted.

And I flew, like a lifeless ragdoll, off the edge of the mountain.

I couldn't see what happened to Gaius; my mind was turned off—blinding my eyes and senses. My ears were clogged with blood, my chest was bruised as if it were hit by a thrashing bull, and all my surroundings were as dark as a black hole... but I knew—I *knew* I was—

Falling—I'm falling fast—what—what's happening—

My burnt cloak and untied hair whipped at my face, sniping at me—waking me up. I suddenly opened my eyes and saw nothing but the burning sunset sky above and the blurring cliffside next to me—flying past me with the speed of an airplane.

Ecuras didn't just toss me away; he blasted me off the cliff!

I was free falling to my death—straight to the bottom with nothing but stone to greet my end. I was going to splatter. I was going to die—

No—Gaius... needs me!

My legs flailed as the wind sucked out of me. The ground only feet away—

I can't let Ecuras win! Those stars are meant for the good hearts in the world—not for Darkness to exploit!

Knotted hair battered my neck and face as my body flipped around—the rocks beginning to show their details to me—

I have to save them. I have to save all the worlds—I have to save myself—I AM NOT DYING LIKE THIS!

The moment I wished to keep living was when my heart started glowing—*literally glowing!* Something inside me heated up like a fire—a warming, blazing flame. The veins in my chest were beaming with rays of purple and orange—the same light as the one from the night the Agapéd fell from the sky and landed in my backyard. A warrior radiance from a Wishing Star.

Aches and burns from Ecuras' attack blazed up and down my body, but I didn't care. I clenched my fist and saw *magic—the same glow from my chest was in my hands!* I was powerful, I was alive, and I had no intention of dying by something as trivial as being thrown off a mountain!

Gaius said I was powerful. Kamari told me I was strong, and for the first time, I *knew* I was.

Letting my heart take control, I didn't hit the ground but pressed off the air beneath me with my feet and hands. Something in me—something with strength and purpose—just told me I could do it. There was a transcendent light inside my heart—the mightiest in the world—and I finally trusted it with all I had.

And I. Started. *Flying.*

I whirled around, saw the rocky floor below, and bolted forward, *truly hovering in the air!*

This—this is real?

When I noticed what had happened, I didn't waste a moment. I saw myself face death and win. Nothing—I mean *nothing*—could stop me, and I had a Keeper who needed my help.

Gaius and Ecuras were at swords, pressed up against each other's chest. In his slithery voice, Ecuras divulged loudly, "You fight for pleasure now! Even if you defeat me—even if you get what you've waited so long for—Darkness has already won! You lost the only thing that could save you!" Ecuras combusted Gaius to the ground. "The Agapéd is *Dead*—splattered and turned to dust!"

The Keeper looked angry and distraught, but he wasn't giving up. He held his sword up high, but Ecuras shot it out of his hand—scything up Gaius' arm and painting it scarlet. He bit back his screams, feeling defeat creep upon him.

Suddenly, Saraqiel's vessel, about to swing at his opponent, noticed a glowing light wisping behind him.

A normal glow wouldn't have made the man of Darkness stop his attack, even one as bright as the sun. The small glow from the heart of a child that seemed to have escaped death would, if she was the only thing in the world that could defeat him.

And that was me.

Gaius was breathing heavily, but I saw him peek a smile as Ecuras stared at me, startled that I was flying above the cliffside in my burnt-up clothing.

My fists were pulsing with magenta magic, starting to collect pieces of the mountain as if they were lighter than dust. I didn't say a word—honestly, I couldn't think of anything witty or vicious to say; I just really, *really* wanted to punch him. He hurt me, hurt Tuff, and most of all, hurt Gaius.

I gathered the rocks from the mountain like a vacuum, watching as they swirled around me, and bolted *fast—right toward Ecuras.* I picked up the soil like a blanket and pulled part of the mountain onto Ecuras. Not only did I land a hit, but a blow so hard that trees flew with it... and Ecuras went *down hard*—a football field's length away!

My strength—it was something beyond powerful. Whatever the power the

Agapéd had, it had been storing it up for this very moment.

I flew up to Gaius and landed by his side. The sight of me being alive seemed to negate all his pain. He was smiling and acting as if his arms weren't covered in blood.

Before I could say anything, a loud bomb went off in Ecuras' direction. Chunks of earth went flying as a column of foreign sigils formed in the sky above him—blue and black magic as bright as lightning, taller than any forest tree. Gaius and I stared at our opponent, but something was changing. The wind blew, and I could feel dark magic absorbing from the earth into Ecuras.

"What's happening?" I asked Gaius, breathing hard but holding my stare toward the dark Mystic a hundred yards away.

Gaius wiped off the blood from his arm like water, grabbing his sword. "He's letting Darkness take over."

Even though I was scared, I trusted in my magic more than ever. I clenched my fists. "You ready?"

"I believe that is my line." Gaius wrapped his arm in the green and yellow roots of the Aeson Spurge plant he had strapped to his belt, the yellowing pollen seeping into his tender cuts and crusted, gaping gashes. A gallant grin slipped as he willed the roots of the spurge to tie tight. "Let's go."

I flew next to Gaius as he surfed the grass on tree roots. Had to admit, I felt as powerful as him at that moment.

When we came upon Ecuras, he was not human anymore. His arms and legs were elongated, bones sticking out like his skin couldn't hold them inside. Blue and gray were the colors of his body, except for his face which was turning as black as the shadows he was casting. His eyes were glowing sapphire like his dark magic, and his jaw was protruding with teeth grimacing like a rabid vorrg. On his back, his shoulder blades had glowing blue thorns sticking out. Dark magic mixed in with his blood—turning black like squid's ink—and the lashes Gaius made to him earlier were glowing from the inside. *He is dying... but not before Saraqiel attempts to stop us first.*

Dark Ecuras glared at Gaius and me as we flew in, summoning a river of explosives toward us. He had placed the magic bombs on the ground, so I swooped down and moved the earth toward the sky as if it was as light as cotton—sigils attached and all. The explosion went off above us, allowing Gaius an opening.

My teacher sprung forward and sent missiles of torpedo-sized thorns toward Dark Ecuras.

Our enemy was too focused on blocking and neglected me. I bolted toward him from the sky, gathering magic in my palms, and spiked his back with the stone form underneath. *I hit him—hard too!*

With him arched over in pain, I landed on the ground with my feet and attempted to grab his chest, but he swung his arm at me. I ducked down, and Gaius came swinging next, using the plants to power his punch. We then took turns whipping magic back and forth—rocks, dark magic, and plants all flying through the air. Gaius had my back, and I had his; Ecuras had no one, and we began to see his strength deplete.

Like a flash bomb, Dark Ecuras slammed the ground with an explosion near my feet.

I flew into the air to avoid the attack, but so did a giant shadow mixed in with all the dusty debris.

It was him—soaring right for me like a hawk toward its prey. He reached out his humanoid arm and went for my neck—sending me farther and farther into the clouds. We were now alone in the sky.

Blue heat from his fingertips singed my neck as he held me tight in the sky. But his moves were sloppy, fearing death approaching him, his eternal lifespan on its last leg. I, on the other hand, felt thunderous despite all the burns and scratches tainting my body.

I bit down on my lip, took out my dagger, and sliced his ribs. Black blood splattered from the cut.

He flinched, his hand releasing my neck, glaring at me as we both were hurtling toward the earth.

"Lisa, now!" I faintly heard below as I saw Gaius—small as an ant—sending four ropes of thorns toward Dark Ecuras' arms and legs.

This is it!

I looked at the foe beneath me as he sent a sigil to my right. It combusted right next to my ear—sending a ringing through my head, my dagger flying out of my hand, and devastating burns on my skin—allowing Ecuras a chance to grab my shoulder.

I didn't have time to be a fancy fighter, so I bit his hand hard like a barbaric animal, penetrating his nasty skin and feeling his black blood hit the corner of my burnt face. I spat it out—its tang like coppery seawater. With Dark Ecuras distracted with pain, I then reached for the left side of his chest—right where his pulsing, blue heart was. His skin was as brittle as ashy wood, and when I tore through his flaking chest, I *grabbed it*. I grabbed it hard as if I was pulling up a root from the ground.

Lisa, this is it! Give it all you have!

I pulsed my magic straight through his heart just like Gaius told me to: strong and with everything I had.

Dark Ecuras tried to stop, but Gaius' thorned ropes finally reached the enemy's arms and bound him tight.

Nothing is stopping me now. I could feel my heart throbbing relentlessly as the ground neared us below.

Gaius was right about my body aching: My legs were on fire, and my muscles wanted me to quit, but my heart surged on. It was valiant—forcing all the magic through my veins and into my right hand like a speeding comet. The pain made me scream a gular battlecry as I felt Ecuras' heart shake—glowing a warming purple with *my* magic.

Finally, magenta beams burst through his chest and out his spine, whipping iridescent ribbons lighting up the sky around us.

I am not letting Darkness win! I clenched harder, feeling my arms about to give out and my head ring violently as my celestial magic continued to jet out of my skin and through his body.

His chest then concaved, and all the warmth and burning from his magic stopped pricking my fingers. There was no more fear slicing my chest—no more horror rattling in my bones. That menacing aura surrounding him had vanished.

And I knew—I knew I did it. His magic pulse was destroyed.

With my magic burning bright like a star through his chest, I looked behind Ecuras and saw a glowing green sword rising as the ground came nearer.

Gaius propelled himself toward us, sword in hand, and used the bound thorned ropes as bungee cords. I immediately flew off Ecuras, knowing his magic was destroyed, and watched as Gaius sliced clean through our enemy—a gash that severed his left arm and head.

He. Was. *Finished.*

The dark corpse of Ecuras fell to the ground with the cover of black and blue mist, and both Gaius and I landed on opposite sides of him—safely with the help of our magic. There was no loud boom, splatters of black blood, or sound of rocks crashing when he landed—no avalanche of power or a band of rattling bones, only a subtle thud and cracks of soil. Once the dust and magic soot cleared, we saw Dark Ecuras becoming nothing but an ashen skeleton and black magic... beginning to dissipate away just like any other dark magic creature.

All fear of Saraqiel's power was vanquished.

I did it... I defeated the Fallen... so why am I feeling... so... w-weak...

GAIUS

I looked up from the carnage of Ecuras, breathing heavily, blood clotting up my arm underneath the binds of the Aeson Spurge, and I ran—ran straight for her.

She was collapsing. She—she was dying—

No—

I threw down my sword and slid through the ashes—keeping her dirtied brown hair from hitting the ground. And I grasped her battered body in my arms.

She wasn't moving, and her once-glowing chest had faded. The warmth in her face was bone-pale—so, so pale—

And my heart plummeted. A darkness I never wanted to feel again.

No.

I curled up her frail, tattered body in my arms, elevating her head. I never knew how small she was until then, her body one thrash away from snapping in half, and I bit back my lip until it bled.

I shouldn't have pushed her to do this...

Her body was feeble, covered in burns and scratches. Her cloak was nothing more than a bib around her collarbone, and her shorts were the color of mud, crusted with blood. Blotches of scarlet dirt tinted her cheeks—the face I was meant to protect.

My throat turned raspy and dry. Lisa still was not moving.

She... she wasn't meant for this... She was just a child...

And that was when guilt bound me to the soil, shackling me to ache and pain. I was the one meant to fight—meant for the wounds and permanent scars—and yet, she was in my arms, covered in an ocean of ruby-red burns that should've been tarnishing *my* hands. She was meant to be out of the way until I had secured him, only using the Agapéd to destroy his pulse, not to fight back. She was meant to stay *safe*. Maybe... maybe there was some way I could have just finished him off myself—crippling his magic—she wouldn't be—

I flinched, staring at her, shaking. *No—she's not dead.*

I pulled her long hair over her shoulder, attempting to wipe away the scuffs tainting her face, when her skin became blurry in my vision. My eyes—I refused my body to ever allow emotions strong enough to penetrate the dam I had built up. I welcomed the drought for 400 years, never letting a trickle of salty liquid escape. But now... its walls were cracking...

"Lisa, come on..." I managed to mutter, trying to remember which parts of her once-rosy cheeks were freckles and not just soot as my thumbs continued to rub her skin. "Not you... Lisa, please... wake up..." I didn't even recognize my breaking voice, hoarse and grating, and I could feel the warmth of tears maneuvering through the hairs of my beard; I hated it—gritted my teeth at it. Hated myself. "Just open your eyes for me..."

I knew that the power it took to destroy a heart was the same amount it took to keep the other alive. I *knew* that, and I should've told her.

My jaw clamped down hard, and my hands pulled her in tighter.

I. Knew. That.

I had seen it over and over again. Centuries of death and life and death and life. I knew the price of being the Agapéd and the price of choosing to train her... with me... at my home. Letting her into my life. I knew the price of being her mentor because I knew my heart, but she was just so excited—so thrilled at the beauty of our world. The beauty of magic. The wonder in her own heart, the day she asked me to train her.

Me. I... I don't remember the last time I was really wanted...

She picked me—a fool with a barricaded heart of stone. She gave me a reason to learn to love magic again, too. She gave me a reason to find joy in this monotonous world of work, sleep, and magic, a purpose for waking up every day. And I had hoped—so *selfishly* hoped—that things would have been different.

I thought—I thought I could make her strong enough to withstand the power the Agapéd gifted her... and I thought I had outgrown the sting of sorrow for when that wasn't the case. But this tang of agony—her being in my arms motionless—was as cold and piercing as a steel sword slithering up and down my throat. I'd prefer that brutal castigation every day for the rest of my life than to see her like this—

My chest tightened, trying to suffocate the words that I couldn't keep down, and my fingers clasped sturdy around her neck and arm. "Please... You can't leave... You can't... die. Not—not like this..." I waited for an answer. "Lisa...?"

She did not respond.

She did not move.

And then, the dam broke in my eyes.

And I wept.

Whatever hope I had left faded like Kalm's setting sun, streaming down my face in watery blood and reminding my skin what tears felt like, but I still kept cradling her body in my arms as if she was a newborn... as if she was *my* newborn, just waiting for life to be gifted to her once again. She had so much more to live for—she couldn't go. Not just yet.

My voice cracked like a pathetic child. "Give her another chance, *please...*"

I gave my heart to her months before, but that pain was *nothing* like the piercing heartbreak I was feeling now. At that time, I was doing my duty as a Keeper—making sure she stayed alive for this moment.

But now... everything was different.

I was losing her, the one thing I didn't deserve... the one precious thing I *swore* I would never let fill my life again. But... she chose me. She—for some reason—wanted me to train her. She wanted me beside her. She made magic worth it. She wasn't mine—wasn't of my blood... and yet, I took her in as if she was my own. Because, deep down, I wanted her there, too...

My head sunk low until my forehead pressed against hers. Cold. Lifeless.

I just didn't know a father's love had already consumed my heart until she—my little, weary girl—had perished in my arms.

I told her I would protect her.

I told her I would be there for her.

I told her I'd make her a Hero.

And I should've never told myself I could be the father she never had because now—this—all of this—

I—I—

"I'm so—so sorry, Lisa..." I cried, my forehead hovering over hers, watching my tears sprinkle onto my little girl's all-too-pale skin.

Hues of pumpkin and magenta—colors her face normally lit up with—began to fade in the sky. The sun had set... and it was time to release the stars. She was so excited about this night, too.

I grasped her tight as I managed to stand, my little girl's legs draped off the side of my arm while her arms folded along her stomach like a doll.

What is the point of a starry sky if she can't be there to see it...

But, I couldn't mourn. Not right now. I had a job to do, and I knew she would be upset with me if I didn't do it.

That was all I had to cling to—to push me forward. And I took a step with Lisa cradled in my wounded arms and walked back through the forest stretch.

Tuff joined me on the way as darkness loomed over Boolavogue's woodlands. I hadn't noticed if he was there the entire time during battle or even at all. Maybe he, too, didn't want to face reality. Or perhaps... he heard her last thoughts—her last words. I'd give anything to be that little dote for even just a moment.

Her little orange glainie didn't float ahead or hover above like a little moon to diminish the shadows of the drooping branches or rooted snags, and I almost tripped a couple of times. But I didn't make him light the way, watching as the dote's glowing warm body sat snuggled up against Lisa's—wishing for a heartbeat to thump against his plump, saddened face.

This... this was probably the first time Tuff couldn't hear Lisa's thoughts since he had met her. A part of him was stripped away, having to imagine she was only sleeping to avoid any more sparkling tears from staining her bloody clothing.

A Keeper and a glainie crying... how utterly gimpish is that...

Twenty... maybe thirty minutes had passed. I didn't know. My arms burned with aches, but I didn't care, holding Lisa close to my heart.

I remained silent, hoping miserably to hear her voice, but only the sound of leaves and twigs crunching beneath my boots permeated the air. In turn, my mind stopped, and my emotions ceased. I didn't want to face the truth—didn't want to feel this pain of losing a child. A child that wasn't mine, no matter how much I wished it were so. *Did Lisa care this much about me?* I hoped... I hoped she enjoyed being in my home. I know I wasn't the best at being her temporary guardian. Didn't know a single thing about raising a kid, let alone a dotish girl who could barely hold a sword.

I bit back my lip again. I'd miss seeing her. Miss seeing her drawing creatures, telling me about Earth. The way she loved the stars—telling me how beautiful they were, amazed how I could make them grow. I'd grow a whole galaxy for her if it meant she wouldn't stop smiling. I'd miss having her laugh, caring for her. I'd miss her being my little girl, padding barefoot around my house, telling me about her days at the castle—telling me about her mother. *How... how do I even tell her mother? How do I tell a woman I never met that her daughter is—*

I pushed out that thought... and let nothing else in. Each new stride across the forest floor was aimless. And my purpose for continuing forward was lying lifeless in my arms.

A breeze came blowing in. Nothing was special about that spring breeze. It smelled like damp grass and was a cool temperature like the many before, leading a couple of wandering leaves to the forest soil. It did refresh my wounds and chill my broken face, and, in truth, I wish it lingered a while longer.

And then, for some reason, Tuff started whistling.

The dote had remained utterly muted, laying upon her chest, so the sudden change in silence startled me. I hadn't looked at him—hadn't looked at Lisa—for the duration of the woodland trek, but now, it was impossible to ignore his hooting. Impossible not to look down.

One glance was all it took.

I dropped to my knees with a thud and couldn't look away from her freckled face. My breathing stopped—my heart began to soar—as my eyes were unsure of what they saw. I freed my right arm, letting her legs dangle on the soil, so I could brush away the mix of blood and dirt from infecting her eyes. It was causing her pain... causing her to squint from the subtle discomfort.

47
WISHING STAR RELEASE

His hand around my jawline and neck was the first bit of warmth I felt, and his green eyes reflecting Tuff's orange glow were the first things I saw, turning glossy the more I began blinking.

Amid Gaius' sniffles, my soft voice muttered. It wasn't a strong mutter, but it was all I could muster at the moment.

"Did... you see that..." I squinted up at him in the middle of the forest floor. "I flew... I really flew."

Gaius smiled down at me before wrapping me back up in his arms, turning his once tears of sorrow into ones of joy.

As my heart slowly woke up, gifting me more strength, the Keeper slid me on his back as we continued through the woods and to his home. He used his Aeson Spurge to heal some of my wounds, but the ones infected with Ecuras' dark magic—the burns in particular from his sigils' explosions—remained, painting my body. I told him I was fine to evanesce and didn't need a piggyback ride, but he didn't want to take any chances. His kindness never ceased.

I had my bloody arms around his neck, talking his ear off about the whole fight, bragging about how cool I thought I was—zooming around and showing Darkness who was boss.

He laughed at me, not believing how I could still be so enthusiastic.

Tuff joined our walk, happily lighting our path with his orange glow. He gave me a plethora of joyous hoots, followed by sudden glittery sobs staining my dirty shoulder. He, too, was beyond grateful I was alive.

"When I was falling and my chest started glowing, what was that? Some type of superpower?" I asked Gaius, my voice a bit weak but too curious to remain silent.

I felt his breath hit my arms. "Sometimes, on extremely rare occasions, the heart of one with Starnate magic will glow when the user produces an extreme amount of magic."

"Really? I just thought about needing to live to save your life, and I started flying."

"I wasn't going to die."

I rolled my eyes. "*Whatever* you say..."

There was a moment of silence before Gaius spoke again. "You did well back there."

I smiled back confidently, though he couldn't see it. "I did, didn't I?"

He huffed. "You survive one toss off a cliff, and you now think you're invincible..."

"Heh—no, but at that moment, I really did..." I leaned my head on his shoulder as I hugged his neck, right up against his right ear. "But I couldn't have done it without you, though. So, thanks."

⁓

We soon made it back to Calendula, its streets mostly empty as many were in Boolavogue for the festivities, and Gaius took me through a back entrance of the Veradome. When we walked inside his hearth, his greenhouse was glowing brighter than I had ever seen it before—blues, pinks, and yellows radiating relentlessly. I remained on Gaius' back until we reached the staritorium's double-glass doors, where I slid off and wobbled atop the floor. Aches crept up my body and my stamina was dreadfully low, but I was too excited for the stars—pushing my pain aside to see the magical plants ready for take off.

When Gaius opened the door, my mind was lost... there weren't words pretty enough to describe the starry ocean above our heads.

Wishing Stars—in the *tens of thousands*—bobbed up and down against the glass ceiling. They rained pastel yellow and crystal blue dust onto the floor, coloring my dirty shoulders with celestial rainbows, humming their ambient joyous songs.

My smile became wide as the aroma of the stars smelled sweet, like cherries, creating a happy feeling all around. *I can't believe Gaius gets to see this every year!*

Before I had time to take another step, a voice emerged from the middle of the room. I had been gawping at the ceiling and noticed nothing besides the Wishing Stars.

"Lisa!" the voice said, and when I looked forward, I saw Inna, her strawberry hair tied beautifully in a waist-long braid. She ran straight for me with a jovial embrace. "Oh, my goodness... I am so happy you're alive—look at you! Your little face is all bloody and burned, but you're here—here and standing. I am so glad."

Gaius spoke before I could. "She did well."

"And Inna—I learned how to fly!" I announced, her hug releasing, standing on my tiptoes. "It was incredible! I just zoomed right off the edge of the cliff, and—"

I had to stop mid-sentence because my mind couldn't focus on the words coming out of my mouth as I saw Kamari, Emunah, and—lo-and-behold—*Vilmad* standing in the middle of the staritorium. I smiled at them while Inna guided me to my mentors.

Emunah grinned big beneath his black beard, extending his arms wide before giving me a gentle pat on my shoulder. Even that small tap nicked my Ecuras burns, but I didn't care. "Now, there's a sight—a true Hero and her mighty companion! If it weren't for the dirt and grime, I wouldn't have believed you were even in battle with a smile like that dressed upon your face."

My clothes were pretty destroyed, but it was true that I couldn't stop smiling; being in a place of magic gave me only emotions of peace and joy.

I looked up at Vilmad and couldn't help but ask him, "How come you all are here? Thought you both were powerless against Saraqiel's magic?"

Gaius snickered at my statement.

Vilmad had his mouth open to refute my assumption, but Emunah butted in first—giving the fellow Guardian a hardy slap—and said with a proud smile, "Doesn't mean we would just stand around and not help our fellow Keepers—Vilmad would've given all he had to save the stars, even if he won't admit it."

Vilmad ignored Emunah and muttered toward me and Gaius, "I knew you would succeed... just didn't know how *much* of you would, so I came. No need to be histrionic about me doing my duty. It was what I was made for."

Kamari came up to me, grinning wide and looking elegant in spring wear, her braided locks still bundled loosely on her head. "I told you—yo' light was strong." She then looked up at Gaius. "Would not have happened widout you."

"I disagree," Gaius replied with his arms crossed.

Kamari hit his shoulder, the one that was bruised and scratched up.

Gaius flinched when Kamari blurted, "*Na so*—can you take a compliment every once in a while? I do not just go handin' dos out fo free."

Vilmad spoke again, "Guess, with Lisa still here, that means the Agapéd isn't finished just yet."

I looked up at him, furrowing my brows. "What do you mean?"

Suddenly, a realm of gold appeared about ten feet from where we were all gathered. It reminded me of evanescing magic, but I had never seen rivers of opaline gold before. A lady's silhouette walked out of the beam of light, and her liquid-diamond wings fluttered softly behind, leaving a trail of gilded dust as she stepped on the stone floor.

"Lady Ariela, you know you shouldn't be this far away from Haim Gana," Vilmad said as the golden Elysian strolled into the staritorium. She glowed like the stars above, with a calming smile on her bronze lips.

"Being away from my realm for only a small moment won't drain the life from my soul," she began, stopping right at me, scanning me up and down.

I looked bad—hair messy, purple cloak in tatters, bloody knees, and burnt ears—but she still smiled. "I had to come and see you. I watched from Haim Gana as you defeated Saraqiel's magic. You were very brave, Lisa, doing what none of us here ever could; for we are feeble beings when opposing the Fallen, and our magic is nothing but a brush of a hand when up against it. You should be very proud—a true Agapéd warrior." She held out her hand, palm facing my chest. "I can't vanquish the scars or seal all wounds from the Fallen's magic, but I can help a bit with the pain. Do you mind?"

"Not at all." I grinned. She could've offered me a cheap bandage, and I would've said yes—anything to help the pain was much appreciated.

In a couple of moments, gold magic from her fingertips began sewing up my clothing and stitching back together my cloak. The length was shorter than before, given she had to use what thread was left; still, she made it beautiful. Her fingers then flicked the air. The scratches Gaius' healing plant skimmed over on my skin, she healed easily, though the aching from the sigil's burns was still there. Some new scars remained from the dark magic, faint burns along my ears and on my chest, Ecuras' handprint around my neck, too, but nothing huge like the vezper claw marks—easily concealable with my Eternling bracelet.

The last thing she did—something she didn't need to do—was remove every spec of dirt from my body, including the patches covering my shoes and the flecks that dusted my hair.

I felt bad that Gaius didn't get the same treatment, and I looked back at him; he didn't like the attention. Lady Ariela went ahead and cleaned his wounds and clothing as well with her magic.

"Vilmad," Lady Ariela said as she fixed up Gaius' bloody arm, the one laced with dark magic, "you were saying something I believe Lisa needs to hear?"

Perplexed how Lady Ariela could hear our conversation from inside her realm, Vilmad stuttered, "Oh—yes..." The Guardian turned toward me, squinting down, the first time his stare wasn't *too* unimpressed. "Seeing as your magic is still with you after defeating one of the Fallen signifies the Agapéd still needs your heart, which means—"

"You get to stick around us a little while longer!" Emunah cut off Vilmad's sentence, excited and loud.

I didn't even think of that... I get to keep being with all of them...

Ariela finished healing Gaius—a new white swirled scar on his arm now— and knelt before me. "As long as the Agapéd gifts you life and power, you are still needed, Lisa. You are alive on purpose, and I am grateful for that. My fallen brethren are silenced, but that doesn't mean Darkness isn't still moving among the galaxies. So, Gaius will still be your instructor, guiding you in magic and making you stronger, if that is alright with you?"

My heart leaped miles ahead. "It is more than alright with me—thank you."

"Can't wait to see what all you become, Miss Lisa," she concluded, beginning to back away along with Emunah and Vilmad. "Well, I think it's about time for the stars to be released now. Thank you... to you all."

The three magic beings walked ahead and disappeared through Lady Ariela's golden rivers of magic until it was only me and the three Keepers left.

Kamari rolled up her sleeves and moved her fingers like a dance. In moments, the gravity around her clothing, shoes, and hair shifted. She started floating above—flying just like I did but with her gravity magic!

In her hardy voice, Kamari said to Gaius, "I dink it is about time we gift da skies deir galaxies of stas—what you say?"

Gaius smiled big beneath his boxed beard, excited to finally release all his hard work. "I agree."

With his muscular hands, the Keeper lifted his palms in front of his chest and began to summon ribbons of green glowing magic. Light swirled like a rushing stream right up to the moment he pushed his hands toward the sky—releasing the concentrated magic into the air. Radiant waves of virescent green soared to the edges of the ceiling, flowing into the glass and unlocking latches that held down the dome.

The ceiling blossomed like a glass flower, releasing all the stars into the night sky.

Kamari flew to the highest bobbing Wishing Star and whipped her hands forward, making her purple Keeper magic flow like cosmic confetti all over the stars.

One by one, the shining floating fruits of magic began glowing brighter as Kamari commanded them to follow her through the ozone and up to space. Their migration was the purest form of beauty, and I couldn't believe I was watching it.

A brawny hand nudged my shoulder.

"Come on," Gaius said. "You can see it better outside of Calendula."

Inna and I followed Gaius out to the secret hilltop entrance of Boolavogue. A billowing sea of stars flooded the sky, sparkling bright and zooming as fast as a school of rainbow celestial starfish. Their dust sprinkled down on top of the cattle fields, coating the rolling hills with a nebula of pinks, blues, and yellows, even painting a cow or two. The stars then shifted and swam over the Inner Kingdom, brushing the brick buildings and white walls with galactic hues. A captivating, ethereal wonderland—impossible to look away from.

"This is the coolest thing I have ever seen," I said, standing on the edge of the clifftop, buffing away some of the stardust soot from my hair.

Inna giggled as she sat on the ground, making some of the stardust float away from the weeds. "Have to say, I agree with you—this year's migration is truly the best so far."

Gaius then sat on one of the broken logs near the ridge. "Don't stand too close, or you'll topple over," he politely warned me.

I shoved my heels into the ground, throwing my chin in his direction. "You know I can *fly* now."

Those green eyes sagged. "Lisa…"

I threw my hands up, surrendering, "Okay, okay, okay." As I turned *away* from the cliff's edge, I asked, "So, can we go ahead to the festival now?"

A brogue, hardy scoff covered in bafflement came from his lungs. "Did you forget you just fought a battle? Your adrenaline won't last long enough for you to even make it down the mountain path. You need to rest."

It was true that a heavy blanket of weariness was beginning to fall on my shoulders, and my legs wanted nothing more than to lay limp. Still, I didn't care.

"But, don't we have to tell the King we won?"

The Wishing Star gardener looked up at his handy work. "The stars are a sign of our success."

I begrudgingly sat on the ground between him and Inna, the grass feeling cool against my thighs.

Gaius' voice was sincere when he said, "Next year."

I peeled my eyes away from the stars, facing him. "Next year, what?"

"Next year, we will enjoy the festival together." His face was happy, the happiest I had ever seen—relieved and at peace. "And the year after and the year after that, if you'd like."

Inna started giggling. "Since when did you become so acquainted with the Boolavogue crowds, Gaius?"

"I'm not…" He then turned his eyes back toward me. "But, I'll go if you insist."

My cheeks perked up, fighting back my tiredness. "Then, you better believe I'm going to want to visit every year."

A soft smirk appeared underneath his facial hair. "Fine."

As we watched the never-ending pool of magical fruits soar in the sky, I did my best to try and fight back my yawns. I didn't want to look away from the skies, but I was getting a bit sleepy.

"You know…" Gaius' voice slowly began as he stared up at the stars he grew. "Bet you can still see a couple of them flying over Earth right about now."

My curiosity was piqued, and my tiredness took a back seat. "You're serious?"

He nodded his head, to which Inna huffed and corrected. "He most certainly is not. Lisa fights off Darkness, and you toy with her?"

"I do not lie. There will be stars flying over Earth tonight, probably have already entered the Milky Way." He dusted the glittery star soot off his shoulder. "I may have asked Kamari to evanesce a handful through Earth's mesosphere." A flash of green sparked as he winked at me. "Consider it a birthday present."

I grinned, suppressing a yawn. "Pretty sure you're just trying to send me home to rest."

A mighty shrug came from his shoulders as Inna giggled.

"But still, thank you... though..." I said. "How did you know... I would have gotten to see them?"

He didn't look at the stars or at Inna, though I felt the blush-blonde Keeper's eyes staring at me from behind. Gaius merely smiled at me covered in stardust and plopped on the grass. "Because I promised you would get to see them, and I don't break my promises even with death standing in the way." That was when he huffed. "And you need to rest on Earth for a while, and this was the only way to get you there."

After dusting more Wishing Star residue off my legs, I stood up off the grass. "Well, I'll be sure to let you know how bright they are next time I see you."

I was about to evanesce away when I remembered my magic stamina was extremely low, and I knew I would probably collapse if I tried to travel trillions of miles in just seconds. "Uh, actually, do you think you could evanesce me? My magic is a little worn out, and I don't wanna get stuck in space, especially since Kamari will be busy for a while."

Gaius chuckled as he stood and released his arms from their crossed position. He held up his palm and gave me one more smile. "See you soon. Stay safe," my teacher told me as blue magic began to rise from his hand.

I landed safely in my forest, and my eyes instantly shot toward the sky. Most of the leaves were in the way of my view, but I did see something bright shoot across space.

They are already here! I gotta tell Mom—

Suddenly, I remembered I had told Mom I would be at Jenny Kim's until the next day. It was very late, like 10:00 p.m., I was wearing strange clothing, and it was my birthday... so showing up through the back door would seem a bit bizarre.

Still, I wanted to see the stars with Mom. I grabbed a sweatshirt out of my orbkit and exchanged it with my cloak, quickly reset the Concealment Charm on my Eternling band, and ran toward the front of the house. *Hope I don't smell too much like dirt and woodland forest.* My legs were about to give way when I made it to our little front porch, but I didn't care.

Like a guest, I rang the doorbell and waited for Mom to answer the door.

She quickly answered and stood in the entranceway, dressed in her usual Friday night pajamas: her oversized Johnny Cash shirt, fluffy slippers, and yoga pants. All her caramel hair was stuffed into a bun, and her makeup was washed; she was as pretty as ever.

I fell into her arms and held her close to me, pressing my face against her.

My embrace left her frazzled, causing her to wobble over. "Sweetie—what are you doing here—and so late? I thought you were having a sleepover at Jenny Kim's. Is something wrong?"

I didn't lie to her. Beaming, I answered, "I just felt like being with you instead—plus, there's supposed to be a *huge* shooting star show tonight, and our house has the *best* view."

"You sure Jenny Kim won't get mad at you for bailing?" She looked the road up and down. "I didn't even see a car come by—"

"Nah—it's my birthday anyway, and I wanna do this instead. I promise Jenny Kim is fine with it."

Seeing her daughter extremely excited to be home with her, Mom accepted my abrupt return without any more questions. "Well... then let me grab my coat and some blankets, and we will watch—is it starting right now?"

I was already heading out the back door. "Yes! Come on! It's going to be *amazing!*"

Outside, Mom and I laid down on our big navy-blue blanket, the one that we designated for picnics. Up above our heads, we began to see the stars—Gaius' stars—flying high and decorating the dark violet sky with light. I always thought those stars were just some hot rocks—nothing but loose space debris I learned about in school. I knew the truth now, and it was *way* cooler.

I wasn't sure what time the stars all found their places in the sky since I didn't bother to count the minutes; I was too distracted. Mom and I went back and forth, making silly wishes each time a star shot by. The best was Mom's when she wished for a better memory so she would stop losing the backdoor key, making me belly laugh a bit painfully. I, though, didn't have a sincere wish to make. I had Mom with me, a star-obsessed Keeper back in Calendula waiting for my return, magic in my heart, and breath in my lungs. Honestly, I was perfectly happy and couldn't wish for a better life than the one I had.

ACKNOWLEDGEMENTS

First, I'd like to thank Jacob, my wonderful husband, for being the one I look up to for creative critique and advice. Thank you for telling me to make doppelganger magic and not time-traveling. I cannot express enough how much clearer and more fun Lisa's experience is with the Echo Ring, even when I tried to defend myself and say, "It works" (it never did). Thank you for the advice on the final battle, Vilmad's character, and the King's demeanor. You were working a full-time job and still gave so much of your time to editing my book, fixing many of my grammatical mistakes, and getting rid of my plethora of semicolons (I still kept a handful). Thank you for guiding me creatively. You've helped me become the writer I am today. I love you so much... so be ready to help me with Book 2. I'm going to need it.

Thank you to my family. Mom, you were the first one to read this, and I'll never be able to express my gratitude for how much that meant to me. Thank you, too, for encouraging me in art and writing in middle school. I started my first book in seventh grade, and ever since you've been supporting me. Dad, thank you for your wisdom and kindness, showing such fatherly love and protection in my life. I am blessed to have been raised by you and Mom. Thank you to my sister and all my extended family. You've always encouraged my art, and my story will have humor and heartfelt moments inspired by you in the books to come. Thank you—my loving family.

I'd like to thank my Instagram followers, the ones who have been with me from the beginning, and the ones who have found me recently. Your encouragement means more than the stars to me. Every single like, heart, and comment on my posts and Instagram stories are special to me, and I do read every one of them. To the ones who have stuck by me since high school and college, watching my art go from K-Pop portraits to random cartoons, thank you for reading this book. To know you read this brightens my heart, knowing my book and characters were worth your time. I promise to continue writing and drawing, growing our Agapéd Bearer world together.

Lastly, I'd like to thank Christ. I never wrote this book because of wealth or because I thought I could write something better than what was on the everyday bookstore shelf. I wanted to create a place for those to go off to and know they are worth living for. We are here for a purpose, just like Lisa, and I wanted to show that aspect of Christ in this book. He gave me my creative abilities and continues to provide me with life each day, and I plan on using that gift to create even more books about the battle between Darkness and Light.

Stay safe and know you are worth living for.

Made in the USA
Las Vegas, NV
19 September 2024

95522643R00340